From stage actor and international ~~to millions throughout the world,~~ selling author, Judy Nunn's career has been meteoric.

Her first forays into adult fiction resulted in what she describes as her 'entertainment set'. *The Glitter Game*, *Centre Stage* and *Araluen* are three novels set in the worlds of television, theatre and film, each of which became instant bestsellers.

Next came her 'city set'. *Kal*, a fiercely passionate novel about men and mining, is set in Kalgoorlie. Then came *Beneath the Southern Cross*, a mammoth achievement chronicling the story of Sydney since first European settlement. And finally, *Territory*, a tale of family, love and retribution set in Darwin, which took Australia by storm and made Judy one of Australia's top-selling female fiction writers.

'I like to write larger-than-life stories,' she says, 'about larger-than-life people, caught up in the historical events of their time. And I can't help it,' she laughs, 'the actor in me always insists on an added plot twist here and there, to keep the reader guessing until the final curtain falls.'

Judy Nunn's fame as a fiction writer is spreading rapidly. Her novels are now published throughout Europe in English, German, French, Dutch and Czech.

By the same author
*The Glitter Game*
*Centre Stage*
*Araluen*
*Kal*
*Beneath the Southern Cross*
*Territory*

Children's fiction
*Eye in the Storm*
*Eye in the City*

# JUDY NUNN

# PACIFIC

RANDOM HOUSE AUSTRALIA

Random House Australia Pty Ltd
20 Alfred Street, Milsons Point, NSW 2061
http://www.randomhouse.com.au

Sydney   New York   Toronto
London   Auckland   Johannesburg

First published by Random House Australia 2004

National Library of Australia
Cataloguing-in-Publication Entry

Nunn, Judy.
Pacific.

ISBN 1 74051 304 5.

1. Motion picture actors and actresses – Fiction.  2. World
War, 1939–1945 – Campaigns – Pacific Area – Fiction.
3. Nurses – Fiction.  I. Title.

A823.3

Cover photograph: Getty Images
Cover design: Darian Causby/Highway 51
Internal design and typesetting by Midland Typesetters, Maryborough, Victoria
Printed and bound by Griffin Press, Netley, South Australia

10 9 8 7 6 5 4 3 2 1

To the next generation,
Brett and Nathan,
Sam and Cory.
Love to you and your families . . . and
to those who will follow.

# ACKNOWLEDGEMENTS

My thanks, first and foremost, to my husband Bruce Venables. Brucie, you are a true gem.

Thank you also to the pals and workmates: my agent James Laurie; my publisher Jane Palfreyman; my editor Kim Swivel; all at Random House Australia; and as always, Robyn Gurney, Colin Julin and Dr Grahame Hookway.

For the provision of 'author's retreats', many thanks Suzie and Grahame for 'the writer's room', and Rob and Dee for 'the cabana'.

And for assistance in the research of this book my sincerest thanks to the following:

In Fareham: Maralyn of the Tourist Information Centre at Westbury Manor Museum, all those at Bembridge House, Ferneham Hall.

In Vanuatu: Roz Rose, Tony Young, Gerry and Jan Smelik of Tamanu Beach Resort, Matthew Erceg of Sea Air Limited, Paul and Helene Gibson, Pat Bochenska and Gillian Mitride.

In Sydney: Suzie Clark of Fox Studios, Gillian Simpson of the Australian National Maritime Museum, and Nick Truswell and his helpful staff at the Quay Grand Hotel.

Amongst my many research sources, I would like particularly to recognise the following:

Reece Discombe, historical papers, Vanuatu Library, Port Vila, 1979.

Lt Colonel Ritchie Garrison, USA (Ret), *Task Force 9156 and III Island Command*, 1983.

Irving and Electra Johnson, 'Yankee Roams the Orient', *National Geographic* (March 1951).

Richard Shears, *The Coconut War*, Cassell Australia Limited, 1980.

Colonial History of Vanuatu, www.vanuatutourism.com.

# Prologue

The elements were peaceful. A cloudless sky, a gentle breeze, an unruffled sea. It should have been a perfect summer morning. And the beach should have been inviting. Terrace houses, some five storeys high, fronted onto the broad expanse of sand, a pretty setting, echoing past holiday-makers' delight. But it was no holiday haven today.

Today black smoke dimmed the sun, and the sea and sky merged to a murky grey as layer upon layer of German aircraft swooped from high to unleash their 1,000-pound bombs on the English destroyers. The elements were peaceful, but mankind was bent on death and destruction.

Martin Thackeray lay on the deck, clinging to the gunwales of the small wooden fishing boat as the Stukas roared overhead. The boat had pulled out to sea and was in the midst of the havoc being wreaked upon the British warships. He looked back at the shore barely a mile away, at the beach and the houses. He thought of Margate where his family used to holiday annually when he was a child and he tried to blot out the smoke and the exploding shells and the bodies bobbing about in the oil-blackened sea. He concentrated on the beach and the houses. It could have been Margate, he thought. And the long V-formation of soldiers marching down to the shore could have been holiday-makers. He clung to the thought as rigidly as he clung to the gunwales, fearful of losing consciousness, for the loss of consciousness meant the loss of his life. Why did death frighten him so? he wondered. He'd seen many men die. Now it was his time. He must accept it. But somehow he couldn't. Guilt mingled with his pain. Had he lost his faith? Why was he so fearful of meeting his Maker? He chastised himself, urged himself to make his peace with God, accept his fate, but even as he did so he couldn't resist the need to fight back. The pain once again engulfed him and, desperately, he thought of Margate and his childhood. Stay alive, his mind urged, stay alive.

Despite the chaos which reigned, there was little panic amongst the troops. Thousands waited patiently on the beach for their turn to march crocodile-style into the sea. Like well-behaved schoolchildren they waded, some up to their necks, rifles held high above their heads, to the flotilla of craft waiting to take them home. In the skies overhead dogfights raged as RAF fighters engaged the Luftwaffe, but still the soldiers kept their orderly files until, one by one, two by two, they were hauled aboard vessels where they collapsed, exhausted, on the deck.

Martin had been unable to wade beyond waist-deep. He would not have been able to make it that far had it not been for the man who had saved him.

The humiliation of the British Expeditionary Force had been total, and the troops had retreated as far as they could when orders had been received to assemble on the beach. Few believed the rumours of a rescue mission. They'd be stranded if they went to the beach, they thought. Slaughtered or taken prisoner. But orders were orders and thousands upon thousands of soldiers scrambled through the bombed-out villages to head for the open and vulnerable shoreline.

Martin Thackeray and twenty others of his unit had been trapped in a ruined church as the enemy advance troops entered the deserted village. They'd left it too late to make their escape. They opened fire. The enemy took cover and skirmishing had continued throughout the entire day and into the night as the Germans tried to ascertain the Allied numbers remaining in the village. Fresh enemy troops arrived and dug in for the morning when they'd storm the church and surrounding buildings.

It was just before dawn when the men had made their escape bid, but they were lambs to the slaughter, mercilessly mown down by the surrounding forces which awaited them. Only Martin and young Tom Putney had emerged unscathed, eventually making it to the coastline a full day later.

'Christ almighty!' Tom had muttered in his thick Cockney accent as they'd ducked through a narrow street which led to the sea. 'Jus' look at that!'

'Don't blaspheme.' Martin's reply had been automatic. Tom's blaspheming and his own remonstration had been a running joke between them for months, but he too had stood dumbfounded at the sight of the myriad vessels churning through the water. There must be hundreds, he'd thought. Too many to count, and of every description. There were troopships and mine sweepers, cruisers and yachts, pleasure craft and fishing boats, and others, little more than dinghies. And on the beach sat thousands of men, patiently waiting their turn for deliverance. Some had been waiting for days.

'I wasn't blasphemin', Marty,' Tom had said, 'I was givin' thanks.' Even in the direst of circumstances Tom was always good for a joke, but this time he wasn't joking at all. 'It's a bleedin' miracle, it is. A bleedin' –'

He'd stopped mid-sentence as the building beside them erupted. A shell had found its mark. But they were out of the battle zone, Martin had thought vaguely as the force of the blast lifted him bodily into the air.

When he had come to his senses, seconds or hours later, he couldn't tell, he had realised that the shell had not been fired from the battle zone. The Stukas overhead were determined to halt the escape mission.

Yet more troops were pouring down the narrow street making for the shore, climbing over the rubble of the building, tripping over the body of Tom buried waist-deep in debris.

'Tom!' Martin had dragged himself over to his friend, a searing pain in his left leg and chest. There was a ringing in his ears and his vision was blurred, but he knew Tom was dead. Tom Putney had been barely twenty, ten years younger than Martin. Too young to die.

'Our Father,' Martin had begun as he crossed Tom's hands over his chest, 'who art . . .' Then suddenly he was grabbed by the wrist and hauled to his knees, the pain screaming through his body.

'Don't waste your breath, boyo.'

'Our Father who art in heaven . . .' Martin had protested, as much for himself as for Tom.

'Come on!' Emlyn Gruffudd had urged. Jesus Christ! He was as religious as the next man, but what was the point in saying prayers for a bloke who had half his head blown off! And at a time like this! 'Come on,' he'd repeated, hoisting Martin to his feet. 'You can make it.'

Martin had found himself half carried, half dragged to the beach. He had no idea who the man was but, as his sight cleared, he knew that he was not from his unit. He had tried to thank the man but waves of pain had engulfed him and the words wouldn't come out.

'Don't you worry, boyo,' Emlyn had muttered, 'you'll make it.'

The ringing in Martin's ears blocked out any sound. Once again he'd tried to voice his thanks and his lips formed the words, but nothing came out, not even a whisper.

The wounded were the first to be shepherded into the queue making its way to the water and Emlyn Gruffudd thanked his lucky stars that he'd rescued the Englishman. He might have been waiting his turn with the others for days if he hadn't. It had not been his intention to jump the queue, but when the opportunity had offered itself he didn't say no. He hoisted Martin higher up on to his hip, ignoring the groans of agony. Perhaps the poor lad was already dying, he'd thought, as he started to wade.

Only minutes later they were picked up by one of the lighter craft which had negotiated its way into shallower water.

'Ten's the limit, room for two more,' the skipper of the small fishing boat had said and he and his young crewman, a lad barely out of his teens, had helped them aboard. There was no disorderliness from the other troops in the water. The men simply waded out further or waited their turn in the shallows, aiding the wounded.

'That's it, Billy-boy,' the skipper had said to the lad, 'we've got our load of pongos, we're off.'

So Martin clung to the gunwales and, whilst the boat chugged out into the channel, he watched the beach of Dunkirk and thought of Margate as he fought to retain his consciousness. But once they were out in the boisterous sea, the motion of the boat sent such pain through his shattered leg and his chest that unconsciousness seemed a blessing. If this was death, he thought, so be it. The pain had become unendurable and he prayed to God as he slipped into the merciful blackness.

'Portsmouth's chaos. So's Southampton. The big boats are all makin' for the docks there.' The voice was authoritative, an older man with a thick Hampshire accent. 'We're headin' for Fareham.'

The ringing in his ears had lessened and, as he came to, Martin heard the words clearly. So he was still alive. He didn't know whether he was thankful or not. He steeled himself to the pain which once again galloped through him like an angry stallion, every part of his body now screaming in agony.

'Where's Fareham?' he heard a Welsh voice query. 'Never heard of it.'

'Roughly 'alfway 'tween Portsmouth and Southampton,' the skipper said. 'About four mile upriver. Home eh, Billy-boy?' The skipper smiled through his grey beard at his young crewman. 'We're headin' home.'

'Aye, Skip,' the lad grinned back.

Martin once again felt the blackness slide over him. But this time he didn't think of God and he didn't think of death. He no longer cared, he simply wished to escape the pain.

He awoke once again to the sound of voices. Many of them this time. Voices of command. 'Easy does it. Gently now.' Others scrambled from the boat, willing hands helping the wounded, and he heard the Welshman say, 'You can make it, boyo,' as he felt himself lifted onto the jetty. He gritted his teeth to prevent himself crying out. They laid him on a canvas stretcher and carried him to a waiting vehicle, one of many in the quayside dockyard. Army Landrovers, private cars, even several horses and drays: the place was a hive of activity.

Martin was delirious, his brain in turmoil. Where was he? The voices were English, all of them. He wanted to ask, 'Am I home?' but he didn't dare try to speak. Then a hand was holding his. A soft hand, but its grip was firm and reassuring.

'Don't worry, you're home now.' A woman's voice. She had read his mind, and she looked like an angel. He fought against the blackness as he felt himself drift away. He didn't want to lose sight of the vision. An angel, with hair so fair it formed a halo around her face. 'You're home,' she said again, 'you're safe. We're taking you to the Royal Victoria Hospital at Netley.' Her voice was gentle and came from very far away. And then she smiled. He held on to the voice and the vision as they lifted him into the Land-rover. His fear and uncertainty had left him now. He was saved, the angel had told him so. 'You're safe,' she'd said, and he believed her.

# BOOK ONE

# CHAPTER ONE

'Nora – can I never be anything more than a stranger to you?'

'Ah, Torvald, the most wonderful thing of all would have to happen.'

'Tell me what that would be!'

'Both you and I would have to be so changed that . . . Oh, Torvald, I don't believe any longer in wonderful things happening.'

'But I will believe in it. Tell me! So changed that . . .?'

'That our life together would be a real wedlock. Goodbye.'

She left, and he sat, burying his head in his hands.

'Nora! Nora!' He looked around. 'Empty. She is gone.' Hope flashed through his mind. 'The most wonderful thing of all . . .?' Then he heard the sound of the door below as it closed.

The final performance of Henrik Ibsen's *A Doll's House* at the Theatre Royal, Haymarket, received a standing ovation. The award-winning production had played for over a year to capacity houses for each of its 431 performances, and its success was in most part due to the young actress who had taken London's West End by storm. 2003 was certainly Samantha Lindsay's year.

In the centre of the lineup, hands clasped with her fellow cast members, Samantha walked downstage to take the final of the curtain calls. There'd been twelve in all. She'd accepted the bouquet from the theatre manager, taken several solo calls and now, as the cast bowed, she glanced to the wings and gave a barely perceptible nod to the stage manager. He acknowledged her message, the lights dimmed, the cast left the stage and the audience was still loudly applauding as the house lights came up.

Backstage, cast and crew hugged each other affection-ately, some with tears in their eyes, and Deidre, who played the maid, openly cried. It had been a long run and a very happy company; they would miss each other. A celebratory supper had been arranged for the entire cast, but for now they continued to mingle in the wings, savour-ing the moment. Alexander embraced Samantha.

'My darling doll-wife,' he said, 'you've been a glorious Nora, it's been wonderful.' Then, when he'd kissed her on both cheeks, he couldn't help adding, 'But why on earth did you call a halt? We could have taken at least another half dozen calls.'

Sam recognised it for the genuine complaint it was. 'Always leave them wanting more,' she replied innocently, 'isn't that what they say?'

He appeared not to hear her. 'We took fifteen on the last night of *Lady Windemere*, and that only ran for a hundred performances, we could probably have stretched it to twenty tonight and created a record.' Alexander had never approved of the fact that the cast had been directed to take their curtain calls from Samantha. The girl gave a stellar performance in the role of Nora, he agreed, but she was far too inexperienced in theatre etiquette. In West End theatre etiquette, in any event.

'Oh well, too late now,' Sam shrugged. Alexander's litany of complaints had become water off a duck's back to her. He was a fine actor and they'd worked well

together, although she'd had to overcome his open antipathy in the early days. Alexander Wright had been
unaccustomed to working opposite a virtual unknown.
However, the reaction of the preview audiences and the
opening night reviews had altered his opinion and, like
everyone else, he'd eventually succumbed, albeit begrudg-
ingly, to Samantha's natural charm and lack of pretension.

'She's a dear,' he'd say to those who asked what
Samantha Lindsay was really like – and, to his secret
chagrin, there were many who did. 'Quite the little
innocent really.' He always managed to make it sound
simultaneously affectionate and patronising.

Sam was not innocent. She was unaffected certainly, but
she had realised that it made things easier for everyone if
she simply pandered to the actor's ego.

'I'm quite sure you're right,' she now added as she
noticed the familiar scowl, 'and yes it's been wonderful.'
She hugged him genuinely. 'I've loved working with you,
Alexander, you've taught me a lot.' She meant it. She'd
learned a great deal from him and she was grateful.
Besides, Alexander couldn't help being Alexander. What
was the saying? *A pride of lions, a gaggle of geese and
a whinge of actors.* After thirty dedicated years in the
theatre, Alexander Wright was a product of his profession.

Recognising her sincerity, he replied with the dignity
befitting such a compliment. 'Thank you, my dear. I feel
it's one's responsibility to encourage young actors.'

He was touched by her remark, she could tell, and was
about to embark upon one of his many, and interminable,
stories of past productions, so she pecked him on the
cheek. 'You have, and I'm very grateful.' She smiled. 'And
now I have to get the slap off.' She grabbed the bouquet of
flowers which the assistant stage manager was patiently
holding for her and headed for her dressing room. 'See you
at supper,' she called over her shoulder. 'I'm bloody
starving!'

Alexander shook his head with exasperated fondness. She was so ridiculously Australian.

Reginald waited ten minutes before tapping on Samantha's dressing-room door. If it had been another of his female clients he would have waited at least half an hour, but it took Sam only ten minutes to 'get her slap off', as she called it. And, as she never ate before a performance, she was always ravenously hungry after the show and impatient to leave. Furthermore, she preferred to eat at one of the small cafes where the food was good, rather than somewhere one went to be seen. Reginald had found Samantha refreshing from the outset, although it had taken him some time to adjust to being called 'Reg'. He accepted it now and they'd become close friends.

'Reg!' Sam was minus her stage makeup but still in a stocking cap and robe at her dressing-room mirror when the dapper little Englishman entered. She jumped up, wig in hand, and hugged him. 'Take a seat,' she said, 'won't be a tick.' She sat, dumped the wig on the wig stand, pulled off the cap and brushed her fair hair, normally curly and framing her face, back into a severe ponytail. Nothing else you can do with wig hair, she always maintained. She refused to start from scratch and coax back the curls, it took too much time and after a show food was far more important. 'We hung around backstage saying goodbyes,' she explained, 'God only knows why. Everyone's coming to supper.' She jumped up once again and started taking off her robe.

'I'll wait outside.' Reg rose.

'Don't be silly, I'm perfectly respectable.' She dropped the robe. 'Look! Thermals!'

Reg smiled but still discreetly averted his gaze. Even in a winter vest and thigh-length, cotton stretch knickers she looked sexy, lean and lithe, with the body of a healthy young animal. He found it a little confronting and he'd much rather have waited outside.

Sam dressed quickly; she hadn't meant to embarrass him. She'd deliberately donned the thermals before he'd arrived in order not to. What was it with the English? she wondered. Australian actors stripped openly in dressing rooms, but even the English acting fraternity seemed prudish, and her immodesty had often been frowned upon.

'Did you check that the beer's arrived?' she asked as she zipped up her cord trousers and grabbed her jumper. She'd arranged the delivery of two cartons of beer for the stage-hands who had to strike the set and 'bump out' in preparation for the next production.

'Yes, they're holding it at the stage door. The doorman was most amused that it was Foster's.'

'Thought I'd make a bit of a statement. All respectable, you can look now.' She grabbed her overcoat from the peg on the door. 'Come on, I'm starving.'

'We'll be the first there.'

'Goody, we'll grab the best table.'

So much for making the grand late entrance, Reginald thought, and so much for dolling herself up. He cast a circumspect glance at the corduroys. They were going to the Ivy after all, the best table had been booked for the past two months, and even on closing night she was still one of the hottest things in town. 'No need to rush,' he said with a touch of irony, 'Nigel's minding the table for us.'

For the first time Sam drew breath. 'I didn't know Nigel was coming.'

'Sam,' he said patiently, 'I told you last week he needs to do this interview before you leave for Sydney.' Nigel was the publicist Reginald employed to promote a number of his top clients and he knew Sam didn't like the man. Which was understandable, most people didn't, but Nigel was very good at his job. 'He says you've been avoiding meeting him for the past five days.'

'I've had to move out of the flat, for God's sake,' she

protested, 'I've been organising the furniture removal, I haven't had time!'

'Then you should have made time.' Sam could be infuriating on occasions. 'You've won the Olivier Award, for God's sake! You have to be fair dinkum about this.' It was a term she'd taught him as a joke, laughing at the way he said it in his pukka English accent, but it usually proved most effective. 'You can't just disappear from London. We need to keep you hot. We need to make the industry aware that you're about to star in a Hollywood movie.'

'I know, I know. But it's the last night!'

It appeared for once that 'fair dinkum' wasn't going to work. 'Fine,' Reg snapped, 'I'll tell him to come to Fareham then, shall I?' She glared back at him, and her hazel eyes held a glint of defiance, but Reginald was fully prepared to stand his ground. 'He'll be happy to make the trip, I'm sure.'

'All right, you bastard, you win.' She gave a resigned shrug and he knew that she wasn't really angry, just as he knew that the language was not intentionally insulting. Sam's voice held no nasal twang and was not particularly Australian, but her behaviour certainly was and Reg had grown to love her for it. She tossed her scarf around her neck. 'Let's go.'

'Lippy,' he reminded her. Then, whilst she slashed the lipstick across her mouth, he added, 'And a touch of eyes.' She glared at him once again in the mirror. 'Well, at least some mascara,' he said. 'It's the Ivy, Sam, and there's bound to be press photographers sniffing around.'

'I don't know why we're not going to Zorba's,' she grizzled, 'the food's much better.'

'Because the others want to go to the Ivy, that's why. Stop being such a prima donna.'

It was a biting night, unusually cold for so early in September, and as they walked up the broad Haymarket towards Piccadilly Circus, Sam turned to look back at the theatre, at the stateliness of the Corinthian columns with their gold embossed motif and the arches and stonework, all perfectly floodlit. A glorious building, its interior was of equal magnificence, with molded ceilings, crystal chandeliers, polished marble, and layer upon layer of English gold leaf. What a privilege it had been to work there.

She remembered the first time she'd been to 'the Haymarket', as the actors fondly referred to the Theatre Royal. It had been December 1994 and she'd caught the train up from Fareham during the two days she'd had free of rehearsals. So many firsts, she remembered. Her first trip to England, her first visit to London, and her first experience of West End Theatre. She'd seen the new Tom Stoppard play, *Arcadia*, and the Theatre Royal had just that year undergone major restoration. She'd been eighteen years old and it had been the most magical experience of her life. And now, nine years later, she'd worked there. She'd played a leading role at 'the Haymarket', the most elegant theatre in London. During the eight performances a week for over a year, she had never once taken the experience for granted. And now it was over.

'It's been a good run, hasn't it?' Reginald had been standing silently beside her for a full minute or so. He knew what she was thinking.

'Ever master of the understatement, Reggie,' she grinned. It was their secret language. He drew the line at 'Reggie' and she only ever used the term in private.

He took her hand and smiled. 'Onward and upward, Sam. Onward and upward.'

'I hope so.' The forthcoming film role was potentially the biggest step yet in her career, but movies were risky business, as they both knew. And she would miss the theatre.

'*Torpedo Junction*. It's a rather old-fashioned title, don't you think?' Nigel sat, pen poised over his notepad, gin and tonic untouched. He'd graciously waited until Sam had finished her supper, a huge steak – God knew where the girl put it, she was built like a whippet – and then he'd insisted the three of them retire from the main arena of the restaurant to one of the more private leather booths.

'Come on, Sam,' Reg had urged, recognising that she was loath to leave the others. 'They'll be partying for ages, you can join them later.' Then, when she'd looked a little rebellious, he'd muttered, 'You promised you'd be fair dinkum.'

'Okay,' she'd said meekly enough.

'Old-fashioned in what way?' she now asked a little archly. She couldn't help herself: she found Nigel such a supercilious bastard.

'It sounds like a war movie from the 1940s.'

'Well, it is in a way, isn't it? Torpedo Junction was the infamous Japanese submarine hunting ground during World War II.'

Nigel adjusted his Gucci glasses and gritted his teeth. He didn't like Sam any more than she liked him. Little upstart. Didn't she realise that, as a journalist with his own PR company and all of the contacts he had to hand, he could destroy her? And if she wasn't on Reginald's books he'd take great delight in doing so. But he couldn't afford to lose the account of Reginald Harcourt Management, so he gave a glacial smile and continued.

'So that's what it is then? A war film?'

'No.' What a waste of time it all was, Sam thought. She hated playing these games. But it was part of the job, she told herself as she took a breath and tried to sound pleasant. 'It's about love really. Human love.'

'Ah,' he pounced like a hungry cat. It was exactly what he was after. 'So it's a similar genre to *Pearl Harbor* then, a war story with a love theme.' Nigel scratched away at his notepad, delighted. At this early stage, before commencement of filming, the production house was releasing no specific details about *Torpedo Junction,* merely the title, the principal cast, and the fact that it was the next big-budget production from Mammoth.

'No, it's not a war story with a love theme,' she said tightly. That wasn't what she'd meant at all, Sam thought, cursing the man. What the hell did it matter anyway? Whatever she said he'd misquote her.

'Who'd like another drink?' Reg asked, giving Sam a warning glance as he rose from the booth. It was the way Nigel often conducted interviews. Offend the subject just enough to make them defensive. That way they gave away more of themselves or, in this case, more of the project. The subject matter of the script was under wraps, and Sam knew that.

'I'm fine, thank you, Reginald,' Nigel said, taking the mildest sip from his gin and tonic.

'Another red for me, thanks,' Sam gave Reg a nod that said she not only knew exactly where she stood, but she was more than a match for Nigel Daly.

'It's not at all like *Pearl Harbor* actually, Nigel,' she said, draining the last of her glass and smiling, she hoped, sweetly.

'What is it like then?'

'Why don't you ask me how I feel about working with Brett Marsdon? It's what everyone will want to know, surely.'

She was right of course, but he'd be able to sell another whole story on the *Torpedo Junction* theme if he could get it out of her. 'So you don't want to discuss the script?' He gave it one last try.

'It's about people, Nigel. One of the best scripts I've ever read. And it's all about people.'

The smug bitch, he thought. She went on to parrot the details which had been generally released. It was an American production, Mammoth's biggest budget movie of the year, they were shooting offshore, interiors at Fox

Studios in Sydney and on location somewhere in the South
Pacific or far north Queensland, the specific details hadn't
been released yet. It was nothing he didn't know already.
Nigel gave up.

'So tell me about Brett Marsdon,' he said. 'How do you
feel about working with Hollywood's hottest property?'

Not all of the questions were trite. In true form, Nigel
questioned her about the fact that she would be playing
an Englishwoman. 'Film critics are very quick to judge
accents,' he said.

'I've been working in the English theatre for the past
two years,' she replied, a fact of which Nigel was fully
aware, she thought. He'd not only seen a number of her
performances, but Reg would have sent him her CV. She
glanced at Reginald but he sipped his white wine and said
nothing. It was not his job to field the questions.

'Of course,' Nigel replied smoothly, 'but this is your first
movie role, is it not?'

*Is it not*, she thought, whoever said *is it not*? But, aware
that he was once again needling her, she gave a cheeky
smile instead of biting back. 'Oh no, I was a prostitute in
a low-budget thriller three years ago.'

'Really?' It was Nigel's turn to glance at Reginald. 'That
wasn't on the CV.'

'I ended up on the cutting-room floor, the whole scene
did. And the movie bombed anyway.'

'I see.' Well, he could hardly use that, could he? He
asked her about her ties to England. After a year as the
darling of London's West End, did she anticipate coming
back to Britain, or would Hollywood claim her? Surprisingly enough, she warmed to the theme.

'I'll go where the work is, of course,' she said, 'but I'd
like to live in Britain when I can.' She grinned at Reg. 'I've
bought a house here.'

'Oh?' Nigel feigned interest. 'Where?'

'Fareham.'

'Fareham!' His surprise pleased her. Had he expected her to say Chelsea or South Kensington? 'Why on earth Fareham? It's miles from anywhere.'

'It's where I did my first panto. Well my only panto actually,' she corrected herself. '*Cinderella* at Ferneham Hall, Fareham, 1994.'

Nigel winced. The traditional Christmas family pantomime was hardly something to boast of, and certainly not a production in a backwater like Fareham. Really, the girl was impossible.

Sam looked at Reg. She had no intention of cloaking her humble beginnings in secrecy and she couldn't give a damn if others wished that she would. But she didn't want to offend Reg. Reg had been responsible for her success and, in the early days, he'd suggested she neglect to mention her lack of formal training to the press. Surprisingly enough, Reginald Harcourt gave an encouraging nod.

'It was the first time I'd ever worked in the theatre,' Sam said, 'although the producers didn't know it. Not that they would have cared, I suppose. I was only hired because of the soapie.'

Nigel looked incredulously at Reginald. He'd known that Samantha Lindsay had started out as a teenager in an Aussie soap, but surely they didn't want to go in that direction?

Reginald made his one and only contribution to the interview. 'I think it's time Sam's background was discussed. It makes her different,' he suggested mildly. 'I think readers would find it interesting.'

Readers maybe, Nigel thought, but hardly prospective producers and casting agents. Oh well, if the girl wanted to hang herself, and if he had the agent's permission, he was only too happy to oblige.

'How fascinating,' he said as he scribbled in his pad.

# CHAPTER TWO

Samantha Lindsay had grown up in Perth. 'Perth, Western Australia, not Perth, Scotland', she was wont to say, having recognised the need for clarification the first day she set foot on British soil.

She'd known she wanted to act from the age of ten but her mother had taken little notice. Sam had been permitted weekly singing and dancing classes at a local amateur theatre because several of her friends went, but she was expected to outgrow her childhood fantasies and attend university. The classes only fed Sam's ambition and, by the time she was sixteen, she was secretly, and impatiently, awaiting the day when she could audition for drama school. She'd made enquiries and seventeen was the minimal age requirement for entry to the WA Academy of Performing Arts, although eighteen was preferable, she was told. Then, in mid-February, shortly after her seventeenth birthday, she read an advertisement in the *West Australian*: 'AUDITIONS for "Families and Friends". Males and females 14–15 years old.'

Sam, who looked young for her age, put her hair in pigtails, wore her old school uniform to the audition and got the job.

'Families and Friends' was a highly successful Australian soap. It had been running for eight years and had sold to over twenty countries worldwide. The only drawback was, it was shot in Sydney. There was little her parents could do, Sam was 'going East' and nobody was going to stop her. It broke her mother's heart.

The publicity machine was set in motion and Samantha Lindsay, like many a teenager before her and after, became a household name, not only in Australia, but in Britain where the series was particularly popular. It shocked her when, eighteen months later, the channel didn't pick up the option on her contract. Her agent knew why.

'You're too old now, Sam,' Barbara said. Barb Bradley was a no-nonsense woman who believed in calling a spade a spade. 'You're not a kid any more, pet, you're past your use-by date.' It was true that in the past eighteen months Sam had blossomed from a pretty, but gawky, schoolgirl into a sensual young woman, and since 'Families and Friends' was aimed at a youthful market, few teenagers found themselves re-contracted once their transition to adulthood became evident.

'Don't take it personally,' Barb advised her, although she knew it was difficult for the poor kid not to. Barbara Bradley had had a number of teenage clients spat out by the system and it cut them up every time. 'You've got the panto to look forward to, pet.' She was glad she'd organised the panto for the Christmas production break, now at least Sam had something to look forward to. 'When you come back we'll concentrate on adult roles.'

The pantomime was of the lower-budget variety and was to be staged at a venue called, unexcitingly, Ferneham Hall, in the obscure town of Fareham, none of which sounded frightfully thrilling to Barbara, but she'd dealt with the producers before and found them honest enough.

The booking of young Aussie soap stars for the British Christmas pantomime season had become a thriving

business, particularly if one cracked the big-budget productions, but Barb hadn't recommended Sam to the bigger
producers. The girl was untrained, she'd never worked in
the theatre, and Barb had been unwilling to risk her own
reputation.

'You *can* sing and dance, can't you?' she'd asked a little
anxiously when the Fareham job had come up.

'Oh yes,' Sam had assured her confidently, and Barb
hadn't pushed any further. It didn't really matter anyway:
who'd see her in Fareham? And Vermont Productions
probably didn't care, they only wanted the face from the
telly.

Ferneham Hall, Fareham, might have held no thrill for
Barbara, but it did for Sam. She was going to England! It
was 1994, she was eighteen years old, and she was going
to work in the theatre! She might as well have been
booked into the London Palladium.

And she wasn't disappointed from the minute she
arrived. Well, that wasn't quite true. She *had* been a little
deflated when the company manager picked her up at
Heathrow Airport on a freezing morning in early
December and she discovered they were driving direct to
Fareham. 'Don't I get to see London?' she'd asked. Pete
Harris, a rather taciturn man in his mid-thirties with a
mild London accent, had given a short bark of a laugh as
he headed south on the motorway. He thought she was
joking and when he realised she wasn't, he wondered
whether he had a true innocent on his hands or whether
she was one of those untalented, arrogant, young Aussie
soap stars who demanded special treatment. He'd met a
number of them in the five years he'd been working for
Vermont Productions. 'London's a bit out of the way,' he
said brusquely.

Sam was a little deflated by the motorway too. Where
was rural England? She realised that perhaps she'd been
naive. What had she expected? *The Wind in the Willows*?

This never-ending ribbon of concrete no doubt led to an industrial jungle where she was to be trapped for two whole months. Flight fatigue was setting in – she'd been warned about that – Pete was untalkative, and she started to feel vulnerable and lonely. But when they turned off the motorway and wound their way through the southern slopes, things suddenly changed. She was enchanted. The English countryside was every bit as magical as she'd imagined: copses of beech trees, elegant in their winter nakedness, briar hedges, streams forded by picturesque bridges, huge oak trees and yews. Then up the hill to Fareham. Her first view of St Peter's and St Paul's Church, its ancient stone tower standing guard over the tombstones which dotted its wooded gardens. Then into the heart of the township: houses tall and imposing with knapped flintstone walls, others tiny with garrets and small bay windows, Sam had never seen architecture like it. A history she'd never known unfolded before her eyes.

'What a beautiful place,' she said, awestruck, as Pete did a quick lap around the town to give her the layout. He felt relieved. Thank God, she's an innocent, he thought, and he turned off Osborn Road into the broad gravel driveway of Chisolm House.

Although Chisolm House had been converted into bed and breakfast lodgings, it bore all the appearance of the grand private residence it had once been. A set of six large bay windows, three downstairs, three upstairs, looked out over a magnificent and well-maintained front garden, complete with manicured lawn and a fountain. The main entrance, to the right side of the house and directly off the gravel driveway, was guarded by two stone lions and an impressive conifer in an earthenware tub.

'Hello there, Pete.' A large, matronly woman in her fifties stood at the door as the car pulled up. She'd obviously been expecting them.

'Hi, Mrs M,' Pete said, heaving the suitcase out of the boot. 'This is Samantha Lindsay. Samantha, Mrs M.' He dumped the case on the steps. 'Welcome to Fareham, Samantha, see you in two days,' he added and took off at the rate of knots. He had a million things to do at the theatre and he'd hated having to interrupt his day to pick up the little Aussie soap star.

Pete Harris had reversed his personal opinion. Samantha Lindsay was obviously a nice girl, and even better looking in the flesh than on TV, but his professional suspicions remained intact. He'd be willing to bet she could neither sing nor dance. None of them could. These kids might draw the crowds but they knew nothing about panto.

'Come in to the kitchen, dear, you'll want a cup of tea.' Before Sam could protest, Martha Montgomery, known to all as Mrs M, picked up the heavy suitcase, and bustled on ahead through the hallway. 'Such a long way to travel, you must be exhausted.'

Sam followed the woman as she crossed through the small entrance hall lined with coat stands and hat pegs. Ahead was a broad wooden staircase leading to the upper floor, but Mrs M turned a sharp right and walked down several steps to the kitchen. Before following her further, Sam glanced briefly through the open double doors to the left of the staircase and glimpsed a magnificent drawing room. High ceilings, ornate furniture, a crystal chandelier brilliantly capturing the light from the bay windows overlooking the garden.

'I don't know how you young things do it, really I don't, I hate air travel at the best of times, but all that way from Australia! Dear me!'

Sam obediently followed the voice and walked down the steps into a kitchen the size of a small ballroom. Mrs M had already deposited the suitcase by the massive wooden table in the centre of the room, and was busying herself at

the equally massive wooden bench which looked out the
side windows onto the driveway. Through the open door
to the left was a narrow staircase which Mrs M explained
led to the upstairs back rooms that had once been servants'
quarters. Pots and pans and utensils hung from wooden
pegs everywhere and, despite the size of the place, it was
warm and cosy.

'You'll want breakfast, I'm sure,' Mrs M said, 'you must
be starving.'

'No, thank you. I ate on the plane.'

'Oh rubbish, they don't serve enough to feed a sparrow
on aeroplanes, and you look like you could do with some
feeding up.'

Was the woman for real? Sam wondered. She seemed
like a caricature. Fat and hearty, an incessant smile, eyes
that crinkled in a jolly face, a gap between her two front
teeth, and the thickest Hampshire hog accent imaginable.
Sam was already practising, in her head, the oblique vowel
sounds, the cadences, the thickly sounded 'r's, but she was
sure if she used that accent on stage she'd be accused of
'going over the top'.

'Now you sit down, Samantha, and I'll cook you some
eggs.'

'No really, Mrs M.' Sam had an insane desire to laugh,
even the name seemed part of the caricature. 'I couldn't eat
a thing. And please call me Sam, I always think people are
cross with me if they call me Samantha,' she found herself
rattling on, 'my mum used to call me Samantha when she
was riled.'

*Riled*, how quaint, Martha Montgomery thought, but
the girl was Australian after all. And she looked so tired.
She must be lonely too, so far from home.

'Sam it is then,' she said. 'Here's your tea. Drink it up
and then we'll settle you in. You do look tired, dear. And
it's little wonder.'

Sam didn't want to laugh any more. She wanted to cry.

The woman's kindness made her suddenly aware that she was exhausted and lonely and very far from home. And Mrs M wasn't a caricature at all. Mrs M was warm and real and Sam wanted to hug her. She blinked away the quick, burning threat of tears and accepted the cup of tea. Flight fatigue, that's what it was, how embarrassing.

Poor little thing, Martha Montgomery thought. So young too. 'How old are you, dear?' she asked.

'Eighteen,' Sam replied, looking out the windows. Damn it, she told herself, don't burst into tears. She felt ridiculous. 'I'll be nineteen in February,' she added, as if that gave her extra status.

'So where do you come from, Sam? What part of Australia?' Mrs M brought the pot to the table and sat. She concentrated on the cup as she poured her own tea, knowing that the girl was fighting hard not to cry.

'Perth,' Sam said.

'Perth?' Mrs M looked up, bewildered.

'Perth, Western Australia.'

'Ah, of course.' Mrs M gave a hearty laugh. 'I thought for a minute you meant Perth, Scotland. Silly me.'

'I live in Sydney now, though. That's where they shoot "Families and Friends".'

Sam quickly recovered from her bout of self-pity and they spent a pleasant twenty minutes chatting. It appeared that Mrs M didn't watch 'Families and Friends'.

'I don't really watch much telly at all,' she said apologetically. 'I prefer a good book myself, but I believe it's a very popular show.'

Sam was rather thankful. She'd been overwhelmed by the reception she'd received from British travellers during the flight, and at Heathrow, when she'd arrived, she'd been instantly recognised, besieged for her autograph and inundated with questions about the series. Relieved to be able to talk of something other than 'Families and Friends', she asked about Chisolm House.

'It was built in the 1850s,' Mrs M said, clearly a full book on Chisolm House. 'A developer called Charles Osborn was responsible for most of the Victorian townhouses along this road. He was in it for the money of course, but he certainly had an eye for architecture; they're in different styles and quite lovely, each and every one. The Chisolms bought the place in 1918. They had only one daughter and Chisolm House was left to her. Would you like another cup?' she asked.

'Yes please.'

'Old Miss Chisolm had a stroke three years ago,' Mrs M went on to explain as she poured the tea from the pot with its hand-knitted cosy. 'She'd lived here alone for ages – well, apart from me and the maid and the gardener, that is. She has no family left to speak of, just some distant relatives who can't wait to get their hands on the house. Poor dear, a tragic life.'

Martha Montgomery had been Phoebe Chisolm's housekeeper and cook for five years before the old woman's stroke, and had been retained as manager when the place had been converted to bed and breakfast accommodation.

'I often think she'd like to see young people enjoying the house,' Mrs M said. 'She's in a nursing home in Southampton now and I visit her regularly. She always knows me and we sit outside and chat over a cup of tea. She seems comfortable and healthy enough, but she's not altogether "with it", poor thing, her mind wanders a lot.'

When they'd finished their tea Mrs M stood and picked up the suitcase. 'We'd best get you settled in now, you'll be wanting to unpack.'

'Please let me take that.'

'All right, dear.' Mrs M relinquished her hold on the suitcase and set off for the door at the rear of the kitchen, talking all the while. 'I'm putting you into the self-contained flat,' she said, 'you'll be more comfy there. We've had actors here for the past two pantos at Ferneham

Hall and they always want the flat. It's probably best for all really, it means they don't disrupt the household when they come home late.'

She led the way through a laundry and then a small enclosed back porch where mackintoshes hung on pegs and Wellington boots and sandshoes were lined up on the floor. 'The gardener keeps his things here,' she explained, 'and I have a maid come in daily to service the rooms and do the laundry.'

Then they were out the back door in a pebbled court-yard surrounded by trellises of climbing roses with an arch in the centre. It was very attractive, Sam thought.

Mrs M still didn't draw breath as she continued through the arch. 'The flat has all the mod cons, if you want to look after yourself, dear,' she said, 'but you're more than welcome to join the other guests for breakfast in the dining room. Not that we have many guests at the moment and they tend to keep rather much to themselves, so I don't think you'll find yourself bothered.' She finally came to a halt and Sam plonked the suitcase down gratefully.

They were standing in the gravelled rear of the property. To the right, the side driveway culminated in twin garages and, directly ahead, several cars sat in marked parking bays. To the left was a quaint two-storey building of sandstone with a slate-tiled roof and multi-paned glass windows. It stood like a proud baby sister to the big grand house, boasting its own impressive and predominant feature – a huge central arch with two heavy wooden doors.

'It used to be the stables,' Mrs M announced. 'The Chisolms had it converted in the forties.' She crossed to the small door at the left side of the building and unlocked it. 'The big doors are only for show,' she explained to Sam, who'd picked up the suitcase and followed her, 'they're bricked up on the inside. Miss Chisolm told me that she wouldn't let her father get rid of them, she'd loved playing in the old stables as a girl. Come along in, dear.'

Sam hefted the suitcase inside and looked about at the open-plan living space with its sandstone walls and heavy timber beams.

'This was the tack room,' Mrs M indicated the kitchen, separated by an island bench, 'and over here,' she crossed to the dining and lounge room area, 'this was the actual stables, four of them, I believe, although the Chisolms themselves never kept horses. Come and I'll show you upstairs.'

They filed up the steep wooden steps and emerged onto a small landing. 'Up here was the loft,' Mrs M said. Light flooded through the large windows with their small glass panes, and a bedroom and study looked out over the courtyard. At the rear of the upper floor were a large store-room and a small bathroom. 'No bath, I'm afraid, only a shower, but when you feel the need for a good soak in a hot tub, you just come up to the house.'

There were oil heaters throughout the flat and, down-stairs, Mrs M showed Sam how to operate the central system. 'It's very cosy in winter,' she assured her, 'and I've laid in a few things for you.' She proceeded to open various cupboards stacked with coffee and tea, cereal packets and tinned fruit. 'I think you'll find yourself quite comfortable.'

'I know that I will. Thank you so much, Mrs M.' Over-whelmed by the woman's thoughtfulness, Sam felt herself once again perilously close to tears.

Mrs M sensed it. 'Well, I'll leave you alone to have a bit of a snooze,' she said patting Sam's arm. 'Here are the keys.' She put them on the island bench. 'One's to the front door of the house, although it's always unlocked during the day, and the other's to the flat. Now you put yourself to bed, there's a good girl.'

When she'd gone, Sam sat in an armchair and cried. Flight fatigue or self-pity or whatever, she decided to allow herself a momentary wallow. It was strange to be sitting all alone in converted stables in an English mid-winter when, under normal circumstances, she would probably be with the gang sunning herself at Bondi Beach.

Feeling much better after her cry, she blew her nose and looked about. God almighty, how lucky could she get? She loved the stables, she loved Chisolm House, and she loved Mrs M. She'd be happy in Fareham, she knew it and, fighting off the fatigue, she decided to go for a long walk.

Rugged up against the cold, she turned left into Osborn Road and walked up the street to where Pete Harris had pointed out the theatre on the opposite side. There it was. Ferneham Hall, a squat, redbrick building surrounded by a sea of concrete parking space. Towering to its left was the stark white square of the Civic Centre, to its right a multi-storey car park and behind, according to Pete, was a huge shopping complex. Seventies architecture and modern convenience sat unattractively in the heart of the pretty little market town.

Sam decided not to explore the theatre; Pete's hasty departure and his 'see you in two days' hadn't been particularly welcoming. Besides, she was now rather enjoying being on her own. She walked up the road to the parish church of St Peter and St Paul and wandered about its many paths, examining the old tombstones and startling two grey squirrels that scampered up a yew tree. Then down the broad residential boulevard of High Street, with its splendid Georgian houses, and a right turn into West Street, the hub of the town. It was market day and the pedestrian mall of West Street was a colourful hive of activity, barrows and stalls offering every conceivable item of produce and hardware. Spruikers were pitching their wares and the conflicting aromas of roasted chestnuts, fried onions and hot doughnuts assailed the senses.

Sam walked and walked until, two hours later, having circled the entire town, she returned to Chisolm House happily exhausted. She'd explored the dockyards and parkland beside the Quay, Fareham's small, thriving port, and she'd walked to the railway station at the far end of West Street. She'd covered the breadth of the town in order to get 'the lay of the land', having decided that tomorrow she would investigate the shopping complex and buy supplies for the flat. At least that had been her initial plan, until the railway station had inspired an alternative which left her breathless with anticipation. Trains left for London on an hourly basis, she'd discovered. She could see a show in the West End.

She was now in a quandary, though. The fine print in her contract said actors were not permitted to travel more than twenty miles from the venue during the run of the season. But she hadn't started work yet, had she? Sam knew that it wasn't the contract's fine print she found daunting, it was the prospect of landing on her own in the middle of London. She'd have to stay the night if she went to the theatre. Did she dare? Yes, she bloody well did, she thought as she unlocked the door to the stables.

She slept like a baby that night, images of yesteryear flickering through her mind. Fareham had enthralled her. 'A town with a history reaching beyond mediaeval times', the brochure she'd collected from the local museum had stated. But it had an innocence which Sydney lacked, Sam thought as she drifted off in her loft bed above the stables.

The following morning, she considered it common courtesy to mention her plans to Mrs M – she didn't want the poor woman worrying about her overnight disappearance – so she dropped into the kitchen via the back door.

'I thought I might catch the train up to London,' she said casually, 'and go to a West End show.'

'Oh that'll be nice, dear.' Mrs M smiled. 'Would you like some breakfast before you leave?'

So it was that simple, Sam thought, people obviously

popped up to London all the time, it was no big deal. 'No thanks, Mrs M, I've had some fruit and cereal.'

An hour later, Sam set off, her heart thumping, her toothbrush and a spare set of undies in her shoulder bag.

When she finally emerged from the tube station to stand in Piccadilly Circus she had never felt such excitement. It was a bleak winter's day, mid-afternoon, and it had taken her hours to get there. She'd had to change trains twice – 'You should have caught the express,' a porter pointed out well after the event – and she'd got lost in the underground. But she'd made it. Here she was, in the very heart of London. She stood on the steps in the centre of Piccadilly Circus, beside Eros's column, and drank in the chaos of double-decker buses and taxis and tourists. Then she reminded herself that accommodation was the prime concern, it would be dusk soon, so she asked a newspaper vendor where the nearest cheap pub was.

'Cheap pub?' The little Cockney man looked confused.

'Or a bed and breakfast, somewhere to stay.'

'You an Aussie, love?'

'Yes.'

'Thought so. "Pub" don' mean the same thing over 'ere. You want the Regent Palace 'otel.' He pointed across the busy roundabout. 'Over there.'

'Thanks very much.'

She booked herself into a poky little room on the fourth floor, 'bathroom down the hall', and then sought out the concierge for advice. He was a theatre buff and extraordinarily helpful.

'The new Tom Stoppard at the Haymarket,' he said, '*Arcadia*. Wonderful play, but then all of his are. I could book a ticket for you, if you like, but it'll be cheaper if you go to the box office.'

She did. And that was the night that changed her life. After the performance, she stood in the chilling wind that swept up the Haymarket and stared at the stately columns of the Theatre Royal, heedless of the crowds brushing past her. One day I'll work here, she told herself. She didn't really believe it for one minute, but it was something to aspire to.

The season of *Cinderella* at Ferneham Hall, Fareham, proved to be the hardest work Sam had ever experienced. Ten days' rehearsal, then two performances daily, seven days a week for five weeks. There were just two days off in the entire run. Christmas Day and New Year's Day.

She surprised them all from the outset. 'Crikey,' Pete Harris openly commented, 'an Aussie soap star who can sing and dance, you're a godsend, Sam.'

She herself was surprised by his reaction. 'What would have happened if I couldn't?' she asked.

'We'd have changed all the choreography and had you miming the songs. Oh believe me, love, we've done it before.'

Pete became her greatest ally and Sam found that she liked him. He was intimidating, certainly, as he barked his orders and people leapt to obey. And, amidst the bedlam of rehearsals, he would accept no excuses. 'Don't give me that bullshit,' he'd say when the costumes didn't arrive on time or there was trouble with the set, 'just fix it.' His authority was essential, however, with so much to accomplish in only ten days, and Sam very much admired his professionalism.

Sam was 'top of the bill', her photo blazoned above the title on posters all over town. 'Samantha Lindsay from "Families and Friends"' it said, which embarrassed her because the rest of the company, both dancers and actors, were all seasoned performers.

'We're not telly stars, sweetheart,' Garry and Vic, the stand-up comics playing the ugly sisters, explained, 'you're the bums-on-seats.' There was no malice intended, they were just stating the case. Like Pete, Garry and Vic were only too delighted that Sam lacked pretension and was a talented 'pro'. Sam didn't dare admit to any of them that she had never before worked in the theatre.

They were a comradely crowd and, despite the gruelling schedule, or perhaps because of it, they dined together between shows and partied regularly. Usually on a Friday and Saturday night, and usually at the Red Lion in West Street. It was one of the most popular of Fareham's many drinking houses, atmospheric and noisy, and Sam loved it. Just as she loved each and every performance at Ferneham Hall. The theatre became her home and the company her family; she had little time to be lonely.

And then Christmas Day approached. It would be the first Christmas she'd ever spent away from her family; she'd returned to Perth the previous year during the 'Families and Friends' production break. Even Sydney would have felt odd on Christmas Day, she thought, and now here she was on the other side of the world. She hoped she wasn't going to get maudlin, but she wondered how she'd fill in the day. It would be strange not dashing across the street to the theatre and working and playing with the gang.

'So what are you doing Christmas Day, Sam?' Flora asked as they applied their makeup for the evening show, the day before Christmas Eve.

Flora Robbie played the fairy godmother. Twenty years previously she'd co-hosted a top-rating television game show and these days earned a living, more or less, singing Scottish ballads and being fairy godmothers in pantos all over England. She was very popular with the older theatre-goers, all of whom vividly remembered 'In for a Penny' on ITV. She was a nice woman, still pretty in her mid-forties with an attractive Highlands accent, and she and Sam shared a dressing room most compatibly.

'I'm having lunch with some friends,' Sam lied. She wasn't sure why, but she didn't want people's sympathy.

'Oh really? Where?' Flora wasn't being nosy. She'd felt sorry for the girl so far from her family at Christmas.

'Somewhere in Brighton,' Sam said vaguely, then hastily added, 'they're coming to pick me up,' in case Flora asked how she was getting there. Sam had actually contemplated catching a train to Brighton until she'd discovered that no services operated out of Fareham on Christmas Day.

'Oh that's grand. I didn't know you had friends in Brighton.'

'Well, they're friends of the family really, I don't know them that well.'

'You'll have a lovely time,' Flora said, pleased, and relieved that Sam was being looked after. 'Brighton's frightfully chic these days.'

'So I believe.'

'I was going to ask you out with Dougie and me and the kids.'

'That's really sweet of you, Flora,' Sam said, glad that she'd lied, 'but I'm on a promise.' The woman hadn't seen her husband and two sons, who'd just arrived from Scotland, for over three weeks. The last thing they'd need would be the little Aussie tagging along.

On Christmas Eve there was a morning and afternoon matinee but no night performance, and the other members of the gang had planned to return to their various homes for the break. Mostly to London, although Vic and Garry were heading all the way to Manchester.

'Don't suppose you fancy a drive do you, sweetheart?' Garry asked. 'You're more than welcome to join us.'

'No thanks, Garry, I'm meeting up with friends in Brighton.' The lie came out glibly now, and she was thankful she'd thought of it.

'Good-oh.'

Following the afternoon matinee, everyone was in a hurry to leave and Sam took her time in the dressing room.

'Enjoy Brighton, happy Christmas.' Flora gave her a hug before tearing off to join her waiting husband and children, and Sam listened to the others yelling 'happy Christmas' to each other as they departed.

When she thought the coast was clear, she donned her coat and scarf and left, only to discover Pete waiting outside the stage door in the freezing cold.

'Pete!' She was surprised. 'I thought you'd gone to London.' She knew he'd been staying at his sister's house in nearby Portchester during the run, but Flora had said that he and his wife lived in London. Sam had presumed he'd gone home for Christmas.

'Not this year,' he said, and there was something in the weary way he said it which didn't invite a query as to why. 'Susan asked me to invite you over for Christmas dinner.' Sam had met Pete's sister and her young family, they'd come to the first matinee of the season. 'I could pick you up, if you like.'

'Oh that's very sweet of her.' Samantha parroted her standard reply and followed up with the lie. 'But I'm going to Brighton with some friends of mine.'

He looked at her closely for a second or so, then said, not harshly and with the shadow of a smile, 'Don't give me that bullshit, Sam.' She was nonplussed. 'I heard you saying that to Garry and I didn't believe it for a minute. I take it you're planning to wallow in loneliness this Christmas.' Despite the touch of cynicism, she had the feeling he wasn't being unkind, so she opted for honesty.

'Yep,' she admitted, 'something like that.'

'Not an unwise decision,' he said. 'Other people's Christmases are pretty trying, and Susan's'll be the full family catastrophe. I'm not looking forward to it myself. So I'll tell her you're going to Brighton, shall I?'

She laughed. 'Thanks, Pete.'

He kissed her on the cheek. 'Happy Christmas, Sam.'

'You too.' He looked rather unhappy, she thought, as he wandered off to his car. She wondered why he wasn't spending Christmas with his wife.

As she walked down the driveway of Chisolm House there was a tapping at the kitchen windows and she could see Mrs M waving at her to come inside. Only seconds later the front door opened.

'Do you have a moment, dear?' Then without waiting for an answer Mrs M bustled her inside. 'I have a little something for you, come along out of the cold.' She led the way into the front drawing room which Sam had glimpsed on the day she'd arrived.

'What a fantastic room.' The crystal chandelier was reflected in each of the four gold-leaf framed mirrors that adorned the walls, and on either side of the mirrors, in ornate wall brackets, were gas lamps, now converted to electricity. A handsome Edwardian escritoire stood in one corner, a table and a set of Chippendale chairs sat in pride of place at the bay windows, and armchairs and sofas were gathered around the open fireplace with its carved wooden mantelpiece.

'Yes it is, isn't it. It was Miss Chisolm's favourite, she spent most of her time here in her last few years.' Martha Montgomery watched as Sam wandered over to the bay windows to look out at the garden. 'She'd sit right there in her armchair for hours. She loved the garden, particularly in autumn. Or when it snowed. She always said the garden reflected life, with its change of seasons.'

As Sam turned back she noticed the portrait hanging over the wooden mantelpiece. 'Is this her?' she asked.

'Yes,' Mrs M said, 'that's Phoebe Chisolm, she was twenty when it was painted. Lovely looking thing, wasn't she?'

Sam crossed to the painting and gazed into eyes which, for one startling moment, she could swear were alive. Phoebe Chisolm was more than lovely, she radiated life. The artist had captured her as if she'd just turned her head, her thick auburn hair bounced with movement, the tendons of her slim white neck were visible, but it was the eyes which captured Sam's attention. They sparkled with humour and yet they held a challenge, perhaps even a touch of rebellion. Phoebe Chisolm had obviously been a feisty young woman. 'It's a magnificent painting,' she said.

'Yes, he was a local lad who went on to become quite a famous portrait artist. James Hampton, I don't know if you've heard of him.' Sam hadn't. 'There are several of his paintings at the Tate Gallery, I'm told.'

'Is this the family?' On the mantelpiece was a framed photograph of a handsome young couple in a formal pose. The man was standing, a proprietorial hand resting upon the shoulder of his wife who was seated in a hard-backed chair. The wife was very beautiful, with dark hair, and she was holding a baby dressed in a christening gown.

'Yes, that's Arthur Chisolm, he was a doctor, and his wife Alice, and of course that's Phoebe as a baby. Miss Chisolm wanted to leave the painting and the photograph here where they belonged, and I keep them on display to give guests a sense of the history of the house, which I think is only right. I serve afternoon tea here for those who wish it and at night it serves as a television room.'

Sam noticed, for the first time, the large television set, complete with video and sound system, which seemed so out of place in its surrounds, even tucked tastefully as it was in the far corner of the room.

'You said she had a tragic life.' Sam's eyes were drawn back to the portrait. 'In what way?' She hoped Mrs M wouldn't be offended, but she felt a need to know what had happened to Phoebe Chisolm.

Far from being offended, Martha Montgomery was delighted by Sam's interest. Both Chisolm House and her former mistress were subjects very dear to her heart.

'She married in 1945.' Having constantly referred to Phoebe Chisolm in her single status, Mrs M was aware of Sam's surprise. 'Yes, an American naval officer she met right here in the borough. Fareham's always had a strong navy history, but in the weeks before D-Day there were hundreds of American servicemen stationed around these parts. After the war he took her back to America and they lived in New York. They had a daughter, but tragically she died of leukemia, the poor little thing. Just fifteen years old, she'd been fighting the disease for two years. Phoebe Chisolm was never the same after that, I believe she had a nervous breakdown of some sort. Anyway, the marriage broke up and she came back to Fareham. She resumed her maiden name and continued to live in Chisolm House after the death of her parents. She never married again.'

Throughout Mrs M's story, Sam had stared at the portrait, she couldn't seem to tear her eyes from Phoebe's. They held such life, such promise. 'How sad,' she said. 'How terribly sad.'

'Oh my goodness,' Mrs M broke the moment. 'I completely forgot why I'd asked you in.' She picked up a small gift-wrapped package from the coffee table beside the sofa. 'A little Christmas gift,' she said as she handed it to Sam.

'Oh Mrs M, you shouldn't have.' Sam was flustered and, even as she uttered the banality, embarrassed. Having decided to ignore Christmas herself, the formality of gift giving hadn't occurred to her. She should have at least bought the woman a card. 'Really, you shouldn't.'

'It's nothing, dear, just a little memento of Fareham.'

Sam unwrapped a small cardboard box, inside which was a silver statuette of a horse in mid-trot, its front hoof delicately raised. 'How lovely,' she said, balancing the miniature in the palm of her hand.

'It's a Frogmorton,' Mrs M said. 'They're local silversmiths who've been here for generations. They have a fine store and gallery at Brighton and the tourists buy a lot of their souvenir spoons, but I thought, seeing you're living in the stables, the little horse was a more fitting memento of your stay.'

'It is. It's perfect. Thank you.' Sam hugged the woman.

'Happy Christmas, dear.' Mrs M returned the hug warmly, then got down to business. 'Now tell me, what are you doing tomorrow? Do you have plans?' Sam hesitated for a moment, she didn't want to lie to Mrs M. 'I thought not. Why don't you come to Portsmouth with me? I'm staying overnight with my daughter and her family, you'd get on famously, I'm sure.'

Sam decided to be not only firm in her refusal, but truthful. 'That's very kind of you, Mrs M,' she said, 'but I'd really rather be on my own.'

Martha Montgomery nodded, she'd suspected as much. There was an independent streak in young Samantha Lindsay.

'I'm going to go for a very long walk,' Sam continued, 'and I'm going to loll around and read a book. Believe me, that's a luxury after two shows a day. I'm looking forward to it, really I am,' she insisted, hoping Mrs M wouldn't press the point.

'I suggest Titchfield.' The girl would probably feel more lonely sharing another family's Christmas anyway, Martha Montgomery thought. 'For your walk,' she added when Sam looked mystified. 'It's a dear little village, right in the centre of the old strawberry farm district, about four miles out of town. You just continue on the road past the railway station.'

'Titchfield it is.' Sam was grateful for the woman's understanding.

'And you must use the house, it'll be completely deserted over Christmas. Come with me.' Sam found herself once again following the ample rear of Mrs M and the sound of her voice. 'The four guests we had have all gone,' she was saying as they walked up the main staircase, 'and there's no-one else booked in until the day after Boxing Day. You'll have the whole place to yourself.'

They crossed through the upstairs drawing room, equal in splendour to its counterpart below. Mrs M was barging on ahead, but Sam peered briefly through the bay windows. She could see the multi-storey car park and Ferneham Hall and the civic offices a little further up the street. It was a pity, she thought, picturing the view as it might once have been. Fields and meadowland, perhaps even crops, since Fareham was a market town.

*Ten-year-old Jane Miller clutched her threadbare coat about her as she took the shortcut past the old gravel pit that had once been meadowland on her way to Osborn Road and Chisolm House. Her woollen hat was pulled firmly down over her blonde curls, keeping her ears snug and warm against the bitter cold of the December morning. It was a Sunday and she and her best friend Phoebe were going to build a snowman.*

Sam's attention was dragged back to the room. 'For guests with musical inclinations,' Mrs M was saying as she indicated the old upright piano in the corner. 'I keep it tuned. We've had a number of good old singalongs up here, I can tell you.'

After bypassing several other bedrooms on the upper front floor, Mrs M led her to the master bedroom with its large en suite bathroom where Sam could have a 'good old soak'.

'Treat the house as your own, dear,' she said. 'You'll be nice and cosy, the central heating switches off at midnight but it comes on automatically at six in the morning.'

Sam looked longingly at the huge bathtub. 'I'll take you up on that, Mrs M,' she said.

It was the first thing she thought of when she awoke the following morning. A long, hot bath, she couldn't wait. Then she looked out of the stable loft windows and gasped. The world was white. The gravel car park, the trellises, the pebbled courtyard beyond, all was blanketed in snow. A white Christmas. She laughed out loud. The gang at the theatre had promised her her first white Christmas.

They'd told her that the weather reports had said it would
snow during the night, but she hadn't believed them.
There'd been heavy frosts each morning but it hadn't
snowed once since she'd been in Fareham. Why should it
choose to do so on Christmas Eve? But it had.

Apart from the crunch of her footsteps, all was silence
as Sam trudged through the whiteness to the front door of
Chisolm House. She'd never seen snow, and she felt a sense
of wonderment.

She went into the front drawing room and sat at the table
by the bay windows. No wonder Phoebe Chisolm had loved
the garden when it snowed, she thought. The trees, the
lawn, the fountain, all cloaked in white, it was magical.

*A snowball caught Jane fair in the face. She squealed.
Her own missile had missed its mark as Phoebe ducked
and weaved about the garden. Both girls dropped to their
knees, hastily balling together more snow in their gloved
hands, and the fight was on. They assiduously avoided
hitting the snowman, however; they were very proud of
their snowman. Jane always maintained it was a cheat
building it over the fountain, but Phoebe said if it meant
they had the best snowman in town, who cared?*

Upstairs, as Sam soaked in the hot bath, she wondered
at the fact that she didn't feel intrusive. Under normal circumstances she would. She'd feel uncomfortable lying in
someone else's bathtub in someone else's house. But it was
as if the house wanted her there. She felt at home. She put
it down to the snow. It had snowed just to give her her first
white Christmas, she decided. So that she wouldn't feel
lonely. And she didn't. The snow and the house made her
feel very special.

Hands shoved deep in the pockets of her anorak, collar
up, scarf wrapped firmly around her neck, Sam set off on
her hike to Titchfield. She wasn't even halfway there before
she took off the coat and scarf, no longer aware of the cold.
A wintry sun was already turning the snow to sludge.

Titchfield was as picturesque as Mrs M had promised and, from the moment she crossed the stream and walked up East Street, Sam felt she'd stepped into the past. Then East Street wound to the left and broadened into High Street and she found herself in the centre of the village, surrounded by Georgian brick houses converted into shops and cafes. She walked down to the end of the broad thoroughfare, to where, like the spokes of a wheel, narrow roads, each lined with little cottages, led away from the village to the farms and surrounding countryside. With the exception of the cars gathered around the Queen's Head pub where a raucous Christmas party ensued, she could have been standing in another time.

*The sturdy white pony plodded across the little bridge that forded the stream, unbothered by the three small girls perched upon his back. Surefooted and confident, he turned off East Street into the lane which led through the church graveyard. He needed no guidance. Beyond the graveyard was the paddock that was his home.*

*Maude Cookson was pleased that Jane and Phoebe liked to ride her pony. Jane was the smartest girl in their class at school and Phoebe's dad was Dr Chisolm, one of the most important people in the whole borough. Jane Miller and Phoebe Chisolm were good friends to have. Particularly Phoebe. Maude so wanted Phoebe to be her friend. There was one thing, however, which Maude found bewildering.*

*'You should have your own pony, Phoebe,' she'd said on a number of occasions. 'You've got stables where you live, and they're not even used.' Maude's father was a strawberry farmer and they had plenty of space to build stables, but they didn't have the money.*

*'Daddy won't let me.' Phoebe's sigh was always one of utter exasperation. She'd pleaded often enough, but she hadn't been able to win her father around as she usually did.*

*So the walk into Titchfield to ride Maude Cookson's
pony had become a regular event for Phoebe and Jane.*

It was four o'clock in the afternoon, the air still and
freezing with the promise of more snow, when Sam arrived
back at Chisolm House to discover Pete, huddled in his
greatcoat, sitting on the steps to the front door.

'G'day, Sam,' he said. It was a running gag between
them, he was always sending her up about being Australian. 'Crikey, you look a mess.'

She knew it. Her hair was glued to her head and,
although her hands were numb from the cold, her body
was sweating with exertion. She was tired but exhilarated.

'What do you expect?' she asked. 'I've just walked ten
miles. What on earth are you doing here?'

'Waiting for you. Here.' He delved into the pockets of
his greatcoat and produced two tinfoil wrapped packages.
'A touch of Christmas,' he said holding them out to her,
one in each hand. 'One's turkey and one's plum pudding,
I've forgotten which is which.'

'Oh Pete,' she laughed. 'It's very kind of you, but it's not
necessary. I'm having the best day, I'm not lonely, you
don't need to worry about me.'

'I'm not. I'm just pretending to.' She looked under-
standably confused. 'I had to get out of that house,' he
explained. 'You were my excuse. Can't we go inside? It's
freezing out here.'

'Of course, I'm sorry. Come and I'll make us some
coffee.' As they walked down the drive to the stables, she
wasn't sure whether she was glad to see him or not. He'd
broken the mood, she'd been enjoying her solitude. But he
looked so forlorn, she had the feeling it was he who
needed comforting.

It was warm in the stables' lounge room, she'd left the
heating on, and she dried her hair with a towel as she
waited for the coffee to brew. He sat in an armchair and
watched her as she chatted away about Titchfield.

'Yes,' he said, 'it's a very pretty village.' Did she know how beautiful she was? he wondered as she dumped the towel on the bench and set out the coffee mugs, not bothering to comb the tousled wet hair that still clung to her cheeks. It was intriguing to meet a woman so unself-conscious, such a change from Melaney. But then Sam was only eighteen; perhaps Melaney had been like that once. Highly doubtful, he thought wryly. Melaney had always been aware of her beauty and the impact it had on others. It had been one of the things he'd loved about her, he had to admit. He'd felt proud of her for it.

'There you go.' She placed two steaming mugs on the coffee table between them and sat in the armchair opposite. 'Do you want anything to eat?' she asked.

'After Susan's Christmas dinner? You're joking.'

'Well, I'm bloody starving, do you mind?' She jumped up from the armchair and started unwrapping the tinfoil packages which sat on the bench.

'They're probably not hot any more,' he said.

'Who cares, it'll be better than the chicken in the fridge. You sure you don't want some?' She brought the open tinfoil packages to the coffee table and squatted in the armchair, legs folded beneath her.

He shook his head. 'So it was going to be cold chicken for Christmas dinner, was it?'

'Yep,' she nodded with her mouth full of turkey.'Chook, that's what we call it back home, and a bottle of champagne. God this is good. And you're wrong, it's still warm.' She shovelled another lump of breast meat into her mouth. 'What's the matter, Pete, why are you down?'

It was a confronting question. He hadn't realised he'd been so readable, and he certainly hadn't intended to bring his problems to Sam, he'd simply wanted to get out of the house with its cacophony of children's chatter and Christmas bonhomie. But he admired her directness.

'Melaney and I have split up,' he said. 'Melaney's my wife.'

Well, that was pretty obvious, Sam thought. In fact everything was obvious, the man looked so sad. 'Do you still love her?'

'Yes.' His response was instinctive and his answer genuine, but he didn't like her asking the question he'd so often asked himself of late.

'Do you want to talk about it?'

'No.' Her directness was becoming intrusive. He rose from the armchair. 'I'm sorry, Sam,' he said stiffly, 'I didn't mean to intrude on your Christmas.'

'Well, you have, so why don't you stay?' She realised that she'd overstepped the mark but she didn't want him to go, she no longer wanted to be alone. 'Let's open the champagne.' She crossed to the refrigerator. 'I promise I won't ask any more questions.' She got out the bottle and started struggling with the foil. 'It's not the good stuff, but it's got bubbles.'

He realised he'd overreacted. Good God, he was often criticised for his own directness, why should he blame the girl for hers? He took the bottle from her and opened it. 'Why not? I can hardly leave you on your own to wallow in loneliness, can I?' He smiled. He was very good-looking when he smiled, she thought, wondering why she hadn't noticed before. 'Not that you seem to be doing much wallowing. In fact you're positively glowing.'

'Yes I am, aren't I?' She grinned disarmingly. 'It's my first white Christmas. I'm having the best time.'

It seemed a catch-phrase of hers, and he wondered whether it was defensive. Perhaps she didn't want him to know how vulnerable she was. But it certainly sounded healthy. He'd love to be able to say 'I'm having the best time'.

'That's good.' He offered her the glass and they sat once again in the armchairs. 'And you're enjoying the show too,' he said, getting things back on a professional keel, very much aware of his own vulnerability and Sam's attractiveness and the fact that they were alone in the stables. 'That's pretty obvious.'

'Oh I do, I love it, Pete,' she said excitedly. 'And I'm learning such a lot!'

He was surprised. It didn't seem to him that Samantha Lindsay had much to learn. She could sing and dance with the best of them and she was a natural actor. 'What are your plans, Sam? After the panto. Do you go back to the soap?'

'Nope. I'm going to concentrate on the theatre, I've decided. That's if they'll have me of course, there's always a bit of a stigma attached to soap actresses, and it's tough breaking into the Australian theatre with no formal training.'

She could see he was surprised by the fact that she was untrained. She wondered what he'd say if she told him she'd never worked in the theatre before. She decided to maintain her silence on that score.

'Why don't you stay in England?' he asked. Sam was taken aback, the thought hadn't occurred to her. 'I could put you in touch with a good agent,' he said. 'Melaney's with Reginald Harcourt, he's excellent. One of the smaller exclusive agencies, personal management really.'

'Why would he be interested in me?'

Pete wasn't sure that he would be, and he didn't want to raise the girl's hopes. She'd need more than talent in this cutthroat industry. More than guts too. You had to be hungry to make it. He wondered if she was aware of that.

'You'd have an outside chance,' he said cautiously. 'In his own quiet way Reginald's a bit of a megalomaniac, he likes to create new success stories. And he's a nice chap, I'm sure you'd get on.' He wondered whether in actual fact they would. Reginald was a private man and he might find Sam's forthright qualities a bit much. 'Mind you, he takes some getting to know.'

Pete realised that he was chatting in order to distract

himself, both from her proximity and her attention. She
was leaning forward on the very edge of her armchair, her
face close to his and, champagne glass forgotten in
her hand, her full focus was directed at him. He found it
most disconcerting. His overwhelming desire to kiss her
shocked him. 'You'd have to take it easy to start with. He's
a bit of an enigma, Reginald, no-one even knows whether
he's gay or not, he keeps very much to himself.'

Sam was experiencing her own sense of shock, having
realised, all of a sudden, that Pete was attracted to her. She
was accustomed to men finding her attractive but she was
rarely attracted in return. Pete's desire didn't come as a
shock, but her reciprocation did. What she'd taken to be
admiration for Pete Harris had undergone a swift change
and she realised that she found him extraordinarily attractive. She wondered what it would be like to kiss him.

'So your wife's an actress?' she asked, her eyes straying
to his mouth.

'Yes,' he drained his glass and rose to get the bottle. Did
the girl know what she was doing? The way she was
looking at him, was it open seduction, or was it just his
wishful thinking? 'A very good one too.' He poured
his own glass. 'You haven't drunk yours,' he said.

'Oh. Sorry.' She drained her glass in three healthy gulps
and held it out to him for a refill.

'I'm not sure if I could get him to come to Fareham.'

'Who?'

'Reginald Harcourt.' Pete sat, putting the bottle on the
coffee table between them. 'He doesn't usually cover
pantos. But I'm sure I could arrange an appointment for
you in London.'

'Is that how you met your wife? In the theatre?'

'Yes.' She was looking at him that way again. 'On tour,'
he said, taking a sip from his glass and staring out the
window, again by way of distraction. 'She thought it was
just one of those flings you have when you're on the road,

but it wasn't. I avoid that sort of thing.' A total lie, he thought. He'd had affairs during every production he'd managed. Until he'd met Melaney three years ago and, as a result, their marriage had been based on mistrust. 'Why can't you stay in London?' she'd insisted. 'You'd get work freelancing.' 'Because I have a career with Vermont Productions,' he'd told her. 'They pay me good money, I'm their top company manager, there's talk of a partnership.' Good God, he'd thought, didn't the woman realise that if they were going to plan a family, as they'd discussed, they needed a reliable bloody income? And then he'd come home to find she'd had an affair of her own.

He looked at the girl. She was desirable certainly, but he'd resisted temptation on numerous occasions since he'd met Melaney. Was that why he so wanted Sam now? To get back at his wife?

'I'd better go.' He stood abruptly.

'Yes.' She also rose, and a silence that spoke multitudes rested uneasily between them. 'Thanks for Christmas dinner,' she said finally.

'Sorry there's no brandy butter to go with the pudding.'

'I'll manage.'

'Susan wanted to put some in a jar but I got sick of waiting around while she tried to find the right sized one.'

'Happy Christmas, Pete.' She put her hands on his chest as she kissed him on the cheek. It wasn't a conscious act of seduction, she only knew that she wanted to touch him, but it was all that was necessary. Suddenly they were kissing, deeply and longingly.

*His arms were around her, feeling the supple young body against his, her hands on the back of his neck, then her fingers, first tracing the outlines of his cheekbones, then running through his hair, her breathing becoming more feverish. He'd fantasised about such a moment for days, but he'd never thought it possible. It was madness.*

*Sunlight streamed through the huge open stable doors, at any moment someone might pass by. But he didn't care.*

Sam's sense of abandon was so sudden it shocked her. She'd felt a similar passion before, six months previously, after a party at the channel when one of the show's directors had driven her home. She'd never been attracted to the young male members of the cast, although she'd received overtures on many an occasion, but the director was in his early thirties and, to Sam, charismatic. She obviously fancied older men, she'd decided, and it was high time she lost her virginity. She'd been embarrassed at still being a virgin, unable to admit the fact to her friends. Whether it was her middle-class Perth upbringing or not, this was the nineties and she was eighteen years old. So she'd been not only willing to succumb to the passion she'd felt in the embrace of the director, she'd welcomed it. But the experience had proved unpleasant. It hurt, it was over before she knew it, and the director, who'd obviously been taken aback to discover she was a virgin, couldn't wait to get out of her flat.

Now, as warmth enveloped her body and she felt her passion mounting, Sam hoped she was about to discover the secret.

*She desperately wanted him to make love to her. Right here in the stables on this summer's afternoon. She ground herself against him. Her mouth against his, her groin against his. She wanted to discover the secret, she needed to know. She could feel the sun hot on her back and a shred of commonsense took over. 'Let's go up to the loft,' she whispered.*

It was Pete who broke free. The girl was only eighteen, he told himself, and obviously inexperienced, perhaps even a virgin, he could sense it in her desperation. He'd be taking advantage of her. He had to get out. It was his wife he wanted, not this girl.

'I'm going, Sam.' He grabbed his coat from the back of

the armchair. 'I'm very sorry,' he said, turning back to her as he opened the door.

'I'm not.' She marvelled at her own bravado as she looked him directly in the eye.

'I'll see you at the theatre tomorrow,' he said.

As Sam lay in her bed in the loft that night, a soft snow falling outside, she felt hot and restless. Her hand wandered between her thighs and she brought herself to orgasm. It eased her frustration and helped her to sleep, but it wasn't like the real thing. It couldn't be. Surely it couldn't.

'G'day, Sam.'

Pete was the first person she bumped into when she arrived at the theatre for the two o'clock matinee the following day, and she was relieved to discover there was no tension between them.

'How was the plum pudding?' he asked. 'Susan's bound to want a report.'

'Tell her it was great. I had it for lunch today. Along with the cold chook,' she grinned.

'That's a terrible word.' He looked at his watch. 'It's the half,' he said. 'Where the hell are Garry and Vic?' He went off to announce the half-hour call through the tannoy system and Sam scampered upstairs to the dressing room where Flora, always early, was halfway through her makeup.

Garry and Vic arrived ten minutes before curtain up, the traffic had been a nightmare, they said, and Pete gave them the standard lecture about unprofessionalism and said if it wasn't Boxing Day they'd be fined out of their wages. But at the Red Lion after the show, it was camaraderie as usual and Garry and Vic had them all in stitches about their hideous Christmas in Manchester.

Flora Robbie, holding hands fondly with husband Dougie, asked about Brighton, a subject which Sam had assiduously avoided in the dressing room. 'Great,' she'd simply said, pretending she was running behind time with her makeup. 'Gosh, I'll never be ready in time.'

'Where do your friends live in Brighton?' Flora now asked, making polite conversation, as she always did.

'Oh,' Sam pretended she couldn't quite remember, 'somewhere on the front, um . . .'

'Arundel Terrace, didn't you say?' Pete prompted.

'Yes, that's right.' She smiled at him gratefully.

'Arundel Terrace, what a coincidence, a dear friend of mine lives there. Stephen Churchett. Actor-writer, very successful, I'm sure your friends would . . .'

But before Flora could continue the interrogation, Pete embarked on a hideous Christmas story to match Garry and Vic's, about monster children and the full family catastrophe. In his own dour way, he was every bit as funny as the stand-up comics and Sam watched him admiringly. She couldn't help herself; she was infatuated, and she knew it.

'What are you doing tonight?' she asked him six days later during the morning matinee. It was New Year's Eve and, with the following day off, the actors were once again going their separate ways after the two o'clock performance, mostly to London. She hoped he wouldn't think she was trying to seduce him. But then who was she kidding? She probably was. She told herself she simply wanted to spend some time in his company, away from the gang.

'Another monster family gathering at Susan's,' he said. 'How about you? Wallowing in loneliness?'

'Actually, no. There's a gathering at Chisolm House. Mrs M's putting on a bit of a party for the guests to see in the New Year. "A supper and a singalong", she called it.' Sam looked doubtful. 'I don't know what it'll be like, but she said I could invite any members of the company who were staying in town and I thought . . .'

'Love to. You've saved my life.'

Mrs M's daughter, Betty, and her family had come up from Portsmouth and were staying the night. The three young children were raucous and Sam cast an apologetic glance at Pete as the proceedings got underway. It appeared he'd swapped one monster family night for another. But Pete gave her a reassuring smile. She'd obviously taken his 'monster family' stories literally, but they were strictly for laughs. They were also a defence mechanism against the fact that Susan's happy household reminded him of the plans he and Melaney had discussed. He was thirty-four years old, he'd have liked to have had kids. Sam watched in amazement as he horsed around with Betty's children, relaxed and evidently enjoying himself.

The house guests were a pleasant lot. Three navy cadets, a middle-aged couple, and two young women who were on holiday together and held hands a lot. They ate informally in the downstairs drawing room, everyone gorging themselves on Mrs M's spread, which could have fed a small army, and, after the children were put to bed, they gathered around the piano upstairs.

Betty was the musician for the night, as she always was at the 'singalongs', and she played with an unapologetic vigour which defied anyone to notice her mistakes. Furthermore, her repertoire was extensive. She thumped out everything from the latest pop songs to old wartime favourites and she knew the lyrics to each and every one.

'We'll meet again, don't know where, don't know when . . .'

They'd just finished the Vera Lynn bracket when it was time to start the countdown.

'Twelve, eleven, ten . . .' Mrs M had turned the radio on to the BBC. They raised their champagne flutes as they chanted. ' . . . three, two, one. Happy New Year!' Then, to the chimes of Big Ben, they hugged each other and clinked glasses, and thirty seconds later Betty was back at the piano.

'Should auld acquaintance be forgot . . .' They sang as raucously as Betty played.

*'Should auld acquaintance be forgot and never brought to mind . . .' Alice Chisolm was a skilful pianist, but tonight she played with a verve she didn't really feel. 1939 had not been a good year, why should 1940 be any better? As the voices rang out she looked at them all. Phoebe and Jane and their gathering of friends. Young people. Happy. As if there wasn't a war at all. And her husband, Arthur, singing loudest of all. When would it end? she wondered. Some said they'd have Hitler beaten within the year, but Alice didn't believe the optimists. This would be a long and wretched war.*

Sam looked about fondly at the assembled company singing their lungs out so tunelessly. This was undoubtedly one of the best New Year's Eves she'd ever had, she thought.

An hour later, the party started to break up. The middle-aged couple had already retired, the two young women trotted off to their bedroom hand in hand, and only the navy cadets and the indefatigable Betty showed no signs of tiring.

Pete gave Mrs M a hug and yelled his thanks above Betty's thumping.  Sam also made her retreat.

'Thanks, Mrs M, it's been a fantastic night.'

'Happy New Year, Sam.' Mrs M enveloped her in a huge motherly embrace and then rejoined her daughter and the singalong, Betty waving a farewell to Sam, losing the beat, and then getting back into her stride. Betty was a mini-Mrs M, Sam thought with affection as Pete shepherded her to the front door.

They stood on the gravel driveway outside. 'Happy New Year,' they said in unison, and they kissed, both knowing it was not a goodnight kiss. And when she said, 'Do you want a coffee?' they both knew that the invitation meant a great deal more.

Inside the stables, she didn't even make the pretence of turning on the electric jug. They were in each other's arms in a second, and then they were upstairs, in bed, their naked bodies setting each other on fire.

Pete tried not to think of Melaney as he made love to Sam. He didn't want to use the girl, and despite the intensity of his desire, he made love to her gently. He ran his lips down her throat and kissed her breasts, feeling her nipples respond to his mouth, his hands caressing her body, her belly, the curve of her hipbone, then her thighs, then the secret place between. All the while touching her, arousing her, and when he finally entered her she was warm and pulsating and meeting his every thrust.

*He could feel the power of her flesh undulating around him, drawing him further and further inside.*

*'Show me, James. Teach me,' she was whispering over and over.*

*He fought to maintain control, but by now she was moaning and thrusting and unwittingly driving him towards his own climax.*

Then, suddenly, the rhythm stopped and she clung to him, her whole body quivering, a tiny gasp caught in her throat, as if she'd stopped breathing, as if time had stopped still.

In her wildest imaginings, Sam had never thought that it could be like this. Fulfilment flooded through her, and with it a sense of ecstasy. Her body was behaving in a way she had never known possible.

Pete could hold on no longer and he groaned as he thrust himself even deeper inside her, giving in to his own release.

*They lay together, exhausted, on the hard wooden floors of the loft. He'd been astounded by the force of her passion and she knew it. She laughed gently. 'So that's what it's like,' she whispered, and she kissed him as she straightened her skirts.*

They lay side by side on the narrow bed, her head in the crook of his shoulder. 'That was fantastic,' she whispered. She couldn't think of anything else to say.

'Pretty good from my point of view too,' he said as he kissed the top of her head.

'I've only done it once before.' She leaned up on her elbow and looked at him. 'And it certainly wasn't like that.'

She looked so incredibly young, he thought fondly as he stroked a lock of her hair, damp with perspiration, back from her face. He'd been thankful to discover she wasn't a virgin; she was in love with him and that was responsibility enough, he realised with a sense of guilt.

His concern must have shown, because she laughed lightly. 'Don't worry, Pete, it's just one of those flings you have on the road.' She knew it was what he needed to hear.

He was grateful to her for saying it, and overwhelmed with affection, perhaps even love, as he drew her to him and kissed her.

He stayed the night and they made love again in the morning. Then she cooked them scrambled eggs and bacon.

'Do you eat like this every morning?' he asked as she piled the plates high.

'Nope, I'm strictly a fruit and cereal girl – this is part of my seduction campaign.' He obviously believed her. 'Not true,' she admitted. 'It was my special treat for a lonely New Year's Day.' But she wondered at the fact that she'd laid in supplies for two; had she been hoping?

Sam checked that the coast was clear and Pete ducked down the driveway with an anxious eye on the side windows. Any moment Mrs M might appear in the kitchen, but fortunately the breakfast rush was over and the lunchtime preparation hadn't yet begun.

He collected his car from the theatre car park where he'd left it and, twenty minutes later, he drove up to Chisolm House where he and Sam greeted each other conspicuously and set off for the day. She wanted to go to Southampton, she said, to look at the docks.

'Why?' he asked.

'I don't know,' she replied. And she didn't, she realised, the impulse seemed to have come from nowhere. 'But isn't that where the big ocean liners go from?'

'Once upon a time,' he said. 'Well, the pleasure cruisers still do,' he admitted, 'but I can show you some prettier tourist spots.' He took her there anyway, but only after they'd visited the village of Netley, nestled amongst the trees on the shores of Southampton Water, a few miles from the town of Southampton itself. Set in beautiful grounds nearby, the white domed chapel was the only remaining evidence of the once magnificent Royal Victoria Hospital which had been built in the nineteenth century.

'It served as a military hospital during both World Wars,' he explained, 'a huge place – they say it was a mile long.'

Not far away rose the stone battlements of Netley Castle, which Sam insisted they visit.

'Incredible,' she repeated time and again as she ran her hands over stonework which had stood for centuries. 'Just incredible.' Pete delighted in her amazement. 'Well, you don't get stuff like this in Australia,' she said, which only delighted him more.

She wasn't disappointed in Southampton either, she found the quayside romantic. She could see it all, she said, the glamour of the thirties and the trans-Atlantic ocean liners setting off for New York . . .

Pete gazed out over the sprawling industrial port at the vast grey dockyards and railway lines, the barges and tugboats and cargo vessels gathered upon the murky waters. It didn't look particularly romantic to him.

*'When I go to America I'm going to live in New York,' Phoebe said.*

*Jane nodded, but she didn't bother replying – Phoebe*

*said it every time they watched the liners depart. It was a regular outing of theirs; every few weeks they'd catch the train to Southampton and trek down to the docks. Jane's father used to accompany them, but now they were thirteen they were allowed to make the trip on their own.*

*'Right in the very middle of Manhattan,' Phoebe added, and Jane nodded again. Phoebe always said that too, and Jane believed her – once Phoebe had set her mind on something she usually accomplished it.*

*They stood on the visitors' balcony and watched the Mauretania being slowly pulled out to sea by the tugs, passengers still waving from her crowded decks, streamers still fluttering from her railings.*

*Standing at the forefront of the hordes gathered on the balcony, Phoebe and Jane had the very best view; they always made sure that they did. Having checked the newspapers, they'd arrive shortly before the liner's departure and they'd stay for only a while, watching the last of the passengers boarding, pointing out the wealthiest and those travelling steerage. Then they'd sprint to the seaward end of the huge Ocean Terminal building, over 1,200 feet long, to take up their position by the railings before others, farewelling friends and family, had the same idea.*

*Phoebe not only fantasised about the ship's destination, but the romance that lay in life on board. 'We'd have morning tea on the promenade deck,' she'd say, 'and we'd have dinner at the Captain's table, and we'd have a stateroom, with a private balcony.'*

*'But of course,' Jane would agree, 'we'd be travelling posh.' They'd read that the wealthiest passengers always travelled 'Port Out, Starboard Home', the favoured cabins gaining the morning sun and costing a great deal more. They knew each ship and whether it was of the Cunard or the White Star line and they fed each other's fantasies as best friends do. The great liners had gradually replaced Maude Cookson's pony in the scheme of things.*

'Can't you see it, Pete? The crowds at the railings and the streamers? Just like the old black and white movies.'

'Not really, I have to admit.'

'No sense of romance,' she laughed, 'that's your problem.'

They drove back via Portchester so that he could collect a fresh set of clothes; it was tacitly understood that he'd stay the night once again at the stables. 'What will Susan say?' Sam asked as they pulled up outside his sister's place.

'Nothing.' Pete was amused by her childlike concern. 'She'll assume I'm having an affair and she won't approve, but she won't say a thing. I'm thirty-four years old, Sam.' He got out of the car, then leaned back through the window. 'She just doesn't need to know with whom,' he added protectively; gossip in village communities was rife. 'Keep your head down a bit,' he said, then laughed as Sam, alarmed, shrank out of sight.

There was only a week of the season to go and Sam counted the days, or more importantly the nights, as the production drew to a close. They managed to keep their affair a secret from the rest of the company, partying with the gang as always, then slipping back to the stables together when the evening broke up. Sometimes Pete stayed overnight, but more often than not he left before daylight. It was impossible to avoid the kitchen windows, he said, and he was convinced that Mrs M had seen him on several occasions, although she'd tactfully pretended not to.

'She knows, I'm sure of it,' he said.

He appeared to be far more concerned about Sam's reputation than she was. 'Who cares?' she said when he first voiced his worries. 'I don't.' Then she felt guilty. The man might be separated, but he was still married. Furthermore, he loved his wife. 'I'm sorry,' she said, instantly contrite. 'I wasn't thinking. I'm really sorry.'

But Pete's concern for her was genuine. She had her career to consider, he told her. 'The London tabloids would have a field day with you, Sam, you're big news over here, don't forget. "Soapie starlet's affair with older married man" wouldn't stand you in good stead with Reginald Harcourt.'

Sam had made her decision from the outset, however. She had no intention of attempting to carve a career in Britain. Not yet anyway.

'That's exactly what I'd be known as, Pete, a "soapie starlet", and I'd get the odd telly guest role if I was lucky.' It was a life in the theatre she wanted. 'And I'm not ready,' she said. 'I'm nowhere near ready.' She'd return to Australia, and start from the bottom. She'd take classes and grab any stage job she could, she'd learn her craft the hard way.

And she'd make it, Pete thought. She had talent and guts and, above all, he realised as she recounted her plans with a passion, she was hungry.

The last night of the panto was an emotional experience. After the performance, they hugged and kissed and exchanged addresses and phone numbers, and the younger members of the dance team cried. It had been a happy and intense season. There was no partying on after the show – some were driving directly to London, others had early morning trains to catch – and by eleven o'clock Sam and Pete were back in the stables. Their last night together.

They shared a bottle of wine and they talked, and they made love. Then, at two o'clock in the morning, they said goodbye. It was only five hours before a driver was to collect Sam and take her to the airport.

She went downstairs with Pete to the front door. He'd told her to stay in bed, but she'd insisted. 'The least I can do is see you out,' she'd said, 'even us Aussies have some sense of courtesy.'

She was determined not to cry, just as she was determined not to tell him that she loved him. But she did, she thought as they shared their last kiss. 'I've had the best time,' she said brightly.

'So have I.'

Then, whilst she clung briefly to him, she said, her voice muffled in the shoulder of his greatcoat, 'I'll never forget you, Pete.' She couldn't help herself, and he probably couldn't hear her anyway.

'I'll never forget you either, Sam.' She heard the words clearly through the greatcoat, and she looked up at him. He stroked her hair back from her face as he did so often after they'd made love. 'Dear Sam,' he said, 'you've taught me so much.'

He was serious; she wondered what on earth he could mean. 'Like what?' she asked.

He smiled his laconic smile. 'Like "chook", for example.' They kissed once more. 'Goodbye,' he said, and he was gone.

'Goodbye, Pete,' she said to the closed door.

In the morning, when the driver arrived to collect her, Sam discovered Mrs M out in full force to wish her farewell, complete with a foil-wrapped package of sandwiches and a small thermos flask of tea.

'I'm sure you didn't have a proper breakfast, dear, and it's a long drive to Heathrow.'

'But what'll I do with the flask?'

'Oh you keep it, we've plenty more.' As the driver lifted the suitcase into the trunk of the car, Mrs M hugged her. 'You look very tired, dear,' she said, then she stood back and surveyed the girl at arm's length, her normally beaming face serious. 'You look after yourself, Sam, you're a very special girl.'

'I will, and thank you for everything, Mrs M.' Sam took the tiny silver statuette from the inside pocket of her shoulder bag. 'See? My Frogmorton horse, I keep it there for good luck.'

'What an excellent idea.' Mrs M's face was once again wreathed in a smile. 'I shall watch your career with interest,' she said as Sam climbed into the car. 'I may even take up the telly.'

Sam wound down the back window as the car pulled out of the driveway. 'Don't bother,' she called, 'keep your eye on the theatre!'

She drank in her last sight of Chisolm House, Mrs M large and indomitable, beaming and waving as she stood between the two stone lions. Then the car pulled out into Osborn Road, past the parish church of St Peter and St Paul and down the hill.

# CHAPTER THREE

'So *Red Centre* at the Royal Court was your really big break?' Nigel Daly had made copious notes throughout the interview, but he was particularly interested when Sam spoke of the Australian production that had toured to London early in the year 2000.

'Yep. *Red Centre*, the Royal Court, the start of the new millennium and my first meeting with Reg.' Sam looked at Reginald, who hadn't said a word for the past forty minutes. 'It was love at first sight,' she added cheekily and he returned the compliment with a fractional lift of the eyebrows.

The successful touring season of *Red Centre* by Nicholas Parslow, one of Australia's leading playwrights, had been staged at the prestigious Royal Court Theatre in Knightsbridge. It had been the perfect showcase for Samantha Lindsay, and Reginald Harcourt, impressed by her performance, had become responsible for her career, which had taken off in earnest from that moment on. But, at the time, Reg had been completely unaware of the true impact their first meeting had had upon Sam.

'How do you do, Miss Lindsay,' he'd said when he'd come backstage after the show. 'My name is Reginald Harcourt. I'm an agent.'

'Yes, I know.' She recalled the name immediately.

'I wondered whether I might arrange a meeting with a view to representation,' he held out his card, 'that is, of course, if you're interested.'

'I'm very interested, Mr Harcourt. What's wrong with right now?'

'Ah.' It wasn't the way Reginald normally did business. He'd actually intended to have his card sent to her dressing room with a message for her to call, but Pete Harris had insisted he go backstage. 'Nothing, I suppose.'

'You don't mind if I take the slap off while we chat, do you?' Even as she asked, she sat and started tying her fair hair back in a ponytail.

'Not at all.'

'Pull up a pew.'

He sat and watched her in the mirror as she applied a liberal coating of cold cream to her face. She was in a towelling robe and completely unself-conscious about her appearance. It certainly wasn't the conventional meeting between actress and agent, he thought, but it was rather refreshing.

'I enjoyed your performance, Miss Lindsay,' he said.

'Thanks.' She smiled at him in the mirror. 'It's a beaut part of course. Please call me Sam.'

'Yes, it's an excellent role,' he agreed, 'but not an easy one. It takes a good actor to pull it off.'

She turned to face him, wiping the cream and the heavy makeup away with a handful of tissues. 'Did you come to the show just on the off chance, Mr Harcourt . . .?'

'Reginald, please.'

'Reg,' she said and he inwardly winced, '. . . or did someone suggest you check me out?'

'I would have seen the show in any event,' he said. 'I see most of what's on around town, but it was definitely suggested I "check you out", as you say, and I'm very glad I did.'

'Pete Harris?' It felt strange saying his name out loud. Strange and slightly exciting.

'That's right. I believe you did a panto season together some years ago.'

'Yes. We did.'

'Well, he's obviously a great admirer of your work. He said to tell you that he thinks you're even more talented than you were then.'

'He was in the house tonight?' She felt breathless at the thought. Reginald Harcourt nodded. 'So why didn't he come backstage?'

'He and Melaney had to get home to the babysitter,' Reginald said. 'But they both thought you were wonderful, and they sent their congratulations.'

She tossed the tissues in the bin, crossed to the washstand and filled the basin with hot water. 'I didn't know they had a child,' she said as casually as possible.

'Two now.'

'Good grief, really?' She slapped on the skin cleanser. 'Well, of course it's been a whole five years since I saw Pete.'

'Yes, a boy and a girl. Susan's just turned four.'

'How fantastic. Are they blissfully happy?' She dived her face into the hot flannel.

'Yes, very much so. It's a bit of a loss for me, of course, Melaney giving up the business. I used to represent her and she was a very good actor.' His smile was fond. 'But I think she's an even better mother.'

Sam put down the flannel and looked directly at the tidy little man in the charcoal grey suit who had no idea that he had just closed a chapter of her life.

'How lovely for Pete,' she said, wondering with a touch of regret whether there would ever be a man in her life who would mean as much to her as Pete had during that magic Christmas at Fareham. She'd certainly met no-one in the past five years. 'He's a beaut bloke and I'm very glad for him.' She was, she realised.

'Hey, Reg,' Sam undid the ponytail and shook her hair free, 'why don't we clinch the deal over supper? I'm bloody starving.'

'An excellent idea.' Her brashness grated a little, but he sensed she was on edge. Perhaps it was a form of self-defence. Regardless, Reginald decided that he liked Samantha Lindsay. 'I'll wait outside,' he quickly added as she started undoing her robe.

The interview with Nigel Daly having finally concluded, Sam partied on with the *Doll's House* gang, and she had a bit of a hangover when Reginald picked her up at the Dorchester at ten o'clock in the morning to drive her to Fareham. She'd been staying at the hotel for the past week since moving out of her rented flat in Kensington.

'You look terrible,' he said. She didn't, but she was obviously tired.

'Thanks.'

'What time did you get to bed?'

'Four o'clock. And if you dare to lecture me I'll catch the train.'

At Reg's insistence, she'd relinquished the hire car she'd driven during the London season. 'You won't need a car in Fareham,' he'd said, 'and I'll collect you the following Monday and drive you to the airport.' It was very generous of him and Sam was grateful. Besides, she was longing to show him the house.

'No lecture intended,' Reg promised. 'You're permitted to get legless on closing nights.'

She nodded. She had. 'And I feel bloody terrible,' she said.

'The drive'll wake you up.'

He was right. She travelled with the window down until Reg complained that he was freezing, but by then the cold blast of air had done the trick, and she was restored to her ebullient self.

'I can't wait to show you the house.'

'If I had ten pounds for every time you've said that . . .'

'I know, I know, but now you're actually going to *see* it! I can't wait!'

Reg had been taken aback when she'd told him, several weeks previously, that she'd bought the old house she'd once stayed at in Fareham. 'Just like that?' he'd queried. 'On a whim?' She hadn't even discussed it with him.

'It's an investment,' she'd said defensively. 'You're always nagging me about investing my money, you've been telling me to buy a property for ages.'

A small flat in London had been what he'd had in mind, he told her a little archly, something practical that she could lease out. A Victorian mansion was a different kettle of fish altogether, he said. 'It'll be a never-ending expense, Sam, you do realise that?'

'I'm meant to own this house, Reg,' she'd insisted. 'I can't explain it, but it's just meant to be, I can feel it.' His look was decidedly sceptical and Sam couldn't blame him. She knew she wasn't making much sense.

Reg was genuinely annoyed that she'd taken such a major step without consulting him, but he was also mystified. It was unlike Sam to eschew commonsense and behave in such a fanciful fashion. Certainly, like many actors, she adhered to theatre superstition – she didn't whistle in dressing rooms or quote from *Macbeth* and she even touched wood each night before she went on stage – but Reg suspected that was due to her love of tradition more than anything else. Sam was, at heart, a practical girl.

'You're lucky *Torpedo Junction* came in,' he'd said, and he stopped nagging. What was the point? The deed was done. But she was damn lucky, he thought. She'd landed the movie at the very last minute, and she'd been a rank outsider.

Now, he glanced sideways at her and proffered a smile which he hoped looked eager. 'I can't wait to see it,' he said, before returning his attention to the road ahead.

Sam was aware that he was humouring her, but she wasn't offended. Reg didn't know the half of it, she thought as she looked out the car window at the countryside speeding by, the frost still glistening on the ground, the trees magnificent in their rusty autumn foliage. Reg knew nothing of the chain of events. How things had all linked together. And she couldn't have told him. Not only because she knew he'd be cynical, but because she knew he'd have every right to be.

It had started with the leaflet. A month ago. It had arrived at the theatre on a Monday, in an envelope addressed to her and marked 'personal'. A glossy little brochure from a real estate firm, with no note included. 'FOR SALE', it said, 'VICTORIAN TOWNHOUSE IN PICTURESQUE FAREHAM', and there was a photograph of Chisolm House with 'open for inspection' printed beneath. She hadn't pondered the identity of the sender. Some enterprising real estate salesperson who'd discovered she'd lived there years ago, she presumed – she'd been approached by many businesses and charities following the play's extensive press coverage. But, as memories flooded back, she wondered why she'd never returned to Fareham. Just for a visit. For old times' sake. She'd intended to, she recalled, during the run of Nick Parslow's play at the Royal Court several years ago. But then perhaps Fareham, like Pete Harris, had been relegated to a past which should remain past.

She'd decided to drive down the very next morning. Early. A leisurely wander about the town and the old house would be enjoyably nostalgic, and she'd have plenty of time to rest before the evening performance.

But, when she turned off Osborn Road into the side driveway of Chisolm House, she was surprised to discover that the property was not open for inspection at all. There was no-one in sight, the doors were closed, the garden overgrown, the house apparently deserted, and there was no 'for sale' sign to be seen. How odd, she thought as she got out of the car.

She rang the bell, no-one answered; she tried the door, it was locked, so she walked around to the front bay windows. It was sad to see the garden so untidy and neglected, buried beneath a burden of early-fallen autumn leaves, the fountain mouldy and choked with decaying foliage. She peered through the bay windows into the front drawing room. There were no drapes and, despite the grime on the panes of glass, she had clear visibility. The room was bare. Only the fixtures remained, the mantelpiece and the fireplace, and, without the chandelier, even the ceiling looked naked.

She walked down the side drive to the gravel courtyard at the rear and her heart skipped a beat when she saw the stables. The huge wooden doors set into the sandstone arch, the slate roof, the multi-paned glass windows. She looked up at the loft and remembered staring through those windows at the snowbound courtyard that lonely Christmas Day. And she remembered Pete and their nights together.

The front door was locked and she peered through the windows. The interior of the stables, like the house, was devoid of furniture, but somehow it didn't seem as abandoned. The sandstone walls and the timber beams were warm and inviting, a cosy assurance that nothing had changed, and Mrs M's voice came back to her. '*This was the tack room,*' she could hear the thick Hampshire accent, '*and over here, this was the actual stables, four of them I believe, although the Chisolms themselves never kept horses.*' Sam's gaze wandered up the staircase, following Mrs M's voice, '. . . *up here was the loft.*'

Having discovered the house locked and deserted, Sam had been prepared to simply drive back to London, but her glimpse through the stable windows changed her mind.

The sales brochure had said the place was 'open for inspection'; well, she'd demand a guided tour, she decided, and she drove to the real estate office in West Street, near the mall. It was one of three listed on the brochure, the others being in Southampton and Portsmouth.

'Yes, Chisolm House is on our books,' the middle-aged man behind the reception counter told her. He was tall and gangly, the sleeves and trousers of his suit too short for his lanky limbs. 'But as it's a deceased estate,' he explained, 'and as the beneficiaries live in London the sale's being principally handled by Holdsworthy Realty in Mayfair.'

'But you're the local agents?'

'We are indeed.' Jim Lofthouse was sure he'd seen the young woman before but he couldn't think where. She certainly wasn't a local, but her face was familiar. 'Excuse me, have we . . .?'

'Then how come you don't have the place open for inspection?' Sam demanded, dodging enquiry, aware that the man had recognised her. She wanted to get straight down to business.

Her tone was brusque, and the secretary tapping away at the computer in the far corner looked up briefly.

Jim decided, with regret, to forgo his questions; the young woman appeared a little annoyed and he wondered why. He smiled to put her at her ease.

'Chisolm House is not on the market yet,' he said.

'Not on the market?' Sam stared blankly at him, then fumbled in her shoulder bag. 'So what's this supposed to mean?' She slapped the brochure down on the counter.

Jim's hand automatically went to his breast pocket for his reading glasses, but he stopped as he recognised the photograph of Chisolm House. 'Dear me, how strange,' he said, 'the brochures haven't been distributed yet. Where did you get hold of that?'

'It was sent to me.'

'By whom?'

'I don't know.' The man's obvious bewilderment only exacerbated Sam's irritation. 'By one of your colleagues, I presume.' She stabbed a finger at the list of agents on the brochure. 'Someone from Southampton or Portsmouth, or maybe someone from Holdsworthys in London. Surely there must be *some* form of communication between the lot of you.'

Jim Lofthouse was an even-tempered man. Ingenuous, mild-mannered and, according to the old Fareham locals, 'just like his father, unflappable'. The girl's obvious slur upon his competence and that of his colleagues intrigued rather than annoyed him. Her belligerence was so at odds with her appearance, he thought. Lovely looking thing, where on earth had he seen her before?

'No, we're not in communication. Not yet.' He ran his fingers through his thick mop of greying hair as he studied her thoughtfully. 'Not until next week when the place goes on the market.'

The man was an imbecile, Sam thought, her irritation turning to anger. His imperturbability was driving her insane, and she wished he'd stop staring at her so blatantly. He was obviously trying to place where he'd seen her before, but it was bloody rude. 'Then why send out the brochures?'

'We didn't.'

'Well, somebody did!' She'd hit him in a minute. 'Maybe one of your colleagues is trying to get a step ahead of you.'

He shook his head. 'It wouldn't be to their advantage, the place isn't ready for inspection yet.' Jim suddenly twigged. 'Of course, that's it,' he said and the snap of his long, bony fingers was startling. '"Families and Friends", that's where I know you from!'

Sam had presumed he'd recognised her from one of the many British television dramas and series she'd appeared in over the past few years. 'Families and Friends' came as a surprise and she found herself momentarily halted. 'That was nine years ago,' she said.

'Oh they've been showing reruns for a long time.' He smiled, happily relieved that he'd placed the face. '"Families and Friends, the Early Years", it's on at five o'clock in the morning. Mind you, they're up to the middle years now. You've just come on air. Little Margie Nielson, and you're wearing pigtails.'

'You watch the show at five o'clock in the morning?' she asked, incredulous.

'Oh I'm up at that time anyway. I'm from a farming family,' he explained, 'always been an early riser.' She didn't seem cross any more. That's good, he thought. It'd be nice to have a chat, interesting to meet a genuine television star. 'It's more of a comfort really, it reminds me of when the kids were little, it was always their favourite show. They've grown up and left home now, and I miss them.'

'Look, why don't we start again.' Sam smiled. Her intense irritation had passed and she realised she'd been rude. She offered her hand. 'I'm Samantha Lindsay.'

'Jim Lofthouse,' he said as they shook. 'I saw you in a panto too, at Ferneham Hall. Took the kids to it. *Cinderella,* you were very good . . .'

'Thank you,' she interrupted before he could go any further. 'Now, Jim, I'd like to take a look at Chisolm House.'

'It's a bit of a mess,' he said doubtfully. 'The cleaners and the gardener are going in on Friday. Couldn't you come back next week?'

'No, I'm afraid not.' Sam decided that, at the risk of being rude once again, she must be firm. 'I'm doing a show in London and this is the only time I can get down to Fareham.'

'What show would that be?'

She gritted her teeth. '*A Doll's House* at the Haymarket. Could we go over there now? I really don't have much time.'

'Right you are then.' He instructed the receptionist to look after the office, took his time finding the keys and, as they drove off in his car at a snail's pace, he started again. 'I don't go to the theatre much, just the pantos . . .'

He seemed understanding, however, when she told him she'd like to have a look around on her own. 'It's a bit of a trip down memory lane,' she said apologetically as he unlocked the front door; she couldn't bear the thought of him chatting on whilst she explored the old house. 'I stayed here when I was doing the panto.'

'Right you are,' he said, 'I'll wait out here.' Jim propped himself against one of the stone lions, more than happy to stay outside: he was dying for a cigarette. He didn't allow himself to smoke in the office, it was his way of cutting down. But, with a surprising display of sensitivity, he gently closed the door behind her, aware that she wanted to explore the house in private.

Sam peered into the kitchen. It was cold and bare, but nonetheless welcoming. She could almost smell the hearty aromas of Mrs M's cooking. She walked into the front drawing room and, although it too was devoid of furnishings, it no longer seemed deserted as it had when she'd peered through the front bay windows. It echoed a warmth and invitation that seemed intensely personal and she felt as she had that Christmas morning nine years ago. The house wanted her. She felt at home.

Then she heard the piano. A light tinkling at first, she thought she'd imagined it. Then the melody became clear. 'Auld Lang Syne'. It was coming from upstairs. Impossible. She followed the sound, slowly climbing each step, half expecting to see Betty at the keyboard. But the hand didn't sound like Betty's, this was a skilful hand with a gentle touch and the rendition had a melancholic ring to it. She pushed open the door. There was no piano and no Betty, the drawing room was bare, and even as Sam stared at the corner where the piano had once stood, the sound dwindled to the light tinkling she'd first heard, then slowly faded away altogether.

She'd imagined it, of course, she'd known from the moment she'd first heard the sound. Her mind was working overtime in the deserted house which held such memories. The experience was not unpleasant, but it was eerie and a little unsettling.

Jim was sitting, lanky-limbed, all elbows and knees, on the steps of the porch when she reappeared. He was finishing his second cigarette and he took one final hefty drag, unfolded himself and rose to his feet, grinding the butt out with the heel of his shoe.

'I'll show you the stables at the back. Converted to a self-contained flat. Very picturesque,' he said, quoting the sales pitch, 'you'll like the stables.'

'No need, Jim. I know the stables.' The house had had enough of an effect on her, she thought, God only knows what the stables would do. She was contemplating the ridiculous, she told herself, but the urge was irresistible.

'Of course, I forgot. You stayed here.'

'Deceased estate, you said?'

'That's right. Old Miss Chisolm died about a month ago . . .'

The portrait of the young Phoebe Chisolm, eyes radiating life, flashed briefly through Sam's mind.

'. . . and the house was left to some relative and his wife, a cousin, I think.' Jim was opening the car door for her. 'He's a businessman and he wants a quick sale.'

'Thanks.' She slipped into the passenger seat.

'It's investment money to him. He hasn't even bothered to come and look at the place. Just sent down an independent assessor and then left everything up to Holdsworthys. I don't think he's even in the country.'

Jim walked around to the driver's side, and Sam smiled to herself. He really was a terrible salesman. As the car crawled around the block into West Street she plied him with questions. What figure had Holdsworthys put on the property? If the owner wanted a quick sale, would he be interested in an offer right now, before the house was officially on the market?

'More than likely,' he said, 'if the offer was right.'

She didn't come into the office upon their return, but accepted his business card and shook his hand warmly. 'Thanks, Jim.'

As she pulled out from the kerb she could see him in the rear vision mirror, standing in the street, lighting a cigarette. She waved to him and he waved back. Then, as she rounded the corner, she picked up her mobile phone. Ridiculous as the idea was, it was also irresistible.

Sam had been amazed to discover that she could afford the house. Just. It would take every penny of the capital she'd accrued, but then that had been her plan, hadn't it, to buy a property? Of course there would be the exorbitant upkeep and the rates to contend with, but she didn't want to think about the impracticalities of the purchase. She didn't want to think about anything but the fact that Chisolm House could be hers.

She knew she should phone Reg, but she didn't – he'd only try to talk her out of it. She rang her London solicitor instead, giving him Jim Lofthouse's phone number and issuing instructions for him to contact Holdsworthys immediately and make an offer. She looked at her watch as she hung up. It was midday.

For the rest of the drive back to London, Sam pondered her actions. She had no second thoughts, she would not renege on her offer, but perhaps she should rethink her career decisions. There was a contract from the Royal Shakespeare Company sitting at the agency awaiting her signature – a six-month season at Stratford upon Avon – but she'd been hedging, hanging out for the possibility of the movie deal. It was a long shot, she and Reg both knew it. Why should the Americans take a punt on an obscure stage actress? This was a leading role in a big-budget production, they'd go for an A-list movie star. The only reason she'd scored a screen test was because of Nick.

Nicholas Parslow had been an Academy Award nominee two years previously for his screenplay of *Red Centre*. At the time the film had been made he'd lobbied heavily for Samantha Lindsay to recreate her stage role, but to no avail. Nick hadn't won his Oscar, but a nomination was a big career boost, and producers had been quick to vie for his screenplay of *Torpedo Junction*. Again, he'd lobbied for Sam and this time his vote had resulted in a screen test. It was a sad fact, however, that writers' recommendations, even writers with a reputation like Nick's, didn't ultimately carry much weight with Hollywood producers. There'd been no word from Mammoth Productions and Reg had advised Sam to sign the RSC contract.

'They won't wait around forever,' he'd warned, 'and a bird in the hand . . .' It was his favourite proverb, and one he quoted repeatedly to ambitious young actors.

Reg was right, Sam decided as she hit the outskirts of London. And the sooner she grabbed this particular bird the better. The movie was obviously out the window, and if the RSC deal fell through, then she'd never be able to keep Chisolm House.

The moment she was back in her flat in Kensington, she rang the agency. 'I'm going to sign the RSC contract, Reg,' she said. 'I'll pop in first thing tomorrow morning.'

'Fine,' he said, 'good decision. But I'm out of the office for a couple of days. Let's leave it till Friday, shall we?'

'Sure, if you think that's all right.'

'Oh yes,' he assured her, 'they've waited this long, they can hang on until the end of the week.'

The purchase of Chisolm House went through without a hitch. The vendor was particularly eager for a quick sale, her solicitor told her. And, as her finances were unencumbered and she could pay up front, he was willing to accept her offer.

Sam prepared herself for Reg's outburst, she knew he wouldn't approve and that he'd be cross she hadn't consulted him. She'd tell him on Friday, she decided, when she went into the office to sign the contract.

But Reg got in first. He rang her on Friday morning. Early by stage actors' standards. 'Did I get you out of bed?' he asked.

'No, I've been up for a while.' She looked at her watch. Nine o'clock. Strange. It was one of Reg's rules never to ring actors before at least ten in the morning. 'What's the matter?'

'Simon Scanlon just called. You got the movie.' Reg sounded as calm and businesslike as usual but Sam knew him well enough to sense the underlying excitement in his tone. 'He came to the show last night and decided you're *it*, the whole thing's cut and dried. Even the Yanks bow down to Simon Scanlon.'

Simon Scanlon, although fiercely Australian, had directed a number of American box-office hits. He was selective and his films had achieved success across the board, both artistically and commercially, a fact which the American producers very much respected.

Sam was slow in assimilating the news – perhaps it was too early in the morning – and she felt confused. 'I didn't even know Simon Scanlon was in London.'

'He wasn't. He rang out of the blue on Tuesday and said he was getting on a plane that night and would I line him up a ticket for Thursday's performance. I didn't tell you,' Reg apologised, 'because I didn't want to raise your hopes.'

'He rang on Tuesday? From Sydney?'

'That's right.'

'What time?'

'Pardon?'

'What time did he ring?'

'Oh.' Now Reg was confused. He'd expected Sam to be over the moon and here she was grilling him for details. 'I don't know. London time, do you mean?'

'Yes, yes, our time. When did he ring?'

Reg thought for a second. 'Greta had just brought my lunch in so I suppose it was about . . .'

'Midday!' she said. Reg always had a chicken and salad sandwich from the next door deli at midday. 'Simon Scanlon rang you at midday!'

'Yes, that's right. Why?'

Exactly the time she'd bought the house! Sam's hoot of laughter was a mixture of amazement and triumph.

'What's so funny? I thought you'd be thrilled, breathless with excitement and all that.'

'I am, I'm ecstatic.' Chisolm House was her good luck omen, she knew it. 'I'm over the moon, Reggie, I'm over the moon.' It was all meant to be, Sam thought. The old house had dictated it so.

'I see what you mean,' Reg said as he drove through the broad gates of Chisolm House. 'It's lovely. And large,' he added with a meaningful look.

But Sam wasn't listening. 'Oh look,' she said, 'they've cleared up the front garden.' The garden was immaculately tidied of its tangled foliage and litter, and the fountain, no longer choked with leaves, was scrubbed and free of mould.

She was further delighted to discover a plant in a white clay pot beside one of the stone lions, right in the spot where the conifer in the earthenware tub had once stood. How thoughtful of Jim to have gone to all that trouble, she thought. It was hardly customary for a real estate agent to tidy a place up *after* the sale had gone through.

She suddenly realised what he'd meant when they'd collected the keys from the real estate office only ten minutes earlier. 'There's a couple of surprises waiting for you,' he'd said. She felt riddled with guilt that she'd so blithely dismissed his offer to come with them.

'No, we'll be fine thanks, Jim,' she'd said. 'I'll give you a ring if there're any problems.'

He hadn't seemed remotely bothered. 'Right you are,' he'd said. But Sam chastised herself now as she unlocked the front door. It was typically insensitive of her, she'd go around and see him tomorrow and she'd take him a present, a bottle of Scotch or something.

'Welcome to Chisolm House,' she said to Reg as she formally ushered him inside.

He walked on ahead to the drawing room as she checked the light switches in the hall. Jim had assured her that the gas and electricity had been connected and she was thankful to discover he was right.

'Good heavens above,' she heard Reg exclaim.

'Yes, it's fantastic, isn't it,' she said as she joined him. She expected to find him admiring the ornate ceiling and coved cornices – he was an admirer of fine architecture – but his gaze was fixed upon the wall above the mantel-piece.

'That's a James Hampton, I'm sure of it.' Reg was an habitue of art galleries, a connoisseur who prided himself on his ability to recognise the work of lesser known artists. He crossed to the painting and studied the signature in the right-hand corner. 'Yes, it's a Hampton all right. There are several of his pieces at the Tate. I love his work.' He stepped back admiringly. 'Just look at the light.'

Sam stared into the eyes of the young Phoebe Chisolm. And as she did so, she heard a sudden burst of laughter. The laughter of a young woman, impish and tantalising. The sound was as clear as a bell, but came from some distance, there was someone in the front garden, surely. She crossed to the bay windows and looked out, but no-one was there.

'Did you hear that?' she asked.

'What?' Reg paid her scant attention as he continued to admire the painting.

'A girl. Laughing.'

'No. You didn't tell me you had a Hampton portrait.

It came with the house, did it? Rather generous of the owners to throw it in with the deal, I must say. It'd probably be worth a bit. Not that he's widely known outside art circles, but he's very respected.'

Sam crossed back to the fireplace and looked once again into Phoebe's eyes. The laughter had gone now. Then she noticed the family photograph sitting on the mantelpiece. Arthur Chisolm, his wife Alice, and baby Phoebe. She stared in bewilderment at both the photograph and the portrait. 'How did they get here?' she whispered.

Reg glanced at her, realising for the first time her complete amazement. 'You mean you didn't know they were here?' he queried. 'Well, I suppose it must be the surprise your friend Jim Lofthouse was referring to.' He turned back to the painting. 'Lucky you,' he said. 'She's quite lovely. Look at the movement, the way he's captured her head turning into that shaft of light. Magic.'

Of course, Sam told herself, this was Jim's surprise. And the laughter had been of her own imagining. A reaction to the shock of seeing Phoebe's portrait. The chain of events that had taken place had left her altogether too keen to read the extraordinary into the perfectly explicable.

'Yes, she is lovely, isn't she?'

As Reg had said, it was generous of the owners to allow the portrait and photograph to stay with the house, but it was also rather out of character, Sam thought, recalling Jim's description of the businessman who couldn't wait to sell the place. Oh well, the full story would have to wait until tomorrow when she could call in to the real estate office. She didn't dare leave the house until the furniture had arrived. The removal company had promised delivery by early afternoon, and she wanted to get fully settled in today.

Reg insisted upon waiting with her. 'What happens if it doesn't turn up?' he argued. 'You can hardly sleep on the floor, we'll have to book you into a hotel.' Which had been his suggestion from the outset. He'd thought it ludicrous she should plan to spend that first night in the house, but she'd been adamant.

Reg's fears were unfounded, however. The furniture arrived at half past two, by which time she'd given him the full guided tour and unpacked the supplies she'd bought en route. As the removal truck pulled up in the driveway, they were leaning on the island bench in the cosily heated stables draining the last of the coffee from the thermos flask and devouring a packet of chocolate biscuits.

The furniture which Sam had acquired for her small London flat would fit perfectly into the stables, Reg had suggested as they'd chatted over their biscuits and coffee. It'd be madness to attempt setting herself up in the main house. She'd nodded agreement as if it was a breakthrough idea, not telling him that it had always been her intention.

She refused to allow him to stay and help. 'You'll be arriving home in the dark if you leave it much longer,' she insisted, and Reg took one look at the two hefty removal men lugging an armchair apiece and agreed there was little he could add by way of assistance.

'Don't forget to do your homework,' he said before he left, patting the script which sat on the island bench. Reminding young actors of the necessity for homework was Reginald Harcourt's standard procedure, although he knew it wasn't necessary in Sam's case.

Outside in the courtyard, he surveyed the vastness of Chisolm House. 'Well, I suppose it could be a whole new career for you if the movie bombs and Hollywood fails to beckon.' She gave him a querying look. 'You could employ a manager,' he said, 'and turn it back into a B and B. I believe they do very well in Fareham.'

'Always an option.' She laughed as she hugged him. 'Goodbye, Reggie, thanks for everything.'

'Enjoy your hibernation, Sam. I'll see you in a week.'

The workmen moved speedily. It was their last delivery

of the day and an easy one at that; they'd be able to knock
off earlier than anticipated. Barely an hour later everything
was in place. The wooden bed base was the only item
which proved a bit of a problem, and the railings of the
staircase bore the scars to prove it.

'Sorry about that, but it can't be helped,' one of the men
gruffly apologised. 'Just as well it's not a queen size, we'd
never have got it up here.'

'No worries, it's fine,' Sam assured him. It was amazing
the men had managed to manoeuvre the heavy wooden
double bed base upstairs at all, she thought, recalling the
small iron bedstead with its single mattress upon which
she and Pete had slept entwined.

'Have a beer,' she said when they'd finished, 'my shout.'

They were bewildered by the term, but not by the tip.
'Anything else we can do for you, love?' they asked as they
pocketed their twenty quid apiece.

'No thanks, you've been great.'

They left, and Sam looked about at her new home. The
four-seater dining table and chairs, the small three-piece
lounge set, the bookcase, the coffee table and other
sundries all sat comfortably in the open-plan living space.
It was as if they'd been made for the stables.

She decided to go for a walk before the early autumn
dusk set in – the unpacking of boxes and suitcases could
wait. As the owner of Chisolm House she was a part of
Fareham now and she needed to reacquaint herself with
the town.

She turned left into Osborn Road. Across the street
was Ferneham Hall, but she wouldn't visit the theatre,
she decided; it was the older parts of Fareham which
beckoned. She rounded the corner at St Peter's and St
Paul's Church and walked down High Street to the broad
avenue of West Street, passing the popular bakery on the
corner and recalling the smell of hot bread and the queues
which had stretched for blocks. But it was Sunday now

and the place was closed. West Street was deserted and she recalled how they used to joke that Fareham 'closed on Sundays'. As always, however, across the road at the Red Lion the lights were on and the windows were opaque with the steam of activity inside. Perhaps she'd call in for a beer and a snack on her way home. But she'd explore the back streets for a while; she still had a good hour before dusk.

She turned into the small laneway of Adelaide Place which she'd never noticed before, her intention being to cut through to the Quay. But she found it was a dead end. A line of mews faced narrow, wire-fenced garden allotments on the other side of the tiny street, a locked gate opposite each front door. Some yards were neglected, some served as large playpens with a kiddy's bike or a sandpit dug in the corner. Others proudly boasted vegetable gardens, or shrubs and carefully tended flower beds, here and there a potting shed at the rear. It was a private world locked away from the mainstream hustle and bustle and Sam felt like a trespasser. She heard a man's voice through one of the half-open windows.

*'Now you two be careful on that train, Jane, no talking to strangers, mind.'*

Quickly she retraced her steps before the door behind her could open and her intrusion be discovered. She turned left into Quay Street and eventually crossed the railway line to arrive at the grassy recreational park beside the water.

Several young boys were kicking a soccer ball around and an elderly couple were seated at a bench. They smiled at Sam and she smiled in return as she leaned on the metal railings overlooking the water. The tide was out and the several dinghies, listing on their sides upon the muddy flats of the Upper Quay, looked stranded and ineffectual, but the nearby ship-building yard with its slipways and hoisted vessels currently under repair was proof of a thriving trade.

She looked across Fareham Creek to the Lower Quay where boats were moored side by side in the deeper water and the large redbrick facade of the old grain store towered over the neighbouring dockyard buildings. Linking both quays was the promenade of Gosport Street which forded Gillies Brook, and she crossed the bridge, passing the Castle in the Air, the old sailors' pub, white-washed, cheery and inviting. From the Lower Quay, she looked back across the creek to the ship-building yard and the wide expanse of public recreation ground. The elderly couple had gone now, but the boys continued to kick the soccer ball about in the gathering dusk and, in the distance, a pair of young lovers walked hand in hand along the railed waterside path which extended the full length of the park. It seemed strange to think that these sleepy quays and dockyards remained an active port; that they had indeed been a hive of industry in years gone by. But then that was Fareham's fascination, Sam thought. It held its own in the modern world, and yet it retained such a link with times past that it was as if she had stepped into yesteryear.

She called in at the Red Lion on her way home. It was as crowded and noisy as ever, but then there was nothing else to do in Fareham on a Sunday night. Things hadn't really changed at all, she thought. People jostled at the bar and crammed their chairs around the packed tables in the back rooms, making movement impossible but nobody minded.

Sam bought herself a beer, queued up to put her order in at the food counter, then managed to grab a spare seat near the front bay windows, others being more interested in scoring the booths on either side. A waiter delivered her plate of crispy potato skins with melted cheese. Even when you could find a place in Sydney that served them, they somehow never tasted the same, she thought. And, as she watched the groups intent upon having a good time, she didn't feel at all lonely.

' 'Ello love, can we buy you an ale?' He was a pleasant-looking young man in his early twenties, a little the worse for drink but harmless. 'Me and me mate are down from London and we've got a bet on. We know you're from the telly, but we dunno which show.' He beckoned to his friend who started elbowing his way through the crowd. 'Bert reckons . . .'

'I'm a local, actually,' Sam said.

'You're joking.'

'No, I'm not.' She swilled back the last of her beer and rose from her chair.

'I don't believe it. You're Samantha Lindsay, that's what I told Bert, I've seen you on the telly. He has too, but he reckons you're . . .'

'I'm a local, I swear it, I live here. G'day, Bert.' She gave them both a friendly smile and, just as Bert reached her side, she ducked out the front door.

That night, she expected to dream of Pete, but she didn't. She dreamed of Fareham instead. Of the private world that was Adelaide Place, of the Quay and the boats and the recreation park and the path beside the water. In the loft above the stables of Chisolm House she was part of it all. And throughout her dreams, she heard laughter. Two young girls. No longer children and not yet women.

# CHAPTER FOUR

'He is, I swear it. He's sweet on you.' Jane couldn't help giggling as she said it. She was deadly serious, but Phoebe's laughter at the mere suggestion had got her started, as it always did — Phoebe's laugh was very infectious. 'Stop it,' she said whilst Phoebe rolled on the floor pretending uncontrollable mirth. 'Why else do you think he's asked us out sailing? It's because he's sweet on you, Maude told me.' As usual, Jane didn't know what on earth Phoebe found so funny, but she was starting to lose control herself and her giggles were turning to laughter.

'Lofty!' Phoebe gasped. 'He's a spider. A daddy-long-legs.'

Phoebe hadn't found the fact that Ben Lofthouse was sweet on her at all surprising, but she could never resist the urge to make Jane laugh, and together they rolled about hysterically on the wooden floor of the loft, safe in the knowledge that no-one could hear them. The stables were their favourite place and the loft their hideout. Every weekend, they'd climb up the broad, wooden ladder, through the open trapdoor and into their own special world.

Both girls attended Wykeham House School in High Street, Phoebe excelling at hockey and Jane at debating, but their differing interests had little effect upon the friendship they'd shared for more than half of their young lives. Neither did the fact that they came from different walks of life. They were inseparable and such trivialities never entered the scheme of things. And now that they were fifteen years old and looking at boys in a whole new light, another dimension had been added to the pleasure they found in each other's company, a complicity and secrecy all of their own.

Jane wasn't jealous that Phoebe appeared to have a serious admirer in the form of Lofty; to the contrary, she was fascinated. Lofty was two years older than the girls and attended Price's, an old and well-established school with a history of achievers. Despite the fact that his family had been, for generations, market gardeners, Lofty was expected to break the mold and go on to university whilst his brothers took over the business, but he didn't really want to.

At seventeen years of age, hormones racing, all Ben Lofthouse wanted to do was kiss Phoebe Chisolm, and hopefully more. He'd tell himself, time and again, that she was only fifteen, and who ever looked at fifteen-year-olds? But there was something different about Phoebe Chisolm.

And there was. Phoebe herself didn't recognise it. Not really. She knew she could get her way if she wanted to, with her father and schoolmates and now boys. And she flirted and teased and promised her friendship. She never considered that she used people, she simply set out to get what she wanted, like Maude Cookson's pony for weekend rides at Titchfield. She took advantage of occasions when they presented themselves, she told herself, that was all.

It was Jane who recognised Phoebe's power. She didn't envy it and she didn't wish to possess it, but she definitely recognised it. Her friend Phoebe could get whatever she wanted if she tried. Phoebe made things happen. That was why she'd danced three times with Lofty at the invitation school dance at Foresters Hall last night, Jane knew it. The following weekend was the Aquatic Games and Regatta, an annual gala event at Fareham, and Phoebe wanted Lofty to take her out sailing. But Jane had to come too, Phoebe had insisted, and now it was all arranged.

'I have to go home,' Jane said an hour later after they'd talked about the next picture that was coming to the Savoy Cinema, and discussed film stars in general, and agreed that, given their current interest in boys, their favourite Greta Garbo had been replaced by Ronald Colman. They'd also come to a decision as to whether or not Lofty should come with them to the Savoy on Friday night.

'I think we'd better let him,' Phoebe said quite seriously, 'it's the regatta the next day.' And that brought about another giggling fit. Phoebe really was shockingly manipulative.

Jane wished she could stay in the loft all morning as they often did on a Saturday. But this was a Sunday and it was eleven o'clock. Time to go.

Every Sunday Jane would come to Chisolm House after the early church service she attended with her father, always popping home to change first. Ron Miller would certainly not allow his daughter to play around in 'those mucky old stables', as he called them, in her best Sunday clothes. And now it was time for her to go home and cook the huge weekend roast. There would be only the two of them, but they'd live happily on cold mutton for the rest of the week.

The family roast had remained a tradition after Jane's mother's death when she was four and, as her father never broke with tradition, it continued to be a weekly event, despite the fact that her two older brothers had long since left home. Twenty-two-year-old Dave had joined his older brother Wilfred in London a whole three years ago. The family was regularly reunited at Christmas, but apart from the brothers' odd brief visits to Fareham, there was little contact. Jane was too young to go to London on her own, Ron maintained, and he steadfastly refused to go himself. He hated the city.

Jane's father was not a martinet, but he was a proud man, and his pride sometimes made it hard for others. A tile worker, prematurely retired from the Fontley Brick and Tile Works due to a back injury, Ron Miller would accept no financial help from his adult sons, apart from the payment of Jane's school fees.

'I've no need for your money,' he'd say gruffly, 'but if you've a mind to help with your sister's schooling, I'd not refuse.'

In the meantime, his frugal household survived on the income he made as a gardener, his principal employer being Arthur Chisolm. Ron had originally refused the doctor's offer. Their daughters having forged a strong friendship from their early school days, he'd presumed it to be an act of charity and he'd have none of it. 'Accept naught for nowhit' was Ron Miller's philosophy and the adage was repeated time and again to his children.

It had taken all of Arthur Chisolm's considerable diplomacy to persuade the man to reconsider. 'A good day's work for a good day's pay, Ron,' he'd said. 'There are few who give value for money these days, but you're one who does and I'd appreciate it if you'd take up the offer.'

Put that way, Ron could not refuse and, over the years, a bond had been formed between the gruff, burly gardener and his employer, a bond principally forged through the friendship of their daughters. Sometimes, after their respective days' hard work, the men would even share an ale at the King's Head or the Red Lion, and only then would Ron, at Arthur's insistence, refer to his friend by his Christian name. At all other times Arthur remained 'Dr Chisolm'.

'A proud man,' Arthur would comment to his wife on many an occasion. 'At times too proud, I think.' He was unaware that his comments were falling upon deaf ears, for Alice Chisolm privately considered it only correct Ron Miller should show deference to her husband.

Fine-looking at forty, with an air of regality and without yet a fleck of grey in her auburn hair, Alice was considered by some to be over-conscious of her image, indeed even 'a bit of a snob'. But in truth it was her husband's image which was of the greatest concern to Alice. Arthur Chisolm was a man of refinement and a benefactor to many. He believed in helping the underprivileged, accepting barter from the poorer market gardeners in lieu of a consultation fee, or visiting their sick children and waiving the fee entirely. His philanthropy met with Alice's approval. Although she thought on occasions he went too far, it was right, she believed, for such a man to do, and to be seen to be doing, good works for the community. But his dignity must be maintained at all costs. The fact that it was Arthur himself who invited familiarity amongst those he treated often displeased her. She chided him on occasions, always gently, always mindful of her position as his wife, but her remonstrations invariably went unheeded.

'Oh my dear,' he'd say with good humour, 'you're too conservative, this is the thirties, you must move with the times.' He knew she was being protective, and he loved her for it, but it really was unnecessary, he thought.

Arthur Chisolm considered himself a modern man and, whilst his and his wife's differing views on protocol rarely caused friction in their marriage, there was one subject upon which they could not agree, and that subject was Phoebe. Arthur knew that he regularly incurred Alice's disapproval when he encouraged his daughter's independent streak, but he couldn't help himself. He was proud of Phoebe. Even in her flightiness, Phoebe had pluck, he thought. Pluck and determination. His daughter was a modern young woman and he admired her for it, much to Alice's consternation.

The morning of the regatta dawned bright and clear and Lofty awoke excited at the prospect of a whole day in Phoebe's company. She'd even let him hold her hand briefly at the cinema last night. He couldn't remember the name of the picture show they'd seen, something with James Cagney in it. He liked James Cagney, but he'd been aware of nothing but Phoebe's presence beside him. He wondered if the fact that she'd let him hold her hand meant she might agree to step out with him. It was all very well being included in Jane and Phoebe's company when they'd a mind to invite him, but it was hardly the same as stepping out. Today would be the test, he decided. After the regatta he'd ask Phoebe to go to the pictures alone with him next Friday. And he'd offer to seek her parents' permission – she'd know he was serious then. He was nervous at the prospect, but nonetheless determined.

Lofty wished he could feel confident with girls. He did with his male friends, he was quite popular at school, an excellent batsman and an asset to the cricket team. But with girls he was shy. Gangly and awkward in their company. Phoebe was different, though: he knew that she liked him. She made him feel special. And she was very much looking forward to going sailing, she'd told him so. Thank goodness Eric Frogmorton had agreed to lend him his dinghy. But then Eric had no need of his dinghy today, since he was crewing on his father's yacht in the official races.

Lofty dived into the bathroom before the rest of the household began to stir – he wasn't going to queue up behind his brothers this morning. He'd get to the boatshed good and early, he decided. Then he'd rig the dinghy and sail her up the creek to the far end of the recreation ground so he'd be ready and waiting when the girls arrived at ten o'clock.

Phoebe called around to Jane's house in Adelaide Place at nine in the morning. She and Jane wanted to get down to the Quay early and watch the first of the greasy pole competitions to be held in front of the Flour Mill. The official yachting races would take place a little later in the day when the wind was brisk, but Phoebe and Jane didn't want to miss a moment of the festivities.

The narrow garden opposite the Millers' front door was the most impressive of the mews' plots, brimming with healthy produce. Ron Miller grew all his own vegetables, and Phoebe loved harvesting the beans with Jane, or unearthing the carrots and turnips. As she knocked on Jane's door, she wished for the umpteenth time that they had a vegetable garden at Chisolm House.

'Hello, Phoebe.' Ron Miller led the way into the poky little kitchen where Jane was drying the dishes. 'Will you take a cup of tea and a slice of toast? We've some excellent marmalade our Jane bought at the markets.' Ron liked Phoebe Chisolm. She'd be a right handful, he thought, she'd a mind of her own, but there were no airs and graces about her. She was personable and polite and a fine friend for his daughter.

'No thank you, Mr Miller, I've just had breakfast. Are you ready, Jane?'

'Can I go now, Dad? I've done the dishes.'

''Course you can, girl. I'll see you down there when the big yachts start up.' Ron was meeting some old mates from the brickworks at the Castle in the Air and they were going to make a day of it. 'You have a good time now.' He looked at them fondly as they dived for the door. Brimming with girlish excitement, one dark, one fair, chalk and cheese in appearance, and both pretty as a picture. He and Arthur Chisolm had every right to be proud of their daughters. He called out, 'You two take care, mind,' but the door swung shut and, as usual, they didn't hear him.

The waters of Fareham Creek were already abuzz. Rowing craft, doubles, fours and eights, skimmed the surface. Sailing dinghies and small yachts milled about, tacking to and fro, miraculously avoiding collision. Whether they were practising for their races later in the day or simply having fun before the official water course was cleared wasn't evident, but Fareham's annual Aquatic Games and Regatta had most certainly begun. All about the quays and the riverbanks spectators were gathering. Children were swimming in the shallows by the recreation ground and families were already laying out rugs to claim the choicest picnic spots before the rush.

The first of the greasy pole competitions was just about to start. Two vertical poles had been dug into the shallows and a horizontal pole extended from each, at the end of which hung a leg of mutton or pork, the prize for the winner who could reach it. The contenders were mostly young men, fit and athletic, but it nevertheless seemed an impossible task. Jane and Phoebe watched for an hour, yelling encouragement along with the other spectators, but every contestant either slid back into the mud or, closer to the prize, landed in the water, much to the delight of the crowd.

Jane suddenly realised the time. 'It's half past ten,' she said.

'Did you see that?' Phoebe cheered and clapped her hands. 'He nearly got there.'

'We said we'd meet Lofty at ten o'clock.'

'Just a bit longer. Bill Pertwee's up next.' Phoebe didn't even look at her.

'All right. I'll go without you.' Jane turned to leave. She knew better than to try to cajole Phoebe; it was much easier to simply take the matter into her own hands.

Phoebe heaved a sigh. Jane was being bossy again. But

she obediently followed, aware that she couldn't always get her way with Jane.

'Sorry we're late,' she said to Lofty with a winning smile, not bothering to invent a reason why, which she would normally do if she thought it was of any importance.

'It doesn't matter,' Lofty replied, thankful to see her. He'd had a sinking feeling for the past half hour that she wasn't going to show up. 'All aboard.'

The girls, both in light summer dresses, took off their shoes and waded into the shallows. Lofty held on to the bow, the sail luffing in the breeze, as they climbed into the boat.

'Sit in the middle,' he instructed and they huddled together on the small centre seat as Lofty pushed the sturdy wooden dinghy out into the water and clambered over the stern. He grasped the tiller and tacked to port, hauling in the main sheet, the sail catching the breeze, the dinghy obeying, sluggishly at first. When he and Eric sailed they put the jib up too, but Lofty had decided against the extra canvas today; the girls had never been sailing before and, if he was to teach them, it was better to keep things simple.

'When I say "going about", you have to duck,' he told them, 'because the boom swings around. I'll show you. Going about!' he said in his best skipper's voice and he turned the dinghy into the wind.

The girls ducked under the heavy boom as it swung over their heads, and the boat set off on a starboard tack into the middle of the creek to join the throng of other small sailing craft.

Lofty handed Phoebe the rope. 'This is the main sheet,' he said, and he told her how to release it when they were going about and then haul in the slack as they started a fresh tack. The breeze was picking up and the dinghy was now zipping through the water. Small as she was, she was a sturdy, well-designed craft, locally built like many of the vessels out on the creek that day.

Lofty taught the girls how to sit on the side and lean out over the water when the boat listed in the wind, and they loved it. They were becoming real sailors now.

'Make it lean more, Lofty,' Phoebe yelled, pulling on the length of main sheet, the spray catching her in the face.

'Yes, make it lean more!' Jane's feet were hooked under the seat, her back arched as she clutched the gunwales, her whole body out over the water. It was thrilling.

'Want a race?' a nearby voice shouted. Another dinghy of similar size was speeding along beside them. It was Billy-boy, sailing on his own. Billy-boy was only fourteen, but he was serving an apprenticeship with Skip Johnston, the boat builder, and was an excellent sailor.

'Yes!' Phoebe and Jane yelled in unison, ignoring the fact that it was Lofty's right to reply.

'First past the boatshed!' Lofty shouted back to Billy-boy. If his power of decision was to be usurped, then at least he'd set the course.

The race was on. They had to tack three times before they could make a straight run for the boatshed and Lofty was slightly in the lead. His was by far the speedier craft and it was all credit to Billy-boy's skill as a yachtsman that the race was such a close one.

'We're winning! We're winning!' Phoebe shrieked and, only seconds later, she and Jane let out a cheer as the dinghy streaked past the boatshed half a length ahead of Billy-boy.

Then, out of nowhere, a rowing shell appeared directly ahead of them. The four had rowed out from behind the slipway, unaware that the dinghy was bearing down upon them.

Lofty made a lightning decision: there was only one thing for it, he had to jibe. 'Going about!' he yelled, pushing the tiller hard to his left, the boat turning with the wind in an instant. He hadn't taught the girls how to jibe, a much faster action than turning into the wind, and as the boom whipped across and the canvas luffed, they were caught off balance. The sail once again quickly gathered wind and the dinghy started to list, but the girls were unable to compensate, they were on the wrong side. The boat was about to capsize.

'Let go the sheet,' Lofty shouted. Phoebe did so, then everything seemed to happen at once. The sheet snaked briefly in the air like a mad thing, the dinghy righted itself, and Jane, unable to maintain her balance, was over the side, taking the sheet with her.

She landed on her back and, before she knew it, was underwater. She rolled over to swim to the surface, but there was something looped around her neck. It was the sheet, and it was tightening.

Lofty had seen Jane go over the side. He wasn't worried, both girls could swim, he wouldn't have taken them sailing otherwise, it was one of the rules. But thank goodness the boat hadn't capsized – it would have been so humiliating in front of everyone. He'd pointed the dinghy hard into the breeze, but the sail was gathering wind and she was starting to come around. There must be tension on the sheet, he realised. 'Let go of the sheet, Phoebe,' he said again.

But Phoebe was leaning over the side, her hand clasped in Jane's. 'She's caught in the rope!' she screamed. 'Help me!'

Jane had reached up and grasped Phoebe's hand. She could see her friend's terrified face as Phoebe leaned over the gunwales trying with all her might to haul her aboard. But the trailing end of the rope was caught under the stern of the dinghy and, as the sail slowly filled, the rope tightened and Jane was held below the water, her face only inches from the surface.

'Help me!' Phoebe screamed again. 'Help me!' Their hands

were above the water, locked together, but try as she might she couldn't pull Jane those precious inches closer. Nevertheless, her hand was a lifeline and she didn't dare let go.

'Jesus!' After one quick look at the stricken girl, Lofty leaned over the stern to free the fouled rope. The sheet had fed itself up between the shaft of the rudder and the transom and the end of the rope was wedged there.

To Jane, her whole world now moved in slow motion. Her body was gliding gently through the water and, beyond the sun-dappled surface, so close, she could see Phoebe's panic-stricken face. She seemed to be saying something, but her mouth was moving slowly as she formed the words and Jane couldn't hear what it was. She looked up through the bottled glass of the water at Phoebe and the world above, and she could hear nothing. All was silence.

She felt no sense of panic. Her mind, like her body, was starting to drift. Peacefully. Far, far away. She wanted to tell Phoebe that everything was all right, and the tension in her hand loosened as she gave herself up to the strangely euphoric sensation of nothingness.

No! Phoebe wanted to scream it out, but she didn't. Jane was giving up, she could tell. In her eyes was a calmness which Phoebe found frightening. She tightened her grip on Jane's hand. Hold on, she thought, but she didn't scream the words. Her own panic had evaporated. It was only a matter of time, any second now Lofty would free the rope. But Jane was giving up. And she mustn't. She mustn't. Hold on, Jane, Phoebe thought, focussing on the glazed eyes of her friend and willing all the strength she could into the lifeline of her hand. Hold on.

Lofty was desperate. The spliced end of the sheet was thicker than the rest of the rope and was firmly wedged, he couldn't pull it through the gap. Once again he turned the boat into the wind to lessen the tension. The top of Jane's head rose to the surface but the loop of the rope was so firmly around her neck that the weight of her body pulled her away from the boat and she still couldn't surface high enough to breathe. Lofty was running out of time. The knife. Eric always kept a knife on board. Under the stern seat, in a leather scabbard. 'Oh Jesus!' Frantically he searched.

As Jane was pulled away from the side of the boat she could no longer see Phoebe's face; she was looking down into the murky depths of the creek now. But she could feel Phoebe's hand, still holding hers in a grip of iron. And Phoebe's hand became an extension of her own, the only connection she had with life. There was power in Phoebe's hand. Phoebe could make things happen, Phoebe could save her. The murky depths beckoned, but Jane's mind had stopped drifting now as she realised she didn't want to die. She held on for all she was worth.

Lofty had found the knife. He started sawing through the rope.

Leaning over the gunwales, her arm fully extended, Phoebe could feel Jane's hand tighten about hers. She hadn't given up. Jane was holding on with every last vestige of strength she possessed. Phoebe did the same.

'Hurry, Lofty, hurry!' she said, her own strength ebbing.

The knife was sharp, and it took Lofty only seconds. Suddenly, the rope was freed.

Jane surfaced from her silence to the chaos above, to a sun that was blinding and sounds which seemed deafening. Phoebe yelling, the sail loudly flapping, Lofty grunting as he hauled her aboard. She lay in the dinghy and tried to breathe but the air she gasped at stuck in her throat. Then, as blackness threatened to engulf her, she felt her chest over the wooden seat and Lofty pressing her hard in the centre of her back with the heels of his hands. 'Come on, Jane, breathe,' he was saying, and he pressed again, so hard that any minute her ribs might break. 'Breathe.' And then she was spluttering and coughing up water, and then gasping air and coughing up more water, until finally, chest heaving, she was gulping in huge lungfuls of air.

'Thanks, Lofty,' she managed to say, her voice little more than a croak, and she looked at Phoebe, who was suddenly quiet. 'Thanks, Phoebe.'

'Are you all right?'

'Yes.' Their eyes locked and neither said a word. Something had happened between them and they both knew it.

All three were silent for a moment or so, as the shock of what might have occurred set in. Then Lofty said, 'We'd better get you to a doctor.' There was an ugly red mark around Jane's neck where the rope had chafed her.

'No.' Jane felt her neck, the skin was tender and sore. Strange, she thought, it hadn't hurt at all when she was underwater. 'I'm fine, Lofty, really.'

'You all right?' a voice called. It was Billy-boy who'd cruised up alongside them. He'd laughed when the dinghy was about to capsize, and would have made a right joke of it if it had. Lofty might have won the race but he couldn't control his boat in a simple jibe, he'd say. He'd laughed when he'd seen Jane go overboard too. Serve Lofty right for having girls on board, he'd thought. And they'd taken their time getting her out of the water. But now Lofty seemed to be in a bit of bother, the sail was flapping uselessly in the wind and they were drifting towards the shoreline. 'Want a hand?'

'Nope,' Lofty grabbed the frayed end of the sheet and hauled in the sail. 'We're fine, thanks, just had a bit of trouble with the main.'

Billy-boy looked at the mainsail and couldn't see any trouble with it at all. Well, that's what happened when you had girls on board, he thought again. 'Right you are then.' And he left them to it.

Lofty sailed them back to the far end of the recreation ground. 'I'm really sorry, Jane,' he said as he helped her out of the boat. 'I don't know how it happened, I'm really, really sorry.'

'It wasn't your fault, Lofty.' Jane smiled reassuringly. She could see he felt wretched. 'Thank you for saving me.' She refused once again to be taken to the doctor. 'I just want to go home and change,' she said, and Lofty watched miserably as the girls set off hand in hand along the railed path beside the water. It had been a freak accident and no-one's fault, but it didn't stop him feeling guilty.

'Good heavens above, Jane, what happened to you?' Mrs Cookson had set the family rug out on the grass and was unloading the picnic hamper whilst her younger children played nearby. She looked at the saturated summer dress clinging to Jane's legs and the ringing wet curls dripping about her shoulders. 'You're soaked,' she remarked, stating the obvious, as Mrs Cookson always did.

Before Jane could reply, Maude Cookson joined them. 'She took a dunking off Eric Frogmorton's boat,' she said. Maude had been leaning on the path railings watching the proceedings. 'And Lofty nearly capsized, I saw him.'

'But he won the race,' Phoebe interjected. 'Did you see that too?' Maude Cookson never meant to be rude, she was just blunt and, in Phoebe's opinion, a bit stupid.

'Yep, I saw that. He beat Billy-boy.' Maude was impress-ed, Billy-boy had been junior champion yachtsman two years in a row.

'You'd better go home and change, dear, you wouldn't want to catch a chill now,' Mrs Cookson said, and Jane and Phoebe made their escape.

Jane was thankful that her father had already left to meet his mates and the house was deserted.

'What will you tell him about that?' Phoebe nodded at the chafe marks around Jane's throat.

'I'll think of a story,' Jane said vaguely, 'an accident with a skipping rope or something. I won't get Lofty into trouble, it wasn't his fault.'

When she'd changed, they sat on the little bench beside the vegetable garden.

'Nobody knows what happened except us.' It was Phoebe who broke the silence. 'They saw it, Billy-boy and Maude and probably dozens of others. But nobody knows what happened.' It was a sobering thought.

'What *did* happen, Phoebe?'

'You nearly drowned, that's what happened.'

'I *did* drown,' Jane said, 'and you saved me.'

'It was Lofty who did the lifesaving, he got you breathing.'

Jane shook her head. 'I'd drowned before that. And you pulled me back.'

'I held on to your hand, that's all.'

'No it's not. There was more than that.' Jane wondered how she could explain to Phoebe the experience she'd had. The drifting feeling, the certain knowledge that she was floating away to another place. And then the knowledge that Phoebe had brought her back. 'There was much, much more than that.'

'Yes,' Phoebe said. 'I know.' And Jane realised there was no need for explanation, just as there was no answer to what had happened.

That night, along with hundreds of others gathered on the recreation ground, Jane and Phoebe watched the procession of illuminated boats parade down the creek. It was the highlight of the regatta. They watched the bonfire on Cams Point across the water, and the firework display, the 'oohs' and 'ahs' of the crowd echoing about them as each fresh spectacle lit up the sky.

As they watched, Jane felt an overwhelming sense of gratitude that she was alive to see it, and beside her she felt Phoebe take her hand. They turned to look at each other. Phoebe knew what she was thinking. Jane had died and come back to life and Phoebe had been with her the whole time. Phoebe had shared in her death, and their lives were now forever linked. They stood side by side holding hands, and together they looked up at the fireworks.

# CHAPTER FIVE

Sam awoke with little recall of the details of her dreams, but the images remained vivid. Two young girls, one dark, one fair, and the sound of their laughter still rang in her ears. They'd been playing in the stables, up here in the loft where her bed now was, but there had been a trapdoor, and a wide ladder had led to the tack room and the vacant horse stalls below. Just the way she imagined the stables might once have been.

She pondered the images as she ate her bowl of breakfast cereal. She'd been affected by the stories of the past, she realised. She remembered Mrs M saying that Phoebe Chisolm had loved to play in the stables as a child. One of the girls must have been Phoebe, or rather her own image of what Phoebe might have looked like as a child, but who was the other?

There was a tap on the door and, as if on cue, a familiar voice with a thick Hampshire accent called from outside. 'Anyone home?'

'Mrs M!' Sam embraced the woman who, despite the passage of nine years, didn't appear to have changed one bit. 'How did you know I was here?' she asked as she ushered her inside.

'You can't keep a secret in Fareham, dear,' Mrs M beamed, her eyes crinkling with pleasure. 'It's all around the borough that you've bought the house. I even heard about it in Portsmouth, I live there with Betty now. Oh you have done the stables up a treat,' she said looking around, 'and in just one day, how extraordinary.'

'Would you like a cup of tea?'

'That would be lovely.' Mrs M sat heavily in one of the armchairs whilst Sam busied herself behind the island bench. 'You could have knocked me down with a feather when I heard. I certainly didn't think it would come to that when I sent you the leaflet, but when I found out –'

'You sent the leaflet?' The electric jug overflowed as Sam looked up from the sink.

'Yes, I don't know why. Just on a whim. Didn't you know it was me?' Sam shook her head. 'Good heavens, I must have forgotten to put in a note. How silly. I've been following your career with such interest, you know. I sent it as a memento really, it had such a nice picture of Chisolm House on it. I certainly didn't expect you to buy the place, though. You could have knocked me down with –'

'But how did you get hold of it?'

'Get hold of what, dear?'

'The leaflet.' Jim Lofthouse had said they hadn't been distributed, Sam recalled.

'Oh, it just landed in my letterbox, somebody obviously knew of my connection with Chisolm House. Now tell me, dear,' Mrs M was off on a tangent once again, 'were you thrilled when you saw them? Did you wonder how they got there? I so wanted to take you by surprise.'

Things were moving too fast for Sam. She felt as if she were in a ping-pong match with a vastly superior opponent. 'How what got where?' she asked.

'The portrait. Phoebe Chisolm's portrait and the family photograph,' Mrs M explained. In the brief silence which followed she gave another expansive beam. 'You didn't guess it was me. Oh I am so glad. I wanted to give you a special moment. I know that you have such a feeling for this house.'

'Yes I do. And I believe the house has a feeling for me.' The words had popped out automatically, and Sam felt presumptuous and rather foolish.

'Oh it does, dear, I'm quite sure of that.' Martha Montgomery found the statement neither presumptuous nor foolish. 'That's why I returned the portrait and the photograph to their rightful home. They wouldn't belong here with someone who felt no affinity with the house and its past.'

Sam had a dozen questions to ask of the woman as they sat drinking their tea but, as usual, Mrs M waxed loquacious and the questions were answered before Sam could voice them. Jim Lofthouse had been more than happy to allow her access to the house, she said, and, at her suggestion, he'd arranged the delivery of the shrub in the white clay pot. 'A little homey touch by way of welcome.' But it had been Jim himself who had organised a gardener to clean up the front garden. 'He's a very nice fellow, Jim Lofthouse,' she said.

The most interesting part of Mrs M's story was how she herself had come to acquire the portrait and the photograph. 'I saw Miss Chisolm in the last days of August,' she said, 'just before the end. She passed over on the first of September, you know, the first day of autumn, her favourite month. And I'm quite convinced in my mind that she planned it, for she was as lucid as you and me in those final days. "Now Martha," she said, "the portrait and the family photograph are to go to you, and you're to do with them as you see fit." She meant something by it, I'm sure she did. I was to be their keeper, that's what she was saying. And when I heard that you'd bought the place, I knew they were meant to come home where they rightfully belong.'

'But the portrait is valuable, Mrs M,' Sam said. 'You can't just give it away, it could be worth quite a sum of money.'

'Oh my dear,' Mrs M was instantly dismissive, 'as if I could ever sell it. And I've no need for money, I'm retired now, I've no need to work at all. Although I do a little child-minding at a preschool just down the road from Betty's,' she added, 'I love the kiddies, and I like to keep myself busy. Miss Chisolm left me with a healthy annuity, you see. Like I said, she had her wits about her right there at the end. Sharp as a tack, she was, as if her mind had never wandered at all. "You've been a godsend to me, Martha," she said, "in these final years".'

Mrs M was suddenly overcome with emotion and fumbled for her handkerchief in the voluminous handbag which sat on her lap. 'And then she said, "You'll be a godsend to me yet, what's more," and I've no idea what she meant, for it's she who's been a godsend to me and that's the truth.' She dabbed at her eyes, blew her nose unapologetically and, fully recovered, returned her handkerchief to her handbag. 'Oh yes, I've no financial worries until the day I die, thanks to Miss Chisolm, God bless her.'

The morning passed quickly over more tea and more chat. They talked about Sam's plans and her career, and Mrs M's grandchildren, now fully grown and, as Martha Montgomery was about to take her leave, Sam suddenly remembered what she'd wanted to ask the woman.

'Mrs M, did Phoebe Chisolm have a particularly close friend when she was a child? A girl about the same age?'

'Oh dear me, yes. Jane Miller was her name. Of course I only knew Miss Chisolm as an elderly lady, but she spoke a great deal of her childhood and Jane Miller. In fact she spoke of little else. She rarely talked about the bad times, and why should she? Poor darling, she'd had her share. Childhood was precious, she said, and a child's happiness sacred. Why do you ask?'

'I had a dream,' Sam said, once again feeling a little foolish.

'Really?' Mrs M was instantly fascinated; she believed very much in dreams and premonitions and the like.

'Two young girls were playing in the stables.'

'Yes, that would have been Phoebe and Jane.' Mrs M nodded in all seriousness. 'Miss Chisolm told me the stables was their favourite hideout. How interesting.' She leaned forward in her armchair, cuddling her handbag to her ample bosom. 'How very, very interesting.'

'Oh probably just autosuggestion on my part.' Sam didn't particularly wish to pursue such a fanciful conversation. Of course Phoebe Chisolm would have had a special friend. What little girl didn't? She was surprised that she'd asked the question of Mrs M at all. But then the dream had been so vivid.

'Autosuggestion?' Mrs M queried with a touch of disbelief. 'Perhaps.' Then she added enigmatically, 'and perhaps not. One never really knows, does one?' She heaved herself out of her chair. She would love to have chatted on, but she'd promised Betty she'd help with afternoon tea for the Ladies' Auxiliary. 'Well, I'd best be off, dear.'

She was catching the next train back to Portsmouth and refused Sam's offer to get her a taxi to the station. 'Good gracious me, no,' she said, 'I need all the exercise I can get, so the doctor says, and I enjoy a healthy walk.'

'Good luck with the film, dear,' she said as they hugged each other outside in the courtyard, 'it all sounds most exciting.' Sam had promised that she would be in touch as soon as she returned to Fareham after the movie's completion. 'And in the meantime,' Mrs M vowed, 'we'll keep an eye on Chisolm House for you, the three of us.' In answer to Sam's querying look, she said with a smile, 'Jim Lofthouse and me, and Phoebe of course.'

It was lunchtime when Sam finally ventured out, and she was ravenous. She devoured a sandwich sitting in one of the myriad cafes in one of the myriad arcades in the huge shopping complex, after which her first planned port of call was to be the liquor store where she'd buy a bottle of Scotch for Jim Lofthouse.

She cut through one of the arcades which led to the West Street mall and, as she did so, she noticed a sign in a jewellery shop window: WE STOCK FROGMORTON SILVER. Beside the sign was a display of exquisitely crafted souvenir spoons amongst which stood several figurines. Lovely as they were, none of them was as fine as her silver horse, Sam thought. The horse now lived in her makeup kit, wrapped in a small velvet cloth, to be taken out and placed upon her dressing-room table whenever she was performing. It had become her good luck charm. She should have told Mrs M that, and she reminded herself to do so the next time they met.

Lunchtime crowds thronged the pedestrian mall as she passed by Westbury Manor, the beautifully restored Georgian building converted to a proud town museum. She'd collected a brochure there on her very first walk around Fareham all those years ago, she remembered. She must pay a more comprehensive visit to the museum, she promised herself as she walked the further block to the bottle shop.

*Jane and Phoebe had wriggled through to the front of the crowd that lined the expanse of West Street as the procession made its way up from the cattle markets. They had the very best vantage point outside the once fine home of Westbury Manor, now shabby and serving as council offices, and they waved their flags and souvenir programmes in the air, calling out to people they knew in the parade.*

*At the head of the procession, clearing the way, was Eric Frogmorton in his father's brand new, shiny green Vauxhall sedan. Mr Frogmorton was seated beside him in the passenger seat, having allowed his son the honour of* driving. Through the open car window, Eric briefly acknowledged the girls before returning his full focus to the task at hand and the crowds. He was terrified that someone might scratch his father's pride and joy and that he'd get the blame for it.

'Phoebe! Jane!' It was Lofty waving a gangly arm above the heads of the Fareham cricket XI as they marched past in their flannels; they'd won the Borough Shield that year.

Then came the brass band and the cadets from the naval academy, then the horse-drawn carriages, and the floats sponsored by local businesses. Some were decked with flowers, some displayed local produce in intricate designs, and on one float the members of the dramatic society posed impressively in period costume.

The Fareham Coronation Celebrations were a sight to behold and, to Phoebe, they held a special significance. One which she had marked upon her souvenir programme. On the front of the programme were pictures of King George VI and Queen Elizabeth, together with the date, 12th May, 1937, and on Phoebe's programme, beneath the date, she had printed, in her very best hand, 'my birthday'.

'To turn seventeen on Coronation Day is an omen,' she had remarked to Jane, and she'd said it with the greatest solemnity. To Phoebe, the coincidental date of the monarch's coronation and her own birthday was no accident. It had been preordained, and was of the utmost consequence. She wasn't sure how, but there was always a purpose in such things, she told Jane.

Jane secretly thought that Phoebe's fancies were running away with her as they often did, but she loved Phoebe far too much to mar her day by saying anything of so practical a nature. Now, as they waved their flags and their programmes and thrilled with the crowds to the excitement of it all, Jane yelled at the top of her voice. 'Happy birthday, Phoebe!'

*And Phoebe, acknowledging the tribute, smiled with all the warmth and self-assurance of one deserving of such homage on this, her very special day.*

Sam couldn't help smiling as she stepped out of the bottle shop. The man behind the counter had welcomed her as a local. 'Good on you Miss Lindsay, you're one of us now,' he'd said. It made her feel very special.

She'd bought a bottle of Glenfiddich. She wasn't sure if Jim Lofthouse was a single malt man or whether he preferred a blended whisky, perhaps he wasn't even a Scotch drinker at all. But the bottle was expensive and in a nice presentation box, and it was the thought that counted anyway.

She crossed the road to the real estate office near the corner of Trinity Street, and opened the door to discover the young secretary hunched over her computer, but no Jim.

'It's his lunch break,' the girl said. 'He's around the corner at the pub. You could pop in and see him there if you like.'

'Oh no,' Sam replied, 'he's probably having a drink with some mates, I wouldn't want to interrupt him.'

Samantha Lindsay seemed nice after all, Peggy Shortall thought. She'd been bloody rude last time she'd come in to the office. 'He doesn't drink.'

'Ah.' Sam glanced down at the bright yellow plastic carry bag which housed the Scotch.

'And he doesn't go there to meet mates, half the time he doesn't even go there for lunch.' Aware that an explanation was necessary, Peggy added, 'He just goes there to suck down as many fags as he can in an hour.'

'Oh well, I still won't interrupt him. How long do you think he'll be?'

Peggy looked at her watch. 'Half an hour.'

'Fine, I'll come back then. Do you mind if I leave this here?' Sam dumped the carry bag on the counter, and Peggy looked at the bright yellow plastic with the eminently recognisable liquor store insignia. 'I bought him a present,' Sam said with a rueful shrug.

'He'll like that.' Peggy smiled for the first time. 'He's got lots of friends who drink.'

Sam decided to walk down to the Quay. It was a fine day, and she sat on a bench in the recreation park, looking at the boats on the water and the dinghies listing in the low-tide mud. It was so timeless, she thought. So timeless and so peaceful.

'Jane?'

The voice was right beside her and Sam turned to see an elderly woman seated next to her on the bench, staring at her intently. She'd been unaware of the woman's approach, her mind had been so blissfully blank.

'No, I'm sorry,' she said, 'my name's Samantha. Samantha Lindsay.'

'Ah yes.' The old woman smiled. A pretty smile. She must have been well into her eighties, her hair was snow-white and her face weathered with the years, but there was an air of refinement about her. 'Samantha Lindsay. You're the young woman who's bought the old Chisolm House.'

'That's right.'

'You reminded me of someone else for a moment.' The woman looked out over the quay at nothing in particular. 'Such a lot of love in that house.'

Sam's attention was immediately captured. Had the woman known Phoebe Chisolm? They'd be roughly the same age, she was sure. 'Did you know the Chisolms?' she asked eagerly. 'Did you know Phoebe?'

'Oh yes indeed.' The woman smiled her pretty smile once again. 'I knew Phoebe well.'

'And Jane?' Sam felt a sense of excitement. 'Jane Miller?'

'Of course. That's who you reminded me of.' The woman was once again studying her intently. 'Jane had such lovely fair curls, just like you. She was a beautiful girl.'

'Tell me about them,' Sam urged. 'Please. Tell me about Phoebe and Jane.'

But the woman had turned away again to stare vacantly across the water. 'Such parties in that house. A big house, just the Chisolms lived there, but the doors were always open to Phoebe's young friends. And in the war years there was a shortage of billets in the borough and Chisolm House became home to a number of servicemen. They were hard times, with the bombs and the rationing, but we were young, all of us, so young.' The old woman seemed to have drifted away into a world of her own. 'And at Chisolm House there were still parties, and the piano still played.' She shook her head as she gazed into the past. 'Such love in that house.'

Sam hadn't dared interrupt but now, as the woman lapsed into silence, she tentatively asked. 'How did you know Phoebe and Jane?'

Dragged back to the present, the old woman turned to her. 'We went to school together, of course.' She said it as if it was a fact of which Sam should have been fully aware.

'Oh.' Resisting the urge to apologise, Sam made a gentle enquiry instead. 'May I ask your name?'

The woman looked vague for a moment, as if she wasn't quite sure of the answer. 'Maude,' she said finally. 'My name is Maude. I must go now.' She eased herself up from the bench. 'It's been a most pleasant chat.'

Sam wanted to say, 'Where do you live, please may I call on you, can we meet again?' There was so much more she wanted to know. But the woman turned and walked slowly and steadily away down the path with such an air of finality that she felt she'd be intruding if she pushed any further.

Surely, though, an old woman called Maude who'd lived in Fareham all her life wouldn't be difficult to trace. She'd ask Jim Lofthouse, she decided. Jim was a local.

'Oh yes, that'd be Maude Cookson,' Jim said as they sat later in his poky little office. 'The Cooksons have been in the borough for generations, strawberry farmers from Titchfield. But old Maude lives with her daughter here in Fareham now. She's famous around town. Harmless enough, but away with the pixies, absolutely barmy.'

'Really?' Sam was surprised. 'She didn't seem barmy to me. A bit vague maybe, but not barmy.'

'Oh she is, believe me. Off her trolley, mad as a hatter. Senile dementia, poor thing. She's always wandering out of her daughter's house and getting into trouble, they're going to have to put her in a home soon. Last time she had a bad fall and she's been quite lame since. I'm surprised she made it to the park at all.'

Sam recalled the woman's slow but steady gait as she'd walked away. 'She wasn't lame,' she said. 'In fact she seemed quite fit for a person her age.'

'Really?' Jim was puzzled. It didn't sound like old Maude at all. 'What did she look like?'

Sam reflected for a moment, the woman had impressed her. 'Elegant,' she said thoughtfully. Yes, that was the word. 'Quite elegant, with silver hair, and she was well dressed . . .'

Jim laughed. 'Can't have been Maude. Maude's nearly bald, and she wanders around in a dressing gown.'

'She said her name was Maude.'

He shrugged. 'Pretty common name. But it wasn't Maude Cookson, that's for sure.' He shook his head dismissively. 'Doesn't sound like a local to me. Maybe she's from out of town, there's a lot of tourists around.'

Sam could tell he was losing interest, but she persisted. 'She said she went to school with Phoebe Chisolm.'

'Did she?' She'd caught his attention again, she could tell. 'That's odd. I should certainly know her if she's a local. I'll make some enquiries, if you like.'

'Would you? That'd be great. I'd really like to talk to her again, I'm very interested in Phoebe and the old days at Chisolm House.'

'Sure, I'll ask around, I'm playing golf on Friday.' Sam looked mystified at the inconsequential remark. 'A lot of the old crowd hang around the club at Cam's Golf Course,' he explained, 'if anyone knows this mysterious Maude, it'll be one of that mob.' As she rose from her chair, he also stood, his lanky form too big for the tiny office. 'Thanks again for the Scotch,' he said.

'The least I can do.' They walked through to the reception area. 'I should have got something else, though. I didn't know you don't drink.'

'Not to worry, I have mates who do.'

'So I've heard.' Sam smiled at Peggy, who gave her a nod.

'My dad knew Phoebe Chisolm,' Jim said casually as he opened the front door for her.

'He did?' Sam stopped in her tracks.

'Yes, very well, he courted her for a while when they were young.'

'And?' She nodded for him to go on. Why on earth hadn't he mentioned it earlier?

'He was mad about her evidently, but I don't think she was very interested.' Jim grinned. 'It was a running joke in our house. Whenever Mum and Dad had a bit of a row she'd say "you should have married Phoebe Chisolm". And he'd say "she wouldn't have me". And then Mum'd say "no wonder". It was all meant as fun, more or less, but I think Mum was actually a bit jealous. I don't know why, Phoebe Chisolm had married her American soldier and left the country by the time Mum and Dad got together. Maybe she thought she'd caught him on the rebound.' Jim shrugged. 'I suspect she probably did, but they had a happy marriage in the long run.' He grinned again. 'Funny isn't it, talking about your parents as young things? I wonder if my kids ever talk about me that way.'

'Quite likely.' Sam gently steered him back on track, she was fascinated. 'And Jane Miller? Did your dad know Jane Miller?'

'Oh yes, the Millers were an old Fareham family. Let's step outside, shall we?' He'd been holding the door open and, realising that Sam wanted a bit of a chat, a cigarette beckoned. 'Do you mind? It's not cold.'

'Sure.'

Out on the pavement, Jim lit up and continued. 'They're not around any more, though, the Millers. One of the brothers was killed in the war and the other one's in a nursing home in London. He'd be in his nineties now.'

'And Jane? What happened to Jane?'

'Dad said she went to some island in the South Pacific and nobody heard from her again.' He took a hefty drag on his cigarette. 'He said it was big news in Fareham in those days, a young local woman going off to live in some heathen place on the other side of the world. Dad liked Jane. He said she was "an admirable young woman", those were his words. He talked quite a lot about the old days, my dad.'

'I don't suppose he's still around?' Sam asked hopefully.

'Nope.' Jim inhaled, then took a look at his half-smoked cigarette. 'He died fifteen years ago, lung cancer.' He ground the butt out with the heel of his shoe. 'I'll make those enquiries at the golf club for you,' he said as he opened the door.

'Good on you, Jim, thanks.' She was still thinking about Phoebe and Jane as she set off down West Street to do her shopping. She hoped Jim's search for Maude would prove fruitful.

Sam spent the next two days settling in to the stables, unpacking her crates of belongings and making a home to return to. She'd be living in hotels or rented accommodation during the studio filming and on location, and she fully intended to base herself in Fareham when the movie was completed. She wasn't quite sure what she'd do about the house itself. It was far too big for her and she'd probably have to rent it out, but she'd worry about that on her return.

Towards the end of the week she visited the museum and the library to study up on the history of the town and its people. The name Arthur Chisolm featured quite often amongst the mentions of Fareham's prominent citizens, as did those of his wife Alice and his daughter Phoebe, but she could find no reference to Jane Miller and her family. She became fixated upon the fate of Phoebe's friend Jane. What had happened to her when she'd left Fareham? How dearly she would have loved to talk to someone who knew. She still had her hopes pinned on Jim's enquiries.

'Well, your mysterious Maude appears to have vanished into thin air,' Jim said when she called into his office on the Saturday morning. 'No-one at the club knows her and no-one's even seen her around town. I did a check on Maude Cookson in case she'd made some miraculous recovery, but she's as bald and barmy as ever.'

They talked for a while and decided between them that the old woman in the park must have simply been on a day's nostalgia trip to the town of her youth. 'No other explanation,' Jim said. 'Sorry I can't be of more help.'

Sam felt distinctly disappointed as she lay in bed that night. How she'd longed to unlock some of the secrets of the past. But she awoke on the Sunday suddenly riddled with guilt. The script! She hadn't even looked at the script and Reg was collecting her the following afternoon to take her to the airport. How could she have been so slack? She spent all day swotting. Not only learning her lines, but getting into the head of the woman she was to play and, as she did so, she felt the familiar anticipatory tingle of excitement at the prospect of a challenging, well-written role. But this time it was more than a tingle. This time, as she worked on the script, she felt her excitement gather until it charged through every fibre of her being. This was the role of a lifetime. She couldn't wait to get into the heart and the soul of this woman.

She went up to the house in the late afternoon to have one last look around before the fade of daylight, and as she wandered again through the rooms of Chisolm House, she felt more than ever its embrace. The past called out to her.

She heard the piano in the upstairs drawing room. Just a tinkling at first, which she again put down to her imagination running riot. Then she heard the melody. Loud and clear. 'We'll Meet Again'. And there was the sound of voices, men and women singing along. 'We'll meet again, don't know where, don't know when . . .'

She looked out of the downstairs bay windows and heard a girl laughing, the same laughter she'd heard on the day she'd arrived with Reg. And when she turned to look at Phoebe's portrait, she could swear she saw movement. In the moment she'd turned, so had Phoebe. And Phoebe had been captured in that very moment of turning. Her eyes were locked into Sam's and they were saying something.

'What are you doing to me?' Sam whispered. Her mind was reeling, her senses were being assaulted from every direction. The piano, the voices, the girl's laughter, and now Phoebe's eyes, alive and beckoning. Mesmerised, she crossed to the portrait and stared into its depths. Was she going mad? she wondered. But even as she thought it, she didn't feel frightened, and she didn't feel threatened. The house was trying to tell her something. Phoebe was trying to tell her something.

'What are you saying to me?' she whispered to the portrait.

*'It's a fine likeness, James,' Arthur Chisolm said, 'a very fine likeness. Indeed, it's a masterly painting, I'm most impressed.'*

*They stood around the fireplace, the five of them, admiring the portrait which Arthur had just hung above the mantelpiece.*

'You have a great future ahead of you, my boy, and I'm sure your father will recognise the fact when he sees a work such as this. If not, I'll have a word with him, I promise.'

'Thank you very much, Dr Chisolm,' James said gratefully. A word from Arthur Chisolm would most certainly help, although he doubted if even the intervention of the venerable doctor would salve his father's disappointment.

'To James Hampton,' Arthur said, raising his sherry glass, 'and to his future career.'

Alice, Phoebe and Jane each raised their glasses. 'To James,' they said.

'You've certainly captured the spirit of our Phoebe,' Arthur continued. He was genuine in his praise. Good God but the boy had a talent, he thought. Arthur never lied, nor did he exaggerate, and he would most certainly do all he could to pacify the disappointment of William Hampton over the loss of his son's naval career. But the boy was duty bound to pursue such a God-given talent. 'Just look at the light in those eyes,' he said. 'That's our Phoebe all right.'

Arthur continued to gaze proudly at the portrait of his daughter as Alice acknowledged the appearance of Enid at the door signalling dinner was ready.

James flashed a guilty look at Phoebe, he couldn't help it. But Phoebe smiled back openly, flagrant and totally unashamed.

'He has, hasn't he, Daddy,' she said. 'He's captured the real me.'

None of it went unnoticed by Jane. She'd been studying everyone's reaction. Phoebe glanced over and caught her eye.

'What do you think, Jane?' she asked in apparent innocence.

'Oh yes, I think he's captured you beautifully,' Jane agreed. Phoebe was truly outrageous, she thought, but as

*always there were no secrets between them, and Jane
relished the brazen moment they shared.*

'*Dinner is served,*' *Alice Chisolm announced.*

'What are you saying to me, Phoebe?' Sam once again
whispered to the portrait. But the eyes were no longer
alive. They were looking far beyond her at something or
someone from a distant time. The moment had passed,
and Sam was talking to a painting.

She went back to the stables and packed her suitcase for
the following day. She kept herself busy, refusing to admit
that she was shaken by experiences which, she told herself,
were purely of her own imagining. She looked at the script
again, but she couldn't seem to work up the intensity she'd
felt earlier in the day.

It took her some time to get to sleep that night and,
when she did, she once again dreamed. But this time her
dreams were those she'd expected a week ago, when she'd
returned to Fareham and the stables. They were erotic. She
and Pete were in the narrow bed in the loft. She could feel
his body. His skin, his breath, his desire mingling with
hers. But suddenly, it wasn't Pete. And there was no bed.
She felt rough boards beneath her back.

'*Teach me. Teach me, James,*' *Phoebe whispered, thrusting herself wantonly at him.* '*Teach me what it's like.*'

In the morning, Sam woke exhausted, as if she hadn't
slept at all. She couldn't remember her dream, but she was
aware of its erotic nature and that somehow, like the strange
sensations of the previous day, it related to the past.

She jumped out of bed and registered, all of a sudden,
that the loft was freezing. What had happened to the
heating? She raced downstairs and discovered that
the central heating had switched itself off during the night
and that no attempt on her part could reactivate it.

For the next half hour Sam's mind teemed with invention. She stood under the hot shower, thinking, 'The house
itself has switched off, it knows that I'm going.' Then,

rugged up against the cold in her heavy woollen overcoat, making herself a pot of tea, she thought, 'No, the house is *telling* me to go. It's telling me that it's time to move on. It *wants* me to go.'

Well, the house was quite right, she thought, even as she chided herself for being foolish. It certainly was time to move on. The house and all its secrets would still be here when she returned from filming. In the meantime she had a career to think of, and the seductive Phoebe Chisolm and the mysterious Jane Miller were becoming altogether too distracting.

# BOOK TWO

# CHAPTER SIX

He was aware of the feel of clean cotton sheets. He was in a bed. But he hadn't known a bed for so long. Where was he? And a soft warm cloth was bathing his brow. What had happened? Had he dreamed the bombs and the beach and the boats?

Martin Thackeray opened his eyes and the first thing he saw was his angel. The angel at the dockyard who had welcomed him home from the horrors, and the same halo of light rested about her fair hair as she leaned over him, bathing his face.

'Who are you?' he whispered. It seemed of the utmost importance he should know who she was. After that, everything would fall into place.

'Jane,' the nurse in the crisp white uniform softly answered, 'my name is Jane Miller.'

Martin had been delirious for two days. Teetering on the brink of death. The crisis was over, and Jane felt an immense sense of relief. Martin Thackeray's recovery seemed to her an omen. A change in the tide of death and mutilation she'd witnessed at the Royal Victoria Hospital following the evacuation of Dunkirk.

'Welcome back,' she said.

'Jane Miller,' he whispered, and he gently smiled as he once more closed his eyes. 'God bless you, Jane Miller.'

Jane had left school at the age of seventeen to take up her training as a nurse and now, after three years' intensive service in the wards of the Royal Victoria Hospital, she was a qualified Junior Sister. Commuting by train from Fareham to Netley, her days were long and gruelling, but she loved her work and she loved the Royal Victoria.

The vast and impressive military hospital had been completed in 1863 following the recognition that facilities for wounded soldiers returning from the Crimean War were sadly inadequate. Standing four stories high on its chosen site near the entrance of Southampton Water, it extended nearly a mile in length and was ornately designed with arched windows, minarets and a white central dome, beneath which lay its chapel. The Royal Victoria Hospital had served the wounded throughout the First World War and was now proving its worth in the Second.

Small as her role might have been, Jane was proud to be a part of such a noble establishment, and she was a good nurse. Strong, practical and efficient. Dr Chisolm himself had openly sung the praises of his daughter's best friend.

'We need your kind more than ever these days, Jane,' he'd said. 'Resilient young women with strength of character – there's no place for the squeamish in a war hospital.'

Since the influx of heavy casualties from Dunkirk, Jane had assisted in numerous amputations and she knew only too well what he meant. There had been several nurses, and even interns, a good deal older and more qualified than she, who, close to fainting, had been forced to leave the operating theatre.

Arthur Chisolm, too, worked around the clock most days at the Royal Victoria, tending patients at his Chisolm

House consulting rooms one morning a week, and making rare house calls only when the need was urgent.

On occasions, when they were leaving the hospital at the same time, he would drive Jane home and they would chat about the events of the day. Jane was like a second daughter to Arthur.

'I hear you've made our Captain Thackeray your special case, Jane,' he said one evening as he opened the car door for her.

It had been two weeks since Martin Thackeray had regained consciousness and Jane had indeed made a daily habit of spending her morning tea break chatting to him, but she didn't want Dr Chisolm to feel that she was favouring one patient above the many others she tended.

'Oh I'm sorry, Dr Chisolm,' she said, feeling herself flush, 'I didn't mean to single him out, it's just that he sometimes seems . . .'

'No criticism was intended, my dear,' the doctor assured her. 'Your visits obviously do him the world of good, he's making excellent progress.' He started the engine and the car set off down the tree-lined driveway of the Royal Victoria. 'But it will be a lengthy road to recovery for Captain Thackeray, and a friend is just what he needs so far from home.'

Jane knew that Martin's home was in Aberdeen, he'd told her so. 'I served in the parish there before I joined the army,' he'd said. She hadn't known that Captain Thackeray was a minister, but when she'd thought about it later, it had come as little surprise to discover that he was a man of the cloth.

Martin Thackeray was highly educated, having graduated from St Andrew's Presbyterian College and the University of Edinburgh with doctorates in both medicine and divinity. Capable of serving two purposes, the Reverend Dr Martin Thackeray was quickly welcomed into the army, given captain's rank and, in 1939, sent to France as a chaplain with the British Expeditionary Force.

He spoke little to Jane of the action he'd seen, but it was obvious that the scars ran deep. 'I know it's a just cause for which we fight,' he said to her one day, 'and that good will win over evil, as it must.' He said it a little too strongly, as if it was something which needed declaration. 'But the cost is so shocking.' She watched as the intelligent grey eyes clouded with anguish. 'So very, very shocking. One sometimes wonders . . .' His voice trailed off and he became despondent.

On his bad days and nights when the dreams and images returned with a vengeance, Martin found his faith severely undermined. How could it happen? How could God allow it to happen? Then he would try to shake himself out of his torpor. Who was he to question the will of God?

Jane was often his saviour during such moments of crisis. Recognising his despondency, she would talk about her own childhood and encourage him to talk about his. His parents were English and he spoke of them fondly. His father had been a Presbyterian minister, he told her, 'retired now', and they'd moved to Edinburgh when he was twelve.

'That explains the accent,' Jane said. Martin had a beautiful voice, and she loved his soft Edinburgh burr. She could have listened to him all day. 'I thought you were Scottish.'

'Yes,' he smiled, 'it's a wee bit confusing at times. I'm really not sure whether I'm a Scot or an Englishman, and I have to be careful who I say that to – some would find it a positively sacrilegious statement.'

It was only when Jane had left to continue her rounds that Martin would realise just how successfully she'd distracted him and, as the days turned into weeks, just the sight of her became enough. The moment she entered the ward his physical pain and mental torment seemed to magically lift.

'Well, well, well,' he'd say lightly, 'it's my angel of mercy, Jane Miller.' It became a running joke, and she always laughed in reply, unaware that deep down he was deadly serious. Jane Miller was, without a doubt, his personal angel. She was a symbol of goodness in the delicate and threatened world of Martin Thackeray.

*'What General Weygand called the Battle of France is over. I expect that the Battle of Britain is about to begin. Upon this battle depends the survival of Christian civilisation. Upon it depends our own British life and the long continuity of our institutions and our Empire.'*

It was a fortnight after the retreat from Flanders, and France had surrendered. Throughout the British Empire, families huddled about wireless sets to listen to the stirring words of the recently appointed Prime Minister, Winston Churchill.

*'The whole fury and might of the enemy must very soon be turned on us now. Hitler knows that he will have to break us in this island or lose the war. If we can stand up to him, all Europe may be free and the life of the world may move forward into broad, sunlit uplands . . .'*

In the wards of the Royal Victoria Hospital, wireless sets were tuned to Churchill's address, and as Jane sat beside Martin's bed, she felt him take her hand. She was comfortable with the contact and, together, hands clasped, they listened in silence.

*'But if we fail, then the whole world, including the United States, including all that we have known and cared for, will sink into the abyss of a new Dark Age, made more sinister, and perhaps more protracted, by the lights of perverted science.'*

In the downstairs front drawing room of Chisolm House, Arthur, Alice and Phoebe Chisolm gathered about the wireless set and with them, listening intently, was the rest of the household. Ron Miller had been called in from the garden and stood in his socks, having left his gardening boots in the laundry. Beside him were Enid the maid and Dora the cook, and beside them was naval Lieutenant James Hampton. Arthur had recently decided to accommodate servicemen at Chisolm House, billets being in short supply throughout the borough. And, having known the Hampton family who had lived locally until Commander William Hampton's transfer to the Admiralty, Arthur had been only too happy to welcome twenty-three-year-old James into his household. Young James had served aboard the HMS *Grenade* which, along with five other British destroyers, had been sunk in the evacuation of Dunkirk. Although not wounded, he had been badly shaken by the events and consequently granted a month's shore leave. Ensconced comfortably in his upstairs bedroom, James felt secure in the warmth of Chisolm House.

'*Let us therefore brace ourselves to our duties, and so bear ourselves that, if the British Empire and its Commonwealth last for a thousand years, men will say, "This was their finest hour".*'

The assembled company at Chisolm House listened solemnly as Churchill concluded his address before the House of Commons and, via the power of the wireless, to the entire British Commonwealth.

The worst is about to come, Arthur Chisolm thought, may God help us all. 'I must be off to the hospital,' he said. He'd completed his morning's consultations and he was far more needed at the Royal Victoria. 'Don't delay dinner for me,' he said to his wife, 'I may be late.'

It was the same most days, he was rarely home for dinner, but Alice appreciated his instructions; she liked a well-ordered house. She nodded to Dora, who in turn nodded to Enid and both of them disappeared to the kitchen whilst Alice, as always, saw her husband to the front door. As she did so, she noted James and Phoebe once again in deep conversation as they so often were these days.

Alice had initially had her doubts about the billeting of servicemen at Chisolm House – God alone knew what riff-raff might end up under their roof – but a young officer like James Hampton from a good family background was a different matter altogether and she was glad now that she had not openly opposed her husband's suggestion. Phoebe was hardly likely to meet eligible bachelors at the Wykeham House School where she taught reading and writing three days a week to the junior students, and James Hampton was a young man with prospects of both a promising naval career and an inheritance.

Alice had baulked at the idea of her daughter teaching, but Phoebe had been insistent. There was a wartime shortage of teachers, she'd said, and she'd been honoured to be called upon by her old school. After all, she could never take up nursing as Jane had done. 'I don't have the spine for it,' she'd laughed, and this way she was serving a purpose. Besides, she was bored doing nothing.

Alice's attempts at dissuasion had had little effect upon her wayward daughter and, as was to be expected, Arthur approved Phoebe's decision. Exasperated with the two of them, Alice Chisolm had curbed her frustration. 'Whatever you think fit, dear,' she'd said to her husband.

She was now delighted that young James Hampton appeared smitten with her daughter. Arthur, as usual, hadn't noticed a thing, but the lad was even painting Phoebe's portrait, which, to Alice, signalled an interest far beyond mere friendship. She had hinted as much to her husband from the outset.

'James is keen to paint Phoebe's portrait,' she'd said meaningfully.

'Yes, he mentioned as much to me. I think it's an excellent idea,' Arthur had replied, missing her point entirely. 'He's most passionate about his painting, he told me so. Wants to become an artist after the war, he says.'

'Good gracious me, and give up a promising naval career?' Alice was shocked. 'How ridiculous.'

'Yes, it would be a little foolhardy, I agree, but then if the boy has talent . . .'

'It would break his father's heart. Heavens above, Arthur, he might even be disinherited.'

'Oh I doubt that, my dear.' Arthur wondered why his wife was so upset. He hoped she wasn't going to make an issue of the subject, he really didn't want to be disturbed. It was Sunday, the one day he had to himself, and he was seated at his escritoire in his study deeply ensconced in the *Daily Echo*. But he didn't wish to offend his wife, so he said by way of mollification, 'It's probably just a passing fancy.'

'I should certainly hope so.'

'Let's wait and see, shall we?' She seemed satisfied with that and he returned to his newspaper.

It was a preposterous notion, Alice decided, and she put it out of her mind. The painting of Phoebe's portrait was the act of a lovesick young man, and she didn't oppose the project at all. James was quite obviously courting her daughter, and it was an excellent opportunity for the young couple to be alone together.

'When are you going to show them, James?' Phoebe asked, aware of her mother's lingering glance as she left the room.

'Soon,' James hedged again as he had for the past two days. 'I told you. Soon.'

'But it's finished and it's wonderful. Jane's coming to dinner tomorrow, can't we show it to them then?' Phoebe couldn't wait for Jane to see the portrait.

'There's a bit of touching up to be done yet, I want to be sure.'

James *was* sure. He was as sure as he possibly could be that it was the finest work he had ever done. The portrait of Phoebe Chisolm had consolidated his belief in his talent and he was now more determined than ever that, when the war was over and he had fulfilled his duty, he would leave the navy and go to Paris to study. But he was faced with a dilemma. He longed for Arthur Chisolm's opinion. Dr Chisolm, whom he very much admired, owned many excellent works and had a fine eye for artistic talent. But, on seeing the portrait of his daughter, would the good doctor recognise his betrayal? James was riddled with guilt. He was convinced that he had captured, in the eyes of the portrait, not only Phoebe's powers of seduction, but his own naked lust. If it was so readable to him, surely others could see it.

Phoebe looked at him knowingly. She was aware that his guilt tortured him, just as she was aware that, the moment she beckoned, he would succumb. 'Shall we have another sitting?' she asked. 'You can finish the touching up today and we'll show them tomorrow.' She didn't bother lowering her voice and her tone was quite innocent, but the innuendo was scandalous.

James glanced at the door through which Alice Chisolm had just disappeared.

'Oh come along, James,' Phoebe laughed as she took his hand. 'The light is perfect, it's your favourite time of day.' And she led him from the drawing room, through the kitchen where Dora and Enid were working, and out the back door to the stables.

The huge wooden doors were open, channelling a shaft of light from the overhead sun into the open space of the stables. She ran ahead and stood there, right in the centre of the pool of light, then turned to look back at him teasingly. He was powerless to do anything but follow.

It was how he'd first seen her, that morning less than three weeks ago when he'd arrived at Chisolm House. Recalling the house from his youth, he'd wandered down the side driveway to admire its various perspectives, taking from his greatcoat pocket the small sketch pad and soft pencil he always carried. He'd circled to the rear of the house and that's when he'd seen her. Caught perfectly in the shaft of light which poured through the open stable doors. She hadn't heard him, despite the crunch of his service boots on the dusty stone courtyard. Or rather, if she had heard him, she'd chosen to ignore his presence. She appeared to be staring up at the roof. He walked to the stable doors. She continued to ignore him.

'Hello,' he said.

She turned her head, neither startled nor frightened, and as she did, the light caught the movement in her auburn hair. Then she smiled, her eyes and her skin radiantly alive in the magical light. She was breathtaking.

'Hello,' she said. 'You're James Hampton.' She held out her hand and was about to cross to him.

'Please don't move.'

He said it with such urgency that Phoebe froze. 'Why on earth not?' she demanded.

'The light's perfect,' he said, sketching frantically. 'You look wonderful.'

'Oh,' Phoebe was always vulnerable to flattery, particularly from good-looking young men, 'that's nice.' She gave him a dazzling smile by way of thanks.

'Excellent,' he said, 'excellent.' Her eyes were so seductive, he thought. What colour were they? Blue? Green? He couldn't tell. He must paint her whilst he was here at Chisolm House. He hoped she'd agree to sit for him.

'We've met before, you know.'

'Have we?' he responded vaguely. 'Can you turn sideways and look up the way you were doing? Yes, that's it. Stay like that for a moment and then turn back to me, I want to get the movement of your hair.'

Phoebe looked up at the trapdoor. She'd been reliving her childhood days with Jane and their secret place up there. She'd lost the battle with her father about the stables. 'We need convalescent accommodation for hospital patients, Phoebe,' he'd said, 'and the renovation is to commence before the end of the month.' Accustomed to getting her own way, Phoebe had sulked for a while. The only other time she'd not got her way with her father had been as a child when he'd refused her a horse, and she'd sulked then too. But Arthur Chisolm had stood firm regarding the stables and she'd finally resigned herself. At least he'd agreed that the wooden doors should stay; he didn't wish to destroy the aesthetics of the place, he'd said.

'We met when I was ten,' she continued, her eyes fixed on the trapdoor. Then she turned to face him. 'I'm Phoebe Chisolm.'

'No, not your whole body,' he said, 'just your head. Turn away and look up again, then back to me with your head.'

Phoebe did as she was told, but she was getting rather bored now. 'You were thirteen,' she said. 'It was just before you left Fareham.'

'Phoebe Chisolm,' he said, concentrating on the page as she turned her head. 'Yes, I remember.' But he didn't really. 'Can you smile again?' She'd stopped smiling.

'No.' She walked over to him. 'May I look?' He handed her the sketch pad. She stared at the drawing for a moment or so and when she looked up her smile was one of genuine admiration. 'You're really very good, aren't you, James Hampton?'

Without the distraction of his sketch pad and the objective view of the subject he'd been drawing, James was caught off guard. Her smile was so bold. It was as if she was throwing out some sort of challenge.

'Thank you,' he said as he took back the sketch pad. 'Would you sit for me?' She arched an eyebrow, but said nothing. 'That is, if you have the time,' he added. For some strange reason she made him feel self-conscious. 'I'm to be here for a whole month.'

'I know. You want to paint my portrait?'

'Very much.'

'Yes, I think I'd like that.' She contemplated the pro-position briefly, then grinned like an excited ten-year-old. 'When shall we start? This afternoon? Now, if you like.'

James laughed, she'd put him at his ease in an instant. What a mercurial girl she was. 'I think I'd better unpack first, I left my things at the front door.'

James was a lost man. From that day on, Phoebe Chisolm had him totally in her power.

Phoebe's seduction of James Hampton had been a con-sciously planned act. The secret conversations she and Jane had were very often about sex, and they always left Phoebe with a burning desire to discover the secret.

'I'm going to have sex before I get married,' she'd shock-ingly announced one day. 'Purely sex for sex's sake, nothing to do with love.'

'Why?' Jane refused to be shocked, but it seemed a dangerous idea to her, and an unnecessary one at that. She, too, felt moments of frustration and desire, but it seemed sensible to hang onto one's virginity for the right man. 'Why not wait?'

'Because I don't want to die having known only one man.' It was a typically Phoebe statement, Jane thought, she was being deliberately provocative. 'It's perfectly acceptable for men to have sex before marriage,' Phoebe continued, 'and I think it should be so for women too. What if my husband isn't any good at it? I'll be left never knowing what it's really like. It seems a very practical solution to me.'

'But what you don't know you don't miss, surely,' Jane countered.

'Oh I'd know that something was missing,' Phoebe said gravely. 'I'd know that all right.' For once Jane was wrong: Phoebe was very much in earnest. 'But then,' she shrugged, 'if I'd already discovered sex, then I'm sure I could live without it. Or without it being the be-all and end-all in any event.'

'This is all based on the assumption that you love your husband, and that he isn't any good at it,' Jane said with a touch of derision. Phoebe's arguments were very often based on assumptions.

'Well, it's perfectly possible, isn't it? Not all men are expert lovers.'

'Aren't the two supposed to go together? Love and sex?'

'Of course, in a perfect world, but I'm not going to take the risk, I'm going to have sex before marriage just to be sure.'

'I don't believe that women can have sex without love, Phoebe. I'm sure I couldn't.' Aware now that her friend's intention was serious, Jane's look was one of concern. 'I'd be very careful if I were you.'

'Don't worry,' Phoebe assured her, 'I'm going to be selective. I intend to wait for the perfect opportunity.'

And the perfect opportunity had presented itself in the form of James Hampton. But the situation became a little more complicated than Phoebe had anticipated. Although she told herself that she was not in love, she was as much in James's power as he was in hers. She was sexually obsessed with him.

'I found out,' she said simply to Jane.

'James Hampton?' Jane had suspected as much. Phoebe nodded. 'Do you love him?'

'No. And he doesn't love me. But it's wonderful.' Phoebe was glowing with a womanliness words couldn't express. She knew it, and she didn't attempt to hide it. 'It's wonderful, Jane.'

Phoebe was fooling herself, Jane thought, and she couldn't help but feel a touch of envy. Phoebe Chisolm was in love in every sense of the word, and Jane longed to feel the same way.

During the afternoon following Churchill's broadcast, James Hampton did not lay a brush to the painting. There was no need, it was finished. And when he and Phoebe scrambled down the ladder from the loft in the broad glare of the summer afternoon, both still breathless from their sexual abandonment, he reluctantly agreed that the following evening he would unveil the portrait to the family. He must take the bull by the horns at some stage, he realised, he couldn't continue to escape the inevitable.

'It's a fine likeness, James,' Arthur Chisolm said, 'a very fine likeness. Indeed, it's a masterly painting, I'm most impressed.'

James's relief knew no bounds. It had been his own guilt working overtime, he realised. No-one was reading anything untoward into the painting. But as the doctor continued, promising to put in a good word with his father, proposing a toast to his talent, James started to feel wretched. What would the man say if he knew that the person whose praises he now sang had seduced his daughter under his very own roof? Then Phoebe was saying, 'He's captured the real me, hasn't he, Daddy,' and James didn't know where to look.

Several days later, when the renovations commenced on the stables, James's situation became even more insidious. Phoebe would visit him in his room in the dead of night and they would make furtive and feverish love, muffling the sounds of their mutual pleasure in pillows and bed linen and each other's bodies, aware that in the bedroom directly below them Arthur and Alice Chisolm lay sleeping. Then Phoebe would slip silently away and, in the morning, James would awaken to his rumpled bed and a sense of shame. Their coupling seemed sordid now, dishonest and unworthy. There had been a form of innocence to their trysts above the stables. A sense of irresponsibility, as if the portrait had them in its control. It had been the portrait which had aroused their mutual passion. But the portrait now hung above the mantelpiece in the downstairs drawing room of Chisolm House. It was complete, and a chapter was closed.

James wished he had the strength to end it, but he didn't. Phoebe's desire was insatiable, and so was his.

'Martin, this is Phoebe. Phoebe Chisolm, Captain Martin Thackeray.' Martin was seated in his wheelchair in one of the front sunrooms of the Royal Victoria when Jane made the introductions.

'Hello, Captain Thackeray, do you mind if I call you Martin?' Phoebe said offering her hand.

'So long as I may call you Phoebe,' Martin replied as they shook. 'I've heard so much about you I feel we're already old friends.' So this was Phoebe Chisolm, he thought. She was certainly beautiful, Jane had said she was. 'Everyone falls in love with Phoebe,' she'd said. Not quite everyone, Martin thought as he smiled at Jane. 'She's exactly as you described her,' he said. But she wasn't as beautiful as Jane Miller, he thought. Nobody on God's earth was as beautiful as Jane Miller.

'The man's madly in love with you,' Phoebe announced half an hour later as she and Jane walked in the hospital gardens. 'You can see it a mile off.'

'Oh don't be ridiculous, Phoebe.'

'Of course he is. He's as madly in love with you as you are with him.'

'I'm not in love with him at all,' Jane said a little impatiently. Phoebe was acting like a schoolgirl.

Phoebe had insisted upon meeting Martin Thackeray, about whom Jane had been talking for weeks. She was convinced that Jane was in love and was now delighted to observe that the feeling was reciprocated. Good heavens, Phoebe thought, the man had barely looked at her. In the full half hour they'd chatted, he hadn't taken his eyes off Jane.

'He's a bit on the thin side, I prefer men more beefy,' she continued, ignoring Jane's irritation, 'but apart from that he's quite handsome. And he's tall, that's always preferable. Well, he looks as if he's tall, it's difficult to tell when he's sitting down, isn't it?' Jane didn't laugh as she usually did when Phoebe discussed men in such a blithely detached fashion, and Phoebe hoped that being in love wasn't depriving Jane of a sense of humour. 'As for the voice, you're certainly right about that. The voice is absolutely gorgeous.'

'Yes it is, isn't it?' Jane said enthusiastically, she couldn't help herself. 'I love his voice, I could listen to him all day.'

'So you've said.' Didn't Jane realise that she'd said as much at least half a dozen times over the past several weeks? It had been a dead giveaway. 'Voices are very erotic, you know.'

Jane hadn't thought of Martin's voice as erotic, but she found herself agreeing. 'Yes, they are, aren't they. Well, Martin's is anyway.' And before she knew it, she and Phoebe were deep in girlish discussion as to the attributes of Martin Thackeray, an older, highly educated man and a minister to boot. It really wasn't right, but then Phoebe always brought out the worst in her.

Jane hadn't considered herself in love with Martin; she admired him tremendously, and perhaps she had a bit of a crush on him, she'd be willing to admit, but . . .?

'You're in love with him, Jane,' Phoebe stated categorically, 'it's quite obvious. And as for him, he's utterly besotted. So what are you going to do about it?'

'About what?'

'Well, he'll be leaving the hospital soon, won't he? You said they'll have him walking in the next week or so, and they need all the beds they can get.'

'Yes, but he won't be able to travel for at least a month. He'll have to convalesce before he can go back to Scotland.'

'Easy,' Phoebe grinned. 'Just leave it to me.' As always, Phoebe had the instant solution.

'Daddy,' she said that very same night, 'the stables will

be finished in a fortnight, and I think the first occupant should be Captain Thackeray.'

'What an excellent idea, Phoebe,' Arthur agreed.

A week later, a small farewell dinner was held at Chisolm House for James Hampton. The following morning he was to return to active service.

'Just au revoir, my boy,' Arthur said as he proposed the toast. He realised that he sounded a little too hearty as he said it, but then what *did* one say to a young man going off to war? he wondered. 'We'll look forward to seeing you back at Chisolm House on your next leave. To James,' he said, and they all raised their glasses.

'We'll meet again, don't know where, don't know when . . .'

Despite the fact that the drapes were drawn in accordance with blackout regulations, they sang with pre-war gusto, determined to make it a party night. Alice was once again at the piano, Arthur by her side, his hand on her shoulder. James, Phoebe and Jane stood beside him, and Dora and Enid had been called away from the dirty dishes in the kitchen to have a glass of port and lend voice.

'But I know we'll meet again some sunny day . . .'

James was touched. He felt Phoebe's hand creep into his. He knew she wasn't looking at him, and he daren't look at her, but he squeezed her fingers in return.

It was well after midnight when she came to his room and there was a desperation to their lovemaking that night. Afterwards, they lay in each other's arms staring up into the blackness, not daring to turn on the light. They were silent for some time, each lost in thought.

Phoebe was questioning herself. Was Jane right? Was it not possible for a woman to have sex without love? It had certainly been Phoebe's intention, and she thought that she'd proved it possible. But now James was going off to war and might never come back, and she was sick with fear. She turned her head into his shoulder and snuggled as close to him as she could.

James held her to him. Her naked body, normally erotic and a source of instant arousal, felt vulnerable and child-like. He kissed her forehead and stroked her hair and cuddled her like a baby. 'I love you, Phoebe,' he whispered. He hadn't thought that he did, but in that moment she was his whole world, something warm and tangible to cling to.

She knew as he said it that he meant it. But he didn't really love her, she was sure of it. He was a man fearful of what lay in store for him. If she said she loved him in return, he would take it as a commitment; he was an hon-ourable man. She had seduced him and used him, aware of the guilt he'd suffered as a consequence. He owed her nothing. She kissed him.

'Come home safe, James,' she said.

In the morning, she stood at the front doors of Chisolm House with her mother and father and Dora and Enid and they all waved at the Landrover as it backed out of the driveway, James waving back through the passenger seat window. Phoebe's grin was as seductively teasing as it had been the first day he'd met her. She made sure that it was.

On the morning Martin Thackeray arrived at Chisolm House, Jane accompanied him from the hospital as his nurse, and Phoebe was there to greet them at the stables.

'You'll be very comfortable here, Martin, I'm sure of it,' she said. 'It has quite a background, the stables, a lot of love has been shared under this roof.'

Jane cast a look of horror at Phoebe. How dare she allude to her illicit affair with James.

But Phoebe's smile was virtuous. 'Jane and I grew up here as children. They were our happiest days, weren't they, Jane?'

'They were indeed,' Jane agreed, her eyes issuing a warning but, as Martin looked about admiringly at the stables, and Phoebe gave her the wickedest of secret winks, Jane had to fight back the impulse to laugh.

'It's charming,' Martin said. 'I'm very grateful to your father, Phoebe. And to you too, Jane tells me this was your idea.'

Phoebe's face was once again the picture of innocence as he turned to her. 'Yes, it was a good one, wasn't it? I'll let you settle in,' she said and she left the two of them together.

The stables had been converted to an open-plan living space with a bed in the corner and a small bathroom at the rear. The loft had been sealed off and Arthur planned further renovations to convert it to a separate living area, either for servicemen or for convalescing patients who could manage the stairs. At the moment, the situation was perfect for Martin, who could walk only short distances with the aid of a stick. There was a small gas stove and an icebox, and Dora kept the kitchen cupboard well stocked for him when she did the shopping for the big house. During the days, Martin looked after himself but, at the doctor's insistence, he joined them for dinner each evening at the main house.

Jane became a constant visitor to the stables whenever she could get time off from the hospital, which was quite regularly, Dr Chisolm himself being her strongest ally in this. Aware of the delicate psychological state of Martin Thackeray, Arthur Chisolm was firmly convinced that Jane was the best cure to hand. And he was right. In the most tortured moments of his restless nights, Martin often contemplated leaving the church. How could he serve God when he had such doubts about His wisdom? Jane was the only person to whom he spoke of such matters, and she, in her simplicity, restored his faith more than she could possibly know.

'Surely God needs all the help He can get these days,' she said. 'And the men who are fighting this war certainly need those who can support them in their faith.'

'How can I support others in their faith when I doubt my own, Jane?'

She didn't have an answer for that, but just talking about it served a purpose, she could tell. Even as he voiced his insecurity, she could see that, by sharing his torment, he was growing stronger daily. 'You can help because you know what they're going through, Martin. You've been there yourself.'

Despite their discussions and the growth of their friendship, as the days became weeks, their relationship continued to be principally that of grateful patient and caring nurse. Jane always queried whether he'd taken his medication, and he'd laugh and remind her he was a doctor, to which she'd reply 'they're usually the worst'. She helped him with his painful stretching exercises, and supported him as he slowly paced the courtyard, determined to do away with his stick.

Phoebe, observing them, was becoming frustrated with their lack of progress. 'Hasn't he said anything yet?' she demanded. He couldn't have, she thought; if he had, Jane would surely have told her.

'About what?'

'About the fact that he loves you of course.'

'No.' Jane was beginning to doubt whether Phoebe was right. She was aware that Martin needed her, and it was clear he enjoyed her company, but that hardly constituted love.

'Then you'll have to take control of the situation yourself, there's nothing else for it.'

'And how exactly do you propose I go about it, Phoebe?' Jane's tone was heavily laced with irony. 'Should I throw myself at him and seduce him the way you did James?'

Phoebe laughed with delight, she wasn't at all offended. 'Hardly. I mean he wouldn't be up to it, would he, in his condition. Just let him know that you care for him.' Jane still appeared unsure, and Phoebe threw her hands in the air, exasperated. 'For God's sake, Jane, stop being a nurse and be a woman!'

That night, upon Phoebe's insistence, Jane agreed to dine at Chisolm House. She prepared her father's dinner in advance, as she always did when she was invited to the Chisolms for the evening. And she sat companionably with him as he ate. It was an inconvenience to neither. Ron Miller always settled down to his dinner on the dot of half past six, and the Chisolms always dined a good two hours later. They chatted about the postcard that had arrived from Dave that morning. Both the Miller brothers had joined the army and were on active duty. Ron was proud of his boys 'doing their bit', as he said, and he never voiced his innermost fears. It was only right for a man to fight for his country, he said. If he was thirty years younger he'd join up himself. 'Be there like a shot, I would.'

He asked about Martin Thackeray. 'He'll be going back to Scotland within a week or so, you say?' Ron liked Captain Thackeray, they'd shared many an amicable chat as Ron tended the Chisolms' garden.

'Yes, he'll be fit to travel by then. Do you want another cup of tea?' Jane jumped up from the table before her father could delve into the subject any further.

'Wouldn't say no.' Ron Miller was of the same opinion as Phoebe. As far as Jane was concerned anyway. His daughter's dedication to the man's wellbeing was far more than that of a nurse to her patient, and he was sure she was in love with the man. But whenever he asked any leading questions she avoided the issue. Ron wondered what Martin Thackeray's feelings were for Jane. The Reverend Captain certainly wouldn't be leading the girl on, being a man of the cloth and all, but if he should care for her, then Ron certainly approved the match. A minister, as he was, and a doctor to boot. By God but his little girl'd be coming up in the world with a husband like that.

'Thanks, love,' he said as she set the cup down on the table. 'You'd best be off then.'

She kissed him on the cheek. 'Bye, Dad.'

'You take care now, and have a good time.'

Over the dinner table, as Arthur carved the roast, Phoebe studied Martin and Jane. Jane wished that she wouldn't. Tonight was the night, Phoebe had instructed her. She wasn't sure how she was to go about making Martin aware of her feelings and Phoebe's close scrutiny wasn't helping.

'Have you heard from James, dear?' Alice asked her daughter.

'No,' Phoebe replied bluntly. Her mother knew very well she'd not heard from James. Alice Chisolm scrutinised the mail as soon as it arrived each morning.

'Oh well, it's been barely a month, and the authorities are very slow delivering mail from the front. Thank you, Enid, that's quite enough.' Enid was threatening to spoon a second serving of brussels sprouts onto her plate.

'I'll have some more, thank you, Enid,' Phoebe said, remarking that the sprouts came from Jane's father's very own garden. She then deftly turned the discussion to the shortage of fresh vegetable produce.

It was a pleasant evening, the conversation always stimulating between Arthur and Martin, both learned men who enjoyed each other's company. Initially the war was the dominant subject: the bombing raids upon London and the fact that, as Churchill had predicted, the Battle of Britain had begun. They were already suffering the effects in the south. German bombers, unable to reach their London targets due to heavy air defence, dropped their lethal loads upon the channel ports before heading for home.

'It's only a matter of time,' Arthur said, 'before they start targeting us directly.' Martin agreed but, recognising Alice's growing consternation, he changed the subject.

Chopin and Debussy became the topics for the next ten minutes until Phoebe interrupted with her views on American swing bands and jazz. When Martin acknowledged, to Alice's surprise, that he loved the big-band sound, Phoebe gave Jane another surreptitious wink.

They adjourned to the drawing room for the rare treat of coffee, courtesy of the resourceful Dora. Coffee was difficult to come by these days but Dora always managed to lay in a supply; no-one knew quite how and no-one asked. After fifteen minutes or so, Martin excused himself. It was his custom to leave early, he tired easily.

'I'll see you to the stables,' Jane said.

'No, you stay here, Jane,' he replied, not wanting to drag her away from the company, 'I can manage on my own these days.'

'It's dark, you can't risk a fall,' she insisted, 'and I'm still your nurse.' She ignored Phoebe's raised eyebrow of disapproval.

'And a very good one at that,' Martin smiled. He wished she was more. A great deal more. But he'd never take it upon himself to tell her so, he must seem a crippled old man in her young eyes.

'Jane's quite right, Martin,' Arthur agreed. A fall was certainly the last thing the man needed. Arthur himself always insisted Enid see Martin home after dinner, and he even briefly ignored the blackout regulations, turning on the outside light to ensure the man's safety. 'Enid will turn on the outside light for you,' he said.

At the door to the stables, Jane was in a quandary. What would Phoebe do? she questioned herself. Phoebe would be bold and flirtatious of course. But Jane didn't know how to go about it.

'I don't suppose you'd like to ask me in for a cup of tea?' she asked brightly. Oh dear, that sounded terrible, she thought. It wouldn't if Phoebe had said it. She really wasn't any good at this. 'No, of course not,' she quickly added, 'you're tired, I'm sorry.'

'I can think of nothing I'd like more,' Martin said.

'Oh.' She hoped he wasn't just being polite.

Martin insisted upon making the pot of tea himself. 'I am master of my own house, Jane,' he said, 'humble as it may be. Now go and sit down.'

Jane hadn't been in the converted stables at night. It was cosy, she thought. Homey and comfortable. She wondered where to sit. Phoebe would choose the sofa of course, so she sat there hoping that Martin wouldn't think her too forward.

Martin shuffled over with the teapot, cursing his bad leg which was paining him dreadfully, and wishing he didn't look like the cripple he was. He daren't attempt to carry the tray with the cups and milk and sugar which he'd set up on the kitchen bench.

As he put the teapot down on the small table beside the sofa, Jane fetched the tray and he made no protest, but waited until she was seated once again before he sat beside her. When he did, he couldn't help a small involuntary sigh escaping his lips.

'Your leg's bad tonight,' she said. It wasn't a question.

'No, no,' he said, 'it's fine.'

Jane poured the tea and he watched her. She looked so extraordinarily lovely.

'Milk and two,' she said.

'Standard army,' he replied. It had been a daily part of their repartee at the hospital, and they shared a smile.

'I'll miss you, Martin.' Jane couldn't play Phoebe's games, she decided. All she could do was tell the truth as simply as she saw it.

Martin knew that the automatic response should have been 'I'll miss you too, Jane', but as he looked into the glorious blue eyes which so directly met his, he could swear he saw something more than mere friendship. Impossible, he thought. Wishful thinking on his part. So why did he seem to be holding his breath?

'Why?' he asked, trying to sound as casual as possible. 'Why will you miss me?' He felt as if he were on a tightrope.

'Because I care for you,' she said. 'I care for you very much.' How could she tell him she loved him? A distinguished and learned man like Martin Thackeray? She'd sound foolish. A lovelorn schoolgirl with a crush on her teacher, and he'd have every right to treat her so.

Of course she cared for him, he thought, and his disappointment was matched by his sense of foolishness that he'd presumed things could have been in any way different. She was a dedicated nurse and she'd been responsible for his health and his very sanity. Of course she cared for him!

'I care very much for you too, Jane,' he said, and he turned his attention to the cup of tea which sat untouched on the table, praying that she hadn't read the futile hope which, in that instant, had surged through him.

But Jane had. Like a story unfolding before her very eyes, she had seen the astonishment, then the hope and then the shattering disappointment. Phoebe had been right, she realised. Martin Thackeray loved her. 'I'll miss you because I love you,' she said.

Martin looked at her. Words were beyond him. But her hand had reached out and taken his, and it was the most natural thing in the world to kiss her. With a sense of wonderment, he felt her soft lips against his. How could she love him? He was old before his time. He was a cripple, a shell of a man.

'I'm too old for you, Jane,' he said as they parted. It was a girlish infatuation, he told himself. A lovely young creature like Jane Miller?

Jane found his confusion endearing, he looked like a worried little boy. 'You're thirty, Martin, that's hardly old.'

'And you're twenty.'

'Is that a crime?'

'But look at me, I'm a cripple, I'm broken . . .'

'Then we'll just have to mend you, won't we?' Jane felt incredibly strong.

'My angel,' he said, and he stroked her cheek with his fingertips, recognising the strength that lay beneath her loveliness. His angel at the docks. His angel who had brought him back to life. Who would have thought it possible? 'I've loved you from the moment I first saw you, Jane Miller.' They kissed again. Gently, tenderly.

'Will you marry me?' It was Jane who made the proposal.

'No, my dear,' he said. There was nothing he would have liked more, but it wouldn't be fair to her. 'You're young and you're strong, and . . .'

'Sssh,' she put her finger to his lips. There was no argument he could offer which she would accept. They loved each other and nothing else mattered. 'Just say yes,' she said. 'Please, Martin, say yes. Say yes, say yes,' she whispered over and over.

If Martin Thackeray needed any further resolution of his faith it was born that night. God had granted him his angel. He would become well and strong because of Jane. He owed it to her. And he would build a life for them both.

For the next hour they talked about their plans. Martin would formally seek Ron Miller's permission for his daughter's hand in marriage first thing in the morning, he said. Jane wasn't sure if he was serious, it sounded so quaintly Victorian, but there was a twinkle in his eye as he said it.

'His permission?' she laughed. 'Dad'll think it's Christmas. I've been dodging hints about what a fine man you are for the past month.'

They would go to Edinburgh and she would meet his parents. 'What if they don't like me?' she said, suddenly worried. Did it matter if she was a labourer's daughter? She'd never thought about that before. It was his turn to laugh.

'They'll love you, Jane.'

They would marry in Edinburgh, as soon as possible, they agreed. A small, quiet ceremony, Jane insisted. And her father would come up to give her away.

'And Phoebe,' she added. 'I couldn't get married without Phoebe, she'd never forgive me.' So Phoebe was to be bridesmaid. Everything was settled. Then Martin changed the tone of the conversation. The marriage part was easy, but the rest of their lives?

'Are you sure you want to be a minister's wife, Jane?'

'I want to be *your* wife,' she said, 'it goes hand in glove, why should I question it?'

He had known that would be her answer, but her own words were coming back at him. *'You've been there yourself, Martin,'* she'd said. *'You can help because you know what they're going through.'* It's what he wanted to do, he realised, he wanted to help others who might doubt their faith. He chose his words carefully, trying to find his own purpose as he did. Until this very night, he'd been unsure of his path.

'I don't want to settle back into some comfortable parish,' he said. 'Not whilst this war still threatens, I feel I'd be running away.' He registered immediately her look of concern. 'Oh don't worry, my darling,' he smiled, 'they wouldn't accept me back into the army even if I begged. But I want to do something that will serve a purpose. Perhaps some repatriation work, I'm not sure, but, as you said, I know what they've been through and I can help them, both medically and spiritually.'

Jane thanked God as she looked into the questioning eyes that seemed to be begging her permission. Martin Thackeray was a man no longer in torment. 'Then I'm sure a nurse would prove immensely helpful,' she said.

Phoebe Chisolm watched from the darkness of her bedroom which looked out over the courtyard. Through

the shuttered windows of the stables, she could see the slits
of light which glowed well into the night.

They wouldn't be doing it, she thought. More fool them,
they didn't know what they were missing. But they were in
love. They'd been in love all the time and they hadn't
admitted it, even to themselves. Phoebe was glad that she'd
been right, she always liked to be right. And she was glad
that Jane's life was fulfilled. Martin was a good man
and he'd make Jane happy. But what of herself? What was
in store for the irresistible Phoebe Chisolm? she wondered.
Phoebe had never felt more alone in her life.

A week later, as if fulfilling the prophecies of Martin and
Arthur's dinner-table conversation, Southampton suffered
two daylight air raids. Whether the area had been deliberately targeted or used as a bomb disposal site was
debatable, but on 13 and 14 August the township and its
surrounds came under direct attack. A section of train
track was demolished, an engine derailed, houses
damaged, and back yards reduced to rubble and craters,
but, amongst the casualties, there was miraculously no loss
of life.

'A perfect time to be going to Edinburgh,' Phoebe
announced over the breakfast table as her father read out
the headlines from the *Daily Echo*.

Alice gave her daughter a frosty look but said nothing,
having decided to make no further comment on the
subject. Phoebe was being selfish to the extreme, in her
opinion, and the fact that Arthur refused to put his foot
down and forbid the girl's indulgence only annoyed her all
the more.

'Yes, it'll certainly be a lot safer in Scotland,' Arthur
said, but his tone was detached and he didn't look at
Phoebe as he spoke. He was disappointed in his daughter,
and if she was seeking justification and approval of her
actions then he wasn't prepared to give it. However, she

was a grown woman now, and he couldn't force her to fulfil her obligations.

Phoebe's airy announcement that she was going to leave with Jane and Martin for Edinburgh and possibly stay in Scotland for a holiday after the wedding, had received an adverse reaction from both her parents, but for differing reasons.

Alice was horrified at her daughter's lack of etiquette. Going to Edinburgh for the wedding in three weeks' time was one thing, but to accompany the engaged couple was quite another. 'For goodness sake, Phoebe,' she said outraged, 'he's taking her to meet his parents, you couldn't possibly contemplate such an intrusion, it's unthinkable.'

But Phoebe shrugged off any suggestion of poor form on her part. 'Jane's my best friend and she wants me to come,' she said. 'And so does Martin, we've all discussed it. You can ask them yourself,' she said rebelliously before her mother could interrupt.

Arthur's objection came from quite a different quarter. 'What about your teaching?' he asked. 'They need you at Wykeham House, you told me so yourself.'

'I gave them a week's notice that I'd be leaving.'

'Not much time to find a replacement and, as you also told me, there's a shortage of teachers.'

She could sense the reprimand in her father's voice. 'But this is a chance of a lifetime, Daddy,' she said. 'I've never been further than Southampton and Portsmouth, it's an opportunity to travel.'

'Perhaps you could wait until the school finds a replacement,' Arthur suggested mildly.

There was nothing else for it, Phoebe decided. 'I'm bored with teaching now,' she said. She hated the look of disappointment on her father's face, she knew he'd been proud of her teaching. But she was going with Jane and Martin, it had all been decided, and nothing he could say would alter the fact.

'I see.'

Alice was appalled at her husband's apparent capitulation and, in private, she uncharacteristically harangued him about it. 'You must put your foot down, Arthur,' she said. 'It's most unseemly. Whether or not Jane and Martin welcome Phoebe's company is beside the point, I dread to think what his parents will make of it.'

'I'm disappointed that she's so cavalier about her teaching,' Arthur said. 'I'd thought it meant something to her.'

'The novelty's worn off,' Alice scoffed. 'It's typical of Phoebe, she's altogether too frivolous, it's shameful.' Alice had no objections whatsoever to Phoebe leaving the school, but if the argument made an ally of her husband, then she was most willing to encourage his disapproval.

'I can't force her into a career for which she has no true vocation,' Arthur said regretfully. 'And she's right in one way: it is most certainly a perfect opportunity for her to travel.'

'But Martin and Jane . . .'

'Quite obviously wish her to go with them,' Arthur interrupted wearily. 'Martin is fully aware of the girls' strong friendship.'

'And the Thackerays? His parents? What on earth will they think of us?'

'Oh my dear, who cares?' They were probably the strongest words he had said to her in their entire marriage. Not the words themselves, but their tone. He was utterly exasperated and he wished his wife would be quiet.

Arthur knew his daughter was frivolous, charmingly and endearingly so, and because of it he'd spoilt her all of her life. If she had become a shallow person, then perhaps it was his fault.

Several days later, well out of Alice's hearing, he gave Phoebe an envelope of money and told her he'd arranged a bank account in Edinburgh.

'You are not to become a burden upon Martin and Jane,' he instructed her. 'Always maintain your dignity, Phoebe. When it comes right down to it,' he added thoughtfully, 'it's all we really have.' Why should he expect more of his daughter than was in her capacity to give? he thought as he looked at her youth and her beauty. She was young and she was free and there was time for responsibility.

In mid-August, the trio set off on the first leg of their long train journey to Scotland. Martin Thackeray, Jane Miller and Phoebe Chisolm.

# CHAPTER SEVEN

Samantha Lindsay stepped out of Kingsford Smith Airport to a sparkling spring morning, pleasantly warm but not hot, the sun shining in a cloudless blue sky. It was good to be back. She hadn't realised how much she'd missed Sydney. But she recalled someone once saying, 'when you've lived happily in another country for over a year you're a person without a home', and these days she found herself agreeing. She loved England and Australia equally; to make a choice would be very difficult.

'Sam!' She didn't hear the yell above the babble of the milling crowd as she steered her obstinate luggage trolley into the lengthy queue at the taxi rank. She was to have been met at the airport and taken directly to her hotel, but when no-one had been waiting for her as she'd come through customs, she'd headed for a taxi. It hadn't bothered her particularly, Reg had given her the necessary details when he'd collected her at Fareham and taken her to Heathrow Airport. She'd been booked into the Quay Grand Hotel in Macquarie Street, he'd told her as he handed over a large envelope with her travel documents and itinerary.

'The penthouse, suite 1102, overlooking the harbour,'

he'd said. 'The view from the other side of the hotel looks out over the botanical gardens, they tell me, with glimpses of the Opera House, but I thought you'd prefer the water.'

'I would. But I don't need a penthouse, and I don't need a five-star hotel. I'd rather be self-sufficient, Reg, you know that. Can't they give me an apartment somewhere?'

'They have. It's entirely self-contained. A kitchen with all mod cons, a laundry, even a guest bedroom and spare bathroom. It just happens to be a penthouse in a five-star hotel overlooking one of the greatest views in the world, poor you.'

'Well, yes,' she'd graciously acceded, 'I suppose I can live with that.'

She'd have two days to get over her jet lag, he'd told her, before she'd be collected for rehearsals at ten in the morning. He had also given her the shooting schedule that the production company had faxed to him, but she hadn't paid much attention to it during the flight, concentrating more on the script instead. There were to be discussions with the screenwriter and director before the commencement of filming and that was of far more importance to her.

'Sam!' the voice once again shrilled, and this time she heard it. She turned to see Nicholas Parslow elbowing his way through weary travellers, much to the annoyance of many, tripping over their luggage, and saying 'sorry, sorry', left and right.

'Nick!' she said as he finally reached her, pushing his glasses back up his nose in a characteristic gesture which sent a rush of affection flooding through her. 'Being met by the writer!' She threw her arms around him. 'I'm honoured, I thought they'd send a runner. Then I thought they'd forgotten about me and I was going to get a taxi.'

'Sorry we're late. Simon's here too,' Nick said trying to catch his breath, he wasn't used to exercise. He wasn't overweight, if anything he was on the lean side, but he was

certainly unfit, with a writer's pallor and eyes that
squinted in the sun's glare, unaccustomed as they were to
natural light. Nick, whom Sam considered one of the
nicest men she'd ever known, was always happiest scrib-
bling in a notepad, or hunched over a computer, or in
intense discussion with fellow collaborators. 'He's parking
the car, we mis-timed it a bit,' he apologised, 'we thought
you'd be longer getting through customs.'

'Simon Scanlon?' Sam had never met Simon. Nick
nodded. 'The writer *and* the director!' she said. 'I'm
doubly honoured.' She was surprised and impressed, it
was most unexpected.

'Oh Simon's dying to meet you. Here, I'll do that.' Nick
was about to take over the trolley as she guided it out of
the taxi queue.

'No, I'll manage, I'm used to it now, it's got a sticky
wheel. Just hang on to the front and give it a shove when
it starts to turn right. And can you grab that for me before
I run over it?' Sam indicated the heavy woollen overcoat
that kept threatening to slide off the suitcases.

'Well, you certainly won't need this for a while,' Nick
said, slinging the coat over his shoulder.

'How are you coping?' Sam asked as they weaved their
way through the crowds and down the street, Nick lending
weight to the trolley every time it veered to the right.

'Fine.'

She halted briefly and gave him a look which said 'are
you sure?'

'I have my bad days now and then,' he admitted, 'but
work gets me through. It always has.'

Nick's devoted partner of ten years had died shortly
after the stage run of *Red Centre* and, as he'd told her at
the time, working on the film adaptation of his play had
been the only thing which had kept him sane in the months
which followed. Shortly after the funeral, Sam had disappeared to London and a new career, and she hadn't seen

Nick in the whole three years since Phillip's death, although they'd been in regular touch.

'I'm sorry I wasn't here for you,' she said.

'You were,' he assured her. 'That's the beauty of emails. You were more help than you could possibly know.'

'I'm glad.'

'It's good to have you back.' He kissed her cheek, and they set off once again with the luggage trolley, chatting nineteen to the dozen.

'Simon was floored by your performance in *A Doll's House*,' Nick said. 'He told me you inspired him, but then that's no surprise. I said that you would. I only wish I could have seen it.'

'Why didn't he come backstage?'

'I asked him the same thing. "Why the hell didn't you meet her?" I said. But he reckons he was buggered after the flight. He'd got in to London that morning, and he was taking off for Sydney the next day. Fair enough, I suppose.' Nick shrugged. 'But actually I think he was mulling you over. Not that he didn't want you for the role – he rang me first thing and told me you were *it*. But you see, Simon has this most amazing overall perspective.' Nick had now forgotten about the wayward trolley which Sam was fighting to control. 'It's his great talent as a director of course. I bet he was awake half the night piecing everything together with you in the middle, he's really intense like that. Total focus. When he's putting the jigsaw bits together he loses sight of absolutely everything around him.'

'Sounds like somebody else I know,' Sam said as the trolley teetered on the edge of the kerb.

'Oh sorry.' Nick came to the rescue.

They waited by the pedestrian crossing opposite the car park, in full view so that Simon couldn't miss them. 'I've no idea where he parked the car,' Nick said, 'it's safer to wait until he finds us. What did you think of the script?'

'Brilliant. Absolutely brilliant.'

'Yes it is, isn't it?' Nick's agreement was in no sense ego-driven. Although a highly talented writer, he was an unassuming man, and when he considered a script the result of a collaborative effort, he was quick to give credit to others. *Torpedo Junction* was, in his opinion, as much a product of Simon Scanlon's inventive input as his own creative skills.

'And I'm over the moon about Sarah Blackston,' Sam said. 'She's the role of a lifetime.'

'Yes she is, isn't she!' Nick beamed enthusiastically. 'Mamma Black! And she was tailor-made for you, Sam.'

'You weren't thinking of me when you wrote her, surely?'

'Not initially,' he admitted; Nick was always honest. 'She's loosely based on a real character and that's what inspired me. But as soon as I started writing Mamma Black you were in my mind.'

They would probably have stood on the kerbside chatting for hours if a voice hadn't interrupted them.

'Samantha Lindsay. At last!'

Sam turned to see a man whom she instantly recognised. The newspaper and magazine photographs were unkind, she thought. Big-boned, craggy-faced, and beaky, he certainly resembled a pterodactyl, just as the newspapers portrayed, but he emanated such a warmth and energy that the overall impression was immensely attractive.

'Simon,' she said before Nick could introduce them, but then Simon Scanlon already had his hand outstretched. 'I can't believe you've come to the airport. I'm a bit overwhelmed, I have to admit.'

'Couldn't wait.' His handshake was bone crushing. 'Thought you were great in *A Doll's House*. Dying to have a chat. Do you need to crash right away or could you handle a coffee?' Simon often spoke in shorthand and always got straight to the point.

'Don't be pushy,' Nick protested, 'she's probably exhausted, it's a hell of a long flight.'

'Have you ever travelled first class?' Sam laughed. 'I've been asleep in a full-length bed for the past seven hours. Thanks for that, by the way,' she said to Simon.

'Don't thank me, thank Mammoth. Terrible waste of production money, in my opinion. Business class is perfectly adequate.' His voice was a bark but his grin was amiable, and Sam found him disarming, in an alarming sort of way. 'Let's make it your place, Nick.'

'She might want to go to the hotel first,' Nick said protectively, aware that Simon could be a bit much on first meeting, particularly with those he'd decided he liked. With those he didn't, he was dismissive, choosing simply to ignore them. 'And there's such a thing as body clocks and jet lag, you know, even if a person *has* slept for seven hours.'

'I can handle the body clock and the jet lag,' Sam said, 'but I'd like to dump my gear at the hotel and check in first, if that's all right. Could you give me an hour?' she asked apologetically.

'We'll drive you there and wait outside.' Simon obviously wasn't going to let her out of his sight any longer than was absolutely necessary.

Sam adored her apartment at the Quay Grand. She was personally escorted to the eleventh floor by the hotel manager, who gave her a guided tour, an operational rundown of the high-tech appliances and equipment, and then tactfully left her to 'settle in'.

Complete with kitchen surfaces of black marble, and a massive spa in the master bedroom's en suite, the place was even more luxurious than Reg had promised, but to Sam, far outweighing the luxury was the spectacular view of Sydney Harbour.

She stepped out onto the balcony. Towering far to her right was the coat hanger of the Bridge, the laughing mouth of Luna Park nestled cheekily beneath it. Directly below her was the ever busy ferry terminal of Circular

Quay, and the broad path, teeming with tourists and sightseers, which led around the point to the Opera House. A gleaming white ocean liner was docked at the far side of the quay and the harbour itself was a kaleidoscope of colour and action. Smartly trimmed green and yellow ferries chugged back and forth; huge catamarans, the less traditional but speedier form of public transport, zoomed effortlessly across the blue water's surface; pleasure craft milled idly about; and dodging and weaving amongst them all like frantic messenger boys on bicycles were the water taxis. I could live on this balcony, Sam thought.

Then the porter arrived with her luggage and there was no longer any excuse to drink in the view. Hurriedly, she unpacked her essentials, cleaning her teeth and washing her face, all the while guiltily aware that Simon and Nick were sitting in the car out the front.

Simon, having been assured that Sam was safely booked in to the hotel, had turned down her offer to come up to the apartment and had even refused to sit comfortably in the foyer.

'We'll wait in the car,' he'd told her, 'you'll be quicker that way.'

'He's a bugger, isn't he?' Nick had said. 'Don't let him bully you, Sam, take your time.'

But Sam had been bullied nonetheless. She would have loved to have showered and changed, but she didn't dare. She brushed her hair and rubbed some moisturiser into her face; travelling first class didn't stop your skin drying out, she thought. A quick spray of the Givenchy she'd bought at the duty free and twenty minutes later, script under her arm, she strode through the foyer to the waiting car.

Nick lived in Surry Hills. A huge gutted warehouse with steps leading to a loft which housed a bedroom and an extensive library.

Downstairs, every available piece of wall space was taken up by whiteboards scrawled with notes in different coloured markers, and corkboards pinned with papers and pictures. There were benches with computers and printers and fax machines, but predominant was a huge wooden table strewn with more papers and literature. Nick did much of his work by hand. 'I like paper,' he maintained. 'It's tactile and trustworthy.'

A potbelly stove was up one end of the vast room, surrounded by old armchairs and sofas, but for the most part people sat around the wooden table on a miscellany of ancient upright chairs garnered from second-hand shops. Despite the fact that Nick now earned top money, he liked to hang on to the past. 'Why change a good thing?' he'd say.

Light streamed through large leadlight windows upon the gloriously creative chaos, and Sam, who had often been to Nick's home in bygone years, felt moved, remembering that half of this huge open space had once been taken up by Phillip's easels and sculptures.

She glanced at Nick who gave a gentle smile of recognition, knowing exactly what she was thinking.

'Down to business.' Simon sat at the table whilst Nick prepared a plunger of coffee in the open kitchen alcove nearby. 'I presume you've looked over the schedule.'

'Only briefly,' she admitted, sitting opposite him. 'I know we're shooting the opening scenes in the English house here at Fox Studios, and then we go on location to Vanuatu. That's great, isn't it?' Sam was excited at the prospect of Vanuatu, she'd never been there before. 'I thought we were shooting in far north Queensland . . .'

'No, no, we're going to where it all really happened,' Simon interrupted brusquely, 'but I don't want you to think about that now. I want you to concentrate purely on the opening scenes.' He leaned forward, elbows on the table, pterodactyl eyes gleaming with excitement, and, like many before her, Sam found herself mesmerised.

'Sarah is two different people,' he said. 'I want you to put Sarah Blackston out of your mind completely. She is Sarah Huxley, and she's locked in the claustrophobic house of her father. It must be beyond all possibility to envisage this colourless creature adventuring to Vanuatu and becoming Mamma Black. Her destiny is locked in this mausoleum of a house, as her father had always predicted it would be. She will look after him until he dies and then she'll live on, an old maid with money but no-one to love her.'

He leaned back in his chair, tapping his fingertips together aware that he'd captivated her. He'd told her nothing she hadn't gleaned from the script, but his intensity was like an electrical charge.

'Her father, Clifford, calls her a mouse, and she is,' he continued. 'We must see no strength in her until the final two scenes in the house. It's only then that we realise she was never really a mouse at all. She was strong from the very beginning, it was only her father's derision that made her a mouse.'

'Oh yes, I agree with that,' Sam said vehemently. 'It's right there on the page. The defiance of her father, the farewell scene, it's all there.' She glanced at Nick. Mesmeric Simon Scanlon may be, she thought, but let's give the writer his due. Nick, however, smiled benignly as he brought the plunger of coffee to the table. He loved seeing Simon at work with actors, the man was inspirational.

'Yes, yes, of course it is,' Simon agreed with a touch of impatience. 'Now, let's concentrate on the set for a minute, the set's very important. Where's the sugar, Nick?' He started pouring himself a cup of coffee. He really was an arrogant man, Sam thought, but she couldn't help herself, she was riveted.

'We could have shot the opening and closing scenes on location in England you know, but I wanted a set. Mammoth thought I was mad; they've got a *Titanic* budget and they thought I was trying to cut corners. Stupid bastards. Typical Hollywood. They shower you with money when it's not needed, and cut you back when it is.'

Nick joined them at the table with the sugar and milk, pouring a cup of coffee for Sam and giving her a reassuring wink.

'There'll be no exterior footage shot in England,' Simon continued. 'We never see the outside of the house, just the claustrophobic interior, mirroring the influence of the father. The set will work very effectively to our advantage.' He swigged down his coffee. He always drank it black and boiling hot, with three sugars. 'That's originally how I wanted to finish the film, Sarah alone in the house once more with nothing but memories, her American lover dead, the mausoleum closing about her. But of course the producers demanded a happy ending, so soldier boy returns having survived the POW camp. Typical.'

His tone was scathing, and Sam again found his contempt an insult to Nick's work. 'I think the final scene where Sarah and her lover are reunited is beautifully written,' she said defensively. 'It's very understated and moving.'

'Well, of course it is, Nick's a genius. Worked his tits off trying to lend a bit of magic to something so trite.'

'And he succeeded.' There was a definite touch of ice to Sam's tone now. Strange how quickly one could go off Simon Scanlon, she thought.

Nick himself was grinning happily at the two of them. Dear Sam, he thought, being so protective, but in fact he never found Simon insulting. The two of them worked together far too well to offend each other, even when they disagreed. He didn't bother saying so, though; Sam would get Simon's measure soon enough. She was a perceptive and creative young woman, and, overwhelming though he might be, Simon Scanlon was no dictator, he welcomed artistic input from actors. He and Sam would make a formidable team.

'The middle-class setting was Simon's idea,' Nick said, in order to put Sam at her ease and also to assure her of the egalitarian working relationship he and Simon shared. 'I thought the Victorian father despising his daughter because she didn't measure up to his dead wife was a bit too much like *The Heiress* myself. I initially wanted to make Sarah working class, but Simon was actually . . .'

'*The Heiress* hardly went off to the New Hebrides to become a heroine to the natives,' Simon scoffed.

'. . . he was actually quite right,' Nick continued, ignoring him completely, 'it gave Sarah a far greater strength of character. A young woman exchanging a comfortable middle-class existence for a remote island in the South Pacific, a pretty brave move in those days.'

Sam was momentarily confused. 'I thought you said Sarah Blackston was based on a real character?'

'No, I said "Mamma Black" was based on a real character. Very loosely. She was known as Mamma Tack actually, and I've no idea who she was, but the stories abound in Vanuatu –'

'Hardly relevant,' Simon interrupted. 'Back to business. Now about the father . . .'

He was possibly one of the rudest men she'd met, Sam thought, wondering why Nick was so unaffected, but then Nick had always been too nice for his own good.

'. . . I really wanted to check this out with you first,' Simon continued. 'I don't like casting actors who might not get on. Harmony amongst the cast. Most important. But your agent said you weren't to be contacted at Fareham. He's very protective, your Reginald Harcourt.'

What on earth was he talking about? Sam wondered, bewildered by his sudden change of mood. No longer overbearing, he seemed to be seeking her approval.

'It only hit me several weeks after I got back from London,' he went on. 'We'd screen-tested for the father, but I hadn't found what I was after. I wanted to cast an

Australian actor of course, but I couldn't find the true . . .
I don't know . . .' he was uncharacteristically fumbling for
the right words '. . . the innate Victorian pomposity that
comes from an ingrained class system.'

Sam was now completely bemused. Simon Scanlon was
not only one of the rudest, but one of the most contra-
dictory men she'd met. Barking orders in shorthand one
moment, then obscurely rambling on the next. She wished
he'd get to the point.

'The father appears a small role in the overall film,' he
continued, 'but Clifford Huxley is a very important character, I'm sure you'll agree. Pivotal to the development of
Sarah. Anyway, I woke up in the middle of the night and I
suddenly realised that I'd already *seen* Sarah Huxley and
her father.' Simon was leaning forward again now, elbows
on the table, eyes once more electric with excitement.
'I swear to you, Sam, I realised that I'd actually been
watching Sarah and Clifford Huxley when I saw the two
of you up there on that stage.'

The penny suddenly dropped. *A Doll's House.* 'Alexander Wright,' Sam said.

'Do you agree?' Simon's query was earnest and concerned. 'The chemistry between the two of you is perfect.
Am I right? Tell me I'm right.'

'Yes of course.' Sam was under his spell again. The man
was a chameleon. Now she liked him, now she didn't. But
he was certainly right. 'Alexander is wonderful casting,'
she agreed.

'Wright by name, right by nature.' Simon gave a bark of
delighted laughter. 'Alexander Wright *is* Clifford Huxley!
I'm so glad you approve.'

'Just as well,' Nick added dryly, 'he's flying in
tomorrow.'

'Samantha! My darling doll wife,' Alexander intoned as
he kissed the air beside her cheeks. He was deeply

grateful to Samantha Lindsay. She was directly responsible for a career breakthrough which, at his age, he'd
presumed an impossibility. Alexander was eager to
embrace Hollywood. He would never have admitted it,
but treading the boards eight performances a week, albeit
in the West End, had become rather tiresome. This was
his big chance at the movie career which had, through no
want of trying on his part, somehow eluded him throughout his life.

'The old team, eh!' he exclaimed, laying it on for all it
was worth. 'Husband and wife, now father and daughter.
We are destined to work together.'

'Alexander! It's beaut to see you, it really is.' She deliberately swung into the Australian vernacular as she hugged
him warmly. She could read him like a book and she
was aware his performance was all bravado, that he
was hoping, indeed praying, she would welcome him like
an old friend.

'Oh my dear,' he said, so overcome that for a moment
he dropped his theatricality, 'it's lovely to see you too. It
really is.'

Standing nearby in the production offices Mammoth
had hired at Fox Studios, Nick Parslow gave Simon
Scanlon an 'I told you so' look. Simon had voiced his
worry about Sam's personal opinion of Alexander Wright.

'Her agent swears she won't mind,' he'd said. 'But what
if she can't stand the man? He's a good actor, but I hear
offstage he's a pompous old fart.' As always, Simon had
made his enquiries.

Nick had been quick in his reassurance. 'You can trust
Reginald, Simon,' he'd said. 'He knows what he's talking
about, and he always has Sam's best interests at heart, he
wouldn't let anything interfere with her work. Or her
personal life for that matter,' he added knowingly. Nick
and Reginald had become close friends, and both shared
the deepest of affection for Samantha Lindsay.

Simon had deliberately called Alexander in first, eager to read Sam's reaction, and half an hour later the other actors involved in the opening scenes arrived at the production office.

'Mickey!'

There was an exuberant reunion between Michael Robertson and Sam the moment he walked through the door. They'd worked together in the theatre on many an occasion, including the production of *Red Centre*, and when Reg had told her that Michael had been cast as her missionary husband, Sam had been 'over the moon'.

'How amazing!' she'd said. 'I'm over the moon! I can't think of anyone I'd rather work with. How utterly, fantastically amazing!'

'Not really,' Reg had said, 'it's the way he operates.'

'Who? How?'

'Simon Scanlon. He'd been favouring another actor over Michael, Nick told me, but when he found out the two of you were such good friends, Michael had the job, simple as that.'

'Oh.' Sam hadn't been too sure how to take it; it didn't sound right to her.

'As far as Nick and Simon are concerned, Sarah Blackston is the crux of this film,' Reg had said. 'It's the woman's story and they want to concentrate on her, despite the lover and the POW camp, and Brett Marsdon and the American market. It's the story of "Mamma Black", Nick told me. And Mamma Black is you, Sam. Simon Scanlon will do anything to keep you happy.'

'Sammy, Sammy, Sammy!'

Alexander Wright watched from the sidelines as the lanky actor whirled Sam off her feet. He had the distinct feeling that his proprietorial relationship with Samantha was being severely upstaged, but he tried his very hardest to look like an indulgent parent.

'Alexander, this is Michael Robertson.' Sam introduced

the men personally, instead of waiting for Simon's official introductions all round. 'Two of my favourite actors,' she said. And Alexander beamed, once again reinstated.

The moment did not escape Simon Scanlon. Samantha Lindsay was more than a bloody good actress, he thought, she was a bloody good diplomat. He couldn't have been happier.

He made the formal introductions. There were three other actors playing the minor roles of household staff: the butler, the housekeeper and the maid.

'Hello, Anthony. Hello, Fiona.' Sam shook hands with them warmly. 'Great to be working together again.' Anthony Cole and Fiona Hedge were character actors who'd been around for years and, although their roles were never large, they were rarely out of work, particularly since the arrival of big-budget overseas movies. They were colourful troupers who, from the radio days of old, could handle any accent thrown at them. Both were thrilled that Sam recalled them from the guest roles they'd had in 'Families and Friends' when she'd been a teenager.

Ada, playing the maid, was unknown to them all, a young actress fresh out of drama school, but Sam greeted her with equal warmth, putting the girl at ease in an instant.

Jesus Christ, but Samantha Lindsay was a gem, Simon thought.

The first two days were devoted to discussion of the script, the characters and their relationships, and in the rehearsal room adjacent to the production offices the actors were encouraged to interact freely. Simon was not going to block any specific moves until they were in the studio set, he told them. He was very receptive to any suggestions from the cast, and was pleasantly surprised by Alexander's perceptiveness.

'Clifford is not unlike Torvald, is he?' Alexander commented, referring to the character he'd played in *A Doll's House*. 'Not a bad man in the true sense of the word. Thoughtless and misguided, and very set in his ways, but even when he appears malicious, he doesn't really intend to be, does he?'

'Spot on, Alexander, spot on!' Simon applauded. Alexander Wright might behave like a buffoon at times, he thought, but he certainly wasn't dumb when it came to interpretation. 'He's a "right" man who sees the world only from his own perspective. It's his insensitivity to those about him, particularly his daughter, which makes him so shockingly cruel.'

Two weeks had been allotted to shoot the opening scenes, after which they would relocate to Vanuatu where the American star, Brett Marsdon, would join them. Simon had deliberately orchestrated the proceedings so that the Huxley household would become a close-knit unit. The opening of the film, he said, was totally isolated. 'A film within a film,' he told them, 'think of it that way.' This was a conspiratorial household where the old servants had known the mistress before she died. They were fully aware of the father's deep-seated dislike of his daughter, and the unspoken reason why: that Clifford Huxley had never forgiven his daughter for robbing him of his beautiful wife in childbirth.

'But they're not going to risk their jobs, are they?' he said. 'They're not going to threaten the comfortable lifestyle they've had for over twenty-five years, so they're conspirators. Only the young, newly appointed maid has no idea why Clifford Huxley is so contemptuous of his daughter. The maid is an innocent in a household destined to emotionally and psychologically destroy a young woman. The maid is, in many ways, the audience. Out there in the dark, discovering the secrets of the past as it's unravelled before them.'

Ada was thrilled – she'd thought the maid was just a bit part. She hadn't realised that her character was of such depth and importance.

It was one of Simon Scanlon's greatest talents. He made every actor, no matter how seemingly trivial their role, feel valuable and indispensable to the production. And he did so because, to him, they were.

Then there were three days of meetings and discussions with designers, hairdressers and makeup artists, followed by costume and wig fittings, and at the end of the third day, Simon announced that they were moving into the set the following morning.

The cast had met the set designer, Rodney, a talented man in his mid-thirties, easygoing and affable, who had worked on the last three of Simon's films. But no-one had been shown a model of the set, or even a ground plan of the layout. It was a deliberate ploy on Simon's behalf.

'We'll meet at ten o'clock outside Stage 7,' he said. 'We'll all go in together, and you'll explore the home where you'll be living for the next eleven days.'

Sam arrived at the studios the following morning a good half hour before the others. She always arrived early, having instructed her regular driver, an eager young runner called Ben, to collect her from the Quay Grand an hour before her scheduled call each day. After Ben had driven through the studio gates and past the guard house, she'd alight at Stanley Crick House.

The picturesque vine-covered building had been the Royal Agricultural Society's members' stand in the days before Fox had taken over the Sydney Showground, once home to Australia's largest annual agricultural exhibition. It stood on the border between the two sectors which now constituted Fox Studios. On one side was the vast professional complex of sound stages and production offices, recording studios and editing suites, workshops, makeup departments and dressing rooms. On the other was Bent Street, the equally vast public area of retail shops and markets, cafes and restaurants, entertainment venues and art-deco cinemas.

Sam enjoyed wandering around Bent Street before the tourists arrived, exploring the shops, having a latte in an outdoor cafe and generally soaking up the atmosphere. To her, the whole of Fox Studios seemed a world unto itself, like a walled city, locked away from the realities of outside.

Today, however, she didn't alight at Stanley Crick House, but instructed Ben to go directly to Sound Stage 7. She wanted to explore the exterior of the huge sandstone building which she'd admired from some distance, unaware that this was where they would be filming the Huxley house scenes.

Stage 7 was housed in a restored heritage pavilion and was the largest and most recently converted sound stage on the Fox lot, having opened for production only earlier that year. Sam looked up at the massive facade that had once been the main entrance to the pavilion. Wide stone steps on either side led to a portico supported by twin Ionic columns, beyond which was a large stained-glass window depicting a map of Australia. High above, in massive letters carved deep in the sandstone, was the inscription: 'AUSTRALIA'S 150TH ANNIVERSARY COMMEMORATIVE PAVILION 1938'. It was a proud building.

She walked up the steps to the portico and looked out over the view. Below her were the myriad streets and shopfronts of the tourist sector, for all the world like a miniature village. Behind them to the right was the old stone clock tower and, rearing over a hundred metres high in the background, modern and strangely out of place, were the giant night lights of the Sydney Cricket Ground.

Sam found the perspective exciting. The odd mixture of styles and shapes, the blending of old and new, past and present, all added to the sense of anticipation she'd had from the moment she'd awoken that morning. There'd been enough discussion. She couldn't wait to start work in earnest.

Half an hour later, when they all met at the rear stage door of the studio, there was the same feeling of anticipation amongst the others.

Simon and Nick led the way inside, followed by Rodney, the set designer, and the actors trooped in after them.

The immensity of the gutted and soundproofed interior was overwhelming. Nissen hut-shaped, 3,600 square metres in area, rising to a height of twenty metres, it looked exactly like an aeroplane hangar. But it didn't house aircraft. Sitting solidly and incongruously upon the huge floor space was a Victorian mansion. There were two sets: the ground floor of the house, and behind it, the upper floor, enabling each to be lit from the lighting grid which was rigged high above.

'Take your time and wander the sets,' Simon instructed after he'd called up the work lights, 'we'll have discussions with Rodney afterwards. I want you to get the feel of the place first before we go into technicalities.'

Alexander, Mickey, Anthony, Fiona and young Ada continued to gaze about, awestruck. They'd never seen a studio so huge. But Sam wasn't looking at the studio at all, she was staring at the set. They were facing the ground floor of the house, and there were three bay windows. She walked around the corner to the right; the main entrance would be on that side, she thought. It was. Several stone steps led up to a porch. She pushed open the front door and entered.

There was a small hallway with a coat stand and pegs on the walls. She crossed through it. The kitchen would be down several steps to the right. And there it was. A big kitchen, the hub of the house, cosy and warm. A large wooden table and bench, pots and pans hanging from pegs, and an open door leading to a narrow staircase. That would go up to the servants' quarters, she thought.

She went back towards the hall and turned right again, into what she knew would be the drawing room. She felt as if she was in a dream. That it wasn't happening, that at any moment she might awake. A surreal experience, dreamlike and yet hauntingly real. She was in Chisolm House.

The drapes were drawn over the bay windows, but there was a chair and table beside them, as if someone made a habit of sitting and gazing out at the garden. There was an escritoire in the corner, converted gas lamps in wall brackets, gold-leaf framed mirrors. She looked about, unnerved. It wasn't happening. It couldn't be. There was a fireplace. There was a mantelpiece with a framed photograph perched in the centre. The only thing missing was Phoebe's portrait. A tapestry hung in its place.

'You seem to know your way around.'

She was startled by the voice beside her. 'Sorry?' she said, shocked back to the present.

'You headed straight to the main entrance,' Rodney said. 'You seem to know your way around.'

Sam heard the other actors. They'd found their way to the front door and were now exploring the kitchen, she could hear their 'oohs' and 'ahs' of admiration.

'I do,' she replied. Her brief sense of panic was gone, but she still felt shaken as she gazed around at the walls and the fireplace and the bay windows. 'I own this house,' she said.

Rodney grinned. 'Taking method acting a bit far, isn't it?'

'I'm not joking, Rod,' she said. 'I bought a house in Hampshire only a month ago. It's identical.'

'Oh, this is a pretty stock Victorian design,' he shrugged, 'there's nineteenth century houses like this all over England.'

'But the electrically operated gas lamps, the mirrors, the escritoire in the corner . . .'

'A lot of them converted their gas lamps to electricity, love,' he assured her. She seemed a bit shaky, he thought. 'Gold-leaf mirrors were all the rage in Edwardian days, and face it, where else would you put the escritoire?'

'Yes, you're probably right,' Sam agreed, trying to sound casual. 'Just a coincidence.'

''Course it is. Don't let it rattle you.' He grinned again; Rodney rarely took things seriously. 'Besides,' he added, rolling his eyes dramatically, 'you can "use it to your advantage", as Simon would say.'

'Yes, I can certainly do that,' Sam smiled. 'But don't say anything to him, do you mind?' She chastised herself. The similarities between the set and Chisolm House were purely coincidental, just as Rodney had pointed out, and it was foolish of her to dramatise the situation.

'Sure, no worries.'

'The set's divine, Rodney. A masterpiece!' Alexander was leading the troops into the drawing room.

'Thanks, Alexander. What do you think of young Clifford?' Rodney crossed to the mantelpiece and picked up the framed photograph. 'It's come up pretty well, I think. Archie spent half the night working on it, he wanted to surprise you.'

Sam, having stood back and drawn breath in order to recover herself, joined the others as they gathered around to admire Clifford Huxley and his beautiful bride. The wedding photograph was an important prop, and the photo shoot had been held just the previous day in a private studio.

It had been a nerve-wracking experience for Alexander. Not at first. At first he'd felt resplendent in his youthful makeup, his impeccable wig and his finely tailored Edwardian costume. The wardrobe and makeup team had spent two hours working on him and he'd been thoroughly convinced that he looked not a day over thirty-five, as was the intention. Then he'd been confronted with the girl who was to pose as his wife. She was all of twenty-two and one of the most glorious creatures he'd ever seen. His confidence had been instantly undermined. Dear God, but he'd look like a stupid old fool, he'd thought. He'd covered his humiliation with bluster, made the customary remarks about 'old enough to be your father, my dear', secretly knowing he was old enough to be her grandfather, and he'd dreaded seeing the final result. Now here it was. He held his breath.

'You look wonderful, Alexander,' Fiona said admiringly, Anthony beside her nodding in emphatic agreement.

And he did. Young and handsome and thirty-five. Alexander glowed with a mixture of pride and relief. 'Yes, it has come up rather well, hasn't it?'

'How did he do it?' With a youthful lack of diplomacy Ada was looking from the photograph to Alexander and back again in disbelief. 'How on earth did he do it?'

Alexander suddenly didn't like the girl.

'Archie's a genius,' Rodney said, and Alexander was about to dislike him too, until he continued, 'Just look at that lighting and the grain of the reproduction, you'd swear that's an Edwardian photograph.'

'Yes, it's a work of art all right,' Alexander agreed.

'Who's the girl?' Mickey asked. 'She's gorgeous.'

'Suzie someone,' Rodney said. 'She's not an actor, hasn't even done any modelling. Simon wanted an unknown and she had the look he was after.'

'What a pity we weren't allowed on the shoot,' Mickey said regretfully, casting a cheeky look to Sam. He was known to have a roving eye and she'd knocked him back on many an occasion in the past. Since he'd accepted their relationship was to remain platonic he'd often shared his lustful feelings with her. They made a joke of it.

But Sam didn't return his glance. She was staring at the photograph, another sense of déjà vu stealing over her. There was no baby Phoebe in the photograph, certainly, but the pose was the same. The formal portrait. The husband standing, proprietorial hand resting upon the shoulder of his wife seated in a hard-backed chair. And the wife was a dark-haired beauty. It was Arthur and Alice Chisolm.

Together, they explored the upper floor of the house, and as they did, Sam tried to ignore the persistent similarities between the set and Chisolm House. The tiny rooms at the rear were the servants' quarters with a shared bathroom and a small communal kitchen. The three large front rooms with bay windows were the master bedroom, Clifford Huxley's study and the upstairs drawing room. An upright piano stood in the far corner of the drawing room, which again unnerved her, but she registered, with a vague sense of relief, that nothing else was familiar to her. Then she reminded herself that this was more than likely the way Chisolm House would have looked in the days of Arthur and Alice, which only added to her nagging feeling of déjà vu.

'Everybody got the feel of the place?' Simon had re-appeared with Nick, takeaway coffee cups in hand, having left the actors alone to explore the set. 'Right. Over to you, Rod.'

Once again they walked each room, Rodney explaining the technicalities, pointing out which walls were 'floaters', removable to allow camera access, and Sam was relieved to find herself back in the make-believe world of film.

They loosely blocked each scene, like rehearsing a stage play, Simon giving them their moves and key marks, encouraging them not to perform but simply to feel their space. It was a relaxing way to start work and Sam felt very much at home with his method of direction. He intended to film in sequence, and tomorrow they would shoot the opening scene.

Sam was called for hair and makeup at seven in the morning and, having arrived a good fifteen minutes early, she sat in her dressing room with the coffee which Ben had obligingly fetched her, and started on the *Sydney Morning Herald*'s cryptic crossword. But it didn't make sense this morning, she was far too excited to concentrate. She picked up her script, but that didn't help either. She knew her lines backwards and seeing them on paper meant nothing. Then finally she was summoned to the makeup room and her day began.

Two hours later she looked at herself in the mirror. The wardrobe and wig fittings, the discussions with Simon, the makeup artist's experiments, all had come to fruition. She was looking at Sarah Huxley.

The hair was a mousy light brown, parted in the middle and tied loosely in a bun at the nape of the neck. The skin colour was pallid, bordering on unhealthy, and the powdered-down brows and lashes robbed her eyes of drama, giving them a timid look. She was dressed in a grey suit, with a high-necked jacket and mid-calf-length skirt. Modest and conventional, it was nonetheless of fine wool and well cut. Despite the year being 1935 and the country being in the throes of a depression, Clifford Huxley was a wealthy man and dressed his daughter in only the finest.

As Sam looked at Sarah Huxley in the mirror, she knew that she had the character. She watched herself shrink. She saw the uncertainty creep into her eyes and, as her shoulders imperceptibly hunched, the suit, now sitting on a defeated young woman, no longer looked well cut.

When she arrived on set, with the wardrobe, hair and makeup entourage, Simon was quick with his compliments. 'Well done, team,' he loudly announced, 'you've turned a beautiful young woman into a mouse,' and they all beamed with pleasure. But Simon could see that the defeat of Sarah Huxley was coming from within. 'Good girl, Sam,' he whispered. And, like the others, Sam found herself beaming with pride. Simon Scanlon had that effect upon people.

Simon called up the lights and the actors gasped in awe. The opening scene was set in the downstairs drawing room and the facade of the set had been wheeled away to expose the interior. A ceiling had been hydraulically lowered; it was a night scene and Simon wanted the effect of the chandelier.

The chandelier. Night-time at Chisolm House, Sam thought. Then she saw the portrait. It was hanging on the wall to the left, perfectly lit between two gas lamps. She walked over to it – they all did – quietly lost in admiration. It was a work of art. Simon had planned it as a surprise for them all.

'The mistress,' he announced when they were all gathered about the painting. 'Clifford's wife Amelia, she rules Huxley House. Isn't she magnificent?'

There was a spontaneous round of applause and everyone turned to Rodney who gave a mock bow, accepting the compliment, but like all of the others who'd received praise from Simon, he too was secretly glowing with pride. He'd worked long and hard on the portrait, the same model who had posed for the wedding photograph sitting for him day in, day out. He might as well have been working for the Archibald Prize, he'd thought. But Simon Scanlon's approval had been all he'd needed. The applause of the cast was just the cream on the cake.

Only Sam remained gazing at the portrait. She was thankful it wasn't Phoebe. She didn't know if she could have taken that. There was no rebellion, no provocation in this woman. She was neither teasing nor tantalising, but there was a power about her. It was a formal studio portrait. Hands crossed on the lap, she was impeccably groomed, her luxurious auburn hair conventionally parted in the middle and drawn back behind her neck. But her eyes met the artist in a steady, confident gaze. There was a strength and serenity in her beauty.

This was Amelia Huxley, Sam thought, not Phoebe Chisolm. But she was in the wrong place.

'She should be over the mantelpiece,' she said.

There was a pause. Sam's voice had been peremptory

and the others were taken aback, particularly Nick Parslow. It wasn't like Sam to be dictatorial.

'She's absolutely beautiful where she is,' Alexander said with a touch of disapproval. It wasn't up to actors to change the set, he thought.

'I put her there so that she's the first thing you see when you come into the room,' Rodney explained. 'I thought that's what Clifford would want.' He looked at Simon who nodded approval. 'Besides, she can't go anywhere else,' he added good-naturedly, 'the lighting's all rigged for her where she is.'

'Amelia Huxley should be over the mantelpiece,' Sam repeated.

There was another pause. They were all starting to feel uncomfortable.

'Sam's right,' Simon announced. Samantha Lindsay was affected by the portrait, he could tell. He didn't know why, but anything that worked for actors worked for Simon Scanlon. 'Amelia goes over the mantelpiece.'

'It'll take us a while to re-light her,' Rodney said.

'Fine by me. Everyone to their dressing rooms. We'll call you when we're ready.' As they trooped out of the studio he whispered in another aside to Sam, 'Good girl. Use it. Use it.'

She looked at him, surprised. Did he know? But he didn't.

'Whatever you're feeling, Sam,' he said urgently, his pterodactyl eyes disappearing into slits, 'use it. It's working.'

She would, she thought, as she went back to her dressing room. She'd use Phoebe and Chisolm House. She would tell no-one, not even Nick. But whatever strange force was coming into play, and there was certainly something, she wouldn't let it frighten her. She would use it in whatever way she could.

Over the ensuing ten days, Simon Scanlon became obsessed with Samantha Lindsay and her performance. Something was driving the girl. He didn't know what it was and he didn't care, but she had metamorphosed before his eyes, and she was taking the others with her. She was inspired. As she looked up at her mother's portrait, longing to be beautiful like Amelia, longing to earn her father's love, she was achingly moving. The portrait became the centre of the household, and Sam had been quite right, Simon thought. Amelia belonged above the mantelpiece.

Sam was aware of the force that was driving her. She found herself living in two worlds. She partied with the others, enjoying their company. She walked around the harbour foreshores and through Hyde Park, revelling in the beauty of Sydney. On the weekend, she browsed through the markets at the Opera House and the Rocks. But the moment she arrived on set, she found herself in that other world. The world of Huxley House where no daylight penetrated. Where the drapes remained closed, upon Clifford Huxley's instruction, and Amelia's chair, a constant reminder of her presence, remained beside the bay windows where once she'd sat looking out at the garden.

The set and its eerie replication of Chisolm House no longer unnerved Sam. She accepted its claustrophobic embrace the moment she entered it, feeling herself instantly become Sarah. The house was her ally.

'May I invite Mr Blackston to dine after the service next Sunday, Father?'

They were seated at each end of the large oak dining table, Sarah and her father. The dining room was adjacent to the downstairs drawing room, just as it was at Chisolm House. It had a similar bay window, and twin doors at the rear led directly to the servants' stairs and the kitchen. Sam was glad that she'd never dined with the bed and breakfast guests at Chisolm House all those years ago, as it meant she held no memories of cosiness or familiarity that might interfere with the awkward distance between herself and Alexander.

'*You are mistress of this house, Sarah.*' Clifford's tone was scathing. '*You have no need to beg my permission. You are free to invite guests whenever you wish.*'

There had been discussion in a previous scene of the Reverend Hugh Blackston. Sarah, skilled in flower arrangement, visited the local church each Saturday afternoon and prepared the floral arrangements for the Sunday services. Clifford had noted that, over the past several weeks, she had come home an hour later than usual. Curiosity had finally won out and he'd asked her why.

'*I take afternoon tea with Mr Blackston,*' she said. '*I hope you don't mind, Father.*'

'*God in heaven, girl, you're twenty-five, you're at liberty to see whomsoever you please.*' Clifford hated her servility.

And now she was asking the man to dine at Huxley House. Clifford was intrigued as to the intentions of Hugh Blackston – surely he couldn't be interested in a mouse like Sarah. He had personally met Blackston on a number of occasions following the Sunday services he and Sarah attended, but he'd taken little notice of the man, just as he took little notice of anything connected with the church. He attended the services simply because it was proper that he should be seen to do so.

'*The Reverend Blackston is a most interesting man, Father,*' Sarah said in response to his enquiry, Clifford suspiciously noting an uncharacteristic animation in her eyes. '*He is shortly to leave for the New Hebrides where he is to serve as a missionary.*'

In accordance with the script, the budding relationship between Sarah Huxley and Hugh Blackston was never seen. Everything was contained in the house. And the buildup to the arrival of the Reverend Hugh Blackston was electric. The tension between father and daughter perfect, the housekeeper and the butler suspicious, like their master, of the Reverend's intentions, the maid simply thrilled by the prospect of romance.

Simon Scanlon was delighted. Alexander was scaling new heights working with Sam. And so were the others. Fiona and Anthony and Ada were equally inspired.

*'Welcome to Huxley House, Mr Blackston.' It was a wintry night and they stood around the cosy open fireplace in the downstairs drawing room, just the three of them, as Clifford proposed the salutary toast.*

*'Thank you, Mr Huxley.' Hugh raised his glass, returning the salutation. 'She's very beautiful, your mother,' he said to Sarah of the portrait which was impossible to ignore.*

*'She was. Oh yes, she most certainly was,' Clifford replied, as if the remark had been addressed to him.*

*'I can see the resemblance.' Hugh smiled encouragingly at Sarah. He wasn't lying, he had seen the same strength in Sarah's eyes that he now saw in the portrait. But she had wilted in her father's presence; he'd noted the same reaction after Sunday services when the three of them had met.*

Sam looked at the love and encouragement which shone in Mickey's eyes. He was a fine actor and he was giving her everything. She felt herself flush. The blood literally rose to her cheeks and she stared at the floor, avoiding Alexander's penetrating gaze. Sarah was fearful that her father might read the love that unashamedly welled inside her.

*Clifford watched his daughter's embarrassment. He felt her cringe. And so she should, he thought. 'I hardly think so,' he scoffed. How dare Blackston pretend to perceive a likeness between Amelia and his mouse of a daughter. The man was a charlatan, he decided there and then. Who would have thought it? A man of the cloth. After his daughter's money.*

The scene in the dining room was even more fraught with tension, the servants hovering, at Clifford's encouragement, as he repeatedly undermined Sarah.

*'We had such dinner parties here in the old days,' Clifford said, 'didn't we, Beatrice?'*

'We did indeed, sir.' The housekeeper smiled, then darted another quick look of warning towards the maid who should have been serving the trifle instead of staring at the Reverend as she had been doing throughout all four courses of the meal.

'We don't any more,' Clifford continued. 'Sarah's not quite up to it. And a house needs a mistress for that form of entertaining. Isn't that so, Billings?' he asked as the butler poured his glass of dessert wine.

'It is, sir,' Billings agreed.

'Perhaps Sarah doesn't wish to entertain,' Hugh gently suggested, deciding that it was time someone took a stand. He ignored Sarah's horrified glance.

The man's tone may have been mild, but the essence of his comment was not. 'What exactly does she wish then, Mr Blackston, can you tell me?'

'I do believe that she wishes to marry me, Mr Huxley, and I'd be most grateful if you'd agree to the union.'

The words were out before Hugh could stop them. He and Sarah had agreed that he would meet her father and then, over the customary port and coffee in the drawing room, delicately approach the subject. But Hugh had decided that Clifford Huxley was a tyrant who enjoyed bullying his daughter and the sooner Sarah was away from him the better. They would marry with or without Huxley's consent.

'That will be all, thank you,' Clifford dismissed the servants, and Beatrice nudged the maid, who was openly gawking. When they had retired to the kitchen, closing the doors behind them, Clifford took a sip of his sauterne before continuing. 'You realise that if I withhold my permission you will be marrying a penniless young woman.'

'So be it,' Hugh replied. 'Your daughter's money is of no interest to me, sir.'

'Pray then, what is?' Clifford sneered, glancing briefly at Sarah, who sat in silence, eyes downcast.

Hugh said nothing, but leaned towards Sarah and reached

*out his hand. She and her father were seated in their cus-*
*tomary places at either end of the table, Hugh in the middle.*
*To clasp his hand Sarah herself needed to lean forward and*
*extend her full arm. It would be a gesture of total defiance.*

*Clifford, who had ignored his daughter throughout the*
*brief exchange, now turned his full gaze upon her, daring*
*her to so openly flout his authority.*

*She didn't hesitate, but reached out her hand. 'I love*
*him, Father,' she said and, as her fingers entwined with*
*Hugh's, she abandoned her father. 'And I will go with him*
*to the New Hebrides as his wife.'*

*Clifford was speechless. Shocked by her brazen*
*audacity. He took another sip of his sauterne as he fought*
*to recover himself. He wanted to throw the glass of wine*
*in her face. The ingrate. She had robbed him of his Amelia,*
*and yet he had done his duty by her throughout her entire*
*miserable existence. She'd had the best schooling money*
*could buy, she wore the finest clothes, ate the finest food,*
*she lived a life of luxury, and now she was going to desert*
*him. Who would look after him in his twilight years? She*
*owed him that much, surely.*

*'I see,' he said finally. 'Well, there's really nothing more*
*to discuss, is there?' He rose from the table.*

They were right on schedule, and the day before the film
unit was to leave for Vanuatu, they shot the brief final
scene between Sarah and her father. Sarah had left Huxley
House with Hugh that same night of the confrontation,
and had been staying with his sister who lived in nearby
Worthing. There had been further scenes shot in the house,
mirroring the decline of Clifford Huxley, a defeated man,
aware of how sorely he would miss his daughter, but too
proud to beg her forgiveness. Now she had returned to say
goodbye before sailing for the New Hebrides.

There was to be a wrap party after the shoot that day,
and the others came in to watch the filming of the final
scene. Huxley House had had its effect upon them all. It

was as if they'd been making a separate film – 'a film within a film', as Simon had instructed – the work had been so intensely personal.

'Sure,' he agreed when they sought his permission to watch the filming. 'Check it out with Sam and Alexander, and stay out of their eyelines of course, but so long as they don't mind, it's fine by me.'

Sam and Alexander didn't mind one bit. Sam thought it was amazing that Mickey, Fiona, Anthony and Ada should come to work when they had the day off, and Alexander was secretly delighted. An audience out there in the dark. He'd missed an audience.

*'You haven't shaved, Father.' Sarah was shocked. She'd never seen him unshaven.*

*'I forgot. I awoke late this morning.' He hadn't shaved in the whole three days since she'd left. 'I'll ring for tea.'*

*'No, please don't bother.' She didn't want to see the servants. 'I only came to say goodbye.'*

*'I thought as much.'*

*She crossed to him where he stood by the mantelpiece, wondering whether he would kiss her farewell, but he didn't. He was a tall man and it was impossible for her to make the gesture without him offering his cheek, so she proffered her hand instead.*

*'Goodbye, Father.'*

*'I shall not disinherit you of course, Sarah,' he said as he shook her hand. 'It was never my intention, I was simply testing the man.'*

*'An unnecessary test, as it turned out, but thank you.'*

*What was it about her? he thought. There was a confidence, even a boldness that he'd never before seen, but there was something else. Then he realised. She was no longer plain. When did that happen? he wondered. And how? His mouse of a daughter. There was life in her eyes, pride in her bearing, she looked womanly and alive.*

*'When do you leave?' he asked.*

'We sail from Southampton the day after tomorrow,' she replied.

'You'll marry in the New Hebrides then?'

'We were married yesterday.'

So that was it, he thought. She'd discovered love, she'd become a woman. Of course that was it. He thought of Amelia. 'I shall miss you,' he said, avoiding her eyes, staring into the fireplace instead.

'No you shan't, Father.' She didn't say it unkindly, but the words sounded brutal nonetheless. 'Why should you miss the millstone you've had about your neck all these years?'

He looked at her then. 'Is that what you were?'

'Yes.' Suddenly, she felt an aching pity for him. 'I'm sorry I couldn't be my mother.'

'You're all I have left of her, Sarah.'

'I'm sorry. I'm so very sorry.' She reached up and touched his cheek, but he didn't lower his face for her to kiss it. 'Goodbye, Father.'

She was gone, and Clifford looked up at the portrait of his wife, tears welling in his eyes.

'Cut!' Simon called. 'That's a wrap,' he announced to the crew. 'Well done, Alexander. Very moving. Well done.'

The final shot had been a closeup on Clifford, and the makeup artist had been standing by with a menthol blower to induce tears, but Alexander hadn't needed it. Sam had joined the others, watching from the sidelines as they'd changed lens for the closeup, and she'd been his inspiration. God but he loved an audience, Alexander thought.

There were cheers from the crew and embraces all round and Simon made the final announcement.

'Party as long as you like tonight,' he said. 'But don't miss the plane tomorrow. Vanuatu, here we come!'

# CHAPTER EIGHT

The SS *Morinda* bucked and rolled her way through the swell of the vast Pacific Ocean, but the elements presented little danger. She was a solid vessel, an inter-island tramp steamer that had weathered many a storm, and today's conditions were nothing to her. The dour skipper had privately assured Jane that the vessel was in relatively safe waters. He considered it only fair, he'd said, that she and her husband should be kept informed, travelling with a child, as they were. Jane noticed, however, that he'd offered no such assurance to the other passengers – four Australians and two New Zealanders – a rough and ready bunch; he obviously enjoyed watching them sweat.

She searched the horizon, barely visible beneath heavy clouds. The skipper had said they'd see the island any moment now but, although the rain had ceased, the steamy vapour still clouded her vision. 'You'll be surprised how quickly the weather clears,' he'd promised her.

Then suddenly, miraculously, he was right. The haze disappeared, the sky became blue, and there it was, like magic, in the distance dead ahead. The island of Efate. Craggy mountains rearing abruptly out of lush tropical forest, breakers rolling relentlessly upon coral shores. And somewhere not yet visible amidst this dramatic landscape was Vila, the capital of the archipelago known as the New Hebrides.

Approximately 840 miles east of Australia, the Y-shaped cluster of the archipelago was made up of four main and sixty smaller islands. Efate lay to the south and, roughly twenty-five miles long and eighteen miles wide, it was the chief, although by no means largest, of the group, Espiritu Santo and Malekula to the north being far larger. But Efate housed the capital of Vila. It was from here that the dual colonial administrations of France and Britain governed the New Hebrides. And it was the capital of Vila that was Jane and Martin Thackeray's intended destination.

It had been a long and hazardous voyage, but one neither Jane nor Martin had questioned from the outset. Jane had had some initial concern for the baby's welfare, but he was strong and healthy and, as Martin himself had said, 'His father is a doctor and his mother a nurse, my love, he could hardly be in better hands.' And Jane had agreed. Little Ronald Thackeray would grow up with the same spirit of adventure which she and Martin shared.

The Missions Committee of the Presbyterian Church of New Zealand had been in urgent need of a doctor for their New Hebrides Mission and the position had been offered to Martin six months after the baby's birth. Unable to find a suitable candidate in New Zealand due to a wartime shortage, the Committee had sought further afield and Martin Thackeray, doubly qualified, a minister of the church and a medical doctor, had proved a perfect choice.

Martin had jumped at the chance, his wife, too, embracing the opportunity. Jane had been overjoyed at the renewal of purpose she saw in her husband. The decision to serve as a missionary doctor on the other side of the world, radical as it might be, was the obvious and final step in the restoration of Martin's faith. He had found his cause. And a month later, Martin and Jane Thackeray, together with baby Ronald, embarked upon the voyage that would change their lives.

The majority of passenger vessels on the England to Australia run had been requisitioned by the Admiralty as troop and supply carriers, but the SS *Themistocles* remained in commercial service for the Aberdeen line, and the Thackeray family had boarded in Liverpool, bound for Australia via the Cape of Good Hope.

It had been a perilous journey, fraught with the dangers of war. At night they had travelled without navigational lights, and there was the ever-present threat of U-boat attacks. But thirty-seven days later, they had arrived in Sydney, where they had travelled by train to Brisbane before boarding the SS *Morinda*.

Now, finally, they had reached their destination, and as Jane clung to the railings she felt breathless with anticipation. Martin was below, minding the baby. They took turns, and he had selflessly insisted she go up on deck for the first view of the island. He and Ronnie would join her, he said, when they came into port and the waters were calm. Then together, all three, they would view their new home.

The *Morinda* neared the promontory beyond which lay Mele Bay and the small protected harbour of Vila, and Jane gazed in wonderment at the beauty that unfolded before her eyes.

Endless groves of coconut palms and vivid green rainforest stretched from the backdrop of towering mountains to the shore. Sandy beaches gleamed, blindingly white. And all was surrounded by crystal-clear water of the lightest aquamarine, broken here and there by shelves of coral reef.

Never had she seen colours of such intensity. It was as if the artist who had painted this landscape hadn't bothered with a palette at all, but had simply dipped his brush into the paint pots, so unblended, so pure and stark were the contrasts.

Then they rounded the promontory into the broad sweep of Mele Bay where, to starboard, tiny islands guarded the harbour entrance and where, nestled beyond, lay the township of Vila.

The main street, with its several stores and businesses that catered to the colonial and expatriate society, ran parallel to the waterfront. Jutting out over the water were a number of piers and boatsheds and, on a small promontory, an intriguing building with shuttered verandahs. Perhaps a hotel or a restaurant of some kind, Jane thought, judging by the activity she could see through the open shutters.

Neat white homes with red roofs climbed the lush hillsides that rose from the shoreline, and within the harbour itself was a tiny, perfectly shaped island upon which stood a fine house.

The overall setting was one of such romance that it might have leapt from the pages of Kipling or Maugham, Jane thought. She noted, with a sense of curiosity, that the fine house on the island was flying the Union Jack.

'Iririki,' a voice said behind her, apparently reading her thoughts. 'Iririki Island, home of the British resident commissioner.' Martin had done his homework.

'Oh, Marty, I'm so sorry.' She whirled about; he was standing behind her, Ronnie in his arms, and he was grinning broadly. 'I was just about to come down and get you,' she said, riddled with guilt.

'No you weren't. I've been watching you for the past ten minutes.'

She kissed him as she took the child. 'I've been shockingly selfish,' she said, 'but I couldn't help myself. I was carried away. Isn't it all so beautiful?'

'Yes. It is.' Martin looked at her as she kissed the wide-eyed child and pointed out the island and the British flag.

'Very, very beautiful.' Her fair hair was in wild disarray and her eyes glowed vivid with excitement. They hadn't always been that colour, he thought, it must be the reflection of the ocean. He could swear they were aquamarine.

He put his arm around her and the three of them looked out at Vila as the SS *Morinda* slowly made her way towards the main jetty. 'Welcome to your new home, my love,' he said.

'*Our* new home, Marty.' She nestled her head into the crook of his arm and the child imitated her, nuzzling his little face against her neck. 'We're going to be so happy here.' Then she jerked her head up sharply, startling Ronnie, who let out a brief wail. 'Oh my goodness,' she exclaimed as she saw the outrigger canoes that had appeared to their left. She'd been so preoccupied with Iririki Island that she hadn't noticed the approach of the natives.

There must have been at least twenty canoes, simple dugout tree trunks with extended bamboo arms to prevent their overturning. They were flimsy, light craft but most proficiently handled, the smaller ones by two rowers, and some of the larger ones by half dozen or more men.

As the islanders drew closer, Jane felt unnerved, she had never seen people so black. Everything about them looked frightening to her, even their hair, which grew in an untamed frizz several inches from their heads. And they were gesticulating excitedly, calling out in an unintelligible language, and waving their arms and their paddles wildly in the air.

She resisted the instinctive urge to clasp Martin's arm, but he sensed her unease nonetheless. 'There's no cause for concern, my love,' he said. 'It's just a welcoming party, the locals are very friendly.'

'I'm aware of that,' she said stiffly, embarrassed at having been caught out. 'I was informed of the fact, if you remember.' Prior to their departure, she had been introduced to the representative of the Missions Committee and he had explained to her, briefly, the government and general customs of the New Hebrides.

Martin wasn't offended. He was aware that she was not annoyed with him at all, but with herself for having allowed her fear to be so readable. 'Of course they weren't always friendly,' he added, 'cannibalism was rife on a number of these islands.'

She glanced sharply at him. The representative had said no such thing to her, and it was sometimes difficult to tell when Martin was joking.

'In fact missionaries have contributed to quite a number of Melanesian feasts over the years, I believe.'

'Stop it, Marty,' she whispered, looking about to see if anyone else could hear, but the other passengers were leaning over the railings waving to the islanders.

'Oh yes,' he continued airily. 'They'd chop up the poor chap, roast his flesh on hot stones and serve him with taros and yams. They'd even invite the neighbouring tribe in for a share, if they were on friendly terms and hadn't eaten them first – they were a generous bunch.'

'That's not funny,' she said, cuddling Ronnie close as if to protect him from such images, although the child was happily mimicking the other passengers and waving at the strange black people.

'Perhaps not, but it's true.' Martin had been fully tutored on the history of the Mission, and had also read every piece of literature he could find relating to the New Hebrides. 'Fascinating, don't you think?'

She looked at him uncertainly, his sense of humour was so often disconcerting. But he once again put a comforting arm around her.

'Don't worry, my love, they don't do it any more.' Then he couldn't resist the urge. 'At least I don't think so,' he smiled.

Martin Thackeray and his family had been assigned a small house tucked into the side of the hill, across the clearing from the Presbyterian Church. The little path that led to its front door was shrouded with cabbage palms and tropical trees, and its verandah overlooked the harbour. Jane found it most charming. Nearby was a playing field, reminiscent of an English village green, which was known as the British 'paddock'. It was in the 'paddock' that every possible form of event staged by the colonial British took place, from official ceremonies to church fetes, football games and cricket matches.

The British were, however, vastly outnumbered by the French throughout the islands in a strange form of colonial government known as a Condominium, the two nations having signed a convention in 1906 which officially married them as joint guardians of the New Hebrides.

It was an uneasy marriage, resulting from the outset in a fiercely competitive stance taken by both, even in the choice of their respective residencies. The French immediately settled upon the ideal spot directly overlooking the harbour of Vila, forcing the British to make do with an inferior outlook tucked amongst the trees half mile away. Not at all happy with the arrangement, the British resident commissioner then decided to build his house on the island of Iririki, completely upstaging his opponent.

The ground rules having been established, the constant game of one-upmanship continued over the years and, to further confuse the issue, both administrations insisted upon dual bureaucracies. There were two sets of customs on arrival in the colony, two law systems, police forces and jails, two departments of education, two health services and two coin currencies, the French franc and the British shilling. Despite logical predictions that such a costly and inefficient government would last little more than a decade at most, tenacity and sheer pig-headedness had paid off. Thirty-five years later, the New Hebrides Condominium remained well entrenched.

'We call it Pandemonium,' Godfrey said as he refilled Martin's glass with the beaujolais he'd provided from his fine cellar stock. 'Some wag coined the term around thirty years ago and it's stuck ever since.'

Godfrey Tomlinson had introduced himself just three days after their arrival. 'Mrs Thackeray?' he'd enquired when Jane had answered the knock at the front door. Then, without waiting for an answer, he'd doffed his Panama hat and proffered his hand. 'I'm Godfrey Tomlinson, how do you do?'

He was an imposing-looking man, silver-haired and grey-bearded, with piercingly intelligent blue eyes. A cream linen suit hung, somewhat crumpled but strangely elegant, on his wiry frame, and as he smiled, his face wreathed into the wrinkles born of a lifetime in the tropics. Jane judged him to be in his seventies. The quintessential South Sea Island Englishman, she thought.

'Do forgive the intrusion, I merely wished to welcome you to Vila. I'll call back at another time if I'm inconveniencing you.'

'Not at all, Mr Tomlinson, it's very nice of you to call, please come in.' She'd led the way into the main room of the house. A large, airy lounge room with wooden shutters that opened out onto the small verandah overlooking the harbour. Steps, which for Ronnie's safety Martin had barricaded with a strip of lattice, led off the side of the verandah to the clearing where, in the distance, stood the church and the house of Martin's superior, the Reverend Arthur Smeed.

'Most attractive,' Godfrey said, admiring the brightness of the curtains and cushions and scatter rugs. 'You've done wonders in only a few days. And this is young Ronald, I take it?' Ronnie was happily amusing himself rattling the cane bars of his playpen in the corner.

'Yes,' Jane replied, wondering how he knew. But then the arrival of the missionary doctor and his family would inevitably be a source of gossip in a small town like Vila. It was disappointing to contemplate, given his old-world courtesy and impressive appearance, that Godfrey Tomlinson might simply be an interfering old busybody.

'I'm afraid my husband isn't here at the moment,' she said, 'he's at the church in discussion with Reverend Smeed.'

Martin had been in discussion with Reverend Smeed for the past three days and next week he was to leave for Malekula. Jane had known that his work would take him to the various islands, but she hadn't expected to be left on her own quite so soon.

'Ah, yes of course, he'll be a very busy man, your husband. When does he leave?'

'At the end of next week.' Again, she wondered how Godfrey Tomlinson knew of Reverend Smeed's plans for her husband, but she said nothing, refusing to ask how he had acquired his knowledge.

'So soon?' Godfrey had suspected as much. The Reverend Arthur Smeed, representative of the Presbyterian Church of New Zealand and a dedicated man, was a hard taskmaster. If Martin Thackeray was a man of equal dedication, and having accepted the appointment he probably was, then he would no doubt find the work rewarding. But it would be hard on his young wife. Which was the reason Godfrey had called upon her. It wasn't his custom. He knew everyone in Vila, and everyone certainly knew him, Godfrey Tomlinson was an institution throughout the islands, but he rarely visited people's homes, and he rarely invited others to his.

Arthur Smeed had told him, however, of the outbreak of measles on Malekula, a common ailment to Caucasians, but one that could wreak havoc amongst the islanders. God alone knew how long Martin Thackeray would be needed in Malekula, and God alone also knew where he'd be sent to from there. Godfrey had decided that the young doctor's wife would need an ally. The least he could do was to offer his support. Perhaps even, if he liked her, his friendship.

'All the more reason for the two of you to accept my invitation. And the baby of course,' he added, smiling his leathery smile at Ronnie, who grinned back and rattled the bars of his playpen more vigorously than ever. 'I would be delighted if the three of you would dine with me at my house before Dr Thackeray's departure. I'm just up there behind you.' He waved a hand airily above his head. 'The bungalow on the ridge.'

Jane had admired the 'bungalow on the ridge'. Situated in a beautifully tended tropical garden of flowering shrubs and bougainvillea, it was surrounded by wide verandahs and wooden-shuttered windows, and was a most elegant home. Several times she'd intended to ask Reverend Smeed who lived there, but the opportunity for conversation had never presented itself; the busy Reverend was not given to passing the time of day. He was well intentioned and most concerned for her welfare, certainly, but each of his visits to the house had been solely for the purpose of ensuring all practicalities were in place and 'teaching her the ropes', as he put it.

'Are you happy with the maid I employed for you?' he'd barked at her in his strange New Zealand accent upon their first meeting. And it had seemed to Jane a rhetorical question as he went straight on to explain that he'd taken great care to choose a girl who spoke passable English, unlike most of the Melanesians, he said, who communicated in Bislama, the local form of pidgin. And the girl was, furthermore, he pointed out, trustworthy and well trained with children.

Yes, Jane thanked him, she was perfectly happy with Mary.

And was she aware of the best shop for both general supplies and speedy delivery of catalogue-ordered items? It was in the centre of town and run by a New Zealander called Harry Bale. And did she know that English currency was of a higher comparative value in the islands than

French? And she must be most wary of Reid's Hotel, that curious building sitting on the promontory which, Smeed warned, was acceptable for afternoon tea but should be avoided during the evening when alcohol was heavily consumed. Ernie Reid's establishment was quite the social centre of Vila but after dusk it catered to the habits of the island's reprobates. And then there were the acceptable, and the not so acceptable, acquaintances. Vila society was such a potpourri there were certain elements she should avoid at all costs.

Arthur Smeed meant well, and Jane appreciated his advice, but she was determined to find her own way and her own friends in Vila. She also found him exhausting and felt guiltily thankful when his whirlwind visits were over. How she longed for simple conversation.

'I've admired your garden, Mr Tomlinson,' she said.

'Ah yes,' Godfrey smiled, 'I'm very fond of gardening.'

In the pause that followed, Jane felt duty bound to make the offer. 'Would you like tea?'

'If you have the time, most certainly, how nice.'

Godfrey played with Ronnie whilst she made the tea. Or rather Ronnie played with Godfrey, engaging in a tug of war with the old man's beard.

And then they sat on the verandah overlooking the tranquil waters of the harbour, and they chatted. About everything and nothing. About the uncomfortable humidity of the monsoon season, about the war and whether the Americans would ever join in, about gardening and Jane's intention to grow her own herbs, and possibly vegetables too.

'An excellent idea,' Godfrey agreed. He asked no leading questions and foisted no advice upon her unless she asked for it. Jane found his company most relaxing.

An hour later, when he took his leave, they had decided upon Wednesday for the dinner party.

'I shall look forward to it,' Jane said as she shook his

hand. She wasn't sure what to make of him. He was charming, fascinating and utterly mysterious. Her first impression had obviously been quite wrong. He was neither a parody of the quintessential South Sea Island Englishman, nor was he an interfering busybody. Whoever he was, she liked him enormously. 'I shall look forward to it, very, very much, Mr Tomlinson.'

'Given the fact that we're neighbours, shall we make it Godfrey?' he suggested, blue eyes sparkling vivaciously. He was aware that she had been reading him, just as he'd been reading her. Jane Thackeray had spine, he decided. Even if she didn't yet know it.

And now here they were, seated in Godfrey's spacious dining room with its wood-panelled walls and timber-beamed ceiling, Ronnie fast asleep in his bassinet nearby.

'Pandemonium? It's a good name for it,' Martin agreed. He'd also taken an instant liking to Godfrey Tomlinson. 'Surely the most bizarre government the world's ever known.'

'Oh it was even worse in the old days, I assure you. I was here when the whole thing started and it was positively ludicrous. The Spaniards were involved then too.' He offered to refill Jane's wine glass.

'No thank you, Godfrey,' she said hastily, already feeling the effects of two generous glasses.

'It was the Spaniards who first put the New Hebrides on the map in the seventeenth century,' he explained, 'hence all the Spanish names about the place. Well, it was a Portugese navigator actually,' he corrected himself, 'but he was in the service of Spain.'

Martin put his hand in the air like an eager schoolboy. 'Pedro Ferdinand de Quiros,' he said, and Godfrey applauded him.

'Excellent, Martin, you've done your homework.'

Jane smiled. Marty looked as if he'd just come top of his class.

'So when they set up the first joint court in 1910, they had a French judge and a British judge, and a presiding president who'd been appointed by the King of Spain.'

Godfrey filled his own glass and gave a hoot of laughter. 'He was a hopeless man. Utterly hopeless. Count de Buena Esperanza.' He rolled the name impressively off his tongue. Godfrey spoke fluent Spanish, along with French, Italian, several Melanesian dialects and the local Bislama. 'He'd plod to and from the courthouse on a wheezing old mule, and then he'd sit up on the bench in his grand judicial robes with a British and French judge on either side.' Godfrey struck a pose and preened his beard. He was in fine form, and thoroughly enjoying himself. 'And all the while he was in blind utter ignorance of everything going on about him, he was as deaf as a post!'

Jane and Martin burst out laughing. Godfrey's enjoyment was very contagious.

'And it wouldn't have made any difference if he hadn't been! The man couldn't speak a word of English, barely understood French, and Melanesian and Bislama were beyond his comprehension. What on earth he was doing there is beyond me. Ah, Leila.'

Godfrey's housemaid and cook, a rather sullen-faced woman in a bright red cotton dress with a matching headband encircling her frizzy black hair, had appeared to clear away their empty main course dishes.

'Would you like some water?' Godfrey asked Jane.

'Thank you.'

'Mi wantem sam kolwata plis, Leila,' Godfrey said to the woman, who nodded and silently disappeared. 'Of course the locals were totally confused by the Condominium,' he continued, without drawing breath. 'Everywhere there were French and British flags, and then photographs of the French President and the British King started appearing on the walls of government buildings, and the islanders didn't know what to make of it. A lot of them thought the President and the King were brothers and lived apart because they didn't like each other. I'm sure many of them still believe it.'

Godfrey sipped his wine, and there was a mischievous twinkle in his eyes when he continued. 'Of course there were some benefits to be had from the Condominium. For traders anyway.'

Before he could go on, Leila arrived with a large glass of water. She stood there, for a moment uncertain.

'Kolwater blong Missus,' Godfrey said, and she placed the glass in front of Jane.

'How do I say "thank you"?' Jane asked.

'Tangkyu tumas,' Godfrey replied.

'Tangkyu tumas, Leila,' she said.

The woman smiled briefly, then ducked her head and concentrated on clearing away the plates. She wasn't sullen at all, Jane realised, she was shy.

The local beef Godfrey had served had been magnificent, but the portions had been huge and Jane had been unable to eat half of her meat, which now sat congealing on her plate. She didn't want the woman to think she hadn't appreciated the meal.

'How do I say, "I've enjoyed my meal"?' she asked.

'Mi laekem kakae ia,' Godfrey said.

'Mi laekem kakae ia,' Jane said as Leila picked up her plate.

'Tangkyu, ta,' Leila said. And this time, as her eyes met Jane's, her smile was broad and infectious. Then she disappeared once more into the kitchen.

Jane wasn't sure why, but the moment gave her the greatest of pleasure.

Godfrey nodded approvingly. 'It's an excellent idea to learn Bislama,' he said. 'Too many don't. It's a simple language, and it gives the locals face if you take the trouble to learn it.'

Martin was very much in agreement. He intended to learn

everything he could to ensure easy communication with the islanders and their ways, he said, and Bislama was his first priority. But, as Martin voiced his intention, Jane remained lost in her own thoughts, still affected by the woman's smile, and how simple it had been to make contact.

'You were saying, Godfrey, that the Condominium served a purpose for some?' Martin enquired, he'd found it most interesting.

'Ah yes. Traders. The two sets of customs could work to one's advantage if one knew how to use them. A trader's property was checked by a pair of British policemen and then by a couple of gendarmes, and if there was anything a little . . .' Godfrey made a balancing movement with his splayed fingers as he searched for the word. 'A little dodgy, shall we say, he'd play one mob off against the other. You see a British . . .' He'd been about to say 'crook', but decided upon an alternative. 'Well . . . someone involved in a slightly roguish activity,' he said with a smile, 'could only be arrested by a British constable, and he could only be tried by the British court. And, as the French and the British despised each other, a trader could now and then work the system in his favour. If, of course, he had the wit to do so.'

It was such an obviously personal admission that Jane and Martin were dying to enquire further, but both were too polite to do so.

Godfrey left the moment hanging in the air, aware that he'd piqued their curiosity. Then he laughed. 'I was a sandalwood trader in those days,' he said, adding vaguely and with an all-encompassing wave of his hand, 'amongst other things.' He was about to wax on with further stories of the Condominium's inadequacies but, noticing that Martin Thackeray was taken aback by his announcement, he realised the man was aware of the sandalwood traders' unsavoury reputation. Which was hardly surprising, he thought, as it had been apparent throughout the evening that Thackeray had made some study of the New Hebrides.

It was time to back down a little, Godfrey decided.

'Oh not all of us were quite the demons that history has painted us, Martin,' he said assuringly.

Jane was intrigued. 'Demons?' she asked innocently. 'How do you mean, demons?'

Godfrey realised that it wasn't going to be quite that easy to drop the subject. 'The sandalwood trade was responsible for the slaughter of thousands of islanders over the years,' he said, 'simply in order to rob them of their forests. When guns didn't have as rapid an effect as the traders wished, they introduced diseases for which the islanders had no genetic immunity. Measles, for instance.' He cast a look at Martin, who was listening attentively. 'Measles meant death to the locals in those days. It still holds a great danger for them,' he said meaningfully.

'Yes, it most certainly does,' Martin nodded, wondering how Godfrey knew of the outbreak on Malekula, as he obviously did.

'Then, towards the end of the century . . .' Godfrey said, returning his attention to Jane, 'that's around my time,' he added, his expression enigmatic '. . . when the forests were close to depletion, many a trader turned his hand to blackbirding.'

'Blackbirding?' Jane asked, not sure if she should, sensing an undercurrent to this conversation, but unable to resist her query.

'The slave trade.' Godfrey had dropped all semblance of bonhomie. His eyes, which had sparkled with humour, were now deadly serious. 'Workers were needed, mainly for the Queensland sugar plantations, and they called it "indentured labour", but it was virtual slavery. Fewer than twenty percent of the islanders sent to Australia, or indeed New Caledonia or Fiji, ever saw their homeland again.' He leaned back in his chair. 'The blackbirders were a vile breed,' he said. Then he turned once again to Martin. 'I, needless to say, was not one of them.'

There was an uncomfortable silence. How had they come to this impasse? Martin wondered. He had made no enquiries, the man owed him no apology. Martin didn't know what to say, he felt most awkward.

So did Godfrey. How had he allowed this to happen? he wondered. He'd been showing off, that's how. The young couple enchanted him. He'd wanted to amuse and impress them, and he'd thrown caution to the winds. And now they were embarrassed.

He took a hefty swig of his wine. 'Oh well,' he said lightly, 'they were the good old, bad old days,' and the bonhomie was back as he raised his glass. 'But they're long gone now.' They weren't, he thought. Not really. There was much injustice perpetrated upon the innocent islanders by the so-called 'patriarchal' colonial society. But Martin Thackeray would find that out soon enough. 'A toast to the future,' he said.

The awkward moment had passed, and the rest of the evening was most enjoyable. Godfrey regaled them with stories of bygone days, colourful and outrageous, Leila served a dessert of lush tropical fruits, and Jane tried out her newfound words of Bislama with great success, Leila giggling when she got it wrong.

'He's been a rascal in his day, our Godfrey,' Martin said when, two hours later, he and Jane were back home and preparing for bed. 'He probably still is.'

Jane laughed. 'Don't be ridiculous, he's an old man who likes living in the past. A charismatic old man, I must say,' she added. 'I find him charming.'

'He's charming all right. A charming old rogue who still works the system.'

'Oh Marty, how can you say that, he has to be well into his seventies.'

'Age wouldn't stop a chap like Godfrey Tomlinson, my love. You can bet your last penny he's got a foot in both

camps, just like he did in the good old days.' He could tell
that she found the notion fanciful. 'He said he's retired,
right?' She nodded. 'And then he said he did a little work
as an agent,' he added with a meaningful look. 'A bit of
import, export here and there?' He made a balancing
movement with his splayed fingers, just as Godfrey had
done. 'An *agent*. That can mean anything. Believe me,
there's life in the old dog yet.'

'Well, I like him. A lot.'

'So do I,' Martin grinned, 'and I can think of no better
person to look after you while I'm away. I'm sure that's
what he has in mind, he's very taken with you, I can tell.
He'll be a valuable friend for you, my love.'

Martin was right. In the fortnight that followed,
Godfrey Tomlinson did indeed look after her and, having
apparently assigned himself as Jane's personal guardian, he
was worth his weight in gold.

It was Godfrey's intention to introduce Jane Thackeray
to the real Vila. Both the good and the bad, and the first
port of call was the club room at Reid's.

Jane had visited the hotel a number of times, taking
afternoon tea sometimes with the ladies from the church
committee and sometimes with her newfound friend,
Hilary Bale, the storekeeper's wife, but heeding Reverend
Smeed's warning, she had avoided Reid's at night.

'Mr Smeed is perhaps a little overcautious in his advice,'
Godfrey said. 'The earlier part of the evening will present
no problem. Besides, you'll be in my company.' Godfrey
was of the opinion that being overprotective would not
serve Jane's better interests. She needed to meet the real
Vila and Reid's was the perfect starting point.

The plan was to stay for just an hour or so, after which
they would dine at the little French restaurant further
along the front. Jane was now perfectly comfortable
leaving Ronnie with Mary, and she blessed the Reverend
Smeed for his choice. A personable girl in her twenties,

Mary was missionary trained, and fitted perfectly into the household. The child adored her and so did Jane. Mary was teaching Jane Bislama, but of far greater importance, it was through Mary that Jane was learning about the Melanesian people, their culture and their way of life.

She learned that the islanders, a happy, carefree people, were deeply religious, for the most part having embraced Christianity. She learned that family was the backbone of their society, that they shared the nurturing of their children and that they revered their elders. So eager was she to discover everything she could about the islanders, that she plagued Mary with questions about tribal customs, traditional dress and ceremonial dances, to the point where Mary ran out of answers and had to check with the elders in her village. Mary was very proud to be a tutor to the Missus, and the two women had become firm friends.

It was a Friday night and Reid's was already doing a brisk trade when they arrived at seven o'clock. Chinese waiters tended the green baize-topped tables where customers sat chatting over their Australian imported beers or their Bombay gins in long icy glasses of tonic water. There was a buzz of comradely conversation and laughter, and, despite the open verandah shutters and the warm breeze that swept in from the harbour waters, the smell of pipe tobacco and cigars hung in the air.

Within minutes Jane had met an eclectic gathering of itinerants, expatriates and colonial servicemen. There were several New Zealanders, two Australians, a number of French and British, and a Dutch couple who lived on a yacht moored in the harbour. Reid's was certainly the place to which everyone gravitated, she thought, but there were few women present. She refused to feel self-conscious, however, and put her trust in Godfrey. And he was certainly her calling card. Godfrey made no overtures, he simply waited for others to come to him. And they did.

'Mr Tomlinson.' A man whom Jane judged to be in his late thirties had tapped Godfrey on the shoulder. 'May I be introduced to your charming companion?' he asked in his heavily accented but perfect English. He was a handsome man, of average height but solid build, with a patrician face, a fine head of hair, the temples of which were flecked with grey, and he bore the confident assurance of wealth.

'Mrs Thackeray, M'sieur Marat,' Godfrey said obediently, but rather charmlessly, Jane thought, which surprised her a little.

'Madame Thackeray.' The Frenchman bent and kissed her hand, his lips lingering just a moment longer than necessary, but not long enough to be offensive.

'How do you do,' Jane said.

'I have looked forward to making your acquaintance. And that of your husband.' Jean-François Marat looked around the club room. 'He is not with you?'

'Dr Thackeray is in Lakatoro,' Godfrey replied brusquely before Jane could answer, and she was taken aback by his tone; Godfrey was normally so courteous. It was not only evident that Godfrey Tomlinson disliked M'sieur Marat, but that he took little trouble to disguise the fact.

'Ah yes, of course,' the Frenchman said. 'I heard there were some medical problems on Malekula. Will you join my table?' he asked Jane. 'The two of you of course,' he added to Godfrey. 'A glass of champagne by way of welcome to Mrs Thackeray?'

'Delighted,' Godfrey said, though he plainly wasn't, 'thank you.' Then he offered Jane his arm before the Frenchman could offer his.

Under normal circumstances Godfrey would not have received, nor would he have accepted, the invitation. He and Marat did not like each other. But he recognised it as an ideal opportunity for Jane to meet the members of 'the other camp', as he referred to them. Seated at Marat's table was the French resident commissioner and several of his upper echelon.

During the following half hour Jean-François Marat was so attentive to Jane that she began to feel embarrassed. The entire table was French-speaking and yet he repeatedly steered the conversation back into English, at one point even chastising the assembled company when they once again broke into a rapid-fire conversation in their mother tongue.

'Shall we pay some courtesy to Madame Thackeray?' he suggested with an icy smile and an edge to his voice that brought the table to a halt. Jean-François Marat was one of the most powerful men in the colony and even the resident commissioner appeared to be at his beck and call.

'Please, M'sieur Marat,' she insisted, feeling herself flush with self-consciousness, 'don't let my presence inhibit conversation. Besides,' she said, trying to laugh the moment off, all eyes upon her, 'it's excellent practice for me. I do speak a little schoolgirl French,' she admitted, 'appalling as it is, and I really must learn to be proficient whilst I'm here.'

'Of course you must,' Jean-François agreed smoothly, 'but this is your first evening in our company.' He was ignoring the others at the table, it was as if the two of them were alone, and 'our' company seemed to infer 'mine'. Jane found his scrutiny most confronting.

'I intend to become proficient with every language which is practised in Vila, M'sieur Marat,' she said, not knowing where to look, the intensity of his gaze was so disconcerting. 'I'm currently learning Bislama.'

'Oh really?' His tone intimated 'why bother'. He spoke it himself, but then it was necessary for communication with the workers on his plantation. 'How admirable,' he said. What a waste of time, he thought. A woman with looks like Jane Thackeray's shouldn't bother herself with the blacks.

Jean-François hadn't been able to take his eyes off Jane from the moment he'd seen her arrive at Reid's on the arm of the interfering old fool Godfrey Tomlinson. So this was the wife of the new missionary doctor. He'd heard she was pretty, but she was more than pretty, he'd thought as he'd watched her in animated conversation. She was exquisite. Fair hair, blue eyes, skin like porcelain, and a smile as fresh as the morning. Jane Thackeray was an English rose.

Now, as she sat at his table and he devoured her with his eyes, he wondered how long it would take before she became bored with her drab English husband. A missionary doctor? Subjugated by the church, working for a pittance? Such a woman deserved far better. In any event, she was bound to become restive during her husband's long absences from home, and Jean-François was quite willing to wait. He'd had many a clandestine affair with the frustrated wife of an absentee husband. It was only a matter of time, he'd found, before women left on their own became restless. Then the heat and the sensuality of the tropics did the rest.

'I very much look forward to meeting Dr Thackeray,' he said ten minutes later when Godfrey and Jane took their leave. Once again he kissed her hand, and once again his lips lingered. 'When your husband returns, you must both come to dine at Chanson de Mer,' he insisted.

He continued to hold her hand and Jane stared back at him, unnerved and not sure what to do.

'My home,' he said. 'The name is my little indulgence.' He smiled and his dark eyes seemed bent on seducing her. 'I am right by the sea,' he softly explained, as if he was telling her a personal secret. 'And the Pacific sings to me. Her own special song.'

'Thank you for your invitation, M'sieur Marat.' She withdrew her hand. 'Au revoir, gentlemen,' she said to the others who had risen from the table.

'You must be wary of Marat,' Godfrey warned as they walked along the front to the restaurant, 'he can be dangerous.' He avoided any mention of the man's detestable behaviour, not wishing to embarrass her further. Godfrey had found Marat's barely disguised lust both contemptible and insulting.

'He's certainly arrogant,' Jane agreed. Her reaction to Marat's attention had gone beyond mere embarrassment, she'd found him extraordinarily unsettling. Never before had she been so studied, as if she was some form of prey. 'Who is he, Godfrey?'

'He's a plantation owner, very rich and very powerful and he has the French officials in his pocket. Marat's is the biggest copra plantation on the island and he uses his money in every corrupt way possible. I suggest you and Martin keep well out of his way.'

Several days later, Godfrey insisted she join him on a buggy ride. 'I'm going to show you the real Efate,' he said. 'But I'm afraid you'll have to leave Ronnie with Mary, an outrigger canoe's not the safest place for a child of his age.'

Jane's eyes widened at such an alarming prospect, but she made no protest, which delighted Godfrey.

The unpaved roads of Vila extended only a few miles to the north and the east of the town, and Godfrey had never seen fit to own a motor vehicle. He'd imported any number of them as an agent, he said, particularly in the earlier years when cars were a novelty and there'd been many an eager client. 'But I can't see the point in owning one myself,' he said, 'there's nowhere to drive. A buggy is vastly preferable.'

The horse, a reliable twelve-year-old bay gelding called Luke, set off at a walking pace down the track and, when they arrived at the bottom of the hill, they turned into the main street. It was Monday morning and Vila was busy. Locals were on their way to work, women in brightly coloured 'Mother Hubbard' dresses, the standard female attire of the islanders, and men in weathered shorts and shirts, hand-me-downs from their colonial employers. Beneath wide straw hats, the Tonkinese labourers, immigrant workers from Indochina, balanced twin baskets on shoulder poles and, at the warehouse of Burns Philp & Company Ltd, local native workers carted sacks of copra, which had been transported by drays from the plantations, to the vessel waiting at the Burns Philp pier.

'The all-powerful BP,' Godfrey said, indicating the export company's sign, 'known locally as "Bastards of the Pacific". Burns Philp virtually control the economy of these islands.'

The copra boat arrived every several months, he told her, when there was a load awaiting collection. Since the depletion of the sandalwood forests, copra, the smoked meat of the coconut from which soaps and oils were produced, remained one of the principal exports throughout the New Hebrides.

Jane held her wide-brimmed straw hat firmly on head as they travelled down the main street; she was enjoying her buggy ride. Godfrey flicked the reins and Luke obediently raised his gait to a lazy trot, unperturbed by the vehicles that passed them by.

'When the cars first appeared,' he said, 'there was quite a to-do about which side of the road they should drive on, yet another competition between the French and the British. In France they drive on the right and in Britain on the left, and it looked as if it could get quite nasty. Then some bright official suggested that they keep their eye open for the next horse and buggy that came around the corner and they'd settle for whichever side of the road it wasn't travelling on.'

'The French obviously won,' Jane laughed.

'They did, confound them.'

The road had become little more than a track by the

time they reached Malapoa Point, the northern headland of Vila's harbour, and soon they were travelling beside the sweeping shores of Mele Bay. Eventually, Godfrey pulled the buggy up at a sandy spit opposite which, only several hundred yards away, was a small coral island, the huts of a native village clearly visible amongst the trees.

'That's where we're going,' he said, offering his hand as Jane alighted. 'Mele Island.' He waved his arms high over his head and only moments later, Jane saw an islander push an outrigger canoe into the shallows of the white sandy beach. As the canoe set out from the island, she watched Godfrey efficiently go about his business. He unharnessed Luke and tethered him to a tree, then he filled a large tin can from the canvas water bag, both of which he kept in the back of the buggy, and watered the animal. It was a ritual, she thought, intrigued. These visits to Mele Island were obviously a regular occurrence.

Five minutes later, the canoe shovelled its nose up onto the sand and the islander leapt out. A strong young man in his twenties, he was bare-chested and bare-footed and wore shorts far too big for him, belted around his stomach by a length of rope.

'Goffry!' he exclaimed in the loudest of greetings, the two men embracing and slapping each other's arms. 'Goffry!' The rest, to Jane, was a jumble. Bislama would not help her here, she thought, they were speaking a Melanesian dialect and at the rate of knots.

When the boisterous exchange was over, Godfrey introduced her.

'Fren blong mi Missus Thackeray,' he said in Bislama, then he stood back and waited for the performance he knew would follow.

The islander gave the broadest of grins and extended his hand, which she accepted.

'Allo, Missus Tackry, allo. Nem blong mi Rama.' The handshake was vigorous and enthusiastic.

'Allo, Rama,' she said, returning his grin.

'Goffry besfren blong mi,' he said, pumping away energetically.

'Yo, yo,' she nodded in fervent agreement, 'Goffry
nambawan.'

'Welkam, Missus Tackry, welkam.'

'Tangkyu tumas, Rama.'

Having established their mutual friendship with
Godfrey, which to Rama meant he and Jane were now
friends, the official greeting was over, the hand pumping
ceased and he pushed the canoe out into the water.

Godfrey gave Jane an approving smile. Her enthusiasm
had been perfect; animation was always the key in such
an exchange. He'd offered her no advance warning of
what to expect, nor any specific advice on how to behave.
'They're good people,' he'd simply said, 'treat them as
you find them.' And, instinctively, she had. Godfrey was
pleased.

Jane took her sandals off and, noticing that Godfrey,
shoes in hand, was making no attempt to roll up his
trousers, she waded knee-deep into the water, ignoring her
calf-length cotton skirt.

Rama balanced the craft and they climbed gingerly
aboard. Then, seating himself in the centre, he started to
row with his single paddle towards the island, chatting all
the while to Godfrey in his Melanesian tongue.

It was a hot, sultry day, the air thick and threateningly
heavy with moisture. 'It'll storm tonight,' Godfrey had
said. But as yet there was no such sign. The sky was cloudless, the sea's surface unruffled by wind and, as the canoe
approached the sandy beach, Jane looked down through
the crystal-clear water to the reef below. She could see the
infinite colours, shapes and patterns of the living coral and
the fish, vivid and exotic, that darted in and out the
intricate maze of nooks and crannies. A world teeming
with life lay just beneath them. She would have loved to

have leaned over the side for a closer look but she didn't dare, she felt very vulnerable in the flimsy craft.

'Can you swim, Jane?' Godfrey had noticed her fascination with the reef.

'Oh yes, most certainly, I enjoy it.'

'Then next time we come to Mele Island I shall bring an underwater mask for you. You'll find a fairyland down there, I promise.'

'I'd love that.'

A group of a dozen or so islanders had gathered on the beach to greet them, and they were most effusive in their welcome as Godfrey and Jane waded in from the shallows, Jane again ignoring the skirt which clung to her knees.

The men slapped Godfrey on the back and arms, the women giggled and took his hand and the children jumped about tugging at his clothes.

It was Rama who introduced Jane and, one by one, the islanders shook her hand. 'Welkam, Missus Tackry, welkam,' each one said, and two small boys started jumping up and down chanting 'Missus Tackry, Missus Tackry', showing off, obviously enjoying the sound. Meeting a friend of Goffry's was a rare and special treat.

Then, as the entire company made its way along the track that led from the shore to the village, a little girl slipped her hand into Jane's and, with a beaming smile, led her up the path. It was a declaration of ownership, and more than the other children could stand. Suddenly Jane was surrounded, each child claiming a part of her. Sharing her other hand between them, tugging her skirt, taking her arm and jabbering away excitedly, big brown eyes in happy, healthy little faces laughing up at her. Jane was enchanted by each and every one of them, but she maintained her hold on the little girl's hand and they shared a secret smile.

The Mele Islanders were virtually an extended family and their village was very small, no more than a series of bamboo-framed huts with thatched roofs of sago palm, and walls of natangora, the painstakingly woven material made from coconut palm, pandanus tree or sugar cane leaves. They had made little use of the Europeans' corrugated iron that was readily available and very popular amongst the locals in the larger villages of Efate.

As Godfrey and Jane arrived with their welcoming party, the villagers sitting on their natangora mats outside the open-framed entrances of their huts waved and called out. Godfrey waved a greeting in return, and those who'd accompanied him from the shore stood back at a respectful distance as he approached the largest of the huts.

A big man, with an alarming head of grey hair that stood out six inches from his head like an outrageous halo, appeared at the entrance. In his late sixties, he was old by islanders' standards, but obviously in good health.

'Goffry!' he exclaimed, holding his huge arms wide, and once again there was much back-slapping as the men embraced and greeted each other in Melanesian. Then Godfrey beckoned Jane over.

'Brata blong mi Moli,' he said in Bislama after he'd introduced her to the big man.

'Welkam, Missus Tackry.' Moli shook her hand.

'Tangkyu tumas, Moli,' she replied, intrigued that Godfrey had called the man his brother and assuming it was intended as a show of respect.

Moli insisted that Godfrey show Jane around the village and she was initially a little self-conscious. She didn't wish to be the centre of attention, and the men were obviously good friends, surely they wanted to talk together. She said so to Godfrey.

'Moli is the village elder and he loves to show off,' Godfrey replied. 'He'd be terribly hurt if you didn't want to explore his village.'

'You called him your brother,' she said.

'Yes.' There was a brief pause. 'He's not really.'

Jane smiled, presuming he was joking, but Godfrey's look was strangely quizzical. 'He's my tawian.'

She shook her head. He was plainly testing her Bislama vocabulary, and it didn't stretch that far.

'My brother-in-law.' Godfrey smiled as her jaw dropped in amazement. 'Come on, Moli's watching. We're being very rude standing here talking English.'

For the next hour, Jane was given a fascinating insight into the lives of the villagers. She watched women weaving the intricate natangora, and men chiselling out the interior of a tree trunk that was to become a canoe. She was shown the proud catch that morning, a huge mahi mahi fish, bright yellow and over six feet long. They would feast on it tonight, over an open fire down by the shore, with baked taros and yams. She watched the women digging up the root vegetables and preparing them, and they invited her to stay for the feast, but she explained it was impossible. She had a pikinini, she said, and she had to go home. They were immediately interested. How old was her pikinini? they asked. A boy or a girl? Then one woman said that her pikinini was sick. In what way sick? Jane asked.

'Sik long samting,' the woman shook her head, 'mi no save.'

Jane shared a look with Godfrey. 'Soem mi,' she said to the woman, and she and Godfrey followed her to a hut at the far end of the village.

A girl of about fifteen sat on the floor and beside her, on a woven mat, lay a boy of five or six, his head resting in the girl's lap. The girl was humming gently and stroking his forehead whilst the child stared listlessly into space.

Jane knelt beside them and the girl cast an anxious glance at her mother. The woman nodded her acquiescence and, as Jane cradled the child's head in her hands, the girl moved to one side.

Jane eased the little boy's head down on the mat and felt his brow, damp with perspiration, his temperature was high. Removing the cloth that covered him, she rested her ear against his bare chest and listened to his breathing. It was laboured. Then, supporting his back, she sat him up and told him to cough.

'Olsem mi,' she said, and she coughed loudly by way of demonstration. The boy obediently copied her. His cough was deep and wheezing. 'It's a bronchial infection,' she said to Godfrey. 'I don't think it's pneumonia. At least, not yet,' she added ominously, looking up at the thatched roofing of the hut. It would storm tonight, Godfrey had said. The child must not be exposed to the elements. 'Do you think they'd let me take him home?' she asked.

'I don't think that would be wise, Jane,' Godfrey replied. She had no idea what she was doing, he thought. What if the child died?

But Jane knew exactly what she was doing. 'He's at risk here,' she said. 'I want to take him home.' Godfrey shook his head, and was about to attempt further dissuasion, but she said firmly and unequivocally, 'It's much easier if you ask them, Godfrey. But if you don't, then I'll ask them myself.'

They stared at each other for a moment and Godfrey couldn't help but admire the strength of purpose he saw in her eyes. He turned to the woman and spoke in Melanesian, the mother and daughter exchanging a fearful look. The girl started shaking her head and said something in reply; she obviously didn't wish to trust her little brother to the care of the white people.

'Tell them he won't be safe when the storm comes,' Jane said. 'He needs to be kept warm and dry. Tell them I'll look after him.'

Godfrey spoke at some length to the woman and her daughter, but both of them still appeared undecided.

Jane pulled the cloth back over the child's chest and rose to her feet. 'Mi lukaotem pikinini blong yu.' Having said that she would look after the woman's child, she wanted to add 'I promise'. But she didn't know the word for 'promise', so she took the woman's hand in both of hers instead and smiled her assurance.

It was enough. She could see that the woman trusted her.

'Nem blong boe blong mi Sami,' the woman said, and she even managed a tremulous smile as she told Jane the name of her son.

'Mi lukaotem Sami,' Jane promised, and the woman nodded.

Godfrey sought out Moli and explained the situation to him, for the woman was a widow and Moli's permission was necessary if they were to take the child from the island.

Half an hour later, Rama and another young islander rowed the three of them ashore in one of the larger canoes, Jane cuddling the child in her lap. And in the buggy on their way back to Vila, little Sami was once again nestled against her. He'd fallen asleep now, lulled by the swaying of the buggy, and it was Godfrey who opened the conversation. The two of them had been silent whilst the little boy's wide brown eyes had stared up at Jane. He'd stared, not in fear but in fascination. Listless as he was, Sami had appeared to find her a great source of interest.

'Will he be all right?' Godfrey asked.

'I hope so,' she said. 'But he wouldn't be if he stayed on the island.'

Godfrey watched her as she gently stroked the head of the sleeping child. He remembered their first meeting. Was it only two weeks ago? He'd thought she had spine but that she didn't yet know it. Well, he'd been right. She certainly had spine, he thought, to take such a risk.

He changed the subject. 'I owe you an explanation,' he said. 'I wasn't trying to shock you when I told you I was Moli's brother-in-law.' He wondered if he had been. There was something about Jane Thackeray that made him want to impress her. 'The fact is, it's true, Moli's sister was my wife.'

In her worry for the child Jane had completely forgotten the bombshell Godfrey had dropped with his seemingly casual statement. She was instantly intrigued. Perhaps this would explain the mystery that surrounded him.

'I was a young man in my thirties, she was ten years younger.' Godfrey concentrated on the reins and Luke and the track ahead; he had told no-one his story. 'They accepted me in the village. Perhaps because I made their life easy,' he said. 'I'd be gone for a long time and then I'd return with money, and gifts they could barter, it was probably that simple. And my wife had a son. She called him Tom.' He smiled. 'Pola was very proud that her son was half English.'

Jane watched him silently. He was reliving the past, speaking as much to himself as he was to her. He looked old, she thought. She often forgot that Godfrey was an old man, there was such an innate energy about him. But he looked his age now, old and tired.

'I liked having a son,' he said, 'but I wasn't a very good father, I was never there. Pola didn't seem to mind, though. She had her family, not just her parents and Moli, but the rest of the village.' He glanced at Jane. 'You've seen what they're like, the whole village is a family.'

'We lived like that for nearly twenty years,' he continued, 'and we were happy. There was a party every time I came home to Pola and Tom, the whole village would celebrate.' He took a deep breath before he went on. 'And then one day the party was over. Just like that. I came home and there was no Tom. I had no son, my wife was a broken woman and the village was devastated.'

'What happened?' Jane asked.

'Blackbirders. Tom wasn't the only one. They'd taken every young buck they could lay their filthy hands on, the murdering bastards.' It had been over twenty years ago;

strange, Godfrey thought, how in the telling he still couldn't disguise his anger. He paused to regain control. What was the point? he told himself. Anger achieved nothing, and at his age it should be avoided.

'I spent the next several years trying to trace him, but it was useless.' He shrugged. 'And Pola died a year later. Diphtheria. Another white man's legacy,' he said with bitterness. 'An epidemic, it wiped out half the village on Mele, and a whole lot of other villages as well.'

They were off the track now and on the road into Vila. 'So there you are, Jane, that's my story,' he concluded. 'I've never told anyone before.'

Jane wondered why she was the person he'd chosen to tell, but she felt privileged. 'I'll keep it a secret,' she promised.

He'd known that she would. 'Oh there's no real need. Feel free to tell Martin if you wish, husbands and wives should have no secrets.'

It was dusk when they reached the cottage. Godfrey alighted and took the sleeping child from her, carrying him inside. 'I'll call back tomorrow and see how he is,' he said when she'd bedded the little boy down.

'Thank you, Godfrey.' She kissed his cheek. 'It's been an extraordinary day.'

'Yes it has. In every conceivable way.' Godfrey knew why he'd chosen to tell Jane his story. Foolish old man he may be, and a good fifty years past his prime, but he was in love with Jane Thackeray. She would never know it of course, but he rather liked admitting the fact to himself. It made him feel so very alive. 'Good night, my dear.'

The next several days were crucial in the recovery of little Sami. He broke into a fever, as Jane had suspected he might, sweating and shivering despite the heat. She bathed him and kept him warm and, when the fever had abated, she fed him the soup Mary had cooked. She'd instructed Mary how to prepare the chicken broth, and how to take Sami's temperature at regular intervals. Mary was now determined to learn every nursing skill she could from the Missus. The Missus was as good as any doctor, Mary thought, and she boasted as much to all her friends.

Mary was not the only one impressed by Jane. Godfrey was lost in admiration and he told her so when he arrived a week later with the horse and buggy to take little Sami back to the island.

'You realise if you hadn't healed the child, you would have been in a shocking predicament,' he said as he watched the boy, squealing and laughing, at play with Mary and Ronnie on the verandah.

'I didn't heal him, Godfrey,' she smiled, 'he's a healthy little boy, his body healed itself, he just needed to be kept warm and dry.'

'Nevertheless, it was a very courageous thing to do.' She'd changed, he thought. That day on the island had changed her. He wondered if she knew it.

Jane did. She'd known it from the moment she'd recognised the trust in the woman's eyes. And she'd sensed, from the moment she'd taken the care of the child upon herself, that her whole life had changed. She wasn't quite sure how or why, but it was Godfrey who now put it into words.

'You can serve a great purpose here, Jane. Not only with your nursing skills, but you have a way with these people. They trust you.'

'Yes,' she said. He was right. That was how she'd changed, and that was why. She now had a purpose.

That night she wrote to Phoebe. Throughout the voyage to the New Hebrides she'd sent regular telegraph messages from various ports of call assuring Phoebe of their safety, as she'd promised she would. But she'd also heeded her friend's more frivolous instruction.

'Don't bother writing,' Phoebe had said, 'you'll only make me feel guilty.' Phoebe never wrote letters, she found it a bore. So, as yet, Jane had curbed the urge to write.

Tonight, however, was different. Godfrey's words had had the deepest impact upon Jane, and she needed to tell Phoebe.

*'Forgive my correspondence,'* she wrote, *'and don't feel obliged to reply, but I have to let you know that you were right. "All things are meant for a purpose." You have always said that, Phoebe, even when we were little more than children, and never more strongly than upon our parting, do you remember?'*

Jane remembered. Her last meeting with Phoebe was indelibly etched in her mind. It had been in Fareham when she and Martin had travelled south for several days to say goodbye to her father and to introduce him to his new grandson before they sailed for the New Hebrides. They had motored down from Edinburgh in Martin's father's car, avoiding London and the chaos of rail travel.

It was strange to Jane, being back in the little mews cottage in Adelaide Place, a married woman with a husband and child. The girl she'd once been was everywhere, and yet that girl seemed a lifetime ago.

One thing remained constant, however: the intensity of her friendship with Phoebe. The first afternoon, they sat outside on the little bench by the vegetable garden. It was a clear autumn day, and Jane was rocking the baby in the wooden cradle her father had presented her with. 'Made with my own two hands,' Ron Miller had proudly announced.

'Remember when I died and you brought me back to life?' Jane asked.

'Yes,' Phoebe said, 'of course I do.'

'We sat right here that day.'

There was so much to remember, so much to talk about, and so little time left to them.

'Soon you'll be living on the other side of the world,'

Phoebe said with a touch of envy. 'I always thought I'd be the first one to travel.'

'So did I.'

Phoebe was teaching full time at Price's school now. To the relief of both her parents she seemed to have developed a sense of responsibility since her return from Scotland.

'Time I grew up,' she admitted to Jane. 'But I still intend to travel, and I'll live in America, just like I said I would.' It was the same rebellious Phoebe of old. 'Right in the heart of Manhattan,' she added, and Jane, as always, had no reason to doubt her.

They talked at length over the next several days, meeting in the afternoons when Phoebe was free of her young pupils. And then, all too soon, it was the morning of Jane's departure.

They stood in West Street whilst Martin packed the luggage into the boot of the car and Ron Miller cuddled his namesake, pulling funny grandfather faces at the child.

'Let me know you're safe, whenever you can,' Phoebe said. 'But don't bother writing, you'll only make me feel guilty.'

'I'll miss you, Phoebe.' Jane felt a stab of fear. Phoebe had inspired her spirit of adventure throughout their childhood, and Martin's newfound calling had instilled in her the same sense of challenge. But she was suddenly unsure of herself. Without Phoebe's influence, was she strong enough? Phoebe had always been the leader. 'I'll miss you so much.'

'Don't be silly, you won't have the time,' Phoebe laughed. 'A husband and child and a whole new world? Heavens above, I envy you.'

They embraced, and Phoebe held her very tightly as she whispered in her ear. 'All things are meant for a purpose, Jane, remember? And your purpose is just beginning.'

Martin returned to Vila the day after little Sami returned to the island.

'Oh Marty, he's the most adorable child,' Jane said. 'They all are. We'll get Godfrey to take us to the island so that you can meet them. The whole village. They're wonderful people.'

She was more excited than he'd ever seen her. And never before had he heard her speak with the passion she had as she'd recounted the story of Sami.

'Well, you obviously didn't miss me too much,' he smiled.

Jane flushed. 'Of course I did.' How unwifely and inconsiderate she'd been to launch into an account of her own activities with barely a query about his work on Malekula. 'You've been gone nearly a whole month, I missed you dreadfully. I'm sorry, it was selfish of me to talk about myself.'

'To the contrary, I'm delighted.' He was. 'And you weren't talking about yourself at all, Jane,' he said. 'You were talking about the people of these islands.'

He'd loved her from the moment he'd first seen her, his angel at the docks in Fareham, and he wouldn't have thought it possible to love her any more. But, right at this moment, he did.

'Oh my love, what work we can do, you and I,' he said as he held her to him.

The week of Martin's homecoming would be a busy one. There was a personal invitation from the British resident commissioner to a luncheon at his home on Iririki Island, the church committee was organising a fundraising fete, and Jane was planning her first dinner party. Just the storekeeper, Harry Bale, and his wife Hilary, and of course Godfrey, and she'd felt obliged to invite the Reverend Smeed. A casual dinner for six, she told herself, nothing to get in a panic about. But she wanted everything to go smoothly, it was important for Martin.

Then, two days later, the commissioner's invitation, the fete, and Jane's dinner party all paled into insignificance.

*'Yesterday, December 7, 1941 – a date which will live in infamy –'*

The whole of Vila was tuned in to the Australian Broadcasting Commission's Overseas Service as it relayed President Roosevelt's address to Congress. Along with the rest of the world, they listened to the news that would change their lives.

'– *the United States was suddenly and deliberately attacked by naval and air forces of the Empire of Japan. Always will we remember the character of the onslaught against us. No matter how long it may take us to overcome this premeditated invasion, the American people, in their righteous might, will win through absolute victory.*'

Pearl Harbor had been bombed and the Americans had joined the war. It would be only a matter of time before they arrived in the New Hebrides.

# CHAPTER NINE

The Boeing 737 turned sharply in preparation for landing. Landing on Efate was always a delicate procedure; the approach to Bauerfield Airport was a tight one, as the pilots of Air Vanuatu knew only too well.

From her window seat, Sam could clearly see the island paradise below. The deep green forest, the crystal-clear ocean, and the white, white beaches. How breathtakingly pure the colours were, she thought. Unreal in their perfection. Like a picture postcard.

Unlike many of her countrymen, Sam had never visited the customary South Pacific haunts popular with Australian holiday-makers, and she was entranced.

She stepped off the plane to be instantly engulfed in a wave of heat. She'd experienced a similar sensation, briefly, during stopovers at Singapore and Bahrain airports en route to or from Europe. It was a different sort of heat from that of an Australian midsummer. All-embracing and suffocating, but at the same time sensual.

The terminal of Bauerfield International Airport was tiny and quaintly reminiscent of the fifties. As the passengers passed through customs and stepped out into the tropical glare of the day, they were met by a quartet of local musicians on box bass and guitars singing a song of welcome. Then several young islander women in colourful dresses with hibiscuses behind their ears greeted them and guided them to their respective transport.

So this is Vanuatu, Sam thought.

'Great, isn't it,' a voice said, 'and it's only the airport – wait'll you see the rest.' Beside her, Nick Parslow dumped his suitcase on the ground.

'I love it already,' she said.

They were soon joined by the others, Simon Scanlon, Michael Robertson, Rodney the set designer, and members of the crew. Half the flight had been booked out by Mammoth Productions.

'G'day, Rod,' said a voice with an unmistakably Queensland twang, and a middle-aged man, dressed in shorts, a white short-sleeved shirt and shiny shoes with knee-high socks, shook Rodney's hand. 'G'day Simon, Nick,' he said, shaking their hands also, 'good to see you again.'

Bob Crawley was introduced to Samantha and Mickey as the film's location transport manager.

'Bob's much more than that, though,' Rodney said. 'Knows everyone in Port Vila, he's been a godsend.'

Bob had indeed been Rodney's right-hand man during the months of meticulous research required for the set layouts and designs. And he'd loved every minute of it. 'Not often you get a chance to work in the pictures, mate,' he'd said time and again to Rod.

His overtly ocker manner was at odds with his crisp, neat appearance, as Sam and Mickey quickly discovered.

'So you're the Hedy Lamarrs, are you?' he said, grinning broadly at the two of them. Sam's bewilderment was obvious. 'Stars. You know, Hedy Lamarr, star,' he explained. 'Pretty exciting, I gotta tell you.' He gave them both a nudge and a wink. 'I've never met any film stars before.'

'Oh no, I'm just an actor,' Mickey assured him. 'Sam here's the star.' There was a cheeky glint in his eye as he self-effacingly acknowledged Sam.

'Oh well, I'll have to take special care of you then, won't I?' Bob said, and Sam could have kicked Mickey Robertson. Bob Crawley would obviously be hard to take in heavy doses.

It appeared that Bob ran a vehicle hire company on the island and had been employed by Mammoth to provide all transport and drivers during the filming. He'd decided to make himself personally responsible for the top end of the hierarchy, however, and, whilst the rest of the crew travelled to the Crowne Plaza in the special bus provided by the resort for its guests, Bob drove Simon, Nick, Rodney, Samantha and Mickey in his Toyota Landcruiser.

'You sit up the front with me, Sam,' he said as he folded out the extra seats in the rear of the Landcruiser. 'Gotta look after the Hedy Lamarr.'

She cringed again. Bob was going to be very wearing.

As it turned out, he wasn't. After politely fielding a question about what it was like to be a film star – this was her first movie, she said, so she really didn't know – she asked him about himself, and he proved to be both an interesting man and a fund of information.

He'd lived in Vanuatu for twenty-five years, he told her. 'Came here a couple of years before they got their independence,' he said, 'when the place was still called the New Hebrides. I was an adventurous little bugger,' he grinned, 'only nineteen, out to see the world. Bummed around the islands for a while, drove trucks for a copra plantation on Malekula, sold diving gear at a shop on Espiritu Santo . . .'

Bob obviously loved a good chat, and Sam was finding everything he said fascinating, but at the same time she was riveted by the sights she was witnessing through the Landcruiser's window.

Huge banyan trees, their aerial roots forming columns, stood like ancient cathedrals amidst the tangle of tropical vines and palms. And every now and then, amongst the wealth of vegetation, they passed a village that appeared little more than a collection of hovels. Rows of shabby huts, made of corrugated iron and thatching and hessian, obviously anything the villagers could lay their hands on. But the islanders themselves seemed remarkably happy and healthy.

Women, carrying baskets and bundled palm leaves on their heads, waved and smiled as the car passed by. Men, hefting woven bags of firewood on their backs, raised a hand in acknowledgement. And any number of children jumped up and down and called out in cheeky high spirits.

'I started up the car hire company in Port Vila about ten years ago,' Bob concluded, 'when I'd stashed up enough dough. And now, I tell you, you wouldn't get me living anywhere else. Not for love or money,' he swore. 'Why would you want to? Just look at that.'

They'd reached the coast and, as they came over the hill, the township of Port Vila was laid out before them, nestled comfortably within its perfect natural harbour.

During the brief drive through the centre of town, Bob gave Sam and Mickey the guided tour of Port Vila that he'd given the others on their first visits.

'Chantilly's Hotel,' he said, 'that's fairly new, good restaurant there, Tilly's on the Bay. And that's Rossi's restaurant.' He pointed out an attractive white building with verandahs overlooking the harbour. 'Still the most popular expat hangout, always has been. 'Course it's been rebuilt and extended over the years, but it's been there forever. Used to be called Reid's in the old days.'

Sam looked at Rossi's with particular interest. Reid's Hotel. She felt she already knew it. Reid's was in the script. It was where Sarah met the French plantation owner.

'And from about here on,' he said, indicating the

remaining forefront of the harbour with its sea wall and yacht club, 'that's all reclaimed land. And the main wharf down the end there, that's where the cruise ships come in.'

Sam wondered what the ocean-cruising passengers thought of Port Vila when their luxury liners hoved to at the wharf. Glamorous as the location was, the town itself was rather shabby. Which somehow added to its charm, she thought, but it would surely leave tourists a little bewildered. She wasn't sure what she'd expected herself, and she said as much to Bob.

'I think I'd expected something a bit more commercial,' she said, 'more geared towards tourism. But I prefer it the way it is,' she hastily added, she didn't want to sound critical.

'Yeah, me too, I like it shabby.'

He'd caught her out. 'Oh I didn't mean . . .'

But Bob wasn't at all offended. 'Port Vila hasn't changed much over the years. It's actually gone downhill since the French and English left in 1980,' he said. 'The locals were a lot better off under colonial rule. They're not very good at running their own dance.'

As they continued at a snail's pace along Lini Highway, he pointed out various other landmarks, the post office to the left, the local markets to the right, but Sam was intrigued by the small, perfectly shaped island in the middle of the harbour.

'Iririki Resort,' he said in answer to her query, 'very popular, just a minute's ferry ride into town . . .'

Iririki. Again the name registered. It was in the script. Iririki Island was the home of the British resident commissioner. Sarah and Hugh Blackston dined there.

'. . . used to be the British commissioner's residence,' Bob continued.

'We'll be filming at Iririki,' Nick said, aware of what Sam was thinking. 'The scene with Sarah and Hugh and the commissioner.'

'We were actually going to book in there,' Simon interjected, 'the whole unit. Either Iririki or Chantilly's, but I thought it was better if we were a bit out of town.'

Nick agreed with him. 'We don't want to annoy the locals – film crews can be a rowdy lot. Besides, there's more room at the Crowne Plaza.'

The Crowne Plaza was less than ten minutes' drive south. It was a most attractively designed resort, situated beside the impressive Erikor Lagoon. From its large, open reception area, paths meandered amongst green lawns and coconut palms to solid stone bungalows with thatched roofs, each overlooking the lagoon.

'We've taken over the whole place,' Simon said to Sam and Mickey as they drove past the nine-hole golf course and up the main drive. 'The second unit's been here for weeks shooting the aerial shots, as well as the visual footage we'll need for computer graphic background. And of course Rod's team's been here for the past month building the sets at Mele Bay and Quoin Hill. We'll drive out tomorrow and I'll show them to you. Fantastic locations, and, if the sets have come up half as well as Rod's sketches and models, you're going to be knocked out.'

'They'll be even better,' Rodney promised him, 'you just wait and see.'

The bus had arrived at the hotel before them, Bob having dawdled on his sightseeing tour from the airport, and the members of the crew were already being treated to the resort's official welcome by a group of islanders in tribal dress.

The moment Sam alighted from the Landcruiser, a necklace of tiny shells was placed around her neck by a young Melanesian woman. Then a nuggetty islander swooped upon her, shaking her hand in his powerful grip and displaying, in his black face, the whitest teeth she'd ever seen.

'I am Chief Joe,' he beamed, 'welcome to our land. Welcome.'

He was an impressive-looking man, a little shorter than Sam, but powerfully built. Bare-chested and bare-footed, he wore the chief's tribal dress of grass skirt with a grass cape draped over one shoulder. Black feathers projected from the back of the wide headband around his shaven skull, woven armbands encased his muscular biceps and he carried a carved wooden staff which he pummelled against the ground from time to time.

'I am Chief Joe, welcome,' he said as he beamed at Mickey and, one by one, he shook everyone's hand and repeated his greeting. Simon, Nick and Rodney had been through the same procedure each time they'd stayed at the Crowne Plaza. Then, the official welcome over, the entire company filed into the reception area to be signed in and taken to their accommodation.

'All this and I'm being *paid* as well? I don't believe it!' Sam said to Nick an hour later when he called by to see how she was settling in. 'Is yours as posh as mine?'

'Not quite, love, you are the star after all.'

Sam had been allocated one of only several bungalows built out over the water. They were larger than the others, near the swimming pool and bar, and were considered the resort's deluxe accommodation.

'They're all fabulous, though,' Nick said. 'I'm number 25, just down there, you can see me from here.' They were sitting on her open verandah, having admired the tiny fish darting about amongst the pylons below, and he pointed further down the lagoon. 'Simon and Brett Marsdon have the other two deluxe bungalows. Simon offered me the choice, said he'd actually prefer to be further away from the pool because the bar could get noisy at night. But I declined.'

'Why?'

'Politics. Writers are pretty low down in the Hollywood pecking order and I think our young Mr Marsdon might get his knickers in a knot if he found out I had accommodation equal to his.'

'You're joking!'

'Not at all. In fact he'll probably be a bit miffed at his director and co-star sharing equal status. Did you know he wanted a Winnebago sent out for his personal use on location?'

Sam shook her head.

'He carried on like a two-bob watch when we told him he couldn't have one. Well, his agent did anyway. "It's a standard clause in Mr Marsdon's contract",' Nick said in an appallingly bad West Coast accent. 'His agent's actually called Mort, would you believe, and Mort wasn't going to budge, threatened to pull Marsdon out of the movie. The producers were terrified, "Give him a Winnebago for God's sake," they said, so we had to take them on as well. We told them it was a physical bloody impossibility, that the roads on Efate weren't built for luxury caravans. I must say I was lost in admiration at Simon's self-control. He hadn't wanted Marsdon in the first place, but Mammoth had insisted, distribution and all that, and I know he wanted to tell both Marsdon and Mort to go to hell, but he kept the peace instead.'

Nick took off his glasses; it was a stinking hot day and the sweat was causing them to slide down his nose. 'It's true about the roads,' he said, wiping the frames on his T-shirt. 'Christ, they haven't been improved since the Yanks built them in 1942 – you need a four wheel drive to get to Quoin Hill.'

'So Brett Marsdon's a monster then,' Sam said lightly, but she had a vague sinking feeling. She'd been naive, she told herself. Like the rest of the world, she'd believed Brett Marsdon's press. 'The golden boy of movies', they hailed him. Both onscreen and off, the press loved Brett Marsdon. But he was obviously insufferable, she thought, and the ensemble camaraderie she'd experienced in Sydney was all about to end. 'Why didn't anyone warn me?'

'What point would there have been? He's the bums-on-seats

and we're stuck with him. Anyway, we'll find out soon enough. He'll be here in a couple of weeks.' Nick put his glasses back on and jumped to his feet. 'Fancy a swim?'

The actors were not needed for the next two days. Rodney was supervising the final dressing of the sets, after which there was to be an intensive fortnight spent shooting the scenes between Sarah and Hugh Blackston prior to the arrival of the American fighter pilot.

As promised, mid-morning the next day, Simon took Sam and Mickey out to show them the sets constructed at Mele Bay and Quoin Hill. Nick came with them and Bob Crawley was once again behind the wheel.

'You blokes haven't seen them yourselves, have you?' Bob said to Simon and Nick. 'Well, you just wait, you're in for one helluva shock. Couldn't bloody believe it myself. Jeez, you movie people, I dunno. The money you spend! Must have cost a mint!'

When they got there, Simon and Nick were not shocked at all, they were delighted. The set had been perfectly realised from the sketches and models they'd pored over for months, and at great length, with Rodney. And the location they'd personally chosen in their earlier field trips had proved ideal.

Stretching along the normally deserted shores of Mele Bay was a small harbour town. There were jetties and boatsheds and buildings fronting on to the water, and behind them was a main street with shops, a post office, restaurants and businesses.

'Vila in 1942,' Simon announced after the moment's silence during which they'd all stared in admiration. Then he turned to Sam, his pterodactyl eyes gleaming. 'The Vila of Mamma Black, Sam,' he said. 'Just prior to the arrival of the American forces in the New Hebrides.' And Sam felt a tingle of excitement.

'You've done a great job, Rod,' Simon said as the set

designer joined them. Rodney and members of his team had been at Mele Bay since dawn.

'Yep. Knew you'd like it,' Rod replied, giving his lazy grin, but secretly basking in the praise, as he always did when it came from Simon Scanlon.

The group of them stood on the sandy spit looking out over the foreshore and Rodney explained the layout to Sam and Mickey.

'That's the Burns Philp warehouse and pier,' he said, 'where the boats came in to collect the copra.' He pointed further along the shore to a building with shuttered verandahs. 'That's Reid's Hotel,' he said, 'and the boathouse just this side of it, right on the water, that's Mamma Black's. We'll be shooting interiors in Reid's and Mamma Black's,' he explained, 'but the other town buildings are mockups. Come and I'll show you.'

No amount of research had been spared during the pre-production phase of *Torpedo Junction*, and the township of Vila, prior to the land reclamation, sea wall and additional buildings, had been recreated to the last detail. But it had been recreated in a way that only the world of film could accomplish.

Sam was in a state of utter amazement. What had appeared from their viewpoint at the spit to be an entire town was a complete deception. The buildings on the foreshore side of the main road were three-dimensional, 'so that we can shoot walk-pasts', Rodney explained. But those on the opposite side were facades. Behind the post office, the stores and the restaurants, so real and solid in texture, there was nothing but frames of steel scaffolding.

'We used stronger framework than usual,' Rodney explained. 'Normally they'd be wooden struts, but it's the monsoon season after all. We chose to film this time of the year because there are less tourists around, but if the worst comes to the worst and a typhoon's forecast we can easily take the facades off the scaffolding and lay them flat out on the street.'

Even the street itself, to Sam's further astonishment, was made of synthetic fibre. 'It breathes,' Rodney said, showing her the holes in what appeared to be a solid paved road, 'so that we don't kill off the grass underneath. And it'll be rolled up when we're not shooting wide shots.'

Mammoth Productions had guaranteed the local government that the location would be left undamaged and, once that stipulation had been agreed upon, gaining permission to film had been easy. It was all a matter of money, Simon told them. 'Not just payment to the government,' he said, 'but to the villages; there's a number of them in this area. Each one gets a whopping fee by local standards, and of course the villagers themselves get paid when we use them as extras, probably more than they earn in a year. Everybody's very happy, believe me.'

The interior of Reid's Hotel was thrillingly atmospheric. Sam could just see the colourful mixture of colonial society milling around amongst the baize-topped tables and spilling out onto the shuttered verandahs. But it was the converted boathouse of Mamma Black's that most excited her. This was where Sarah had discovered herself, Sam thought. This was where Sarah Blackston had become Mamma Black.

It was a solid timber building with a corrugated-iron roof and an outside water tank. 'British built,' Rodney told her, 'used to belong to an English trader who converted it into a makeshift home for himself, hence the water tank.'

Huge doors opened onto the shore where small boats had once been slipped into the shed, and large shutters on the upper half of the other three walls could be lifted by rods that then wedged into the window ledges, opening the building up on all sides. Benches and a sink were set down one end, two narrow beds at the other, matting on the floor. Sarah's work area, Sam thought, where she tended her flock.

Rodney flicked a switch and, in the centre of the wooden beamed ceiling, a large electric fan slowly started to rotate. 'Generators are connected, we're ready for action,' he grinned. Then he showed them all, as he had at the Reid's set, how whole sections of walls were 'floaters' that could be removed for camera access.

An hour later, they piled back into the Landcruiser to set off for the other location at Quoin Hill.

'What's that island?' Sam asked Bob Crawley as she looked out across the sandy spit.

'Hideaway,' he said. 'Used to be Mele Island in the old days. Do you swim?' he asked.

'Of course.'

'Well, you'll find some great snorkelling over there. You should give it a burl if you get the time. Coral reef only twenty metres from the shore, the fish are unreal! Hideaway Island's very popular with the tourists, and the Kiwi chef does a beaut chicken coconut curry.'

As they slowly wound their way up the hill, Bob avoiding huge potholes and ruts where he could, Rodney explained to Sam and Mickey that the other sets to be used in the location filming were 'actuals'.

'We've hired the real thing,' he said. 'The Blackstons' cottage, the church, the plantation owner's home, they're all actuals. It'll make shooting without floaters more diffi-cult and the lighting'll be tricky, but with a bit of extra dressing from the art department they'll be very effective and authentic.'

The views from the top of the hill were spectacular, but as they continued down towards the coast around the back of Mount Erskine, Sam noticed again the blankets of purple-flowered vine that seemed to have such a stranglehold. She'd seen it everywhere they'd driven, in some places it had even crept its way up to the topmost heights of the giant banyan trees. It looked like the morning glory vine that was such a menace in Sydney, she thought, and she said so to Bob.

'It is,' he said. 'A smaller leaf variety but same thing really. It's not indigenous to the islands at all, it's a legacy from the Yanks.'

'The Yanks?' she queried. 'How come?'

'They planted it as camouflage during the war, called it mile-a-minute vine. It grows much faster than the local lantana. Bastard of a thing. It can smother a whole coconut plantation.'

A little further along the road they pulled up at Port Havannah, a huge natural harbour protected by two islands.

'Havannah Harbour,' Simon announced as they got out of the car, 'where the American fleet was based. We'll be filming here.'

The southern channel between the coast and the smaller of the two islands, Lelepa, had been mined as protection against attack, Rodney told them. 'No problem with the northern channel between Moso Island and the coast,' he said, 'that's all shallow reef, but they netted the gap between the two islands, lowering the net to take their own ships out. The big threat of course was Jap submarines.'

It was two o'clock in the afternoon by the time they approached Quoin Hill and everyone was starving.

'The Beachcomber,' Bob said. 'They've got good tucker there.' And fifteen minutes later he pulled up beside a weathered building on the wildest coastline imaginable, where pandanus trees grew horizontal to the ground from the sheer force of the wind, and where angry surf churned over treacherous reef as far as the eye could see.

A sign said 'Beachcomber Resort', and several bungalows stood apart from the main building, forlorn but brave in their defiance. The Beachcomber Resort obviously catered to only the hardiest of guests, those who were genuinely seeking a remote outpost.

'G'day, Bob.' The Australian who owned the place was

as weathered as his surroundings. Tall and gaunt, he leaned at an angle like the pandanus trees, as if his whole life was a battle. He welcomed the six of them effusively and chatted nineteen to the dozen whilst he opened bottles of ice-cold Tusker beer, the local brew that was popular throughout the islands. They all guzzled from the bottle, except for Bob Crawley, who was being very professional and sticking to water.

'Told you,' Bob said half an hour later as they tucked into the white, firm-textured poulet fish cooked in lime. 'Good tucker.'

'Why *poulet*?' Sam queried, recalling from her school-days that 'poulet' was French for chicken.

'Jeez I dunno,' Bob shrugged. 'But it's always been poulet and it's always been bloody good.'

Everyone agreed, and they all voted the meal one of the best they'd ever eaten.

'Kakae ia nambawan,' Bob said to the chef, an islander in his twenties who'd served them personally and appeared to run the place.

'Tangkyu, ta,' the young man said, pleased with the compliment.

When it was time to leave, the Australian was loath to let them go. Starved of company, he tried to ply them with more beer. 'One for the road,' he said with a touch of desperation.

But Bob was emphatic. 'See you next time, mate.'

Their last image of the Beachcomber Resort was the Australian, standing amongst the pandanus trees, the wind straining his cotton shirt against his ribs as he waved goodbye.

'Lonely place,' Bob said.

Two sets were constructed at the Quoin Hill location: the American airbase and the Japanese prisoner of war camp.

'It's a bit of an MGM backlot,' Rodney said as they

wandered amongst the barbed wire enclosures and bamboo huts of the POW set, 'having the two sets side by side like this. But it's eminently practical, good for transport, and the terrain's spot on for both of them.' He waved an arm around at the barren landscape of grasses and hardy scrub.

They chatted with several of Rodney's team who'd been working there since the early hours of the morning, before driving the further kilometre to the airstrip.

'This is for real,' he told them, 'this was the actual airbase and the landing strip was still here, we just cleared it a bit. With permission of course. And we added the revetments.' He indicated the three-sided, flat-topped embankments. 'They're aircraft protection against enemy bombs,' he said. 'The planes were housed in the revetments and camouflage hauled over the top – netting and vines – to prevent visibility from the air.'

'Allo! Allo!' A group of islanders had appeared from nowhere, mainly women and children, and they were waving to the group and smiling excitedly.

'Allo!' Bob called, encouraging the others who all waved back. 'They're from Epule village,' he told them, 'it's just nearby.'

'Ah yes,' Simon said, 'Epule village, we're recruiting extras from there when we film the airbase sequences.'

As they returned to the Landcruiser, Bob asked them if they wanted to go back to Port Vila the way they had come or continue on the round trip, since they were by now nearly halfway around the island anyway. 'Be a little bit longer,' he warned them, 'and the roads are rough until the last few k's.' They voted unanimously for the round trip.

Nearly three hours later, when they arrived back at the Crowne Plaza after the gruelling drive, they agreed it had been worth it. The whole of Efate was a scenic wonder.

Simon and Nick joined Sam on her verandah at dusk to

share a cold Tusker before meeting the gang for dinner.

'Now you tell me how a Winnebago could be expected to make that trip,' Nick said after they'd toasted each other.

'Did you tell her?' Simon asked with a disapproving scowl. 'About Marsdon?'

'Why not? Best to be warned. Don't you reckon, Sam?'

'Too right,' she agreed.

Simon didn't. Harmony amongst the cast at all costs. He intended to personally field any prima donna behaviour from Marsdon, and he expected there'd be some, but he didn't want Sam fed with a sense of antagonism before he'd even arrived. He glared at Nick, who shrugged back.

Too late now, Nick thought, aware that Simon would take him to task when they were alone. Besides, he was glad he'd set Sam straight. Forewarned was forearmed.

But over the next fortnight Sam had little time to dread the arrival of Brett Marsdon. The work was intense, tiring and thoroughly exhilarating. Most of her scenes were with Mickey and the actors who had been flown in from Queensland to play the smaller roles of the British commissioner, the church minister and various prominent colonials and expats. There was also the key support role of the village girl who befriended Sarah, teaching her Bislama and the ways of her people. A young islander called Elizabeth, who worked for the local radio station, had been cast and the affinity between the two women was so immediate that Simon quickly dispensed with the official Bislama coach he'd hired for Sam, recognising that Elizabeth's coaching from the sidelines only strengthened the bond.

They shot the montage sequence denoting the passage of time, and Simon marvelled at Sam's skill as he watched the emergence of Sarah Blackston, transformed by her purpose into a woman of strength and beauty.

Ten days into the shoot the Frenchman who was to play Phillipe Macon, the plantation owner, arrived from Paris.

Louis Durand was a highly respected and popular actor in the world of European art-house cinema. He was in his early forties but answered to thirty-five, not through vanity but for casting purposes, and his latest movie, *L'Homme qui a Perdu son Honneur*, had won that year's Academy Award for Best Foreign Film. *Torpedo Junction* was to be his first major Hollywood movie, and Simon considered the man a casting coup.

'He's top box-office whichever way you look at him,' Simon had said. 'Europe already loves him and America's keen to welcome him with open arms.'

Louis was an arresting presence. A charismatic mixture of ugly and handsome that the camera loved, he was destined to play powerful characters, usually of the more unsavoury kind. In reality, however, he was a highly intelligent actor who loved his craft. Following the Academy Awards, he had been inundated with offers from America but he hadn't agonised over his choice. He had decided to make his Hollywood debut playing Phillipe Macon in *Torpedo Junction* because the film was to be directed by Simon Scanlon. Louis was an avid fan of Scanlon's work.

The feeling was mutual. Simon found a soulmate in Louis Durand, a man equally dedicated to the world of film. And, as with the other members of the cast, the all-important rapport between Louis and Samantha was perfect. Everything was progressing so smoothly, Simon thought, that something simply had to go wrong.

'Oh man, what a place! Let's party!'

And this was it, Simon realised, the moment he'd dreaded. All his nightmares were answered with the arrival of Brett Marsdon.

Simon had gathered the principal cast in the hotel reception area to greet the American upon his arrival, and both

he and Nick were unimpressed by Marsdon's flashy exuberance. But to the others, Sam included, Brett Marsdon
appeared as handsome and personable as one would have
expected from his onscreen persona and the press that had
preceded him.

He seemed younger than his twenty-eight years, Sam
thought. Boyish in his enthusiasm. He was very American
and very showy, certainly, but his handshake, freely offered
to all, was warm and firm and his dazzling smile appeared
genuine. This was neither a jaded actor working purely
for his eight-figure fee, nor an ego-driven superstar who
believed his own publicity; this was a young man happy to
meet his co-workers. Why judge him for the very American-
ness that had given him his worldwide popularity?

'I can't tell you how great it is to meet you guys. God,
I'm looking forward to this.' He turned to Sam, dimples
flashing beguilingly. 'And we get *paid* to be here?'

Sam laughed. 'That's exactly what I said.'

Perhaps the all-American enthusiasm was fake, she
thought, or perhaps he was merely excited, an eager puppy
wagging his tail. She decided upon the latter. And he was
certainly good-looking, even more so than the camera gave
him credit for. But she was surprised to discover that he
was only a few centimetres taller than she was.

Like a number of leading male stars, Brett Marsdon was
below average height, but he was in such perfect propor-
tion that the tall, muscular onscreen image was an easy
deception for the camera. Lean-hipped, he moved with the
grace and agility of a boxer in training, and beneath his
open-necked silk Armani shirt, his compact body was
toned to perfection. The smile, the dimples, the piercing
blue eyes that the women's magazines swooned over, were
all as electric offscreen as on, but it was the very force of
his energy that made him compelling. He was like a coiled
spring, body and mind alert, in love with life and ready for
action.

'Man, I've been to some places,' he grinned at Sam, 'but this is it! We'll have a ball here, you and me, Sam.'

Sam sensed Simon's disapproval, and Nick's too, but she couldn't rid herself of the eager-puppy impression; they were being a little unfair, she thought.

'We'll do some work first, shall we?' She smiled a subtle warning to Brett, who immediately took the hint.

'Oh man!' he said, turning the full force of his attention on Simon. 'This role! I can't tell you how much I'm into this role. He's a hero, man, they don't write them like that any more.'

'Well, you can thank Nick for that,' Simon said a little woodenly. 'Nick's the writer, you know.' Simon wasn't sure whether Marsdon had twigged to that fact during the introductions.

'Oh yeah, man, I know.' Attention swung to Nick. 'Your work is fantastic. I love the script, I wanted the role the moment I first read it. But then Mort would have told you that.'

'Mort was a bit too busy telling us about the Winnebago.' Nick wasn't sure why he'd made such a bitchy remark and he sensed the daggers from Simon the moment he'd said it. But he hadn't liked the innuendo in Marsdon's 'you and me, Sam' comment. He realised that to everyone else it had seemed innocent, and perhaps, given his own relationship with Sam, he was being overprotective. Perhaps it was simply because he was gay. Maybe he was a little more alert to sexual predators. Whatever it was, he'd be willing to bet that Marsdon was on the make. And within only minutes of meeting his co-star. Nick didn't like the man.

'The Winnebago!' Brett's laugh was genuine. 'Shit, man, you didn't take that seriously.'

'Well, we did at the time,' Nick's reply was arch, 'given the fact that Mort was going to pull you out of the movie.' He was aware of Sam beside him and knew that she was taken aback, just as he knew that he was behaving totally out of character; it was unlike him to be so discourteous and unfriendly.

'In the past now, Nick. Neither here nor there,' Simon said with a withering look and a voice like ice. 'Good to have you aboard, Brett, I look forward to working with you.'

'But it's just so much bullshit, you know?' Brett appeared desperate to clear the air. 'Just agent stuff. They have to keep up with the agreements of the previous contract, it's their job. I couldn't give a shit about a Winnebago.'

'Fair enough,' Nick said, aware that he'd gone too far. 'Not my call anyway. Sorry.' The apology didn't sound heartfelt, but it was enough.

'Come on, Brett.' Simon whacked a solid arm around the smaller man's shoulder. He hadn't reversed his initial reaction to Marsdon, but he was willing to give the young man the benefit of the doubt; it was to his own advantage to do so. 'Everyone to the pool, drinks are on Mammoth.' And the others all trooped off after them.

'That was a bit rough,' Sam said to Nick as they followed.

'I know. I'll cop it from Simon. But the bloke's going to try to crack on to you, I can tell.'

'So? I can look after myself, Nick.'

'Sorry.'

He looked so dejected that she took his hand as they walked down the stone steps to the pool.

Brett watched them from his position propped against the bar, Simon Scanlon and Louis Durand on either side. The writer had come on pretty strong, he thought, and he'd sensed it had something to do with Samantha Lindsay. But, as they walked hand in hand down the steps, he sensed something else. The guy was a fairy, he was sure of it. No competition there then.

The conversation inevitably turned to film and, in discussing European cinema, Brett Marsdon raved about *L'Homme qui a Perdu son Honneur.*

'It should have won Best Picture,' he said to Louis, 'not just Best Foreign Film. It's a work of art, man.'

As it turned out, Brett was an avid admirer of the great French film directors. Furthermore, he'd seen every one of Louis's major films, and preferred to watch the original versions without their subtitles which he found very distracting.

'Parlez vous francais?' Louis queried and suddenly, to everyone's astonishment, Brett started chatting away to him in rapid French.

Simon stared dumbfounded for a moment or so before turning to Nick, who was the only other French-speaking person present. 'What the hell is he saying?'

'His grandmother's French, he grew up in Menton on the French Riviera and he visits her every year after the Cannes Film Festival.'

'Hey, I'm sorry, you guys,' Brett apologised, halting midstream. 'I didn't mean to be rude. It's just so wild to be working with Louis Durand, you know?' He punched the big Frenchman's arm lightly. 'Man, your work is great!'

'Merci beaucoup,' Louis smiled, aware that his ego was being pandered to, but finding the young man's passion for French film most gratifying.

Simon, delighted by the rapport established between the American and the Frenchman, was rapidly reassessing his initial impression of Brett Marsdon. Nick, however, was not impressed. So Marsdon was bilingual and had a knowledge of French cinema, so what? He still didn't like the man.

Brett had the rest of that day and the next to get over his jet lag, but it was obvious jet lag meant nothing to him. He stayed up late that night after dinner, talking first to Louis Durand until the Frenchman retired, then to anyone else who was in the mood for a drink and a chat, and the following day he insisted upon coming out to location to watch the filming.

'The old Marat plantation,' Simon told Sam. 'Once the wealthiest property on the island, I believe. Pretty rundown now, leased out to a New Zealander, but the location's glorious.' They were shooting a scene between Sam, Mickey and Louis in the home of the French plantation owner, and the set was an 'actual'. It was just beyond Port Havannah Harbour and the house overlooked Undine Bay.

'Just look at that! Man, what a place!' Brett said yet again as they pulled up in the Landcruiser beside the still waters and the sandy white beach.

'Good spot, eh?' Bob Crawley agreed. He was thrilled beyond measure to be driving Brett Marsdon. A true blue Hedy Lamarr if ever there was one, he could dine out on this for the rest of his life. And what a beaut bloke into the bargain.

During the filming, Brett curbed his exuberance and watched intently. Making sure he was well out of the actors' eyelines, he observed every move Sam and Mickey and Louis made, his eyes darting between them, noting even the tiniest nuance.

He himself was also being observed. Simon Scanlon was pleased with Brett Marsdon's interest. So the kid wanted to learn, he thought with a sigh of relief. Thank God for that. Marsdon wasn't going to be any trouble at all.

'Action,' he called.

*'A toast, Mr Blackston.' The Frenchman gave a dismissive wave to the black maidservant who was hovering beside the dining table, having poured the wine. 'To you and your beautiful wife,' he said raising his glass. 'Welcome to Vila.'*

*'Thank you, M'sieur Macon.' Hugh exchanged a brief*

*glance with Sarah as they both followed suit and raised their glasses. 'To your very good health, sir.'*

*Macon gave another peremptory wave and the maidservant, who had stood by the servery awaiting her orders, picked up the tureen of soup. 'I can be a valuable ally, Mr Blackston,' he said, studying the girl carefully as she ladled the vichyssoise into Sarah's soup bowl, terrified of spilling a drop. 'I carry much weight in the colony.'*

*The man's charm was impeccable but his words inferred that he could also be a formidable adversary. His eyes continued to follow the maid as she moved on to Hugh. 'Please do not hesitate to call upon me,' he said smoothly, 'should you need any assistance. As I mentioned to your wife, I am at your disposal.'*

*Beneath the lace tablecloth Sarah's hand sought Hugh's.*

*'We are obliged to you, M'sieur,' Hugh said, 'both for your offer and for your hospitality. Tangkyu tumas,' he said to the maid.*

*There was silence whilst Macon's soup was served and, when the maid had retired, he smiled, the perfect host.*

*'Bon appetit,' he said as he raised his spoon.*

Brett Marsdon had not been present during the previous scenes they'd filmed at Reid's when Sarah had met Macon, and in the presbytery cottage when she'd warned her husband of the danger she'd felt in the Frenchman's presence. But, as he watched the dinner scene progress, the tension between the three characters was palpable.

Christ, they were good, he thought. Durand, he'd expected, the man was a cinematic genius, in his opinion. But Mickey Robertson . . . So economical, so understated. And Sam . . . Well, Samantha Lindsay was a star in the making. She'd had little dialogue in the scene, just several lines at the end, but her eyes had said it all, particularly when she'd taken her husband's hand beneath the tablecloth.

He'd have to lift his own game, he realised, couldn't get by on tricks this time. He'd need to do more than just please the fans. The critics'd be watching *Torpedo Junction* like hawks; it was a Scanlon film after all. And up against competition like this lot they'd roast him alive if he just laid on the charm.

As they set up for the reverse shots, Brett studied Sam's relationship with the two men. She wasn't sexually interested in Louis, he was sure of it. Much as she admired the man, theirs was a strictly professional relationship. But he sensed a deeper friendship with Mickey Robertson. Were they an item? he wondered. Only one way to find out.

'The chemistry between you two is so fantastic,' he said to Mickey and Sam after he'd joined the actors during the lunch break and congratulated them all on the scene. 'Have you guys worked together before?'

'Oh yes, tons of times,' Sam said. 'We've run the gamut, siblings and spouses and lovers, you name it.'

'I preferred the latter,' Mickey said, putting a lanky arm around her, then adding suggestively, 'but we never seemed to get enough rehearsal,' his fingers snaking towards her breast.

'Lecher,' Sam laughed as she pushed his hand away.

'I know,' he happily agreed.

Well, that was easy, Brett thought.

Dinner back at the Crowne Plaza that night ended up a rowdy affair. The Australian stunt pilot who was to double for Brett had arrived that morning and he described, in detail, the Second World War fighter aircraft that were sitting out at Bauerfield Airport.

'Grummans and P-41s and Mustangs. Warbirds lined up like there's no tomorrow. Fan-bloody-tastic. And just you wait'll you see your Corsair, mate,' he said to Brett. 'Beautiful-looking thing, in mint condition, can't wait to take her up.'

Highly susceptible as he was, Brett Marsdon was soon carried away on his own wave of excitement. 'I tell you, man, this movie is going to be the greatest,' he raved to the stuntie and anyone else in earshot, 'today's filming really blew me away.' And before long everyone, the crew included, was infected with his enthusiasm.

As they all left the dining room, Brett suggested an impromptu party down by the pool. 'Open bar,' he said, 'drinks on me.'

The idea was welcomed by the crew, but Simon quashed it immediately.

'Big day's shoot tomorrow,' he said to everyone. 'Early start. And your first day on set,' he added to Brett with a warning tone.

Who did the guy think he was? Brett wondered. He was only the director, when all was said and done. If I want to throw a party, man, he thought, I'll throw a party, I don't need your goddamn permission. He wanted to say it, but he knew it wouldn't be a wise move.

'Hey listen, Simon,' he said, taking the director aside. 'I think it might be a really cool idea if you let me pick up the tab for a few drinks.'

Simon looked at him through slitted eyes. Was Marsdon trying to put one over him?

'It's de rigueur, man,' Brett grinned, dimples working overtime, 'the star always picks up the tab,' but he quickly abandoned the smile when Simon failed to respond.

'Look, I know you don't buy this whole star-system shit,' he said in all seriousness, 'and neither do I. But it keeps me on side with the gang, you know? I don't want them to think I'm full of it. Gets us off to a good start, the crew and me. All buddies. You know where I'm coming from?'

Simon did. It actually made sense. If there was any antagonism amongst the ranks towards the American superstar and his multi-million-dollar salary, it would dissolve, in true Aussie tradition, once Marsdon had shouted the crew a few beers. And if there were some hangovers around tomorrow, did it really matter?

'Okay, Brett,' he said. 'Very generous of you.'

'Thanks, Simon. I appreciate your understanding.' Oh thank you very much, Brett thought. Big deal, I have Daddy's permission. He hoped the guy wouldn't stay long.

Simon didn't. He had two beers at the pool and left at ten o'clock.

''Night all,' he said. 'Don't forget, sparrow's tomorrow.' 'Sparrow's fart start' was his reminder that their call time was dawn.

''Night Simon,' they all chorused like obedient children, and he grinned, aware they were sending him up.

Nick left shortly after. If Brett Marsdon wanted to ingratiate himself with the crew and give himself a hangover into the bargain, then let him. But Nick hoped he wouldn't lead Sam astray. The scene they were shooting first thing in the morning was between Sarah and the American fighter pilot. It was crucial to the film and the characters, and Nick was angered at the thought that Brett Marsdon could jeopardise it.

'Go easy, Sam, won't you,' he whispered to her.

She didn't say anything, but raised an eyebrow by way of reply; it was the first time he'd ever lectured her.

'I know, I'm sorry,' he said. 'It's just that it's a big scene first up.' He wanted to say 'and I don't trust Brett Marsdon', but he knew it would sound foolish. She'd only tell him she could look after herself, and she'd be quite right.

'Of course it is,' she said simply, wondering why he was behaving the way he was. ''Night, Nick.' She kissed him on the cheek.

''Night.' And he slipped away quietly, feeling like a fussy old aunt.

Brett watched him go. Good, he thought. He knew the writer didn't like him. The way was now clear.

'Hey, Sam,' he called. 'Over here. Louis just told a great

story about Gerard Depardieu and his first Hollywood gig. Come on, Louis,' he urged as she joined them, 'you have to tell it in English now.'

The stuntie left at eleven o'clock, tired of mineral water and cursing the fact that he had to fly the next day when it was turning into such a beaut party. Several of the crew ended up in the pool, some clothed, some not, and Mickey remained seated at a table overlooking the lagoon, in deep conversation with Elizabeth from the local radio station. She was teaching him Bislama and, always good with accents, he was getting it right, which delighted Elizabeth. But Mickey was wondering what it would be like to go to bed with her. He loved the glossiness of her skin and he wondered if she was that colour all over. He'd never made love to a black woman. She was so bloody attractive, and a really nice bird, would she be offended if he chatted her up? He looked at his watch surreptitiously. Couldn't afford to have too late a night, he thought, he was second scene up for the day. Perhaps he should ask her how to say 'I find you sexy' in Bislama.

Louis Durand begged off at midnight. He would have retired much earlier if he'd been filming the next morning, but he had the day off and was going snorkelling at Hideaway Island instead. He wasn't the least bit critical of the others partying on. They'd get by the next day with their thumping heads, they were ten years younger than he was – a little more actually, he reminded himself – and he'd done the same thing a decade ago.

'Bon nuit,' he said.

Sam looked about. She and Brett were the only cast members left; she'd noticed Mickey leaving with Elizabeth a good half hour ago. She glanced at her watch. Midnight. The crew were still skylarking about in the pool, an impromptu game of water polo in progress, others bar-racking from the sidelines. They were in for the long haul, she thought, as crews always were when it was an open tab. And Jimmy, the islander serving behind the bar, was still dishing out his cocktails, along with the Tusker, champagne, wine and anything from the top shelf.

Time for bed, Sam thought. The taste of wine was turning sour, she'd had more than enough.

'Thanks, Brett,' she said, 'it's been a good night.'

'Hey, Sam, don't leave me.' He was in full party mode and wasn't about to let her go. 'How about a quick line,' he said, taking a small leather pouch from his pocket. 'Just a bit of a hit, c'mon now, I really want to talk to you.'

So that explained his constant energy, she thought as she watched him tap the white powder out of its tiny plastic bag onto the small square mirror. She should have known.

'No thanks, I'm not into coke.' She smiled as she said it, she didn't want to sound censorious.

'Oh well, each to his own poison,' he grinned, taking the already rolled fifty-dollar note from the pouch. 'One more drink for the road then. C'mon, Sam,' he pleaded as she shook her head, 'I'm the host, I can't leave yet, keep me company.'

'If I have one more glass of wine I'll puke,' she said bluntly, 'and besides, I'm busting for the loo.'

Brett gave a joyful hoot of laughter. 'God, how I love you Ossies,' he said. 'I really do.'

'It's Aussies, Brett,' she corrected him. 'Aussies with a zed.'

'A *zed*?'

'Well, a zee to you.'

'Aussies,' he said correctly, 'and we'll make it a cocktail, something exotic. C'mon,' he urged, 'you'll never sleep with this racket.'

Sam looked at the pool awash with semi-naked crew, all laughing and yelling. Her bungalow was only twenty metres away. He was right, she thought, she'd never get to sleep, and sleep was the most important thing. One strong cocktail'd do the trick, then she'd go to bed and pass out for a good five hours.

'Okay,' she agreed, 'something strong and sweet. I'll be back in a tick,' and she went off down the path that led to the toilet block.

'Strong and sweet it is,' Brett said when she returned five minutes later to discover a huge rainbow-coloured cocktail sitting on the bar.

'What the hell is it?'

'Don't ask me. Jimmy's special, whatever that is.'

'It's strong all right,' she said taking a sip, 'should do the trick.'

'Let's get away from the noise,' he suggested, and they took their drinks to the table that Mickey and Elizabeth had vacated, overlooking the lagoon. Behind them the noise remained as loud as ever but, as they gazed out over the dark water at the lights still twinkling on Erikor Island, they could have been alone, just the two of them.

'Beautiful, isn't it?' she said.

'It is,' he agreed, staring at her. 'To us.' He raised his bottle of Tusker. She looked at him quizzically. 'To *Torpedo Junction*.'

Well, she'd drink to that, she thought, and she clinked her glass against his beer bottle.

'I can't wait to work with you, you know that? Watching you today, man,' Brett shook his head in admiration, 'I really mean it, you are fantastic and I'm not bullshitting, I swear it.' He wasn't, he meant every word he said.

'Are you trying to get into my pants?' He was so intense that Sam couldn't resist sending him up.

He didn't laugh, but he wasn't offended. 'I sure am,' he said.

'Oh.' She took another sip of her cocktail, buying time. Well, that was certainly direct, she thought.

'I told you we'd have a ball here, you and me, and I meant it.'

'And I said we'll do some work first, if I remember.'

'That's right.'

'Well, we haven't yet.' Why did she feel he had control of the situation? He no longer seemed like an eager puppy, his eyes were burning a hole in her skull. Maybe he was too coked up, maybe she was a bit drunk, but he was confusing her. 'I mean we haven't worked together yet.'

'And that's exactly why we should make love.' Brett was accustomed to having sex with his female co-stars. As far as he was concerned it went with the territory, particularly when they were filming on location. It was a buzz and it helped his performance, added to the onscreen electricity.

'I have a theory,' he said. 'I believe audiences can tell when people are lovers, there's a chemistry that translates onscreen. I like to use everything, you know? Like all of this,' he looked out over the lagoon, 'and us,' he looked back at her, 'and the attraction we feel for each other.'

Why was such a clichéd argument sounding so persuasive? Sam wondered. There were any number of responses on the tip of her tongue. She could send him up about taking 'method' too seriously, or tell him to 'just act' — wasn't that what Laurence Olivier had once said? But she realised that she did find him very attractive and, even as she considered a suitable retort, she was wondering what it would be like to go to bed with him.

He knew she was weakening. 'Besides, it'd be fun, wouldn't it?' he said, his smile cheekily daring her.

Sam stared into the eyes that made female audiences swoon, and part of her wanted to laugh. She could see that same come-to-bed look in closeup on the screen, and she felt as if she was in one of his movies. Yet, at the same time, she was aroused. How extraordinary, she thought. She grinned rather inanely back at him and took a swig of her half-finished cocktail.

'Your place or mine?' he asked.

'Mine,' she said, 'so that I can pass out.'

'You lead the way, I'll bring the drinks.' He picked up her glass. 'You want another one?'

'No way.'

Brett grabbed a beer from the bar, instructed Jimmy to stop serving in an hour and followed her to her bungalow.

They sat out on the verandah and drank for the next quarter of an hour or so, in between kissing and fondling and teasing each other.

'Let's go to bed,' Sam whispered. Her brain was spinning, either from the effects of the alcohol she'd consumed or the lust that now consumed her, but either way she desperately wanted sex.

'Not just yet, in a minute.' Brett was enjoying the seduction. She was getting hotter by the minute and that was the way he liked it, her desire was a real turn-on. 'Finish your drink.'

She drained the glass, and moaned as she felt his hand go to work once again on her nipple. She felt utterly abandoned as she opened her mouth to his. We'll be doing it out on the verandah in a moment, she thought vaguely, as his other hand found its way between her thighs, but she didn't really care, the verandah would be fine. She moaned again and parted her legs.

Then, suddenly, everything went wrong. The hand that was thrusting itself through the crotch of her panties was vile and invasive. The fingertips that had been teasing her nipple were pinching it now, torturing her. And the tongue that had been gently exploring her mouth was threatening to choke her. Everything that had been erotic was hideous. She was under attack. She was being raped. She fought back.

For a moment Brett thought it was part of the game, that she was turned on and wanted it rough. He fought back briefly himself, enjoying the struggle, but within seconds he realised she was serious.

She was pushing against him with all her might and, as he broke away, she fell to her knees on the deck of the verandah. He went to help her up, but she backed away from him.

'Get away from me, you bastard.' Her voice was angry, but she was frightened, he could tell. Then he saw the paranoia in her eyes.

'Oh shit,' he said, recognising the signs. 'Come on, Sam, get up.' Once again he tried to help her, and once again she backed away.

'You come near me, you creep, and I'll scream rape!'

'Sssh, keep your voice down, for Chrissakes, they'll hear you.' He squatted on the verandah deck, staying a safe distance away in order not to alarm her. 'I wasn't trying to rape you, Sam. You're just having a bad trip, that's all.'

She glared at him, still paranoid, still not trusting him, but listening.

'Your drink had an e in it. Come on, baby, I didn't mean to scare you, just a bit of fun.'

'What have you done to me?'

'I crushed up a pill and spiked your drink, and I'm sorry, okay? I'm really sorry.' She was staring at him, horrified, but at least he was getting through. He was relieved that she wasn't going to have a fit; she'd frightened him there for a minute. 'Just one little e, that's all it was. You're having a bad trip. The thing is not to worry, it'll wear off soon. Come on now, get up, there's a good girl.'

She allowed him to help her to her feet. 'You bastard.' Her heart was pounding. She was going to have a heart attack, she was sure. 'I've never taken one of those things in my life.'

'Yeah, that's pretty obvious.'

'I think I'm having a heart attack.'

'No you're not. It's just panic, that's all.' Jesus, he certainly hoped it was. She was spaced out all right, he could tell. 'You need to move around. Want to go for a walk?'

She stared at him, saw the concern in his eyes. He was a puppy again. A frightened puppy this time, trying to make things better. How on earth could she have considered sleeping with him? 'Bugger off, Brett, I'm going to bed.'

'Not a good idea, baby,' he spoke soothingly, trying to talk her down. 'Better to keep moving, helps the paranoia wear off.'

'I'll look after my own paranoia, just go.'

'Hey c'mon, Sam, I'm only trying to help.'

'You've helped enough. Piss off.'

'Okay, okay.' He backed away. 'Drink plenty of water, and a lot of deep breathing, you got that?'

'Yes, yes, I've got that, now get out, go away.' She had to lie down, the world was spinning, she was going to fall over any minute.

'Water and deep breathing, you'll be fine baby, trust me.'

She didn't answer, but after she'd locked the door behind him she took his advice. She guzzled water from the bottle in the refrigerator, then lay down on the bed and concentrated on her breathing. In, two, three, four, out, two, three, four, she counted, her hands on her diaphragm. She tried to practise the meditation exercises she'd learned all those years ago at drama school. But nothing worked. Panic seized her. Her heart was pounding more wildly than ever.

Just a bad trip, she told herself, that's what he'd said. Just one little e, he'd said that too. It was only a pill, and people popped pills all the time, didn't they? Yes, and people died too. What the hell was in the pill? Stop it, she told herself, stop it. Just a bad trip, that's all, just a bad trip.

But no matter how hard she tried to reason with herself, something in her brain told her that the darkness engulfing her was death. She concentrated on the chink in the curtain. Through it, she could see the lights of the pool. As long as the lights were on she was safe. The lights were her life and she focussed on them. She didn't dare sleep. Sleep meant blackness and blackness meant death. Stay awake, she told herself as she stared, fixated, at the chink in the curtain, whatever you do stay awake. Then she heard the last of the revellers making their farewells. Oh dear God, she thought, any moment now they'll turn off the pool lights.

Then silence outside. All was still and quiet. And suddenly the lights went out.

She lay in the dark, listening to the sound of her laboured breathing and waiting for the moment of her death. Images and sounds formed in her mind: faces unrecognisable and barely human; voices, distorted and incoherent.

Gradually they took shape to become one, and a face she knew appeared before her. It was the face of the old woman she'd met in Fareham. Maude. Maude with her silver hair and her pretty smile. But Maude wasn't smiling now, she was stern and disapproving. She spoke, and her voice was the same as it had been that day in the park, well modulated, and refined. But this time it was not gentle. This time there was a hard, admonishing edge to her tone.

'You foolish girl,' she said. 'You'd jeopardise everything? All that we've worked for, you and I?'

The face drew closer and closer, the eyes stern, the mouth a thin hard line, and the voice grew harsher. 'Foolish girl! Foolish!' Closer and closer it came until Sam could see nothing but the old woman's eyes.

'You owe it to me,' the voice said. 'Never forget that. You owe it to me.'

What did she owe? What? The eyes were engulfing her now. Then the two became one. They merged, the blue of the iris, the black of the pupil, one huge eye, coming closer and closer, any moment it would devour her. The voice softened a little.

'Don't be foolish and throw it all away. We're a team, you and I. A team, don't ever forget that. A team, dear. You and I. A team.'

The voice echoed all around her, the blue iris disappeared, and everything became black as Sam felt herself swallowed up by the pupil of the eye.

# CHAPTER TEN

The face of war in Europe had changed, as President Roosevelt had assured the world it would.

'*The Americans have arrived,*' Phoebe wrote to Jane. '*They've set up a camp not far from Fareham, and when I ride my bicycle out of town (bicycles have become most popular due to the petrol rationing, and I've discovered I enjoy it, so very good for the figure) I see them marching all over the countryside. And when they come into Fareham they're a frightfully friendly bunch, very generous. They dish out items that even Dora can no longer acquire through her black-market connections, chocolate and coffee and things. Several officers dined at Chisolm House the other night and they were awfully polite. And very smartly done out, I must say, I adore their uniforms. But I do so wish they wouldn't give the children (who follow them about like puppies) chewing gum, it's such ghastly stuff.*'

Phoebe's response to Jane's letter had been spontaneous.

'*How dare you apologise for writing,*' she'd said.'*Oh Jane, you shouldn't have taken me seriously when I told you not to correspond, I simply didn't want you to feel obligated. I am thrilled that you have discovered your purpose and I expect to be kept well informed of the developments. In the meantime, I promise, my dearest friend, that I shall override my reluctance to put pen to paper and keep you well up with all the excitement of Fareham, which, apart from the bombs and the Americans, could hardly compare with the drama of the New Hebrides.'*

Phoebe was quite wrong, Jane assured her in the reply she sent post-haste, delighted to be once again in contact with her friend. The events in Fareham sounded far more dramatic than the climate that prevailed in Vila. Since the address of President Roosevelt three months previously, little had changed in the New Hebrides.

*'The Japanese have reached the nearby Solomon Islands,'* she wrote, *'and we are fearful that we may be their next target. For the moment, however, life simply goes on as usual.'*

But although military activity in the Pacific had, as yet, had little direct effect on Vila, a whole new world had opened up for Jane Thackeray.

Martin had spent the past three months principally stationed in Vila, with only several days away now and then, and Jane felt more than ever that she was truly settled, in both her marriage and her new home. She and Martin led a social existence. They had dined several times at Iririki Island with the British resident commissioner and had thrown a number of dinner parties of their own. Christmas Day had been shared with the Bales and Godfrey, and New Year's Eve had been celebrated in style at Reid's Hotel with a party of raucous expatriates, after which they'd watched the fireworks on the foreshore. They had become a part of the colony, both of them adjusting to the heat of the tropics and to the violent and unpredictable storms of the monsoon season. But, far more importantly, Jane had become a part of Martin's work. They were partners in every sense of the word. The best of friends and the perfect team.

When he visited a local community in his capacity as

minister, she went with him. Sometimes they travelled by car, but more often than not they used the church's horse and buggy. Sometimes she left Ronnie with Mary, but mostly she took the child with her, carrying him native-style in a sack-like harness tied around her neck and waist. Martin loved her for it.

'A true islander, my love,' he'd say time and again with pride.

The fact that they travelled as a family won the trust of the villagers, who themselves were very family-oriented. The minister and his missus and their baby were quickly accepted into the islanders' homes, and Jane would play with their children whilst Martin held services or spoke on behalf of the Mission. Alternatively, when he was tending the sick, the old women of the village would mind Ronnie whilst Jane assisted her husband in his medical work.

Shortly before his first birthday, Ronnie spoke his first word, and Jane was convinced he'd said it in Bislama.

'How can you possibly tell?' Martin laughed. 'Mummy and mami sound the same.'

'No, it was definitely mami,' Jane said, refusing to budge on the issue.

Several days later, they celebrated the birthday with a small party, inviting Godfrey and Mary. Mary had cooked a cake. It wasn't a very good cake, sagging in the middle, but then Mary had never baked a cake before. Jane, Martin and Godfrey all vowed it was delicious, and fortunately it did taste much better than it looked. Mary, a buxom, good-natured young woman, who adored both Ronnie and the Missus, flushed with pleasure.

Despite the fact that Ronnie had been officially christened in Edinburgh, Godfrey was declared the child's honorary godfather, and it was obvious he took the position very seriously. It was in the middle of his humble, but lengthy speech, as he held his godchild in his arms, that Ronnie uttered his second word.

'Dadi,' he said quite clearly, and his little fingers reached out for the old man's beard, always a source of fascination.

Again Martin was unconvinced that the child was speaking Bislama, and again Jane was adamant that he'd said 'dadi' and not 'daddy'. Godfrey didn't care either way. The word had been directed at him, and that was all that mattered.

In mid-April, Martin was sent to Espiritu Santo, the archipelago's largest island, well to the north.

'I don't know how long I'll be away all told,' he said. 'Two months, I would think, possibly three.'

They made love the night before he left. Tenderly and considerately, as they always did. From the outset, their sexual relationship had been founded rather on an extension of their mutual love and respect than on an all-consuming passion.

'I'll miss you,' she said as she lay in his arms.

'And I you.' He kissed her forehead. 'But at least I won't worry about you this time. You've certainly found your niche, my love. I do believe Godfrey will be quite happy to see the back of me, though,' he added lightly, 'he told me that he hardly sees you any more.' He kissed her gently once again. 'You'll have time on your hands to make a fuss of him whilst I'm gone. I think he's lonely, old Godfrey.'

But Jane had no time on her hands at all when, only two days later, early in the morning, Mary arrived with Sera Poilama.

'This my friend Sera, we come from the same village.'

The young woman Mary introduced was in her mid-twenties, just a little older than Jane, and quite beautiful. Her black hair, flattened and pulled back from her face in a severe bun at the nape of her neck, accentuated her handsome features, and beneath the cotton dress her body was lithe and graceful.

'Allo, Sera.' Jane extended her hand.

'Allo, Missus Tackry.' Sera gave a respectful bob as she shook Jane's hand. Her voice was smooth, well modulated, and in keeping with her appearance, Jane thought. There was something inherently elegant about Sera. As it turned out, she spoke little English but was fluent in basic French.

'I'm sorry,' Jane said with an apologetic smile as Sera started rapidly explaining her predicament, 'my French is not very good.' So they conversed in Bislama instead.

Sera's four-year-old son was ill. At first he'd just had a cough and a runny nose, she said, and she hadn't worried too much. But over the past three days he had become sick.

'Sik, tumas,' she said, her face stricken with worry. She was sure it was bad. Even her husband didn't know how bad, her husband thought the sickness would pass. But she was a mother, and something in her blood told her that her son was in danger. She hoped that the Missus might come and visit him.

What were the symptoms, Jane asked. 'Hao nao sik?'

'Hem taed, les. Hem no wantem kakae.'

'Hem gat soa we oli harem long bodi?'

Sera looked uncertain. She wanted to get the facts right for the Missus and she wasn't sure if her son was in actual pain. Sometimes he whimpered, but mostly he was very, very tired. That was what worried her so much, he was normally such an active little boy.

'Hem soa lelebet,' she said.

The child was lethargic and off his food but he was not suffering severe pain. Jane enquired why Sera had not brought him to see her. The village was very nearby, Mary walked into town each day.

Sera explained that she no longer lived in the village. She was a maidservant on a coconut plantation, she said, and she and her family lived in a house on the property. Not far away from the big house, she added with some pride.

It didn't really answer her query, Jane thought. Having made the trip herself, why had Sera not brought her son with her? Jane sensed that Sera was avoiding the question.

Had she been worried that her little boy was too ill to travel? she asked.

Sera looked at Mary. It was Mary who had suggested she come and see the Missus, and she wasn't sure whether she should speak her mind. But Mary nodded.

'Masta no bilif pikinini blong mi sik.' Sera shrugged helplessly. 'Masta bilif hem jes taed, no wari.'

How could Sera's employer be so heartless? Jane thought. How could anyone tell the mother of a sick four-year-old not to worry, that her child was just tired? Whoever it was simply didn't care whether the child lived or died.

Sera went on to explain that the Masta would be angry if he found out she'd gone against his wishes and taken the child to a doctor. But everyone knew that the Missus visited villages everywhere. And if the Missus was simply to call upon them, then no-one would know that she had been asked to do so.

Jane asked who Sera's master was.

'M'sieur Marat,' Sera replied, then automatically she broke into French, 'Je suis la bonne a Chanson de Mer, la maison de M'sieur Marat.'

'Oh.' The reply was quite within the bounds of Jane's limited French, but Sera took the Missus's hesitation as a lack of comprehension.

'Mi haosgel, big haos blong Masta Marat,' she said.

But Jane barely heard her. She was wondering whether she should seek Godfrey's help. She would visit Sera's child, certainly, but she didn't welcome the prospect of bumping into Jean-François Marat on her own.

She had encountered the Frenchman on a number of occasions since their initial meeting, mostly when she'd been shopping unaccompanied in town, and each time, as he'd kissed her hand and exchanged seemingly innocent pleasantries, she had found him disturbing. Fortunately, upon their last encounter, she had been with Martin. They'd walked out of the post office together and literally bumped into the Frenchman.

'Ah Dr Thackeray, I have so looked forward to our meeting.' Jean-François had been at his most charming as he shook Martin's hand. 'You have been back in Vila for some time now, I've heard. Perhaps at long last you might persuade your lovely wife to accept my invitation. I insist that the two of you dine with me at Chanson de Mer.'

He'd tried to arrange a date there and then as they stood in the main street but Martin, aware of Jane's reluctance, had managed to evade the issue. He would be only too delighted, he said, but he had many church commitments and would need to check his diary first.

They'd parted, Jean-François insisting that they contact him with a date of their preference, and at home Martin had queried Jane's reticence. She had previously told him of her aversion to the Frenchman upon their first meeting, and also of Godfrey's warning, and Martin himself had sensed the arrogance beneath Marat's charm. But it was hardly reason enough to refuse any contact with the man, he said. Vila was a small town, it was wise to avoid any unpleasantness.

'M'sieur Marat will think it the most frightful snub if we don't accept his invitation, my love.'

'Perhaps we can just leave it until the next chance meeting?' she'd suggested. She didn't know how to express the unrest she felt in Marat's presence, even to herself, let alone to her husband. 'And he may have been making polite conversation, when all's said and done. We wouldn't wish to appear too keen.'

'Yes, there is that,' Martin had agreed. 'But if he invites us again we shall simply have to accept.'

Sera had noticed Jane's hesitation. Indeed she had noticed

the Missus's reaction the moment she'd mentioned the Masta's name. The Missus was frightened of the Masta. Sera understood. Everyone was frightened of the Masta. She looked at Mary. She shouldn't have listened to Mary, she shouldn't have come to see the Missus.

The young woman's bitter disappointment was palpable, and Jane realised that Sera had misread her momentary indecision.

'Of course I shall visit your little boy,' she assured her. 'What is his name?'

'Pascal.' It was the first time Sera had smiled. 'Nem blong pikinini blong mi Pascal.'

She truly was the most beautiful-looking woman, Jane thought. 'We'll all go together,' she said. 'Mary, you'll carry Ronnie whilst I drive the trap.'

Mary grinned triumphantly at Sera. 'See? I told you so,' her eyes said. She had known that the Missus would take care of everything. The Missus never let Mary down, the Missus was Mary's personal hero.

Even as Jane had contemplated asking Godfrey to accompany them, she had quickly dismissed the idea, recalling the antipathy she'd sensed between the two men. Any irritation Marat might feel at her intrusion would be multiplied tenfold if the Englishman was with her.

She needed the Reverend Smeed's permission to use the horse and buggy and, as she walked over to the church, she told herself that, as Sera's family lived away from the big house, it would be most unlikely she would encounter Marat in any event.

The Reverend Smeed was quite happy for her to take the horse and buggy. It was most admirable of her to visit the sick child, he said, but surely someone should accompany her. He was rapidly thinking who on earth he could send; he was far too busy himself.

'Mary is coming with me,' Jane said. 'We can manage perfectly well on our own, I assure you.'

And the Reverend Smeed thought, as he had for some time now, what an extraordinarily modern young woman Martin Thackeray's wife was.

It was a long ride out to the plantation at Undine Bay, several hours in the horse and buggy, and Jane wondered how Sera had made the trip into town.

She'd hitched a lift with a dray delivering copra to the Burns Philp warehouse the previous day, she said, and she'd stayed last night with Mary in the village. Her sister, who lived with her and her husband and who also worked as a maid at the big house, was looking after her son and her eighteen-month-old daughter, Marie.

The poor woman must be desperate, Jane thought, and, as the drive progressed, she tried to put her at her ease, asking about her family and her home until finally Sera was chatting away in the most animated fashion.

Her husband's name, it appeared, was Savinata, although she referred to him as Savi, and every time she mentioned his name she glowed; it was clear she loved him very much. Savi had been working for the Masta for more than six years and he was a boss himself. He organised the labour teams from his village for the harvest. Savi was very clever. Savi could speak French and it had been he who had taught her. He could even speak English. Savi was the Masta's nambawan man and he was paid in French francs, she said proudly. The Masta didn't pay the village workers real money, but gave them their huts and a bullock a month.

Sera felt happier than she had for the past three days, ever since Pascal had become so sick. Missus Tackry was a fine person. Warm and caring. And Missus Tackry would make Pascal better, just as Mary had promised she would.

Savi had taught her to speak French when they were courting, Sera said, so that she could get a job at the big house. That was why the Masta had given them their very own house when they'd got married. And he'd given her sister Selena a job too, even though Selena's French wasn't very good.

Sera's face clouded slightly as she spoke of Selena. She knew why the Masta had given Selena a job, and she knew why Selena didn't work hard to improve her French. She didn't need to. Selena was sleeping with the Masta, and Sera didn't approve of the fact.

But she was once again happily smiling as she spoke about her house. Sera was proud of her house. No-one else she knew had their very own house, with three rooms, and a sink.

The change in the woman was remarkable, Jane thought, as she watched Sera chatting away. The worry had left her face and she was childlike, carefree in her happiness. Charming as it was, it only added to Jane's own worry. It was obvious that Sera had placed her entire trust in Jane, convinced that the Missus would save her son. But what if she couldn't? Jane thought. What if the little boy was truly ill and beyond help?

At Undine Bay, they pulled off the rough coastal track and Jane drove the buggy up the road that led to the plantation homestead only five hundred yards away. So this was Chanson de Mer, she thought. A large timber bungalow with a shiny silver corrugated-iron roof, it was surrounded by verandahs and stood in a wide, cleared ground of rough grass overlooking the ocean. Behind it, stretching as far as she could see, was the coconut plantation.

So much for avoiding Marat, Jane thought, wondering if he was watching them through the windows as they trotted boldly up the drive.

But, halfway to the house, Sera directed her to the right and she pulled the horse up to a walk as they drove off the road to the wooded area of trees and palms several hundred yards away. Nestled amongst them was Sera's 'house'. It was little more than a hut, with a rusty corrugated-iron roof, an open-framed entrance and open windows.

It would probably not be visible from the homestead, Jane thought, but she guided the horse through the trees and around to the rear, just to be sure.

The Masta was not home, Sera said, as if she had read Jane's thoughts, his motor car was not out the front of the big house.

Jane breathed a sigh of relief and, as they alighted from the buggy, she took her medical bag from the back and instructed Mary to stay outside with Ronnie whilst she examined the child.

The hut was a far more solid building than those Jane had seen in the villages she'd visited, and the interior was much more sophisticated. There were three separate rooms with open-framed doors and windows, but blinds of natangora matting could be rolled down for privacy. There was matting on the floor also, and a table and chairs in the main living area and a bench where Sera prepared food. In one corner were large containers of water and a sink that sat in a bamboo frame, the hose beneath it disappearing through a hole in the wall. The sink was self-draining, Sera proudly explained, and they fetched their water each day from the tank at the big house.

The little hut was neat and tidy and obviously tended with care. Sera had every right to feel proud of her home, Jane thought.

Sera led the way into the larger of the two rooms at the rear of the main living area. The little room was where Selena slept, she said, and this room was hers and Savi's and the children's.

A young woman was sitting on the floor, a sleeping infant cradled in her arms, and a little boy lay on the bedding beside her. His head was turned to one side and his eyes were shut tight, but his breathing was fitful and Jane could tell that he was not asleep.

The woman, who appeared around twenty, was a younger version of Sera. Not as arrestingly handsome in facial features but, in a voluptuous way, just as attractive.

'Sista blong mi Selena.'

'Allo, Selena,' Jane said.

Sera then introduced Jane as if she were royalty itself. 'Missus Tackry,' she said to her sister with the utmost reverence.

'Allo, Missus Tackry.' Selena was about to scramble to her feet; it was wrong that she should be sitting whilst Missus Tackry was standing.

Jane gestured for her to stay seated and, as Sera herself sat and took the infant from her sister, she knelt beside the little boy.

'Allo, Pascal,' she said.

The child turned his head slightly at the sound of her voice and, as he opened his eyes, she saw his flicker of interest in the white woman with the fair hair who was leaning over him. But he quickly closed his eyes again, squeezing his lids shut as tightly as he could, and again he turned his head away from the light that streamed through the nearby open window.

Jane instructed Selena to pull the blinds down, over both the window and the door that led to the main room. The child was photophobic, the light distressed him, it was not a good sign. She took the pencil torch from her medical bag and lifted the boy's eyelids to check his pupils, talking softly to him all the while. The pupils were normal, there was no sign of brain hemorrhage. She checked for the other symptoms, which she feared might confirm her suspicions, testing his spine for any stiffness or irritation. He whimpered in pain as she turned his neck. Then she stripped him of the light cotton shirt he was wearing and searched for the ominous evidence of bacterial rash. To her relief, there was none.

The child had meningitis, she was sure of it. But it appeared to be viral. She certainly hoped so. Oh God, why wasn't Martin here? He would know. But then would he?

How could anyone be sure? She so desperately needed another opinion. If the meningitis were to prove bacterial, it could be catastrophic.

She questioned the women. Had Pascal been in contact with other children? Oh yes, Sera and Selena answered. Savi's parents and his brothers and sisters lived in the nearby village, and they regularly took Pascal there to see his grandparents and to play with his cousins and the other children.

And had any of the other children had coughs and runny noses? Jane asked. Yes, they had, the women said. And had they recovered? she queried. Oh yes, the children had all got better, they told her.

It had to be viral, Jane thought, it simply had to. Everything pointed to it, surely. But how could she be positive?

She instructed Sera that Pascal must be kept away from the light. The room must be dark, she said. And he must be kept cool at all times, and he must be fed plenty of fluids.

'Plante kolwater,' she repeated as she prepared to take her leave. She would come back tomorrow, she said. She told Sera that she believed Pascal would recover, but that the next twenty-four hours were vital, and that they must all pray.

Outside the hut, Sera had tears in her eyes as she farewelled Mary and Jane. 'Tangkyu ta, Mary,' she said, hugging her friend fiercely. But when she turned to Jane, words couldn't suffice. 'Oh Missus Tackry,' she said, 'oh Missus Tackry.' And suddenly she was crying, all the pent-up worry about her little boy flooded out in a wealth of tears. Jane embraced her, wondering as she did at her own audacity in giving the woman hope when her diagnosis could prove wrong.

During the ride back to town, she prayed fervently for the boy's safety, but beneath her prayers, anger seethed. Blind, cold anger at Jean-François Marat. If little Pascal

Poilama's meningitis proved to be bacterial, not only would the boy die, there was the risk of an outbreak amongst the villagers, perhaps even a localised epidemic. And all because of the Frenchman's utter disregard for the people who served him. Sera Poilama had told him of her son's illness and Marat had dismissed it out of hand. The man was a monster.

As she'd driven the trap down the main drive Jane had rather hoped to meet Marat on his way home. She'd have liked to have confronted him whilst her anger was at its peak.

Now, half an hour later, as they plodded their way back home, she was glad that she hadn't. Creating an enemy of a man like Marat would be to no-one's advantage. He would no doubt vent his own anger at her interference upon Sera and her family.

Beside her, Mary had lapsed into silence. For the first ten minutes after they'd left the plantation Mary had been most talkative, eager to chat about her friend Sera and the miracle of their visit to Pascal, but she'd soon realised the Missus was deep in her own thoughts and Mary respected that. So she chatted to Ronnie instead, and he answered back in his strange mixture of Bislama and English and gibberish as he happily punched the air with his fists.

By the time they arrived home in the early dusk, Jane had made her plans. Tomorrow, after she had visited Pascal, she would drive out to the village and examine the children for any sign of bacterial meningitis, and she would travel on her own; she could not afford to expose Ronnie to any possible danger. But she wondered how the villagers would receive her. Would they trust her? It was different when she was with Martin and her baby son, they were accepted as a family, but the local people were not accustomed to a white woman travelling unaccompanied. Again she contemplated seeking Godfrey's help, and again she dismissed the idea. These were Marat's workers and she must move cautiously. Under no circumstances must she arouse the Frenchman's anger.

Early the following morning, when she once again sought Reverend Smeed's permission to use the horse and buggy, she allowed the man to presume Mary was accompanying her, aware that he would forbid her to travel alone.

'The child will make a speedy recovery, I hope,' Reverend Smeed remarked as he wished her well.

She had been deliberately vague as to the boy's specific illness. He was lethargic and off his food, she'd said. She wondered what the good Reverend's reaction would be if she told him there was the possibility of an outbreak of bacterial meningitis on the island. Of course, if it were to come to that, Martin would be immediately recalled to Efate, and Jane wished for the hundredth time, as she had throughout her sleepless night, that Martin was with her right now.

'I hope so too, Reverend Smeed,' she replied.

Mary had been disappointed to discover she was being left out of the adventure this time.

'I need you to stay home and look after Ronnie,' Jane told her.

'But Ronnie want to come too.' Mary tried a little subtle blackmail, indicating the child who was waving his arms about and yelling 'mami' over and over in the hope that either Jane or Mary would pick him up.

'I'm going to examine the children in the village after I've visited Sera,' Jane explained, 'and I don't want Ronnie with me.'

The response puzzled Mary. The Masta and the Missus often took Ronnie with them when they visited villages. 'But I help you,' she said. She was a very good assistant, the Missus had often told her so.

'You are not coming, Mary, and that's that,' Jane said in a tone that defied any further discussion.

Mary sulked for a while, but nevertheless packed a

lunch that she insisted Jane take with her. 'Not right you go on your own,' she said as Jane climbed into the buggy.

'Goodbye, Mary.'

It was close to midday by the time she reached Undine Bay and, as she turned off the track and into the drive, she was relieved to notice there was no vehicle parked outside the big house.

She drove the buggy to the rear of the hut just to be safe and Sera, who was waiting to greet her, once again seemed to read her thoughts. The Masta had not come home last night, she said.

'Allo, Missus Tackry.' Selena appeared at her sister's side, the baby girl slung over one hip, and as Jane returned the greeting she wondered who was looking after Pascal. But obviously the child's condition must have improved, she thought, Sera was beaming as she ushered her into the hut and through to the bedroom.

On the bedding in the corner of the darkened room, a man was seated leaning up against the wall, and the child was in his arms. He was gently rocking the little boy from side to side, and the little boy's arms were hooked around his neck. As soon as the women entered, the man carefully laid the child down on the bedding and rose to his feet.

Jane could see, even in the gloom, that the little boy's eyes were open and that he was watching everything.

'Man blong mi Savi,' Sera said, and Jane turned her attention to the man.

Savi didn't wait for his wife to make the further intro- duction. He took Jane's right hand in both of his. 'Missus Tackry,' he said, 'is an honour. From Pascal I tank you. I tank you so much from my son.'

Jane was touched, not only by the man's profound gratitude, but by his determination to communicate it in English. She wasn't sure what to say, though, she hadn't even examined the child yet. 'He's improved then, I take it?' she said, which sounded rather abrupt, she realised.

'He is live,' Savi said. 'He is much sick in night. We is much worry.'

'Perhaps I should look at him,' Jane suggested.

'Oh yes,' Savi dropped her hand instantly, 'oh yes, plis.'

She knelt, and Savi crouched beside her, watching her every action as she examined the child.

'Allo, Pascal,' she smiled. 'Nem blong mi Missus Tackry. Olsem wanem?'

The little boy gave the faintest of smiles and nodded as she asked him how he was; it was obvious that he found her intriguing.

She chatted to him throughout the examination, telling him everything she was doing and why, aware that she was really explaining it all to Savi whose face was only inches away, his eyes darting from the pencil torch, to the stethoscope, to her, to the boy. Savi was missing nothing.

She was very sorry if it hurt a little bit, she said to Pascal as she tested his neck and his spine. But this time, as she turned his head gently to the side, he didn't whimper – he was far more interested in continuing his own examination of the white missus.

The photophobia had lessened considerably, the spine was more flexible, the neck less tender and, although the child was still very lethargic, his interest in her was an excellent sign of his recovery. Jane rose to her feet and Savi jumped up beside her.

'He is good, yes?' he asked.

'He is still very tired, Savi, and it will take him some time to recover his strength,' she said, 'but yes, he will get better.'

She didn't need to say it in Bislama for Sera, Savi said it all. He picked his wife up bodily and whirled her about, nearly bowling over Selena who was standing by the doorway, the baby in her arms.

'Ssh,' Jane said, trying to calm him down. 'Ssh.' She put her finger to her lips. 'Too much excitement, Pascal must be kept calm and quiet.'

Savi put Sera down guiltily. 'Sorry,' he whispered. 'So sorry, Missus Tackry.'

Jane knelt once again beside Pascal. He was a very good boy, she told him, and he was going to be strong again soon. She was going now, she said, but she would come back and visit him in one week's time.

Savi, who had instantly crouched at her side, smiled at his son. 'Yu talem Missus Tackry tangkyu, ta, Pascal.'

'Tangkyu, ta,' the boy said obediently, his voice little more than a whisper.

Jane smiled and stroked his head gently as she said goodbye. 'Siyu, Pascal.'

Pascal smiled back at the nice white missus, he liked her a lot. 'Siyu, Missus Tack,' he said.

Selena remained with Pascal whilst Sera and Savi accompanied Jane outside.

'Missus Tack,' Savi grinned. 'Is good name.' He decided right then to adopt it. The Missus was special to them, she deserved a special name, and Missus Tack it was.

Savi was not at all happy, however, to discover Missus Tack had driven the buggy all the way from Vila on her own. It was not right she should travel without an escort, he maintained.

In the daylight, where she could see him properly, Jane was further impressed by Savi. He was a good-looking man, around thirty, with a lean, fit body, and he wore his hair cropped very short, like a woolly cap on his finely shaped skull. But it was his vitality and the intelligent enquiry in his eyes that struck her above all else. Sera's proud comment about her husband had been no mere boast. Savi was clever.

Sera tried to ply Jane with some of the special yam soup she had made for Pascal. And there was fish that Savi had caught that very morning. She would cook for Missus Tack, she said. She smiled at Savi, she too liked the nickname.

Jane thanked her but apologised, saying that she didn't have time to stay and eat, she was going to the village to examine the children. Whereupon Savi immediately announced that he would go with her and introduce her to his people.

'I take Missus Tack my village,' he said, 'meet my people.'

'Thank you very much, Savi,' she replied, 'I would be most honoured.' She was delighted, it solved all her problems.

The horse having been watered and tended to, Savi took the reins and, during the fifteen-minute ride to the village, Jane insisted he share the chicken sandwiches and fruit that Mary had packed for her. He ate a little but was far more interested in speaking English. Such an opportunity for practice was rare, and Savi didn't intend to waste one minute of it. 'No Bislama,' he said, 'we spik English, I learn.'

When they arrived at the village, Jane could not have asked for a better reception. The moment they drove up to the cluster of huts and lean-tos, they were surrounded. Savi was obviously very popular amongst his people, and many called him 'bos', Jane noticed, another form of 'masta' commonly used by workers towards their employers, but the term was most affectionately applied in Savi's case.

Savinata Poilama was the villagers' direct link with the 'big bos'. In their eyes it was Savi who created employment. It was upon his direction that they harvested and delivered the coconuts. It was Savi who allotted the jobs at the smokehouse where the coconut meat was dried to become copra and packed into sacks. And it was Savi who organised the labour required to load the sacks and take them by dray to the Burns Philp warehouse. And they were rewarded for their efforts with homes and chickens and sometimes, most valuable of all, pigs. And once a month the village received a bullock. Savi was their hero.

Furthermore, it appeared to Jane, Savi was related to half the village. Brothers, sisters, nephews, nieces and a multitude of cousins and their families were all introduced. And then he took her to his parents' house. This was where she could examine the children, he said. He had given orders, upon Jane's instruction, for all children under the age of twelve to report for examination.

A queue stretched for a hundred yards as mothers obediently lined up with their babies and young children, and one by one they filed into the open hut which was larger and more accommodating than the shanty dwellings that constituted the rest of the village. It was not grander, however, no more opulent. It was the same mixture of thatching and hessian and rusty corrugated iron abandoned by the Europeans. But it was certainly bigger, as befitted the fact that Savi's parents were elders of the village, and had a very large family. Many of the Poilama family remained housed in their parents' home with their own children until it became so crowded that they moved out to build their own shanty huts.

Savi's parents were kind and most welcoming to Jane, but like the villagers who were now entrusting their children to her, they were simple people. And, as Savi continued to ask questions in his broken English about the examinations and what they meant, Jane was intrigued by his thirst for knowledge. Who or what had inspired him?

Pascal's illness, she explained, was easily spread. 'Contagious,' she said. It was a new word for Savi, and he practised it, he liked to learn new words. It was a disease that attacked children, she told him, particularly babies and infants, and she needed to make sure it was not going to spread through the village.

'No con-tay-jus,' he said.

'Yes.' If she'd had the time she would have explained in more depth, and she knew he would have understood. But as she examined endless ears and eyes and chests, at the same time fielding Savi's questions, it was best to keep it simple, she thought.

To her relief she discovered no sign of bacterial meningitis and, as in the other villages she'd visited with Martin, she found the children for the most part healthy and well nurtured.

No thanks to Jean-François Marat, she thought as, several hours later, Savi gave her a guided tour of the village. She was not shocked by the conditions, she'd seen it before in outlying villages. Most had no access to education for their children, no fresh water supply apart from the local stream which, used for every necessity, could be a source of disease. And mostly their houses were constructed from the remnants discarded by Europeans and garnered from rubbish dumps. But this was the village that supplied Marat's personal workforce and these were the people to whom he paid not one franc.

Jane had been surprised when Sera had told her the villagers were unpaid for their labour. The government rate of payment for native workers was twenty shillings a month, and she had presumed the same payment rate had been adopted by the private sector. Which was probably naive of her she now realised. Perhaps if the villagers had been housed well, she thought, their needs tended to, their children offered some form of education, it might be a fair exchange. But, as she looked around at the primitive conditions, it appeared plainly evident that Marat cared nothing for the welfare of his workers. It was disgraceful, Jane thought.

As they left, the villagers again crowded around, smiling and waving goodbye, and children followed the buggy down the track calling out 'siyu Missus Tack', until it disappeared amongst the trees.

Savi was insistent upon travelling all the way back to Vila with her. He would stay the night at Sera's village and hitch a ride home with a work dray the following morning, he said, and he refused to take no for an answer. It was a long trip and she would not reach town until after dark. It was unthinkable that Missus Tack should travel alone at night.

Jane finally gave in, admitting to herself that she was thankful for the offer, she was thoroughly exhausted. They drove back to Savi's house in order for him to tell his wife of their plans, and along the way Jane queried him about his knowledge. How had he learned French and English? she asked. Had he been to school?

No, but a cousin of his had. 'My cousin name Pako,' he said, 'that mean "shark".' Jane nodded, she knew the word. 'Ah yes.' Savi had been so carried away with his English that he'd forgotten Missus Tack's Bislama was very good.

Savi was proud of his cousin Pako Kalsaunaka. Pako was a sergeant in la police de Surete, he boasted. Pako had education. He could even read and write. Savi was a great believer in education. He would have liked to have gone to school himself, but no-one in his village ever had. Pako's mother had moved to her husband's village near Vila when she had married, and Pako had gone to a school set up by the French on the outskirts of town. Pako often visited Savi, they were very good friends. Pako was his inspiration.

'Pako learn me French,' Savi said. 'And Bos, he learn me French, I work long time Bos.'

'M'sieur Marat taught you French?' she asked, thinking it sounded most unlikely.

It was, and Savi laughed at the notion. 'I listen Bos. And Bos friends, you know? I listen. Is easy. English?' He shook his head. 'English much hard. When I go Vila I listen English. Man spik English, I listen much, you know?' He shook his head in frustration. 'But English, much hard.'

'When I come to visit Pascal I will give you an English lesson,' Jane promised.

Savi's face lit up at the prospect. 'You learn me English?' he said.

'No.' He was instantly crestfallen and she laughed. 'I will teach you English. I will *teach*, and you will *learn*.'

'Ah.' He grinned. 'You *teach*,' he pointed at her. 'And I *learn*,' he said, jabbing his chest with his forefinger as he slowly sounded out the words. 'Is good. You *teach* Pascal along me?'

'Yes, I will teach Pascal as well.'

'Well?' Savi was confused. 'Well' meant 'not sick'. Missus Tack had already made Pascal well; what did that have to do with learning English?

'*As* well,' she explained. 'I will teach Pascal too.'

But 'too' was a number, Savi thought. One, two, three . . . He could count English good, right up to twenty.

She registered his bewilderment. 'Also?' she asked hopefully.

He remained puzzled, 'also' was a word he didn't know at all.

'Aussi,' she said finally in French.

'Ah,' he nodded going over the words in his brain. 'As well' and 'too' and 'also' all meant 'aussi'. So many words, he thought. 'English much hard,' he said.

'Yes, very difficult.' Again the brown eyes keenly searched hers, demanding a translation. 'Très difficile,' she said, wondering how long her limited French would see her through.

'Ah.' More nodding. 'Yes.' Then he spoke his newfound phrase with the greatest of care. 'English verree diff-i-cult.'

'Well done.' They were pulling into the drive to Chanson de Mer and, as he opened his mouth to query the further use of the word 'well', she called a halt to the lesson and clapped her hands instead. 'Bravo,' she said, and he beamed with pride.

Sera tried to force a meal upon them before they left but Jane was relieved when Savi said they should waste no time in setting off. Best they reach the roads into Vila before nightfall, he told Sera. It was not good for the horse to travel rough tracks in the dark, the animal might stumble.

They waved goodbye to Sera, and Savi drove the buggy down the main drive away from Chanson de Mer and out onto the coastal track.

They had travelled less than half a mile when they heard the vehicle coming towards them. Savi heard it first and knew exactly who it was. He gave a loud, piercing whistle, startling Jane. And then she, too, heard the vehicle. It was travelling fast, considering the state of the road, and the track was narrow and winding, there would be no room for it to pass. She gripped the side of the buggy and stared, terrified, at the bend up ahead.

But Savi assured her there was no need for fear. 'Bos come,' he said. The Bos would have heard his whistle, it was a regular signal they used.

Then the Landrover appeared around the bend. It slowed to a more reasonable speed before stopping a mere ten yards in front of them, Savi having pulled the horse up to a halt. He shushed the nervous animal with a few soothing words and alighted from the buggy as Jean-François Marat got out of his car.

'Bonjour, Bos.' Savi joined his master, and the two men exchanged several words, which Jane couldn't hear, but Marat's eyes were focussed upon her. Then the Frenchman walked over to the buggy.

'Madame Thackeray,' he said. 'What a pleasant surprise.'

He was smiling, but was he angry? Jane wondered. It was impossible to tell. 'I do hope you don't mind,' she said, 'but Savi has kindly offered to drive me back to town.'

'So he told me. He is a good man,' Marat redirected his smile briefly in Savi's direction, 'mon ami Savi.'

Savi was surprised that the Bos should refer to him as his friend in front of Missus Tack. The Bos never called him 'friend' in the presence of Europeans. He did so quite often in front of the villagers, though, and Savi knew why, he'd worked it out a long time ago. At first he'd thought the Bos was giving him face and it had pleased him. But then he'd realised that the Bos wasn't paying him respect or being friendly at all. The Bos wanted his workers to fear Savi, to be afraid that Savi might report them to his 'good friend' if they didn't work hard. It was not necessary and Savi didn't like it, but he always smiled when the Bos called him 'mon ami'. No-one could afford to offend the Bos. They needed the Bos, not only he and his family, but the people of his village.

He smiled now, but the Bos was no longer looking at him, he was looking at Missus Tack.

'I will drive you to your home,' he said to Jane. 'It will be far quicker and far more comfortable, and Savi will follow in the buggy in his own good time.'

'No really, I couldn't possibly put you to so much trouble.' Jane cursed the fact that her heart seemed to be pumping at twice its normal rate. It was merely the shock of the Landrover's appearance, she told herself.

'It is no trouble at all, I assure you, Madame Thackeray, any gentleman would do as much, allow me.'

And she was compelled to accept his outstretched hand as he assisted her from the buggy. He held on to it for just a fraction too long, or so it seemed to Jane.

He barked an order to Savi in French and opened the Landrover door for her, taking her elbow as she climbed into the passenger seat, quite unnecessarily, she thought. Then he backed the Landrover around the bend to a clearing where there was sufficient space to turn and they were off at a healthy speed, despite the rough track, Savi and the horse and buggy already out of sight.

Marat made no enquiry as to why she was on his

property, which surprised her, she'd expected him to. Instead, his conversation was relaxed and casual.

He'd had this track purpose-built for his work drays, he said, but it was useless for motor transport other than four wheel drive vehicles. He intended to build a proper road one day so that he could use trucks for the copra transportation, so much speedier.

'The roads on Efate are non-existent. One of the prices one pays for a Condominium government,' he smiled, 'the French and the English can never agree upon anything.'

'Oh yes,' Jane said, 'the one consistency in the Condominium is its state of continual disagreement.' Her mild panic had been overreactive, she'd decided. Much as she disapproved of the way Marat conducted his business, there was nothing to fear personally, the man was no threat to her. And, for the next ten minutes, they chatted convivially about the more ludicrous aspects of the joint colonial government.

'I must admit,' she said finally in the silence that followed, 'this is a far more comfortable mode of travel, I do appreciate your trouble.'

'Had I known you were contemplating a visit to Undine Bay I would have insisted upon driving you,' he said. 'I am appalled to think that you made that long trip in a horse and buggy.'

He sounded neither critical nor accusatory, but Jane realised it was time she offered an explanation. Had his preamble been designed for that purpose, to place the onus upon her? Once again her guard was up. She must tread carefully, she thought.

'I wish to continue my husband's work in his absence,' she said, 'and I have taken it upon myself to visit various remote villages and offer my medical services.' As she said it, she realised it wasn't a lie. It was her intention to do exactly that.

'On your own? Unaccompanied?'

She glanced at him expecting to see scepticism, but was met with admiration.

'If I feel I will be welcomed, yes,' she answered. 'Of course it is advisable to have a contact, the villagers are unaccustomed to a European woman travelling on her own.'

'And who was your contact at Undine Bay?'

There was no interrogative edge to his voice, he appeared merely interested, but Jane knew she was walking on thin ice.

'In a roundabout way, my housemaid Mary,' she said, 'surprisingly enough,' and she was astounded at the ease of her response. It was after all, the truth. 'She is a very close friend of Sera Poilama, they come from the same village.'

'Ah yes?'

Here was the tricky part. 'Mary had heard that Sera's little boy was not well, and I decided I would pay him a visit.'

'How very kind of you,' Marat said. How had the housemaid heard? he thought. Who had told her? Who was talking behind his back?

'Little Pascal was extremely ill, I discovered.'

He seemed surprised. Surely it was a performance, she thought. He had been told of the child's illness. Jane started to feel insecure; was the man playing games with her? But she had no intention of backing down now. Jean-François Marat should know of the dire consequences that could have resulted from his own inaction. She steeled herself.

'I feared, from the child's symptoms, that the illness might be contagious and that, if it was, it could result in an outbreak amongst the village children, perhaps even a localised epidemic. So Savi very kindly offered to take me to the village in order to examine the children. Upon my request,' she hastily added, realising, as she did, that it was the only outright lie she had yet told the man.

'I am most indebted to you, Madame Thackeray.' As he

had listened to her, Jean-François had slowed the vehicle to half the speed they'd originally been travelling in order to give her his full attention. 'And how is little Pascal now?' he asked.

'He will recover.' Jane was bewildered. The man's concern seemed genuine.

'And the children of the village?'

'Healthy. I found no symptoms of the disease, thankfully enough.'

'I am most relieved to hear it,' he said. 'How shockingly remiss of me.' In response to her querying glance, he added, 'You see, I was told that the child was not well.' Behind his facade of guilty concern, he watched her keenly; did she know he'd been told?

'Really?' Jane feigned surprise. 'You were told?'

Oh yes, she knew all right, Jean-François thought. Jane Thackeray was intelligent and had spirit, both of which made her more desirable than ever, but she wasn't a particularly good actress. He could read her like a book. But then he found most women eminently readable, which made them so easy to manipulate. It all came down to sex, and Jane Thackeray was no different. He had known from the moment he'd first met her that she was a woman as yet unawakened and ripe for the picking, although she herself was unaware of it. And the fact had been confirmed when he'd met the good doctor: he could sense no passion between them. He must be wary of deliberately communicating his desire, however; it frightened her. Pity. Many women responded quite differently to the knowledge they were desirable. But it had been a misjudgement in this case. He must try a different tack.

'Oh yes,' he said. 'Sera herself told me that her son was not well.' Obviously it had been Sera who had summoned Jane Thackeray's assistance, he thought, but he would take no action. He was grateful to Sera, she had handed Jane Thackeray to him on a platter. 'I visited the boy of course, but to my shame,' he shrugged regrettably, 'I thought that the mother was overreacting. Even the boy's own father, my good friend Savi, didn't seem to believe it was too serious.' Well, of course that's what Savi believed, Jean-François thought. Savi believed everything the Bos told him.

Jane registered a ring of truth as she remembered Sera's words of the previous morning. Her husband thought the sickness would pass, Sera had said. But she was a mother, and something in her blood told her that her son was in danger.

'I take full responsibility, however,' Jean-François continued, 'I should have sought medical advice.' And he certainly should have, he now realised, it was a lesson learned. It hadn't occurred to him that the boy's illness could be contagious. Good God, if the village children had become ill, his workers would have been severely affected. 'I will know better next time,' he said in all honesty. 'Meanwhile, Madame Thackeray, you have my sincerest thanks.'

Jane was flummoxed. The man's remorse was evident and she was left with nothing to say.

'You will be visiting Pascal again, I trust?' Marat enquired.

'Yes,' she said. 'I promised Sera I would return in a week.'

'Then of course you will allow me to drive you there and back. I insist,' he said when she hesitated, 'it is the least I can do.'

'Thank you, M'sieur Marat, that would be most kind.'

It was dusk when Mary, who had been anxiously awaiting the return of her mistress, heard the approaching Land-rover. She opened the door of the cottage and stood frozen to the spot at the sight of Marat. She had had no dealings with the Frenchman, but she knew who he was. Everyone knew Masta Marat.

Jean-François escorted Jane to the front door. 'You must be Mary,' he said without waiting for an introduction.

'Say hello to M'sieur Marat, Mary,' Jane prompted gently as the young woman remained, immobile and dumbstruck, on the doorstep.

''Ow do you do,' Mary murmured in her very best English, eyes downcast, staring at her feet.

'I believe it was you who informed Madame Thackeray of Pascal Poilama's illness,' Jean-François said.

Mary was terrified. She looked at the Missus. Why had the Missus told the Masta that? But the Missus was signalling her with her eyes. The Missus wanted her to say yes. So she nodded.

'You did the right thing, Mary,' Jean-François smiled. 'You have been a good friend to Sera, and you have helped to make her little boy better. I am obliged to you.' He was obliged to them both, he thought. Sera and Mary had done him a great favour.

Mary breathed an audible sigh of relief. 'Missus make everyone better,' she said proudly. 'Missus very good doctor.'

'Yes, yes.' Enough chat with the housemaid, he thought, and he gave her a brisk nod.

Recognising the Masta's dismissal, Mary obediently retired inside, but she left the door open in case the Missus should require her.

Jean-François and Jane agreed upon the day of her visit the following week and he promised that he would pick her up at nine in the morning.

'Would you like some tea?' she asked. 'Or something to eat before your journey home? It will be dark before you reach Chanson de Mer.'

He liked the familiarity with which she said 'Chanson de Mer'. So she remembered the name of his house, it was a promising sign.

'I would not dream of imposing,' he replied, 'you must be exhausted. I suggest you retire as soon as possible.'

'It is no imposition, I assure you.' She was rather hoping he would refuse, she didn't wish to entertain him. Marat no longer frightened her, but she was still not entirely comfortable in his presence, and she was indeed exhausted. She felt obliged to make the offer, however. 'In any event I cannot retire until Savi arrives, I must return the horse and buggy to Reverend Smeed.'

But Jean-François had it all planned. 'I shall dine at Reid's,' he said, 'and wait for Savi there. He will need to drive right past the hotel and I will be watching out for him. We will return the horse and buggy and then I shall drive Savi home.'

'I couldn't possibly allow you to . . .'

'Of course you could *allow* me, Madame Thackeray, and you must. You must allow me to repay at least a little of the debt I owe you.' The Frenchman's tone was authoritative and final, and Jane, suddenly overwhelmed with fatigue, longed to accept his offer. The thought of waiting for Savi for the next two hours and then returning the horse and buggy to Reverend Smeed, who would no doubt demand a full explanation as to the lateness of her return, was more than she could bear.

'But Reverend Smeed will be expecting me,' she protested weakly.

'I shall visit the Reverend immediately and inform him of our arrangements.' He could see that she'd already given in. She was grateful for his concern. Excellent. He was winning her trust. 'Mr Smeed must surely have been worried about your travelling unaccompanied,' he said, 'and he will become even more so as night approaches.'

'I'd be obliged if you neglected to mention my travelling alone,' she said. 'Reverend Smeed believes that Mary was with me.' She felt herself flush as the Frenchman raised an eyebrow. 'I didn't lie,' she assured him, 'it was merely his presumption.'

'Then of course I shall say nothing,' Jean-François

promised, 'apart from singing your praises for the deed you have done me.' He studied her closely. Did Smeed know that she had visited his workers?

Again Jane flushed. 'I saw no reason to alarm the Reverend before I had made my examinations,' she said. 'He knows only that I was visiting a sick child.'

So she was capable of deception, most interesting, Jean-François thought. 'How wise,' he replied, 'one would always wish to avoid unnecessary panic.' Smeed knew nothing, that was good. And how lovely she looked when she flushed. He smiled thoughtfully at her for a moment, and Jane started to feel self-conscious.

'Most women are content to be housewives, Madame,' he said finally. 'You are obviously not one of them.'

Jane saw in the dark eyes that were studying her so astutely something which, at first, she took to be mockery. Then she realised it was approval.

'No, M'sieur, I am not.'

'You are a most admirable woman.' He held out his hand and she took it. 'And now I must bid you good night.' This time, as he kissed her hand, Jane found nothing intimidating in the gesture. She blamed her own ignorance and unfamiliarity with the French custom. How foolish of her to have been unnerved, she thought, and how unfair of her to have judged the Frenchman for a simple common courtesy.

'Thank you for driving me home, M'sieur.'

'Bon nuit, Madame Thackeray.'

He had sensed her relax as he'd kissed her hand. It was always the same with Englishwomen, he thought as he walked to the Landrover. They were unaccustomed to physical contact because of their men; Englishmen were so cold and aloof. But once an Englishwoman relaxed, she found she enjoyed being touched. A masculine hand to the elbow. A manly arm about the waist. Brief, tasteful, and always in the guise of courteous assistance.

He climbed into the car and started the engine. English-women were so susceptible once they relaxed, he thought. That's what made them putty in his hands.

She was standing on the front doorstep and she waved him farewell as he slowly drove off. She looked magnificent, he thought. Even more so than the day he'd first met her. Her fair hair framed a face now tanned by the sun and her slim body was fit and youthful. Everything about Jane Thackeray was vital and alive. Everything except her sexuality, he thought, and the prospect of awakening her filled him with the utmost excitement. He was tired of black velvet, Selena bored him now, she was too easy, as was the French trader's wife he bedded from time to time. He'd been missing the thrill of the chase, he realised. To conquer Jane Thackeray would be the ultimate triumph.

He waved through the open car window. 'Nine o'clock,' he called, and he watched in the rear vision mirror as she closed the front door behind her. It would take time of course, she was an intelligent woman who could not be rushed, but the prize would be worth the wait.

'Missus Tack!' Pascal was excited to see Jane. She was his friend. None of his cousins in the village had a white missus for a friend.

Upon examination, Jane found the boy's condition remarkably improved. He was still tired and weak, but the photophobia had gone completely and he was feeling no pain. He was eating now, Sera told her. He was enjoying his food, she said, and he was taking an interest in things. So much so that they had had to shift his bedding into the front room by the doorway, so that he could watch what was going on outside, and so that he could play with Marie who would toddle about, making him laugh when she fell over.

Marat had left Jane at the Poilamas' hut, telling her that he would return when she had completed her examination of the child.

'I do not intrude upon their privacy,' he'd said as they'd turned off the coast track and into the main drive to Chanson de Mer. 'It would not be right for the master to come into their home. They report to the big house for work each day. It's the way it should be.'

Jane agreed, but was surprised by the man's tact, it didn't seem in keeping with the lack of care he displayed to his workers. She was cautious as she broached the subject of Savi's English lesson, however, realising that the offer she'd made with such largesse had been a rather thoughtless one. Savi was Marat's foreman, he could hardly take a morning off at his leisure. Moreover, why would the Frenchman be interested in his number one worker learning English? He might even be opposed to the idea.

'It was a little foolish of me to make such a promise,' she admitted.

'Not at all, it was most generous of you. I see no problem in Savi having an hour or so away from his work.' Jean-François was quite happy to foster Jane's relationship with the Poilama family. The more often she visited them the better, he thought as he drove across the open scrubland towards the hut. 'Savi has an enquiring mind which I believe should be encouraged.'

When they'd pulled up, he got out of the car and walked around to the passenger side. 'I shall send him to you,' he said, opening the door and taking her hand as she alighted, 'and I shall return to collect you at one o'clock.'

The woman's offer to teach Savi had certainly been presumptuous, he thought whilst he drove back to the house, but the more Jane Thackeray interfered in his personal affairs, the more she was playing into his hands. Besides, it would do no real harm for Savi to learn English. It was, after all, the man's enquiring mind that made him such an invaluable worker. Savi was as skilled in the plantation's management as any white overseer would be.

But at heart he was the same as the rest of the blacks, Jean-François thought. Simple and easy to control. They all were. Even the smart ones. In fact, the smart ones were the easiest of the lot. The smart ones were prone to corruption. Savi's cousin, Pako Kalsaunaka, of whom he was so proud, was a prime example. Pako was firmly in Jean-François's pocket and the Frenchman encouraged the cousins' friendship – it was a valid excuse for the Sergeant's regular visits to the plantation. Jean-François had plans for Pako. Through his connections with the French authorities, he would see to it that the young man rose to power in the police force. The Condominium could not last forever; one day the New Hebrides would claim its independence, and when it did, Pako Kalsaunaka would be an obvious candidate for a prime position in the new government's hierarchy. He would also be Jean-François Marat's personal ally.

But, easy as the Melanesians were to manipulate, he thought, they were lazy labourers. He would have preferred to employ Chinese or Tonkinese. Hard workers, the Asians. But Asians were also canny, you couldn't trust them. They learned quickly and before you knew it they were setting up their own businesses. In Jean-François's opinion, the blackbirders had had the right idea. Round up the islanders' young bucks and put them to work. It was a simple fact that men worked harder and stole less when they were separated from the distractions of family and village life.

Alas, blackbirding was no longer legal, but he had an ace up his sleeve with Savi. Jean-François's villagers worked hard by Melanesian standards, and they did so because of Savi. Theft was at a minimum too; the villagers would not steal from their good friend Savi.

Savinata Poilama was worth his weight in gold and Jean-François knew it. Which was why he'd done his best to keep his hands off the man's wife. By God there was a beauty, he thought. He'd lusted after Sera from the moment he'd first laid eyes on her, and he still did. Now more than ever, her grace and bearing and sheer unavailability drove him mad with desire. But he'd had to satisfy himself with the sister instead, Savi was far too valuable to lose.

Selena had proved a satisfying distraction. A highly sexual creature – as most of them were, Jean-François had found – she was good-looking and her body was luscious. But several years down the track she now irritated him. Slothful and lazy, except in bed, Selena obviously believed that servicing the Masta was enough to keep her employed. It wasn't, and Jean-François would certainly have replaced her with another sexually compliant housemaid if it were not for the fact that she was Savi's sister-in-law. She also served as a convenient babysitter for Sera, who was an excellent worker. The Poilama household must be kept smoothly run and intact, he had decided.

Given his current state of dissatisfaction, the fresh challenge which had presented itself in the form of Jane Thackeray was most timely, he thought, as he pulled the Landrover up outside Chanson de Mer.

Sera had waited for the Landrover to drive away before going outside to greet Jane, having no wish to feel the Masta's lust here on her own home ground. She watched fondly as the Missus examined her son, Pascal enjoying the attention and chatting animatedly to his best friend Missus Tack.

Every day at the big house Sera was aware of the Masta's desire, and she avoided physical contact whenever she could, although he was forever inventing reasons to touch her. He'd ask her to fetch something for him and stroke her hand as she gave it to him, or he'd admire a dress she wore and caress her shoulder as he did so.

She never told Savi that the Masta touched her. Even that time two years ago when the Masta had been drunk and had tried to force himself upon her, she hadn't told Savi.

She'd fought the Masta like a tigress when he'd tried to rape her. She'd bitten him and torn at him with her nails until he'd given up. He'd called her a black slut and told her to send her sister to him. The next day he'd pretended that nothing had happened. Or else he'd been so drunk that he didn't remember.

Sera couldn't understand how Selena could bear the Masta touching her. But Selena liked sleeping with him, the Masta was very good in bed, she boasted. Very sexy. So Sera kept her disapproval to herself. She presumed her husband knew that Selena was sleeping with the Bos, but then Savi believed in people minding their own business and, just as she had never mentioned the Masta's attack upon her, so the two of them had never discussed Selena's relationship with the Bos. Nothing was worth risking Savi's job and the security and comfort they had all come to depend upon.

Jane had finished her examination now and was playing an 'I spy' game with Pascal. The Missus spoke Bislama like a local, Sera thought. Most white women knew only enough Bislama to issue orders to their servants. How lucky they were to have found such a friend as Missus Tack.

'Missus Tack!' Savi had arrived. As eager and excited to see Jane as Pascal had been. It was time for his English lesson and he couldn't wait.

Sera insisted upon showing Savi the fish and yam meal she had made with coconut milk for Missus Tack's lunch. He didn't need to light a fire, she told him, it was good to eat cold, but Savi was paying scant attention, he was too keen to get started on his lesson. Then, leaving the children in their care, Sera walked up to the big house to help Selena.

Sera would have liked, very much, to stay for the lesson.

Like Savi, she longed to learn English. But it was washday
and she was worried that Selena would be slovenly in her
work. When the Masta was away, as he often was, Sera
would take the children with her to the big house whilst
she worked. More and more, lately, she didn't trust Selena,
and washday was the most important day of the week. If
the Masta's clothes were not scrubbed spotlessly clean, if
they were not hung to dry properly, if they were not impeccably ironed, he would get very, very angry. And she'd had
to teach Selena about the money he occasionally left in a
pocket. The Masta had put it there deliberately as a test of
their honesty, she'd told her sister right from the start, but
Selena hadn't listened and one day she'd stolen five francs.
Sure enough, the Masta had confronted her, and Selena
had said that she hadn't seen the money, it must have fallen
out of the pocket. Then she'd pretended to find it behind
the washtub. But the Masta had beaten her anyway; he
hadn't believed her. And when Selena had told Savi she'd
been beaten, Savi had said that it served her right for
stealing. Sera loved her younger sister, but Selena could be
very stupid sometimes, and stupidity was dangerous.

Savi, aware of his wife's disappointment in missing out
on the lesson, promised her, as she left, that he would
teach her what he had learned that day. 'I *teach*,' he said,
'you *learn*.' Then he looked to Jane for confirmation. 'Is
right?'

'Yes, quite right, Savi,' she said. 'Very good.' And she
promised Sera that she would come back again, with
M'sieur Marat's permission of course, and they would
have another lesson just for her.

Savi proved an exhausting but rewarding pupil, not only
relentless in his own desire to learn, but eager for his son
to be given the same opportunity.

For the first ten minutes, they sat on the floor in the
front room near the little boy's bed, Marie toddling about
beside them, and Jane was pleased to note Pascal's genuine

interest. Like father, like son, she thought. The child listened attentively as she translated the meaning of a word from Bislama into English.

'I come, you come, we come, they come,' she recited and he repeated the words.

It wasn't long before he tired of the game, however, and as he drifted off to sleep, she and Savi moved to the table where the lesson started in earnest until, an hour and a half later, a shrill little voice sounded out from the open doorway.

'Bos come!' Pascal called, now wide awake, as he watched the Landrover drive away from the big house.

Jane was surprised by the boy's retention. Perhaps he was simply imitating his father, she thought, but then she'd noticed that Savi did not speak English to his wife and son. It was no coincidence, she decided. The four-year-old had understood and retained the word in just one ten-minute lesson. She was very impressed.

Savi was neither surprised, nor impressed. Savi was alarmed. He'd suddenly remembered Missus Tack's lunch.

'Missus Tack no eat,' he said. 'Sera much angry.'

'Sera *very* angry,' she corrected.

'Yes, Sera *very* angry. Eat, eat. Quick, quick,' he said, thrusting the bowl and a wooden spoon at her.

Jane laughed – it was obvious that Sera ruled the roost in the home – and she dug into the cold stew with relish, discovering that she was famished.

She managed about half a dozen mouthfuls before the Landrover pulled up beside the hut and the Frenchman got out.

'Thank you, Savi,' she said, hastily swallowing the final mouthful. 'Tell Sera it was delicious.'

'Dee-lish-us.' Savi grinned, happy that she'd liked the food, but happier still that he'd learned another word.

Jane knelt to say goodbye to the children. The toddler tottered about, waving her brown, chubby arms in the air, and Pascal hugged Missus Tack as hard as he could.

When Savi accompanied her outside, Marat told him that Selena would shortly return to look after the children and that Savi was to get back to work as soon as she did. But the Bos said it in French and Savi recognised a warning in the way that he said it. Savi was not to practise his English in the Bos's presence, he realised. He would not have done so in any event, since the Bos never encouraged him to speak English. Savi had been most surprised when the Bos himself had told him to report for his lesson; he had presumed that Missus Tack would teach him in secret.

'Oui, Bos,' he said, and he waved goodbye to Missus Tack as the Landrover turned right and set off across the rough open ground towards the big house.

They were going in the wrong direction, Jane thought.

'You'll have some refreshment before the journey home, I trust?'

For some strange reason her mild sense of panic returned. Perhaps it was simply because she hadn't been prepared for the invitation, which was a perfectly natural one, but she didn't want to be alone with the Frenchman in his house.

'It's very kind of you, M'sieur, but if you don't mind, I'd prefer to get back to my little boy. I'm not normally away from him for such a long period of time.'

She'd been away from the child for a whole day, Jean-François thought, and she'd been prepared to be away from him well into the night too, when she'd come out in the horse and buggy.

'But you must be starving,' he said, 'I insist you take lunch.'

Thank goodness for Sera, Jane thought. 'I have already taken lunch,' she replied. 'Sera had prepared a cold dish of fish and yams for me.'

Most annoying, he thought. He hadn't taken Sera's hospitality into consideration. Next time he would tell her that the Missus was to dine at the big house.

'How extremely unpalatable,' he said.

'To the contrary, it was delicious.'

'I'm sure it was,' he acceded with good grace. 'Sera is an excellent cook, although I prefer her French cuisine myself. Cold fish and yams,' he remarked as he turned left into the main drive and made for the coast road, 'I fear, Madame Thackeray, that you are becoming quite native.'

He said it jokingly, and she laughed in reply, once again cursing herself for her overreaction. 'I do believe I am,' she said. 'My husband calls me "a true islander".'

Jane wondered what the sophisticated Frenchman would think if he could see her squatting with the village women, her son in a carrying sack slung around her neck, as she had done so often on her trips with Martin. She relished the image, and missed Martin more than ever.

Up ahead, a group of villagers, women and children, were wandering along the track. On their heads, the women carried palm leaves tied in bundles and, recognising Jane as the vehicle passed them by, they smiled and waved, and the children yelled 'Missus Tack! Missus Tack!' at the tops of their voices.

'Your newfound friends,' Jean-François said, 'you appear very popular, I'm impressed.'

She doubted the sincerity of his remark, but she smiled at him anyway. He was right, she thought as she waved through the open car window. The children of Efate were indeed her friends. Wherever she went, their exuberance and the uninhibited affection they displayed towards her filled Jane with a sense of love and purpose.

The drive back to Vila was most enjoyable. It was the first day in May and the weather was perfect. 'Hot, but not too hot,' as Jean-François said, 'and a gentle breeze from the sea. Efate is beautiful this time of the year.'

The Pacific Ocean was glorious in its tranquillity, and as they passed sandy coves where coconut trees leaned over white beaches and waves rippled across coral reefs, Jane marvelled at the beauty, realising with a sense of surprise how little she thought of England these days. She missed her father and the Christmas reunions with her brothers, and most of all she missed Phoebe. But she didn't miss England. Efate was her home, she thought. She belonged here.

'You have a special feeling for this place,' Jean-François said; he had been watching her.

'Yes, I do.'

'And for its people, I think.'

'Very much so. I wish I could do more to help them.'

'In what way?'

He appeared most interested, and Jane felt suddenly bold. She would tell him exactly what she thought, she decided.

'I believe they should be remunerated for their labour,' she said. 'And I believe that their conditions should be improved and education made available to them.' There. She'd made her statement. Plain and simple. She waited for him to disagree.

'Remunerated?' He seemed amused by the idea. 'You mean they should be paid a weekly wage for their services?'

'Well, not exactly, not necessarily weekly.' Jane was disconcerted. His smile was not sardonic, rather it was indulgent, as if he were talking to a child. 'But yes,' she emphasised firmly, 'they should be paid. They should be financially remunerated.'

'And what would they do with the money?' The question was rhetorical, he didn't wait for her reply. 'They have no need of money, they live by a barter system, money would confuse them. They principally value live-stock and they are well rewarded for their labours with chickens, sometimes pigs, which they value most highly of all, and the village receives a bullock a month. They are more than happy with the arrangement, I assure you.'

Jane felt like an ignorant schoolgirl being taught a lesson

as he progressed smoothly to the next point she'd raised, neither irritated nor insulted, his intention simply to inform her.

'As to their conditions, they live as they wish. If I were to provide special dwellings or modern conveniences, I would be altering the very fabric of their existence. Who am I to interfere with their culture and their way of life?'

There was little she could refute in anything he'd said, and she was starting to feel rather naive.

'The same principle applies to education,' he continued. 'Which is, after all,' he reminded her, 'the government's responsibility, not mine.'

She sensed a gentle reprimand, and she had to acknowledge that he was right. 'Yes,' she said, 'the responsibility of education does indeed rest with the Condominium, and I feel they are sadly lacking in their efforts. Both the French and the English.'

Jean-François decided to keep his personal views on the islanders' education to himself. He firmly believed that the blacks should be kept in their ignorant state, except for those chosen few who could be relied upon to do the white man's bidding.

'Mind you,' he pointed out, 'education, too, can intrude upon their way of life. It can court confusion and disruption.'

'But one cannot halt progress,' Jane argued. 'Their lives have already been intruded upon, they have been introduced to the white man's ways.'

He nodded his acknowledgement, as if she'd scored a point. He was very much enjoying the conversation, it was always enjoyable to converse with an intelligent and desirable young woman, and the obvious fact that he was impressing Jane Thackeray was making the experience doubly pleasurable.

Jane couldn't understand how he could acknowledge her comment without agreeing with her argument. 'Then surely it follows that they should be offered the opportunity of improvement,' she said emphatically. 'That is, of course, if they wish it. They should at least have the choice. My husband and I are strongly of this opinion.'

At the mention of Martin Thackeray, Jean-François felt a surge of irritation. Of course the insipid Englishman would believe in educating the blacks. What would such a man know of the real world?

He stifled the retort that sprang to his lips and said very mildly instead, 'Your husband is a man of the cloth, Madame Thackeray. Dedicated as he is to the spiritual wellbeing of these people, he is perhaps at times unaware of the more practical aspects of their daily lives.'

Jane looked sharply at the Frenchman, sensing a slur upon Martin's masculinity in his words, but he was smiling respectfully. Nevertheless, she felt the need to retaliate.

'My husband is also a doctor of medicine, M'sieur Marat,' she said stiffly. 'He is an eminently practical man.'

'Of course, of course.' He'd offended her, how stupid of him. 'I meant no disrespect, I assure you. I deeply admire the doctor's work, as does everyone on the island. My sincere apologies if I've caused any offence, it was certainly unintentional.'

'The apology is mine, M'sieur.' Jane regretted her sharp reply; the man had clearly meant no harm. 'I was perhaps being a little overprotective of my husband.'

'As every good wife should be,' he said, 'most admirable.'

They shared a smile and Jean-François thanked his lucky stars he'd got out of that one. No more cheap jibes cloaked in sincerity, he told himself. The woman was not a fool, and he couldn't risk undermining her newfound trust in him.

He asked her about her little boy, and she said his name was Ronnie. He was fourteen months old now, she said. Very talkative, and starting to walk, which made him quite a handful.

'The next time you visit us, you must bring Ronnie with you,' he suggested, and the idea pleased Jane.

'I would like that very much,' she said. 'He and little Marie Poilama are nearly the same age, it would do them good to play together.'

'Excellent.'

He missed his own son, he said, deciding that it was the opportune moment to share a sense of parenthood.

Jane had heard that Marat's wife had left him a few years previously and that she'd taken their son with her. Gossip was rife in Vila and it was common knowledge.

'Simone never really adjusted to the tropics,' he said. 'Even after ten years she found the heat unbearable. It was perhaps wrong of me to have inflicted such a life upon her. But like you, Madame, I fell in love with the New Hebrides from the outset.'

And he'd fallen in love with its women, he thought. It had been his lust for black velvet that Simone had found unbearable, the stupid bitch. Not once in the ten years they'd been here had he cheated on her with a white woman. But she hadn't been able to get it through her head that sleeping with the blacks was par for the course. Everyone did it, it didn't count as infidelity. Good God, he'd had endless affairs in Paris during the previous five years of their marriage, not that she'd known of course, but she should have been thankful his newly discovered lust for black women kept him faithful.

'Our son, Michel, was thirteen when she returned to Europe,' Jean-François said, 'and I agreed that the boy should go with her to complete his education. War had just broken out and it was too risky to return to Paris, so she now lives in Lucerne, and Michel attends boarding school. It was all for the best really, his education is of sole importance, and Swiss schools are amongst the finest, in my opinion.'

By now they were travelling beside Mele Bay and he

looked wistfully out at the little island, so picturesque in the calm waters. 'But I miss him very, very much.'

And he did, he thought, realising that his conversation had become more than a ploy. He was enjoying unburdening himself to Jane Thackeray, he hadn't spoken to anyone like this in years. Certainly he'd been glad to see the back of Simone, she'd become tiresome in her discontent, but he had enjoyed having a son, particularly as the boy had grown older. He'd been a hero to Michel.

'He didn't want to leave,' he said, 'but what sort of education is there in Vila for a boy on the verge of manhood?' There was a touch of irony in his smile as he added, 'Even for the *white* population, Madame.'

Jane said nothing. There was nothing she could say, she thought, surprised by the intimate turn of the man's conversation.

'I wanted my son schooled in Europe. Just as I want him to return and claim the inheritance I have built for him.'

Jean-François wasn't lying. The day before the boy had left, the two of them had ridden on horseback into the heart of the plantation at dawn. 'This will be yours, Michel,' he'd promised, 'one day you will be the wealthiest man in the New Hebrides.' He'd felt very proud that morning. Both of himself and his achievements and of the son he'd sired to inherit it all.

'Barely a day passes when I do not think of my son,' Jean-François said, 'and wish that he was with me.' Which wasn't exactly true. He did think of Michel a great deal, but he certainly didn't want the responsibility of parenting. It was far more convenient for the boy to remain in Switzerland until he reached maturity.

Jane was bewildered. Why had Marat chosen her as a confidant? It was as if he'd been longing to talk about his life and had finally found a person in whom he could place his trust. But why her? She'd nonetheless found herself feeling sympathetic to the Frenchman as she'd listened.

'He's growing into a fine young man,' Jean-François said. 'He is nearly seventeen now, next year he will be attending university in Zurich.'

'You must be very proud of him.'

'I am. Most proud indeed.'

They had reached Vila and, as they drove along the main street, he enquired when she might next wish to visit the Poilama family. He would naturally drive her there and back.

She accepted the offer; she had promised another English lesson, she said, which she hoped might include Sera.

The woman's presumption was extraordinary, Jean-François thought. Did she intend to set up a school for his servants, and did she expect them to be at liberty to attend whenever they wished?

'How considerate,' he said. 'I know that Sera will be most appreciative.'

They made an arrangement for two days later and he insisted that, as Ronnie would be with her, the two of them were to take luncheon with him at Chanson de Mer.

Jane laughed at the thought of Ronnie 'taking luncheon'. 'We'd be delighted,' she said.

He helped her from the Landrover and, a protective hand at her elbow, escorted her to the front door of the cottage.

'I have very much enjoyed our conversation,' he said.

'I too, M'sieur.'

'The day after tomorrow, at nine o'clock.' He kissed her hand. 'I look forward to your company. And of course, to Ronnie's.' He smiled.

'Thank you so much, M'sieur Marat.'

'Perhaps, given the fact that we are to become regular travelling companions, we might dispense a little with the formality,' he laughingly suggested. 'Why don't you call me Jean-François?'

He was still holding her hand and Jane suddenly recalled the night at Reid's Hotel when she'd first met him. How she'd felt like some form of prey as he'd studied her. And Godfrey's words that the man was not to be trusted. Did she have cause to fear him? But his smile was engaging, his laugh humorous, and the idea seemed ludicrously melodramatic.

'Of course,' she said. But she withdrew her hand.

He would have preferred her to have returned the compliment. She should have said, 'and you must call me Jane', but as she didn't, he decided to expedite proceedings.

'Au revoir, Jane.'

'Au revoir.' She couldn't quite bring herself to say 'Jean-François'. She didn't know why, and she felt rather foolish, but somehow it didn't seem right.

Jean-François smiled to himself as he left. He knew exactly why she was reluctant to embrace any form of familiarity. She was sexually attracted to him but couldn't admit it, even to herself. She would find out soon enough. But he would take his time. He would become her friend first and foremost, until she herself became aware that she wanted far more from him. He'd have her begging, he thought.

During the drive out to Undine Bay, any possible misgivings Jane might have had two days previously were forgotten. Ronnie was wriggling uncontrollably on her knees, excited with a sense of adventure, and Jane found herself looking forward to the afternoon.

Following her English lesson with the Poilama family, Jean-François collected her and Ronnie from the hut.

'It's extremely generous of you, M'sieur Marat,' she said, 'to allow both Savi and Sera time free from their work.'

It certainly was, he thought. 'Nonsense, I'm pleased that they have been granted such an opportunity to learn. And it's Jean-François, don't forget,' he prompted with a smile. 'Did the children get along?' he asked, looking at Ronnie who was chattering away excitedly.

'Oh yes, he and Marie became great friends, but she's thoroughly exhausted him. She's further advanced in the toddler stage, and he kept falling over trying to keep up with her. He'll sleep like a log this afternoon.'

How convenient that will be in the future, Jean-François thought.

'Allo, Missus Tack.' Selena greeted Jane at the front door of the big house, taking Ronnie from her and making a fuss of the child. She was pleased to be serving lunch for Missus Tack and her baby; Sera usually waited table when the Masta entertained. Selena had even made a special dish of mashed banana and papaya for Ronnie, just the way baby Marie liked it.

The interior of the house was simple but elegant, designed for life in the tropics. A huge, timber-floored living space was surrounded by shuttered windows, which remained open to the verandah on hot, still days, and locked firmly shut when the monsoons threatened. To the right was a solid, twelve-seat dining table, to the left a miscellany of sofas and lounge chairs in rattan and bamboo, and two ceiling fans whirred continuously from the exposed beams overhead.

The bedrooms and bathroom were through to the rear of the house, Jean-François said, and he sat on a rattan sofa bouncing Ronnie on his knee whilst Jane visited the bathroom.

'What an extremely amiable child,' he said when she returned, and he continued to play with the baby whilst Selena served luncheon, Ronnie chortling away all the while.

Jane was touched to discover that Selena had prepared a special dish for the baby.

'But of course,' Jean-François said, as if he'd personally

instructed it. For once Selena had done something right, he thought.

'It was hardly necessary, Jean-François,' she laughed, 'I did bring my own supply of baby food.' The name sprang quite easily to her lips as she watched him dandling her son on his knee. Indeed 'M'sieur Marat' would have sounded quite ridiculous under the circumstances.

'I wouldn't hear of it, I invited you *both* to luncheon, if you recall.'

The food was simple but delicious, thinly sliced rare roast beef and a salad with an exotic lime juice dressing.

'In the heat of the day,' he said, 'I presumed that you would prefer something light. And the beef is home-grown,' he boasted. 'We rear prime cattle on the plantation.'

Jane congratulated Selena on the meal, but Jean-François corrected her. 'Selena doesn't cook,' he said. 'Sera prepared the meat last night and the dressing is of her own invention.'

Selena left the room scowling. It had been she who had prepared the meal. She had taken great pains to slice the meat thinly, and she had made the salad herself. Why did Sera always get the credit?

For Jane, the luncheon at Chanson de Mer proved a most pleasurable experience, and the drive home equally relaxing. She said as much to Jean-François as he bade her farewell at the front door of her cottage, the Frenchman having refused the offer of a cup of tea.

'Thank you, Jean-François, it has been a lovely day.'

He noticed no reticence as she said his name.

'Perhaps we should make it a weekly event,' he suggested. 'I wouldn't want Savi and Sera to miss out on their lessons.' In the slight hesitation that followed, he gestured to the child fast asleep in her arms. 'Besides, Ronnie and Marie have obviously embarked upon a lifetime friendship.'

She laughed and agreed to the same time next week, and

he wondered, during the drive home to Chanson de Mer, whether he might accomplish the seduction before her husband returned. Not that it really mattered, Martin Thackeray's work would always require his absence. But it was an interesting possibility to contemplate.

Jean-François's pursuit of Jane Thackeray was rudely interrupted, however, when the very next day Vila was reduced to a state of utter confusion.

They arrived unannounced, in the dawn light of 4 May, and the local population awoke in terror at the sight. The vast, peaceful waters of Mele Bay were massed with warships.

Many islanders fled to the hills in fear. The Japanese had secretly invaded and were about to attack, they thought, and it took some time to convince them otherwise.

Of the five huge warships, surrounded by scores of naval escorts and attendant vessels, four bore the US flag and one the Dutch. The Americans had finally arrived in Vila.

# CHAPTER ELEVEN

The US Navy Advance Base TF-9156, under the command of Brigadier General William Rose, was code-named 'Roses' and, the very day of the troops' arrival, headquarters were set up in the large, two-storey, red-roofed building on the hill overlooking Vila which had once been the home of the British judge.

The vast task force set about its work immediately. An entire infrastructure was needed to support the military population and its tens of thousands of tons of machinery. There were roads, wharves and airfields to be constructed; barracks, depots and a hospital to be built; refrigeration units, support installations and defences to be organised, and all with lightning speed.

The mammoth undertaking was carried out with all the efficiency typical of the indefatigable US Army Construction Battalions, affectionately known as the Seabees, and the US Army Corps of Engineers. Within days, it appeared, the Americans had taken over not only Vila, but the whole of Efate.

Airstrips were being constructed on the north-east corner of the island at Quoin Hill; the safer anchorage of Havannah Harbour had been selected for the fleet; a naval camp had been set up at Malapoa Point; and a road, intended to circle the entire island, was already under construction.

Local labour was required by the military to assist the Seabees, principally in the clearing of land for the airstrips and roads, and for the never-ending task of unloading cargo as fresh troops, supplies and machinery arrived. Over one thousand islanders were recruited, many of them travelling from neighbouring islands when the word spread like wildfire that they could get rich working for the Americans.

The US military, displeased by the inefficiency of the colonial agents, quickly undertook their own recruitment and supervision of labour, which in turn displeased the government.

If the islanders were to work directly for the American forces, the colonial authorities maintained, then they must be paid no more than one and a half shillings a day. The standard rate of pay was twenty shillings a month at most, and it was feared that any more would cause postwar inflation.

Whilst agreeing amongst themselves that the strange Condominium government was a joke, the Americans adhered to the rules, but they also lavished upon their new native friends gifts of US food rations, clothes and cigarettes.

The islanders became eager recruits, despite the fact that they were unaccustomed to working so hard and that the labour was difficult and tedious. The Americans fascinated them in every way. They could do God's work. To the New Hebridean natives, the bulldozing of trees could not be comprehended as the work of man. And there were black soldiers, just like them. The Negro servicemen were a source of great interest, and the apparent equality they shared with their white brothers was astounding. And the American bases were places of huge excitement. In the domed quonset huts of corrugated iron that had sprung out of nowhere, loud music played from speakers in the walls and food was

kept in iceboxes. To the islanders, the Americans repre-
sented a whole new magic way of life.

In turn, the Americans, upon discovering the poor living
conditions of the natives, became even more lavish in their
generosity, their gifts extending from food and tobacco to
radios and iceboxes and furniture. The colonial authorities
strongly disapproved, but there was little they could do
about it.

'Jane!'

Jane was coming out of the post office with Hilary Bale
when she heard her name called, and she looked across the
road to see Jean-François waving at her through the chaos.

The main thoroughfare of Vila, with its cacophonous
noise and seething activity, was barely recognisable these
days. Crowds of off-duty American servicemen competed
for bargains, teams of labourers marched by on their way
to work, and a constant stream of trucks and machinery
laboured its way through the centre of town, swirling dust
in the air and scattering the jostling hordes in its wake.

She watched as Jean-François crossed the road,
narrowly avoiding a jeep, to arrive breathless beside her.

'If the Japanese don't kill us, the Americans will,' he
laughed. 'I haven't seen you for over a month, it has been
far too long.'

'Hello, Jean-François.' Jane was about to introduce
Hilary, but Marat had already grasped the woman's hand
in both of his.

'And Madame Bale, how lovely to see you.' He hadn't
noticed the storekeeper's wife; he'd had eyes only for Jane
Thackeray. 'I had the pleasure of your good husband's
company over a card game last night at Reid's,' he said as
he kissed Hilary's hand.

'I know, Harry told me,' she beamed, enjoying the experience. Jean-François Marat was devilishly handsome and
he made her feel so attractive. 'He also told me that you
won as usual.'

'Only a harmless amount, I assure you.' He always flirted with Hilary Bale, he knew she enjoyed it. In her mid-thirties, a little overweight, with an easygoing manner and a New Zealand accent slight enough not to be grating, he found her quite attractive. Prior to the war in the Pacific, her husband had often been out of town on purchasing trips, and Jean-François had had his eye on her for a while. It would have been so easy to lure her to the little apartment above his office in Vila, where he conducted most of his casual liaisons. But he was no longer interested in Hilary Bale, just as he was no longer interested in casual liaisons. He turned to Jane.

'Savi and Sera ask after you constantly. They miss you, and so does little Pascal.'

'Yes,' Jane said. She'd been thinking a lot about the Poilama family, and felt that she'd let them down. They were her friends and she'd promised them regular English lessons. 'Do tell them how sorry I am,' she said, 'but my work with the US medical corps has left me so little time to spare.'

Something had happened, Jean-François thought. When she had cancelled their previous arrangement, saying that she had offered her services to the Americans as an interpreter and that she would contact him after the chaos had settled, he had respected her wishes. But as the weeks had passed, he'd wondered whether she was avoiding him. He had thought of calling upon her, but had decided that an accidental meeting would better serve his advantage, and he knew that she regularly visited the post office.

'How is Dr Thackeray?' he enquired, making pleasant conversation as he studied her. Yes, she had been avoiding him, he thought, her manner was different, she was once again on her guard. Why? Jean-François was puzzled. What had turned her against him? 'He has not yet returned, I hear.'

'No, he's staying a little longer to assist the Americans.

There are some health problems with the native recruits on Espiritu Santo, just as there are here.'

A second American base had been established on Espiritu Santo, the 100,000 troops that had arrived doubling the island's population almost overnight, and five hundred native workers had been employed to assist the Seabees.

'We're in regular contact,' Jane continued, 'and we both agree that much of the illness is due to the issue of military rations and the islanders' change of diet.'

'How very interesting,' he said. It was. He could use the information as further ammunition to keep his workers. If they went to the Americans, they would get sick, he'd tell them. 'It is fortunate then, for my own workers' sake, that they have remained loyal to me.' They hadn't remained loyal to him at all, they'd remained loyal to Savi, and at Savi's suggestion he'd even started paying them. A pittance in comparison with military pay, certainly, but enough to keep most of them. Savi had been right when he'd said a bullock a month was no longer enough. Jean-François was sick to death of the Americans, they were disrupting his life.

'The Americans have a lot to answer for, do you not agree, Madame Bale?' He smiled at Hilary, taking care to include her in the conversation.

'They have certainly taken over Vila,' Hilary agreed. Not that Harry was complaining, she thought, business was booming, and she personally loved the presence of the Americans. Vila had never been so exciting.

'I think the dietary issue will resolve itself,' Jane said. 'The medical corps are aware of the problem.'

She didn't go into any detail about the role she had played, but Jane Thackeray had been indispensable to the Americans, firstly as an interpreter, then as a medical authority on the New Hebridean natives and their dietary habits. Captain Porter, Commander of the US Navy Base Hospital Unit, and his team had decided a vitamin deficiency was causing the outbreak of diarrhea and, more worryingly, beri-beri. Jane had suggested, just as Martin had done on Espiritu Santo, that the islanders be returned to their traditional staple fare of fish, yams and coconuts. Captain Porter's team had followed the advice, also adding unpolished rice to the natives' rations and, already, the beri-beri rates were dropping.

'I am to visit the base at Havannah Harbour tomorrow,' Jane said, 'to address the labour recruits on the importance of avoiding American rations.' She felt the need to stress how busy her itinerary had become, aware that Jean-François was wondering why she'd avoided him. And she did owe him an explanation, she thought, since they had parted on such amicable terms. But what could she say? She couldn't very well tell him about Godfrey.

'You were alone with Marat in his house?' Godfrey Tomlinson had been openly shocked when she'd told him she'd lunched with Jean-François at Chanson de Mer.

'Not exactly alone, Godfrey,' she'd replied, amused by his outrage. 'Selena, his maid, was there and Ronnie was with me. It was just a simple luncheon.'

'A housegirl and an infant hardly qualify as chaperones. It was most unseemly of you to accept such an invitation.'

She'd laughed out loud. He sounded so quaintly Victorian that she'd even wondered for a moment whether he might be joking. 'Why unseemly? I've dined alone with you in your house.'

'I am not a libertine, Jane,' he'd said, ignoring her flippancy. 'Marat is. And he has designs upon you.'

Although he still sounded old-fashioned, she was no longer laughing.

'I never spoke of it at the time,' Godfrey continued, 'because, frankly, it was embarrassing, but Marat's intentions were evident the night you first met him. You felt it yourself. Do you not remember?'

Yes, she remembered. She remembered feeling

confronted, but she had dismissed her reservations. She'd decided that she'd been wrong. The Frenchman was considerate. He was charming and thoughtful, his company was interesting and his conversation stimulating. She felt defensive. Godfrey's intense dislike of Jean-François was colouring his argument.

'He drove me to the Poilamas' house so that I could give Savi and Sera the English lesson I promised them,' she said rather primly. 'It was quite natural he should offer me lunch.'

'And I presume these English lessons are to become a regular ritual?' Godfrey asked with more than a touch of sarcasm.

'Yes,' Jane answered rebelliously, the lecture beginning to annoy her. 'Savi and Sera welcome the tuition, both for themselves and for their son, and as they are my friends, I'm more than happy to oblige.'

'And have you asked yourself, Jane, why Jean-François Marat would welcome his servants learning English?' The old man's steel-blue eyes glared into hers as if he was trying to drill commonsense into her skull through the sheer force of his will. 'It is the very last thing he would want.'

Godfrey had left without drinking his tea. And he'd left disappointed, perhaps even disillusioned. Were Jane's behaviour and defence of Marat a sign of her naivete, as he'd initially thought, or was she perhaps welcoming the Frenchman's attentions? He told himself it was none of his business, but the sooner Martin Thackeray got home to his wife the better, he thought.

And Jane was left in a state of confusion.

'Well, Jane, if you are to visit Havannah Harbour tomorrow,' Jean-François said, 'we should make the most of today.' He turned the full force of his charm upon Hilary Bale. 'Can I tempt you ladies to an early lunch at Reid's?'

'That was exactly our intention,' Hilary replied before Jane could answer. 'We'd be delighted if you joined us, wouldn't we, Jane?'

'Yes, of course.'

'I have an even better suggestion. Why don't we lunch at Chanson de Mer?' Again the invitation was directed to Hilary. 'Perhaps Harry could join us, we could make it a party?'

'Oh no, Harry is working at the store, we each have one day off a week.'

'How sad for Harry,' he smiled, 'but not for me. It means I shall have the ladies' company all to myself. I insist you agree.'

'It's a wonderful idea,' Hilary applauded, thrilled at the prospect of a visit to Chanson de Mer. She'd been hoping for a long time that Marat might ask Harry and her to dine at his house, but Harry had said that the Frenchman was exclusive with his personal invitations.

'Mainly Frenchies, Hil,' he'd said. 'He's good company at Reid's but he only invites his own kind back to the plantation.'

'We accept,' Hilary said, 'don't we, Jane?'

'I'm afraid not,' Jane apologised, much to Hilary's horror. 'It's a long drive to Undine Bay and I promised Mary she could have the afternoon off. Mary is looking after Ronnie,' she said to Jean-François.

'Then Mary and Ronnie must come too,' he answered. 'I'm sure Mary will welcome the opportunity to see her good friend Sera. And even better,' he said as the idea hit him, 'you can give Savi and Sera their long-awaited English lesson. That is,' he added, turning again to Hilary, 'if Madame Bale can put up with my company for an hour whilst you do so.'

Hilary beamed again. It was a fait accompli.

'Mary may have other plans for her afternoon off,' Jane said weakly.

'Then we'll leave it all in Mary's hands, shall we? She shall decide. Now come along mesdames, enough chattering in the street, I'm parked over at Reid's.' And he took their arms, protectively guiding them across the road and through the stream of servicemen, workmen, traffic and machinery that constituted the current mayhem of Vila.

Twenty minutes later, they were on their way. Hilary was seated in the front of the Landrover with Jean-François, and Jane, at her own suggestion, in the back with Mary and Ronnie.

'An excellent idea,' Jean-François had said. Whatever put her at her ease, he thought. 'Madame Bale can enjoy the view. You've not driven to Undine Bay before, Madame?'

'No, indeed not,' Hilary answered. 'In the whole four years we've been here, I've never driven further than Malapoa Point, I'm always too busy in the store.'

'It will be a far more comfortable ride this time, Jane,' Jean-François said, smiling at her in the rear vision mirror, 'the Americans have built my road for me.' He was pleased when she smiled back at him.

Upon their arrival, they discovered the Poilamas' hut deserted. 'Sera will have taken the children to the big house,' Jean-François said. 'She quite often does so when I'm gone for the day.'

He was right. It was washday, and Sera and Selena were at the old wooden table that stood under the shade of the back porch, both of them scrubbing away at the clothes in the big tub whilst the children played on the ground beside them.

The women were taken aback when the Masta appeared unexpectedly, but he seemed in an affable mood, so they decided not to worry. And then Pascal noticed Jane.

'Missus Tack!' he yelled, and for several minutes chaos reigned before Jean-François called things back into order and started issuing instructions in French.

He told Sera to send one of the work boys to the

smokehouse where Savi was working and tell him to go home. She and Savi were to have their English lesson with the Missus, he said.

Sera looked uncertain. She would have liked nothing more, but it was washday and Selena couldn't be trusted on her own; Selena would just dunk the clothes in the water and then hang them on the line. But it appeared Selena's duties lay elsewhere.

'And Selena, you will prepare lunch for our guests,' Jean-François instructed. 'The freshly smoked leg ham – thin slices, remember – a salad with Sera's dressing, and the fresh bread I bought from the bakery this morning.'

Selena nodded, happy to escape the hated washtub, but Sera was confused. Had the Masta forgotten?

'It is washday,' she reminded him.

'Leave the clothes to soak, you can do them tomorrow,' he said.

Sera was astounded. Tomorrow? But today was washday. Washday never changed.

Mary accompanied Jane and Sera to the hut to look after Ronnie and Marie whilst the lesson was in progress, and Hilary was left quite content in Jean-François's company, sitting on the front verandah sipping the iced tea that Selena had made for them.

'What an idyllic view,' she said, looking out admiringly at Undine Bay.

'Yes, it is pretty,' he agreed, but his mind was on Jane and why she'd been avoiding him. He'd wondered whether perhaps she'd discovered one of his questionable business dealings; her work with the military would certainly have brought her into contact with the local authorities. If so, he would explain it away easily enough. But he needed to find out the reason in order to combat it, and Hilary Bale might well be able to shed some light on the mystery.

'I worry about Jane,' he said with concern. 'She has been working so very hard of late.'

'Indeed she has,' Hilary agreed.

'Military and government authorities can be so demanding, I do hope she isn't placing the islanders' health above that of her own.' He was about to enquire which particular government official might be responsible for overworking Jane and placing her at risk, but Hilary interrupted.

'Oh dear me, no,' she said heartily, 'Jane thrives on the pressure, she's never been healthier. It's we who suffer.' She smiled.

'In what way?' Jean-François returned her smile, but he was irritated. The stupid woman was going to talk about herself, he thought.

'We, her dearest friends,' Hilary explained good-naturedly. 'She has quite neglected us, I'm afraid. I've barely seen her myself, and neither has Godfrey. He was complaining most bitterly just the other day.'

Of course, Jean-François thought. It wasn't some unsavoury piece of information Jane had uncovered that had led to her altered opinion of him, it was the interfering old Englishman. Godfrey Tomlinson had turned her against him. She'd been with Tomlinson the night they'd first met, he remembered. He hadn't realised they were such particularly close friends.

'Ah, Godfrey Tomlinson,' he said with affection, 'a true eccentric.'

'Yes, I suppose he is,' Hilary replied. She hadn't previously thought of Godfrey as eccentric; courteous and old-fashioned perhaps, but upon reflection, she decided Jean-François was right. 'He's certainly a man of mystery,' she said, 'one knows so little of his past, only that he's been here forever and seems to have money, but no-one knows how he came by it.'

The same way everyone else who'd used their brains came by it, Jean-François thought. By wheeling and dealing and turning the inadequacies of the Condominium to his advantage. Godfrey Tomlinson had been a crook in his day just like the rest of them, which was why Jean-François had presumed they were one of a kind when he'd voiced his views on blackbirding.

There'd been at least a dozen of them, quite drunk at Reid's, the year before Simone had left. They'd been mostly French and most had black mistresses and he'd been espousing the joys of Selena who had newly arrived on his property. He hadn't noticed that the Englishman, who spoke fluent French and mingled quite comfortably in their company, had gone noticeably quiet.

'She knows all the tricks,' he'd boasted, 'but then most of them do, they're highly sexual creatures. If we could just keep the women to ourselves and put the men to work, it would be an ideal society. Bring back blackbirding,' he'd laughed, 'and we'd have it all on a platter.' And the others had laughed along with him. All except Godfrey, who had turned on him like a rabid dog. He'd called him every name under the sun and, if the others hadn't held him back, the stupid old fool would have physically attacked him. It had been laughable, Jean-François could have flattened the puny Englishman with one blow. He'd dismissed Godfrey Tomlinson from that night on. The old man was a native-lover, soft and weak, and Jean-François had no time for such men.

'He's an admirable gentleman, Godfrey,' he said, 'but as you quite rightly commented, Madame Bale, he has been here for so very long . . .' there was the shadow of concern in his voice '. . . that I feel the tropics may have affected him.'

'In what way?' Hilary was fascinated. She was not a malicious woman, to the contrary, she was gregarious, and generous in her friendship. But she loved talking about other people, just as she loved becoming involved in their lives. There was very little else to do in Vila.

'He has lost touch with reality,' Jean-François said

sympathetically, 'as can so sadly happen when one lives a lone life, as Godfrey has, in a place like the New Hebrides. He has become obsessive in his opinions, and, how do the English put it? A little "dotty" perhaps.' He smiled. 'English expressions can be so apt, can they not?'

'Yes,' Hilary said, 'perhaps he is a bit.' She'd never found Godfrey dotty at all, but she didn't wish to disagree. Jean-François meant no harm and Godfrey was, after all, an unusual man. It was quite plausible that some might find him dotty.

'Maybe it's just age, he must be well over seventy,' Jean-François said, 'and age of course affects us all. Except you, Madame Bale, you never seem to grow a day older. May I call you Hilary?'

'Of course you may.' The Frenchman was flirting with her and she loved it. She was also flattered that he considered her a friend on a first-name basis. She couldn't wait to tell Harry.

'And I am Jean-François,' he said. 'More iced tea?'


'This come from education,' Savi said; his cousin Pako had joined the New Hebrides Defence Force and Savi was fiercely proud. They'd finished their lesson, but he always insisted upon speaking English to Missus Tack. It was another lesson in itself, he thought, just to practise. 'Pako look so good in his uniform. Much men join Defence. *Many* men,' he corrected himself.

Savi was right. Two hundred natives had joined the New Hebrides Defence Force, mostly from the island of Malekula, and amongst those who held rank were a number of policemen.

'One day Pascal have education,' he said. 'English is good start. One day Pascal be policeman maybe.'

Jane agreed that Pascal should go to school when he was old enough. Like many very young children, he was quick to assimilate a new language, she had noticed, but there was more to it than that. He was a clever boy, she told Savi and Sera, he would be a good student.

When the Landrover arrived to collect her, Jane said her farewells to the Poilama family in the hut, and then Savi accompanied her outside to where Jean-François was waiting.

Marat's curt nod to his worker indicated that Savi was to return to his duties immediately, but as he drove to the big house, the Frenchman was effusive to Jane. He had very much enjoyed Mrs Bale's company, he said, and as it was not every day of the week he found himself in the company of two such attractive ladies, he insisted that they open a bottle of his best wine and make it a party.

Jane couldn't help feeling a little uncomfortable. Productive and enjoyable as the English lesson had been, she had nonetheless been coerced into visiting Chanson de Mer and Godfrey's warning still echoed in her mind.

Throughout the luncheon, she was thankful of Hilary's presence and the fact that Jean-François directed much of his attention towards the New Zealand woman. But as Hilary herself was definitely in a party mood, and as the conversation was animated and the food delicious, Jane forced herself to relax, she didn't wish to spoil Hilary's enjoyment.

'The ham is home-grown and home-smoked,' Jean-François boasted in response to Hilary's compliment, 'my own secret recipe.' But when he added, with a special smile to Jane, 'we rear fine pigs on the plantation,' her smile in response was politely guarded.

During the drive back to Vila, Jean-François was pleased when Hilary suggested he drop her off at Jane's cottage.

'We always have a cup of tea together after our lunch out,' Hilary told him, 'I need to make the most of my one day off a week.'

Excellent, Jean-François thought. The garrulous New Zealand woman was bound to chat on to her friend about the conversation they'd had, which could only serve his cause. And as she had been such an easy conquest, he knew she would paint him in glowing colours. All of which was necessary, he thought, he had sensed a continuing uncertainty in Jane Thackeray.

'Will you join us?' Jane asked him at the front door, rather hoping that he would decline.

'Good heavens, no,' he said. 'You must have a great deal to talk about. I have disrupted your day quite enough as it is.'

'To the contrary, Jean-François,' Hilary insisted as he kissed her hand, 'you have made our day most pleasurable.'

'The pleasure was mine, I assure you. Don't forget,' he said to Jane, 'I am at your disposal whenever you wish to visit the Poilamas, you have only to contact me.'

He would have kissed her hand too, but Ronnie was fast asleep in her arms, so he patted the child's head instead. 'Marie has exhausted him once again,' he smiled. 'Au revoir, mesdames.'

And he left Hilary to convince Jane that any fears Godfrey Tomlinson may have instilled in her were the ramblings of a dotty old man. But if Hilary didn't succeed, he decided, then he would simply start from scratch. When Martin Thackeray returned, he would invite him and his wife to Chanson de Mer and he would dispel all doubts by winning the approval of the good doctor himself. Jean-François had no intention of giving up on the chase.

'He has to be the most attractive man in Vila,' Hilary said as she watched him drive off.

'More attractive than Harry?' Jane smiled.

'Well, he's certainly more handsome.' Hilary followed her into the kitchen. 'And he's so French and flirtatious.'

Jane laughed as she filled the kettle, she knew Hilary was teasing. Unlike many in the colony, the Bales had an excellent marriage and Hilary would be the last person to place it under any threat.

'Flirtation's an art lost on the New Zealanders and the Australians,' Hilary lamented, 'and, for that matter, the English too. You must admit, Jane, he makes one feel terribly attractive.'

'Yes, he does,' Jane replied. Hilary, in her uncomplicated and straightforward way, had put her finger right on the problem that troubled Jane.

Godfrey's lecture had not instilled fear in her, as he had intended it should. But it had instilled guilt. She'd been aware of his disappointment in her as he'd left and she'd pondered the situation deeply that night. Had she behaved in an 'unseemly' fashion, as Godfrey had put it? She'd decided that she had. She'd succumbed to the Frenchman's flattery and charm. She'd enjoyed his conversation and his company and, in doing so, she had been disloyal to Martin in the extreme.

The Frenchman's harmless flirtation might be fun to Hilary, Jane thought as she filled the teapot, and perhaps that was the healthy way to view it, but she was riddled with guilt at having been so susceptible.

They sat on the verandah and Jane poured the tea.

'I do hope he asks us again,' Hilary said. 'Just the two of us. You must contact him, Jane. He asked you to, remember? "Any time", he said.'

Jane had no intention of contacting Jean-François. She had already decided that she could visit the Poilamas on her own. The Americans had built the road right through to Quoin Hill. Martin had taught her how to drive, and with the Reverend Smeed's permission, she could borrow the car belonging to the church. It would be a hair-raising experience, but she'd manage it.

Hilary obviously wasn't going to leave the subject alone, however, so Jane decided to put an end to the discussion of the Frenchman.

'Godfrey can't stand him, you know, he thinks Jean-François's not to be trusted.'

'Well, Godfrey would, wouldn't he,' Hilary said dismissively. 'Godfrey's judgement shouldn't be taken seriously, he's been far too long in the tropics.' She registered Jane's surprise at her remark. 'He's a dear of course,' Hilary said, 'but he's terribly old-fashioned, you know that yourself. Jean-François thinks he's dotty.'

'Does he indeed?' How interesting, Jane thought. She wondered if Jean-François had guessed at Godfrey's interference. Not that it really mattered. 'Godfrey Tomlinson is one of the wisest men I know,' she said. Then she changed the conversation to the surefire distraction of the US forces.

The next morning at dawn, Corporal 'Biff' Jackson of the navy medical corps called to collect Jane; it was planned that she should arrive at Havannah Harbour before the workday started. Biff Jackson had been assigned as her regular driver for the past month or so and he and Jane had developed a comfortable relationship. She liked him despite the fact that, unlike most of the other Americans she'd met, he was a dour young man who took life very seriously.

'Hello, Biff.'

'Hi, Jane.'

They exchanged greetings as she climbed into the staff car and, during the drive, they talked about the progress of the US Navy Base Hospital. Currently under construction on the Bellevue plantation about three miles inland from Vila, it was intended to be the principal medical facility in the region, but it was a slow process in the making.

'I don't see it being completed before August – 186 quonset huts,' Biff shook his head, 'that's one hell of an ask.'

'How many beds do they think it'll staff?'

'They're aiming at around 600, I think. Well, that's for a start.' He looked out across the endless Pacific. 'If things hot up out there, who knows, we might have wounded pouring in from everywhere.'

They were silent for a while. It was a sobering thought, particularly for Jane, as she recalled the Royal Victoria Hospital following the evacuation of Dunkirk. The endless stream of wounded and dying, the packed wards, and yet more arriving each day. The mutilations, the amputations, the screams of haunted, shell-shocked men. Was it all about to start again? She had been lulled into a sense of security here on this idyllic island.

There were whistles of admiration when Jane arrived at the Havannah Harbour naval base, and she tried not to show too much leg beneath her calf-length cotton dress as she climbed out of the staff car. She was accustomed to the Americans' show of approval, however, recognising it as good-humoured and harmless. The troops were lounging around the mess hut eating breakfast, and she waved back as they saluted her with their pannikins.

Biff introduced her to the commanding officer and, as he did so, several other officers gathered nearby. Unnecessarily, Biff thought. If it hadn't been a good-looking woman he had in tow, they wouldn't have given a second glance.

'Lieutenant Colonel Kempsey, Jane Thackeray,' he said. '*Mrs* Jane Thackeray,' he emphasised for the others' benefit, and Jane smiled. Biff was always protective.

She suggested to the Lieutenant Colonel that she mingle casually with the islander recruits, who were squatting around their own mess area eating breakfast, rather than address them formally.

'Whatever you feel is best, Mrs Thackeray,' Kempsey agreed. 'But perhaps I should introduce you first.'

'I'd rather introduce myself,' she said, 'that is, if you don't mind.'

Rather unorthodox, he thought, but then she was a civilian, and he'd been told she had a way with the natives.

As it turned out, no introduction was necessary. Although the majority of the workers at the base were from other islands, there were a number of locals, most of whom recognised her and, as she approached, the cry went up, 'Missus Tack! Missus Tack!'

Within minutes the men were all crowding around her, those from elsewhere interested in meeting the white missus who was so popular on Efate.

She chatted to them in Bislama, asking them their names and where they were from, and discovered that most came from Tanna to the south. She asked them if they liked the food and they said yes, the food was good. Then one man said, 'Mi laikem Merika kakae,' and that started it. Several others agreed. 'Yo, yo, Merika kakae mo gud,' they said and before long everyone was grinning and nodding. 'Merika kakae nambawan.'

'Nomo,' Jane shook her head firmly, 'Merika kakae nomo gud. Merika kakae makem yufala sik.'

They'd been told that it was the American food that was making their people sick, that they must eat their own special rations, which the military now prepared for them. But they hadn't wanted to. The American food tasted good, and there was a lot of it, and their new army and navy friends were happy to share it with them.

'Yu mas kakae aelan kakae,' Jane stressed. 'Aelan kakae em i impoten tumas.'

The local men, aware of Jane's reputation, were the first to be convinced. If Missus Tack said it was important they eat the local food, they said, then she must be right. Missus Tack was 'nambawan dokta', they told the others. She made everyone better when they were sick. Missus Tack knew everything.

Many of the American servicemen had gathered around to watch. It was an impressive sight, the slim English-woman holding command over the islanders who surrounded her.

'Now she is *gorgeous*!' Charles 'Wolf' Baker murmured to his buddy Chuck Wilson.

'She's married,' Chuck said; he'd been amongst the officers who'd lined up near the commander hoping for a personal introduction.

'Just my luck,' Wolf grinned. But he watched her with admiration. They could certainly do with her out at Quoin Hill, he thought. The team of workers at the remote airbase refused to eat their special rations and a number of them had become ill. Wolf himself had explained they'd get sick if they kept eating American food and they'd appeared to understand, but they didn't believe it. Or they didn't want to, he thought. American food was 'number one', they kept saying, and the army cooks in the mobile kitchen, who were black themselves, didn't have the heart to refuse them.

'We can't discriminate, Lieutenant,' they said, and the islanders played on their black brothers' sympathy. It was a delicate situation.

The workers gave Jane an enthusiastic farewell and Lieutenant Colonel Kempsey walked her to the staff car where Biff was already waiting.

'I'm most impressed and most obliged, Mrs Thackeray,' he said as he shook her hand.

'Oh I'm sure there'll be a bit of cheating,' Jane warned him, 'they've certainly discovered a taste for your food. But perhaps a treat now and then,' she suggested. 'One meal a week on American rations wouldn't do too much harm.'

'An excellent idea.'

'Excuse me, sir.' A young officer had appeared beside them. He saluted the commander. 'Ma'am,' he said, acknowledging Jane.

Kempsey returned the salute. 'Yes, Baker?'

'I was wondering whether Mrs Thackeray might visit Quoin Hill, sir.'

Kempsey nodded. The Lieutenant had informed him of

the trouble they were having with the recruits and the rations. 'That's entirely up to Mrs Thackeray and her driver,' he said.

'I'd be more than happy to do so,' Jane agreed. But Biff looked uncertain, he was supposed to return the staff car by ten o'clock.

'I could drive you there myself, ma'am,' Wolf said, 'and escort you back to Vila.'

'In that case, what are we waiting for?' Jane smiled.

'An introduction perhaps,' Kempsey replied. 'Mrs Thackeray, Lieutenant Wolf Baker.'

'At your service, ma'am.'

'How do you do, Lieutenant.'

Chuck watched as his buddy drove off with Jane Thackeray in the jeep. So did most of the others and they grinned and nudged each other. How the hell did he do it? they all thought. Wolf had a way with women and the men respected him for it. That guy could charm the birds right out of the trees, they said. Wolf Baker sure was something else.

'How long have you been in Vila, ma'am?' Wolf asked as they drove up the hill.

'Nearly eight months.'

'Is that all? Wow,' he said, deeply impressed, 'I thought you'd been here for years, you speak their lingo like a native.'

'It's a very simple language, Lieutenant,' she assured him, 'it doesn't take long to learn.'

'But the way they all respect you, that was an amazing thing to watch.' He grinned at her. 'You were really great back there, you know that?'

She found his admiration highly suspect. His grin was too engaging, his manner too personal. Was he admiring her communication skills or her appearance? she wondered. He wasn't eyeing her up and down and there was nothing lascivious in his behaviour. There was not one thing to which she could openly take offence. But Wolf Baker was too rakishly good-looking to be true. And he knew it, she decided. It was quite apparent how the nickname 'Wolf' had come into being, the man obviously made a habit of playing on his looks. He was laying it on for all it was worth, as he no doubt did with every woman he met, and Jane wasn't having a bar of it.

'My husband is a missionary doctor, it's my job to become a part of the islanders' lives,' she replied, not rudely but with the intention of putting him in his place.

'You're kidding,' he said, undeterred. 'You don't look like a missionary's wife.'

'Really? And what does a missionary's wife look like?' This time her tone was icy.

'I don't know,' he said with disarming honesty, 'I've never met one.'

She didn't know what to make of him. He clearly intended no offence. A change of subject was called for, she decided. 'Tell me about yourself, Lieutenant.'

'Sure,' he said amiably, 'what do you want to know?'

'Well, where do you come from for a start?'

'Boston, Massachusetts.'

'And?'

She was grilling him, and he wondered why. But it was okay, he didn't mind. '*And* I'm twenty-six years old, *and* I graduated from Harvard School of Engineering in '39, *and* I joined the United States Army Air Force, *and* I got my bars in '41.' His grin was irresistibly boyish. 'Name, rank and serial number, Charles Wolfgang Baker, Lieutenant 2nd Class, United States Army Air Corps, 97352402, at your service, ma'am.' He saluted her, and she couldn't help but laugh.

'Wolfgang?'

'Yeah, my grandmother was Austrian and she and my mom were big Mozart fans, so . . .' he shrugged.

'So you were nicknamed "Wolf".'

'Nope, I was nicknamed "Chuck". I got saddled with "Wolf" at the army airbase in Montgomery, Alabama. The guys thought it was a hoot when they found out my middle name was Wolfgang.'

'Wolf suits you.' She said it without innuendo and with a smile. It did suit him, she thought.

'You reckon so, ma'am? Me too, I like it. Every second guy I know's called Chuck.'

She laughed again, her suspicions already fading. Charles Wolfgang Baker was eminently likable.

'And what is your job at Quoin Hill, Wolf? Please call me Jane,' she added, 'I've never quite adjusted to the American habit of "ma'am".'

'Sure thing, Jane.' He was pleased that he'd made her laugh. Gosh but she was a good-looking woman. Damn shame she was married. 'I'm adviser on the construction of the US Army airstrips,' he explained, 'they transferred me here because of my degree in civil engineering.'

'Transferred you from where?'

'45th Fighter Squadron.'

'Fighter Squadron?' she queried. 'So you've seen action?'

'Yeah, in a way,' he said. 'I was on fighter plane duty in Hawaii when the Japs bombed Pearl Harbor. They blew the crap out of everything . . . sorry, ma'am . . . Jane.' The smile had disappeared, the humorous glint in the hazel-brown eyes had faded and his face no longer looked boyish. 'There were a few Curtiss P-36s and P-40s undamaged and our squadron CO ordered them fuelled and armed. About ten of us managed to get up there, but it was too late.' He shook his head as he recalled the images. 'Jesus it was a mess. One big, horrible, burning mess. And not a Jap in sight. We searched the area for forty-five minutes, dodging our own flak half the time. The AA crews were firing at anything in the sky and that meant us. They had the jitters and they could hardly see through the smoke, they didn't know who the hell it was they were trying to blow away.' His shrug was one of resignation. 'But it was all over.'

He'd been staring at the road ahead, and now he smiled once more; he hadn't intended to sound so sombre. 'I tell you, Jane, I can't wait to get back up there.' His eyes were gleaming with excitement. 'Right up there in the thick of it.' He gazed at the sky as if for a moment he saw himself there. 'We'll show them who's boss, just you wait and see.' Then he turned back to her. 'And it won't be long. Any moment now.'

Jane was amazed at the sight that greeted her when they reached Quoin Hill. Laid out before her very eyes in this remote north-east area of the island was a virtual airport. But it was disguised. Aeroplanes of every description, fighters, bombers, and cargo planes, sat in revetments covered by netting and vines. Ammunition stores, mechanical garages and an ordnance depot, 'stacked to the ceiling with weaponry', Wolf said, were all similarly camouflaged.

'There's not much we can do about the airstrips themselves.' The runways were constructed of crushed coral, he told her, and they'd certainly be visible from the air. 'But as for the rest?' He gave her a cheeky wink. 'The Japs'd have no idea what we've got hidden away up here.'

Jane's introduction to the islander recruits proved as unnecessary as it had been at Havannah Harbour. Two of the men, brothers, were from Savi's village and she had examined their children during the meningitis scare. The brothers approached her enthusiastically, well before she had time to mingle and introduce herself to the others.

'Missus Tack, olsem wanem, i gud?' they asked, shaking her hand, first one brother, then the other.

She replied that she was very well thank you and shook their hands with equal effusiveness, then she asked after their families. They said that they'd had to leave the village when they started working for the Americans. The Bos had said that he wasn't giving a bullock a month to families whose men didn't work for him, and they hadn't wanted to cause trouble for the others who'd stayed with the Bos out of loyalty to Savi.

The brothers didn't seem worried about the change in their circumstances, however. The wife of the older brother came from Epule village, right here near the airbase, he said, and they had all moved in with her family. Everyone was very happy because of the presents they brought home from the Americans. They had furniture in their huts now, and new clothes, and a radio.

The animated conversation between Jane and the two brothers quickly drew the interest of the other workers and before long she was once again surrounded by islanders eager to meet Missus Tack. She introduced the subject of rations and diet, and the brothers, proud to be 'besfren' with Missus Tack, 'nambawan dokta', told their workmates that they should listen to Missus Tack because Missus Tack knew what was best for them.

Wolf, as before, had watched from the sidelines. 'You are *fantastic*,' he said when she rejoined him. 'You really are, Jane, you are *something else!*'

His open admiration was no longer suspect. If he was a puppy, she thought, he'd be wagging his tail, he was so beguiling.

'I'm just doing my job, Wolf,' she laughed.

They chatted as he gave her a guided tour of the base and she told him all about Martin and their work together.

'He's a lucky man, your husband,' Wolf said. And he meant it. He'd never met a woman like Jane Thackeray.

Lunch was called at midday and they decided to eat before the drive back to Vila, both agreeing they were starving, but Jane insisted upon eating the islanders' rations.

'Have to set a good example,' she said. 'Why don't you join me?'

'Okay.'

The brothers had mysteriously disappeared, perhaps to eat at their village nearby, Jane thought, so she and Wolf sat amongst her newfound island friends, who were impressed to see the white Bos eating 'aelan kakae'.

'What is it?' he asked Jane.

'Fish and sweet potato,' she said, 'with coconut pulp and lime juice.'

'It's great. How do I say "I like it"?'

'Mi laekam kakae ia.'

'Mi laekam kakae ia,' Wolf said to the men who laughed their approval and nodded and slapped each other on the back.

Just as the two of them had finished eating, the brothers returned, and with them were their wives and three children who had come to see Missus Tack. The older brother's two sons chattered nineteen to the dozen, both vying for Jane's attention, but the younger brother's little girl of around eight was shy. Clutching a fistful of her mother's cotton dress, she peeped out from behind the woman's legs, interested in the proceedings but far too timid to say anything.

Wolf smiled at the mother and knelt down beside the little girl. 'Hello,' he said.

'Talem allo, Lela,' the mother coaxed.

The little girl remained silent, grabbing a bigger fistful of her mother's dress, but she didn't dodge away. Her lips parted in wonderment and she stared wide-eyed back at Wolf.

'Her name is Lela?' Wolf questioned the mother.

'Yo,' the woman nodded.

'Hello, Lela.'

'Allo,' the little girl whispered.

'You're very pretty,' he said. Then he looked up at Jane who had been watching him out of the corner of her eye as she'd chatted to the boys. 'How do I say "you're very pretty"?' he asked.

'Yu luk naes tumas.'

'Yu luk naes tumas, Lela,' he said and he smiled at the little girl.

Lela's eyes didn't leave his as she returned his smile. 'Yu luk naes tumas tu,' she said, her voice a little bolder this time.

Wolf laughed and looked again to Jane.

'Yes,' Jane said. 'Lela thinks you're pretty too.' She was amazed. When she had examined Lela at the village she hadn't been able to get a word out of her. She hadn't even been able to get the child to look at her. The little girl had been so painfully shy that she'd clung to her mother and stared at the ground throughout the entire examination. The mother had said that Lela was always like that with strangers. Even strangers like Missus Tack, she'd said apologetically.

'How did you do it?' she asked ten minutes later as they walked to the jeep.

'Do what?'

'Lela. She never talks, she never looks people in the eye.'

He grinned again and gave a jaunty shrug. 'Charisma, I guess.'

He was joking, but he was right, she thought, that's exactly what it was. Wolf Baker was far more than good-looking, he was charismatic. When he was interested in someone the full focus of his attention was extraordinary. She had felt it herself, and so had Lela. She wondered whether he was actually aware of the effect he had on others. Quite possibly not, she thought.

'Excuse me, sir, we have a bit of a problem.'

They were met at the jeep by a corporal who sprang to attention, eyes front, and smartly saluted.

'Yes, Jack?' Wolf returned the salute, but was casual in his manner, a signal to the corporal, whom he knew well, that the full military show was not necessary in Jane's presence.

The young man got the message and visibly relaxed. 'It's Big Ben, sir, he's sick as a dog.'

'In what way?'

'Threw up his lunch . . . beg pardon, ma'am,' he said in deference to Jane. 'And he's come over dizzy.'

They followed the corporal to the mess hut where a number of men were gathered around a large black American soldier. He was seated on a camp stool, his head in his hands.

'I'll be okay,' the big man was saying over and over. 'I'll be okay, I'll be okay.'

'What's the trouble, Big Ben?' Wolf asked, and the man tried to get to his feet and salute. 'Sit, sit,' Wolf said putting a hand on his shoulder.

'I'm sorry, sir,' the man said, 'I don't know what . . .'

Jane knelt beside him, her hand to his forehead, then she checked his pulse and his eyes. He was a giant of a man, strong and fit, but he was as weak as a baby, his energy sapped. He was shaking and sweating, his eyes were rolling and his temperature was high. He'd be delirious any minute.

'Blackwater fever,' she said as she stood. 'He needs quinine. Intravenously and as soon as possible.' She stated the case in a matter-of-fact way, not wishing to alarm Big Ben and the men, but her eyes told Wolf that the matter was urgent. 'We have to get him to Vila.'

The two of them followed as the men half carried and half dragged the protesting Big Ben to the jeep. Wolf looked at the young Englishwoman who seemed to him a never-ending source of amazement. He'd presumed that she worked as a local interpreter for the medical corps.

'I didn't know you were a doctor,' he said.

'I'm not,' she replied. 'I'm a nurse.'

'You could have fooled me.'

'Cover him with a blanket,' she said to the men when they'd put Big Ben in the jeep; he was lying on the back seat, his legs hanging over the side. 'And bring me a bucket of cold water and a towel.'

As they set off for Vila, she leaned over the back and bathed his face. 'How long have you been feeling sick, Big Ben?' she asked, 'I'm Jane, by the way.'

'When I woke up this morning, ma'am. Didn't say nothin', didn't want to let the team down, you know?'

'Well, you just lie there quietly.' The fever was upon him and he was shivering now. 'We'll have you at the hospital in a couple of hours,' she kept soothing him as she bathed his face. 'You'll be all right, Big Ben,' she said over and over.

'Don't wanna be no trouble, ma'am.'

'Ssh, you're no trouble at all, you're going to be fine.'

But by the time they'd reached Havannah Harbour, Big Ben was muttering incoherently.

'Jesus, will he be okay?' Wolf asked.

'I don't know, it depends if we can get him there in time.'

Wolf tried to step up the speed, although he was already driving like a maniac.

'Blackwater fever's a malignant form of malaria,' she explained. 'It attacks the kidneys and it's a killer if you don't catch it in time. If only he'd reported in sick this morning we could have got the quinine into him first thing.'

Wolf nodded, it was typical of Big Ben. Big Ben never wanted to cause trouble. Big Ben was a gentle giant from Alabama who'd joined the army as a private to fight for a country that had not treated him kindly. Big Ben was a friend to everyone.

'You've had no cases of malaria yet?' Jane asked, squeezing out the towel and soaking it again, continuously bathing the man's face to keep his temperature down.

'Not at Quoin Hill. I guess we've been lucky. Several guys came down with it at the Havannah Harbour base, but not like this. The medico gave them some pills and they seemed to be okay.'

'Vivax malaria,' Jane nodded, 'it's benign, it can be treated orally.'

Until the completion of the navy hospital at Bellevue, the military had an arrangement with the French and English hospitals on the island, and many malaria cases were presently being treated, she told him.

'They're starting to pour in,' she said, 'it's going to be a problem.'

Jane had become personally involved in the malaria predicament. The medical corps believed that malaria could become a bigger killer than the enemy itself and they had urgently requested supplies of quinine. Mass malaria treatment would be necessary for both military and islanders, they said, and Jane had agreed to work with the locals, distributing tablets and stressing their importance to the natives.

The military had recognised in Jane Thackeray a veritable gold mine. The special trust she had with the local population was proving invaluable.

The jeep bounced and skidded dangerously along the rough, pitted road and Wolf kept darting admiring glances at Jane as she tended to Big Ben calmly, professionally, with no thought of her own safety. What a remarkable woman she was, he thought.

'I'd say you got him here in the nick of time,' the doctor told Wolf, who had been anxiously pacing the waiting-room floor of the English hospital for over an hour since Big Ben had been wheeled away, Jane, too, disappearing with the medical team.

'Mrs Thackeray can take credit for that,' Wolf said, acknowledging Jane who had reappeared with the doctor.

He was thoughtful as he drove her home. 'You saved Big Ben's life, Jane,' he said after a moment or so. 'And I'd like to thank you on behalf of the men.'

'Just doing my job, Wolf.'

But for once he wasn't in a frivolous mood. 'Big Ben's

one of the best. The men are going to love you for what
you've done.' He smiled but he was still in deadly earnest.
'You're a hero to the local people, and you're a hero to us.'

He saluted her as he said goodbye. But he was grinning
his ridiculously boyish grin as he did so, and she wasn't
sure whether he was joking or not.

He was back the following week. 'Got a minute to visit
the hospital?' he asked. 'Big Ben wants to say thanks.'

Fifteen minutes later, the two of them walked into the
ward.

'Hello, Big Ben,' she said, 'I'm Jane, remember me?'

The bare, black skin of his arms rested over his massive
chest, stark against the white sheets. Big Ben was
enormous, and the bed was far too small for him.

'Oh yes, ma'am.' Big Ben remembered Jane vividly. In
fact she was the first thing he'd remembered when he'd
regained his senses only several days previously to find
himself in this little bed. The soft, soothing voice, the
pretty white face, the damp towel bathing him, he remembered it all. But he remembered before that. He remembered watching her with the islanders. Even as he'd started
to feel really sick, he'd kept watching her. How she spoke
their language and how they respected her and called her
Missus Tack. And then they'd brought their families to say
hello. Missus Tack was a saint to his black brothers here
in the Pacific, Big Ben thought, and she was a saint to
him too.

'How are you feeling?' Jane asked. 'You're looking
good, except you need a bigger bed.'

He laughed. 'I'm feeling just fine.' He wasn't really, he
was as weak as a kitten, but the doctor said he'd get his
strength back. And it was all because of this itty-bitty
white woman standing beside him. He reached out his
hand. He wanted to say thank you. But he couldn't call her
'Jane', that wasn't respectful enough. And he couldn't call
her 'Missus Tack'. 'Missus' was islander talk. He needed

something special, something that came from his own people.

'Thank you, Mamma Tack,' he said as she shook his hand.

# BOOK THREE

# CHAPTER TWELVE

S am awoke to the insistent ring of the telephone, and
automatically picked up the receiver. The recorded
voice told her it was five o'clock in the morning, her
pre-arranged wake-up call. She laid her head back on the
pillow, trying to recall the events of the night. There'd been
the party at the pool. And then she'd been out on the
verandah with Brett, and they'd been about to go to bed
together. God, how had she let that happen?

Suddenly it all came swimming back into her brain. The
ecstasy pill. The overwhelming panic. The terrifying sense
of imminent death as she lay in the dark. Then the hallu-
cinations. The vision of the old woman from Fareham.
The clarity of her voice. 'We're a team, you and I, dear,' the
old woman had said, 'a team.' Then the giant eye, getting
bigger and bigger and finally swallowing her.

She shivered at the memory. How bizarre, she thought,
what extraordinary tricks the mind can play when it's
tampered with. Then, after briefly cursing Brett Marsdon
for his stupidity, she resolved not to dwell on the strange-
ness of it all, but to repair the damage instead.

She threw the light cotton doona aside and tentatively
stood, surprised that she didn't feel worse. Surely she

should have a hideous hangover, but she wasn't even tired. She went into the bathroom and turned the mirror lights on for a close inspection. How much sleep had she had, three hours, four? But her skin was tight and her eyes were clear. The after-effects appeared to be minimal, she thought thankfully.

'G'day, Sam.'

'Morning, Bob.'

The Landcruiser was parked out the front, and Bob Crawley was waiting in the open, hotel reception area. Bob was always punctual. As 'personal chauffeur to the stars', a term he intended incorporating in his brochures, Bob considered it his duty to provide top professional service.

He and Sam sat in the deserted lounge chatting amicably as they waited for Brett Marsdon. Bob was to drive the two actors to Mele Bay, the crew having left in their trucks and vans a full half hour earlier to set up. Simon Scanlon would arrive at location an hour and a half after the actors who, by then, would have been through the lengthy process of makeup, hair and wardrobe.

Morning call times were tightly scheduled, strictly adhered to, and any tardiness or inefficiency met with the disapproval of all. Not only did a late start put them behind schedule, but it meant they lost the best part of the day, for it was the clear morning light that was most effective on film. In fact, Simon and Kevin Hodgman, the director of photography, considered the early light so precious that they went to great pains to select which scenes and shots would be filmed first up.

'Bit late, isn't he?' Bob Crawley said, finally breaking the silence and stating the obvious, but Sam didn't reply. Their conversation had died down over the past quarter of an hour. They'd now been waiting twenty-five minutes, and she was angry. She didn't want to take it out on poor Bob, however, so she strode up to the night clerk seated behind the reception desk and told him to go and knock on Mr Marsdon's door.

'And don't stop until you've woken him up,' she said grimly.

The clerk, a young islander called Henry, checked his list of wake-up calls and said that Mr Marsdon had already been woken up.

No, he hadn't been woken up at all, Sam said, but Henry nodded emphatically and assured her that he had made the wake-up call himself.

'Yes, I believe you,' she replied with a touch of exasperation. 'But, you see, he didn't wake up, he slept through the call.'

Henry stared at her, pleasantly but blankly.

'We need to wake him up!' Sam desperately urged.

'Ah.' Henry smiled and nodded and picked up the phone.

'No, no, that won't do!' She curbed her annoyance, but she wanted to scream; sometimes the islanders' incomprehension of the concept of urgency was infuriating. 'I want you to go to his door, and I want you to keep bashing on it until he wakes up.' She thumped her fist on the desk by way of example.

Henry wanted to say that it wasn't his job, that he was on reception duty. The early morning shift was his favourite, always easy, nothing to do. He didn't want to walk all the way down the hill and then back up again. But if he rang through to William who was on security, it would take a long time – William was usually asleep. Henry sensed that the young woman was getting angry and he never liked being hassled, so he gave in.

It was a full fifteen minutes before he ambled back, and Sam was beginning to wish she'd sprinted down the hill herself.

'Mista Marsdon is woken up now,' he said.

'Thank you.' She tried to make her smile as gracious as possible.

Several minutes later, Brett raced breathlessly into the reception area doing up the buttons of his open-necked cotton shirt.

'Sorry I'm late,' he panted, 'slept through the wake-up call. Just as well for Henry here, eh?' He smiled at the clerk, and from behind his desk Henry returned the smile, glad that his trouble had been so appreciated.

Sam said nothing, but marched out to the Landcruiser, the other two following.

Bob had presumed that the actors would sit together in the back seat as they usually did. He respected their passion for their work. Sam and Mickey and Louis would always listen to each other's lines, or discuss their characters and the scenes they were about to shoot. This time was different, however.

'I'll sit in the front with Bob,' Sam said to Brett, 'and you take the back seat.' It was nothing short of an order. 'You can get a bit more sleep on the drive out there.' He looked terrible, she thought. His skin was puffy, his eyes bloodshot, and the bags underneath them made him look ten years older. What was the man doing to himself?

'Great idea, thanks, Sam.' Brett jumped into the back and lay down immediately.

His apology for being three-quarters of an hour late had been perfunctory to say the least, and he hadn't registered her annoyance at all, both of which made Sam even more angry. She climbed into the car, Bob started the engine, and as they pulled away from the kerb, she leaned over the back seat.

'You look bloody terrible, you know that,' she said accusingly.

'Sure, sure,' he said as he closed his eyes. 'They'll fix it, don't you worry, that's what makeup artists are for. We're going to be great today, you and me, Sam.' And he was asleep in a matter of seconds.

Sam looked out the window at the dawn sky as they drove, the normally talkative Bob respecting her silence. She was probably getting into character, he thought. God, he loved working in show business.

Brett Marsdon appeared to have no recall of last night's events, Sam thought. Not that she would have expected him to say anything in front of Bob, but surely she should have read some recognition in his eyes, in his general behaviour. It was a worry. A very big worry, she thought. Did they really have a junkie on their hands?

Bob drove fast, trying to pick up some of the time they'd lost, but they were still half an hour late when they arrived at Mele Bay, where the trucks and vans were all parked on the spit overlooking the mock township.

Maz raised a critical eyebrow as Sam and Brett stepped up into the makeup van reserved for the principal actors. Which one of them was responsible for the hold-up? she wondered as she studied them for the obvious signs. Of course, she should have guessed.

'Come on, Brett,' she said. He looked a mess. 'Into the chair, you're mine.' Maz was the boss, and personally responsible for Samantha Lindsay's hair and makeup, but, recognising Brett Marsdon as an urgent case, she gave a nod to Ralph, her second-in-command. She shoved Sam's kit and makeup charts along the bench to him, muttering under her breath with a glance at Brett, 'This could take a while.'

'Sorry we're late, Maz.' Sam took the onus of apology upon herself. There was none forthcoming from Brett, who'd climbed into the makeup chair and was about to fall asleep.

'No worries.' Maz winked an assurance that she was well aware of the guilty party. 'We'll get you both done in time.' And as she quickly cleansed, toned and prepared Brett's face, she talked Ralph through Sam's makeup and the requirements of the day.

Maz was a highly experienced makeup artist. A tough-talking, good-natured little woman in her mid-thirties, who worked hard and partied hard, she was well liked and respected by actors. She in turn liked and respected them, with the exception of a handful whom she considered spoilt brats, and Brett Marsdon appeared to be one of them. She hadn't worked with him before, but she knew his kind.

She lifted back his eyelids and inserted the drops that would clear the redness. His kind were the insolent little shits who partied all night, then relied on makeup artists to undo the damage. She didn't actually mind that part of it, she thought, laying the infused eyepads over his eyes to reduce the swelling. She rather enjoyed the challenge of restoring their looks for the camera, but when they were unapologetically late, and arrogant to boot, she wanted to belt the crap out of them. A late start meant she had to rush her work, and she bloody hated that.

To Maz, makeup was far more than a technical and artistic skill, it was a psychological affair. The relationship between makeup artist and actor was intimate. She started their day, both physically and mentally. She relaxed them with hot face towels, and refreshed their skin with toners before applying their makeup, she massaged their scalps before starting on their hair or their wigs. She liked to take her time. She listened when actors wanted to chat, and she was as silent as the grave when they didn't. She gossiped when they wished and, if they sought her advice on personal problems, she told them exactly what they wanted to hear. Maz was very good at her job.

And then pricks like Brett Marsdon came along and buggered things up, she thought, gently patting the elasti-cising cream in with the tips of her fingers and watching the skin tighten as she did so. Selfish little shits who arrived late, forced her to rush her work and thereby stuffed up her day. She invariably got them on set looking perfect and with no halt to production time, but she was never thanked for it. And on the rare occasion when it was an impossible task and the director and crew were kept waiting, the cry was always the same. 'What the hell's going on with hair and makeup?'

Once the puffiness was reduced enough to apply makeup, she started under Brett's eyes with the masking stick. She was on the downhill run. Clever masking, a special base, intricate use of highlights and shaders, the rest was easy. She'd have him ready on time, and she'd do it with good grace, but she didn't like Brett Marsdon.

It was all very well to be a party person, Maz thought – Christ alive, she was one herself, she could pop e's and snort coke with the best of them – but actors had to be careful. And if they couldn't be careful, they could at least arrive on bloody time and be grateful when she undid the bloody damage.

'Fantastic!' Brett grinned into the mirror. 'Absolutely fantastic!' And Maz had the distinct impression that the compliment was directed at himself, not her.

'Can we have Mr Marsdon on set, please.' Even as the first assistant director's voice crackled over the two-way radio set, the makeup van door opened and the second AD popped his head in. 'They're ready to go,' he said.

The second disappeared and Brett bounced out of the chair, revitalised. 'Thanks, babe,' he said, 'you've done a great job.'

'My pleasure.' He hadn't even bothered to remember her name, she thought.

Sam was already waiting on set when Brett arrived. They were filming at Mamma Black's, and she was sitting beside the boathouse in a director's chair, script in hand, the extras who had been brought out in the mini-bus milling around drinking mugs of tea.

Brett leapt in front of her and struck a pose. 'Looking good,' he said, flashing his perfect smile, teeth gleaming in the crisp early light, 'what did I tell you?'

'Looking very good,' she agreed. 'Maz is a genius.'

'Looking good yourself, Sam.' He stepped back and appraised her admiringly. He hadn't paid any attention to her when he'd been sitting in the adjacent makeup chair – he'd been too busy drifting off to sleep – and he hadn't even heard her leave the van. He'd seen her as Sarah Blackston before, when he'd watched the filming at Undine Bay, but this was a different Sarah entirely. Her hair was blonder, bleached nearly white by the sun, and her skin was tanned and healthy. Gone was the restricted, demure woman he'd watched in the scene with the husband and the plantation owner. This woman was a free spirit, a very part of the environment that surrounded her.

The montage depicting Sarah's transformation had been filmed before his arrival and Brett was looking at the Sarah Blackston who had become Mamma Black, saviour to the local people and valuable ally to the American forces. He was most impressed.

'You're looking better than good, you're looking fan-bloody-tastic!' he said, with an attempt at an Australian accent that was so awful Sam laughed.

'Action,' Simon called five minutes later.

*'So you're Mamma Black.'*

*Sarah was in the boathouse. Having lifted up the second of the large shutters, she was wedging the rod into the window ledge when she heard the voice in the street, and turned to see the lieutenant watching her.*

*'Yes.'*

*Wily Halliday looked the young Englishwoman up and down. 'You're not what I expected.'*

*Sarah found the man's manner impudent. 'Really?' she replied archly. 'And what exactly did you expect?'*

*'Well, someone older, for a start.' Again he looked her up and down, taking in the lithe brown arms and slim body, his eyes resting momentarily upon the pert breasts*

*evident beneath the light, sleeveless shirt.* 'Someone . . . I don't know . . . bigger, I guess.' *He grinned suggestively.* 'Hell, Mamma *Black, what was I supposed to expect?*'

'Cut!' Simon called. He took Brett aside. 'Less lascivious, mate,' he said quietly.

'How do you mean?' Brett was on the defensive in an instant. He hadn't been playing it lasciviously at all, he thought.

'I mean that he's not on the make. He's not undressing her with his eyes, he's simply surprised and he's honest about it.'

'But he lusts after her,' Brett countered. 'Shit, man, look at her! What guy wouldn't?'

Simon heaved an inward sigh. Brett Marsdon was going to be trouble, but he always placated his actors. 'Yeah, I'm sure he does, but let's keep that hidden for a while, shall we? Let's just play it simple for starters. Genuine surprise, genuine admiration.' He smiled encouragingly. 'Okay?'

Brett shrugged. 'Okay.' But he wasn't very happy. This was the scene where the stars of the movie first met. Surely there should be sparks. Instant chemistry, that's what it was all about.

They started again and the scene progressed.

*'No offence intended, ma'am, I assure you.' Wily apologised in earnest, realising that she'd found him too forthright.*

*'None taken, Lieutenant . . .?' She waited for him to introduce himself.*

*'Lieutenant Wily Halliday, at your service, ma'am.'*

*His smile was disarming as he saluted, and Sarah smiled back, realising that she'd overreacted. The young lieutenant might be brash but he meant no harm. She started levering up the next shutter.*

*'Let me give you a hand.' He took the rod from her.*

*'Thank you, Lieutenant. Wily . . . that's short for*

*William, is it?' she asked, keen to make up for her brusqueness.*

*'Nope. I was named after Wily Post.' It was a proud announcement, and when he'd wedged the rod into the window ledge he stood waiting for her to be impressed. But there was no reaction at all. 'You've never heard of Wily Post?' he asked incredulously.*

*'Sorry.'*

*'One of America's great heroes. Pioneer aviator. Created airmail routes from Alaska to Florida.'*

*'Ah.' She nodded.*

*'First man to fly solo around the world, seven days, eighteen hours and forty-nine minutes. He was my dad's best friend at school.' He grinned with inordinate pride. 'Wily Post was the reason I became a pilot.'*

'Cut!' Simon called. Once again he took Brett aside. 'You're laying it on a bit thick, mate,' he said.

'Laying *what* on thick?' Brett was bewildered.

'The charm,' Simon said as gently as he could, although he wanted to throttle the man. Marsdon wasn't relating to Sam at all, he was simply pulling out every trick in the book. From the sparkling eyes to the million-dollar smile, he looked like a toothpaste commercial. 'Like I said, mate, he's not trying to score, he's genuinely proud of being named after Wily Post.'

This time Brett was more than defensive, he was rebellious. 'I wasn't playing him like he's trying to *score*, Simon! I was playing the character for what he is. He's a hero, man! And what the fuck's wrong with a bit of charm anyway?' And why the fuck was Simon Scanlon considered such a crash-hot director? he thought. Jesus, what does he want from me? I'm a number one box-office star, I've been hired for my onscreen charisma, and he's asking me to act like a wimp.

But Brett could feel the beads of sweat forming at his temples. He remembered how impressed he'd been as he'd watched the other actors at Undine Bay. He'd told himself not to rely on the old charm. Was Scanlon right? Was that what he was doing, just playing the star? He hadn't intended to, he'd been giving it his best shot. He was getting jumpy. Careful, he told himself, don't let the paranoia set in.

It was just as he'd feared, Simon thought, Marsdon could no longer act without his tricks. It was why he'd fought against the man's casting from the outset. Brett Marsdon was basically a good actor, Simon knew it. Indeed in his early films, when he'd been little more than a teenager, he'd displayed an extraordinary natural talent. But for the past several years his box-office successes had been realised on the strength of his good looks and personality. So much so that his tricks had now become second nature, the man wasn't even aware of his mannerisms. Or was he? Simon wondered. Beneath the actor's belligerence, he had recognised a strong sense of insecurity. Brett Marsdon was afraid. Was he doubting himself?

Very patiently, Simon started to spell out the character of Wily Halliday as he saw him.

'Wily's *not* a hero, Brett. Not *yet*. And even when he *does* become a hero, it's only through his actions, there's nothing inherently heroic about him as a man. And he certainly doesn't see himself as hero.' Brett was sulking, it wasn't getting through. 'Look, mate, you're right,' Simon said trying to bolster the actor's confidence. 'You're dead bloody right, he's charming. But it's the sort of charm that comes from within. Wily's not trying to sell himself.'

It wasn't working at all. Brett's sulky pout had now become a baleful glare. He hadn't been trying to *sell* himself, for God's sake. Fuck you, Scanlon, he thought.

The man had closed off completely, Simon realised. He switched to another tack.

'I tell you what,' he suggested, 'let's try a bit of improvisation. No cameras, just you and Sam.' Perhaps Sam could get through to him, he thought. Marsdon obviously couldn't, or wouldn't, take direction. Not from him anyway. An instinctive approach might prove more productive.

Brett continued to glare, so Simon slung an arm around his shoulder. 'Come on, mate,' he said, 'relax and give it a burl,' and Brett reluctantly allowed himself to be led back to the boathouse. 'You blokes take a break for a while,' Simon said to Kevin, 'we're going to do a bit of impro,' and the director of photography and his team disappeared for a coffee.

'Right,' Simon instructed, 'a different scenario. We'll take it from where you introduce yourself, Brett. Sam, you take the piss out of him about being called Wily, and Brett you convince her it's your real name.'

Sam nodded, she enjoyed improvisation, but Brett didn't look too sure. He wasn't accustomed to working without a script.

'I don't want you to stay in character,' Simon told them. 'I want you to go whichever way you want, do whatever you like, say whatever comes into your head, I'm just after interaction.' He gave Sam a meaningful look, which she instantly understood. Simon wanted her to push Brett, perhaps even to unnerve him, anything to elicit an instinctive response.

Brett looked at Sam. Did she approve of this bullshit? But she smiled encouragingly. 'Come on, Brett, have a go,' she said, 'it's fun.'

'In your own time,' Simon called.

'Lieutenant Wily Halliday, at your service, ma'am.' Brett wasn't sure how to start the ball rolling, so he stuck to the script.

Sam looked him up and down, then raised a scornful eyebrow. 'Wily?' she said. 'That's apt.'

'How do you mean?' He was confused. Sam didn't look like Sarah Blackston any more. She didn't look like Sam either. She was brassy and brazen and provocative.

'It suits you,' she said. 'Wily, as in cunning. Wily, as in crafty.' Her smile was wicked. 'It's a very good nickname.'

'It's not a nickname,' he protested. He was more than confused, he was well and truly out of his depth.

'Really? Pity. I found it attractive.'

'In what way?' He couldn't think of what to say.

'Well, you're trying to chat me up, aren't you?' She grinned seductively and he couldn't take his eyes off her. 'You're trying to get into my knickers, Wily Halliday.' She put her hand on his shoulder and gently trailed her fingers down his chest. 'I'd say that makes you one wily bastard, wouldn't you?' And the tip of her tongue slid lazily across her upper lip.

Christ, she was coming on strong, he thought, and the memory of the previous night returned. He recalled the excitement he'd felt when they'd been on the verge of making love. Jesus, but she'd turned him on. Then she'd had that bad trip and he'd gone back to his bungalow. He'd felt pretty jumpy so he'd smoked a joint to calm down and then he'd hit the wall.

Brett hadn't thought about last night's events all morning, apart from a vague sense of relief that Sam was fine. So, she'd had a bad trip, so what? Everyone had a bad trip now and then. But here she was, coming on to him so strong, and it all flooded back.

He tried to concentrate on the improvisation. 'Wily's not a nickname,' he said. Her other hand was on his chest now. Her mouth, lips parted, was coming closer, and he couldn't drag his eyes from hers. 'Wily's who I am.'

'Wily is who you are?' she whispered, and she started to unbutton his shirt.

'Wily Post,' he said, mesmerised.

'Wily what?' She stopped and drew back, surprised.

'I was named after Wily Post.'

'Who the fuck's Wily Post?'

The vulgarity shocked him. And her eyes were cold. No longer bent on seduction, she was mocking him now.

'Wily Post was one of America's great heroes.' Brett had no option but to return to the script, he was completely rattled. 'First man to fly solo around the world. And my father went to school with him.'

'Cut!' Simon called. 'Well done, you two. Thanks, Sam.' He kissed her cheek, but the gentle pressure of his fingers on her shoulder was a far greater expression of his gratitude. 'Good on you, Brett,' he said giving him a hearty pat on the back, 'that was great.'

What was? Brett wondered. He hadn't done anything. But Simon's praise had a profound effect on him and, his belligerence now forgotten, he beamed like a child being congratulated by a favourite teacher.

'We'll do a dry run,' Simon said. 'No cameras. Go from the top of the scene. And take it from Sam, Brett. Relate to her, she'll give you everything.' Another look, which Sam acknowledged with an imperceptible nod, assured Simon that she would.

They ran the scene twice and Brett was starting to relax. Without the pressure of the cameras he was happy to concentrate on reacting purely to Sam's performance.

'We're ready to roll,' Simon announced and, whilst makeup was called in for touch-ups, he took Kevin aside for a quiet discussion which no-one heard. Then as Kevin left, he called Sam over to him.

Brett watched Simon Scanlon, his arm around Sam, the two of them in intense conversation. Thank God for that, he thought, his paranoia no longer a threat, Sam was getting notes from the director too, he wasn't the only one.

'It's not working,' Sam said.

'It is, believe me, he's relaxing by the minute.'

*He's* relaxing, Sam thought, what about *me*? 'But he can't keep taking the lead from me, it's unbalancing the scene.' Surely Simon could see that, she thought. She wished that Nick Parslow was there; Nick certainly wouldn't allow his script to be so wrongly interpreted, she thought. But Nick had gone to Brisbane to meet some obscure research person who had flown out from England. Today of all days! Damn it, Sam thought, it wasn't a researcher she needed, it was an ally.

Sam's survival instincts had come into play. Her own performance was being undermined. She was bolstering Brett's inadequacies at Simon's request, and it wasn't fair of him to ask it of her. 'I'm trying to give him too much when I should be holding back. I keep coming out of character.'

'I know, I know,' Simon said quite happily.

'Well, bugger that.' Sam was irritated. She felt suddenly exhausted and fed up, and she wanted to hit Simon Scanlon.

'Sam, listen to me.' His arm was around her, his fingers gripping her shoulder. 'We're not rolling film, we're doing a dry run, I just want to see how he reacts to the camera.'

She stared at him. So the whole thing was a setup? In her tiredness, she was confused. But the old Svengali gleam was in Simon's eyes and she found herself, as always, intrigued. When Simon Scanlon was fired up there was a madness about him that was mesmeric.

'No-one's going to ruin your performance, Sam,' he said. 'No-one! But if we can't find a truthful balance with Brett we're in deep shit, and you're the only one who can get it out of him.'

'And after the dry run?' She was still bewildered by his tactics. Was she supposed to alter her performance in the instant he decided to roll film?

'Relax, we're not shooting this scene at all today.' He gave a casual shrug in response to her surprise. 'We've lost the early light anyway. We'll reschedule it for first up tomorrow.'

The pressure suddenly off, Sam felt a mixture of relief

and fatigue, but she still wasn't sure about Simon's overall plan.

'I'm going to call a break after this run and we'll set up for the scene with you and Brett and Mickey.' He could see she was tired and confused. 'Everything'll be fine, trust me, Sam,' he assured her, and she had no option to do otherwise.

Maz had completed touching up Brett's makeup and was standing by to do Sam's, but she made an announcement instead.

'I want Sam in the van,' she said to Simon, 'we need more than touch-ups.' Sam needed the full overhaul, Maz thought, she looked buggered.

'Touch-ups'll be fine,' Simon said.

Maz, who never feared fronting directors, was about to argue, but Simon muttered in her ear. 'We won't be using any of these takes.'

'Oh. Okay.' She shrugged, but she was puzzled. Why were they rolling film if they weren't going to use it? Sheer bloody waste, in her opinion. Still, it wasn't her place to say anything.

'Action!'

It was as Simon had suspected. Once they were rolling, or once Brett *assumed* they were rolling, he again couldn't resist acting for the camera. His performance was certainly more truthful than it had been at the outset, but he was still trying to make an impact. Marsdon was fixated upon the fact that this was his first appearance in the film, Simon realised, and more importantly that it was the scene where he first met Sarah Blackston. How could he make the man realise that his own charisma and the chemistry between the two of them was already there, that there was no need to work at it?

'Cut!' he called. 'That's it for Mamma Black's,' he announced. 'Take a break everyone whilst we set up for the scene at Reid's.'

Maz was at his side in a second. 'I'll need a good hour and a half for Sam,' she said.

'No worries.'

Whilst Sam was whisked away to the principals' makeup van, Simon and Kevin walked towards the nearby set of Reid's Hotel.

'But Simon . . .' Brett followed them.

Simon stopped. 'What's up, Brett?'

'We haven't finished the scene.' How could they call a halt after only a few takes? he thought. 'What about the reverse shots?' he asked. 'What about the closeups? When are we going to . . .?'

'Oh I'm not using any of this morning's stuff, mate.' Brett's jaw gaped. Why on earth not? he wondered. 'We've lost the early light,' Simon explained, 'and it's such an important scene, I want you both looking good. Not to worry,' he smiled, 'we'll shoot the whole thing first up tomorrow. Damn good rehearsal though, Brett, well done.' Another pat on the back, and Brett was left standing there, bewildered. Was Simon mad at him, he wondered briefly. But no, the director seemed quite happy. Strange guy, Brett thought.

As they walked to the Reid's set, Simon told Kevin his plans. Tomorrow they would reverse the tactic, he said. They would tell Brett they were not rolling film, that they were using the cameras simply to set up angles and shots. Then they would roll without Marsdon knowing it.

'Any trick we can use, Kev.'

'Fine by me.'

Kevin Hodgman was a man of few words who lived his life through a camera lens. Everything that caught his attention – a face in a crowd, a bird in flight, a reflection on water – constituted 'a great shot'. Over their respective twenty-year careers, he and Simon Scanlon had worked together many times, and he'd often seen Simon resort to tricks when he couldn't get a performance out of an actor through the force of his own inspiration. Somehow he always managed to make it work, and Kevin had no reason to believe that this time would be any different. But he could tell that Simon was worried.

'She'll be jake, Simon,' he said comfortingly.

Ralph had just finished Mickey Robertson's makeup when Maz and Sam arrived back at the van.

'G'day, Sammy, how's it going?' Mickey leaned lazily back in the chair.

'Fine. Hello, Elizabeth, I didn't know you were called today.'

Elizabeth was seated nearby. 'I'm not,' she said. 'Mickey asked me if I'd like to come out and watch the filming.' She and Mickey exchanged a smile that spoke multitudes.

Sam had noticed the two of them huddled together at the party last night. Well, they'd obviously had a good time, she thought, I'm glad somebody did. She plopped, exhausted, into Maz's makeup chair.

'I'm looking forward to seeing the experts at work.' Elizabeth's pretty brown face beamed unashamed pleasure as she leaned forward and took Mickey's hand. She'd been delighted last night when he'd asked her how to say 'I find you sexy' in Bislama. She'd set her sights on him a week ago and she'd wondered what had taken him so long.

'Everyone out, please,' Maz broke up the chat. 'Brett'll be here for touch-ups, we need both chairs.'

'Maz the Militant,' Mickey said, but he obediently rose, stooping as he did, his lanky frame too tall for the van. 'Come on, Liz, let's get a cup of tea.'

'You can grab a quick cuppa too if you like, Ralph,' Maz said.

The offer was casual, but Ralph knew she wanted him out of the van for a moment. He closed the door behind him.

'You've hit the wall, haven't you,' Maz said to Sam as

she poured a glass of water. Then she delved into what she referred to as 'the help kit', her stash of remedies and drugs, many of which were illegal without a prescription.

So that was why she'd felt so suddenly exhausted, Sam realised. Of course! It hadn't been simply lack of sleep catching up with her. She'd wondered why she'd felt so good this morning, why she hadn't looked hungover, and why she hadn't felt tired after a fair bit of booze and only several hours' sleep. The bad trip might have passed, but the pill had still been working. Now the effects had worn off and she'd crashed.

'Yes,' she said, 'you're right, I've hit the wall.'

'Drink this,' Maz handed her an ugly-looking concoction in a glass.

'What the hell is it?'

'A bit of everything, but basically a massive dose of vitamin B.'

The mixture had a surprisingly instant effect. 'Wow,' Sam said as she felt her eyes spring open.

'Good stuff, eh? Maz's miracle cure. Lie back, we've got time to go from the top.' She tilted the chair and started cleansing Sam's face.

They were silent for a while, Sam relaxing under Maz's expert ministrations.

'I took an ecstasy pill,' she finally admitted. Maz hadn't asked for any explanation, but given all the extra work inflicted upon her, Sam felt that she was owed one.

'Thought so,' Maz said, placing the cool, soothing pads over Sam's eyes. 'And you're not used to them, right?'

Sam shook her head.

There was a tap at the door, Ralph being tactful. He popped his head in. 'All clear?'

'Yep,' Maz said. Ralph had Brett Marsdon in tow, and she looked shrewdly at the American as he stepped up into the van. She knew damn well where Sam's e had come from. The little prick, she thought.

Fifteen minutes later, her makeup fully restored, her body and mind revitalised by Maz's 'miracle cure', Sam sat with Mickey and Brett in the Reid's set awaiting Simon's call of 'action'.

'*Wily Post, eh?*' *Hugh was impressed.*

'*Yes, sir.*' *Wily flashed a smile at Sarah, pleased that Dr Blackston knew of Wily Post's fame.*

'*Thank goodness, Hugh.*' *Sarah laughed.* '*You've saved the Blackston name. When Lieutenant Halliday first introduced himself to me I had no idea who Wily Post was.*'

'*One of the greatest aviators the world's ever known, my dear.*'

*Hugh Blackston had recently returned to Vila after a month's absence, and the three of them were sitting in the lounge at Reid's Hotel, Sarah having introduced the American to her husband.*

*Hugh turned to Wily with a smile.* '*So your destiny was preordained, Lieutenant. Given a name like that, you were of course duty bound to become a pilot.*'

'*I guess I was, sir.*' *Wily grinned, he liked the doctor.*

*Hugh had taken an instinctive liking to the young pilot too, it was difficult not to, he was so ingenuous. But he rather wished the fellow wouldn't call him 'sir'; there would, after all, be little more than ten years' difference in their ages. He decided to nip it in the bud.*

'*Shall we dispense with the "sir", Lieutenant?*'

*Wily was nonplussed. Had he caused offence? He'd intended only respect. The guy was a doctor and a reverend one at that.*

*Hugh realised that the young man thought he'd offended him, and he laughed out loud.* '*Good heavens, man, you make me feel so old!*'

The scene was progressing beautifully and Simon couldn't have been happier. Brett was relaxed. No longer set upon making a personal impact, he was responding to Mickey and a relationship was developing between the two men. A relationship that Brett himself wasn't fully aware of, Simon thought, just as Wily Halliday wouldn't be. The subtleties of the scene lay in Mickey's performance. The older man was studying the Lieutenant's good looks, aware that the young man was the same age as his wife. He was aware, too, that his wife had developed a friendship with this man, as she had with many of the military with whom she worked. Hugh Blackston trusted his wife implicitly, and felt like a traitor as he pondered his misgivings.

*'Time to go, my dear.' Hugh rose from the table. They'd been there for some time, discussing Sarah's work with the military, and the indispensable place Mamma Black's now served in Vila. Hugh was proud of his wife, and ashamed of the feelings he wrestled with. 'Perhaps, Lieutenant, you might care to join us for dinner?'*

*'What an excellent suggestion, Hugh.' Sarah smiled from her husband to Wily and back again.*

*'I'd be honoured, Dr Blackston,' Wily said.*

*'Shall we make it Hugh?'*

'Cut,' Simon called.

'Brett's responding to Mickey like there's no tomorrow,' Simon said to Sam on the way back to the hotel. He'd suggested she go with him in his Suzuki hire car instead of travelling in the Landcruiser with Bob Crawley and the others. She'd had a feeling she knew why: he wanted to talk about Brett. She'd been right.

'Yes, he is,' she agreed, 'but then Mickey's so easy to respond to . . .'

But Simon wasn't listening. 'The first scene between you two is the worry. In fact the whole relationship between Sarah and Wily'll be a worry if we can't break through this Hollywood star syndrome shit. Has he got the hots for you?'

The question had come out of nowhere and she looked

at him in astonishment. But he was concentrating on the rough, rutted road and simply waiting for her answer.

Sam knew Simon Scanlon well enough now not to find him offensive. Every personal intrusion was for the good of the movie, she'd discovered, so she decided to be honest.

'He tried to chat me up last night,' she admitted, 'but I don't know how serious it was. He was a bit grog-affected. We both were.' She made no mention of drugs.

'Yes, he fancies you all right, I could see that in the impro this morning. Which of course could work to our advantage.'

The slits of his eyes were still focussed on the road, but Sam could tell his brain was working overtime. She didn't know whether to feel outraged or not.

'Are you asking me to sleep with him for the sake of the movie?'

'Well, stranger things have happened.' Simon shrugged. Then he turned to meet her eyes, which were wide with astonishment. 'Good God, no, woman,' he laughed. 'I'd prefer it if you didn't. Torrid affairs amongst actors can make for a shitload of trouble.' His smile vanished as quickly as it had appeared and he concentrated again on the road, swerving to avoid the potholes when he could. 'But you have an effect on him, Sam. It may be sexual, it may be your per-formance — I suspect it's a mixture of both. All I know is that he relates to you on some level. I don't know what it is, and I don't intend to try to find out. If I do he'll close off from me altogether.' His eyes met hers again, and he said in all seriousness, 'I need you to get through to him, Sam.'

Oh great, she thought, and how the hell am I supposed to do that?

'Basically he's insecure,' Simon continued. 'He's got it all there to play Wily Halliday, he just doesn't know it, so he uses the tricks.'

Sam agreed wholeheartedly. But what did Simon expect her to do?

'How do I go about it?' she asked.

'I've no idea. Bloody awful road, isn't it?' he said as they hit another unavoidable pothole.

The crowded dining room at the Crowne Plaza was as lively as always that night and the discussion, as usual, was of the day's filming. It was a hot, sultry evening and the general consensus was to meet at the pool after dinner for a dip and a drink before crashing early. Many were still feeling the effects of the previous night's party.

'Fancy a drink at my place?' Sam asked Brett. She'd decided to take the bull by the horns.

'Sure.' Christ, it was the full come-on, he thought.

There was no mistaking his eagerness, so Sam set him straight. 'I want to talk about tomorrow's scene,' she said.

'Yeah, yeah,' he grinned impishly, 'we can do some more impro. See you there in ten, I'll just call by my place first.'

Ten minutes later there was a tap at her bungalow door and she opened it to discover him brandishing a bottle of Bollinger and two chilled glasses.

'Called in at the bar on my way,' he said.

His eyes were bright, he was in full party mode, and Sam suspected that he'd snorted a quick line in preparation for some action. But she said nothing as they walked out onto the verandah where they sat, Brett opening the champagne.

'To us,' he toasted when he'd filled the glasses.

'To the movie,' she said automatically as they clinked.

'Now, where do we start?' He put his glass on the table, ready to close in.

'We don't. I meant what I said, Brett, I want to talk about work.'

'Sure, go for it.' Plenty of time, he thought, they had all night.

'You were terrific in the three-hander scene today. Mickey thought so too.'

'He did?' Seduction was momentarily forgotten at praise from Mickey Robertson. 'That's great. I love working with him.'

'Me too. He always manages to bring out the truth of a scene. That's why you two were great together today, the scene was so bloody truthful.'

Brett looked suspicious. Was there criticism intended? 'And it's why our scene didn't work, is that what you're saying?'

'Yes, that's what I'm saying.' Sam could see the defensiveness spring into play, but she was going for broke. Subtlety was not her forte, she could only be direct and say things the way she saw them. Damn you, Simon, she thought, I'm no psychiatrist, I'm probably doing irreparable damage.

'I see.' Brett's paranoia leapt to the fore. She didn't like working with him. Just like Scanlon, she thought he was full of Hollywood bullshit. Well, fuck her. He was a star and this was her first fucking movie. What would she know?

'Do you realise how attractive you are, Brett?'

He'd drained his glass and was about to leave, but the non sequitur confused him and he stared at her suspiciously. What was she playing at?

'I was knocked out when I first met you,' she said. She had to get through to him quickly, she thought, he was on the verge of walking out. 'Not just the good looks and all that, it was your eagerness that stunned me. I hadn't expected you to be so . . . I don't know . . .' she fumbled for the word '. . . so enthusiastic, I suppose, so unaffected. I remember thinking you were like a puppy wagging his tail.'

'How cute,' he said coldly. And how patronising, he thought.

'Oh you were much more than cute.' She could tell he was insulted, but she refused to be deterred. 'You were disarming. You were magnetic.'

'Was I?' Brett rose. 'Pity I turned out to be such a disappointment.' He'd asked for it, he supposed. What an egotistical idiot he'd been, arriving with champagne, assuming she wanted to pick up where they'd left off last night. It was his humiliation she was after, and she'd succeeded. She was pissed off, and he couldn't blame her, she had every right to be.

'I'm sorry about the party,' he said. 'I shouldn't have spiked your drink. I was high and I wasn't thinking. It was a stupid thing to do.' He had to get out whilst he still had a vestige of dignity. 'I'll see you in the morning.'

'Oh for God's sake, sit down.' She picked up the bottle and refilled his glass. 'Stop taking this personally.'

'How am I supposed to take it? You want to piss on me for taking advantage of you? Fine, you've done it, and I've said I'm sorry. Good night.'

'I don't want to piss on you, that's not what I'm saying.'

'Then what the hell *are* you saying, Sam?'

'I'm saying Brett Marsdon is Wily Halliday,' she explained, exasperated. 'Sit down and drink your champagne and stop being so bloody defensive.' He sat but he didn't drink his champagne, he watched her instead.

'The Brett Marsdon I first met was Wily Halliday,' she said. 'He wasn't out to make an impression, he was an excited, eager puppy. Don't you see, Brett? That's Wily!' She was so passionately earnest that Brett forgot the perceived insult. 'Wily's completely unaware of the effect he has on people,' she continued. 'That's his true charm. He honestly doesn't know that he's charismatic.' She picked up her glass, sat back and studied him. 'And that's the impression I had of you when we first met.' She raised the glass in a silent toast, then downed the champagne in one hit. 'And that's why you're going to be the perfect Wily Halliday.' Had she got through? She hoped so, she'd meant every word she'd said.

Brett was silent for a moment. It was just the boost his shaken ego needed. 'Thanks, Sam.' He couldn't think of anything else to say.

'Just stating the facts.' She put the glass on the table and took a deep breath. 'One other thing, though . . .' She wasn't sure how he'd react, but she knew she had to say it. 'Go easy on the coke. It can make you forget that we're all batting for the same team.'

She was the only one who could have said it to him. If anyone else had offered him such advice, he would have told them to mind their own goddamned business. But deep down Brett knew that she was right. He'd been jumpy a lot lately. He could have punched Simon Scanlon's lights out today, and it was all because of his own drug-induced paranoia. And the party last night. How the hell could he have done that to her?

'I nearly blew it with you, didn't I?' He shook his head. 'I must have been crazy. I'm really sorry.'

'You've already said that.' He looked like a worried little boy. He looked like Wily Halliday, she thought. Boyish and ingenuous. She smiled as she rose to her feet. 'It's over. Forgotten. Never happened.'

He stood and hugged her. 'We're going to be great, you and me, Sam,' he whispered in her ear, and this time there was no bravado, just relief.

'Yes we are,' she said, returning the hug.

'So I was an eager puppy . . .' His expression was quizzical as he held her at arm's length. 'You want to know my first impression of you?'

'Sure.'

'I thought you were one helluva hot little number and I couldn't wait to get you into the cot.' He smiled and gave a helpless shrug. 'So sue me, it's the truth.'

Sam laughed. He was incorrigible. He was brash, cheeky, and disarmingly honest. He was Wily Halliday.

'Go to bed, Brett,' she said pushing him to the door. 'On your own!'

'So you're Mamma Black.'
'Yes.'

'*You're not what I expected.*'

'*Really? And what exactly did you expect?*'

'*Well someone older, for a start. Someone . . . I don't know . . . bigger, I guess. Hell,* Mamma *Black, what was I supposed to expect?*'

'What have you done to him?' Simon whispered to Sam when they'd completed the first take. 'No,' he said, raising his hands in the air, 'don't tell me, I don't want to know. Just keep doing what you're doing, you're a genius, Sam.'

At the end of the day's filming, Sam felt elated. Simon's 'genius' tag might have been going a bit far, she thought, but he'd been right. Whatever she'd done to Brett had certainly been effective. Sarah and Wily had come alive that day and, all her qualms forgotten, she now looked forward to working with Brett Marsdon.

As the Landcruiser pulled up at the hotel, she spied Nick Parslow waiting for them in the hotel reception area.

'G'day, gang, how did it go?' he asked, joining the actors as they piled out of the car.

They walked into the hotel together, chatting animatedly, everyone having something to say about the day's filming. Ten minutes later Mickey and Brett disappeared to shower before dinner.

'Where the hell were you when I needed you?' Sam demanded once she and Nick were alone. She had determined to say nothing in front of the others.

'Oh really? Trouble?' He looked concerned.

'Nothing that hasn't sorted itself out,' she admitted, 'but what a bugger of a time to desert me.' He raised an eyebrow. 'The opening scene between me and Brett?' she said, spelling it out.

'I thought the timing was rather good myself,' Nick replied, easing his glasses up the bridge of his nose as he often did when he saw a confrontation coming. 'If I'd been here I wouldn't have come out on location anyway.'

'Why on earth not?'

'My presence on set wouldn't have helped, Sam, I can read Brett's antagonism a mile off. He doesn't like me.'

'That's because he thinks you don't like him.'

'Really?' Brett's feelings were of little concern to Nick, but he was pleased that Sam was being protective of the American, it augured well for their working together. 'So what happened?'

Sam paused for a moment. Although she hadn't intended to tell Nick about the ecstasy pill and the disastrous night with Brett, she had certainly anticipated discussing the difficulties they'd had with the American. But it was too complicated, she now realised. How could she explain the astonishing change in Brett's performance today without giving Nick, who knew her so well and was also so perceptive, the reasons why? She decided on evasive action instead.

'Some teething problems,' she said. 'It's probably best if Simon fills you in.'

'Right you are,' he nodded. 'Now let's have a drink, there's someone I want you to meet.'

She was relieved that he didn't appear interested in pursuing the conversation, but also a little puzzled. She'd expected him to grill her further. 'What teething problems?' he would normally have demanded. He seemed rather distracted, she thought.

'Not now, Nick, I have to have a shower, I'm filthy.'

'No shower, you're as fresh as a daisy, and I want you to meet him before the others congregate. Come on, he's waiting at the bar.' Arm linked firmly through hers he started marching her out of the reception area.

'Can't you give me twenty minutes . . .?' she started to protest.

'Nope, the gang'll be turning up and I want you to meet him on your own, it's important. Now listen to me, Sam . . .'

She allowed herself to be led. He was so intensely excited, the way he was during script discussions and workshops and play readings. What was going on? she wondered.

'You remember I told you Mamma Black was loosely based on a real character?' he asked.

'Yes. You said her name was Mamma Tack, but you didn't know who she was.'

'Exactly, apart from the fact that she was an English-woman married to a missionary doctor.' He shrugged. 'Writer's licence, I was inspired by the stories about her, simple as that. I didn't research the woman herself, it was never going to be a true story, Mamma Tack was simply an inspiration.' He'd slowed his walk to a snail's pace as they started down the hill to the poolside bar, but he was talking at the rate of knots.

'Well, some British journo busted us. There was a huge feature in the *Times* weekend supplement about the theme of Mammoth's new big-budget production in the South Pacific. Pictures of you, pictures of Brett. That's fine, great publicity. But there was also a detailed breakdown of *Torpedo Junction*'s plot. A bloke called Nigel Daly. Don't ask me how he did it. There must be a spy in our midst and he paid them off for a look at the script or whatever . . .'

'Yes, that'd be Nigel's style,' Sam agreed. 'If there's a way, he'll find it.'

'As it turns out he's done us a favour,' Nick said. They were fifty metres from the pool now, and he'd come to a standstill. 'At least I think he has. I hope you won't find it confusing.'

'Find what confusing?'

'I promise I'm not going to make any radical changes to the script,' he assured her. 'Simon'd kill me if I tried anyway. But it might give you an added insight. You know? You might even find it inspirational. It's inspired me, I can tell you . . .'

'Nick, what the hell are you on about?'

'Sorry,' he said, 'got carried away,' and he started slowly

from the beginning. 'Someone responded to the *Times* feature and got in touch with Mammoth. He said he was related to Mamma Tack. At first I thought he was a sensation-seeker, and then, when Mammoth put him onto me and I discovered he was for real, I thought he was after money. Either rights for the story, or the threat of a libel suit, neither of which would have held water, but it would have been an unnecessary hassle.'

'So what did he want?' She wished he'd get to the point.

'He wanted to help us in any way we might need,' Nick said. 'He's really interested in the project. He flew out at his own expense, said he was planning a trip anyway, and he's here right now.' He took her arm again and started walking towards the pool.

'It's incredible stuff,' he said, and again in his enthusiasm his words tripped over themselves. 'Mamma Tack was a woman called Jane Thackeray and she died in 1994. The locals called her Missus Tack because they couldn't pronounce the name, and it was the Americans who christened her "Mamma". She came from the south of England and she was married to a missionary doctor called Martin. Well no surprises there,' he admitted, 'apart from her real name, that much I knew of Mamma Tack. But I tell you, Sam, the parallels with the script and the story of the real Jane Thackeray are uncanny. She even knew the French plantation owner whose homestead we're filming in!'

They were nearing the pool and he lowered his voice, but his words tumbled out even faster as he told her of the similarities in the deaths of the husbands. 'Isn't it extraordinary? Hugh Blackston and Martin Thackeray died the same way.'

By now Sam was finding Nick's excitement contagious and, as they arrived at the pool, she looked about expectantly. The place was deserted, with the exception of a lone man seated at a table, and Jimmy behind the bar polishing the glasses in preparation for the 'hafmad filem bigfala grup', the crazy movie crowd.

The man rose from the table. He was in his early thirties and most intriguing-looking. Straight-haired, fine-boned and lightly olive-skinned; European, but with perhaps a touch of island blood.

'Jason, sorry to keep you waiting,' Nick said, 'this is Samantha.'

'Hello, Samantha.' Jason held out his hand. 'I've heard a great deal about you,' he smiled. The accent was very British, and Sam thought that she had never seen eyes so piercingly blue.

'Sam, this is Dr Jason Thackeray, Mamma Tack's grandson.'

# CHAPTER THIRTEEN

The medical corps' worst fears had been realised. Malaria had struck with a vengeance and both troops and islanders were falling victim to the killer disease. The mass distribution of quinine was essential, and doctors were urgently needed to treat the hospitalised patients who were fighting for their lives, far too many of them losing the battle. Martin Thackeray was called back to Vila.

'Good heavens above, Jane, I don't believe it!' Martin hefted a delighted Ronnie onto his shoulders and, holding the infant's hands, he stared in amazement at the open-shuttered boatshed on the other side of the busy street. He'd arrived that very morning and she'd said she had something to show him, mysteriously refusing any further explanation, and he hadn't known what to expect. Certainly not this, he thought. How extraordinary . . .

A large wooden sign, hanging above the boathouse door, said in bold black letters 'MAMMA TACK'S', and an orderly queue of islanders patiently waited for the supply of quinine tablets that Mary dispensed to them as they slowly filed past.

'My clinic,' Jane announced.

'Mamma Tack's?' he quizzed.

'Yes. Mamma Tack. That's me.'

'How in the world did this happen?' He meant the boathouse and the clinic, but she took him literally.

'It's a nickname the Americans came up with,' she said, 'and the locals have adopted it. I must say I rather like it myself.'

Wolf Baker had put the sign up as a joke, but it had been immediately accepted by locals and troops alike. The islanders loved the American term, it made Missus Tack even more special, and the servicemen derived great amusement from the idea that the pretty young Englishwoman was known as 'Mamma'.

In the several weeks of its existence, Mamma Tack's had proved itself far more than a clinic; it had become a significant social centre. Jane maintained the interior as her personal workplace, storeroom and dispensary, but all around the exterior, beneath the sporadic shade afforded by the elevated shutters, were chairs and camp stools and matting. Here people gathered to chat and consume the endless mugs of tea Mary made, or the cold drinks she proudly supplied from the icebox. Mary was Mamma Tack's personal assistant and took her new career very seriously.

'It's wonderful, my love.' Martin put an arm around her, and Ronnie, seated precariously on his shoulders, momentarily lost his balance. But the child's chubby little legs locked themselves around his father's neck in a stranglehold; Ronnie had no intention of falling.

'So the medical corps set this up for you,' Martin said as he disentangled himself and repositioned the child. 'It's very impressive.'

'Well, no, they didn't really,' she corrected him. 'Oh they furnish whatever medical supplies and equipment I need, I can have whatever I like. But it's the servicemen themselves who supplied the furniture and the icebox and the stove, and heaven only knows what else, all requisitioned from military stores. I doubt whether the paperwork's in order,' she laughed, 'but the quartermaster obviously turns a blind eye. Every day they arrive with something new.'

It had been Wolf, together with Big Ben and a gang of cohorts, who had adopted Mamma Tack's as their personal cause, and the boathouse had become a meeting place as much for servicemen as it had for islanders.

'They even put in a ceiling fan,' Jane said. 'Come and I'll show you.'

Martin took Ronnie from his shoulders and hugged the child firmly to his chest as they crossed the street, avoiding the jeeps and the trucks and the troops and work teams.

There were cries of 'Allo, Mamma Tack' from the islanders in the queue and Jane waved to them all, those she knew and those she didn't. Mary acknowledged the Missus and the Masta with a smile, but maintained her station, handing out supplies and giving instructions as she did so.

'But you'll never guess the strangest thing of all, Marty,' Jane said as she opened the door. 'Do you know where the boathouse itself came from?'

'Requisitioned by the military, surely,' he said. 'It's been abandoned for years, I don't even know who owns it.'

'I own it,' she grinned. 'He's given it to me. "Lock, stock and barrel", that's what he said.'

'Who?'

'Godfrey.'

'Godfrey?' Martin put Ronnie down as they stepped inside and the child galloped off, clumsy and fearless, falling and picking himself up, eager in his newfound mobility. 'You mean Godfrey Tomlinson?' Martin's tone was one of disbelief.

'He's the only Godfrey we know.'

Jane had been equally astonished when Godfrey had

made the offer. They'd been taking afternoon tea at Reid's when she'd told him that the medical corps planned to set up some form of temporary clinic for her to cope with the islanders' mass malaria treatment. 'They want somewhere near the centre of town,' she'd told him, 'but I've no idea what they have in mind, and I don't think they do either.'

'I have the perfect solution.' Godfrey had taken her by the hand and marched her out of Reid's, forgetting to pay for the afternoon tea.

'Godfrey,' she said, trying to keep up as he charged down the street. Despite his age he was striding purposefully, a man with a mission. 'Godfrey, don't you think we should pay for the tea?'

'Ah yes,' he said, 'later, later.'

Then they came to the boatshed. Jane had passed by it often. It was in good condition, but it was always closed and she didn't know who owned it.

'This is your clinic,' he said.

What a good idea, she thought. 'Well, yes, I suppose the medical corps could find out who . . .'

'It's yours, I'm giving it to you. Lock, stock and barrel.'

It had been as simple as that. There had been no paperwork involved, but Jane had no doubt it was his to give.

'I built it myself,' Godfrey said, 'as a warehouse in my trading days. I even lived in it from time to time. It's strong and durable and will serve your purpose well.' He'd told her nothing more. Godfrey told no-one any more than he felt was absolutely necessary about his properties or his business activities.

'Good old Godfrey, ever the man of mystery,' Martin said, looking about, impressed. The boatshed was bigger than it appeared from the outside. Shelves and cupboards, a stove, sink and icebox all stood around the walls, and at the far end, which had once been a slipway, was a curtained-off section with bedding on the floor.

'My examination room,' she explained. 'I've been promised two beds, they're arriving today.'

'You're a miracle, my love,' he said, taking her in his arms, regardless of the eyes of those filing past the open windows. He held her close. It had been a whole four months. How good it was to be with her again. 'You and your clinic, you're an absolute miracle.'

'I didn't do it,' she said. 'Godfrey and the Americans, it's all thanks to them.'

'No it's not, Jane.' He looked at her with profound respect. 'It's not them at all. It's you, my love.'

The pride in his eyes was her greatest reward. 'It's good to have you home, Marty,' she said. 'I've missed you.'

'Hey, Mamma Tack!' The voice was a deep American baritone and they looked out into the street to the jeep that had screeched to a halt in a cloud of dust, the orderly queue of islanders scattering.

'Big Ben!' Jane called as she walked to the window and leaned out beneath the shutters.

'Got 'em right here for you, Mamma Tack,' Big Ben yelled, and Wolf jumped out from the back of the jeep where he'd been balancing the two narrow bedsteads during the chaotic drive.

'Just like we promised, Jane,' Wolf shouted out to her and he and Big Ben started unloading the beds, the locals gathering around to help.

Martin dodged out of their way as two islanders helped the huge black man and the young lieutenant carry the bedsteads into the boathouse.

'We've got a couple of mattresses and pillows too,' Wolf said, 'and another crate of soft drinks. Hi, Mary.'

Mary gave the men a wave and kept on working as they dumped the beds behind the curtain.

'And hey,' Wolf said to Jane, as Big Ben and the islanders disappeared for the rest of the supplies. 'I'm lining up a radio. You could do with some music around here, liven the place up.' He clicked his fingers and did a quick-step around the boathouse. 'A bit of big-band sound, what do you say?'

'Wolf, I'd like you to meet my husband,' she interrupted. As usual Wolf's exuberance could be overpowering.

'Oh.' He stopped in his tracks. He hadn't noticed the tall man standing unassumingly in the corner.

'Darling, this is Lieutenant Wolf Baker. Wolf, my husband, Dr Martin Thackeray.'

'Hello, Lieutenant.' Martin held out his hand.

'How do you do, sir.' Wolf all but sprang to attention as they shook hands.

'My wife's told me of the incredible generosity of you and your men,' Martin smiled, 'and I must say,' he added glancing around the boathouse, 'the result is amazing.'

'Anything for Mamma Tack and her clinic, sir, she's one in a million.'

'And this is Private Coswell,' Jane said. Big Ben had reappeared, two thin single mattresses draped over his massive shoulders and two pillows sitting on the crate of drinks he was carrying. 'Big Ben, this is my husband, Dr Thackeray.'

'Private Coswell.' Martin once again extended his hand.

Big Ben was flustered. The mattresses had wedged in the doorway and he didn't want to drop the drinks crate. He shoved his way clumsily forward, the mattresses fell to the floor, he put the crate down with an almighty clatter, and accepted the doctor's hand.

'How do, sir,' he said.

Martin and the two men exchanged pleasantries before Wolf and Big Ben had to return to duty, and Jane was amused to see Wolf Baker on his very best behaviour. She'd recently accused him of being a larrikin.

'What the heck's a larrikin?' he'd asked.

'It's an Australian expression, used quite a bit here in the colony.' She'd found the term most colourful when she'd first heard it herself, she remembered. 'A larrikin is a man who behaves inappropriately. A man with no taste, no manners and no sense of occasion,' she'd said, being deliberately facetious. 'In other words, a bit of a lout.'

'But I have a great sense of occasion.' He'd seemed genuinely insulted. 'I come from Boston where good manners were born. I've been to Harvard. They don't allow louts at Harvard.' Oh dear, he's offended, she'd thought, and she was about to explain that she'd been joking. 'I swear to you, Jane,' he'd said, his hand on his chest, 'taste and good manners ooze out of my every pore.'

It was impossible to take Wolf Baker seriously, she'd decided.

And now here he was meeting Martin, and his behaviour was impeccable. Perhaps too impeccable, she thought, noting the highly respectful 'sir' tacked on to every second comment he made. Was it a mockery? she wondered briefly. But it wasn't, she realised. This was Boston good manners. Wolf Baker was meeting an older man who was a doctor and her husband, and the respect and sense of occasion he was showing were utterly appropriate. He'd stopped playing the larrikin in deference to Martin Thackeray, and she liked him for it.

Wolf and Big Ben took their leave.

'Goodbye, sir.' Whilst Big Ben stepped out into the street, Wolf once again shook Martin's hand. 'It's been an honour to meet you.'

'The pleasure's been mine, I assure you, Lieutenant. You must come and dine with us some time.' The young man's respect was flattering and his earnestness engaging but Martin wished he wouldn't call him 'sir', particularly given the familiarity between Baker and his wife. He felt he was being treated like Jane's father rather than her husband.

'I'd love to, that'd be great, thank you very much, sir.' Wolf grinned from Martin to Jane, delighted by the invitation. 'I'll see you later, Jane, we'll be back with the radio and some fresh supplies in the next day or so.'

'Bye, Wolf! Bye, Big Ben!' Jane called as she and Martin stood in the street, Ronnie slung over her hip, waving to the jeep as it roared off down the main street dodging the endless traffic.

'Seems a nice chap,' Martin said, and Jane smiled at his typically British reserve. 'He is, believe me,' she replied, 'but he can be quite exhausting at times. He was on his very best behaviour with you, my darling.' She leaned up and kissed him on the cheek. 'He obviously finds you impressive, and so he should.'

Martin had been surprised at the easy relationship between Wolf Baker and his wife. It wasn't like Jane to encourage such familiarity, he thought. But then perhaps it was. He had noticed a change in his wife after his four-month absence. There was an added assurance in her, a sense of independence and an authority which he was aware had evolved through her work with the military. He respected her for it and he was not critical of her friendship with Wolf Baker. But deep down he had to admit that he would have preferred it if the man were a little older. Or at least not so devilishly good-looking.

'So what will we do with our afternoon, my love?' he queried as they walked back to the cottage. Martin was to report to the newly completed Bellevue Hospital the following day where his work would commence in earnest, and Jane had left Mary in charge of the clinic so that they could spend time together.

'I could take you for a drive around the island,' she casually suggested.

'You could take me for a drive?' He stopped in his tracks.

'Oh yes,' she said, ignoring his astonishment. 'The Americans have built a road around the whole of Efate. Some areas are a little difficult to negotiate, but for the most part . . .'

'Since when have you been driving?'

'For ages,' she said airily, enjoying showing off.

'But, Jane, you hate driving,' he said. 'I had to nag you every day, remember?' He'd insisted upon teaching her to drive for safety purposes. 'In case of an emergency, my love,' he'd said time and again.

'Oh not any more. Reverend Smeed lends me the church's baby Austin and off I go, free as a bird.' In the face of Martin's incredulity she could no longer keep up the pretence and she burst out laughing. 'I've driven only the once,' she said, 'to Undine Bay and back.'

'Undine Bay, but that's miles.'

'Yes, and I hated every minute, it was a ghastly experience. I'm really not very good,' she admitted.

'What on earth were you doing at Undine Bay?'

'It's a long story,' she said, handing Ronnie to him as they climbed the hill. 'It all started when Mary brought a friend of hers to see me. Sera Poilama. Sera's little boy was sick.'

Back at the cottage as Jane prepared lunch she told him about Sera and Savi, and also about Jean-François Marat.

'Jean-François?' Martin queried an hour later when they'd finished eating. He'd been surprised by her constant use of the man's Christian name. 'And you dined alone with him?'

'That's exactly what Godfrey said,' she replied, assuming that her husband disapproved, but determined to be honest nonetheless. 'Godfrey considered it most unseemly of me to accept the invitation, and I believe he may have been right.' Jane still lived with the sense of disloyalty Godfrey's words had instilled in her, and her guilt could not be absolved until she'd admitted to the fact. 'I'm sorry, Marty, I'm really very sorry if I behaved incorrectly.'

'Good heavens, my love, why apologise?' Martin replied. 'You must dine with whoever you wish. I'm simply surprised, that's all. You were so determined to avoid an invitation to Marat's home before I left that I presumed you couldn't stand the man.'

The simplicity of his response touched her deeply. His trust in her was absolute. Unquestioning and unreserved.

'You're right, I didn't like him,' she said, 'but he was so obliging in driving me out to see Sera and Savi, and I found him . . . well, entertaining, so I suppose I changed my opinion.' How superficial she sounded. And she had been, she decided. Like Hilary Bale, she had been flattered by the man's attentions, and she had not even been aware of it until Godfrey's admonishment. The thought made her feel more guilty than ever. She looked at Martin for his reaction, but he just nodded, readily accepting her explanation.

They were leaning back in their chairs sipping their cups of tea, and she rose and crossed to sit on his lap.

'Whoa,' Martin said, nearly spilling his tea. He put down the cup. 'What brought this on?'

'I love you, Marty,' she said, her head nestled into his shoulder.

'And I you, my dearest.' He put his arms around her, stroking her hair and rocking her gently in silence. 'What is it, Jane?' he asked after a moment or so.

'I've felt guilty,' she said. 'Godfrey made me feel as if I'd been disloyal to you.' She lifted her head and he could see the distress in her eyes. 'I would never be disloyal to you, Marty, you know that.'

'Of course I know it, my darling, ssh.' He cradled her to him. 'Godfrey had no right to make you feel that way. Ssh.'

She loved him as much as it was humanly possible to love, Jane thought, reassured and comforted as he continued to rock her gently in his arms. Marty was home, and any guilt or confusion she'd felt about the Frenchman was a thing of the past. She broke the moment and jumped to her feet.

'We're wasting time,' she said. 'This is your first day home, your one day off, and there's so much to show you.'

Martin didn't think they were wasting time at all, he could have cuddled her all afternoon, but he agreed nevertheless, and twenty minutes later, having borrowed the Austin from Reverend Smeed, they set off on their drive. Martin was most keen to see the American bases at Mele Bay and Havannah Harbour.

'Shall I drive or you?' he asked in apparent seriousness, and Jane simply climbed into the passenger seat, placing Ronnie firmly on her lap by way of reply.

She'd told him, in humorous detail, of her hair-raising drive to Undine Bay. 'It wasn't at all funny at the time,' she'd insisted, enjoying his laughter. 'I risked life and limb, and I swear I shall never drive again unless it's totally unavoidable.'

She had not, however, told him of her encounter with Marat that day. She had no wish to keep secrets from her husband, but her feelings remained too complicated to analyse, even for herself.

Jane had left Ronnie with Mary and driven alone to the Poilamas' house, not wishing to endanger any life other than her own, and throughout the journey she'd been thankful that she had. The constant stream of American trucks and jeeps and bulldozers and tanks dwarfed the Austin and she'd arrived at Sera's quite unnerved by the experience.

She'd noted the Landrover parked out the front of the big house as she'd turned off the coastal track, but she had her speech all prepared for Jean-François. She would simply tell him that she wished to be independent, and now that the roads were negotiable, thanks to the Americans, she would say that she enjoyed driving.

Which was the farthest thing from the truth, she thought as she climbed shakily from the Austin.

Pascal and Marie ran out to greet her, closely followed by

Sera, who was surprised but delighted to see the Missus.

As was to be expected, Savi was not at home. He was working with the harvesting team, Sera said. And when the Masta came home, which could be at any minute, she would have to report to the big house.

But surely the Masta was already home, Jane remarked, indicating the Landrover in the distance.

'Masta is horseback ride,' Sera said, very proud that they were communicating in English. She and Savi practised constantly and he made her speak English at every opportunity.

'Oh I see.'

'Today no English lesson,' Sera said regretfully.

'No matter,' Jane replied, she had simply wanted to say hello. She would try to come and see them when she could. Perhaps a Sunday, when they were not working, she suggested. Daunting as she'd found the drive, she was determined to fulfil her obligation to the Poilamas, and she told herself hopefully that perhaps there would be fewer military vehicles about on a Sunday.

Sera looked shrewdly at Jane. The Missus had come in her own car, unannounced, and Sera knew what that meant. The Missus did not want the Masta to know. Did she, too, fear the Masta? Sera had also registered Jane's relief as she'd got out of the car. The Missus did not like driving. The Missus was brave, but it was not right for her to risk so much for them.

She had another idea, she said, breaking into Bislama, the conversation had become too complicated for her to continue in English. When Savi went into town, she suggested, he could bring Pascal with him.

'Visitim Mamma Tack,' Sera smiled. Although she rarely left the plantation herself, she had heard of Mamma Tack's. Everyone had. Then perhaps, she tentatively asked, the Missus could give Savi and Pascal their English lessons?

It was a very good suggestion, Jane agreed, but what about Sera's lessons. 'Yu visitim tu, Sera?' she asked.

Sera shook her head. She would not dare arouse the Masta's anger by going into town, but she didn't tell the Missus that. 'Savi tijim mi,' she said. Savi was a very good teacher.

Jane sensed Sera's true reason for choosing not to accompany her husband and child into town, but she said nothing. There was a wealth of things unspoken between the two women, all of which both recognised.

'I will come and see you when I can, Sera,' Jane said in English as they embraced.

'You good friend, Missus Tack,' Sera replied.

Pascal and Marie begged her to stay longer, but having successfully avoided Jean-François, Jane decided to leave whilst the coast was clear. Sera understood implicitly, and didn't insist upon preparing a meal for the Missus, as she would ordinarily have done.

But they were too late. Sera and the children were still waving goodbye to the Austin as it turned off the rough ground and onto the main drive, when the horse and rider appeared from out of the dense plantation.

'Bos come!' Pascal was the first to notice.

The horse, a large bay, had broken through the coconut trees at a gallop and, urged on by its rider, it increased its pace, Sera watching from a distance as it raced at break-neck speed towards the Austin.

Marat had seen them through the trees from afar as he'd held his spirited stallion back to a walk. At first he'd been irritated by the sight of the Austin. Who was secretly visiting his workers? And how dare they, he'd thought. Then, still tiny specks too far away to identify, he'd seen the women embrace, a white woman and a black. It meant only one thing. The white woman was Jane Thackeray, and he'd allowed the eager animal to break into a canter, dodging dangerously amongst the coconut trees. Then, at the edge of the plantation, he'd given the horse its head and it had thundered out into the open space at a gallop.

Now at full pace, he caught up with the Austin as it reached the open main gates and, aware that he cut a fine figure on horseback, he raced past and pulled the animal to a jarring halt directly in front of the car.

Jane was startled. He'd appeared out of nowhere, she hadn't noticed his approach. She was travelling slowly and there was no fear of collision, but she was nervous and shaken as she jammed her foot down on the brake.

Jean-François dismounted athletically, proud of his horsemanship, and the stallion stood beside him snorting and tossing its head and pawing the ground. He waited until she'd turned off the engine before sauntering over to the driver's window, holding the excitable animal tightly by its bridle.

'Jane,' he said, 'a surprise visit, how delightful.'

'Hello, Jean-François.' She leaned out the open window waving a hand to disperse the dust that still swirled in the air. 'You gave me a terrible fright, I didn't see you coming.'

'You were about to leave without calling on me?' he queried. She would surely have presumed he was at home, he thought, the Landrover was parked right outside the house. 'Shame on you,' he said with good-natured censure.

'Sera told me you were out riding.'

'Ah well, in that case you are forgiven. It is nearly lunchtime, you'll join me?'

'Thank you, but no,' she said, 'I must get back to Ronnie.'

Excuses again, he thought, the child would be in the company of the ever-reliable Mary. 'So to what do we owe the honour of this visit? Hardly an English lesson, Savi is harvesting and Sera has a full workday ahead of her.'

'Yes, it was silly of me, I know, but I just thought I'd call in and say hello on the off chance.'

'What a very long way to come "on the off chance".' He

tried to sound nonchalant but it was difficult.

'An excellent opportunity for me to practise my driving skills,' Jane said, recognising the trace of mockery as she launched into her prepared speech. 'Now that we have negotiable roads, thanks to the Americans, I've decided I rather enjoy driving.'

A lie, he thought. 'Really?' he smiled. 'I find the military traffic rather unsettling myself.'

'I'll get used to it,' she said.

'Jane . . .' He released the horse's bridle, slipped his wrist through the loop of the reins and, resting his hands either side of the car window, he leaned down towards her. Beside him, the stallion, with its extra freedom of movement, danced restlessly. 'You know that my offer is always open, I am more than happy to collect you and take you home whenever you wish.'

'Yes, I appreciate that,' she said, 'and it's most generous of you, but I don't wish to be an imposition . . .'

'You are never an imposition, I assure you.'

'The fact is, I wish to be independent, Jean-François.' She met his eyes with an honesty that she hoped he would understand. 'It's very important to me.'

'I see.' It was a fait accompli, he realised. There was little he could say in response to such an unequivocal statement. But he must not allow her to sever the ties.

Jean-François Marat's conquest of Jane Thackeray was no longer a game and no longer a challenge. It was no longer even a conquest. He was determined to possess her entirely. She was to be his, and whether it took a year, two years, he didn't care. He was obsessed with the woman, and he knew it.

'As always, Jane, I admire your spirit,' he said, 'but how will Savi know when to report for his lessons if you are to arrive unexpectedly? Surely we should come to some arrangement regarding your visits. I would hate to disappoint both Savi and Sera, they so look forward to their English lessons.'

His smile was magnanimous, but Godfrey's words returned to Jane. '*Have you asked yourself, Jane,*' Godfrey had said, '*why Jean-François Marat would welcome his servants learning English?*' And the old man's tone had been scathing. '*It is the very last thing he would want.*' There was nothing untoward in the Frenchman's manner, but Jane was suddenly fearful that Godfrey might have been right.

'I hate to disappoint them too, Jean-François,' she said firmly, 'but I fear the lessons will have to be deferred for a while. With the malaria programme underway I'm very busy at the clinic.'

He sensed her reserve. Was he being too persistent? He mustn't frighten her off. 'Ah yes,' he said with a light laugh of amusement, 'Mamma Tack's. A typically irreverent American name, in my opinion, for a facility as admirable as yours.' He turned his attention to the stallion, gripping its bridle and calming the animal as it pulled on the reins, eager for action. 'Well, I mustn't keep you, Jane.'

She was relieved to be free of his scrutiny. Bent down to the car window as he had been, his face close to hers, she had found her confidence undermined.

'But I'm not letting you get away altogether,' he said jovially as he brought the horse under control and turned back to her. 'When Dr Thackeray returns next week I insist you both accept my longstanding invitation.'

'We'd be delighted,' she agreed, resisting the instinctive impulse to ask how he knew of her husband's imminent return. The Frenchman obviously made it his business to know everything that was going on in Vila. He would have to have made enquiries, either of the Reverend Smeed or the medical corps, in order to hear of Martin's recall to Efate.

She turned the ignition key, the engine started up, and, as Jean-François mounted the bay, which pranced impatiently, she leaned through the window to wave goodbye.

'Shall we say a week from Saturday?' he asked, the stallion wheeling on the spot.

'I shall look forward to it,' she called up to him, 'and I know my husband will too.'

Jean-François waved a farewell, and Jane watched as the horse broke directly into a canter, then only seconds later galloped full pace across the open ground.

'By the way, we're more or less committed to dine with Jean-François at Chanson de Mer this coming Saturday,' Jane said, as she and Martin returned from their afternoon's drive, Ronnie fast asleep in her lap.

'Is it "more" or is it "less"?' Martin smiled, aware of the answer.

'Well "more",' she admitted. 'I felt duty bound to accept. You told me yourself that we must,' she said in protest as he laughed. 'Before you went away. You did, Marty, remember?'

'Of course I remember, and of course we must. I look forward to meeting the Jean-François Marat who's no longer an enemy to the people.' She had told him during the drive of her initial reaction to Marat's treatment of his workers, and how naive she had felt when he'd expounded his own views on the disruption of the islanders' lifestyles and culture. Martin wasn't sure if he entirely agreed, but it would be interesting to spend an evening in the Frenchman's company, he thought.

Jean-François had gone to a great deal of trouble. The table, although laid only for three, was a work of art. A Venetian glass vase filled with hibiscus blooms sat in the centre and silver candlesticks stood at each end. The cloth was of French lace, the cutlery of the finest silver, the wine goblets of cut crystal, and the napkins damask. He was self-effacing when Jane expressed her admiration.

'A legacy from Simone,' he said, 'she acquired so many lovely things during our trips abroad, and she always insisted upon a well-laid table.' Which was a lie. It had been he who had demanded only the best at all times, and his taste was impeccable. 'Where would we be without our women, eh Martin?'

'Indeed,' Martin agreed.

Jean-François had quickly cut to the chase regarding Christian names. 'Please call me Jean-François,' he'd said as he'd warmly shaken Martin's hand. 'Your wife and I have already achieved first-name basis through our mutual involvement with the Poilama family. I am deeply indebted to Jane,' he'd added with a smile in her direction, 'for all the help she has offered my good friend Savi and his family.' Thackeray would respond well to the idea that he had a personal relationship with his servants, Jean-François thought contemptuously. Just like Godfrey Tomlinson, the man was a native-lover.

'I look forward very much to meeting the Poilamas,' Martin said.

'Fine people,' Jean-François replied vociferously, 'fine people. A sherry? Or would you prefer Scotch?'

Jean-François was bent upon impressing both the Thackerays this evening. He would establish a man-to-man relationship with Martin, he'd decided, which would be easy; men were always flattered when he made them feel they were his masculine equals. Particularly when, like Thackeray, they were not. The impression upon Jane would be of a more subliminal nature. The table was indicative of his opulence, and he'd already hinted at the trips abroad, all of which would represent an enviable lifestyle to the wife of a missionary doctor. But he was sure, as the evening progressed, the message would become even stronger. Jane Thackeray would recognise not only the difference in the world he could offer her, but the difference between her husband and a real man.

'This is Sera,' Jean-François said to Martin as Sera entered from the kitchen with a tray of hors d'oeuvres.

'Sera is the wife of my good friend Savi.'

'How do you do, sir.' Sera put the tray down and addressed Martin with grace and assurance. 'I am most pleased to meet you.' Then she darted a quick sideways glance at Jane, who smiled her congratulations. Sera's English had been faultless.

Martin was struck by the woman's poise and beauty, and enchanted by the fact that she had obviously rehearsed the phrase. Even more so that she had rehearsed it in preparation for meeting the husband of her good friend Jane; he had noticed the women's exchange.

'How do you do, Sera,' he said, extending his hand. 'I have heard so much about you and your family.'

Sera's assurance faltered. She looked at the outstretched hand, then at the Masta, fearful and unsure what to do.

A flash of irritation surged through Jean-François, but he covered it in an instant. 'Go ahead, Sera,' he said with an encouraging smile, 'shake hands with Dr Thackeray.'

'I look forward to meeting your husband and children,' Martin said as they shook.

'Thank you, sir.' She didn't dare look at the Masta, but stared at the floor before disappearing once again into the kitchen.

'I must apologise,' Martin said to Jean-François.

'Why, my dear Martin? Why must you apologise?' The Frenchman gave a bewildered shrug, although he knew why Thackeray was apologising, and so the man damn well should.

'My behaviour was not within the boundaries of the protocol established in your house,' Martin said formally. 'It was wrong of me, and I sincerely beg your pardon.' He didn't really wish to beg Marat's pardon; he wished to beg Sera's. It had indeed been wrong of him to adopt such a casual manner with a servant in another man's house, but Marat had professed to a personal friendship with the Poilamas. If such had been the case, Martin thought, then his own untoward behaviour would have caused merely a minor embarrassment. But he had seen the annoyance in Marat's eyes, and he had seen the fear in Sera's. The man was lying, Martin realised. The Poilamas were no more to him than servants. Why was he pretending otherwise?

'Sera's English was perfect,' Jane said, wishing that Martin would relax. He was being so stiff and formal and typically British. 'She's been practising that phrase to impress you, my darling. I'm sure Savi has had her saying it over and over.' She turned to Jean-François. 'Savi's English is excellent these days.' Savi had called in at the boathouse with little Pascal only three days previously and they'd had an extensive lesson. Jane didn't notice the flicker of interest in Jean-François's eyes as she continued. 'He has the most astonishing ear for languages.'

When had she seen Savi? he thought. And where? 'All due to your excellent tutelage, Jane,' he said.

'Oh no, he's a natural,' she laughed. 'I can claim no credit for that.'

The meal was superb, as was to be expected. Jean-François had gone to great pains to ensure it.

'The beef is home-grown and of prime quality,' Jane parroted and she and Jean-François laughed.

'You must take your wife in hand, Martin,' the Frenchman said, 'she is making fun of me.'

'Oh really? In what way?'

'I have a tendency to boast of my livestock,' Jean-François admitted, 'as Jane well knows. And indeed Mrs Bale,' he said, wary of appearing too exclusive. He looked to Jane who gave a smile by way of confirmation. 'Our good friend Hilary has also been witness to my . . . what is that wonderful English expression . . .? To my "bragging".' He smiled. But Martin didn't return the smile, he simply nodded politely, and Jean-François was aware that, despite his best efforts, he wasn't winning the Englishman. Not that perhaps it mattered. He sensed that

Thackeray was coming off second best in his wife's eyes this evening, but strangely enough he would have preferred the man to admire him.

'Oh yes,' Jane agreed, 'Hilary thought the ham was the most delicious sensation she'd ever experienced.'

'That may be going too far,' Jean-François replied with a modest laugh.

'The beef is certainly excellent,' Martin said.

The conversation turned to the war. The Guadalcanal campaign raged to the north and casualties were arriving in increasing and alarming numbers at the Bellevue Hospital. It was malaria, however, which could well prove a bigger killer than the Japanese bombs, Martin remarked. 'Malaria is currently at a crisis point and most urgently in need of address.'

'The Americans are fortunate to have you and your lovely wife at hand during such a time,' Jean-François said.

'Yes, I am very proud of Jane and her work.' For the first time since he'd arrived Martin appeared to relax, smiling and clasping Jane's hand. 'My wife is an extraordinary woman.'

'She most certainly is, Martin. You're a lucky man.'

Then, as if to avoid any topic that touched upon the personal, Martin introduced the subject of the government's relationship with the military.

Throughout the evening Jean-François was at a loss as to how to approach the Englishman. His attempts at masculine camaraderie met with little success.

'You must come riding with me, Martin,' he said. 'In the plantation at dusk.' He waxed rhapsodic for Jane's benefit. 'The moon through the coconut trees, then out on to the flat at full gallop, nothing before you but the sea.'

'I don't ride,' Martin said. 'I'm rather frightened of horses actually, I have the feeling they don't like me.'

Jean-François was amazed by the man's admission. Didn't he realise what a weakling he sounded? Didn't he care how he must appear in the eyes of his wife?

Jane wanted to laugh. It was just like Martin, his sense of humour was so unpredictable, and she waited for him to share the moment. But he didn't, and it fell rather flat. The Frenchman hadn't realised he was joking, she thought and then she wondered herself whether he had been. She sensed that Martin didn't like the Frenchman, and she decided that he was being deliberately impolite. It was so unlike him, she thought.

'I must admit I'm a little fearful of horses myself,' she said, simply to fill in the awkward pause. She'd had no experience of horses at all, apart from the days when she and Phoebe had ridden with Maude Cookson in Titchfield, all three of them perched on the old white pony, and she'd had no fear of horses then. 'I suppose it's just a lack of experience,' she said, and the conversation then turned to the safer and more impersonal subject of the Americans and the tumultuous effect their presence had had upon the islands.

It was the after-effects that were of far deeper concern to Martin. 'The war cannot last forever,' he said, 'and I fear for the islanders when the Americans leave.'

To Jane's relief it appeared that Martin and Jean-François had finally found a topic upon which they were in mutual agreement. They were both of the opinion that the disruption to the islanders' lives would leave them in chaos when the American forces finally withdrew from the New Hebrides.

'It will be difficult for them to adjust to their old way of life,' Martin said. 'The government will be unable to offer them the luxuries afforded them by the Americans.'

'Nor should the government attempt to do so,' Jean-François adamantly replied. The islanders had become greedy in his opinion, and the sooner they returned to the old status quo, the better. But he added, in case he'd sounded uncaring, 'It would be a corruption of their basic lifestyle and values.'

'I agree,' Martin said, although he suspected the Frenchman's motives were far from altruistic. 'However, their lives were corrupted well before the arrival of the Americans. The colony owes the local population education on all levels and the chance to achieve, should they wish. Certainly they are owed the opportunity to have a say in their society, instead of being subjugated and used merely as a labour force.'

'Oh yes, indeed,' Jean-François nodded. Thackeray was not only a native-lover, the man was an idealist. The worst kind, he thought.

Jane said nothing, aware that Jean-François's views on the islanders' education did not concur with hers and Martin's, and that the Frenchman was agreeing simply to keep the peace. But she couldn't really blame him. Martin had been far from personable all evening.

An hour later, when they took their leave, Jean-François shook her hand instead of kissing it. Had Martin inhibited him that much? she wondered, and she felt a mixture of annoyance and embarrassment.

'Thank you, Jean-François,' she said, 'I have had a most enjoyable evening.' A quick glance to Martin. 'We both have.'

'The pleasure has been all mine, Jane.' She was annoyed with her husband, he thought. Excellent.

The evening had not gone as Jean-François had planned. Martin Thackeray was not as impressionable as he'd assumed. But perhaps the outcome would serve an even better purpose than his original intention, he thought, revising his tactics. He would continue to be gracious towards Thackeray at all times, and the more the man closed off, the greater would become his wife's annoyance. The seeds of discontent had been sown.

'It has been an honour, Martin,' Jean-François said as the two men shook hands. 'I have for so long admired your work.'

'Thank you for your hospitality,' Martin replied. Not once had he called the man by his Christian name.

'What on earth is the matter with you, Marty?' Jane asked as they drove away from the house. 'Why were you so insulting to Jean-François?'

'I wasn't.'

'Yes you were.'

'In what particular way?'

He was being pig-headed in demanding specifics, she thought. 'You were so remote,' she said.

'That's hardly insulting.'

'And you didn't call him Jean-François once all night.' There, she thought, that was specific enough.

'Which is surely my prerogative. Where's the insult in that?'

Jane was silent as they turned onto the coast road. It was a glorious still night, the sky was cloudless and the moon nearly full, its light rippling across the ocean's surface. Under normal circumstances she would have been leaning out of the car window, drinking in the balmy air and admiring the view, but she was studying her husband instead. His profile in the moonlight was quite clear to her, and she knew that he was deep in thought. He adopted the same furrow-browed intensity when he was solving a problem, and she usually left him alone and waited for him to come up with the answer, which he invariably shared with her. But this time she didn't leave him alone.

'You don't like him, do you?' she demanded.

'No.'

'Why? He was charming to you the entire evening.'

Martin ignored her question. 'Godfrey was right, Jane. I don't want you to see Marat again, except in the normal social course of events.'

'Good heavens, Marty, why on earth . . .'

'Promise me,' he said, his eyes not leaving the road, 'that

in my absence you will not be alone in that man's company.'

'Very well,' she said stiffly. Never before had he given her an order. 'Of course I promise.'

They said nothing for quite some time, both staring fixedly through the windscreen at the road that dipped and wound its way around the coast, eerily illuminated by the car's headlights.

After five minutes or so, Jane stole a glance at him. His face was still stern, deep in thought. What was it? she wondered. Her initial annoyance had faded and she wondered what problem he was trying to solve. Then she sat back and waited for him to share the answer with her, as he always did.

But Martin had no answer. Only questions. Questions that reared themselves in his brain, one after the other, relentlessly. Why couldn't Jane see the Frenchman for what he was? Jane, who was normally such a fine judge of character. Her initial reaction to the Frenchman had been one of dislike. So what had changed her opinion of the man? Many women were susceptible to flattery and charm, but Jane had never been one of them. Her lack of vanity, refreshing in one so beautiful, prevented it. Was she attracted to the man, perhaps without knowing it herself? And then the questions became a torment.

Martin remembered how they had made love on the day of his return to Vila. It had been when they'd come home from their drive in the late afternoon and Jane had initiated it. They'd been hot and sweaty and they hadn't even washed, but she'd aroused him with her desire. There, in the living room, the sleeping child in his cot, she'd whispered, 'I've missed you, Marty,' and her open mouth had been against his, her body pressing close, and then suddenly they'd been in the bedroom. They'd never before made love during the day. It was not modesty, but rather mutual consent that dictated their lovemaking take place under the cloak of darkness. Then they would caress each other and whisper their endearments and share their bodies as they shared their very souls.

Martin had presumed Jane's urgency, and his own arousal, had been the result of his long absence and their mutual desire. But they had made love twice since, both times initiated by Jane, and both times she had been more intense, more sexually urgent, than in the past.

Martin had noticed many changes in his wife, all of which he respected. The growth of her independence, her strength of character and command, all a result of her work with the Americans and her deep commitment to the islanders. He had presumed the emergence of her sexuality might also be a result of this change. But now a far more ominous question presented itself. Was she dissatisfied with that aspect of their marriage?

She was a young woman, barely twenty-three years old, and he was the only man she'd known. Did she need more than he had to give? He'd not been a virgin himself when they'd married, but his fumbling sexual experiences as a young man had left him feeling guilty, sinful. And then his life had been devoted to his studies, to the church and medicine. Sex had meant little to him until it could be shared in a loving union. He had found that union with Jane. He loved her with all his heart, as he knew she loved him. But had a man like Marat aroused a need in her that could not be satisfied by their marriage?

He remembered her saying she'd felt guilty, disloyal even, for having dined alone with Marat. He'd been surprised at the time. Why should she feel guilty? he'd wondered. Unless, he now asked himself, she was aware of a sexual feeling between herself and Marat. The Frenchman was handsome, virile, masculine. A potent mixture. And Martin had been aware of the man's attraction to his wife. Had Jane fallen victim to his allure? Was that the cause of her newfound sexuality and her restlessness?

Martin was overwhelmed by his own sense of disloyalty at such a notion. How dare he question his wife's honour and veracity. He didn't, he told himself. He didn't for one moment. He trusted Jane implicitly. But the questions kept whirling like dervishes in his brain.

Her voice broke into his thoughts. 'Did we just have our first fight, Marty?' Jane was now worried by his preoccupation. Was he angry with her?

He took his eyes from the road for the first time since they'd left the plantation and, in the half light, she was looking up at him like a worried little girl.

'No, my love,' he smiled reassuringly, 'we did not.'

'Oh good.' She relaxed. 'So what is it exactly that you don't like about Jean-François?' she asked, genuinely interested.

'You really wish to know?'

'Yes.'

'Well, I found him rather vulgar.'

Jane was surprised. Vulgar? The sophisticated Jean-François Marat? How horrified he would be to hear such a term applied to him.

'Now really, my love,' Martin said playfully, 'were you impressed by that show of excess? Three people dining and the table laid for royalty. Who was he expecting, King George?'

Jane laughed. 'Yes, you're right,' she said, 'it was a bit excessive.'

'And the horseback riding. Galloping out onto the flats in the moonlight. Didn't you find that a little much?'

She hadn't at the time, but she supposed she did now and she was getting a fit of the giggles. 'Well, you certainly did. Oh, Marty, you were so rude, I didn't know where to look.'

'Neither did Marat. The man thought I was totally spineless and despised me even more for admitting it.'

'Yes, he did, didn't he?' The giggles overtook her as she recalled the look on Jean-François's face, which she hadn't really understood until Marty had explained it.

He waited until her laughter had subsided. 'The man's also a liar, Jane,' he said, 'and not to be trusted. He cares nothing for your friend Sera and her family.'

'Yes,' she said, suddenly sober. 'I know that. It's why I want to help them.'

'And you must, my love. But you can do so without being alone in Marat's company.' His concern was not born of jealousy. Martin sensed more than the Frenchman's attraction to his wife. He sensed that Marat was a man accustomed to getting what he wanted and that, in the pursuit of it, violence would present no barrier. Godfrey Tomlinson had been right, Martin thought. Marat was dangerous. 'You will promise me?'

'I already have, Marty.'

Over the ensuing weeks, Martin put aside the questions that tormented him. They were disrespectful to his wife, he decided, and during the fierceness of his days at the hospital, he indeed had little time to ponder the sexual aspect of his marriage. But occasionally in the dead of night, after they'd made love, his insecurity returned to plague him and, delicate as the subject was, he decided finally to confront it.

'Do I make you happy, Jane?' he asked.

'What a question at a time like this,' she said teasingly, cuddling herself into the crook of his arm and nuzzling her head against his shoulder as she always did after they'd made love. He could feel the soft silk of her chemise against the bare skin of his chest and her breath fanned his neck.

'I mean it, my love,' he said, turning his face to hers, although she was barely visible in the darkness. 'Are you happy with our marriage?'

'Oh my darling,' she said, puzzled by the seriousness of his tone and the depth of his question, 'of course I'm happy with our marriage.' She raised herself onto one

elbow, her other hand stroking his cheek. Why was he torturing himself? she wondered.

She hadn't understood, he thought, feeling awkward and
self-conscious, but determined to continue nonetheless. 'I
would wish to satisfy you in every aspect of our marriage,
Jane,' he said, thankful that the darkness cloaked his
inability to express himself; he'd never felt more inhibited in
his life. He took her hand and held it against his chest. 'I
want to make you happy, my love . . .'

'You do make me happy,' she whispered. She had to
interrupt him, she couldn't bear the pain of his query. 'You
make me happy in every possible way.' She kissed him
with all the love that she hoped he would recognise and
when their lips parted he could see the glimmer of her tears
in the darkness. 'It would be impossible for me to love you
any more than I do, Marty,' she said. 'You are my life.'

They never spoke of the subject again, and as Jane
worked ceaselessly at Mamma Tack's, she became less
sexually demanding, to the point where Martin persuaded
himself that perhaps he had been a victim of his own
imaginings. That perhaps Jane's increased desire had
been, as he'd first suspected, a direct result of their lengthy
separation.

Jane had been horrified at the agony of self-doubt she'd
recognised in her husband, and even more so by the realisation that she was responsible for his torment. She was
aware that she had initiated their lovemaking, as she never
had in the past, that she had made overtures to him when
he'd least expected it, that she'd been more urgent and
more responsive. She didn't know why. She herself had
wondered at her restlessness since his return. What was it
she wanted? she'd asked herself. Was it the frenzy of
passion Phoebe had spoken of?

She remembered Phoebe's words with the clarity of yesterday. 'I found out,' Phoebe had said, 'and it's wonderful.
It's wonderful, Jane.' Phoebe hadn't needed to say more,

her face had glowed, wanton and womanly, and Jane remembered, even as she'd been critical, her sense of envy.

Was that what she'd been demanding of Martin? The rapture that Phoebe had experienced? But why now? Why all of a sudden this desire for discovery? And what right did she have to demand Phoebe's secret? She wasn't Phoebe. Rapture would come easily to the sensual, flirtatious, sexually liberated Phoebe Chisolm. Martin was considerate, their coupling was warm and tender, and Jane felt content in her womanliness and the fact that she was so loved. It was selfish in the extreme to desire more.

Now, riddled with guilt that her demands had raised such doubt and insecurity in her husband, Jane quelled her desire and concentrated her energies upon the all-consuming tasks that awaited her daily at Mamma Tack's.

Jane and Martin Thackeray's marriage remained one of abiding love, and if there was something unspoken between them, something that each occasionally recognised, they refused to allow it to become an issue as they addressed the mutual commitments that claimed their every waking hour.

More and more casualties were arriving from Guadalcanal and the fight against malaria continued. But it was a fight that was slowly being won, and the end was in sight.

'Fatalities have dropped by forty percent,' Martin said as he helped Wolf unload the crates of supplies from the jeep.

It was Saturday, Martin's afternoon off from both his church duties and the hospital, although he was on call should he be needed. Jane had received word from one of the men that Wolf Baker was back and that he'd call in to Mamma Tack's, and Martin had been there to greet him.

Martin Thackeray had initially felt threatened by the Americans who flocked to Mamma Tack's. The men socialised amongst themselves at the boatshed, certainly, and mingled with the locals, but they were really drawn

there because of Jane, he was sure of it. There was no
question that they respected her, indeed if anyone had
stepped out of line he would have been physically attacked
by his compatriots; and Jane, in turn, treated them like
brothers. She knew every man's name, quickly memorising
that of a newcomer, and she would talk to them about
their homes and their families and sweethearts. They were
lonely, she told Martin. Her own brothers were serving in
North Africa and she would like to think that there was a
woman in whom they could confide.

Pure in purpose as Mamma Tack's was, Martin couldn't
help being painfully aware of the fact that Jane was
surrounded, daily, by virile young men.

These days, however, he refused to see the servicemen as
a threat. He couldn't afford to. Just as his views on
Marat's sexuality had been disrespectful to Jane, so too
was his concern about the Americans, he'd decided.
Besides, what was the point in worrying? Most of the
young men were quite possibly in love with his wife, or
thought they were, and there was little he could do about
it but admire their taste. He had even befriended the man
who most openly wore his heart on his sleeve. Wolf
Baker's devotion to Jane was plainly evident and he took
no pains to disguise it, for which Martin respected him.

The two men had become firm friends although it had
been a whole fortnight since either Jane or Martin had
seen the American. He looked different, Martin thought.
Tired. And he'd lost some of his boyish bounce.

'Forty percent?' Wolf was impressed. 'That's great,
Marty. You deserve a medal, the whole damn lot of you.
Hell, the guys have been saying who needs the Japs when
we've got malaria.'

No-one apart from Jane called Martin 'Marty', not since
his army days anyway, and at first Martin had been
nonplussed by Wolf Baker's free use of the nickname.
His natural reserve hadn't allowed him to say anything,

however, and Jane, sensitive to his feelings, had broached the subject.

'I'll correct him if you like, Marty,' she'd said, 'but you mustn't be offended, nicknames are a way of life to the Americans, it's a sign of affection.'

'Well, I suppose anything's better than "sir",' he'd said, and now he wouldn't have had it any other way. Martin liked Wolf Baker.

'Are you all right, Wolf?' he asked. 'You look tired.'

'Sure,' the American grinned, 'forty-eight hours leave up my sleeve, couldn't be better.' But as Martin looked knowingly at him, his smile faded. 'I've had a tough couple of days, Marty.'

'Dinner tonight?'

'Great. You're on.'


'Wolf kambak!' Ronnie's robust eighteen-month-old voice shrilled from the playpen in the corner as Mary opened the door wide to Wolf. 'Wolf kambak! Wolf kambak!' The child bounced up and down on his sturdy little legs, his arms in the air, and it was obvious he wasn't going to stop yelling until he was picked up.

Wolf obliged, crossing the lounge room and hoisting the excited infant high in the air. 'What's he saying?' he asked Mary, but before she could answer, Jane bustled in from the kitchen, a bowl of salad in her hands.

'He's glad you've come back,' she said, 'he's been asking after you every day for the past two weeks.'

Wolf sat on the wooden floor with the child and they played, Ronnie charging at him and Wolf falling flat on his back from the pretended force of the impact.

'I'm going to have to start learning this lingo,' he said as Ronnie gabbled away excitedly in his mixture of English and Bislama.

'Yes, I'm afraid so. Mary, will you get Wolf a drink whilst I make the salad dressing? He spends so much time with us at Mamma Tack's,' Jane called over her shoulder as she returned to the kitchen, 'that the locals have adopted him. Mary says he's part-islander.'

Mary grinned at Wolf. 'He sure is,' she said. She was very proud of the Americanisms she was picking up and was forever adding a new phrase to her repertoire. 'You want a beer, Mista Wolf?' He'd asked her to call him Wolf, but she'd thought it was a little disrespectful so she'd added the Mista.

'Great, thanks, Mary.'

'Marty's at Godfrey's,' Jane's disembodied voice called from the kitchen, 'they're choosing some wines for dinner, at Godfrey's insistence, he wants to show off to you.' Her head popped through the door. 'Oh, I forgot to tell you Godfrey's coming to dinner. You don't mind, do you?'

'Good God no,' Wolf yelled above Ronnie's squeals. He'd met Godfrey Tomlinson a number of times at Mamma Tack's, and the Englishman had been present at a previous evening he'd spent with Martin and Jane. Godfrey had held the floor throughout the entire dinner, and Wolf had found his stories of the old days fascinating. 'I could listen to Godfrey all night,' he called from under the child's body, which was smothering his face.

'Just as well,' Jane said wryly. 'Now for goodness sake stop overexciting Ronnie, I can't stand the noise.'

But that night the talk was not of the old days and Godfrey didn't hold the floor. He was wise enough to know when it was his time to be silent.

The evening started off frivolously enough, with much discussion of the wine carefully selected from Godfrey's cellar, and the old man accepted the compliments, enjoying his moment of triumph. But towards the end of the meal, when Martin asked Wolf about his trips to the fleet, Godfrey, like Jane, listened in silence.

'They're having a bit of a rough time, aren't they?' Martin said with his typically British talent for understatement. He knew that the American had flown out to the fleet during the past fortnight, men from Wolf's unit had told Jane so at Mamma Tack's.

Martin Thackeray recognised the signs of stress in Wolf Baker, he'd seen them before many times, and the alacrity with which the American had accepted his dinner invitation led him to believe he might want to talk about what troubled him.

'Please don't feel obliged to speak of the campaign if you don't wish to,' he added, rather regretting the presence of the older Englishman. Fond as he was of Godfrey, it hadn't been his intention to invite him. Jane had issued the invitation without his knowledge, but then she hadn't known he wished to talk privately with Wolf.

'I'd like to,' Wolf said. He needed to, he realised. It wasn't something he could talk about with his buddies. They all respected the unspoken pact: you didn't tell the other guys when you were rattled, everyone had their own case of the jitters, you didn't need to share yours.

'It is pretty rough out there,' he admitted. 'Well, you'd know that, Marty, you've seen the wounded coming in.'

Martin nodded, but said nothing, aware that the American had welcomed the opportunity to unburden himself.

'I made a couple of trips. First time in a Dauntless. She's a two-seater,' he explained for the others' benefit, 'and I was taking a journalist out to the USS *Wasp*. Just him and me, and it was a quiet day, pretty uneventful. I dropped the guy at the carrier, refuelled and came back. Easy,' he shrugged. 'But two days ago I flew a Dakota cargo plane out to the Solomons. We were carrying fresh medical supplies and two battle surgeons, emergency stuff, the guys had been copping it heavy.'

Wolf took a sip of his wine. His voice was matter-of-fact and unemotional as he told his story, but the growing tension in him was evident to the others.

'Well, there was some Jap activity about, but mainly reconnaissance, I figured, and we landed at Henderson Field okay. Coming back was the hard part. We'd unloaded and refuelled and we were preparing for takeoff when everything went crazy. The sirens were screaming and our guys were jumping into their fighters and we had to get up there as quick as we could to clear the airstrip. Then the moment we took off they seemed to come out of nowhere. High-level bombers, dive bombers, fighters. Jap planes everywhere you looked. I tried to hightail it for home, but within seconds there were dogfights all around us, and we were in the middle. A cargo plane's a pretty easy target and we were copping fire from every direction.'

This time Wolf didn't sip his wine, he drained the half glassful that was left. He needed to calm down, he was starting to get the jitters.

'So we had to take evasive action,' he said, his voice still steady. 'I tell you, man, I was trying to dodge and weave that damn thing around like it was a Dauntless. I only wish to hell it had been, a Dauntless has got guns.' He couldn't help it, he was feeling shaky again, and the frustration was now showing in his voice. 'That was the real bastard! We couldn't fight! No bombs, no guns. We were just up there, a sitting damn duck in a sky full of flak.'

He automatically reached for his glass again only to discover it was empty. Martin picked up the wine bottle, but Wolf shook his head. 'No thanks, Marty, I'm fine.'

He wasn't fine, Martin thought, putting the wine bottle down. Wolf Baker wasn't fine at all.

'We made it back to base eventually,' he concluded, 'but my two crew had been hit. My cargo master was shot up pretty bad, and I lost my co-pilot.' It was a simple statement and his tone was detached, but there was no disguising the pain in his admission. 'He was a buddy of mine from back home, and I have to admit it hit me a bit hard.'

The others were all watching him in silence. Then Martin said, 'Shall we have a pot of that wonderful coffee Wolf generously supplied, my dear?'

Godfrey Tomlinson was appalled. The offer of coffee seemed so jarringly out of place.

But, as Jane rose unquestioningly from the table, he realised that Martin wished to talk to the young man alone. He quickly stood himself, before Jane could suggest he give her a hand in the kitchen.

'If you don't mind,' he said, 'I'll forgo the coffee, it disagrees with me late at night.' It was not yet ten o'clock and, although Godfrey did eschew coffee of an evening, he was well known for talking, over copious glasses of his favourite red, well into the wee hours of the morning. It was hardly late at night for Godfrey. 'So I shall take my leave, my dear.' He kissed Jane on the cheek. 'Thank you so much for a beautiful meal. Martin. Wolf.' He shook hands with both men. 'Good night to you. And I'm sorry, Wolf,' he said, holding the American's hand in both of his for a moment. 'I'm very sorry to hear of the loss of your friend.'

'Thanks,' Wolf replied brusquely. He didn't intend to be rude; he'd registered the old man's sincerity, but he'd rattled himself in the telling of his story.

Jane saw the Englishman to the front door. 'You're a love,' she whispered as she kissed him again.

'I hope Martin can help him,' Godfrey whispered in reply.

'I think a bourbon might be the go, don't you?' Martin suggested when Jane had disappeared to the kitchen.

'But you don't like bourbon,' Wolf said.

'No, I can't abide it, filthy stuff.' Martin crossed to the dresser in the corner. 'That's why the bottle you brought last time is intact. I meant for you, I'll have another wine, if you don't mind.' He poured the drinks. 'Shall we go out onto the verandah?'

When they were seated outside, Martin got directly to
the point. 'You blame yourself, don't you?' Beneath Wolf's
anger, frustration and grief, all of which had been apparent
from the outset, Martin had recognised a far more dangerous emotion. The man was torn apart by guilt.

In the dim verandah light, Wolf stared down at the glass
of straight bourbon in his hands, and nodded. 'He was a
good guy, Marty. His name was Joe, but we called him Sonny
because his dad's a big wheel back in the States. Sonny was
my buddy, and I should have brought him home.'

'But you did,' Martin said softly.

There was a strength and authority in his three simple
words, and Wolf looked up from his glass.

'You did bring him home, Wolf. You brought both your
men home. You flew that plane through that battle zone
and you landed it safely back at base. It's not your fault
Sonny died.'

It was the truth and Wolf needed to hear it, grief had
clouded his perspective, but he was still unable to free
himself of his guilt.

'I know his folks,' he said shaking his head. 'I often
stayed weekends at their country place. His old man's
a senator and he's loaded, but he's not a bad guy, and
his mom's really great.' He stared distractedly down at his
glass again, swirling the bourbon about. 'Sonny was their
only kid. He was their whole world. They'll be torn apart.'

'And after the shock of their loss?'

The American looked at him, confused.

'Think how grateful they'll be that you brought him
home. There's a lifetime of agony in "missing in action",
Wolf.'

Martin's words were pragmatic and to the point, but
there was something in the way he said them that reached
beyond the mere truth of his statement. There was compassion and understanding, and something else. Something
that Wolf recognised as faith.

'People need to grieve,' Martin said. 'And when there's no tangible evidence of their loss, no earthly body, the process is very hard. You've helped Sonny's parents more than you could possibly know by bringing him home.'

Wolf had never thought of Marty as a priest, although he knew he was ordained. Hell, the guy was a missionary. But he'd seemed too practical somehow to be a priest. Wolf wasn't sure what his idea of a priest was, he didn't know any personally, but Marty was so real, so direct, so approachable. Perhaps it was because he'd been an army chaplain. Not that Marty himself ever spoke about his army days; it had been Jane who'd told Wolf.

Now, for the first time in their friendship, Wolf Baker was aware that Martin Thackeray was a man of God, and the practicality and wisdom of his words took on a special significance. Wolf felt a weight lifted from him, as if he'd been absolved of his guilt.

'Thanks, Marty,' he said inadequately. Did the man know what he'd just done? he wondered, and he took a swig of the bourbon, the raw liquor stinging the back of his throat, as he sought how better to express himself.

But there was no need. Martin registered that he'd been of some help and he was glad. 'So what do you want to do now?' he asked. 'Do you want to talk some more or just get drunk?'

'What about both?'

Jane delivered the coffee, although she doubted they'd get around to drinking it. Martin was opening another bottle of wine and Wolf had placed the bourbon bottle on the verandah table. So she left them to it and went to bed.

Whilst Wolf talked and got drunk, Martin sipped his wine and watched, commenting only when it seemed to be called for.

'It was the sheer goddamn helplessness of it, Marty,' Wolf

raged, 'sitting up there with no goddamn guns.' He was pacing the verandah now. 'Flak, flak, flak, everywhere,' he said, firing into the air with his right hand and spilling bourbon from the glass he was holding in his left. 'I thought we were going to blow up any second. Boom! I thought, there'll be nothing left of us. Jesus Christ, I was scared. Sorry.' He was suddenly conscious of blaspheming in front of Marty, though he never had been before. But Martin took no notice. 'I can't wait to be up there with guns. I swear to God I'll blow the bastards to hell.' Wolf was aware that it probably sounded like bravado, but he didn't care, it was all pouring out of him. 'I will, Marty, I'll blow them to bits, Jesus, I will. Sorry.'

'Oh for goodness sake, stop being so reverent,' Martin said. Wolf's blaspheming was of no consequence to him, and neither was his talk of retaliation, which he would normally have disagreed with. Wolf was simply letting off steam, and it was doing him good. Martin sat quietly drinking his wine, aware that he was getting a little heady himself, whilst Wolf worked it out of his system.

But when the American sat down, by now quite drunk, and started talking about the death of his friend, Martin could no longer be objective.

'He was sitting right next to me, Marty, when those bullets ripped through the starboard side of the cockpit. They missed me by inches and they blew the back of his head off. One minute he was there, we were screaming at each other through the R/T, and the next minute he's slumped over the control panel, dead.'

'I wasn't blasphemin', Marty,' Tom Putney had said. 'I was givin' thanks. It's a bleedin' miracle, it is. A bleedin'—'

Martin was back in Dunkirk. The explosion roared through his brain as he remembered. One minute Tom had been there, and the next minute he'd been dead.

'A quick death,' he said, 'he wouldn't have felt any pain.' Martin wasn't sure whether he was referring to

Tom Putney or to Sonny. He was getting drunk, he thought, he wasn't accustomed to heavy drinking.

'Yes, that's what I keep telling myself,' Wolf agreed. 'I mean, Jesus, I've seen enough dead bodies.' He'd given up worrying about his blaspheming, it obviously didn't bother Marty. 'Pearl Harbor was a massacre, blood and guts everywhere. But when it's your buddy, and he's right next to you. You know what I mean?' The bourbon bottle was empty and he was starting to slur his words.

'Yes, Wolf, I do. And I think it's bedtime. You're in the spare room. Come on.'

Less than a week later, Martin made his announcement. It was a humid evening in early September, and he and Jane were sipping their cups of tea on the verandah, both having returned from a hard day's work.

'A patient arrived at the hospital today,' he said, having decided to broach the subject circuitously. 'A leg wound, badly septic, they flew him in early this morning. He's a chaplain aboard the USS *Wasp*. Or rather he was. It's a nasty wound. We can save the leg, but he'll be out of commission for some time. So the *Wasp* is without a Protestant chaplain.'

Jane felt a stab of alarm. Where was this leading? Martin wasn't thinking of offering his services, surely.

'Some of the troopships are too, there's a shortage of Protestant chaplains. Reverend Hemmings, that's the fellow's name,' he added unnecessarily, 'was visiting one of the troopships, and that's how the accident happened, his leg got crushed in the transfer from a small boat.'

She was looking at him strangely. Behind the growing suspicion and fear in her eyes was something unfathomable, and he found himself rambling, as if to avoid the final announcement.

'He's a good chap, Hemmings. Very stoic. He kept quiet about the seriousness of his injury for far too long. It was brave of him really, albeit stupid, but he obviously knew how much he was needed.' He wished she'd stop looking at him like that, it was most disconcerting. 'So as you can see, they're rather desperate, and they need someone out there as soon as possible.'

He tailed off lamely. 'Anyway,' he shrugged, 'I volunteered for the post. I leave in two days.'

Two days! Fear gripped her. 'Why, Marty?' She asked after a moment's silence. 'Why?'

'I told you, my love, the men need a chaplain.'

'But why you? Why now?' Jane tried to keep calm. 'This has something to do with Wolf, doesn't it? Something to do with the other night.'

His old nightmares of Dunkirk had returned that night he'd talked with Wolf; he hadn't had them for a long time now. He'd laughed them off in the morning, saying that he'd been drunk. 'Godfrey's fine reds don't agree with me, my love, not in excess anyway,' he'd said. But he'd told her all about his conversation with Wolf, and the agony of guilt the American had been suffering. The evening had obviously triggered Martin's memory, and Jane had thought no more about it, apart from her gratitude that Martin had been able to help the American. Now she cursed Wolf Baker.

'It is, isn't it, Marty? It's because of Wolf Baker.'

He realised it was anger he'd seen behind her fear. The last thing he'd expected was anger. 'No,' he said, bewildered. What on earth did Wolf have to do with it? he wondered. Did she think Wolf had suggested him for the post? 'It has nothing at all to do with Wolf. Wolf doesn't even know that I've volunteered.'

'It's because of him you feel the need to prove yourself.' The words were out before she could stop them and they shocked her. Her anger evaporated in an instant. She hadn't meant to sound cruel. 'I'm sorry, I shouldn't have said that.'

'Is it what you believe, Jane?'

'I don't know.' He appeared neither angered nor hurt by her outburst, but it was obvious he was seeking her truthful answer, and she wondered herself what she'd meant in the heat of the moment. Did she truly believe he was trying to prove himself? And if so, to whom? To her? Did she think he was trying to prove his manliness by going off to war? No, she didn't. That wasn't Martin's way.

'I truly don't know, Marty. All I do know is that you had no desire to volunteer your services before that night with Wolf.'

He was relieved by the honesty and simplicity of her reply. 'I wasn't needed,' he said. He put his arm around her. 'Coincidence is a fine thing, my love. That's all it is, I swear, my volunteering has nothing to do with Wolf Baker.'

He kissed her lightly, then sat back once again with his cup of tea. 'But you may be right, Jane, perhaps I do feel the need to prove myself.' He saw the worry that sprang into her eyes.

'Oh not to you, my love.' He smiled reassuringly. 'Not even to myself. Perhaps I feel the need to prove myself to God. I only know that He's called me and I must answer.'

He sat sipping his tea, as they did every evening whilst they discussed their day, and Jane wondered how he could be so calm when he'd just shattered her peaceful existence.

'If I asked you not to go, Marty, would you stay?'

'But you wouldn't ask me that, would you, my love? Not when Christian men are about to be called into battle and they have no chaplain of their faith to bless them. You wouldn't ask me that, would you?'

'No,' she said, 'I wouldn't ask you that.'

Two days later, early in the morning of 10 September, they held each other close as the young corporal waited patiently outside in the jeep. Martin didn't want her to come to Quoin Hill.

'A long drive to no purpose, my love,' he'd said.

'Godspeed,' she whispered. And she stood at the door of the cottage, Ronnie in her arms, as she watched them drive off, Martin smiling and blowing a kiss first to her, then to Ronnie.

When he arrived at Quoin Hill, amongst the scores of khaki-uniformed servicemen, a familiar figure was waiting for him.

'Wolf,' he exclaimed with pleasure as the jeep pulled up. 'I'm so glad you're here, I wanted to say cheerio before I left, but everything happened so quickly.'

'No need to say cheerio just yet, Marty, I'm your pilot.'

The corporal bade them farewell, the jeep took off and the two men stood chatting, oblivious to the activity that surrounded them.

'You're my pilot?' Martin said, incredulous. 'What a wonderful coincidence.'

'Not really. Chuck Wilson was assigned to fly you out – that's how I heard you were going – he's a buddy of mine, so I volunteered to swap places, Chuck didn't mind.'

'Oh.' Martin was extremely touched. 'That's grand of you, Wolf. That's really grand.'

Wolf gave a nonchalant grin, but he was delighted by Martin's reaction. 'No big deal,' he said. 'Come and I'll show you the drill.'

Martin shouldered his kitbag and followed the American to the gleaming blue two-seater plane standing beside the airstrip ready for takeoff.

'A Douglas SBD Dauntless dive bomber, she's a little honey.' Wolf affectionately caressed the wing of the aircraft. 'And she's got guns. Thirty calibre,' he said, pointing to the two machine guns mounted on the fuselage. 'I feel a lot happier with guns, Marty.'

His wink was personal and cheeky, and Martin was

pleased to note that Wolf Baker was back on form. His bounce fully recovered, the American was as irrepressible as ever.

'And she can travel over 900 miles in four hours without bombs attached,' Wolf added as he loaded the kitbag into the hold. 'Like I said, she's a honey.'

Twenty minutes later they were ready to go, Wolf having rigged Martin out, first with his Mae West lifejacket, then his parachute, meticulously checking every buckle and attachment of the harness. 'Got to be careful with you amateurs,' he said.

The rear seat of the Dauntless faced aft, the passenger or crew member seated with his back to the pilot, and as Martin was about to climb into it, Wolf stopped him.

'Something I want to say, Marty, whilst there's just you and me.'

Martin looked around at the hive of activity that was the airbase: islanders loading and unloading cargo, mechanics working on aircraft, troops going about their duties. He raised a humorous eyebrow, but Wolf wasn't to be deterred, he was serious now.

'It'll be noisy up there,' he gave a vague skyward glance, 'and when we get to the *Wasp* we won't have any time together. I'll be refuelling and they'll have the welcoming committee out for you, so I want to say it before we take off.'

'What is it, Wolf?' Martin asked. The American seemed unsure of what he wanted to say.

Wolf Baker wasn't unsure of what he wanted to say at all, but he was unsure of the words with which to say it. He admired Martin Thackeray more than any man he'd met.

'You don't know what you did for me the other night, do you, Marty?' he asked.

Martin answered carefully, aware that it somehow seemed important, although he wasn't sure why. 'I think I gave you some peace of mind, Wolf, and if I did, I'm glad.'

'Oh you did that all right,' Wolf nodded. 'You sure did that. And that's what you'll do for those guys out there.' Wolf wasn't accustomed to struggling with words, he'd always had the gift of the gab, but then he'd never addressed a topic so beyond his comprehension.

'I'm not a religious guy, Marty, and I think in a wartime situation guys like me often envy those who are. But you bridge the gap. I don't know how you do it, but you do. You'll get through to those guys out there, just like you did to me, and I can't think of any man better for the job.'

'Thank you, Wolf.' It was the perfect endorsement and Martin welcomed it. He had no doubts about what he was doing, just as he'd had no second thoughts when he'd volunteered. God's will was not to be questioned. But the thought that he might be of some comfort to men like Wolf, men who had not embraced the faith, gave him an added purpose.

'I hope you're right,' he said as they shook hands.

'Oh I'm right, you can bet your bottom dollar on that.' Wolf grinned. 'Now let's get up there, shall we?'

# CHAPTER FOURTEEN

Wolf's prediction proved correct. The moment they landed aboard the USS *Wasp*, there was no opportunity for them to say their goodbyes. Martin was instantly greeted by the Executive Officer who awaited him on the observation deck of the conning-tower.

'Dr Thackeray, boy are we glad to see you!' Commander Dickey enthused as he introduced himself. 'The men have been sorely missing a chaplain. You're most welcome aboard, sir, I assure you.'

Just before he was whisked away to 'meet the men', Martin looked for Wolf. But the American wasn't standing idly by; he, too, had been pounced upon. The Flight Commander, who had also been awaiting their arrival on the observation deck, had taken him to one side.

'Good thing you're here, Lieutenant,' the Commander was saying, 'we need a transport plane. Every aircraft aboard is covering operations for the convoys and resupply units headed for Guadalcanal . . .'

Martin couldn't hear exactly what was being said, but it was clear that Wolf was receiving orders, so he gave his full attention to Commander Dickey.

'Thank goodness the *Wasp* is bigger than she appears

from the air,' he joked, looking about at the massive aircraft carrier. 'I was rather worried there for a minute.'

The Executive Officer laughed, he'd heard it before. Most novices were visibly shaken upon landing, some were even physically ill. He liked the new chaplain for making a joke of it.

Martin hadn't actually been nervous at all. He'd found the experience exhilarating. From the moment he'd seen the USS *Wasp*, far below in the distance, sitting like a miniature toy on the Coral Sea, the watchful destroyers mere dots nearby, he had found the whole process extraordinary. What a miracle of man's invention, he'd thought, minutes later, as Wolf prepared the Dauntless for landing. He'd twisted his body about in the rear seat, craning his neck for the forward view, determined not to miss a thing, and then it had all happened with such breathtaking speed. One moment Wolf was flying low, making his steady approach, then they'd touched down, the far end of the carrier's runway frighteningly close. Then the hook beneath the aircraft's fuselage had grabbed the wire, and in only seconds they'd come to an abrupt halt, the Dauntless stationary, quivering like a dragonfly having alighted upon a lily pad.

As Martin followed the officers from the observation deck, he cast another look back at Wolf and this time the American caught his eye. They waved to each other, and just before Martin disappeared through the hatch, Wolf grinned and his wave became a salute. Martin smiled to himself as he descended the ladder.

Wolf turned once again to the Flight Commander, and his grin disappeared. He was finding his orders somewhat daunting.

'We'll bring him up in an hour when your aircraft's refuelled and checked for takeoff,' the Commander said. 'Grab yourself a cup of Java in the meantime. Dr Redmond will be with him and he'll give you instructions.

And we've been in contact with Bellevue, they'll have transport waiting as soon as you touch down at Quoin Hill. You should get there by dusk.'

'Yes, sir.' Wolf saluted, and the Flight Commander, having returned the salute, left him to ponder the task at hand.

He was to transport an injured naval officer back to Efate, a fighter pilot whose plane had been badly damaged in a dogfight. The rear gunner had been killed and the pilot had made a successful crash landing at sea. He'd got clear of the sinking aircraft, but he'd been in the water for twenty-four hours before they'd picked him up.

'Surprisingly little physical injury,' the Flight Commander had said, 'but a bad case of battle trauma, I'm afraid. He's going to be repatriated as soon as possible, but Bellevue's the first step.'

Battle trauma, Wolf thought as he waited on the observation deck swigging the mug of coffee he'd grabbed from the officers' wardroom. That could mean anything, poor bastard. The guy might be catatonic or he might be a gibbering mess. What if he threw some sort of fit when they were up there? Wolf didn't know what to expect and he didn't welcome the responsibility.

'John, this is Wolf Baker.' The pilot's uniform bore the stripes of Lieutenant Commander and he outranked Wolf, but the doctor made his introduction with no recognition of rank. 'Wolf, this is John Stubbs.'

'Hi, John.' Wolf took his cue from Dr Redmond, a tough, wiry little man but obviously sympathetic. Redmond had arrived before John Stubbs in order to have a 'quick chat', as he called it, and when Stubbs appeared several minutes later, he was assisted by two medical orderlies. The guy could walk okay, Wolf noted, although he was tentative, distracted.

'His mind's closed off, he doesn't know where he is,'

Redmond had explained. 'I don't think he'll cause you any trouble,' he'd added, aware of Wolf's concern. 'He's mobile, and he can understand and obey simple instructions, but he's unable to make any decisions or choices.'

Wolf offered his hand as they were introduced, but the pilot didn't even notice; he was looking out over the flight deck at the tidy rows of fighter planes. Not frightened, but bewildered, his eyes were wide, and his mouth slightly open, like a child, unsure of himself and his surrounds. John Stubbs was a big man, fit and strong, in his early thirties, and it was a pathetic sight.

The doctor and orderlies accompanied them down to the flight deck, and John stood obediently still whilst one of the ground crew rigged him with his Mae West and parachute. Then the orderlies, whom he obviously knew and trusted, helped him up onto the wing and into the rear seat, talking him through each action and placing his limbs in the right spot. 'Put your hand here, John, and now your leg here, that's right.' Wolf wanted to look away, it was so sad.

'Will he be all right?' he asked Redmond.

'In a peaceful environment I'm sure he'll make a recovery,' the doctor replied diplomatically. He could tell young Baker was moved. 'Psychiatrists can do wonders these days.'

Satisfied that the patient was settled, Redmond and the orderlies prepared to leave the flight deck, but Redmond had one final piece of advice.

'Avoid any action if you can, Lieutenant. I worry that further stress of combat could render him catatonic.'

Wolf gave a laconic smile. 'I'll do my best, Doc,' he said. Jesus, did the man think he was going to go hunting Japs?

Before he climbed into the cockpit, Wolf checked that John Stubbs was safely buckled in, but the orderlies and ground crew had taken care of all that. His flying cap and R/T headset were on, his harness fastened, and he was sitting quietly, his hands folded in his lap, his eyes darting around warily.

'You all set, John?' Wolf smiled, patting the man's shoulder. 'Ready for a trip?' John looked up at him and nodded trustingly. Perhaps the guy liked him, Wolf thought, kids always did.

During takeoff he tried not to be distracted by the thought that the experience might disturb John Stubbs. He wished he was flying an aircraft where he could see the guy's face in the co-pilot's seat, but he couldn't afford to think that, he told himself. It was just him. Just him and the Dauntless.

And then they were off.

He climbed steadily to 20,000 feet and headed east for Efate. 'You right, John?' he called through the R/T over the throb of the engine. 'You okay back there?'

'Mmmm. Mmmm. Mmmm.'

He heard a series of humming noises through the headset. What the hell was he supposed to make of that? he thought. But there didn't seem to be any hysteria in the sound.

'How's that for a view? Some sight, huh?'

'Mmm. Mmm.'

Wolf was sure it was a signal of agreement, and he started to relax.

John Stubbs was actually rocking back and forward in his seat, his hands still clasped in his lap, not tightly, not distressed, but he wasn't looking at the view. He was somewhere else entirely.

They'd been travelling for nearly three hours when Wolf saw the Japanese aircraft below him. It was a Pete, a two-man float biplane, slow-flying and no match for the speed of the Dauntless. There would be no need for a showdown so long as he held his course. The Pete wouldn't dare chase him this close to the Americans' New Hebridean bases. Christ, what was it doing here anyway? They must be only fifty miles from the coast of Malekula. It would have to be a special reconnaissance plane, surely.

Wolf was about to report the Japanese biplane's position to Quoin Hill, but he hadn't reckoned on the escorts. He'd been distracted by the continuous humming through the R/T. John Stubbs seemed to be singing a song, he'd thought, and he'd been lulled by the sound and the evident safety of their flight. They were not far from home now.

The two Zeros had seen him well before he'd seen the Pete, and they dived from above, a patterned attack.

Wolf saw them in the same instant he saw the tracers cross the nose of his aircraft and he banked sharply, feeling the jarring thud of bullets hit the stern of the Dauntless. He wheeled the aircraft, chose one of the Zeros and dived. He had guns this time, he thought. This time he could attack. No need to run this time.

He felt no bravado, no thoughts of revenge, just a cold, clinical thankfulness that this time he could fight back.

The humming he could hear through his headset was now high-pitched and continuous, like an electrical saw reverberating in his skull, but he had no time to think of John Stubbs. The Zero was in his sights, and he fired. A direct hit, flame burst from its fuselage and it started to spiral, but Wolf didn't wait to watch it plummet into the sea. He climbed fast, the other Zero on his tail.

Together they climbed. Together they wheeled. Wolf fired, he missed. The Zero fired, Wolf dived, bullets streaking through the air only feet above him.

Again they banked, and wheeled and fired, then dived only to climb again, dodging and weaving, a macabre dance in the sky.

John Stubbs was no longer humming. He'd opened his mouth and the sound through the headset was a primal scream.

The scream, far from distracting Wolf, became an outlet for his anger and terror. It was the scream he would have

liked to have let loose himself, but didn't dare. John Stubbs
was doing the screaming for them both.

The dance continued. Once more, Wolf climbed and
wheeled with his deadly partner, and for a second there
was a loss of synchronicity, a moment when they were out
of step. It was the moment Wolf needed. He fired. Orange
flame burst from the Zero's fuselage, and this time he
watched as it spiralled into the sea.

The Pete was on its own now, flying low, escaping to the
north. Wolf knew that the Dauntless was damaged, not
critically, but he was aware of a faint shudder in the
aircraft. If he was to have any hope of reaching Efate, he
needed to maintain a slow, steady pace. But he had to
down the Pete. God knew what information the Japs
might have gathered from their reconnaissance; they'd
sure taken some risks getting it.

He took up the chase. The Pete was desperate to escape,
but it was no match for the Dauntless, and finally, John
Stubbs's screams ringing in his ears, Wolf pulled the Dauntless into one more climb. Then he wheeled and dived.

He wanted to scream along with John as he fired a burst
at the Pete. He scored a hit. Not fatal, but the biplane
turned in an attempt to limp its way home. The fight was
over.

Wolf had paid a price, however, as the Japanese pilot
well knew – his own gunner had also scored a hit. The
American would not follow them, there would be no
further attack, the American's aircraft was useless.

The 7.7mm machine-gun fire from the Pete's rear gunner
had perforated the engine of the Dauntless. It started to
sputter. The engine was dying, and Wolf knew that he
couldn't make it to Quoin Hill. But he could see land in the
distance. Not Efate, he was sure, they were too far north,
probably Malekula, he thought. Although God only knew
where the dogfight had taken them, he'd lost all perception
of direction and distance.

He tried to make radio contact with the base at Quoin Hill, but there was no reply, just an ominous crackling in his headset. He repeated over and over an approximation of his position in the hope that he might be getting through. Then the crackling ceased and the radio went dead. Above the engine's sputter, all was silence, and it was only then he realised the other sound that was missing, the sound that had been missing from the moment they'd been hit. John Stubbs had stopped screaming. Was he catatonic as the doctor had feared? Was he dead?

Wolf pulled off his headset. 'John!' he yelled with all the lung power he could muster. 'John, are you okay?'

Silence.

There was no time to think of John Stubbs.

Wolf put the aircraft into a long, shallow dive. He had to ditch her, but the closer he could get to land, the closer he would be to the possibility of rescue.

He focussed on the island up ahead and as he flew, barely a hundred feet above the clear blue water, the aircraft shuddered more violently and the sputter of the engine became more erratic in its death throes. But he was getting closer. Closer and closer, he could see the shapes of distant coconut trees now.

The water loomed. He was skimming above its surface. He had to keep the nose up.

'Brace yourself, John!' he yelled, just in case the man could hear him.

Then the undercarriage of the Dauntless hit the water. The aircraft bounced and skipped. Once, twice, three times. It was a stone thrown by a child, skittering across the sea. But each time it bounced, the water felt like concrete. Keep the nose up, keep the nose up. Wolf fought to maintain control. And then finally, jarringly, they were down and shuddering to a halt. A sluggish metal weight sitting in the middle of the sea. Any minute the aircraft would tilt nose down and, once she did, she would plummet to the ocean's depths.

Wolf struggled with his seatbelt and parachute harness. He told himself not to panic, as water bubbled into the cockpit. Panic made for clumsiness. Slow, steady. That's it. And he was out, standing on the wing, desperately trying to free John Stubbs. The man was alive, and he appeared uninjured, but he was unconscious. Probably just as well, Wolf thought, freeing the seatbelt and fighting with the buckle of the parachute harness, he'd be either catatonic or raving mad otherwise.

Oh Jesus, he thought, oh Jesus, he couldn't get the buckle undone, and the plane was half submerged, any second she'd start to tilt. He tried to drag Stubbs out, parachute pack and all, but he was a big man and he seemed to be wedged into the seat. Finally the buckle gave way, but it was too late, the plane was tilting now. She was starting to go down, and Stubbs was going down with her, his head disappearing beneath the water's surface.

Wolf dived and, as the submerged plane continued to tilt, everything became slow motion. There were only seconds before the Dauntless would plunge for the bottom, and those seconds seemed a lifetime.

With one hand, he held on to the side of the cockpit to keep himself anchored, whilst with the other he slipped the harness from Stubbs's shoulders and fed his arms through the straps. Freed of the parachute, he managed to pull the man half out of the rear seat, but Stubbs was tall, and his legs remained locked in the cockpit. Without traction, his body floating freely, Wolf didn't have the strength to pull him free. The nose of the plane was pointing downwards now, her tail clear of the water, and as she started her dive, Wolf yanked on the cord of Stubbs's Mae West. The lifejacket inflated. Then, with a firm grip on Stubbs, he let go his hold of the aircraft and inflated his own lifejacket and, as the plane plummeted to the ocean floor, the two men rose to the surface.

They bobbed about in the water like corks, Stubbs now semi-conscious, coughing and spluttering.

'You okay, John?'

But he didn't reply. His body having instinctively fought for the breath to survive, John Stubbs soon lapsed once again into a state of unconsciousness, and, grasping the man's lifejacket, Wolf started to swim for the distant shore.

It was probably a futile exercise, he thought, unless the wind and the tide were in his favour, in which case he'd be better off just drifting anyway. But swimming gave him something to do.

Then he noticed the fin. The black dorsal fin slicing the water and heading straight for them. He stopped swimming. The shark circled them inquisitively, not bent on attack. Wolf cursed the fact that he'd had no time to grab the survival kit – there was a vial of chlorine in it which served as a shark repellent and it had gone down with the plane.

He twisted his head about, following the shark's every movement, intermittently darting glances at John Stubbs, searching for the wound that might have rendered him unconscious. Was there blood? He couldn't see any ominous leakage from beneath the man's flying cap. He was suddenly aware of a pain in his chest. Had he himself been wounded on impact? Was he bleeding? But the pain felt internal, maybe a fractured rib. He hoped so. They didn't need blood in the water.

In the gathering dusk, the shark kept circling. Soon there might be others. And soon it would be dark, and Wolf would no longer be able to see their fins.

Two days later, aboard the USS *Wasp*, Martin heard the news. Second Lieutenant Charles Wolfgang Baker and Lieutenant Commander John Stubbs were missing in action.

The Executive Officer had approached Martin as he was leaving the hangar deck following early morning prayers.

An area of the hangar deck, known affectionately as 'the chapel', had been allocated for Sunday services and prayer meetings, regularly conducted by both the Protestant and Catholic chaplains aboard.

'I thought you should know,' Commander Dickey said sympathetically; it had been apparent to him that Baker and Thackeray were friends.

No, Martin thought. No, not Wolf. 'What happened?' he asked.

Quoin Hill airbase had received a radio message from the Dauntless as Wolf was preparing to ditch the aircraft, the Commander told him. They hadn't been able to make contact themselves and the aircraft's position had been vague, although Wolf had reported that he was in sight of land. Two Corsairs had been dispatched to search the area where they presumed the plane had gone down, but they'd found nothing and darkness had rendered the exercise futile. The following morning, however, they'd remounted the search and, in covering broader territory, they'd sighted a Japanese amphibian aircraft downed thirty miles off the coast of Espiritu Santo. A naval patrol boat had picked up the two-man crew from the Pete and, upon interrogation, it had been discovered that Wolf had shot down their Zero escorts and incapacitated the biplane. But, according to the Japanese pilot, the Dauntless had been badly damaged herself and would certainly have had to crash land.

'The Japs were very helpful,' Commander Dickey said. 'The interpreter reported that the Japanese pilot greatly admired Baker's skill.'

'Just as I admire his resourcefulness,' Martin replied. 'He was in sight of land, you say?'

The Commander nodded. 'Malekula, he seemed to think. The Pete was discovered off Espiritu Santo, but it was heading north and it had covered quite a bit of ground before it ditched, so we're also presuming it was the shores of Malekula that Lieutenant Baker sighted.'

Something told Martin that Wolf had made it ashore. He didn't know why, but he had a strong presentiment that both men had survived. 'I believe he's alive,' he said. 'And John Stubbs too.'

'I hope so, Dr Thackeray,' the Commander replied. 'I hope so.' He certainly wouldn't bet on it himself, but he admired the man's faith.

Jane heard the news from Chuck Wilson, whom she'd met a number of times with Wolf. She knew they were close friends and she liked the man.

Chuck arrived at Mamma Tack's early in the morning, just as Jane was opening the clinic for the day. He'd decided to deliver the news personally, rather than allow her to hear it via the grapevine.

'Can I have a word, Jane?' he asked through the open-shuttered window.

His face was grave, and Jane felt a sense of dread as she nodded to Mary to take over, and to keep an eye on Ronnie, who was playing with some local children nearby. She ushered Chuck inside and they retired to the examination area at the rear of the boatshed, Jane pulling the curtains across for privacy.

'I have some bad news, I'm afraid,' he said.

The breath caught in her throat. 'Marty.'

'Oh no. No, no,' he quickly assured her. She'd gone suddenly pale, and he was horrified that he'd aroused such fear in her. 'Your husband's on the *Wasp*. Hell, the *Wasp* is impregnable. He's fine. Really he's fine.'

She sank thankfully onto one of the beds. She knew Martin had arrived safely at the aircraft carrier, they'd told her that much, but she lived in constant fear.

Chuck sat on the other bed, facing her. 'It's Wolf. They've reported him missing in action.'

'Oh.' Her face remained ashen.

'It happened on the return trip.'

'What return trip?'

'After he'd flown Dr Thackeray to the *Wasp*.'

'Wolf flew Martin to the *Wasp*?'

'You didn't know?'

No-one had told her that. She shook her head.

'It was supposed to be me,' Chuck said, feeling wretched. 'I was assigned the job and Wolf swapped places.'

Chuck Wilson was plagued by conflicting emotions. He couldn't stop thinking that if it hadn't been for Wolf Baker, he'd be the one missing in action. He felt burdened with guilt and yet at the same time thankful to be alive, and he hated himself for it.

He explained what had happened. They knew the full story, he said, because of the Japanese crew aboard the Pete. 'There was no sign of the Dauntless,' he concluded. 'And they couldn't find the bodies of Wolf and his passenger.'

He'd told the facts in a clinical fashion, but he was starting to crack up now.

'Wolf wanted to fly your husband out there and when he volunteered I didn't see any problem. I mean, I thought it was a pretty straightforward transport flight. Just there and back, you know? I didn't think . . .'

'And why should you?' Jane felt deep sympathy for the man. He held himself responsible for Wolf's death, just as Wolf had blamed himself for the death of his co-pilot. 'It's not your fault, Chuck.'

'Yeah, I know that.' Chuck was embarrassed, he'd been on the verge of tears. He stood. 'It's fate, I guess.'

'That's exactly what it is.' She wanted to take his hand, to offer some physical comfort, but she was aware of his self-consciousness. 'It's fate and there's nothing you or anybody else could have done to prevent it.'

'Yeah. You're right.' He gave a weak smile and tried to sound jaunty. 'Well, I'll see you around, Mamma Tack.'

And he beat a hasty retreat, thankful that no-one but Jane had seen him cracking up.

She sat for several minutes, absorbing the news. Wolf Baker was dead. And he was dead because of his devotion to Marty. If he hadn't volunteered . . . if he hadn't flown Martin to the *Wasp* . . . But she knew she couldn't afford to think like that. It was indeed fate. Or the will of God, as Marty would say. She only hoped Marty would see it the same way. She hoped he wasn't blaming himself and suffering like Chuck Wilson.

Martin thanked the Executive Officer for bringing him the news personally, and then returned to the chapel. He sat by the bulkhead where he normally stood to address his congregation. He didn't pray, not at first anyway, he asked himself questions instead. Why did he believe Wolf was alive? Commander Dickey was clearly of the opinion that both men were dead, and why shouldn't he be? That's what 'missing in action' invariably meant.

Martin questioned his own positivity. Did he believe Wolf was alive because he had to? Because he was the reason Wolf Baker had been flying that aircraft? No, he was sure that wasn't the case. His deepest instincts told him Wolf had survived, and so had Stubbs. Was God sending him a message? he wondered, and he knelt before the table, which served as his altar.

Martin Thackeray's instincts were more than accurate. Even as he knelt to pray, Wolf Baker and John Stubbs were bidding farewell to Soli and Tura and their families before setting out from the village.

It had been Soli and Tura who had rescued them.

The brothers always fished at dusk well out off the coast of the cape, where there was a deep shelf in the reef and the big fish gathered. It was also a favourite feeding place for sharks and they'd frightened three of them off with their paddles before they'd hauled the white men aboard their outrigger canoe.

The men were lucky, the brothers thought. Lucky they weren't wounded. There was plenty of feed around for the sharks, and they would rather eat fish than people. The islanders themselves often dived amongst the sharks to collect shellfish from the reef. But the islanders were careful not to cut themselves on the rocks, for if they drew blood the sharks would attack. Many a diver had been taken that way. The men were lucky they were not wounded, the brothers agreed.

Soli and Tura had taken the men to their village. They'd had to carry the bigger one because he was unconscious, but he was alive. And the women had given the other man fish and roasted coconut as he'd squatted with them around the cooking fire. He'd been very hungry. They'd fed the sick man some water as he'd muttered and drifted in and out of consciousness, but he'd been unable to eat any food. Then they'd bedded the men down in one of their huts and left them to sleep, wondering if the sick man would be dead in the morning.

Wolf, exhausted, had slept soundly that night. He'd been awoken now and then by groans from John Stubbs, and he'd heard the terrible gnashing of teeth as the man had writhed beside him on the floor of the hut. He hadn't been able to see Stubbs in the blackness, but several times Wolf had reached out to grab an arm or a shoulder to try to comfort him.

'Ssh, John. Ssh, it's okay. Everything's okay,' he'd said repeatedly, until Stubbs's groans had died down and he'd returned to a fitful sleep. Everything wasn't okay, Wolf had thought, God only knew what hideous torment the man was suffering.

Wolf had still been fast asleep when the first rays of sunlight had streamed through the open doorway, and it was then that he'd felt the hand on his shoulder.

'Leonard?' he heard a voice say. The hand was shaking him now, and his ribs were hurting. He heaved himself groggily onto one elbow.

'Leonard!' the voice said. 'Jesus Christ, man, I thought you were dead.'

Wolf stared up at John Stubbs. Stubbs, still wearing his canvas flying cap, was on his knees leaning over him, and he appeared to have regained not only his consciousness, but his sanity.

'You're alive, Len!' Stubbs's expression was one of utter incredulity. 'I don't believe it! It's a miracle! You're alive!'

Then Wolf realised. The man was not sane at all. John Stubbs thought Wolf was the rear gunner who'd been killed. What should he do? Surely it was best if he played along with the delusion.

'I sure am, John,' he said. 'And you're conscious. You've been out to it since we crashed yesterday.'

'Have I? Was it yesterday? Christ, I've been having some dreams. You remember the sharks, Len?'

Of course he did, Wolf thought. He'd been terrified. But how could John Stubbs remember the sharks? He'd been unconscious.

'Yeah, 'course I do, I was scared as all hell.'

'I thought they'd got you. I was so sure . . .' John's voice trailed off and a haunted look crept into his eyes. The images were there, quite clear in his mind. They were in the water. Miles from anywhere, no land in sight, just him and Len. And Len was wounded, bleeding badly.

'I've been hit, John,' Len had said.

'Hang in there,' he remembered saying. 'Hang in there, buddy.' He could see himself saying it. And as they'd bobbed uselessly in their lifejackets, he'd kept on saying it. He'd fed Len water from the survival kit and when the sharks had arrived, he'd chucked chlorine everywhere, but it hadn't done any good. They were surrounded by Len's blood and the sharks had gone wild. He could still hear

Len's screams. But he hadn't let go. It had become a tug of war. Whilst the sharks had ripped away in a feeding frenzy, he'd held onto Len's lifejacket, yelling and screaming himself. Long after Len's screams had stopped, he was still yelling, and the sharks were still feeding. He'd wondered why they didn't attack him, but it seemed they were only interested in the bloodied meat.

He didn't remember the rest of the night, or the next morning. But he remembered when they'd picked him up. He'd still been holding on to Len. He'd had his arm around his lifejacket and Len had looked so white, so very, very white. 'Hang in there, buddy,' he'd said as the patrol boat approached them. 'Hang in there just a bit longer, we've made it, okay.'

And then he'd heard someone say 'Jesus Christ!' and he'd heard someone else being sick as they hauled the torso aboard. The little that was left beneath the lifejacket had been drained of all blood.

Wolf sat up quickly, ignoring the jab of pain in his ribs. John Stubbs was shaking uncontrollably and there was an inexpressible horror in his eyes. Was he about to throw a fit? Wolf thought. Was he going to become catatonic?

'It's okay, John,' he said, kneeling and clasping the big man firmly by the arms. 'It's okay. I'm here. See? I'm right here.'

The horror in John Stubbs's eyes faded to relief, and he slumped back on his heels. 'Oh Christ, Len,' he said, putting a hand to his forehead and shaking his head. 'I've had such dreams, such terrible dreams.'

'Well, you put them right out of your mind. I'm here and we're safe, and that's all that matters.'

'Yeah. Yeah you're right.' Stubbs nodded emphatically, and then he smiled. 'Hell, it's good to see you, buddy.'

'You too, John.' Wolf returned the smile. If he was to get the man to safety, he realised, it was imperative to continue the delusion. 'You had me worried when you were unconscious. It's good to have you back.' Wolf rose to his feet. 'Now let's find out where we are, shall we?'

'Any idea?'

'New Hebrides, one of the islands to the north. My guess is Malekula.'

Stubbs stood, and Wolf noticed that he was rather shaky on his feet, which was hardly surprising. 'You okay?'

'Yeah sure.'

A small group of women and children were waiting outside the hut, curious to see the white men. As Wolf and John appeared, the children gathered around them and the women giggled and chatted amongst themselves in their strange tongue. John swayed unsteadily, about to fall, and, whilst Wolf propped him up, one of the women ran for help.

They were in the communal centre of the village, the blackened remnants of an often-used cooking fire in the middle, logs strewn about, and the open doorways of a dozen or so primitive thatched huts facing onto the gathering place. Wolf sat John down on one of the logs.

'Sorry, buddy,' the big man said, 'just a bit dizzy, that's all.'

'Let's have a look at you.' Wolf started to ease off John's flying cap, but stopped when he noticed the congealed blood that had seeped through the back, realising that the canvas had stuck to the man's scalp. Hell, he thought, they were lucky the cap had contained the blood when they were in the water. But he didn't voice his thoughts. It had been the talk of sharks that had brought on John's near seizure.

'There's an injury where you smashed your head,' he said, 'it's congealed.'

'Right. Cap stays on.' John pulled the sides firmly down over his ears. He knew the drill in the tropics, they all did, he'd be asking for infection if the wound was exposed, and the cap would act as a form of bandage. 'Now let's have a look at you.'

'I'm fine.'

'Bull. I saw you holding your chest, you've probably got a busted rib. Take your shirt off.'

The women giggled as Wolf obediently stripped, and he gave a saucy wink to one pretty girl who covered her mouth with her hand.

There was an angry bruise across his chest. John examined it. 'Does it hurt when you breathe?' he asked.

'A bit, but not much.' Wolf took a deep breath, then he twisted from side to side. 'It's more when I move.'

'The harness,' John said. 'Just a bruise. I don't think you've busted anything.'

Wolf could see flashes of the old John Stubbs emerging, strong, authoritative and not to be messed with. He liked John Stubbs, he decided as he put his shirt back on.

The woman who had gone for help returned with the two brothers, one of whom was her husband.

Wolf had not seen the men's faces in the darkness as they'd paddled the outrigger back to the island, but he'd seen them quite clearly at the cooking fire. These were the men who had saved their lives. He'd watched them whilst they'd held John's head and fed him water from a coconut shell.

'Thank you,' he said, nodding and patting his chest and gesturing at John. 'Thank you, thank you,' he repeated, and he offered his hand.

The brothers didn't understand the greeting of the hand, but they knew what the white man was saying and they grinned and nodded in return and slapped him on the arm. Then they slapped John on the arm and grinned at him too. They were pleased that the other white man hadn't died during the night.

Wolf decided that introductions were called for. 'Me,' he said, placing his hand once again on his chest. 'Me . . .' He'd been about to say 'Wolf', then he quickly remembered. 'Len.' He jabbed his forefinger into his chest, ignoring the stab of pain from his bruising. 'Me, Len,' he repeated, feeling as if he were in a Tarzan movie.

The men understood immediately. They pointed to each other and introduced themselves, the older as Soli, the younger as Tura. Then Wolf introduced John.

'Him, John,' he said, patting John Stubbs's shoulder. John was still sitting on the log. He'd tried to stand when the brothers had appeared, but he'd quickly sat down again, he was still very shaky.

'Imjon,' the brothers grinned, repeating the name, and Wolf decided that was good enough. They were Imjon and Len and everyone was very happy.

By now all the villagers had gathered around them, even the elders. Theirs was a small village, tucked into a protected bay on the north-western coast of the island, with hills to the south-east, and it housed an extended family of little more than thirty people.

The village itself was very primitive. Wolf had noted no use of European materials as he'd seen in a number of villages on Efate. There was no corrugated iron or hessian. The huts were pole-built with thatched roofs and walls of natangora. Where the hell were they? he'd wondered. Miles from civilisation, it appeared.

It was time to discover their position, he decided, and his mimed enquiries became ludicrous. As was to be expected, 'where is this village?' met with no response, so he strode about pointing to the huts, picking up pieces of earth, gesturing all-embracingly to the sky, and the more he asked them 'where is this place?' the more his audience laughed. The children jumped up and down, clapping their hands, the women giggled and the men grinned. The white man was very, very funny. Even John Stubbs was finding him amusing, and Wolf was getting frustrated.

'I give up,' he said finally, sitting beside John, the children squatting all around him, happy little faces cupped in hands, elbows resting on bony knees, eyes shining expectantly as they waited for the next performance.

The laughter had died down, and John Stubbs took over. He stood, determined to ignore the dizziness that still threatened.

'Soli, Tura,' he said respectfully. He had correctly assessed that the brothers, although not elders, were well placed amongst the village hierarchy. Besides, they were the only ones whose names he knew.

Standing six foot and three inches and powerfully built, John Stubbs was an impressive figure. Soli and Tura listened very carefully to what he had to say.

'We,' John spelled out very carefully, gesturing to himself and Wolf. 'We, Len and Imjon . . .' The brothers nodded. So far so good. 'We are from far away.' The brothers looked puzzled. Not so good. He gave a clumsy sweep of his arm to denote the other side of the world. 'Far, far away,' he repeated.

Wolf smiled, John's mime was far worse than his.

'We are from,' John gave another dramatic sweep of his arm, 'America.'

He was astonished by the instant reaction. 'America,' a number of the islanders repeated, and it seemed they'd understood. John glanced triumphantly at Len, and was about to ask the natives where *they* were from, but Len had suddenly leapt up, and was gesturing for him to be silent.

The islanders were not repeating John Stubbs at all, and Wolf knew it. They were saying 'Merika', and they were pointing south-east, towards the hills. Then somebody said 'Johnny from Merika', and several others took up the chant, still pointing to the hills.

Wolf had heard the phrase at Mamma Tack's. 'Johnny from Merika' was quite popular with the locals, along with 'okay' and 'sure thing'.

'There are Americans over there,' he said to John, 'probably an observation post.' Wolf nodded his understanding to the islanders and, when the chatter had died down, he addressed the brothers. 'How far? How long to travel?' he enquired, miming short and long distances with his hands. He couldn't understand their reply, but by the looks on their faces, and their dismissive shrugs, the observation post was not far away at all.

John instantly took command. 'Let's go,' he said, stepping forward, as if he was about to set off on the trek there and then. But he again swayed unsteadily, and Wolf made him sit down.

'Tomorrow,' he said. 'We'll go tomorrow.'

'You're in command now, are you, Len?' There was a sarcastic edge to John's voice. Buddies they might be, but he was not accustomed to accepting orders from his rear gunner.

'I'm afraid so.' Wolf decided to take the bull by the horns and he ignored the dangerous glint in the man's eyes. 'You've suffered a wound to the head, you've been unconscious for fourteen hours and you're no doubt concussed. It's my job to take command.'

'I see.' John looked him up and down. It wasn't like Len to be so assertive.

Wolf wondered whether he'd overstepped the mark. Was it suspicion he could see in Stubbs's eyes?

'Come on, John,' he said reasonably. 'You haven't eaten and you're suffering dizzy spells, you need food and rest, man.'

Good old Len, John thought. He'd never make it to the top brass, he lacked leadership skills, but he could always be relied upon for downright commonsense.

'You're right, buddy,' he said. 'We'll leave first thing tomorrow.'

Wolf Baker didn't dare sleep that night.

As soon as they'd kipped down in the hut, John was out to it, and at first Wolf was assured by the sound of gentle snoring beside him. But, as he felt himself drift blissfully off, it started. The writhing body, the gnashing of teeth, the groans. And then John was suddenly sitting bolt upright, and he was screaming.

'Get away!' he was yelling at the top of his voice. 'Get away! Get away, you bastards!' Then the screaming became unintelligible.

'It's all right, John.' Wolf reached out in the blackness and grabbed the man's arm. 'It's me. Len. It's okay. We're safe.'

'Leonard? Len! Oh Christ, buddy, you're alive.'

'Of course I'm alive, John,' Wolf said calmly, 'I'm right here beside you.'

'Oh. Oh Christ.' John Stubbs was panting, his voice trembling in the dark, fighting for control. 'What happened to us? Dreams. Crazy dreams.'

'Nothing happened, John. We're here and we're safe. Nothing happened. Go back to sleep.'

'Sorry, buddy.' A deep, shaky breath. 'Sorry, didn't mean to wake you.'

'That's okay. I wasn't asleep anyway.'

And for the rest of the night, he wasn't. He propped himself up against the wall of the hut, occasionally dozing off a little, but never allowing himself to fall so deeply asleep that he wouldn't hear the first danger signs. The moment the writhing started, at the first gnashing of the teeth, before he heard the groans, he spoke. He didn't dare wait for John Stubbs to start screaming.

'It's all right, John,' he said. 'It's okay, I'm right here.' Over and over he said it until, in his sleep, the man calmed down and the screech of grinding teeth stopped. Then he sat and waited for the next time, worried that if the dreams took over, John Stubbs would awaken once again a broken man. It was essential to maintain the delusion. If John Stubbs was not in control of his faculties in the morning, it would be impossible to take him over the hills.

Wolf must have nodded off just before dawn, because when he awoke, the sun was up and John Stubbs was standing, motionless, at the doorway of the hut. His back was to Wolf and he was staring out into the clearing.

Wolf cursed himself. He hadn't heard Stubbs rise. What condition was the man in?

John turned. 'You're awake. About time. Christ you can sleep. Come on, let's get started.'

John Stubbs appeared unaffected by the images of his dreams; he'd obviously forgotten them. Wolf breathed a sigh of relief and dragged himself wearily to his feet.

They ate before they left, and the villagers gathered to bid them farewell, the brothers giving them water in a bag made of pigskin, and a machete to cut their way through the undergrowth.

Although Stubbs now seemed steady on his feet, Wolf was worried. The brothers had seemed to indicate it was not far to the observation post, but then he didn't know the islanders' views on distance. 'Not far' might mean a couple of hours or it might mean a day's walk, and Stubbs was certainly not up to a full day's trek across the hills. John Stubbs was, furthermore, a stubborn bastard and it would be difficult to persuade him to take regular rest breaks. Then there was the possibility they might need to camp overnight. Wolf didn't relish the nocturnal fits and the awful possibility that the man might wake completely insane.

Wolf would far rather have set out on his own, but when he'd suggested it as an alternative, Stubbs had adamantly refused. It seemed there was no alternative but to make a joint bid to reach the observation post and radio for help. John Stubbs was in desperate need of medical attention.

The two men bade a cheerful farewell to the islanders, John eager to get going, and Wolf full of misgivings.

They walked and climbed for three hours, heading for the distant landmark Soli had pointed out, a spiral of rock that sat like a beacon atop one of the hills. The observation post would be on high ground with a full view of the surrounds, Wolf thought, perhaps it might even be at the rock itself. At any rate, from the top of the hill they would be able to observe their position.

It was tough going in places, and John insisted upon taking his turn with the machete, cutting a swathe through the undergrowth as they made their way forward to the base of the hill. And then they'd started the exhausting climb, Wolf calling a stop now and then to swig from the water bag, pretending to need a rest break himself when John insisted they keep pushing on. The big man was sweating profusely. He was driving himself too hard, and Wolf was worried.

They were not far from the top now, they could see the rock. They'd lost sight of it during the climb, but Wolf had kept their direction steady, following the sun's arc. He was feeling the effects of his lack of sleep and his bruised ribs were aching, but John Stubbs remained indefatigable.

'Come on, Len,' Stubbs said impatiently as they sighted the rock, 'we're nearly there, you can have a rest at the top.' He took the machete from Wolf and surged ahead and, as he did so, Wolf saw the blood seeping through the flying cap, leaking its way out onto the collar of his shirt. The heat and exertion and sweat had reopened Stubbs's wound. If the man kept driving himself like this he'd collapse. Christ, what the hell will I do then? Wolf thought.

'Hey, Len! Come and look at this!' A triumphant yell came from twenty yards ahead. Stubbs had reached the rock. Wolf struggled up the final rise to join him.

'Some observation post!' Stubbs gave a roar of laughter.

They were on a peninsula overlooking a broad bay and, resting at anchorage in the perfect natural harbour, sat scores of ships of every description. Wharves and jetties reached out into the water, and nestled amongst the coconut trees on the flat coastal area was a veritable city of quonset huts.

They weren't on Malekula at all, Wolf thought and, still

gasping for breath and feeling slightly hysterical, he joined in Stubbs's laughter. Before them, barely two miles away, lay a vast American base. They were on Espiritu Santo.

'Let's move, Lieutenant.' Stubbs was the first to recover himself and he took full command. As he started marching down the hill, Wolf followed at a more leisurely pace, prepared to sprint for help if Stubbs collapsed on the way. But he had a feeling John Stubbs wouldn't.

At one o'clock in the afternoon of 12 September, John Stubbs reported to command headquarters on Espiritu Santo.

'Lieutenant Commander John Stubbs, USN, sir,' he said as he saluted, 'and this is my rear gunner, Lieutenant Leonard Mitchell.'

It was only then John Stubbs collapsed.

# CHAPTER FIFTEEN

'He's alive!'

The following morning, Chuck Wilson burst into Mamma Tack's unannounced. When he'd arrived at the clinic, he'd seen Ronnie being bounced around on the shoulders of a serviceman who was standing by the open window chatting to Mary. Jane, however, had been nowhere in sight and, before Mary could stop him, he'd thrown wide the door and simply barged in.

The curtains of the treatment area were open, and Jane was tending the ulcerated leg of a twelve-year-old boy. They were both startled by the American's sudden appearance.

'Evri samting oraet,' she said, patting the boy's shoulder as she rose from her bedside chair.

Reassured, young Thomas sat back and watched the exchange between Mamma Tack and the 'man blong Merika' with avid interest.

'Wolf's alive!' Chuck announced, and he swept her off her feet in a bear-like embrace which she returned, both of them laughing as he whirled her about.

'Is he well?' Jane asked when he'd finally released her

and she'd regained her breath. 'He's not hurt, is he?'

'Nope. He's fine. Hell, he's more than fine. He shot down three planes, he saved a guy's life, he's a goddamn hero!'

Jane laughed again. Pure elation surged through her. 'Is he back? Why hasn't he come to see me?'

'He's on Espiritu Santo, they're keeping him there for a few days until they repatriate the guy he saved. Gee, he'll probably win a medal, I hadn't thought of that. Maybe I should have done the trip myself after all.' He grinned happily. Chuck Wilson was in a state of euphoria. 'But then I'm not Wolf, I wouldn't have pulled it off.'

'I'm so glad, Chuck,' she said. 'I'm so very, very glad.'

His excitement finally died down, and his grin slowly faded. 'My best buddy's alive,' he said, 'and that's the main thing . . .' Given his previous meeting with Jane, Chuck felt the need to make an admission. 'But there's something else . . .'

'Yes, I know there is.'

She did know, he could tell, but he had to say it anyway. Just to her. 'I'm not sure how I could have lived with it, Jane. And now . . .' He shrugged, unable to find the right words. 'Well, I'm off the hook now.'

'You were never on it, Chuck.'

'Yeah, maybe . . .' He gave a gauche shrug.

'I know,' she smiled. 'Easier to say.' Then she hugged him again. 'I'm happy for you, and I'm happy for Wolf. I'm happy for us all,' she said, breaking the embrace and pushing him towards the door. 'Now go away. I have a patient to tend to.'

She was happy for Marty too, she thought as she returned her attention to young Thomas who was sitting on the bed, enthralled by the incomprehensible drama that had unfolded before him. Just like Chuck, Marty no longer had grounds for self-recrimination.

'It seems you were right, Dr Thackeray.' Commander Dickey had the broadest grin on his face, and why not?

During wartime one was rarely in a position to impart good news.

They were once again on the hangar deck, Martin about to conduct the early morning Sunday service in the chapel area.

'Wolf Baker. He's alive, isn't he?'

'He most certainly is.' The Commander noted that Thackeray was relieved but not really surprised, and he marvelled once again at the man's faith. 'John Stubbs too. They're on Espiritu Santo. Baker's remaining there until Stubbs can be directly repatriated to the States; it appears your friend Wolf has a stabilising effect on Stubbs's mental condition. Don't ask me how.'

'Nothing about Wolf would surprise me,' Martin smiled. 'Thank you for bringing me the news.' He shook the Executive Officer's hand and, as the troops gathered about the chapel for morning prayers, he walked over to the table by the bulkhead.

Despite his conviction that Wolf had survived, Martin felt a huge weight lifted from his shoulders and, whilst he led the men in prayer that morning, he gave personal thanks to God.

Aboard the USS *Wasp*, Martin Thackeray felt a greater sense of purpose than he'd ever known. His faith, badly shaken following Dunkirk, had been restored during his time in the New Hebrides. Martin believed implicitly that it was the love he and Jane shared, above all else, that had strengthened him, and he greatly missed her, as he always did when they were apart. But to serve God's purpose, here amongst these men so sorely in need, was a mission for which he had been chosen. Indeed, he had been trained for just such a task. The very experience of Dunkirk, which had threatened his downfall, had prepared him for this. He knew what these men faced. He knew their inner fears and the doubts that beset even those with the strongest of faith, and he felt imbued with a God-given strength to help.

Wolf Baker had been right. In his few days aboard the *Wasp*, it was already obvious that Martin Thackeray was the best man for the job. The troops had instantly embraced him as one of their own. They knew he'd seen active service – it was even rumoured that he'd been at Dunkirk – and they knew that he'd volunteered to join the *Wasp*. They deeply admired him for that. Even the non-devout amongst them, and those of other denominations, not in need of Martin's services as a chaplain, admired him. Hell, the guy could have stayed safely in Vila, they all agreed.

The Reverend Dr Thackeray became known as Marty. The immediate adoption of the nickname, although pleasing to Martin, puzzled him at first, as did the know-ledge of his background the men appeared to possess. Then he realised it was Wolf's doing. Wolf, in his inim-itable fashion, had decided to pave the way, leaking infor-mation that had spread about the ship like wildfire, as anything of any interest always did.

After his early Sunday service, Martin breakfasted in the officers' mess, then before the midday service he held several private consultations in his small cabin. He always made himself available for men who sought personal counsel, and already he had found there were many.

The rest of his Sunday was uneventful. He took his daily constitutional during lunchtime. It had become his routine to skip lunch, enjoying a solitary wander about the ship instead, and he always finished up on the flight observa-tion deck to admire the view.

The vast aircraft carrier, over 740 feet long, the extreme width of her flight deck 109 feet, dwarfed her protective destroyers, always in sight a mile or so away. Intermit-tently over the past few days, Martin had seen the line of troopships far in the distance, and on occasions the battleships and destroyers of Task Force 16, escorting the 7th Marine Regiment to Guadalcanal.

The sight always impressed him. But, for all the might of the American forces, Martin thought, they remained mere dots on the Pacific Ocean. Even the 14,700 tons of the *Wasp*, a vessel massive and powerful beyond belief, appeared a toy in God's scheme of things.

Martin felt very close to God on the observation deck, but he also felt very close to man. He wasn't sure whether he admired man most for his presumption, or for his ingenuity. Probably both, he decided. And as man was also a product of God's creation, surely He must admire him too? Martin always stopped his musings at that point. He was not here to question why God allowed men to war against each other; such thoughts had been his undoing in the past. He was here to offer his own faith as an example to others who might be doubting theirs. Man, admirable though he was, was his own enemy, not God's.

He returned to his cabin and wrote a lengthy letter to Jane for the following day's mail dispatch. It was the first time he'd written to her since he'd been aboard, and he expressed himself freely, as he always could to Jane. He wrote about Wolf Baker and the strange knowledge he'd had of his survival, and he told her of the strength of purpose he felt aboard the *Wasp*. It was as if they were chatting.

He held two more private consultations during the late afternoon, and in the evening, following dinner, he played a lengthy game of chess in the officers' wardroom with Commander Dickey and then retired.

The next day he followed a similar routine, again admiring the view from the observation deck as the *Wasp* inched her way inexorably towards Guadalcanal. He could see a distant battleship with her destroyer escorts and, upon enquiry, he was told it was the USS *North Carolina*.

By Tuesday, they were some 150 miles south-east of San Cristobal Island, Torpedo Junction, dangerous territory, and the carrier was in a state of alert, planes constantly refuelling and rearming for anti-submarine patrol. There was no contact with the enemy during the morning, but shortly after noon a Japanese four-engine flying boat was downed by a *Wasp* Wildcat.

Martin remained on the observation deck much longer than usual that day, enthralled by the action. The sight of planes taking off and landing on the carrier's runway never ceased to intrigue him, and this afternoon they were busier than ever. He could still see the USS *North Carolina* and her escorts. She was a little closer now, barely five miles away.

At 14:20 hours, the carrier turned into the wind to launch eight fighters and eighteen SBD-3s, and to recover another eleven planes that had been airborne since noon. Having completed the recoveries, the ship turned easily to starboard, heeling a little upon the change of course, the air department continuing to work coolly and efficiently, refuelling and re-spotting the carrier's planes for the afternoon mission.

At 14:44 hours, aboard Japanese submarine I-19, Commander Kinashi, his eyes trained through his periscope, gave the order to fire. The command was carried out, and Torpedoman Ohtani heard the hiss of air that signalled the launch of the tin fish. All six Type 95 torpedoes were fired in a spread, the USS *Wasp* their principal target.

'Torpedoes!' The lookout's call from the *Wasp*'s conning-tower rang out loud and clear to the bridge. 'Three points forward of the starboard beam!'

From his position on the observation deck, Martin could see them with shocking clarity. Three torpedoes were headed directly for the *Wasp*. He watched in horrified fascination as one of them broached, jumping above the water like a flying fish.

Captain Sherman ordered the *Wasp*'s rudder hard-a-starboard, but it was too late. In quick succession, the torpedoes hit the carrier amidships, gasoline tanks and magazines igniting, fiery blasts ripping through the forward part of the ship. On the flight deck, planes were thrown about like a child's toys, and on the hangar deck, aircraft triced up in the overheads fell upon those below.

Fires broke out simultaneously in the hangar and below decks, the intensity of their heat detonating the ammunition of the anti-aircraft guns on the starboard side, fragments showering the crew. The number two 1.1-inch gun mount was blown overboard and the corpse of the gun captain was flung onto the bridge to land beside Captain Sherman.

Five miles away, two other torpedoes found their marks. The USS *North Carolina* and one of her accompanying destroyers, the USS *O'Brien*, were both hit.

Within only six minutes of their launching, five of the Japanese torpedoes had struck, and three US warships had fallen victim to the onslaught. But aboard the *Wasp*, the damage that had been inflicted was fatal.

Martin raced down to the flight deck to help a wounded crew member. The man had been struck by one of the aircraft as it had skated across the runway. A glancing blow only, but his right leg was useless, and he was trying to drag himself to safety, away from the planes careering about him.

Grasping the man under the armpits, Martin dragged him to the conning-tower and, beneath the protection of the observation deck, he examined the leg. There was no loss of blood, it was a simple break, and he told the man so.

'You'll have to hold up here for the moment, I'm afraid,' he said. The man was in no immediate danger, and Martin knew that he must get to the medical station where there would be badly wounded men in urgent need of attention. 'I'll send a stretcher for you as soon as I can.'     .

The man called out his thanks through teeth gritted in pain, but Martin, having dived for the ladder to the deck below, didn't hear him.

As he made his way through the hangar deck, all was bedlam. Fires had broken out, men were attempting to control them, others were shouting 'keep clear'. But he kept barging forward through the smoke towards the hatch and the ladder that led below decks. He had to get to the medical station. Then he tripped over something. A body. And the body sat up and spoke.

'Marty, is that you?'

Martin peered at the face of the young officer. 'Huck?' It was Charlie Finn, known as Huckleberry. Huck was a regular at the church services, a devout young Baptist from Ohio. 'Are you all right, Huck?' he asked.

'Yeah, I'm fine. I can't walk, though, my left foot's gone numb.'

Martin bent over the man's leg. Part of Huck's boot appeared to have been blown away. Possibly part of the foot as well, he thought; through the smoke and the blood it was difficult to tell the extent of the injury.

'Not surprising,' he said, taking off his belt, 'you've sustained a rather nasty wound, we need to stem the bleeding.' He pulled the belt tight below the knee. 'Right, now let's get you to the medical station. Can you stand on your right foot?' He helped the young man up, then, levering his shoulder under Huck's armpit, he half carried and half dragged him, feeling his own bad leg buckle under the strain; his old injury still caused him trouble on occasion and he was not accustomed to carrying weights.

The men who had been unsuccessfully attempting to fight the fires were backing away now, scrambling for safety. Then one of them saw the chaplain through the smoke.

'Hey, Marty,' he yelled. 'Get away! Keep clear!' He was waving frantically. 'Over here! This way!'

Martin recognised Ted Foreman, one of the men who had sought private consultation with him. A frightened man, a man who doubted himself.

At that moment, Ted Foreman had neither fears nor doubts. When he realised that Martin was struggling with the wounded young officer, he started instinctively to race to their aid. But the others held him back.

'It's too late, Ted!' Martin heard a man scream. 'It's too late!'

Huck's arm firmly linked over his shoulder, Martin saw the other men drag Ted Foreman to safety before, seconds later, a wall of flame blocked them from view.

The ship was listing to starboard, and oil and gasoline released from the tanks were spewing out to ignite and burn on the water's surface. Martin realised that they were trapped, the fires had encircled them. Flames and smoke belched from the open bulkheads on the starboard side. He dragged Huck as far away from the intensity of the heat as he could, and sat him down with his back against the portside bulkhead. Then he sat beside him. And they waited.

Both men could smell the aviation fuel. All about them gasoline tanks were leaking, and the flames were out of control. They were in a tinder box.

'This is it, isn't it?' Huck said.

'Yes.'

'I'm scared, Marty.'

'Don't be.' Martin was amazed at his own sense of calm. It would be quick, he thought, the whole place would ignite any second, well before they could be burned to death. There would be no pain. He was so glad he'd written that letter to Jane. What a pity he wouldn't be around to watch Ronnie growing up . . .

He took the young man's hand in his. 'The Lord is my shepherd, I shall not want . . .' And Huck joined in. 'He maketh me to lie down in green pastures. He leadeth me beside the still waters. He restoreth my soul . . .'

A moment later, the explosion. It was only one of many aboard the USS *Wasp* as she lay dying, a mere dot on the surface of the boundless South Pacific.

At 15:20 hours on Tuesday 15 September, Captain Forrest Sherman gave the order to abandon ship. He had no alternative. Water mains had proved useless, broken by the force of the explosions, and fire-fighting was ineffectual. The survivors needed to evacuate the vessel as quickly as possible.

Badly injured men were lowered into rubber boats, and most of the able had to abandon from aft, the forward fires were burning with such intensity. But the departure was orderly. There was no panic. And forty minutes later, at 16:00 hours, satisfied that no living crew member remained on board, Captain Sherman swung over the lifeline on the fantail and slid into the sea.

The crew of the *Wasp* had numbered 2,247. The destroyers, persistent in their rescue missions, despite the inherent danger, picked up all 2,054 survivors, whilst the abandoned ship drifted with her dead.

Further violent explosions erupted on the *Wasp* as night started to fall, and the USS *Lansdowne*, allotted the duty of destruction, fired five torpedoes into the carrier's fire-gutted hull. Floating in a burning pool of gasoline and oil, the *Wasp* finally sank by the bow at 21:00 hours.

The shocking news was received on Espiritu Santo early the following morning. Word spread like wildfire about the base. The *Wasp* had gone down, and, it was rumoured, the dead and wounded were numbered in the hundreds. Wolf Baker went straight to command headquarters.

The official estimate and details were not yet being released, he was informed, operations were currently underway to identify all casualties. But Wolf was persistent. He appealed directly to the Commander who finally agreed to radio through an enquiry regarding Dr Martin Thackeray.

The Commander found it difficult to refuse Baker's passionate request. The man had, after all, performed far beyond the call of duty – he'd no doubt receive a citation – and, hell, it seemed only fair to grant him a favour.

The facts were readily available: Martin Thackeray was already listed. He had been killed instantly whilst assisting a wounded officer. The deaths of both men had been witnessed. Details would not be officially released, however, until all casualties were accounted for, probably some time tomorrow, the Commander said.

Wolf immediately requested permission to return to his unit at Havannah Harbour. John Stubbs was to be repatriated that very afternoon, he told the Commander, and so his services on Espiritu Santo were no longer required.

Permission was granted, and it was mid-morning when Wolf's Corsair touched down at Quoin Hill. But he didn't report to the base at Havannah Harbour. He commandeered a jeep instead, and headed straight for Vila.

Jane was not at Mamma Tack's. She was at the house, Mary told him.

'The Missus worry, Masta Wolf,' she said. Everyone in Vila had heard about the *Wasp*, and Mary too was worried for the Masta. 'The Missus wait at home to hear what happen.'

The cottage door opened the moment he tapped on it.

'Wolf!'

Her eyes met his, and for a split second he wasn't sure what to make of her reaction. Then she flung her arms around him.

'I was so happy to hear that you were alive. Chuck brought me the news. The poor man, he'd been sure you were dead. Everyone had thought you were dead. Everyone except Marty, that is.'

She seemed unnaturally bright, he thought as, clasping his hand, she led him through the lounge room.

'I had a letter from him just yesterday,' she said, leading the way out onto the verandah where Ronnie was sitting on a rug playing with his building blocks. 'He said he had a premonition you were alive.'

'Wolf kambak!'

Wolf knelt on the wooden decking as Ronnie charged at him. The collision jarred his bruised ribs a little, but he picked the child up and placed him on his lap as he sat in the wicker chair opposite Jane.

'He said he was so sure!' she continued. 'He didn't know why. He didn't know whether it was his admiration for your resourcefulness or whether God was telling him something.' Her laugh was brittle, strained. 'But then, that's Marty, such a wonderful mixture of practicality and faith.'

'Wolf, where you bin? Where you bin, Wolf?'

Ronnie, more robust than ever, was playfully kicking and punching, and Jane noticed Wolf wince every now and then.

'You're hurt,' she said.

'Just bruising, it's nothing.'

'Come along, Ronnie.' She took the child from his lap and put him back on the rug. 'You play on your own for a while, darling.' And Ronnie was soon absorbed once again with his building blocks.

'You've heard the news of course.' Jane returned to her chair. 'About the *Wasp*?'

'Yes. They won't tell me anything. Not yet. They said "as soon as they know". So here I am waiting. It's been driving me insane.'

Now was the moment. He steeled himself. But she didn't give him the chance. Before he could draw breath, she chatted on, as if she couldn't bear a moment's silence.

'It's so good to see you, Wolf. You know, until Chuck told me, I had no idea you'd flown Marty to the *Wasp*.' She knew she was talking too much, but she couldn't stop. 'Chuck said you'd volunteered to replace him. The poor fellow, he felt so guilty when you were reported missing.'

Why wasn't she asking him if he'd heard anything? he thought. It would make it a lot easier if she did. But then why should she presume he had inside information? She was simply pleased to see him, he was a distraction. How was he to tell her?

'I was worried that Marty might be feeling guilty too. Well, not guilty, but in some way responsible. And then his letter arrived, saying that he'd always believed you were alive.' She smiled. 'It was such a wonderful letter, Wolf.'

Her eyes welled with tears, and there was a quiver in her voice. The woman was at breaking point. He had to tell her.

'He was fulfilled aboard the *Wasp*. He said he felt honoured to have been chosen. That he was serving God's purpose.' She was no longer talking merely to fill in the silence, and she made no attempt to control the tears that now spilled down her cheeks. 'He said he'd never felt closer to God. I was happy for him.'

Her eyes locked onto his. It was the first time she'd looked directly at him since she'd opened the cottage door, and the realisation suddenly hit Wolf: she knows.

And, as if she'd read his mind, she said, 'He's not coming back, Wolf. I don't need them to tell me, I know it.'

'How?'

'Something in his letter. So beautiful, but so final, perhaps Marty knew it himself. Just like he knew you were alive. And then when I opened the door and you were standing there . . .' She stared at him, hardly daring to ask. 'You know it too, don't you?'

'Yes.'

In the pause that followed, Jane mustered the last of her strength.

'Officially?' Her voice was breathless.

He nodded. 'Officially.'

'Oh.' She froze, like a bird poised to take flight.

'They'll inform you tomorrow, when all casualties have been accounted for.' The statement was harsh, brutal in its irrevocability, but Wolf wanted no confusion. Nothing that she could cling to with the last vestige of hope, when there was none.

Jane's final defences crumbled and she sank her head into her hands. 'Oh Marty. Oh Marty, Marty, Marty.'

Her anguish was painful, her body wracked with sobs, and Wolf wanted to hold her, to cradle and comfort her, but he knew it would be wrong to intrude upon her grief. What would Marty do? he wondered. Marty would be practical.

He didn't have a handkerchief, so he went into the kitchen and fetched a clean tea towel from one of the drawers. Returning to the verandah, he squatted beside her chair as she fought to regain control, her sobs quickly becoming silent gulps for air. Then, when she'd taken the tea towel from him, he told her what she needed to hear.

'He died instantly, Jane.'

She looked at him, the tea towel held tight against her mouth as if to stifle her anguish, her eyes desperate with the desire to believe him.

'That's official too. His death was witnessed. The report said that he was assisting a wounded officer, and that he died instantly. Both men did. Marty wouldn't have felt any pain.'

Wolf hoped he was right. Was instant death painless? Who could tell? It was a presumption they all clung to. But the details of the report were factual, and he could see that she knew he was telling the truth.

'Thank you.' She mopped at her face, still gasping a little to regain her breath. Then she clasped his hand. 'Thank you, Wolf, I'm so grateful.'

Ronnie was by their side. He was whimpering for attention, upset by his mother's tears, and Wolf picked him up. He sat in the wicker chair, bouncing the child on his knee and Ronnie, always good-natured, was quickly pacified.

'Would you like me to go?' he asked.

'Oh no. Stay. Please. Stay.'

'Okay. Shall I make us a cup of tea?'

'You hate tea.'

'Any of that bourbon left?'

'Of course. You're the only person who drinks it.'

'Tea for you, bourbon for me.'

He returned Ronnie to his playing blocks, and when he came back with the drinks, Jane had recovered her composure. Her eyes were red-rimmed, but she gave a wan smile and gestured at the tea towel.

'Thank you for the handkerchief,' she said.

'Well, at least I picked a clean one.' He put the drinks on the coffee table between them and sat.

'So tell me about your adventures, Wolf. You're a hero, Chuck tells me.'

'Not really.'

'He said you shot down three planes and you'll probably get a medal.'

'I was just protecting my back,' he shrugged, 'it was them or me.' She was making conversation, bottling up her emotions and it was wrong, he thought. He remembered the night when Marty had encouraged him to get it out of his system. That's what Jane needed to do. She needed to let it all pour out.

'But you saved a man's life, Chuck said.' She sipped automatically at her tea, as if it was an afternoon on the verandah, just like any other. 'That certainly sounds like a hero to me.'

'I'm not a hero, Jane. Marty was a hero. Marty saved men's souls.' Wolf was out of his depth when it came to religion, but Martin Thackeray had had a profound effect upon him, and he needed to tell her so. For her own sake. 'Well, maybe he saved their sanity, like he saved mine. Or maybe their belief that there was still something decent left. I guess it all depends on your perspective.'

He'd hit home. He could see that she'd dropped the pretence of polite conversation and was hanging on his every word.

'Marty was the true hero,' Wolf said. 'He was aware of the dangers out there, and he didn't have to volunteer. Christ, if anyone had served his time, Marty had. He didn't need to prove himself.'

'I know he didn't.' The tears were welling again. 'It was God's will, he said.'

'I don't know much about God's will, but I know Marty's. And I know the effect he would have had on those men. Just like he had on me. Marty was the best man I ever knew.'

She was crying again now, but gently. It was healthy. She needed to cry. 'He was the best man I ever knew too, Wolf.'

They sat for two hours talking about Marty, laughing and crying and telling anecdotes, until Wolf suddenly registered the time.

'I came straight from Quoin Hill,' he said, 'I have to report to base for a debriefing. Will you be okay?'

'Oh.' She'd been immersed in their conversation and she was caught out, confused. 'Yes. Yes of course. I'm sorry. I've kept you far too long. I'm terribly sorry. I completely lost track of . . .'

She looked so lost, so vulnerable.

'I can come back if you like. If you don't want to be alone.'

She didn't want to be alone. Marty had been with them as they'd spoken of him. She couldn't bear the thought of being alone.

'Yes. Yes, I'd like that.'

After he left, she didn't fall apart. She did things instead. There were rituals to be observed. It was Wednesday, and she always did the washing on Wednesdays, usually during a lunch break from the clinic. She preferred to address her domestic chores midweek, somehow managing to squeeze them into her busy schedule. It left her time with Marty on Saturdays when he was free from his hospital duties, and of course she always attended his Sunday church services. The weekends were very special to them both.

She washed the bed linen and hung it on the line. Far to the south, angry clouds were gathering, but it would be some time before the storm broke, and in the light breeze and without the severe humidity of the monsoon season, the bedding was dry within an hour. She ironed the sheets and pillowcases, remade the bed and Ronnie's cot, and then she cleaned the house, which didn't need cleaning, and tended the herb garden, which didn't need tending. She did everything she could to keep herself mindlessly active. And it worked. Her brain seemed somehow mercifully blank. And then, in the late afternoon, Mary returned, having closed Mamma Tack's. She wanted to cook dinner for the Missus, but Jane told her to go home.

'You okay?'

'I'm all right, Mary, yes. Thank you. You go home now.'

But Mary was worried. The Missus didn't look well. And why should she? Not knowing whether the Masta was alive or dead. Mary didn't want to go home. She wanted to look after the Missus.

'I stay, Missus. I cook you dinner. I make sure you okay.'

'Please, Mary, go home.' Jane couldn't bring herself to tell Mary the news. The good-hearted woman had loved the Masta and she would probably wail her grief. She would wish to share it with Jane. And Jane could share her grief with no-one. No-one but Wolf.

Mary reluctantly left, and Jane fed Ronnie. They played together for a while, hide and seek, dodging amongst the furniture. And then, when the child was tired and ready for bed, she tucked him into his cot in the main bedroom and sang him to sleep, as she always did. And then there was nothing left to do. The emptiness started to creep in around her.

By the time Wolf arrived in the early evening, she was agitated. Everywhere she looked Marty was there. And yet he wasn't. And he never would be. How could she keep going? What would she do? The merciful veil of blankness that had enveloped her during the afternoon was disintegrating.

'Wolf!'

She once again embraced him as soon as she opened the front door, but this time there was no pretence. No attempt at social discourse. By now she was approaching a state of panic.

'Thank God you came back!' She clung to him desperately, and he could feel her shaking. 'I don't know what to do, I think I'm going mad.'

'No you're not.' His arms around her were comforting, but his tone was practical. 'You're suffering delayed shock. You know that.'

'Yes.' Commonsense prevailed. Of course, he was right. 'Yes.' She backed away. 'I'm sorry.' She smiled shakily and ushered him inside. 'I didn't mean to pounce on you like that.'

'Pounce away, whenever you like, it's what I'm here for. I think you could go a stiff drink. Do you have any brandy?'

'No. There's dry sherry.'

'No good. It'll have to be bourbon.' He sat her down and poured them both a healthy slug from the bottle on the dresser. Then, joining her on the sofa, he clinked his glass against hers. 'Marty always told me it was "filthy stuff", but it'll do the trick. Come on, drink up.'

She took a tentative sip and winced at the taste.

'Okay, you don't like it. But then I can't understand your passion for tea. Now take a proper swig, it'll do you good.'

She downed half the glass in one gulp, then gasped as the raw liquor assaulted her system.

'See?' he grinned. 'Very effective.'

Jane wasn't at all sure whether it was the effect of the

alcohol, or the presence of Wolf, but she could feel her panic recede.

'Marty was right. It's filthy stuff.'

'I bet you haven't eaten.'

She shook her head.

'Right. I'll see what I can rustle up.'

'No.' She took his hand as he rose from the sofa. She didn't want to eat, and she didn't want him to leave her. 'I couldn't. Really.'

'Okay. At least let me get you some water. You're not used to that stuff.'

He returned from the kitchen with a tumbler of water and she sipped it as they sat in companionable silence, until finally she said, 'I don't know what to do, Wolf.'

'About what?' he asked carefully.

'Everything. Marty was my life. I don't know what to do without him.'

She seemed quite calm now, and he remained silent. That's what Marty would do, he thought. Marty would wait and listen before offering advice. Although Wolf was unsure about what advice he could possibly come up with.

'I don't know whether to go back to England.' Her father would expect her to, she thought. She pictured Fareham. And the Royal Victoria Hospital. She had enjoyed working at the Royal Victoria. She pictured her life the way it used to be. And of course there would be Phoebe. They still corresponded regularly and she longed to see Phoebe. It all seemed so safe. And yet so foreign. 'I don't know whether I'd fit in there any more,' she said.

She was speaking her thoughts aloud, Wolf realised, so he said nothing.

'But without Marty, I'm not sure if I fit in here either.' She finally turned to him. 'I don't know what to do.'

This time it appeared an answer was called for. A practical answer. 'Why would you not fit in here without Marty?' he asked. 'You worked without him all the time.

Marty was away from Vila more often than he was here, you told me that yourself.'

He was trying to be helpful, she knew, but his response was naive. She was in the New Hebrides as Marty's wife, the wife of the missionary doctor, she had no official position. She didn't point that out, though, and responded to his ingenuousness instead.

'Oh yes,' she smiled, 'Marty was often away. But only in body, never in spirit.' It was good to see her smile, he thought. 'In spirit Marty was always right here with me.'

It seemed to Wolf that she had answered her own question. 'And isn't he still here? Isn't that what Marty himself would say?' She looked at him blankly. 'Wouldn't he say he's still here in spirit?' Her smile had faded, and her face looked drained, but Wolf was sure he was on the right track and he didn't let up. 'He is, isn't he, Jane? He's still here.'

'Yes,' she whispered. 'Yes, he's here. He'll always be here.' In his innocence Wolf had answered all of the questions she had asked herself. She knew she must stay.

'Then this is where you belong,' he continued to urge, aware that he'd made some sort of breakthrough. 'You belong here with Marty and everything you've worked for.'

'Yes. Yes, I do. You're quite right.' She raked a weary hand through her hair. 'I suppose it's the practicalities that are frightening me.' She tried to sound constructive, but she felt so tired. 'I mean I'll have to leave the cottage, the Mission Committee will appoint another minister . . .'

'Oh.' He hadn't thought of that. He'd simply wanted to inspire her. The situation was more complicated than he'd assumed. He felt rather stupid.

'. . . and I can't seem to picture the future . . . I can't seem to . . .' Her voice trailed off, she looked utterly exhausted.

'Don't think about it now,' he said as he stood. 'Come on, you need to sleep.'

'Yes.'

She took his hand and allowed him to lead her to the bedroom, but she halted at the door.

'You'll stay, won't you?'

'Of course I will. I'll be right next door in the spare room. Now you get yourself ready for bed, and I'll come back in ten minutes to tuck you in.'

For all of his rakish charm the paternal role suited Wolf, and Jane, childlike, did as she was told. She performed her nightly ritual without thought, washing her face, brushing her hair, cleaning her teeth. She checked on Ronnie, fast asleep in his cot; he rarely woke during the night. And then, in her light cotton nightdress, she slipped between the sheets.

Surely sleep would come easily; she had never felt so tired. Like dripping water sucked into parched sand, all energy and emotion seemed to have leaked from her body. But it had not leaked from her mind. Her mind was refusing to obey the dictates of exhaustion. It was telling her how empty the bed was, how empty it would always be. In the many months of Marty's absence from home, the bed had never felt like this, there had always been the knowledge that he would come back. Now the realisation that he would never lie beside her again made the bed the loneliest place on earth. A crisp white desert of cotton.

She wished she hadn't washed the linen this afternoon. Why had she done that? Just to keep busy. Just because it was Wednesday and Wednesday was washday. How stupid! She might still have been able to smell him on the sheets, or at least to feel the shape of his body in the crumpled linen. He had left last Thursday, early in the morning, and they had made love the night before. Wednesday night, washday night, Marty always commented on the feel of fresh bed linen. It was only a week ago, she thought. One short week since he'd left. Just one washday to the next, that was all. And now she lay in this sterile, meaningless bed with its meticulous hospital corners of which she was so proud. How stupid of her to have washed the linen. She buried her head in his pillow and smelt the fresh soap powder. It angered her, and anger lent her energy.

She threw back the covers and crossed to the wardrobe where his clothes hung in a neat row. There was his favourite jacket, the threadbare one with the houndstooth check, a little frayed at the cuffs. He'd refused to relinquish it, despite her regular requests. 'It's a good fabric, my love,' he'd said, 'and it doesn't matter if a good fabric is a little shabby.' She took the 'good fabric' in her hands, it wasn't a good fabric at all, it was simply Marty's excuse to hang on to the jacket, and she buried her face in it, breathing deeply. She could smell him, her Marty. He was there.

A tap at the bedroom door. She turned. It opened just a fraction.

'Jane? You okay?'

'I'm fine.'

He peered in. 'Hey, you're not in bed.'

'I was. It's just that . . .'

'Come on now. There's a good girl.' He crossed and took her hand, leading her to the bed. 'I'll tuck you in.'

But she didn't want to get into the bed, not that lonely place. Perhaps she'd take Marty's jacket to bed with her. Perhaps that would help.

'Come on, Jane,' he sensed her baulking, 'you have to sleep, you're exhausted.'

His hand on her shoulder, he gently tried to coax her to lie down, but suddenly her arms were around his neck, her face reaching up to his and she was kissing him.

Jane didn't know how it happened. She didn't know what made her do it. But she couldn't stop. She felt such longing. A longing to be held, to be loved, to be safe, to belong.

Wolf was shocked, but unable to resist. He returned the kiss, his arms around her slender body, feeling the ache of his own love. He remembered Marty's shock question, not long after they'd met: 'You're in love with my wife, aren't you, Wolf?' Marty had said it light-heartedly, without accusation, a statement more than a question really, but his expression had been enigmatic as he'd awaited an answer, and Wolf had felt jarringly confronted. 'Who isn't?' he'd said. But he hadn't sounded glib, and his admission had been as much to himself as to Marty, he'd realised. Marty had smiled, respecting the honesty of the reply. It was apparent that Wolf had passed some sort of test, and they'd become good friends after that.

Wolf took her head in his hands, feeling the soft texture of her hair between his fingers and, even as her lips continued to urge him on, he eased her gently away.

'Go to bed, Jane,' he said quietly, but authoritatively, fighting to disguise the strength of his emotions. And this time she obeyed him.

Silent, breathless, she climbed between the awful crisp sheets. She knew she should apologise, she could tell he was shocked. She was shocked herself. But never had she felt so lost, so utterly deserted and, as she lay there, still and compliant, she wanted to scream, 'Don't leave me! Please don't leave me!'

He pulled the coverlet up under her chin. 'Good night,' he said and kissed her on the forehead. Then he quietly closed the door behind him.

In the spare room he lay, elbows crooked, head resting on hands, staring up at the overhead light fitting, studying the glass bowl of its encasement. The shapes of the dead insects captured inside were clearly visible in the lamplight that spilled through from the lounge room. He'd left the door open and the lounge room table lamp on, in case she should call out during the night. Then he would go to her, and he'd comfort her as he'd comfort a child having nightmares.

Twenty minutes later, when the storm that had been threatening throughout the afternoon broke, he was still

staring up at the light fitting. The first crack of thunder
was swiftly followed by rain, a deluge smashing relentlessly upon the tin roof. Angry wind buffeted the cottage
until it rattled, and jagged streaks of lightning flashed
through its windows.

The storm was not of cyclonic proportions. The solid
little house would withstand its force, and it would vanish
as abruptly as it had appeared. But its anger was enough
to provide a welcome distraction for Wolf as he stared
sleeplessly up at the ceiling.

Then, in a flash of lightning that illuminated the room,
he saw her standing there, silhouetted in the open door, a
fragile figure in her light cotton nightdress. He rose and
went to her.

# CHAPTER SIXTEEN

She was sleeping soundly when he awoke early the next morning, her breathing deep and rhythmic, fanning his shoulder. Twice during the night she'd slipped quietly from the room, and he hadn't expected her to return. But both times she had, and wordlessly she'd snuggled against him, assuming he was asleep. She'd been checking on the child, he realised. He had presumed she would go back to her own bed and that, perhaps, in the morning she might even pretend it had never happened.

If that had been her intention, Wolf would have played along. He would behave however Jane wished him to behave. But now as he watched her, fair hair strewn carelessly across the pillow, one lithe tanned arm draped possessively over his chest, he hardly dared move. He didn't want to lose the moment. He didn't feel guilty. He couldn't. He didn't think of Marty. He didn't feel disloyal. He could think of nothing but the love he felt for this woman beside him, whose breath caressed his skin.

She stirred, and her arm trailed from his chest as she rolled away, turning in her sleep. Her breathing was shallower now. She would wake soon.

The moment broken, Wolf wondered what to do. It

might be easier for her if she awoke on her own. He'd get breakfast, he decided. Well, at least toast and coffee. No, tea, he reminded himself. Tea. And then he'd figure where to go from there. He rose very gently, careful not to disturb her, then he pulled on his trousers and silently left.

In her half sleep, Jane sensed movement in the bed. Marty? She'd been dreaming. Beautiful dreams, of Phoebe and her childhood. She would tell Marty about her dreams, she thought, as she felt herself drifting off once more, she wasn't ready to waken yet. She didn't know how much later it was when she rolled onto her back and the fog of sleep lifted. Ten or fifteen minutes perhaps, and the dreams were still in her mind. She opened her eyes and blinked up at the ceiling. But it wasn't her ceiling, and it wasn't her bed. And she realised that the movement beside her had not been Marty.

Wolf! She was instantly awake. She sat bolt upright. He'd gone, and the dull, numbing knowledge of Marty's death returned. The empty nothingness of her life was still there. But it had disappeared last night. How could that be?

She knew she should feel guilty, traitorous. She had betrayed Marty. It had been the storm, she'd told herself. The storm had frightened her. But in the clinical light of early morning, reason suggested otherwise. She'd experienced cyclones of alarming ferocity during the monsoon season, so why had a quick tropical storm driven her to his bed? Surely she had known what she was doing when she came into the spare room. Hadn't she? No, she couldn't believe that. She'd needed to be held, comforted in her intolerable isolation. But it had been more than that, and she knew it.

She lay back on the bed. She'd wanted him to make love to her, she'd wanted to lose herself. And she had. In a way she'd never thought possible. Her restless cravings, her wild imaginings of the raptures Phoebe had described, all had been answered last night. She'd been transported to a world of physical sensation where nothing had mattered, where her mind had been blank to all but the delirium of her body's responses.

She'd felt no shame after they'd made love. She'd been too distracted, too overwhelmed to feel shame. She'd dozed off, and when she'd awoken she'd returned to her own room. She'd checked on Ronnie, and it was only when she'd climbed between the crisp, white sheets that everything had felt so terribly wrong. It was wrong to be lying in this bed with the smell of Wolf Baker on her body. She could get up and wash herself, she thought. She could scrub herself clean and pretend it had never happened. But she didn't want to do that. And she couldn't stay in this lonely place. She'd returned to the spare room and snuggled up beside him. And later, when she'd again gone in to check on Ronnie, it hadn't even occurred to her to stay.

As she lay there, she could still feel his warmth in the crumpled sheets. But he'd gone. He had the decency to be ashamed. She'd shocked him with her wantonness, and she couldn't blame him. She pulled her nightdress up under her armpits and ran her fingers down over her breasts, her belly, to her thighs, aware of new sensations. Her familiar body, to which she'd previously paid scant attention, now seemed foreign and exciting, as if newly discovered. She remembered his hands on her, gently exploring, charting fresh territory, opening fresh horizons. God forbid, she wanted him to make love to her again.

She sat up, forcing her mind back to the real world, wondering why Ronnie wasn't yelling out to her; he normally woke her around now. She pulled her nightdress down over her knees, refusing to think about the shame she knew she should be feeling, and was about to get out of bed when the door opened.

'Breakfast.' Wolf was there with a tray. 'Tea, and toast with marmalade.' He put the tray on the bedside table, toppling the lamp that sat there, but he rescued it in time and sat it on the floor. 'I warmed the pot just like you always do,' he said with his irresistible grin. 'Don't get up,' he added, although she'd made no move to do so; she was simply sitting there staring at him. 'There's no need. Ronnie's had his breakfast, and made one helluva mess, I can tell you, and he's back in his playpen now.' Wolf, unsure of how she might wish him to behave, was covering extraordinarily well.

'Good heavens, look at you!' she said finally, her eyes fixed upon his bare torso. She was staring at the mottled purples and blues tinged with yellow that formed a rainbow across his chest. She hadn't registered the bruising as they'd made love in the half light.

She jumped out of the bed. 'Stand up straight, Wolf,' she said as he bent over the tea tray, setting out the cups, 'let me look at that.'

The nurse had taken over, and he did as he was told, watching her as she placed her hands on his ribcage.

'Breathe in,' she ordered, and he did, feeling her trace the outlines of his ribs. 'Does it hurt when you breathe?' she asked.

'Not much.' The touch of her fingers on his skin was exquisite.

'There could be a hairline fracture. I think I should strap your ribs.'

'No need, Jane,' he smiled, 'really.'

'I'll get some ointment for the bruising then.'

'No, don't,' he stopped her as she turned to leave, 'have your tea instead.' She hesitated. 'It looks a lot worse than it is,' he insisted. 'Honest. It doesn't hurt nearly as much as it did a couple of days ago.'

'I bet it hurt last night,' she said.

It was the first reference to their lovemaking. 'No,' he said, 'not at all.'

It had. It had hurt quite a bit, but he'd used the

discomfort. It had kept him in control, each stab of pain hauling him back when he'd threatened to lose himself in her. He'd been free to relish every quiver of her pleasure, to savour her final abandonment, so much so that, as he'd taken the precaution to withdraw safely, he'd barely been aware of his own release.

He was lying, she knew. It had hurt. 'I'm sorry,' she said.

They were both aware that her words were all-encompassing. She was sorry for far more than his bruised chest.

'I'm not,' he said, and he kissed her.

As their bodies melded, he realised, thankfully, that there were to be no pretences.

Their lovemaking was gentle to start with, Jane wary of his bruised ribs but at the same time revelling in her lack of inhibition, exploring his body as he explored hers. But once again she was soon lost. Her own pain, the emotional rawness that consumed her, was obliterated in a sea of sensuality.

Wolf, too, lost himself. Carried along with the tide of her pleasure, oblivious to all but the feel of her, he no longer fought to keep himself in check. At the last minute, however, he was mindful enough to once again withdraw. Wolf Baker was a very experienced lover, and there must be no mistakes.

Afterwards, as she lay in his arms, his forgotten ribs now aching, he longed to tell her that he loved her. That he always had.

'Now *that* hurt,' he said laughingly instead.

He knew it would be wrong to tell her. Their lovemaking left him surprisingly guiltless, even thankful that he was part of a healing process, but to declare his love would be the ultimate betrayal to Martin Thackeray, and a burden to Jane.

'Oh, I'm sorry.' She sat up, concerned.

Wolf grinned broadly as he stroked her cheek. 'Honey, if that's pain, then give me more.'

She laughed. And quickly stopped. Had she just done that? she wondered. Had she really laughed? Her laughter seemed far more disloyal to Marty than the emergence of her sexuality. Her body's responses were somehow beyond her control, but her laughter was not. She jumped out of bed before she could start hating herself.

'I must look after Ronnie,' she said, 'and Mary'll be here soon.'

She disappeared, and Wolf knew it was time to go. He dressed slowly. He didn't wash, wanting to keep the scent of her with him. Then he made the bed up neatly; perhaps later on she might wish to strip back the linen, but all must be in order for Mary.

When he emerged from the spare room, Ronnie was still happily content in his playpen in the lounge room and Jane was nowhere to be seen. Then he heard the sound of the shower, and wondered whether he was supposed to leave before she reappeared. He didn't want to.

He waited, and five minutes later she emerged in a skirt and blouse, the wet curls of her freshly washed hair clinging to her face, somehow adding to her fragility.

'I'm sorry,' he said, awkward, uncertain of himself; her departure from the spare room had been so abrupt. 'I wasn't sure if I should go, or . . .' He shrugged. Where to from here? he wondered.

'I'm glad you didn't.'

She said it with ease, and Wolf's uncertainty vanished in an instant. 'I'm due some leave, a whole week if I want to take it.' They both knew what he meant.

'I need a few days on my own, Wolf.'

Fragile, young, even childlike as she looked with her wet hair, Wolf recognised a newfound resolve in her.

'Official word will come through today, you said?'

'I would think so,' he replied. 'Probably in the late afternoon. They try to inform the next of kin within twenty-four hours, if they can.'

'I'm going to tell Mary and Godfrey straight away,' she said. She'd made the decision as much for her own sake as theirs. The sooner she got it over and done with the better, she thought, although she dreaded the prospect. 'And I need to be alone to . . .' she didn't falter, rather the words simply didn't seem necessary, 'well, to deal with all of it.'

'Sure. I understand.'

'But I'd like you to come back. That is, if you want to.'

'Of course I want to.' How simple it would be to tell her he loved her. That he'd love her for the rest of his life if she'd let him, that he'd shield her, he'd look after her . . . How simple, and how wrong. He was a distraction, he realised, and he must remain so. His love was of no help to her.

'I'll see you in three days then.' He didn't embrace her, much as he longed to. Instead, he kissed the damp fringe of curls that rested on her forehead. 'You know where I am. Send word if you need me before then.'

'Thank you,' she said a little absently. Her mind seemed elsewhere now.

Mary's reaction was predictable. She wailed, and Jane comforted her. They didn't open the clinic. Jane pinned a notice on the door to the effect that Mamma Tack's was closed as a sign of respect for those who had lost their lives aboard the *Wasp*. Then she visited Godfrey at his bungalow on the rise.

Godfrey's reaction was less predictable, but then apart from his loquacity over a bottle of red, Godfrey was rarely predictable.

'Are you all right?' he asked. He didn't seem at all surprised by the news.

'Yes.'

The moment he'd heard about the sinking of the *Wasp*, Godfrey Tomlinson had set about making his own enquiries. Through his many contacts, he was usually able to ferret out information, but this time the military had closed ranks. Until all casualties were accounted for, details were being withheld even from the next of kin, his reliable informant told him. It would be twenty-four hours before they heard anything. But, from the outset, Godfrey had expected the worst.

'How did you find out?' he asked.

'Wolf Baker told me. Marty's death was witnessed. An explosion. He was helping a wounded man, they both died instantly.'

It was just as Godfrey had feared: Martin Thackeray was not a man gifted with a natural instinct for self-preservation.

She had refused tea, and was perched rather stiffly on the edge of the rattan sofa. She looked tired and drained, but seemed very much in control, and Godfrey wasn't sure if it was a good or bad sign.

'Do you need company, my dear? Do you wish to talk?' he asked.

'No,' she said. She was grateful for the offer, but she couldn't talk any more, she couldn't even seem to think beyond each moment as it presented itself. 'Thank you for offering, but no.'

Godfrey respected her wishes and didn't push any further, apart from telling her that he was available whenever she needed him. And she would, he thought as he saw her to the front door and kissed her cheek. When the shock had died down and she was confronted by the practicalities of her existence, she would certainly need him.

Mary insisted upon staying with the Missus throughout the entire day, and Jane wished wholeheartedly that she would leave. The maudlin sniffles, more audible as the morning wore on, the constant handkerchief dabbing at the brown face, the sorrowful, sideways glances from reddened, cow-like eyes, all stretched Jane's nerves to breaking point. She wanted to hit Mary, and she longed for the distraction of Savi and his English lesson.

Savi arrived at the cottage on the dot of half past twelve with little Pascal, Savi carrying his notebook and pencil. He was learning to write English now. French and Bislama remained his principal languages of general communication, but with Missus Tack he spoke only English and he was very proud of his fluency.

Thursdays had become a weekly ritual for father and son, Savi managing to coincide his visits to Vila with a copra delivery or the purchasing of plantation supplies or the repair of equipment: there was always some legitimate reason for a trip to town. The Bos was none the wiser, and Savi had overcome his sense of guilt. In all the years of his employment with Marat, his English lessons were Savi's only act of disobedience, but he craved to learn and they were, after all, only one hour a week out of his endlessly hardworking days.

Initially the lessons had been conducted at Mamma Tack's, but the chaos there made concentration difficult, so Jane had suggested they meet at the cottage. She always took a break from the clinic around midday. It was good for Ronnie to be away from the Americans, she'd decided, if only for an hour or so; the servicemen spoiled him dreadfully.

Savi never arrived empty handed. Sera insisted upon supplying lunch, not only for her husband and son, but for Missus Tack.

'Is right, Savi,' Sera had said, 'Missus Tack give very much time for you and Pascal. You much make sure she eat good.'

'You *must* make sure,' he had corrected her.

'Yes. That is right.'

Jane enjoyed her weekly meetings with Savi and Pascal, and so did Ronnie. Despite the three-year age difference between the children, Ronnie and Pascal revelled in each other's company. After twenty minutes or so, his initial interest in his lesson having waned, Pascal would turn his attention to Ronnie and the two would have a glorious time. They'd chatter away in Bislama and English and then Ronnie would energetically career around the place trying to find Pascal in his favourite game of hide and seek, the breakables having been safely put out of reach, while Jane and Savi got on with their writing lesson.

Jane's only regret was that Sera couldn't be with them, but it was tacitly understood why. Although he never mentioned it, Jane knew that Savi himself was there without the permission of Jean-François Marat. She also knew that he lived in fear of the Bos. They all did. It would be far too risky to include Sera.

Sera *was* there, though, in the form of the steamed fish wrapped in palm leaves, or the fish and yam stew in the wooden bowl that Savi presented. They always talked of her, Savi telling Jane that Sera's English was very good now, and Jane looking forward to the lunches so lovingly prepared.

Today Savi arrived with two coconuts that he'd carefully carried in the cloth sack Sera had provided. Their husks peeled back, the tops of their shells cut off to form lids, they contained finely sliced raw fish which, marinated overnight in the residue of coconut milk and the juice of fresh limes, had become soused and extremely flavoursome.

Savi was beaming as he knocked on the door of the cottage. The marinated fish was Sera's specialty, and he was looking forward to presenting the coconuts to Missus Tack.

But it was Mary who opened the door, which surprised him; Mary was usually at Mamma Tack's when the Missus took her lunch break.

'Hello, Mary,' he said.

'Hello, Mary,' Pascal chimed.

'What you do here, Savi?' Mary was outraged.

'We have come for our English lesson,' Savi answered, bewildered.

'No English lesson today,' she hissed. Then, recognising his confusion, she said a little more gently. 'You don't know 'bout the ship? You don't know 'bout the Masta?'

What ship? Savi wondered. Working on the plantation, he'd heard nothing about the *Wasp* and the tragic events that had every tongue in Vila wagging.

'The Masta is dead,' Mary whispered, hoping the Missus couldn't hear. 'The ship blow up. You go home now, Savi. You go home.'

But Jane was suddenly beside her.

'Hello, Missus Tack,' Pascal called excitedly; he was always the first to greet Missus Tack when she came to the door.

'Hello, Pascal. Come in, Savi, please.'

Pascal trotted eagerly inside to seek out Ronnie, but Savi stood shocked, looking from the Missus to Mary, who was jabbing her head to one side telling him to go, the whites of her brown eyes flashing dramatically.

'It's true, Savi.' Jane ignored Mary's frantic and none-too-subtle signals beside her. 'My husband was killed in a battle at sea.'

'I am very sorry, Missus Tack.' Savi couldn't think of anything else to say, and he was about to call Pascal; they must go home.

'So am I. Please come inside.' Jane turned to Mary, who was still ludicrously rolling her eyeballs. 'Sera has prepared lunch for us, Mary.' She took the cloth bag that Savi had been holding out so proudly, and that now hung, dejected and forgotten, at his side. 'Will you see to this, please? Thank you,' she added, not waiting for Mary's reply, and Mary had no option but to take the bag and retire to the kitchen.

'Please, Savi,' she said, 'please come in.'

'I do not wish to intrude.' Savi chose his words with care.

'You are not intruding, Savi, you are helping. Do you wish to help me?'

'Yes.' Savi pictured his life without Sera. What would he

do? The Missus and the Masta had loved each other, just as he and Sera did. 'I would like very much to help you,' he said.

Jane took a deep breath. Behind her she could hear Ronnie's exuberant squeals at Pascal's appearance, and she thought vaguely that she'd forgotten to put the breakables out of reach.

'Then please come in and have your English lesson.'

Savi stepped inside and Jane knew that he would ask no questions, that he understood, and she was grateful that at least this part of the day could be conducted with some form of normalcy.


As Wolf had predicted, the official news arrived later that same afternoon. Captain Porter, Commander of the US Navy Base Hospital, appeared at the front door, an envelope in his hand, and beside him, solemn-faced and sepulchral, stood the Reverend Arthur Smeed.

Captain Porter had volunteered for the unenviable task, he and Jane having worked closely together, and the military authorities had agreed that it would be kinder for Mrs Thackeray to receive notification of her husband's death from someone she knew. The Reverend Smeed was present not only as representative of the New Hebrides Mission, Martin's employers, but to offer spiritual support in his capacity as minister.

'Jane, I'm so sorry,' the Commander said, his tone sensitive and caring, 'but I'm afraid I have bad news.'

He was a kind man and it was sensitive of the military to send a high-ranking officer who was also a work colleague, Jane thought, but she wished to avoid both his announcement and his sympathy.

'Yes,' she said, and she took the envelope from him before he could get another word out. 'Thank you.' She knew she sounded shockingly abrupt. 'I appreciate your visit.' She was about to close the door.

Both men were taken aback, particularly Reverend Smeed, who had definite views on how such delicate matters should be conducted. Was there anyone present in the house who would be able to assist Jane Thackeray in her emotional need when she'd read the contents of the letter? he wondered.

He glanced behind Jane at the young islander woman in the background. Mary, the child hoisted over her hip, was comically appearing and disappearing, pretending to be busy, but actually gawking at them with wide, worried eyes.

Mary would be of no assistance at all, Arthur Smeed thought. In fact she might well be harmful to the poor woman. Knowing the islanders the way he did, she would probably wail at the news of the death of her master.

'I think we should stay with you whilst you read the letter, Jane,' he said, kindly enough, but unable to eradicate his characteristic officiousness. 'It's about Martin.'

Arthur Smeed had been the bearer of bad tidings on a number of occasions, and he invariably found spiritual counsel was most helpful to the bereaved. Particularly when, as in Jane's case, there was no family present.

'I know,' she said. 'I'm aware of its contents, I know of my husband's death.' Again she regretted her brusqueness, but she felt she couldn't stand there a minute longer. 'Thank you both for your concern.'

The men left, the Commander curious as to how Jane Thackeray had received prior notification, but thankful to be relieved of his onerous task, and the Reverend Smeed struck by a vague feeling that Jane's lack of emotion and need for spiritual counsel was somehow a little unseemly.

Jane told Mary to go home. Mary was rebellious at first. The Missus needed her, she said. And then Jane made it an unmistakable order. The white missus ordering the black servant. She could tell Mary was surprised and hurt, but she no longer cared. She wanted the young woman out of the house. She couldn't open the envelope until Mary had gone home, and she needed to open the envelope.

But she didn't open it after Mary had gone. It sat on the sideboard for the next two hours whilst she fed Ronnie, and played with him, her eyes all the while flickering to the envelope where it lay. It was only when the child was fast asleep in his cot that she opened it.

'. . . *The vast debt that the US military owe the Reverend Dr Thackeray for his noble sacrifice . . .*' The words meant little. It was the brutally efficient, standard stock phrases that leapt off the page. *'Regret to inform'. . . 'killed in action' . . . 'sincerest condolences' . . .* The words, in all their finality, branded themselves, red-hot-poker-like, in her brain. It was as if he had died all over again.

She sat in Marty's chair, the piece of paper on her lap, her face buried in his old jacket, and she rocked back and forth, bereft anew.

The following day and the day after that became a blur for Jane. Escorted by Captain Porter, she attended the memorial service conducted aboard the destroyer in Mele Bay, where wreaths were cast upon the water and a mournful cornet played 'The Last Post'. She accepted, mindlessly, the well-meaning commiseration of others with dull thanks and the response that she was fine.

Her remoteness worried Hilary and Harry Bale, and the Reverend Smeed tried to convince her that she must come to church, that prayer would help. Mary offered to move into the cottage. The Missus shouldn't be on her own, she said. But Jane was adamant. She wanted Mary to keep away from the cottage, she wanted to be alone. She was aware that she had once again hurt the young woman's feelings, but Mary's doleful mourning had become unutterably depressing. She wished they would all leave her alone. Or just ignore her. Why couldn't they do that?

The nights were even more unbearable. Sleep evaded her, and the wasteland of the double bed seemed huge. She cuddled Marty's jacket to her, but it somehow made her feel lonelier than ever, and she knew deep down, shameful though it might be, that she longed for Wolf's return.

On the third day, she reopened Mamma Tack's, desperate for some form of escape, but the sympathetic looks from the servicemen who gathered there, and the respectful tempering of their customary swearing, suffocated her.

Then, in the late afternoon, Wolf arrived, just as they were about to close for the day.

'How are you doing?' he asked.

'Fine.' The response was so rehearsed by now that it came out automatically.

'Like hell,' he said. There were dark shadows under her eyes; she'd obviously not been sleeping. 'I have a full week's leave, I've booked a room at Reid's. What say I take you and Ronnie out for an early dinner?'

'That would be nice.'

They spoke quite openly. There was nothing untoward that anyone could read into their conversation. But they knew they wouldn't go out to dine that night. And they didn't.

They didn't leap straight into bed either, although their desire was palpable. They took their time, comfortable in each other's company, Jane feeling the unbearable tension of the past several days gradually ease. Wolf played the obligatory game of hide and seek with Ronnie whilst she prepared a chicken salad, and as they ate they drank the wine he'd brought.

'Not quite up to Godfrey's standards perhaps.' Wolf raised his glass to the light, swilled its contents, then inhaled the aroma, adding, in an excellent imitation of Godfrey's fruity tones, 'But a fine bouquet nonetheless,' and Jane felt herself smile.

Finally, when Ronnie was tucked in his cot, fast asleep, she prepared herself for bed. She left the door open should the child cry out in the night, and went to the spare room where Wolf was waiting for her.

He was naked, clearly visible in the light from the bedside lamp, and he stood unashamed, watching her hesitate for a split second, before he reached out his hand.

She joined him, and meekly raised her arms as he slid her nightdress up over her head. Then, when he eased her panties down over her buttocks and they slid to the polished wooden floor, she stepped out of them, pushing them to one side with her foot.

Jane had not seen a naked man before. Her husband had always come to bed in his pyjamas. And she herself had never been seen naked. If Martin had accidentally come upon her undressing, he'd averted his eyes to save her embarrassment. She had always accepted such behaviour as the essence of propriety, the very backbone of her upbringing. So why was she not confronted by this brazen exposure? Why did their nakedness seem so perfectly natural? More than natural, complementary, she thought a minute later as they lay on the bed, the first of his gentle touches striking chords that reverberated through her whole being.

Then, when he entered her, never had she felt so in tune with the moment, so centred. Her body was a symphony of pure sensation, her mind transported by the melody. It built to a crescendo, only to recede and then build again, and again, until she was close to exhaustion.

Wolf held back each time, even as the fresh waves of her excitement threatened to engulf him, but finally he was no longer able to control the dictates of his body and at the crucial moment he once again withdrew.

They lay on their backs, their chests still heaving, the sheets damp with their mingled sweat.

Then after a moment or so, having regained her breath,

Jane said, 'You're very experienced, aren't you?' and he was taken aback. She sounded so clinical.

'Yeah, I guess so.' It was true, but he would have liked to have told her it was different with her. That he'd never been really in love until now. He said nothing.

'I'm not. I'm not at all experienced.'

He'd thought as much. He'd sensed it the very first night. She'd been shocked by her own sexuality. But the admission of her inexperience was also an admission of Marty's, and Wolf didn't want to go down that road.

She seemed about to say something, then stopped and rolled away from him onto her side.

'What's the matter?'

'Nothing.' She was about to turn off the bedside lamp.

'Don't, Jane.'

Her hand faltered upon the switch.

'Please look at me.'

She rolled back to face him.

'What is it?'

She knew she'd sounded brittle, and she knew he was awaiting an explanation. Well, she owed him one, didn't she? If she was going to use his sexual expertise to escape the pain of her husband's death, she owed him that much surely.

'You're angry,' he said. 'Why?'

She was angry, but at herself, not him. 'I'm feeling guilty, which is hardly surprising.' Her voice was still brusque, and he waited silently for her to go on. It was a while before she spoke. 'I'm guilty because I respond to you sexually in a way I could never respond to Marty.' Her anger was gone now, replaced by bewilderment. 'Why is that, Wolf? Is it just because you're experienced? Shouldn't love mean more than expertise? I loved Marty with all my heart, and I don't love you.'

The words hurt, even though he was aware it was not her intention to be brutal, that she was simply desperate for the truth. But she had brought Marty into the room.

Perhaps she was right to do so, Wolf thought. For all of his avoidance, perhaps it was important to include Marty, even in their intimacy.

'Marty was a priest, Jane, sex would have held a very different priority in his life.'

'Different from a man of experience,' she said with a faint smile.

'You got it,' he grinned. Let his past be the scapegoat, he thought. Let him be the butt of the joke if necessary, it didn't matter. She was talking and that was good.

'I tried to change that priority for a while,' she said, her smile fading. 'It was wrong of me. I hurt him. I undermined his belief in himself.'

Having just scaled the heights of sexual delirium, Wolf found it ironic that he would have swapped every erotic moment to hear her speak about him the way she spoke about Marty.

'You didn't, Jane.' He pushed her damp hair gently away from her forehead. 'He knew how much you loved him. He told me you were his life. Just like you told me he was yours. And you know what? I envy him.'

She looked at his face on the pillow beside her, so close, and the thought suddenly occurred to her.

'Are you in love with me, Wolf?'

'That's exactly what Marty asked.'

'Did he really?'

'Uh huh.' He nodded, aware that the immediate vitality of her interest lay in Marty's question, not his own response to it. But, a second or so later, she made the enquiry anyway.

'And what did you say?'

'I said "who isn't?"' This time his reply was glib, and she smiled. She hadn't taken him seriously, which was just as well. Strange how her husband had seemed to know that he was telling the truth, Wolf thought.

Jane turned away, relieved. She didn't want the burden

of his love. She looked up at the ceiling, at the captured insects in the bowl of the central light fitting; she'd been meaning to clean them out for months now.

'I'm using you,' she said.

'I know. Do you want to stop?'

'No.'

'That's good.' He leaned over and kissed her gently. 'I like being used. Go to sleep now.'

She turned off the light, and in the dark he heard her voice, soft now, vulnerable. 'Good night, Wolf.'

'Good night.' It took him a long time to get to sleep.

The conversation was not mentioned the following morning and, as Jane made breakfast, the atmosphere was relaxed. There was a new understanding between them, Wolf thought, as if somehow they had Marty's permission.

Ronnie barged around the kitchen trying to catch him in a game of tag, but as Wolf dodged the child, his mind was on other things. He would embrace the situation, he decided. Despite his love for Jane, he would provide the escape she needed. If their time together was to be merely a distraction, then he would show her a good time. In any and every way that he possibly could.

'Fancy a joy-ride?' he asked.

'A what?'

'A flight in a Dauntless. I can show you the whole island from the air. What do you say?'

Her eyes lit up, the prospect obviously excited her, but she hesitated.

'Come on, Jane,' he urged, 'it's Sunday. You don't open the clinic on a Sunday, and Mary can look after Ronnie.'

The Reverend Smeed would consider it shocking if she didn't attend the church service, but she didn't want to go into the church without seeing Marty at the pulpit. 'I've never been in an aeroplane,' she said.

*

It was thrilling. She'd never experienced anything like it and, through the headset, her screams of terrified delight spurred Wolf on to greater heights in his aerial gymnastics.

They careered through canyons, then up and over volcanic mountains and ridges, to dive again into the deep valleys below. Just as it seemed there was no way out, that they were hemmed in by mountainous rainforest rearing on all sides, the aircraft would soar like a bird high into the patch of blue that had been invisible to Jane. And then suddenly they were out over the clear blue sea, so high that the patterns of the coral reefs and the changing colours of the water over sand and weed looked like a giant patchwork quilt. Another dive, and they were skimming across the surface beside the broad stretch of white sand, then a sharp turn to the right and they were heading directly for the island.

Jane craned her head around in the rear seat as the coconut trees loomed alarmingly close. Closer, and still closer.

Wolf's voice through the headset, 'I don't reckon we're going to make it,' then her scream and his laughter as they banked sharply to zoom above the trees and up, ever up, into the burning blue, her laughter now mingling with his.

They returned to Quoin Hill, and as soon as they landed Wolf leapt from the pilot's seat to assist her.

'That was the most extraordinary experience I have ever had,' Jane said, still in a state of amazement, as she climbed out onto the wing and took his hands.

'Were you scared?' He grinned.

'I was terrified.' She jumped to the ground, tumbling into his arms. 'I'm not sure I can walk.' She was breathless with excitement. 'Oh Wolf, that was astonishing, truly astonishing.'

'We'll do it again. Next time I'll take you to Espiritu Santo.'

He drove her back to the cottage where Mary was babysitting Ronnie, and they all had a cup of tea, Wolf spiking his with bourbon, much to the two women's horror. Then he took his leave and returned to Reid's Hotel.

Jane allowed Mary to prepare dinner for her that night. It was Sunday, and Mary usually prepared dinner on a Sunday. She'd been so hurtful to Mary, she thought, dear, ever-loyal Mary, who only wished to help.

'I'm sorry, Mary,' she said, 'I didn't mean to close you out, but I needed to be alone. Do you understand?'

'Oh yes, Missus.' Mary glowed, all was forgiven in that split second. 'I unnerstan'. I sure do, you bet. I unnerstan' very much.' It was good to see the Missus smile again, she thought. Going up in that aeroplane with Masta Wolf had done wonders for her, although Lord only knew how. Nothing in the world would get Mary into an aeroplane.

The two women ate together and Mary left at half past eight, agreeing to meet Jane in the morning at Mamma Tack's. She now happily accepted the fact that her presence wasn't required at the cottage during the mornings. The Missus still needed to be alone, and Mary understood that.

As arranged, Wolf arrived at ten o'clock. The door to the cottage was shrouded by trees and bushes, out of view from the street; no-one would see him enter. And he had walked from Reid's, along the main street and then up the hill, so that no vehicle would be in evidence outside. In the morning he would leave discreetly, circle up over the brow of the hill, behind the church, and return to the hotel from a different direction. They must be very careful, they agreed.

They made love, and slept in each other's arms. The bed in the spare room was not large, but their bodies fitted perfectly in the confined space. In the morning Jane made them breakfast – fruit and toast – which they ate at the kitchen table, Ronnie beside them in his highchair.

'You can't start the day on an empty stomach, Wolf,' she'd insisted when he said he only wanted coffee.

'You sound like my mother.'

'And my father,' she smiled. She could still hear Ron Miller. 'Now you sit right down there, girl, and you eat,' he would say when she was impatient to run off and meet Phoebe, 'no good startin' a day on an empty stomach.' It had been porridge then.

Jane was preparing Ronnie for his day at the clinic, and Wolf was about to leave when there was a knock on the door. They looked at each other.

'Godfrey or Hilary,' Jane whispered.

Wolf looked about guiltily. Should he hide in the kitchen? Should he leave via the verandah, the only other exit from the cottage? But the verandah's side steps were in full view of the church and the Reverend Smeed's house.

Jane glanced at the clock on the wall and curbed her own quick flush of panic. It was nine o'clock, a perfectly respectable hour, particularly if someone wished to call upon her before she was due at the clinic at nine thirty.

'You came by to see if I was all right,' she said quietly, 'like any good friend would. It's exactly what Godfrey or Hilary are doing right now.'

He nodded. Of course, it was stupid of him to panic. He sat in a lounge chair, and she opened the door.

But it was neither Godfrey nor Hilary who stood on the front doorstep. It was Jean-François Marat, an enormous bouquet of flowers cradled like a baby in his arms.

'Jane,' he said, his face a picture of concern, 'I was so sorry when I heard the news. My dear, you have my deepest sympathy.' He held out the flowers. They were truly magnificent. Far too magnificent, she thought, encircling her arms about them, and she resisted a ridiculous impulse to smile as she heard Marty say, 'Rather tasteless, my love, under the circumstances.'

'Thank you, Jean-François. Please do come in.'

'I deliberately delayed calling upon you to offer my

condolences,' he said, following her inside. 'I did not wish to intrude upon your grief.'

Savi's words exactly, she recalled. How different they sounded coming from the Frenchman.

'Most thoughtful,' she said through the flowers.

Marat quietly closed the door behind him. He had allowed several days for her to get over the worst of whatever hysterical reaction might have resulted from the news of her husband's death. He could now offer himself as her dearest friend, a tower of strength, a man she could lean on. Who else did she have? Old Godfrey Tomlinson? Her girlish middle-aged friend Hilary Bale? No, Jane Thackeray needed a man in her life. And she seemed in control of her grief. His timing was perfect, he thought.

'I believed it wiser to call upon you at your home. I hope you don't mind, but Mamma Tack's, I have noticed, is always so crowded.' He turned from the door as a figure rose from a lounge chair.

'Yes, Wolf was of the same opinion,' Jane said. 'I don't think you two have met, have you?'

'Nope,' Wolf said with a lazy grin.

Ronnie, thrilled at a new presence in the room, barged his way over and collided with the Frenchman's legs, but Jean-François barely noticed, the smile of sympathetic concern freezing on his face as he stared at the American.

'Lieutenant Baker, M'sieur Marat.' Jane made the introduction from behind the flowers that all but obscured her face.

'Howdy,' Wolf offered his hand.

Jean-François tried to resurrect his smile to one of courteous greeting, with little success.

'Lieutenant Baker,' he said as they shook.

'I'll just put these in some water. They're certainly magnificent.' Jane disappeared to the kitchen, dumped the flowers in the sink and quickly ran the tap on them, bent on returning as soon as possible to rescue Wolf.

But no form of rescue was necessary. Wolf chatted away, quite at ease in her absence.

'A terrible thing,' he said. 'Did you know Marty well? He was a great guy.'

Marty, Jean-François registered. Of course. Baker was a friend of Martin Thackeray's.

'Oh yes, a very fine man indeed,' he agreed, looking the American up and down. Handsome bastard, he thought. It had been a shock seeing him with Jane, and his suspicions had run foolishly rife.

'I flew him out to the *Wasp*, you know. Christ, who would ever have believed it!' Wolf shook his head in genuine consternation. 'Aboard the *Wasp* you always felt like you were on land, you know? Hell, she was a floating city, no-one expected her to go down.'

The Frenchman was now totally assured. 'A tragedy,' he said, 'such a tragedy.' He wished the American would shut up. He didn't give a damn about the *Wasp*, and he had welcomed the news of Martin Thackeray's noble death, it was most convenient to his cause. Why didn't Baker just leave?

'You bet,' Wolf agreed. '193 dead, and 85 wounded.'

'Shocking, most shocking.' Jean-François nodded sympathetically, wishing that the whole tiresome war was over and that the disruptive Americans would go back to their own country so that business could return to normal.

Jane reappeared from the kitchen, and he turned his full attention to her.

'How are you, my dear?' he asked. 'Is there anything I can do? Anything at all, I would so like to be of assistance.'

'Thank you, Jean-François, it's very kind of you to offer, but I've had many friends rallying around. There's Godfrey and Hilary, Mary of course, and Wolf.' The glance she cast at Wolf was one of gratitude and friendship. It was quite obvious that Jean-François was trying to ingratiate himself and she wanted him to know that she was surrounded by friends and didn't need his help.

Something was wrong, Jean-François thought. Why was she so strong, so assured? He'd expected a frightened, broken woman. And there was something else too. What was it? There had been nothing untoward in her glance to the American, but there was something different about her, a confidence that glowed from within.

'I'd better be off, Jane,' Wolf said. 'Glad to see that you're coping. Any time you need me.'

Good, Jean-François thought, he'd be left alone with her, and he watched her closely as she shook hands with the American. She was still giving nothing away. Surely it was his own imagination running riot.

'Thank you for your concern, Wolf. Oh my goodness, look at the time,' Jane had no intention of being left alone with Jean-François Marat, 'I'll be late for the clinic, poor Mary will be waiting. I'm so sorry, Jean-François.'

What was the rush? Marat thought. The black woman often tended to the clinic on her own. That's what servants were for.

'We'll all leave together,' Jane said, slinging her large cloth bag over one shoulder and bending to gather Ronnie in her arms.

It was as she bent down that Jean-François caught sight of the expression on the American's face. Apart from registering the man's good looks, he'd been too busy studying Jane to pay any real attention to Baker. But Baker had dropped his guard as he watched Jane pick up the child, and his look was one of far more than friendship.

Jealousy stabbed through Jean-François, and he stood frozen to the spot. Of course she glowed. Of course she was different. The two were lovers. She couldn't hide her sexual awakening and the American couldn't hide his dog-like devotion.

Marat's jealousy turned to rage as he realised that his timing hadn't been perfect at all: he'd left it too late. He should have come to her as soon as he'd heard the news of her wretched husband's death; she'd obviously been only too eager to jump into bed with the first man on offer.

'Everyone ready?' She was bustling them out of the house. Wolf was offering to carry the child. 'No, no,' she said, 'thanks all the same. I need to be independent.'

Marat followed them out the door, barely trusting himself to speak.

'Thank you so much for the flowers, Jean-François,' she said.

'May I drive you?' he asked stiffly.

'No thank you,' she said. 'The walk's good for me, and it's downhill.'

'As you wish.'

He climbed into the Landrover and watched them for a moment or so as they strolled down the hill.

Jean-François Marat did not return to Chanson de Mer that day. Nor did he return the following day, nor the day after that. He stayed in the small apartment above his office in town. The apartment which was reserved for casual liaisons, and which had not been put to use since his obsession with Jane Thackeray had consumed him.

He spied on her, and that very first night his suspicions were confirmed. The American returned well after dark. Marat watched him from the Landrover, parked some distance away, well out of sight. He couldn't see the man's face, but he could tell it was Baker: he recognised the athletic build, and the easy confidence of his gait.

He watched the American glance about, then disappear amongst the trees and bushes that masked the path to Jane's front door, and the venomous anger that had been building in him throughout the day threatened to explode. After all the groundwork he'd put in, he thought, after all the patient planning, the endless waiting games, this cocky young upstart had beaten him to it.

Marat wasn't sure who he hated most, the American or

Jane. She was a whore, he thought, and a stupid one at that. He, Jean-François Marat, had been prepared to offer her his world, to wait as long as it took for her to bore of her spineless husband, and yet she'd jumped into bed with a common young stud. The woman who had obsessed him, who had tantalised him with her grace and style and apparent inaccessibility, was no more than a slut.

He continued to watch the house well into the night, tortured by his imaginings. The passion that he'd sensed in Jane Thackeray was being unleashed at this very moment. He pictured her. As he watched the darkened windows, he could see her writhing beneath the American, moaning, wanton, finally awakened, and the image induced a jealousy bordering on insanity. It should have been his body she was writhing beneath, she should have been moaning for him. He'd been the one destined to awaken her, he'd had it all planned. He'd paved the way, and now this bastard American was reaping the benefits. Marat wanted to kill them both.

It was after midnight when he left, driving the short distance back to his apartment, where the images continued to haunt him throughout his sleepless night.

Marat's jealous rage did not abate; it grew to all-consuming proportions as he continued to spy on Jane, studying her every movement.

On the Tuesday, she left Mamma Tack's at around midday, just as she had done on the Monday. She walked up the hill to her home with the child, sometimes carrying him, sometimes encouraging him to walk. Was a rendezvous planned? Marat wondered. But the American did not appear, nor did anyone else. She spent an hour or so alone with the child, as she had the previous day, and then she returned to Mamma Tack's.

The American arrived again that night, and again Marat watched the cottage in the darkness, his frustration and blind hatred festering.

The Wednesday was the same. Like clockwork, the patterns of her days and nights repeated themselves, and by Thursday Marat could stand it no longer.

Ronnie was playing outside on the verandah and Jane was in the kitchen, ironing the bed linen from the previous day's wash, when she heard the knock at the door. She walked through to the lounge room and glanced at the wall clock. A quarter past twelve. Savi and Pascal were fifteen minutes early. How unusual. Unlike most islanders, Savi had a meticulous sense of time, as far as his lessons with Missus Tack were concerned anyway. She opened the door.

'Jean-François.'

'I thought I'd call by and enquire how you are,' he said smoothly. There was a moment's pause and Marat raised an eyebrow at her lack of courtesy. 'May I come in?' he smiled.

'Oh I'm so sorry. Yes of course.' She had no option but to usher him inside. 'Forgive my distraction, it's just that I'm due back at the clinic in five minutes . . .'

She wasn't, he thought. She'd arrived home barely ten minutes previously, and she always stayed at the cottage for at least an hour before returning to Mamma Tack's.

'. . . not even time enough to offer you tea, I'm afraid,' she smiled apologetically. She must get him out of the house at once, she thought, before Savi arrived. It would cause shocking problems for the Poilama family if Marat caught Savi visiting her when he was supposed to be working. 'It's very kind of you to call, though.'

'Not at all,' he said, seating himself in an armchair. 'I am most concerned for you.' He wondered why she was so keen to be rid of him. Guilt, perhaps? Did she suspect he had guessed at her affair with the American? Marat was enjoying her discomfort.

Dear God, he was settling himself in, she thought. Hadn't he heard what she'd said? And the arrogance that she'd so disliked upon their first meeting was suddenly evident; he was taking no pains to disguise it with his customary charm.

Jane started to worry. At this very moment, Savi was probably walking up the hill with little Pascal. Then she reasoned to herself that of course Savi would recognise Marat's Landrover. He would never call upon her whilst the Bos's car was parked outside.

Her worry subsided. Indeed, she thought, it would probably be wiser to entertain Marat long enough for Savi to assess the situation and disappear. If Marat left now he would no doubt see father and son as they walked up the hill.

'Perhaps I can delay my return to the clinic,' she said, sitting in the armchair opposite him. 'I have become so obsessed with work lately, it occupies my every hour.'

Not quite your every hour, slut, he thought. 'Natural under the circumstances,' he said.

Jane registered the sneer in his voice. It mystified her, but she chose to ignore it, her worry was for Savi, not herself. 'I shall make us some tea after all, and you must forgive my rudeness,' she said. 'Then perhaps, Jean-François, you might drop me back to the clinic. That is, if it's not too much trouble,' she added with all the charm she could muster.

She was humouring him now. He wondered why.

'I didn't drive,' he said abruptly. 'I walked from my apartment.' He had. He'd wanted no-one to witness his calling upon her. He wasn't sure why. He didn't know what the outcome of their meeting would be, but he'd decided to play it safe in any event.

No car, she thought, alarmed, no Landrover outside as a warning to Savi.

'You've not seen my apartment, have you, Jane? You should allow me to show you, it's very much your style.' Reserved for sluts, he thought.

She barely heard him as she looked at the clock. Nearly twenty-five past twelve. She rose and crossed to the front windows, although there was little purpose: the street was not visible from the windows, she could hardly signal Savi from afar. All she could do, she decided, was wait for his knock. Then she would open the door just a little and play out a charade for Marat's benefit, pretend an unwanted visitor was calling. It would probably work. The Frenchman would be flattered that she wished to be alone with him, and Savi would immediately recognise trouble. Pascal would be the problem. As soon as he saw her Pascal would yell 'hello, Missus Tack'. In fact, if the child saw her at the window, he'd probably yell out before she had a chance to open the door at all. Jane hastily edged away.

She was nervous, he thought. Why? Had she recognised his inference about the apartment? And she was fluttering around near the door, perhaps prepared to take flight. He couldn't have that.

'You seem a little edgy, my dear,' he said, rising from his chair to join her.

'Not at all. Please do sit down, Jean-François, make yourself comfortable. Would you prefer a drink? The sun's over the yardarm, as Godfrey Tomlinson would say.' She crossed to the sideboard. She couldn't possibly leave him here in the lounge room whilst she went to the kitchen to make tea, he might answer the knock at the door.

How mercurial her behaviour was, he thought. She was being girlish now, even flirtatious.

'I'm afraid I have only sherry and bourbon,' she offered.

Of course she'd have bourbon, he thought. Laid in especially for the bastard American.

'That's what he drinks, I take it?' He gestured at the bottle.

'Who?'

'Your American friend.'

She was so thankful that he'd followed her away from the door that she failed to notice the irony in his tone.

'Wolf? Oh yes, he drinks far too much bourbon altogether.'

It was a blatant admission, and Marat was taken aback, momentarily flummoxed into silence.

She picked up the bottle, raised a glass, and when he didn't respond to the query in her eyes she accepted his silence as a yes.

'Wolf brought it as a gift for my husband,' she said as she poured the bourbon, 'but Martin always maintained it was filthy stuff.' She smiled as she held the glass out to him, hoping that he wouldn't ask for any water.

She could mention the name of her husband and her lover in the same breath? Marat was astounded. How brazen. And then the thought struck him: she was openly acknowledging that he knew of her affair. And her smile as she handed him the glass: she was flirting with him.

'I am of the same opinion as your American,' he said seductively. 'It is a *man's* drink, do you not agree?' He took the glass from her with both hands, his fingers encompassing hers. The bourbon was an apt symbol, he thought. Her ineffectual Englishman had drunk tea, but he and the American were made of stronger stuff. He stroked her fingers; he would share her with Baker if he had to.

Jane froze, unable to relinquish her hold on the glass. She was horrified more by the innuendo in his voice and in his eyes and the leer of his smile, than she was by the hideous caress of his fingers.

Marat knew, she thought. All her worry about Savi disappeared. Marat knew about her and Wolf. Quickly she withdrew her hand.

Oh yes, she wanted him, Marat thought. She'd allowed her fingers to linger that fraction too long. It was why she'd been edgy from the moment he'd arrived. Who would have thought it? Jane Thackeray was anybody's.

He carefully put the glass down on the small coffee table beside the sofa. He no longer wished to own her, she was tainted goods, just another slut, but he was willing to share her, at least for the moment.

'Don't worry, my dear, it's perfectly natural that you should seek some outlet, some distraction from your loneliness. I understand.'

She backed away from him.

'And I will say nothing, you can be assured of that, no-one will know.' He reached out his hand for her. 'I just wish to comfort you, Jane, like your friend Wolf Baker.'

She was sickened. 'Get away from me,' she hissed. 'Get away from me, Marat.'

He could see the loathing in her eyes, the disgust and repulsion, and he knew that he'd been incorrect in his assumption. She had not been flirting with him. She did not desire him. But he'd have her anyway, he decided. What could she do by way of complaint? Who could she go to? If she accused him of rape he'd make it public knowledge that she was a whore who'd dived into bed with the first man available within twenty-four hours of her husband's death.

'What's the matter, Jane, are we locals not to your liking?' His lip curled scornfully. 'Are you keeping yourself in reserve for the Americans?' He lunged at her. She was about to dive for the verandah to make her escape, but she hesitated: Ronnie was out on the verandah.

It was the moment Marat needed, and he grabbed her, ripping at her blouse, dragging her to the floor.

'You love it, slut,' he grunted as he hoisted her skirt up over her thighs. 'Admit it, you love it.'

Jane fought back with every ounce of her strength, clawing at his eyes with her fingers, but he pinioned her wrists against the floor. She kicked out ferociously, sending the small coffee table spinning across the room, the glass shattering loudly as it hit the sideboard.

Then, as if the smash of the glass were a signal, everything happened at once. Ronnie careered clumsily in from the verandah, alarmed by the sound; Jane stopped flailing about, fearful that the child might be hurt in the struggle; Marat smothered her with the bulk of his body; and at the same instant the front door flew open.

Savi dived upon the man who was about to rape Missus Tack, grabbing him under the armpits to haul him off her.

Pascal grasped Ronnie's hand, and the two of them raced into the kitchen where they hid under the table.

The man was powerfully built, strong. Savi could feel the weight of him as he dragged him clear. But Savi was strong too.

Marat came to his senses as he felt himself hauled to his feet. He was alarmed. Who had discovered him attacking the slut? Thrown clear of Jane, he staggered, off balance, and crashed against the sideboard. Then, as he steadied himself, he saw who it was. His outrage at the audacity of his servant was mingled with sheer relief.

'Get out of here, Savi!' he snarled.

Savi stood motionless, staring at the Bos. When he'd dragged the man off Missus Tack, he hadn't known it was the Bos.

Surely Savi wasn't disobeying him. Impossible, Marat thought. Then he realised that he'd spoken English.

'Dehors!' he ordered. A command he would have given to a dog.

The Bos had been about to rape Missus Tack, Savi thought. Still dumb with shock, he helped Jane to her feet.

The sight of his servant going to the slut's assistance further angered Marat.

'Dehors!' he yelled. 'J'ai dit dehors!'

Never had Savi disobeyed the Bos, but he stood his ground as he finally found his voice.

'No, Bos, I will not go,' and he moved protectively in front of Jane, 'I will stay here with Missus Tack.'

The man's perfect English was not lost on the French-
man, in fact it seemed the ultimate act of insubordination.
But Marat found Savi's stance ludicrous, laughable even.
No black disobeyed Jean-François Marat. Least of all Savi.
Compliant, subservient Savi, who knew better than to bite
the hand that fed him.

'Now you listen to me, Savi,' he hissed. 'You get out of
this house and back to your work where you belong.'

'No, Bos. It is you who must leave.'

Marat was incensed. 'You do as you're told, you black
bastard, or you'll no longer work for me.'

'I do not work for you. From right now I no longer
work for you.' The words surprised Savi as much as they
did Marat. All these years he had protected the welfare of
his family. Even when he'd known that the Bos was wrong
he'd advised Sera, more prone to rebellion than he, that
her masta must always be obeyed. But the Bos had been
about to rape Missus Tack. There were some things one
could not turn away from. 'You must go now. You must
go right now, Bos.'

'You don't tell me what to do, you black scum!'

All of Marat's rage was suddenly centred upon Savi, and
Jane, now forgotten, sidled quickly towards the kitchen to
protect the children.

'You hear me? You don't tell me what to do!' Marat
strode the several paces that distanced them and shoved
Savi in the chest. Savi staggered a pace back. 'You get out,
boy! You get back to the plantation and you get your
family off my property or you're all dead.' Another shove,
and Savi staggered another pace.

Savi didn't want to fight the Bos. But he knew it was the
only way. He darted a glance towards the kitchen. He
could see the Missus peering through the crack in the door.
His son was with the Missus, and little Ronnie too, it was
the only way to protect them all.

'You hear me, boy?' The black was frightened, Marat

could see it in his nervous glances, in the whites of his eyes. Each shove sent him another step back, he was nearly at the front door now. 'Get out, you black bastard.' One final shove would do it.

They were at the open door, as Savi had planned. He must get the Bos away from Missus Tack and the children. He grabbed the Frenchman and hauled him outside.

'Fermez a clef! Les enfants!' he yelled to Jane, unaware that he'd instinctively used his opponent's language, as he wrestled Marat to the ground.

Jane raced from the kitchen and slammed the door shut, locking it. Then she locked the door to the verandah and held the children close to her as she listened to the men doing battle outside.

They crashed about amongst the trees and bushes. Marat was the stronger and the heavier of the two, but Savi was younger and far fitter.

He landed repeated blows to the Frenchman's face, dodging nimbly aside when Marat tried to pinion him in a vice-like embrace. On and on he went, jabbing and dodging, catching the Frenchman off balance, infuriating him further. And then finally, when he had him in the perfect position, he used Marat's body weight to his own advantage, charging him into the trunk of a tree. There was a loud crack as Marat's shoulder dislocated. Then, as he staggered backwards with a howl of pain, Savi charged again smashing him into another tree, and this time it was Marat's head that connected.

It was over in less than two minutes. Behind the locked door, Jane listened to the silence, no longer frightened for herself, but terrified for Savi. She held the children tightly, Ronnie bewildered, Pascal crying. Had Marat killed Savi? Then she heard his voice.

'Open the door, Missus Tack. It is safe.'

Savi was panting heavily, but apart from a cut above his eye he was unharmed. Jean-François Marat lay sprawled on his back on the front path, his face a bloodied mess, his right arm at a grotesque angle to his body.

Jane told Ronnie to stay inside as Pascal ran to his father. Savi picked his son up, and the boy instantly stopped crying, then he looked down fearfully at the body of Marat. He had killed the Bos. A black man had killed his white master. 'If they find out I have done this . . .' He faltered.

Jane knelt beside Marat and checked his vital signs. 'He is alive, Savi, you have not killed him.'

But Savi kept shaking his head.

'You were protecting me. I will tell them that.'

'It will do no good. The Bos is too strong.' She did not understand. Even Missus Tack did not understand, none of the white people did.

Jane did understand. Savi's fear of his corrupt white master was eminently justified. But Marat would need to admit to what had happened in order to lay charges against his servant. She herself would make sure of it. And Marat would admit to no such thing.

'He will not tell anyone that you fought him, Savi. He will not want anyone to know that he attacked me.'

But even if what the Missus said was true, Savi thought, it would make no difference in the end. 'He will kill my family, Missus Tack. He will kill my family for what I have done.'

She could see his desperation. Savi's bravery had deserted him. He was frightened now. Frightened and lost. He had risked everything for her, even, it would seem, the life of his family, and she must take charge now. She must convince him that he was safe, and tell him what to do.

'You must go home, Savi. You must go home straight away. And you must collect Sera and Marie and all of your belongings. The others will help you, won't they?'

Savi nodded. Yes, he could borrow the donkey and cart from the village, and his cousins would help. He was listening attentively, the little boy's arms entwined about his neck, he would do whatever Missus Tack said. Missus Tack always knew best.

'But you must not go to your family's village. You must come in to Sera's village, well away from the plantation and close to town. I can help you then. I can find work for you both.'

Marat groaned, he was regaining consciousness. Savi's eyes rolled with alarm as he looked down at the Bos.

'He will not hurt your family, I promise you,' Jane said. 'But you must leave the plantation this afternoon.'

Marat stirred, then groaned again. And again Savi stared at him, petrified in his fear.

'He will not be able to follow you, Savi, he is too hurt.'

Savi longed to do as Missus Tack suggested. He wanted to turn and run for all he was worth. But how could he leave Missus Tack with the Bos?

Jane understood his quandary. 'And he is too hurt to do me any harm,' she assured him. 'Go now, Savi. Look after your family.'

He needed no further bidding. 'You take care, Missus Tack.' And he left before the Bos could open his eyes and see him standing there.

Jane's courage didn't falter when he'd gone, but she was uncertain about what to do next. She examined Marat. A dislocated shoulder, numerous abrasions, a nasty wound to the back of the head, and no doubt concussion. She could contact the hospital, but what sort of questions would be raised? Why had Marat been beaten to a pulp at her front door? She could simply lock the cottage, return to the clinic with Ronnie and leave the man where he lay, in the hope that when he regained consciousness he would stagger home to his apartment. But she dismissed the thought even as it occurred, her medical training could not allow such an option. And, most important of all, what of her promise to Savi that Marat would not harm his family?

She needed a guarantee, and the only one who could give it was Marat.

She fetched a bowl of warm water and her medical kit and set about tending his wounds. She started with the shoulder first, she would relocate it whilst he was still unconscious. Both hands locked around his wrist, she lifted his arm, then she planted one foot firmly on his chest.

Marat was shocked into consciousness by a searing pain. He gasped and his eyes shot wide open. Jane Thackeray was standing over him, her foot on his chest. What had happened? The slut was doing something to him. He tried to move, but blackness engulfed him.

He'd fainted. Good, Jane thought, as she knelt beside him and prepared a sling for his arm. She worked quickly. When the arm was correctly positioned, she wedged a tightly rolled towel at the base of his neck to prop his head forward whilst she treated the wound, cutting away the surrounding hair and disinfecting it. She would bandage his head when she had bathed the lacerations and abrasions on his face.

It was a little over ten minutes later, as she was bathing his face, that he regained consciousness. Slowly this time, his eyelids flickering, his head turning slightly from side to side. Then his eyes opened and he stared at her. Jane put down the bowl and sponge and watched him warily.

He said nothing; he was trying to piece together what had happened. What was he doing lying here, his arm in a sling, the slut kneeling beside him? And she'd been bathing his face, he'd felt it. Then he remembered. Savi.

'I'll kill him!' he said, sitting up, ignoring the pain in his shoulder. 'I'll kill the black bastard!'

He struggled to his feet, Jane scrambling up beside him, alarmed. But as soon as he was upright, he started to sway, the world swimming giddily about him.

'Sit down.' He was about to faint again. He sank onto

the front doorstep. 'Breathe,' she said, 'breathe deeply,' and she pushed his head between his knees. He grunted with pain as the movement jarred his shoulder, but she took no notice. She needed him conscious now. 'You're concussed,' she said, 'another sudden movement like that and you'll probably faint.'

He breathed deeply and the giddiness gradually cleared, leaving a dull aching throb behind his eyes. He raised his head and looked up at her where she stood beside him.

'He'll pay for this. His whole family will pay for this.'

'No they won't, Jean-François. If you attempt to harm Savi, or a member of his family, I will report your attempted rape.'

He snorted derisively. 'And who would believe you, slut?' Looking up into the sunlight was hurting his eyes. He stared down at the path, nursing his arm in its sling and rocking slightly to and fro. 'You and your American stud! Who's going to believe you, slut!'

'What exactly is this fantasy you seem to have created, Jean-François?' She maintained her composure, her voice icy, her eyes cold, but she was riddled with fear. Did anyone else know about Wolf?

He defied the stinging sunlight to stare up at her again, his ravaged face twisted with jealousy and hatred. 'I've watched you, bitch. I've watched you for the past three nights. You and your husband's "friend",' he sneered. 'Don't deny it.'

'Of course I don't deny it.' He'd been spying on them, no-one else knew, she was sure of it, and she amazed herself with her confidence. 'I don't deny for one moment that Wolf Baker was my husband's friend.'

He laughed, the laugh turning into a wheeze as the pain slid from his shoulder down his arm. 'And he's yours now, isn't he.'

'He most certainly is. And if you attempt to cast any slur upon me and my relationship with Wolf Baker, I will report your attack on me.' She squatted beside him, careful to keep enough distance should he attempt to grab at her, and prepared to leap away if he did. But she was determined to make an impact upon him.

'Who do you think they will listen to, Jean-François? I am Mamma Tack. What do you think they would do to you if you called Mamma Tack a slut? You'd make yourself a laughing stock, you'd never be able to hold your head up in this colony again.' Jane had never felt so strong. 'You say one word about your fanciful notions and I'll destroy you. And if you attempt to harm Savi or any member of his family, I will tell them, Jean-François. I will tell them all that you tried to rape me, and Savi will be my witness.'

He knew he was powerless, and he hated her for it. He glared at her. His English rose, that's how he'd thought of her. Jane Thackeray, his own English rose. Now the very beauty that had obsessed him was detestable. He wanted to destroy it, rip it apart petal by petal and grind it into the dirt where it belonged.

Jane stood. She had won, but she had to distance herself from the murderous look in his eyes. His hatred unnerved her, although she dared not let him know it. She busied herself with her medical kit, taking out the crepe bandage and the gauze.

'Your head needs to be bandaged,' she said.

'Leave it.'

'Very well.' She replaced the supplies and closed her kit. 'I'll borrow the church car and take you back to your apartment.'

She intended to cut from the verandah across the clearing to the Reverend Smeed's, but she needed to step around Marat to get into the house.

As she did so, he grabbed her ankle with his left hand. She didn't scream, and she didn't struggle, but she was terrified. Surely the man wouldn't dare attempt to harm her further.

'You won't take me anywhere,' he snarled.

To her vast relief, he released her ankle. She stepped back. Calm, careful that he shouldn't read her fear. Then slowly he stood.

'You can't walk,' she said, 'you'll probably faint if you try. Let me get the car.'

'I don't need your help, bitch.' He steadied himself against a tree, his eyes once again fixed upon her. 'You'd best watch your back from now on, Jane.'

She met his gaze unflinchingly.

'You'll pay, you know that? I'm always willing to wait, and if it takes me years, no matter. You'll pay, I swear it.'

She said nothing, but she watched him as he turned and made his way unsteadily along the path through the trees. Then she followed him out onto the street to watch him walk down the hill, expecting to see him fall. But he didn't. He stopped now and then, bending down, his hand on his knee, breathing deeply, willing himself not to faint. Then slowly, painfully, he continued on his way, ignoring the curious looks from the few passers-by.

She watched until he was out of sight before returning to the cottage where she sat at the kitchen table deep in thought, Ronnie gambolling about, the afternoon's drama forgotten.

She expected the fear she'd so successfully quelled in Jean-François's presence to return now that she was alone. She expected to feel shaken by her ordeal and frightened by his threat. But she felt neither. She was relieved to have escaped unharmed certainly, but beneath her relief was a resolve to fight, both for herself and for Savi and his family. Marat had warned her to watch her back. Then that was exactly what she would do, she thought.

Where had her strength come from? Jane wondered. Exactly when had she become so strong? So tough? She'd changed. She remembered the young Englishwoman who'd first arrived in Vila, little more than a girl, completely reliant upon her husband. That girl had gone.

She'd changed because she had to, she realised. Marty was no longer with her, and she would need to stay strong, even tough, for the times that lay ahead.

# CHAPTER SEVENTEEN

When Jane returned to Mamma Tack's, she sent Mary to Reid's Hotel with a sealed note for Wolf Baker saying that he was not to visit her that evening. She gave no reason why.

He appeared in the late afternoon as they were closing the clinic.

'Got your note,' he said, 'just thought I'd give Ronnie a ride up the hill.' He didn't wait for an answer, but hoisted the child onto his shoulders where Ronnie bounced around happily. They said goodbye to Mary and the three of them set off for the cottage.

'I meant what I said in the note.' Her pace was brisk and she didn't look at him.

'You didn't say anything.'

'I said you weren't to come around tonight.'

'I haven't,' he said facetiously. 'I've come around this afternoon.'

'You know what I mean.'

'No I don't. Ouch.' He tried to disentangle Ronnie's hands that were threatening to pull his hair out by the roots. 'Telling me not to visit you doesn't say anything, I don't know what you mean at all. Can't you slow down a bit?'

'It means we must stop seeing each other.'

'In what way? As friends?' He was serious now. 'I'm first and foremost your friend, Jane.'

'I know.' She slowed her pace and looked at him. 'And I'm thankful for that. You're a very good friend.'

'Then let's leave it that way, shall we?'

'All right,' she agreed, and they walked on in silence.

Jane had no intention of telling Wolf about Marat. Wolf might insist she go to the police, or God forbid, threaten to confront the Frenchman himself. She didn't need the complication. But Wolf Baker was inextricably connected with the events of that day, and for the first time in their brief affair she felt a true sense of shame.

Throughout the afternoon, Marat's words had kept coming back to her. *'Don't worry, my dear, it's perfectly natural that you should seek some outlet, some distraction from your loneliness. I understand.'*

She could hear the contempt in his voice and see the lust in his eyes, but even as she'd relived her repulsion, the words had taken on a ghastly ring of truth. Wasn't that exactly what she had been doing? Seeking an outlet through Wolf to distract her from her loneliness?

They arrived at the cottage door, where Wolf untangled Ronnie from his hair and deposited him on the front doorstep.

'Play hidey, Wolf, play hidey.' The little boy tugged at his trouser leg.

'Shall I?' he asked Jane. 'Shall I come in, old pal, old buddy? Just for a cup of your fabulous tea?' He rubbed his hands together with pretended delight. 'Yum, yum.'

He looked ridiculous, his hair sticking up like a cockatoo's crest, and she laughed. 'Of course. You can even have a bourbon.' Her laughter quickly died as she fought to quell the image of Marat. *'I am of the same opinion as your American. It is a* man's *drink, do you not agree?'* And she felt the touch of the Frenchman's fingers around hers.

'I'll do the hide and seek thing while you get the tea,' Wolf said. But his heart wasn't in it as he dodged behind the armchairs and the sofa, escaping the indefatigable Ronnie. Something had happened. What was it?

He confronted her as they sat in the lounge room over their respective tea and bourbon.

'What is it, Jane?'

'What's what?'

'Something's happened, that's what. Tell me.'

Never, she thought. Never as long as she lived would Wolf, or anyone else, know what had taken place in this very lounge room. She looked about. There was no evidence of the day's drama. She'd cleared up the mess.

'Guilt,' she said. 'Simply guilt.'

'Okay.' He could see she'd closed off. She was different, he thought. Less vulnerable. Surely that was a good thing, he told himself, but he wondered what was going through her mind, and he wished that she'd share it with him. 'But I'm your friend, Jane, and I intend to stay that way.'

'Good. I need friends. What about something to eat? I'm starving.'

They raided the larder, but she hadn't done the shopping and there were only tins, so they had baked beans on toast, sitting beside Ronnie in his highchair, sharing a smile as he dribbled beans all over his tray.

They put the child to bed together and she saw him to the door; it all seemed so natural.

'Good night, Jane.' His hand gently upon her shoulder, he bent to kiss her forehead.

But even that was enough. The warmth of his fingers through her light cotton dress, the deep tan of his neck teasing her with the intimate knowledge that his chest was a different colour, the tantalisingly familiar smell of him.

His lips brushed her forehead and, as if drawn by a magnet, she leaned forward and kissed the cleft at the base of his throat.

'Stay, Wolf,' she whispered, 'please stay.' She couldn't help herself. Perhaps she did love him, in a way she'd never known. Perhaps she needed the escape of him, the sheer sexual escape. But her body seemed to have a will of its own. And if her actions were shameful, she thought, then so be it, she was damned.

Savi joined the army labour recruits. Jane recommended him for a position of authority, and the military readily agreed that Savi Poilama, bilingual, with a wealth of experience as a plantation foreman, was a valuable asset.

The native work gangs were a common sight in the streets of Vila, singing as they trooped off to work, 'God Bless America' or island versions of the big swing band melodies that were popular at the time. Jane regularly saw Savi, proudly heading his own team, and she waved to him as they marched past Mamma Tack's.

She found shift work with the military for Sera too. As a cook. It remained imperative that island labourers be fed traditional staples and discouraged from a diet of American rations. Good local cooks were eagerly sought after and Sera, given her choice, chose the lunchtime shift so that she could spend the early mornings and evenings with her children.

With two army pays coming into the household, the Poilamas were more affluent than they had ever dreamed possible, and both Savi and Sera were happy in their work.

Sera's sister, Selena, had not fared so well. When Savi had returned to his home to gather his family, Selena had refused to accompany them. She did not fear the Masta, she said. The Masta was different with her, she was special.

Savi refused to remonstrate with her, there was no time. He told Sera to talk some sense into her sister, and went to the village for the donkey and cart, and to enlist the help of his cousins.

Sera, horrified as she had been to hear of the Masta's

attempted rape of Missus Tack, was not altogether surprised. She had lived through a similar experience herself.
She was proud of Savi for saving Missus Tack, it was very
brave of him, she thought. But she was unable to convince
Selena of the dangers of staying.

'The Masta will take out his anger upon you, Selena,'
she said.

'He will not,' her sister replied sulkily. 'The Masta loves
me.' Selena wasn't proud of Savi at all. She thought her
brother-in-law was a fool for having disrupted their lives.
Selena respected Missus Tack like everyone else, but
Missus Tack was white. Savi was not brave at all, in
Selena's opinion, Savi was stupid for interfering in white
people's business.

Savi returned with his cousins, and they started loading
everything they could into the cart. One of his cousins had
suggested that Savi take the Bos's dray with its two-horse
team; he could return it later. Then they could all ride, the
cousin said, instead of having to walk beside the donkey.
It was a long trek and they would have to camp out
overnight as it was.

But Savi would take nothing that was not his. Even if he
were only to borrow the dray, he said, the Bos could
accuse him of stealing. Besides, he was never coming back
to this place.

When they were ready to go and Selena still refused to
accompany them, he washed his hands of her. She could
look after herself, he said. He refused to argue any longer;
the Bos might arrive home at any minute.

But the Bos didn't arrive home for three days.

Marat stayed at the apartment, his dizzy spells clearing,
but his shoulder giving him incredible pain.

When he finally returned on the third day he found
Selena waiting, eager to comfort him and tend to his
wounds. Her presence was intolerable; the mere sight of
her angered him.

He yelled at her to get out, and when she continued to plead that he let her stay, he gave her a backhander with the full force of his strength, sending her spinning across the room with a fractured jaw. In doing so, he reactivated the pain in his shoulder and bruised the knuckles of his left hand, which angered him all the more. He'd kill her, he roared, if she stayed one second longer, and Selena scuttled away, terrified.

She didn't rejoin the family, however; she moved into the local village instead, where she nursed her jaw and planned her future. She would find another white masta who wanted a black mistress, she determined. Selena didn't like to work.

Jane was sympathetic to Selena's predicament and wished to help, but Sera herself told the Missus that any attempt would be useless. Her sister, she said sadly, had severed all ties with her family.

The Poilamas and Jane became closer than ever. A few days a week, in the mid-morning, Sera would drop Pascal and Marie at Mamma Tack's on her way to work. Even though her family in the village could have cared for the children daily, Sera was keen that Pascal and baby Marie have the opportunity to more regularly hear and absorb English. Jane was pleased too, since it meant Ronnie now had close friendships with children his own age. It had been a solitary existence for a little boy surrounded by American servicemen, much as they spoiled him.

The children began to see themselves as siblings, and when Pascal re-christened Missus Tack 'Mamma Jane', the others took up the nickname, including Ronnie. The three were inseparable, and Pascal, several years older than the others, was fiercely protective of his little brother Ronnie and his sister Marie.

Busy as she was, Jane continued to find her work at the clinic fulfilling and deeply rewarding. Mamma Tack's was now indispensable to the locals and, surrounded daily by the love and gratitude of her island friends, she felt a growing sense of peace in their easygoing company.

Wolf's visits were less regular now that he was back at the Havannah Harbour base, but they were no less passionate. Each fortnightly leave he would book into Reid's Hotel. He would come to Mamma Tack's during the day and make the children laugh with his antics. Then, under the cover of darkness, he would come to Jane and they would spend the night together, their need for each other becoming more insatiable as the weeks turned into months.

'What are you doing a fortnight from now?' he asked one early December morning after they'd made love.

'Seeing you, I would think.'

'Yes, but where?'

Was it a puzzle? she thought. What was she supposed to answer? He seemed in a very cheeky mood, something was afoot.

'I give up,' she said. 'Where?'

'Espiritu Santo.' He bounced up to hunch over his knees like an excited twelve-year-old. 'Remember I told you I'd fly you there? Well, there's a Christmas concert on. Artie Shaw's big band. We can stay the Saturday night, and I'll fly us back on Sunday.'

'I hardly think so, Wolf.'

'Mary can stay here at the cottage and look after Ronnie, it's only for one night, and it'll do you good to get away.'

'Oh for goodness sake, don't be ridiculous. How could I stay overnight with you?'

'You wouldn't be staying with me, you'd be staying in the nurses' quarters.' He winked. 'I've got it all set up. "The famous Mamma Tack from Vila visits the nurses on Santo",' he gestured headlines in the air. 'Great public relations exercise. They want to do a story on it for the army bulletin, you know, boosting morale and all that. I've run it by them, and they can't wait to meet you.'

'You've what?'

'I've run it by them. The CO on Santo thinks it's a great idea.' He beamed with an enthusiasm that was over- whelmingly infectious. 'And I've volunteered to be your pilot. What do you say, Jane? You and me and Artie Shaw's big band!'

How could she possibly say no?

'Begin the Beguine' blared out across the open amphi- theatre with all the magic that only an eighteen-piece American swing band could deliver. The concert itself was over and it was dance time now. Women were in a minority and the nurses were danced off their feet, Jane included, as hundreds of servicemen vied for their favours. In the balmy evening, beneath a tropical night sky, coconut palms swaying in the breeze, it was an exhausting, exhila- rating and thoroughly heady experience.

Jane had been officially welcomed by the CO in the afternoon and interviewed by a journalist who'd made shorthand notes in a pad at lightning speed, after which she'd been given a guided tour of the base. She'd told Wolf she felt like a celebrity. 'And a terrible phony,' she'd added.

'Rubbish,' he'd said, 'Mamma Tack *is* a celebrity, and she deserves to be. You're as famous on Santo as you are on Efate – all the guys come back here with stories about you.'

He had accompanied her to the nurses' quarters where she had been warmly welcomed, but where Wolf himself was the star. He flirted effortlessly and outrageously with the nurses, who loved every minute of it, even the stern- faced, middle-aged major putty in his hands. Jane was reminded of her own first impression, that day a lifetime ago when they'd met. Wolf Baker was quite simply charis- matic, she'd thought, and she'd been right. She watched him, at ease with the attention and revelling in it. Wolf was the one born for celebrity, she thought fondly.

And now it was the last number for the evening, 'Moonglow', and Wolf had finally managed to claim a dance with her. She'd been jitterbugged into a state of fatigue and it was a relief to sway gently to the melody, one of her favourites.

'Thank you, Wolf,' she said. 'I don't know when I've had a more exciting time.' She laughed at herself. 'Well, I never have. I haven't had such an exciting time in my whole life.' It was true. The afternoon's flight to Espiritu Santo had been even more thrilling than her first experience, then the personal guided tour of the military base, and now tonight, to top it all off, the incredible excitement of Artie Shaw's big band!

Wolf wanted to tell her that he'd make the rest of her life just as exciting if she'd agree to spend it with him. Now was not the time, he realised, but he was starting to live in hope. He suspected that he was beginning to mean more to Jane Thackeray than a distraction from her loneliness.

'It will soon be Christmas.'

It seemed a rather obvious statement, Jane thought as she sat drinking tea with the Reverend Smeed in her lounge room a week before Christmas Eve.

'Yes,' she agreed, wondering where he was leading. Something to do with the church's Christmas pageant, she presumed; she and Hilary had already agreed to help with the decorations.

'And you still intend to stay in Vila?'

Of course, she realised wearily, the same old subject.

'Yes I do, Reverend Smeed.'

'Ah.'

Both the military and the New Hebrides Mission had been concerned about Jane's plans. She had been assured by each that her return to England would be taken care of, together with any relocation expenses she might incur. It had been a surprise to all when she had declared her intention to remain in Vila.

Arthur Smeed had made the offer, somewhat awkwardly, Jane had thought, that she was welcome to stay in the cottage until the new minister was appointed.

'Thank you, Reverend Smeed,' she had said; she had expected such an offer. And Arthur Smeed had left somewhat daunted. The independence Jane Thackeray displayed was unseemly in a young widow, he thought.

Now he was back. And the conversation seemed to be progressing along the same lines, except that he appeared more awkward than ever.

'It's about the new appointment . . .' he said.

'Yes?' It was just over three months since Marty's death and she had been expecting the news at any moment. She had made enquiries in town about renting a small apartment, and then Godfrey had made his outrageous offer.

'You will move in with me,' he had announced.

She'd laughed initially. 'Don't be ridiculous, Godfrey,' she'd said, 'I'd be the talk of Vila. What on earth would people say?'

'My dear, I am seventy-three years of age, old enough to be your grandfather. This is a large house, you would have your own quarters, and I would expect Mary to move in with you as your personal maid. Let Vila say what it will.'

It was an offer she could hardly refuse, and Mary had been thrilled at the prospect, although Jane had sworn her to secrecy for the moment.

'Well, there have been delays,' the Reverend Smeed continued, 'due to the war, you understand.'

'Yes of course.'

'But I'm led to believe that the appointment will be confirmed some time in the new year. Possibly late January, so given the travel time . . .' He tried to put it delicately. '. . . I'd say we'd be looking to vacate the cottage around the end of February. Would that be convenient?'

Jane was surprised. She had far more time up her sleeve than she'd anticipated.

'That would be perfectly convenient, Reverend Smeed,' she said. She didn't dare tell him of her arrangement with Godfrey, aware that he would find it scandalous, that she was already far too non-conformist for his liking.

It seemed laughable now as she recalled how intimidating she'd found the Reverend Smeed upon her arrival in the colony, with his litany of 'do's' and 'don'ts'. She felt sorry for him now. He simply didn't know what to do with her, she realised. She was no longer the wife of his minister, she refused to go home to the mother country, she didn't conform to his ideas of widowhood. The Reverend Smeed found her confusing.

'Thank you so much for coming,' she said as she farewelled him at the door, and the poor man left more confused than ever.

'I'm having a New Year's Eve dinner party,' Godfrey announced to Jane as he fought, with little success, to rescue his beard from Ronnie who was sitting on his knee, 'and you're the first person on my invitation list.'

'I'm flattered.'

Wolf had invited her to the military's big open-air 'bash', as he called it, but she'd refused. He'd assumed she was uncomfortable about their being seen publicly together, and accused her of being oversensitive.

'Jane, there'll be a thousand people! And you've worked for the military yourself, you're personally invited, everyone is!'

When she'd remained steadfast in her refusal, he'd insisted that they spend New Year's Eve alone together. 'Who the hell needs a party anyway? Just the two of us. What do you say?' Wolf had thrown caution to the wind lately. He hadn't actually told her that he loved her, but he was wearing his heart on his sleeve a lot these days.

'Please, Wolf, go to the party with your friends,' she'd urged. New Year's Eve wasn't particularly important to her, she told him, it was just a night like any other, in her view.

It was true, she thought, remembering how she and Marty had usually been in bed fast asleep by midnight, then how, in the morning, he would say, 'a happy New Year to us both, my love'. But she didn't tell Wolf that. She didn't tell him that she didn't want to think about the New Year at all.

Jane had accepted Marty's death and the knowledge that she must go on without him, but she feared for her future and Ronnie's also. Despite the fulfilment of her work at Mamma Tack's and the love of her friends, she felt somehow displaced, as if she were in suspended animation. The strength and resilience she'd experienced after the incident with Marat seemed to have deserted her as she contemplated her future. Without a place to truly call her own, she felt neither English nor islander, and 1943 loomed dauntingly ahead.

Now, however, she decided that she could not possibly refuse Godfrey's invitation. The old man was lonely, she was sure, and she'd seen little of him over the past weeks.

'Who else are you planning on inviting?' she asked, trying to sound enthusiastic.

'I thought I'd leave that entirely up to you.' Godfrey was aware that she was accepting his invitation under sufferance, that she thought he was lonely. But he was happy to blackmail her with his perceived loneliness, having decided it was his mission to rescue her from her own. He suspected that 1943 was not a year Jane Thackeray was eager to embrace and he was determined to distract her from the worry in any way possible.

'The Bales and who else?' he asked. 'The Reverend Smeed?'

'I think not,' she smiled, aware that he'd made the offer tongue in cheek.

'Wolf Baker?'

There was no inference in the old man's tone, and why should there have been, Jane thought, as she quelled a guilty start. Godfrey knew that Wolf had remained a close and supportive friend following Marty's death.

'I believe Wolf's going to the big military bash,' she said, 'but I'll ask him if you like.' She knew he'd say yes.

'Please do. And who else? Who would you most like to see the New Year in with?' Godfrey was feeling quite excited now, he hadn't had a dinner party for a long time, and since the arrival of Jane in the colony he had discovered a love of dinner parties. 'I want to make it special.'

Jane suddenly realised that she had been inveigled into Godfrey's dinner party because he felt sorry for her, and she was about to tell him that she didn't want to see the New Year in at all. Then a thought occurred to her, and she answered honestly.

'I would most like to see the New Year in with the Poilama family,' she said.

Godfrey had met Savi and Sera and their children several times through Jane but, although he knew of their close friendship, it had not occurred to him that she would suggest the Poilama family. Good heavens above, he chastised himself, in his assumption that she would choose from her white circle of friends he'd behaved just like one of the us-and-thems. Godfrey had always referred, most derisively, to the white colonials who considered themselves superior to the islanders as the 'us-and-thems'.

'What a splendid idea,' he said. 'A family affair. The New Year should be welcomed in with children; they are the future after all.'

'The children will be well and truly asleep by midnight, Godfrey.' She smiled and lifted Ronnie off his lap, rescuing the old man from the child's murderous attack.

'Ah yes, of course.' Godfrey stroked his beard back into position. 'But they'll be there nonetheless. The symbolism will not be lost. We can toast the children as we toast the future.'

Jane laughed. Godfrey's dinner parties were an endless round of toasts, any excuse to top up guests' glasses with his finest reds. Which reminded her, she thought as she put Ronnie down on the floor, she must bring along plenty of soft drinks, not only for the children but for Savi and Sera, neither of whom drank alcohol. It would never occur to Godfrey to lay in soft drinks for a dinner party.

'You must invite Mary of course,' Godfrey said.

'She'll be delighted.' Jane found herself rather looking forward to the party.

'And the meal will be strictly island cuisine. Leila will love the opportunity to show off.'

'She'll have some competition with Sera, I'm afraid,' Jane said. 'Sera will insist upon bringing food and she's a superb cook.'

'Better and better,' Godfrey was inspired now. 'We'll make it just that. A competition, points allotted each dish!' He did so love a dinner party with a theme. And an island theme at that.

'Perhaps, on second thoughts,' he said, 'we won't invite the Bales.' The Bales were a nice enough couple, but underneath they were us-and-thems like the rest; Godfrey had found very few whites who weren't.

'That's probably a good idea,' Jane agreed.

Savi had learned to play the guitar. The only problem was stopping him, Sera said. But no-one minded as they sat on Godfrey's balcony raucously singing along, the children stamping the floorboards and clapping their hands to the rhythm.

The guitar had been a gift from the Americans, and Savi had practised with his new friends endlessly. The songs were hits of the day, and as Savi played, Wolf led the sing-along. Cole Porter, Irving Berlin, George Gershwin: Savi knew all of the melodies and Wolf knew all of the lyrics. He yelled out each line in advance, the others grabbing at the words and bawling them at the tops of their voices. It was not a melodious sound, Godfrey thought, but who cared?

He looked about at them. Savi playing for all he was worth, his gloriously beautiful wife, Sera, shaking her head in fond exasperation, their son Pascal thumping the floor in perfect rhythm. He looked down at their daughter Marie, who was sitting on his lap tugging at his beard. What *was* this destructive fascination children had with his beard? And his thoughts flew back forty years, to Mele Island. To his son and his wife and her extended family. *His* family, he thought. His only true family. Godfrey had little recall of the hideous childhood he'd run away from to sign up for the merchant navy, lying about his age. His life seemed to have started after he'd jumped ship to become a trader in the South Pacific. He belonged to these people more than any white person he knew, he thought. Then he looked at Jane Thackeray, her arms around Mary and Leila, singing out of tune along with the rest of them. Perhaps not more than any white person, he realised. Jane Thackeray served a purpose for them. He did not.

Godfrey Tomlinson was feeling older than ever lately. He was tired, and not very well these days. But none of that mattered tonight. Tonight he was having the time of his life. He decided to get drunk. Thank goodness Wolf Baker was a healthy drinker, he thought. Alcohol was a white man's vice that Godfrey clung to. He'd never been able to share the islander's love of kava. Abominable muddy muck, he thought. And it never did the trick.

Godfrey was getting drunk, Jane thought fondly as she watched him topping up Wolf's glass of red wine. And they hadn't even eaten yet. Leila and Sera had retired to the kitchen, Mary having been mollified for her exclusion with the duty of setting the table. Savi was entertaining the children, strumming on his guitar, quieter now.

Jane had tried to help in the setting of the table, but

Mary had been adamant, so she'd retired to her chair to watch Godfrey and Wolf in animated discussion.

She was grateful to Godfrey. This dinner party had been for the sole purpose of rescuing her, she realised, and it had worked. She felt surrounded by love and friendship. She would miss Marty saying 'a happy New Year to us both, my love' in the morning but, for tonight, she was happy.

Leila and Sera had prepared a veritable feast in an effort to outdo each other, and the cooking competition was diplomatically declared a draw.

The children were all comfortably bedded down well before midnight, but as the hour approached, Godfrey insisted upon toasting the future generation. Then, as the impressive grandfather clock in the corner rang out the first of its throaty chimes, the countdown began and, when the final chime hung in the air, they embraced and once again, upon Godfrey's insistence, raised their glasses.

'To 1943!' he boomed at the top of his voice and Jane found herself joining in the toast as loudly as the others.

Through the open doors to the balcony they could hear the whole of Vila celebrating, the military bash was in full swing. Wolf grabbed Savi's guitar and played 'Auld Lang Syne' boisterously and badly. Despite the guitar lessons he'd had back home, he wasn't the natural musician Savi was, but then Savi didn't know 'Auld Lang Syne', and they had to sing it, Wolf insisted. Hell, it was New Year's Eve.

Savi rescued his precious guitar, inspected it for damage and, relieved that there was none, instigated another sing-along, waking Pascal who trotted out from the bedroom, bleary-eyed with sleep but determined to be a part of it all.

It was two o'clock in the morning when the Poilamas left, Mary with them, to return to the village. Pascal was slung over Savi's shoulder like a sack of potatoes, exhausted, and Marie, in Sera's arms, was sleeping as soundly as she had been for the past six hours.

'She will wake as soon as we are home,' Sera said with a grimace, 'and she will make sure we are awake also.'

Leila busied herself in the kitchen when the Poilamas and Mary had gone, leaving the Masta alone with his friends. It was only correct, she thought, she had had her party. In fact she didn't know any other masta or missus who invited their servants to parties. But then who else worked for a bos like Masta Tomlinson or Missus Tack?

Godfrey wanted to talk on throughout the rest of the night, but Jane and Wolf took their leave shortly before three. Wolf would walk Jane home, he said, on his way back to Reid's. Godfrey, quite bleary by now, had presumed the American was returning to his base at Havannah Harbour. He'd been about to offer him a bed for the night, 'you're far too drunk to drive,' he was going to say, and he'd looked forward to an all-night binge. He hadn't had one of those for a very long time. Disappointed, he saw them to the door, weaving a little as he did so, and Jane hugged him warmly.

'That's the nicest New Year's Eve I've ever had,' she said.

'Yes, it was rather good, wasn't it.' Godfrey shook the American's hand. 'Drive carefully,' he said, only remembering that they were walking after he'd closed the door.

As he slumped on the sofa, he wondered vaguely whether Jane and the American might be having an affair. Lucky man if they were, he thought, nodding off into a fuddled sleep. What a wonderful dinner party. He couldn't wait for Jane to come and live with him. They'd have dinner parties once a week then, he decided.

Leila smiled ruefully. She was glad the Masta had had such a good time, but she worried for his health. She took off his shoes and covered him with a blanket before she went to bed.

A month after Godfrey's dinner party, Wolf arrived in town on his fortnightly leave and, as usual, he called in to

Mamma Tack's during the afternoon. But, even as he played with the children, he seemed a little preoccupied, Jane thought.

'Is something the matter?'

'I have to return to base first thing in the morning.'

She was busy examining a baby with a high temperature and didn't enquire further, but later, when they'd fare-welled Mary and Sera and the children and were walking up the hill, Ronnie on Wolf's shoulders as always, she noticed that he was uncharacteristically quiet.

'What is it, Wolf?'

'We need to talk.'

They sat openly on the verandah. They often did these days, Wolf always leaving before it was dark, to cross the clearing in full view of the church and the Reverend Smeed's house. He would then return late at night through the trees that masked the front door, Jane as meticulous as ever about avoiding gossip.

'I've received a citation.'

'Oh, Wolf, that's wonderful. Chuck always said that you would.' She wondered why he looked so solemn. He'd told her months ago that his CO had recommended him for a citation, and he'd been excited about it then.

He took an envelope from his pocket and handed it to her. She opened it and unfolded the piece of paper inside.

'*For conspicuous heroism above and beyond the call of duty in aerial combat with enemy Japanese forces on September 10th, 1942, and undaunted courage and self-sacrifice between September 10th – 12th, 1942.*'

She looked up and smiled, but he merely nodded for her to read on.

'*Lieutenant Baker engaged three Japanese military aircraft in aerial combat in the area of the Solomon Islands and, despite suffering the extreme physical strain atten-dant upon protracted fighter operations, he shot down all three enemy planes. When forced to ditch into the sea off the coast of Espiritu Santo in the New Hebrides Islands, Lieutenant Baker displayed great intrepidity by keeping his injured and unconscious fellow officer afloat until rescued by local inhabitants. Furthermore, for a period of two days, he sustained the life of his companion in the harshest of environments, and managed to escort him to safety.*

*'His outstanding airmanship skills and his personal valor reflect great credit upon Lieutenant Baker's gallant fighting spirit and upon the United States Army. For his actions, Lieutenant Charles Wolfgang Baker is awarded the Congressional Medal of Honor.*

*FRANKLIN D. ROOSEVELT*
*President of the United States of America.'*

'Good heavens above!' She looked up from the letter. 'The Congressional Medal of Honour!'

He nodded.

She was utterly mystified. 'But, Wolf, that's the highest award they can bestow. Why aren't you thrilled?'

'Oh it's a great honour all right.'

'Then why . . .?' She shook her head, mystified.

'They're sending me back to the States the day after tomorrow.'

'Oh.'

'Yeah, it's pretty common practice. They like to show off their heroes. They tour them around the country as morale boosters, you know, raising money through war bonds and all that.'

'You'll love it, Wolf,' she said gently, 'you'll be a celebrity.'

'Yeah, I know.' He smiled. 'Pretty heady stuff.' Now came the important part. He'd wondered how to broach the subject, and she'd unwittingly given him an opening.

'Jane, do you remember the trip to Espiritu Santo?'

'How could I ever forget it? Artie Shaw.'

'You said it was the most exciting time of your life.'

'It was.'

'Well, that's the sort of life I could offer you.'

She was silent. Why hadn't she seen it coming?

'Marry me, Jane. Come to the States with me.'

'The day after tomorrow?' She kept her reply light.

'Yeah, okay. Well, then meet me there as soon as you can. But marry me.' He was suddenly eager and alive, the way she'd seen him so often, a ball of energy and vitality. 'Marry me, Jane, and I'll give you a life like you've never imagined!' He jumped up from his chair and paced the verandah. 'I'm going to use this, you know. It's the best possible platform for a political career, America loves its war heroes. Hell, I'm a walk-up start. A Boston boy from a good family, good educational background, served his country, awarded the MH. I mean, what more could they want?'

Jane laughed loudly. 'I can just see it. Charles Wolfgang Baker, President of the United States.'

'Why not?' he said. 'You have to aim high in this world and America loves winners. Why the hell not?'

She was instantly sober. He was serious. 'And you can do it, Wolf, I believe you can do it.' She was serious herself, she realised.

'But I'd need a first lady.' His grin was electric but humorous. Wolf wasn't really sure if he was serious or not, but one thing he did know: he wanted to spend his life with Jane Thackeray. 'So what do you say, Jane, you want to be First Lady?'

'You love me, don't you, Wolf?'

All laughter died away; they were both serious now.

'Yes. I always have.'

'And Marty knew it, didn't he?'

'Yep.' Wolf realised what her answer would be, simply by the way she said his name.

It was Jane's turn to wind back the clock. 'You remember you said that I belonged here with Marty?'

Of course he did. He'd been trying to comfort her at the time, to say the right words. They were coming back to haunt him now.

'Sure.'

'And I do, Wolf. Not here with Marty, he's gone, but our work isn't. This is truly where I belong.'

And she did, she realised all of a sudden. Wolf had unwittingly given her the answer. In painting a life that she knew she could never live, he had undone all of her misgivings. The islanders were her people, her very purpose for living, and she belonged right here amongst them.

He was silent for a moment, knowing that her answer was irrevocable.

He looked out over the clearing at the church and the Reverend Smeed's house. The light would be fading soon.

'I guess it's time to keep up appearances,' he said. Then he turned to her. 'Can I come back tonight?'

'To hell with appearances. Stay.'

Later that night, knowing it was their last, their lovemaking took on a whole new meaning.

'I'll always love you, Jane,' he said as they lay exhausted in each other's arms. He found a great freedom in finally being able to tell her.

'I know. And I love you too.' Although she'd been denying it to herself for far too long, in her own way she did love Wolf Baker, she realised, and she felt no disloyalty to Marty in admitting it. 'But not enough,' she added as she saw the flicker of hope in his eyes. 'Not enough to accept the life you offer me. It wouldn't be right for either of us. I think you know that.'

He did. She belonged to the islands, and he knew it.

'I've been so lucky, Wolf. I've been loved by two wonderful men, and that's two more than many women can claim in a lifetime.'

'I don't want to lose you, Jane. And I don't want you to forget me.' He propped himself up on an elbow and looked down at her, earnest, boyish. 'I'll write all the time, you promise you'll write back?'

'I promise.'

'And I'll come back to the New Hebrides some day. I will, I swear it.'

She smiled, although she didn't believe him.

They made love again, and he left before dawn.

# BOOK FOUR

# CHAPTER EIGHTEEN

The Rossi Restaurant, fondly known to all as Rossi's, laid proud claim to the fact that it had once been Reid's Hotel, and its walls bore the framed and faded photographs to prove it. Rossi's and, more importantly, the promontory upon which it stood, were indeed the face of Port Vila in bygone years, all other structures along the town's harbourside having been demolished in land reclamation and the erection of a sea wall in the 1960s.

An attractive white building with wide terraced verandahs and surrounding green lawns, Rossi's was a gathering place for resident expatriates, and maintained an air of colonialism despite the fact that the New Hebrides, renamed Vanuatu, had been free of British and French rule for twenty-three years.

As the filming of *Torpedo Junction* progressed, the actors quickly gravitated to Rossi's during the days when they were not required on set. Many of the crew, when off duty, gathered at Chantilly's Hotel or one of the other more modern establishments in town, or they simply remained at the Crowne Plaza and partied around the pool, but the actors were attracted by the atmosphere at Rossi's.

The local expats were welcoming enough, although it was tacitly understood that no attempt be made to take over the large central table. This was the personal domain of the New Zealanders, Aussies and Brits who lounged around daily, drinking their Tusker beer, poring over their three-day-old Australian newspapers delivered from Brisbane and sharing in a sense of elite camaraderie. Happily, the actors posed no threat, for they were far more content to sit outside on the terrace overlooking the harbour and discuss, as they always did, the no less elite business of film.

Much as Sam loved Rossi's and the intense discussions with her fellow actors, the true Reid's Hotel existed for her in the set at Mele Bay, alongside Mamma Black's. Sarah Blackston now consumed her. But Sarah Blackston had become Jane Thackeray, and Mamma Black's had become Mamma Tack's. Samantha Lindsay was living in yesteryear, and Jason Thackeray was making the past more tangible by the day.

'Mamma Tack's grandson', as Jason had been introduced, not only to Sam but to the actors and crew in general, had inspired in them all a sense of history, just as Nick Parslow had intended. The character of Sarah Blackston had a true identity now. She had become very real to them, and the grandson of the actual Mamma Tack was accepted as part of their team.

Jason found it most odd to start with. He'd been prepared to help in any way that he could regarding the history of his grandmother and her life. Indeed, he had offered his services in order to make sure that they 'got it right'. But, after reading the script and conferring with Nick in Brisbane, he'd discovered that the film was a work of pure fiction. It didn't bother him. He considered it flattering that his grandmother's life had inspired a major Hollywood movie. Mamma Jane would no doubt have been amused by the notion, he thought. But, although he found the process of film-making most interesting, he couldn't understand why he himself was considered so important in the making of a film that was set in a period prior to his birth. Nick was adamant in his assurance.

'Trust me, Jason, your mere presence is an inspiration.'

And Jason put it down to the peculiar intensity of those in the movie-making business.

As the days passed, however, even Nick was surprised by just how much of an inspiration Jason was becoming to the very core of the film. Both he and Simon Scanlon agreed that the presence of Mamma Tack's grandson was spurring Samantha Lindsay on to even greater heights.

Jason Thackeray was an intriguing man, intelligent, with aristocratic features and a faint touch of the exotic in the suggestion of mixed blood. But upon first meeting, his eyes, a piercingly light blue in contrast with the olive tone of his skin, could be somewhat disconcerting.

Nick, having broken through the remote exterior, found Jason an engaging person, and he'd expected Sam, always at ease in forging new friendships, to make a similar break-through when he'd first introduced the two of them. But, initially, Sam had not had Nick's success. She'd found Jason disinterested when she'd tackled him about his views on the script.

'You've read it, how did you find it?' she'd asked in her usual direct fashion. After introducing them at the poolside bar, Nick had shared several moments of super-ficial chat, and then left them alone together, hoping that Jason would have the same stimulating effect upon Sam that he'd had upon him.

'Nick says he didn't do any research on Mamma Tack,' Sam said, 'he didn't even know her real name.' Despite the brilliance of Nick's script, she thought, Jason Thackeray might well be offended by the cavalier attitude to his grandmother's life of dedication. He might view the script as shallow and typically Hollywood. She felt a personal need to assure him of her passion for the project. 'Your grandmother was Nick's source of inspiration. *Torpedo Junction* wasn't intended to be her true story.'

'Yes, he told me the same thing.' Recognising her defensiveness, Jason smiled politely to put her at her ease. 'Nick was quite amazed when he found out that he'd got so much of it right.'

Relieved that he wasn't offended, Sam allowed her excitement to take over.

'I know, he said the parallels between the script and the real Mamma Tack were uncanny. And they are, aren't they? I mean your grandfather died in a battle at sea, and so did Hugh Blackston. But it was pure invention on Nick's part. Isn't that incredible?'

'Not really.' He respected her passion, but he refused to be carried away by it; film people were so easily overexcited, he'd decided. 'It was an educated guess,' he said. 'My grandmother was a widow and her husband was killed in the war, Nick knew that much. Pretty automatic to assume he died at sea. After all, the New Hebrides didn't experience conflict on land; theirs was an air and sea battle.' He shrugged. 'Common sense.'

Sam refused to give up. Fired by Nick's enthusiasm, she felt the need to convince Jason Thackeray of the extraordinary coincidences between fact and fiction.

'But your grandmother knew the plantation owner whose very homestead we're filming in, Nick told me. Don't you find that amazing?'

'Not particularly. The Marat place is the oldest plantation owner's house on the island, it's the natural choice for a location. And of course my grandmother came into contact with the most influential people in town, including Marat. Everyone knew everyone in Vila in those days.' His smile was a fraction patronising, she thought. 'Let's face it, they still do. Nick simply wrote what he perceived to be the truth and it was. Nothing strange about that.'

Sam found the electric blue of his eyes, which had impressed her upon their first meeting, cold now. 'Yes, I suppose so,' she said, deflated.

Jason was aware that he'd disillusioned her, but he was a practical man. He'd come up with a plausible explanation for every apparent coincidence that had appeared in Nick Parslow's script, and Nick himself had found the reasoning fascinating. It appeared, however, that Samantha Lindsay was romantically fixated on the idea that the similarities between her fictitious character's circumstances and those of his grandmother were somehow incredible. Jason refused to fuel any such fanciful notion.

At the end of their discussion that night, Sam was left with the disappointed feeling that Jason Thackeray wasn't really one of the team at all.

But the following morning, when the cameras rolled, Jason found it difficult to retain his objectivity. He watched as they shot a scene between the Reverend Hugh Blackston and his wife Sarah. Hugh was telling Sarah that he was going to war. They were short of chaplains, he said, and it was his duty to offer his services to the military. Again and again they shot the scene from different angles, and each time they did, Jason felt a faint chill down his spine. Could this be the same script that he'd read? The words and the images were so different off the page. He told himself that it was simply the craft of film-making. The set, the lighting, the costumes, the incredible eye for detail that so authentically recreated the past were affecting him, that was all it was. But it wasn't, it was far more.

Jason felt that he was living through one of his grandmother's stories; there had been so many over the years, and this one was the story of Marty. The past unfolded before his eyes, and he could hear her voice as she told him about his grandfather. 'My Marty,' he could hear her say; she'd always called him 'my Marty'. And, as he watched, Hugh and Sarah Blackston became Martin and Jane Thackeray.

At the end of the day's filming he tried to shake off the
feeling that he'd watched history repeating itself, and he
congratulated Nick Parslow and Simon Scanlon on their
excellent work. But although the cameras had stopped
rolling and the lights were turned off and the set was no
longer a magic view of the past, there remained one feeling
that Jason could not shake off. He could not deny the fact
that he had been affected, above all, by Samantha Lindsay's
extraordinary portrayal of the woman who had been of
supreme importance to him throughout his life.

'Would you like to come out to dinner with me?' he
asked. He'd been waiting for her in the foyer of the hotel.

'Oh.' She was disconcerted. She'd noticed him watching
from the sidelines throughout the day's shoot, and when
she'd left to take off her makeup she'd seen him talking
to Nick and Simon. Now, as he'd approached her, she'd
expected some comment on her work. She felt the customary stab of actor's anxiety. Had he hated her performance?
He must have. Why wasn't he saying anything? She looked
around the foyer. The gang would be congregating to dine
soon; they always ate early when there was a dawn start
the following day.

'Please come. There's something I want to show you.'

No longer distant, the eagerness in the compelling eyes
that she'd found so cold the previous night now intrigued
her.

'Sure, why not?' How rude that sounded, she thought.
'Sorry,' she grinned, 'I'd be delighted.'

He took her to Vila Chaumieres, a little further down
Erakor Lagoon. The restaurant wasn't visible from the
street, and Sam was mystified when they got out of Jason's
hire car and wandered along a tiny path that weaved its
way through a miniature forest of tropical ferns and
palms. And then suddenly there it was, tucked away
behind its lush gardens on the water's edge, the most
romantic restaurant setting she'd ever seen in her life.

Candles flickered on tabletops, and in the delicate flood-lighting along the banks of the lagoon, trees dipped gracefully towards the lazy ripples of the outgoing tide.

'This is a movie set,' Sam said. 'We should be shooting here.'

The place was deserted; it was an early hour to dine by Port Vila standards. They sat at a table on the small jetty built out over the water, and she was surprised when he told her to throw some pieces of her bread roll over the railings. She obediently did so, and swarms of fish, all shapes and sizes, broke the water's surface in a feeding frenzy.

'Hey, did you see that?' She leapt from her chair to lean over the railing, scrunching up more bread and scattering it wide. The water seethed with action, slim silver fish leaping above the surface like miniature trained dolphins. 'Hey, Jason, did you see that!'

He put his own bread roll onto her plate and quietly signalled the waiter to bring some more.

When she'd recovered from the excitement of fish-feeding, she sat down, her face glowing, unashamedly childlike. 'What a magical place. It's a fairyland,' she said, looking around, wondering why he'd brought her here; he barely knew her.

'Good food too.'

'Is this what you wanted to show me? I love it.'

'No, it isn't what I wanted to show you at all. I just thought it was a good idea for you to get away from the resort and try some of Port Vila's restaurants. We have some very good ones, you know.'

'So I've heard. But when you have a five o'clock start in the morning, it's tempting to dine in.'

'Yes, I suppose it is,' he agreed. 'Shall we order?'

They ordered their meal and as soon as the wine arrived and their glasses were poured, he raised his in a toast.

'To your performance, Samantha,' he said.

There was genuine admiration in the way that he said it, and she breathed a sigh of relief. 'Oh I'm so glad,' she said. 'You did like it then? Did you feel that I . . .'

But he interrupted. 'This is what I wanted to show you.' He rose from his chair, taking another nearby candle and placing it beside the one that sat on their table. Then he took his wallet from his pocket and produced a small black and white photograph, which he placed before her. It was an old photograph, but unfaded, and in it Sam could clearly see the sunlight that bounced off the fair curls of the beautiful young woman who stood smiling, radiant, holding the hand of a small boy, a frail elderly man with a long silver beard standing beside them.

'Jane Thackeray,' Sam breathed softly, picking up the photograph as if it were something so delicate it might break.

'Yes.' Jason leaned over beside her and looked at the photograph. 'Mamma Jane, I called her. She was the most amazing person I've ever known.'

She glanced up at him, and he was gazing at the photograph with such unabashed love that when his eyes met hers she felt she should look away. That perhaps the practical, somewhat remote man with whom she'd discussed the script the previous night might not wish to be caught out. But she was wrong. Jason had chosen to share the moment with her.

'Mamma Jane was a true mother to me, she brought me up. My own mother left when I was ten.' He smiled, then returned his attention to the photograph. 'This was taken not long after the war. That's my father, he was about five at the time.'

'And the old man?'

'Godfrey Tomlinson. An English trader. He was Mamma Jane's best friend, and she talked about him a lot. I always felt as if I'd known him.'

'Have you shown Nick and Simon this photograph?'

Sam couldn't take her eyes off the young woman, there was such strength in her beauty.

'No, I haven't shown anyone else and I don't intend to.' She looked at him, surprised.

His reply was once more practical and to the point. 'Nick and Simon are making their own film about a woman called Sarah Blackston, loosely based upon my grandmother. The script is there, it's written, they don't need any added information.' Jason found it far more difficult to explain why he had shown the photograph to Sam, however, and he knew she was wondering.

'It was your performance today,' he said, studying the photograph as he took it from her. 'I felt I'd stepped into the past. You *became* her, Sam.'

He looked at her, and his eyes were green now. How extraordinary, she thought. How could someone's eyes be blue one minute, then green the next? It must have been the reflection from the floodlights on the water.

'I was seeing Mamma Jane as a young woman,' he said. 'And I was seeing her past, so many things that she'd told me.'

'How come your eyes change colour like that?'

He threw his head back and laughed. Samantha Lindsay was delightful, he decided. She spoke her mind and he liked her for it.

'I don't know,' he said finally as he sat and leaned back in his chair. 'It happens a lot. Something to do with a change of mood, I think.'

'I'm sorry.' She cursed herself for her stupidly girlish interruption. He was about to return the photograph to his wallet. 'Please? May I have another look?'

'Of course.' He handed it to her.

'Godfrey looks like George Bernard Shaw,' she said.

'Yes, he does a bit.'

His open laughter had encouraged her. She wanted to ask him about Jane Thackeray, and about the boy in the photograph, his father. Her mind was reeling with questions, but she didn't know where to begin. It was all too personal, she thought, and too soon. She didn't know him well enough. Godfrey was a safer bet, she decided.

'Tell me about him,' she said.

'It was not long after the war, the time that photograph was taken . . .'

The waiter arrived with their steaming bowls of French onion soup, and Sam hoped that the moment wasn't about to be broken, but Jason was very relaxed and seemed quite happy to share the past with her.

'. . . It was around then that Godfrey changed my grandmother's life. Mamma Jane always called him her guardian angel.'

Whilst they ate their soup, Jason talked. And Sam forgot that they were sitting in the pretty surrounds of Vila Chaumieres, she was transported to the Vila of Mamma Tack in 1945.

*The Americans departed the islands as swiftly as they had arrived, and they left behind them a postwar state of utter lunacy. But the fault did not lie with the US military. The New Hebrides Condominium government, with all its customary indecision and inadequacy, created its own havoc.*

*The American government had provided vast quantities of machinery and equipment to the Allied forces throughout the conflict, but at the end of the war, it was feared that the return of such hardware to the US could create economic chaos. It was therefore suggested that the Condominium government might wish to purchase the goods. Plant equipment, bulldozers, modern workshop machinery, cranes, trucks, office equipment and much, much more was offered for only seven cents in the dollar of its real value.*

*Instead of jumping at the opportunity to acquire unprecedented wealth and opportunities for development,*

*the New Hebrides government procrastinated, and finally
replied that, as the Americans were leaving the goods
anyway, why should the Condominium pay for them?*

*Rightfully disgusted by the response, the US military
bulldozed every movable object into the ocean.*

*The knowledge that the wanton destruction of such
luxuries had been brought about by their own government
angered the New Hebrideans, but the postwar Condominium authorities ignored the growing resentment. In
their opinion, they had been left with a legacy of overpaid,
over-ambitious natives who needed to be returned as soon
as possible to their pre-war conditions. Adding insult to
injury, the authorities confiscated, wherever they could,
the gifts that had been showered upon the locals, visiting
homes and simply taking away the precious treasures of
iceboxes, radios, furniture, and even clothing.*

*It was in this period of unrest and anger that Jane
Thackeray proved her true worth to the disillusioned
islanders. She was a white person who could be trusted,
she healed their children when they were sick, and
Mamma Tack's was their favourite gathering place. A
haven where they could talk freely, and eat and drink and
listen to the music that played on the radio.*

*Mamma Tack's had become a sort of cafe for the locals,
serving a dish of the day – bowls of soup or stew –
together with endless cups of tea from the urn in the
corner, and even soft drinks. Those who had some money
in their pockets deposited a few coins in the bowl on the
counter towards the upkeep of the place, some arrived
with fresh produce as barter, and those who had nothing
ate for free. It was run on an honour system and at a loss,
but through her work three days a week at the hospital,
Jane was able to pay full-time worker's salaries to both
Mary and Sera.*

*At first, Mary didn't approve of Sera's employment. She
was plainly jealous. 'We don' need help, Missus, we a good*

*team, you and me. And Sera don' need work, Savi got that job at Burns Philp now.' But when Jane promised her that she would remain the boss of the clinic, and that Sera would be in charge of the cooking and kitchen, Mary was quickly appeased. Being the boss of the clinic was a far more important position, in her opinion, and the two women ran Mamma Tack's between them most harmoniously during the days Jane worked at the hospital to make ends meet.*

*The authorities, although disapproving, turned a blind eye to Mamma Tack's, but a number of local businessmen, led by Jean-François Marat, called for its closure. Mamma Tack's encouraged the islanders' love of the indulgences provided by the Americans, Marat and his cronies maintained.*

*It was Jean-François Marat's personal determination to see Jane Thackeray ruined. He had not forgotten his humiliation that day, and he held her directly responsible for the trouble that had ensued with his plantation labourers as a result of Savi's departure.*

*When Savi had left, so had many others, following his example and joining the military workforce. Marat had employed a new foreman, a South African who knew how to keep the blacks in place through sheer fear, but there was no sense of loyalty as there had been under Savi's reign. The men were lazy and pilfering had become rife. Marat's workforce remained in a state of disarray and, in his view, it was all Jane Thackeray's fault. She had cost him dearly, and she would pay for it. Without the support of the military, she had nothing, and Marat intended to send her running home to England with her tail between her legs.*

*But much as Marat pushed for the closure of Mamma Tack's, and much as the authorities would have liked to oblige, they found their hands tied. They could hardly confiscate the stove and the icebox, the radio and the tea urn and furniture, all of which had been gifts from the Americans, for the gifts had been made to Jane Thackeray. Furthermore, Jane Thackeray personally owned the boatshed, they told him, it was hers to do with as she wished. And, as there was no profit made from the business – indeed it was impossible to comprehend how she kept the place operating – there was no real justification for its closure. In truth, the authorities realised that they might well have a riot on their hands if they tried.*

*Marat was thwarted. It appeared that Jane Thackeray was to remain a thorn in his side. But he did not intend to give up. There would come a time, he vowed. One day, there would come a time.*

*Jane's ability to survive was simple. She had a silent partner in Mamma Tack's, a mysterious benefactor about whom the authorities knew nothing. His identity was no mystery to Jane, but the source of his supplies was. Godfrey Tomlinson never ceased to amaze her. Soft drinks, canned goods, tea, rice, cooking utensils and bowls, even fresh linen and blankets for the two-bed treatment area she still ran out the back, everything but the medical materials which the hospital provided her with, was supplied by Godfrey.*

*He refused any payment. 'There is no cost involved, my dear,' he insisted. 'You must simply accept the fact that you have a benefactor.' He also refused to divulge the source of his supplies. 'Ask me no questions,' he'd say, time and again, tapping his nose and looking very smug.*

*Godfrey was only too pleased that he could be of some help. She refused the financial assistance he offered, and even insisted upon paying a weekly rental for the share of his house, which he kept to a nominal amount.*

*Jane knew that she owed her very existence to Godfrey, her 'guardian angel', as she referred to him, a term which gave the old man great pleasure, but she worried about him these days. He looked frail, and she knew that he was not well. She tried to persuade him to come to the hospital for a full check-up, but he refused.*

*'The fragility of old age, my dear, that's all, the price one pays for reaching seventy-five. Do stop fussing.' What was the point of a check-up? he thought. He was dying and he knew it, just a matter of time. Besides, he'd made his own plans, and he didn't want anyone else interfering, not even Jane.*

*Despite his frailty and his constant weariness, Godfrey Tomlinson had not felt such contentment for over forty years. He had a family again. He relished waking up to the sounds of Ronnie's squeals and Mary and Leila arguing in the kitchen as to who would cook dinner that night. But above all, he relished the sight of Jane Thackeray. Little did she know, he occasionally thought with a rush of pure happiness, that she had probably extended his life by several years. He would quite willingly have given up a while back, but then she had moved into his lonely house and made it a home. He loved her immeasurably.*

*'I'm going to Brisbane,' he said one morning. It was March, 1946, not long after Ronnie's fifth birthday; he'd made sure he was around for that. As always, it was an announcement and planned to surprise. Godfrey always liked to surprise.*

*'What on earth for?' Jane asked.*

*'For a while,' he said enigmatically. 'Probably not all that long.'*

*'I don't think you're well enough to travel, Godfrey. I do wish you'd come to the hospital.'*

*He ignored her. 'I'm leaving tomorrow and I would like Mary to take a photograph of the three of us. I have purchased a camera specifically for the purpose. Come along, Ronnie.' He held out his hand and the little boy grabbed it.*

*'Why are you going to Brisbane, Godfrey?' Ronnie asked as they went outside.*

*'Because one needs to travel, and I've become very sedentary.'*

'Very what?'

'Look it up, Ronnie, you know where the dictionary is.' They regularly delved into the dictionary together, and they had such mature conversations that Godfrey often forgot Ronnie's age.

Godfrey was choosy about where they stood. He wanted the light to be exactly right. Then he taught Mary how to use the camera, which took some time, as he wasn't sure how it worked himself.

'I shall have the photograph developed in Brisbane,' he said. 'And I shall send you a copy.'

The following day they stood on the jetty and waved farewell to the Morinda, all four of them, Jane, Ronnie, Mary and Leila. And Godfrey waved back to his family. He knew that he wouldn't see them again.

He'd spoken privately to Jane the previous night. He would give her no address, and he'd appreciate it if she did not try to find out his whereabouts, he said, he would prefer it that way.

It was only then that Jane realised he was going away to die. Like an old dog, privately, on his own, and that it was the way he wished it.

'You will send me the photograph?' she asked.

'Oh yes, I promise I'll send you the photograph.'

As she waved to the fragile figure on the foredeck of the Morinda, Jane waved goodbye to the man who had become both her family and her best friend.

Her eldest brother, Wilfred, had been killed in the Normandy landings and her father, Ron Miller, had died just a year ago. A stroke, her brother Dave had written, it had been mercifully quick. Dave had moved to London and was Jane's one remaining link with her mother country, Phoebe having settled in New York with her American husband.

Jane and Phoebe continued their regular correspondence and Jane had been delighted to hear that Phoebe had given birth to a baby daughter, but she had resigned herself to the fact that it was unlikely they would see each other in the flesh again. Phoebe's life was a social whirlwind, she loved the New York set, and Jane knew that she herself would never leave the islands.

Jane continued to gaze out at the distant Morinda, although she could no longer see Godfrey on the foredeck. How sorely she would miss him, she thought, and she wished he'd allowed her to be with him at the end.

The photograph arrived a month later, forwarded from a firm of solicitors in Brisbane. With it was a brief personal note from Godfrey, and the urn with his ashes which, he instructed, were to be scattered upon the waters around Mele Island. She would shortly be hearing further from his solicitors, he wrote, and he formally thanked her for the pleasure she had given him in the twilight years of his life. There was a touch of humour at the end, however. In a hand which was surprisingly strong he signed himself 'Your friend, Godfrey Tomlinson, Guardian Angel'.

Godfrey had written the note shortly after his arrival in Brisbane and had left it, together with the photograph and list of instructions, with his solicitors. Everything had gone exactly as planned. He hadn't suicided. He had simply stopped eating. He'd stayed in one of his properties outside Brisbane – he owned two – and then when he was reduced to a mere skeleton, he'd signed into a hospice and continued his refusal to eat, maintaining it was his right to do so, and his right had been respected. It had all been very simple.

Notification arrived from the solicitors barely a fortnight later. Godfrey Tomlinson owned far more than the bungalow on the hill. He had properties all over Efate, two near Brisbane, interests in any number of businesses, and various stocks and shares, all of which he had left to Jane Thackeray.

'My grandmother was a wealthy woman,' Jason said, 'thanks to Godfrey Tomlinson.'

'Her guardian angel.'

'Yes, that's right,' he smiled. 'The authorities and those who'd tried to close her down didn't have a leg to stand on. Not that she was very good with money, mind you; she gave a lot of it away. But she sent my father through law school, and I went to Oxford to study medicine, so she obviously had an overall plan.'

They had eaten throughout his entire story, the soup and then their main courses, but although the food had been delicious Sam had barely tasted it. She'd been spellbound by the past. What a broader fabric there was, she thought, and she wished that the film delved deeper into the life of Jane Thackeray.

A group of tourists had arrived, choosing to sit at the jetty over the water, always a favourite spot, and other diners were starting to appear, so Jason and Sam had retired for coffee to the small pebble-stoned courtyard surrounded by trees. She'd declined dessert and sat sipping her long black whilst Jason, admitting to a sweet tooth, devoured a work of art laced with finely spun toffee.

'Doesn't it annoy you that this film is basically a love story when there's so much more to tell?' she asked.

'Not at all. It's a work of fiction, as Nick said.'

'Yes, but it was inspired by your grandmother, and she led such a full life.'

'With a lot of love in it. Are you sure you won't try some of this? It's delicious.'

She shook her head.

'That's what Mamma Jane was all about. Love.' Sam was leaning on the table giving him her full attention and Jason pushed his dessert to one side. He'd lost interest in it now; her desire for communication was too distracting.

'My grandmother was a strong woman. And she was tough too – she had to be. But she was so full of love. The love of her husband, her son, her grandson, the islanders. Her whole life was about love, Sam, and that's what counts. It doesn't matter if the script only deals with a small portion of her life. It's the essence of the woman that's important, and you have it. Her strength and her compassion, I saw it today.'

Sam glowed with pleasure, but her expression was comical nonetheless. 'You sound like a film director,' she said.

'I'm learning,' he grinned.

She finished her coffee. 'What about the love affair with the American?'

'What about it?'

'Well, don't you find it insulting?'

He gave a careless shrug. 'Why should I? It's a fictional story.'

'Yes, but it's inspired by your grandmother,' she said more insistently than ever.

'You keep harking back to that. Why?'

'Because she's important to me. And so is the truth.' The piercing eyes had changed colour again, but she decided not to comment; she stared into them instead. 'And because you showed me the photograph.'

'Yes, I did, didn't I?' He'd asked for that, he thought, he'd invited her into his world. 'Do you want another coffee, Sam?' The waiter had arrived at the table. She hesitated, thinking of tomorrow's five o'clock call, but he nodded to the man. 'Two thanks. Long black.'

'So,' he said with an easy grin as the waiter disappeared, 'you think I should be insulted by the suggestion that my grandmother had an affair with an American serviceman.'

'No! Good God, I didn't say that at all!' Sam was horrified. 'It's a fictional work, you said so yourself, no-one's suggesting she had an affair, I simply meant that . . .'

'I think she did.'

'What?'

'In fact I'm sure of it.' As her eyes widened and her jaw

gaped in astonishment, he again threw back his head and gave a loud, throaty laugh.

She liked the way he did that, she thought, even as she recovered from the shock of his statement. So sudden, so uninhibited. What a mercurial man he was.

'You're not serious!' He was still laughing. 'Come on now, Jason, you're not serious!'

His laughter stopped abruptly. 'Oh yes, I am. Mind you, there was no fairytale ending like the film. He didn't survive a POW camp and come back to claim her after the war, but I believe he loved her for the rest of his life.'

She interrupted. 'How on earth could you . . .' but he ignored her and simply carried on.

'His name was Charles Wolfgang Baker, and he was a friend of my grandfather's. He actually flew my grandfather out to the fleet, Mamma Jane told me, and he was shot down on the return flight. She called him Wolf and he was a war hero, they awarded him the Medal of Honour.'

'She told you that they'd had an affair?' Sam couldn't help herself, she was aghast.

'Oh good grief no,' he smiled. 'I think she only told me about him to explain the letters. They wrote to each other throughout their lives, and I collected the stamps from the envelopes that arrived from America.'

'Why does that mean they had an affair, just because they wrote to each other? People do, you know.' Sam felt the need to defend Jane Thackeray; Jason seemed altogether too disrespectful. 'Well, they certainly did in those days, before faxes and emails and all that.'

'I met him, that's how I know.'

'You *met* him?' Sam's early morning call was forgotten. She was prepared to listen to Jason all night.

He could see that he not only had her full attention, but that she was awaiting an explanation and, having dropped such a bombshell, he knew that he owed her one.

'Just the once,' he nodded. 'I was ten, but I remember him vividly. He was an impressive man, silver-haired and very successful-looking, just the way I pictured Americans should be. I felt quite in awe of him, but I liked him. He was a senator, Mamma Jane told me, and an important one, some even considered him a possible candidate for the presidency.'

The coffee arrived. Jason was silent as he dosed his with liberal quantities of sugar, and Sam hoped he wasn't about to leave the subject there. But he wasn't.

'It was early 1980, six months before the New Hebrides was officially granted its independence, momentous times. Wolf Baker came to see Mamma Jane when he heard the news about my father.'

'So you're Jason,' the American held his hand out to the boy. 'I'm Wolf Baker, your grandmother's written me all about you.'

'I've heard about you too,' the boy said as they shook.

Jane smiled. 'Jason saves the stamps from your letters, Wolf.'

'Well, then I must make sure I send you some special ones the next time I write.' Wolf was impressed by the boy's eyes, so clear and intelligent, yet so full of pain. He leaned down, hands resting on bended knees, his face level with the boy's. 'I was very sorry to hear about your father, Jason.' The boy nodded but said nothing. 'I only knew him when he was a child, much younger than you, but I know he grew into a very fine man, just as you will one day.'

The boy blinked sharply a couple of times, determined not to cry, and Wolf, respecting the fact, talked to him as an adult, aware that it was the way the boy wished to be treated.

'I guess it's up to you to look after your grandmother now. And your mother.'

'Yes.' The boy's eyes met his squarely. 'We've talked

*about it, Mamma Jane and me. We're a team, she says.'*

*'Good. That's the way it should be.'*

*They conversed openly in front of the boy who sat solemn-faced at the kitchen table whilst Jane made coffee. Wolf refused any lunch, saying he'd eaten, although he hadn't.*

*'I'm sorry there's no bourbon,' she said, 'but at least I'm not inflicting tea upon you.'*

*She seemed in less pain than the boy, Wolf thought. So contained and emotionally in control.*

*'It's good to see you again,' she smiled. 'I never thought I would, you know.'*

*'It's a pity it has to be under such circumstances. How did it happen, Jane? You just said an accident in your letter, and I wondered why . . .'*

*'Yes, an accident.' She'd jumped in altogether too quickly, he thought. 'An unnecessary, silly accident. He drove the car off the road and into a tree. Utterly senseless, but then that's so often the way things happen, isn't it?'*

*She didn't want to talk about it, he realised, which was understandable. But her response had been too glib, as if there was something she wished to avoid telling him. He was disappointed; he would have liked to have been of some help.*

*'It was kind of you to come all this way, Wolf, I certainly didn't expect you to when I wrote the news about Ronnie . . .'*

*'I know, but I wanted to see for myself that you were all right. I'm only sorry I couldn't come to the funeral.' It had been two months since Ronnie's death.*

*'How on earth did you find the time at all with your busy itinerary?'*

*'It's not so busy these days. I'm thinking of retiring.'*

*'Retiring? You?'*

*'I'll be sixty-four soon, and once you've missed your run at the big one . . . well,' he shrugged, 'time to step aside.'*

*She was genuinely pleased to see him, he could tell, but he wished she would talk more openly, the way they did in their letters. Welcoming though she was, she seemed, for the moment, to be holding back.*

*The rear door of the kitchen opened and Wolf turned to see one of the most beautiful young women he'd ever laid eyes on. She was carrying two bags of groceries and the boy ran to take one from her.*

*'Leipanga,' Jane said, 'this is Wolf Baker, my old friend from America, you've heard me speak of him. Wolf, this is Leipanga.'*

*Ronnie's wife, he realised. Jane had written of her; they constantly exchanged news about their respective families. Leipanga was the product of an English father and a Polynesian mother, Jane had written, and extraordinarily beautiful. Well, it had been no exaggeration, Wolf thought as he shook the young woman's hand.*

*'I'm so sorry about your husband, Leipanga,' he said, 'you have my deepest sympathy.'*

*'Thank you very much, Mr Baker.'*

*'Wolf, please.'*

*'Yes.' Her eyes locked onto his for a second or so, as if she was challenging him in some way. Flirting even. Wolf was nonplussed. Then she turned away and started unloading the groceries onto the kitchen table.*

*Jane appeared not to notice, setting the coffee percolator and cups on a tray. 'Shall we go out onto the verandah?' she suggested.*

*They sat looking over the view of the harbour, and all the yesterdays came back to Wolf. He'd been visited by his yesterdays from the moment the jet had turned so sharply in preparation for landing at Bauerfield Airport that morning. A difficult approach, he'd thought at the time and he'd commented upon the fact to the pilot, who had informed him that Bauerfield Airport was renowned for its tricky approach. Wolf had thought of Harold then. Harold*

W. Bauer, 'Indian Joe', the best pilot he'd ever known.

Harold Bauer had been killed in November 1942, towards the end of the Guadalcanal campaign, and he should have been awarded his Medal of Honour at the same time as Wolf. In Wolf's personal opinion, anyway. But because Harold Bauer had been reported 'missing in action' he'd had to wait a lot longer. Probably because a dead man wasn't much use to the war effort, Wolf thought; he'd become very cynical lately. Harold Bauer's MH had been awarded posthumously in 1946, and Port Vila's international airport now bore his name. Indian Joe would rather have enjoyed the fact that pilots required a particular skill in approaching his runway, Wolf had thought with a sense of satisfaction as the jet touched down.

The yesterdays had continued to wash over him during the drive into town, past the expanse of Mele Bay, then up over the hill and the first view of Vila. Port Vila, he'd corrected himself, they called it Port Vila these days. It had all come flooding back.

But now, on this verandah with Jane, the yesterdays threatened to engulf him entirely. Thirty-seven years had dropped away. She hadn't really changed at all, he thought, as he watched her pour the coffee. Oh she'd aged, just as he had. Her hair was grey, she didn't dye it or highlight it like her American counterparts, and her skin was possibly more weathered than theirs, but she hadn't changed.

'Milk and two,' she said, placing his coffee on the table beside him. She'd remembered.

'You got it.'

The vitality of her body, her eyes, her smile, the sheer strength of her. She was the woman he'd farewelled before dawn in that little cottage that was no longer there. He'd visited it on his way to see her and discovered, sadly, that it was gone.

'You must have noticed a lot of changes,' she said as if reading his mind.

'In the town, yes; in you, no.'

She laughed. 'Oh, Wolf, you're incorrigible.'

'In what way?' he asked innocently.

'You don't even know your own charm, do you? It's your greatest gift, it always was. No wonder you're such a good politician.'

'I mean it, Jane, you haven't changed. You haven't changed at all.'

'I know you mean it,' she said in all seriousness. 'And I'm saying that you haven't either.'

'Great,' he grinned. 'I'm twenty-six again, that's wonderful.'

'Yes, it is, isn't it?'

They sat in silence for a moment, and then he said, 'Leipanga's every bit as beautiful as you painted her.'

'Yes, she's a lovely looking creature, but not a very good mother, I'm afraid.'

Harsh as the statement was, she said it with a quiet resignation, and Wolf was intrigued.

'In what way?' he asked.

The letters they'd shared over the years had always been open and honest. They'd written about their children, and their children's spouses, and eventually their grandchildren, and Jane had no inhibitions about discussing her daughter-in-law with him. But she checked that Jason was nowhere in earshot this time.

'Leipanga will disappear any day now,' she said quietly. 'She'll desert her son, just as she was deserted when she was a child. Like her mother, she'll sell her beauty to the next highest bidder.' Again, though her words were harsh, her tone was not. She was simply stating the facts.

Jane had had her doubts about her future daughter-in-law from the moment she'd first met her, but Ronnie had been infatuated, and she'd felt she had no right to criticise *his choice. Besides, the girl no doubt loved him in her own way, and as long as he remained successful and provided well for her, she would stay with him. But Ronnie was dead now.*

*She'd tried to persuade Leipanga to stay and be a mother to her son, promising that she would support her and her child, but the proposition had held no attraction. Leipanga needed a man, and she'd been very open about it.*

*'Soon I will be thirty-five,' she'd said to Jane, 'there is little time left. No man wants a woman who is old, and no man wants a woman with a child.'*

*She meant no rich white man and Jane knew it. Just as she knew that, to Leipanga, no other option was worthy of consideration. Like her mother before her, the girl had relied upon the commodity of her beauty throughout her life.*

*'It's sad, Wolf,' she said, 'but there are many like Leipanga.'*

*'Very sad for the boy,' Wolf agreed.*

*'Yes. To lose both parents so quickly.'*

*He was glad that she was now communicating freely as they did in their letters, and he decided to broach the subject that she'd so assiduously avoided. 'Why don't you want to talk about it, Jane?' he asked.*

*'What?'*

*'Ronnie's death. There's something you're not telling me.'*

*It was perceptive of him, she realised. She'd thought that, with her dismissal of the senseless car accident, he'd presumed she simply didn't wish to speak about it, but he'd sensed something deeper. She supposed she should have expected it. During their short time together all those years ago, he had come to know her well, and he obviously still did. She was not skilled at deception.*

*She would have liked to have told him about Ronnie, but she didn't dare. Wolf, in his impetuosity, which she sensed had not lessened with age, might try to address the situation, and that could be dangerous.*

*She would once have confided in Phoebe, she thought. But, for a different reason altogether, she had not even informed Phoebe of Ronnie's death. Phoebe's letters, rare these days, had become progressively distracted. Since the death of her daughter, over twenty years ago now, and the subsequent break-up of her marriage, Phoebe's emotional state remained fragile. She had returned to the safety of Fareham, and Jane, in her letters, encouraged the talk of their happy childhood days which seemed more and more to preoccupy Phoebe.*

*There was no-one from the past in whom she could confide the true facts of Ronnie's death, Jane thought. Not yet anyway. Perhaps, one day.*

*'You're right, Wolf,' she admitted, 'there is more to tell, and I wish I could share it, but it's too soon.'*

*Assuming she was referring to her anguish, he felt guilty for having pushed further. 'I'm sorry, I didn't mean to cause you any further pain.'*

*'No, it's not that,' she said briskly. 'It's not that at all, I would honestly like to talk about it, especially to you of all people. But given the present climate, I daren't.' Her voice was even, and she paused for a moment, prepared to say only as much as she felt she could. 'Ronnie's death was an accident of his own making, and that's the way it must remain. For the moment anyway. One day I'll tell the true story, particularly to his son, but for now . . .' She shook her head. 'Other lives could be in danger.'*

*Wolf was shocked. Someone else had caused her son's death, and yet there was to be no enquiry? How could she bear it? 'Is there anything I can do, Jane? I'm a powerful man, please let me . . .'*

*'No,' she said hastily. 'That's exactly why I can't tell you.' She picked up the percolator. 'More coffee?'*

*She had taken his cup and started pouring without even waiting for a reply, and he knew that the subject was closed.*

*They talked comfortably for a while, about the past and the present, about their lives and their families. But when Wolf brought up the subject of the islands' forthcoming independence, he was puzzled by her reaction.*

*'The end of the Condominium, Jane,' he said. 'Cause for celebration, I'm sure.'*

*'I hope so.'*

*She seemed a little doubtful. How extraordinary, he thought. 'But it's what you've always believed in, the rights of the islanders to choose their own government, to lead their own people.'*

*'So long as the right people are chosen, and for the right reasons. There's a lot of influence being brought to bear from foreign businessmen who've had a hold in the islands for years.'*

*'You fear corruption?'*

*'Oh yes. Oh yes, I do.'*

*Well, of course it was natural, he thought, human nature, greed. Regrettable, but a fact of life. He'd been about to pursue the conversation, a country's politics were always of great interest, but once again, abruptly, she changed the subject. It appeared this was another area of discussion that she did not wish to engage in.*

*They talked on and on, well into the late afternoon, and Jane was surprised when he rose, announcing that it was time to leave.*

*'But surely you'll stay for dinner,' she urged.*

*'No, no, I'll dine at the hotel and get an early night. I leave first thing in the morning.'*

*'How? There are no flights out of Port Vila tomorrow.'*

*'I hired a jet in Hawaii,' he said. 'Just a brief visit, I'm afraid.'*

*'Heavens above, a private jet, I'm very impressed.'*

*'That's good.' He grinned broadly. 'I like to impress.'*

*The age in his face had dropped away and to Jane he looked as boyish as the day she'd met him.*

'Oh, Wolf, I can't tell you how good it is to see you.' She took his hands. 'You are so dear to me.'

'As are you to me.' He realised that he sounded quite stilted as he said it, but the touch of her hands had caught him off guard. How he would love to hold her, he thought, to feel her body close to his, just once more. But it would have been wrong. His loyalties belonged back home, and she was not his anyway. She never really had been. Besides, through the open verandah doors, he could see the boy.

'It's wonderful to have had a great love in one's life, Jane,' he said softly. 'Marty was yours. And you were mine.'

She didn't know what to say by way of reply, so she leaned up and kissed his cheek instead, and then they went into the lounge room.

Jason was seated with his homework spread out on the coffee table before him; there was no sign of Leipanga.

'Goodbye, Jason.' The boy rose as Wolf offered him his hand, and they shook. 'I won't forget those stamps, I promise.'

'Thank you.'

Poor lonely little boy, Wolf thought. Still, he would have Jane in his life, and Jane Thackeray was strong enough to fulfil the role of both parents.

Jason accompanied them to the door, Jane holding the boy's hand.

'Goodbye, Jane.' Wolf lingered for a moment, his eyes drinking their fill, knowing that this would be the last time he would ever see her.

'Goodbye, Wolf.'

'You keep those letters coming, mind.'

'I promise.'


'I've no idea what they talked about all afternoon,' Jason said, 'but it was the look in his eyes when he said goodbye to her. I was only ten, but I could tell that he loved her.'

It was close to midnight, but Sam had lost all track of time. The other diners had gone, with the exception of the tourists who remained on the jetty, partying over liqueurs.

'So Jane and Wolf had an affair,' she breathed.

'Yes, I believe so.' He smiled to himself. She was completely unaware, he thought, that she'd automatically adopted their first names. 'And I got the stamps,' he added.

'Oh really?' She'd forgotten the stamps.

'Yes, an amazing collection, filled half my album. I was an avid stamp collector in those days. I still have them somewhere, and they're probably worth a fortune now. Don't you have to be up in five hours?'

She glanced at her watch. 'Hell! Yes!'

'Let's go.'

# CHAPTER NINETEEN

'Well, that's me gone to a watery grave. What a shame, I never end up with the girl.'

It was Sunday and the film unit was gathered at the Crowne Plaza pool, having an impromptu farewell get-together for Mickey Robertson. They'd completed filming the death of Mickey's character, Hugh Blackston, the previous day and Mickey was flying out of Vanuatu first thing in the morning.

It was a hot afternoon, and most of the gang were in their bathing costumes. Sam looked at the lanky actor lounging against the bar, one gangly arm draped around Elizabeth's naked brown shoulder, and she laughed. Mickey always ended up with the girl. In nearly every production he'd worked on — stage, film or television — Mickey Robertson invariably had an affair with the leading lady. Sam herself had been one of the very few exceptions, but he'd still managed to attract the favours of some other female cast member, and this time was no different. Unlikely looking Lothario though he was, women seemed to find Mickey irresistible. He caught her eye and winked.

The death of the Reverend Hugh Blackston had been

spectacular. Mammoth Productions had hired a number of decommissioned US naval vessels from a company in San Diego that specialised in the supply of naval equipment for movie-makers, and the scene had been filmed at sea aboard a US destroyer.

Jason had accompanied Sam and the other two principal actors on the shoot, both Louis Durand and Brett Marsdon also keen to watch the filming, and he'd found the whole process astonishing. Even without the sound effects of heavy explosives, overhead aircraft and machine-gun fire, all of which would be added in post-production, the scene was terrifyingly real. The explosions didn't appear fake, he couldn't see where the black smoke was coming from, and the cameras were shooting through walls of flame. The whole vessel seemed ablaze. Everywhere, desperate men fought the inferno, hoses fired blasts of water showering debris into the air, a man ran screaming from out of the flames, his body a fireball.

Then the call for meal break, and it all stopped. The smoke pump, the gas-controlled fires in their safety containers, everything was simply switched off. Suddenly they were sitting peacefully on the aft deck of a destroyer in the middle of the Pacific Ocean – all of them: actors, crew, extras, stuntmen and safety officers – and the caterers were serving up lunch. It was sheer madness, Jason thought.

Now, as they partied around the pool, he suggested to Sam that they have an official farewell dinner for Mickey at a little French restaurant where he knew the host well. They could make a private booking, he said, and have the place to themselves.

There was no dawn call for the cast and main crew the following day; Simon would shoot the aerial dogfights with the second unit, and the stunt pilots would bear the brunt of the morning's work. Sam put the dinner idea to the vote and everyone agreed with alacrity.

The evening at L'Houstalet was a raucous affair, most of the gang boldly choosing the chef's famous and highly recommended gourmet specialty of stuffed fruit bat. Jason, who knew better, decided on the boeuf bourguignon. Mickey Robertson, in order to avoid a hangover, had determined that he would remain drunk for his early morning flight, and they partied until well after three in the morning. The staff were thrilled by the presence of none other than Brett Marsdon, who good-naturedly signed autographs, and the host was only too happy with the amount of money that was changing hands.

Jason enjoyed the company of the film crowd, but they were not the reason he had changed his plans. His intention had been to remain no longer than a week in Port Vila, as he did each year. He always returned briefly to his childhood home to catch up with his old friends, but since the death of his grandmother, he rarely stayed longer than a week or ten days.

It had been a fortnight since his evening with Samantha at Vila Chaumieres, however, and he was toying with the idea of staying much longer, perhaps for the duration of the filming. Having recently resigned his residency at the medical clinic in Bournemouth where he'd worked for several years, he was undecided upon his future. He had time on his hands, he thought, why not enjoy it?

He was fully aware that it was far more than the world of film-making which attracted him, but he wasn't sure exactly what it was that intrigued him the most. Was it the portrayal of his grandmother by Samantha Lindsay? Or was it Samantha Lindsay herself? The two had by now become inextricably entwined.

Sam didn't analyse her feelings about Jason at all; she simply spent every moment she could in his company, dining with him most nights and gravitating towards him during filming breaks. He was her link to the past and Jane Thackeray, and she didn't look beyond that. There was so much more Jason knew, she thought, and so much more she needed to find out.

Brett Marsdon's jealousy was patently obvious to all, although he wasn't prepared to admit it. 'We're an ensemble, Sam,' he complained, towards the end of Mickey's farewell party. 'You should be spending more time with the cast.' He meant him. 'But you're always with that doctor guy.' He pretended to forget Jason's name. 'Come on now, we're a team.'

'Research, Brett,' she said diplomatically, 'that's all it is. Research. Jason is Mamma Tack's grandson, remember?'

'Yeah, well, I'm the one you're playing opposite,' he sulkily replied. 'Don't forget that.'

'I don't. I love working with you. You know I do.'

He wished she wouldn't treat him like some kind of kid brother. He knew he wasn't going to make it with her, he accepted that, but he was damned if he was going to let anyone else score, least of all a goddamn doctor! What did Thackeray have to do with the movie business? It wasn't fair.

'And you're brilliant.' She gave him a brief hug. 'I can't think of anyone who could play Wily Halliday better.'

It mollified him somewhat. And she was right, he thought, it was undoubtedly his best performance to date. And he'd cut down a lot on the coke and the party pills. But Jesus, he cursed inwardly, that guy Thackeray was a pain in the ass.

With the departure of Mickey, the filming concentrated upon the love affair between Wily and Sarah, and Sam, as always, was eager for Jason's opinion.

'What do you think of Brett?' she asked as they sat apart from the others, having a pre-dinner drink, Brett scowling at them from across the hotel lounge.

'He seems nice enough.' Jason, like everyone else, thought Brett Marsdon was a spoilt brat.

'No, I mean his performance.'

'Well, I'm hardly an expert,' he said, amused that she should ask, then he realised that she was seriously seeking his opinion. 'I think he's an excellent actor, and he's certainly good-looking.'

'But is he Wolf Baker? I mean is Wily Halliday Wolf Baker?'

Jason gave one of his loud hoots of laughter. 'Good heavens above, Sam, Wolf Baker must have been in his sixties when I met him, and I was ten years old. How on earth would I know?'

She looked so disappointed that he felt he'd let her down. She was always intense when she discussed her work, which was probably why she was such a good actress, he thought, but her intensity sometimes seemed at odds with the girl she really was. Jason thought that he'd never met a young woman so relaxed and free of self-consciousness as Samantha Lindsay.

He didn't like to disappoint her, and he looked across the room at Brett, trying to formulate an opinion, but Brett had heard his laughter and was once again glowering in their direction. The spoilt brat, no answers there, Jason thought.

'He's very different in front of the camera,' he said.

'Yes, he is, isn't he?' She was leaning forward eagerly, aware that he was giving some consideration to her query now.

Jason recalled the day's filming. There had been a strong chemistry between the two of them. It had been completely believable that a woman like Sarah Blackston was attracted by the boyish cheeky charm of Wily Halliday. Could it have been that way between his grandmother and Wolf Baker? He remembered the easy assurance of Wolf Baker's manner and the air of success that he'd worn like a mantle. Would Wily Halliday be like that as an older man? It was eminently possible.

'I think it's quite likely that Wolf Baker was similar to Wily Halliday,' he said.

'Do you think so?' Her face split into the widest grin. 'Do you really, really think so?'

'I really, really do.' He shook his head, bemused. 'It's strange, isn't it, this movie business? If you think about things hard enough, fact and fiction can become quite blurred.'

'Yes!' she exclaimed, punching the air in her enthusiasm. 'That's what makes it so exciting.'

Over the next several days, Jason began to feel strangely uncomfortable watching the love scenes between Sam and Brett. He wasn't sure why; probably just self-consciousness, he thought. Then the morning loomed when they were to shoot in a closed set.

'What does that mean? A closed set?' he asked Sam the night before the shoot.

'We're doing the sex scenes tomorrow. There're only two in the whole film, and they're very tasteful.' Sam had no inhibitions at all about working naked; she'd done so on stage in two previous productions. The scenes were not gratuitous; they were imperative to the script and she had total trust in Simon's direction.

'Oh.' Jason was taken aback.

'Simon's quite happy for you to be there, though. So long as Brett and I don't mind, of course. I've checked it out with Brett, and he doesn't care.'

Brett had actually liked the idea of Jason being on set. 'Might give him a few ideas about how it's done,' he'd said petulantly, 'the guy's a loser.' Sam had ignored the remark.

'No, no,' Jason said hastily, 'I think I'll give it a miss.'

'Oh don't be such a prude.' She grinned reassuringly; she'd forgotten how new he was to the film business. 'It's only acting and I get to keep my knickers on. No simulated sex, I promise you, just a lot of kissing and heavy breathing. It'll probably be difficult to keep a straight face.'

But he didn't return her grin. 'No, I'll sit this one out, if you don't mind.'

'Oh hell.' The reason for his reluctance suddenly occurred to her. How shockingly crass she'd been. He had always associated the filming with his grandmother – when the cameras were rolling she was Jane Thackeray. 'I'm sorry, Jason, I wasn't thinking. I'm really, really sorry.'

'For what?'

'Well . . .' she said awkwardly. 'Your grandmother . . . a sex scene . . . I'm sorry, how tacky of me.'

'Oh for God's sake, Samantha, it has nothing whatsoever to do with my grandmother.'

Sam was startled; he sounded quite snappy.

'Why then? What's wrong?'

'I'm a prude, that's all. You said it, I'm a prude. The others are going into dinner, let's join them before Brett has some form of fit.'

Jason knew he'd been terse, but he also knew, very suddenly, that the portrayal of his grandmother was no longer of paramount importance. It wasn't his grandmother he was in love with. It was Samantha Lindsay. His instinctively 'prudish' reaction had shocked him with the truth. He simply did not wish to see the woman he loved half naked in bed with another man, and his annoyance, he realised, lay in the fact that she didn't recognise that.

'We were great, Sam. The A team.' Brett gave her the thumbs up. The sex scenes had gone very well, he thought. Pity the doctor hadn't been there, he'd been looking forward to that. I'm the one who's in bed with her, buddy, he'd have thought, not you, and you never will be. Doc Thackeray didn't stand a chance, Sam's only interest in the guy was research.

'Yep,' Sam agreed, 'the A team.' The scenes had gone well, she thought, although she was becoming just a little weary of

Brett's constant need for assurance. It was a pity Brett Marsdon had so little real confidence in himself as an actor and a man, she thought. She was glad now that Jason hadn't been on set. He would have been a distraction, and she supposed that she shouldn't have asked him in the first place.

Simon Scanlon had coaxed the perfect performance out of Brett, who now trusted him implicitly, just as Sam did.

'It's an awakening, Brett,' he'd said from the outset when he'd realised the standard stud performance was about to take over. 'A gentle awakening. You love her, you're tender, and she is sexually awakened. You're the one who makes this happen.'

It made sense to Brett. He had the power. And he gave every bit of tenderness he could, whilst Simon, unbeknownst to him, kept the camera trained on Sam.

'So how did it go?' Jason asked when he met her in the hotel foyer. He'd spent the day playing eighteen holes with Louis Durand at the golf course not far from the Mele Bay film location. The two men got on extremely well, communicating more often than not in Louis's mother tongue. Jason, brought up in Vanuatu, where English and French remained the two principal languages, was bilingual.

'It went very well, thank you,' she said coolly. She hadn't forgotten how snappy he'd been last night and she wasn't going to offer any details about the day's filming. She was going to wait for him to ask.

But he didn't. 'Louis tells me you're not called tomorrow. Do you want to go for a drive?'

She hesitated. Tomorrow was Louis's last day on location. They were shooting the confrontation scene and the fight sequence between Wily Halliday and Phillipe Macon. A pivotal scene, it would show the defeat and subsequent downfall of the plantation owner who had pursued Sarah Blackston following the death of her husband. Sam had intended going out to Undine Bay to watch the shoot.

'All right,' she said, aware that her hesitation had lasted for all of two seconds. A drive sounded fun, and she could do with a Brett-free day, she decided.

'Where are we going?' she asked, the following morning. She noticed that he'd loaded flippers and snorkels into the boot of the car, and he'd told her to bring her bathing costume.

'Have you done any of the tourist stuff?'

'No, there's been no time.'

'Thought not. Cascades first then, in you get.'

Cascades, true to its name, was a stream of freshwater rapids that coursed its way down the mountain in a series of falls. On his advice she donned her bathing costume in the change rooms at the car park before they started their trek, and then they set off in their T-shirts and walking shoes, carrying a towel and a bottle of water each.

It was a laborious climb to the top of the mountain, but the scenery was spectacular. The narrow track wound its way through luxurious rainforest to emerge at regular intervals upon the picturesque falls, each culminating in a clear blue pool, the rapids then pursuing a rocky course to the next fall and the next pool. Nature's landscape of terraces was laid out, in all its perfection, down the entire side of the mountain.

They arrived at the top, both sweating profusely. The view was magnificent, Sam thought, sucking the air into her lungs as she looked over the endless sweep of forest that surrounded them. But Jason gave her no time to recover.

'Come on, I need a swim.'

And before she knew it, they were starting the climb down.

The pool was icy and inviting, and Sam swam beneath the waterfall. Holding on to the rock face, she leaned her head back, eyes closed, mouth open, and drank the crystal-clear water.

'It's like swimming in champagne,' she shrieked as she rejoined him.

'I wouldn't know, I've never swum in champagne,' Jason replied in his usual wry manner.

They had a dip in several of the pools, laughing and splashing each other, larking about like children, and then, disappointingly soon, she thought, they were at the bottom of the mountain.

'What an incredible place,' she said, after they'd changed into their clothes and were about to leave. She looked back at the falls and the forest and the first of the rocky pools. 'Absolutely incredible.'

'More to come. I told you we were doing the tourist bit.'

They spent an hour or so at the Botanical Gardens, and then he took her to Hideaway Island. It sat just off the sandy spit in the middle of Mele Bay and she'd seen it often from the film location site.

'It used to be called Mele Island,' he said as they sat in the little open tin ferry that ran like clockwork every few minutes from the island to the sandy spit and then back again.

'Where Godfrey's ashes were scattered.'

'That's right.' He was glad she'd remembered. But he was also glad that, for the first time in his company, she wasn't plying him with questions about his grandmother, that she appeared to simply be enjoying his company.

'Hideaway's about the most popular tourist attraction on Efate these days,' he said, 'apart from the game fishing of course. But it's worth it.'

It was. They donned their flippers and snorkels and joined the other tourists, of whom there were a dozen or so, despite the fact that it was the off season.

Less than twenty metres from the shore, Sam found herself in a fairyland of coral reef teeming with fish of all shapes, sizes and hues. She was surrounded by every colour of the spectrum. It was an underwater paradise.

She swam out beyond the pontoons, which were moored as resting spots, to where the reef dropped away and the water was deeper. The colours were less vivid now, but the fish were bigger. A huge blue groper followed her inquisitively for a while, and then she decided to head back for the shore.

'Oh wow!' she said as she picked her way over the narrow beach of bleached coral to where Jason sat beneath the thatched shade of the restaurant, sipping from a bottle of Tusker. 'Oh wow!' It was all she could manage.

'You're a very good swimmer,' he said.

'I'm Australian.'

They sat amongst the holiday-makers eating poulet fish and drinking Tusker as the clouds gathered and a gentle rain started to fall.

She insisted they have another swim before they left.

'In the rain?' he queried.

'Why not? Frightened you'll get wet?'

The crowd had just returned from filming when Sam and Jason arrived back at the resort in the late afternoon, and Brett was obviously miffed that Sam hadn't come out to the Undine Bay location.

'Where did you get to?' he said. 'I thought you were going to watch the confrontation scene. Hell, it's Louis's last day.'

'We've been to Hideaway Island,' she said with an apologetic glance to Louis.

'You went snorkelling?' Louis asked, his face lighting up. 'It is extraordinary, is it not? So close to the shore! Amazing!' Louis wasn't at all offended. He always took advantage of his days off and he'd visited every tourist spot on the island.

'And we went to the Botanical Gardens and Cascades.'

'Marvellous,' the Frenchman beamed. 'Did you walk to the top?'

'Oh yes, and swam in the pools on the way back down.'

Brett scowled as they chattered on; it was unheard of that they weren't discussing the day's filming, and it was all because of Thackeray. It appeared that Jason Thackeray was more to Sam now than just a source of research, and Brett didn't like it one little bit.

But at dinner that night, as always, the conversation revolved around film, particularly the scenes they'd shot that day, and everyone was very complimentary. There was a series of impromptu speeches, being Louis's last night, and Simon Scanlon announced that the denouement between Wily Halliday and Phillipe Macon had been a triumph. The crew applauded their agreement and Brett, seated beside Louis, basked in the praise.

As soon as Simon sat down, Brett jumped to his feet, eyes bright from the line of coke he'd snorted earlier, and made his own announcement.

Louis Durand, he said, had been his hero for years, and he deemed it a privilege to work with an actor of such stature.

He said it in French, and it went over the heads of most, but when Louis stood and embraced him, there was another round of applause.

The evening continued with much back-slapping and 'au revoir' toasts to Louis, who was leaving Vanuatu the following morning.

Simon Scanlon retired early, as he always did, and Sam said her goodnights not long afterwards. The schedule the following day would be a gruelling one. They would be filming the scenes between Wily and Sarah prior to Wily Halliday's departure on the bombing mission from which he would not return. But she could see that Brett was in full party mode, and decided to give him a gentle reminder.

'Big day tomorrow, Brett,' she whispered, after she'd hugged Louis and wished him a fond farewell.

'Each to their own, babe, each to their own,' he said

with an enigmatic sneer. He could see Jason Thackeray nearby shaking the Frenchman's hand. So he was leaving too. Brett wondered if they were doing it yet. They probably were, and they'd probably be shagging away half the night. What right did *she* have to lecture *him*!

Each to their own? She had no idea what he meant, but he'd obviously snorted a line or popped a pill. He really was his own worst enemy, she thought. Poor Maz would have her work cut out in the morning.

'I didn't know Brett spoke French,' Jason said as he walked her back to her bungalow.

'He's a bit more complicated than he appears,' she said. She had the feeling Jason didn't like Brett much, which was understandable, most of the others didn't either, particularly the crew, but she felt the need to defend the American. 'He's actually insecure underneath all that Hollywood bullshit. What exactly was it that he said about Louis?'

'That Louis Durand was his hero and it was a privilege to work with him.'

'Good on him, he would have meant it too.' They'd arrived at the bungalow. 'He's not a bad bloke really.'

'You're a very nice person, Sam, you know that?'

'Why? Because I stick up for Brett when the others can't stand him?'

'That's part of it.'

She wondered what the other part was, but she didn't ask.

'Gosh, that was a fantastic day, Jason. A really, really *fantastic* day. I loved every bit of it.'

'So did I.'

He kissed her. Very gently, without their bodies touching, just his lips on hers, and for only a moment. So fleeting she hardly had time to register her surprise.

'Good night, Samantha.'

She'd been about to ask him in for a nightcap or a

coffee, but he was already walking briskly down the path, and she felt a bewildering sense of disappointment. Had the kiss meant anything? It had been so brief, so polite, as if he'd simply shaken her hand in bidding her good night. Had their relationship just taken on a new significance, or was she imagining it? Was she perhaps hoping that it had? Sam was very confused as she closed the bungalow door.

Sam didn't see Jason the following day, and she had no time to ponder the subject further. His absence on set was, however, commented upon.

'The good doctor's not fronting up today, I take it?' Brett said when he emerged from the makeup van to join her. She'd been waiting for half an hour whilst Maz did the repair job.

'It would appear not.' She refused to respond to the edge in his voice.

'Goddamn it, how the hell will we cope?'

'Don't be bitchy, Brett,' she said pleasantly.

He took the hint. It wasn't productive to start the day off on a sour note. He gave her one of his special grins.

'Missed you at the party,' he said.

'I didn't know there was one, but you obviously created your own.' She didn't make it a dig and she smiled as she said it.

'Don't I always?' Then he dropped the grin and asked anxiously, 'It doesn't show, does it?'

'No, Brett,' she laughed, 'it doesn't show, you're looking good, really good.' It was amazing, she thought, but he did. Maz, the miracle worker again.

The second assistant director arrived. 'Miss Lindsay, Mr Marsdon, you're required on set.' And the long day began.

Sam was exhausted during the drive back from location. She sat in the front of the Landcruiser with Bob Crawley who chatted on nineteen to the dozen, whilst Brett slept in the back. In the mornings, Bob was very considerate when driving the actors to location; he always kept quiet, knowing they were preparing for their day's work, going over their lines, getting into character. Bob was proud of the way he understood actors. But on the way back, he liked a good chat. Sam, drained, wanted to sit quietly and she wished he'd shut up.

Jason was nowhere in sight when they pulled up at the Crowne Plaza and she made her apologies to Simon and the gang. She wouldn't join them for dinner, she said, she was knackered.

She had a hot shower and ordered room service in her bungalow, half expecting a tap at the door. Then she went to bed early, but, tired as she was, she lay for some time, unable to sleep.

Sam felt a bit down, and she knew why. The feelings Jason evoked in her were unsettling. Was it a relationship she was seeking? After all these years? She'd had the odd affair now and then, but she'd avoided any heavy involvement: her career had always been her first priority.

She chastised herself for overreacting. It was just fatigue, she thought, as she urged herself to go to sleep. Jason was intriguing, certainly, but she had no idea where she stood with the man, he was an enigma. She must stop over-dramatising the situation, she told herself.

The following day, the main unit was relocating to Quoin Hill on the opposite side of the island to shoot the scenes in the POW camp, and they would remain there for a week. The location manager, having decided that the original plan to commute daily from the Crowne Plaza would prove a logistical nightmare, had come up with the perfect solution. On the wild northern coast of Efate, the only accommodation available was the remote and rundown Beachcomber Resort, and he'd booked the entire place out for the week. It would suffice, he said. The film unit would supply their own caterers; all they needed was a roof over their heads, clean beds and decent toilet facilities.

The lonely Australian who ran the Beachcomber had ordered in dozens of crates of Tusker and was eagerly awaiting the film unit's arrival.

The supporting actors, who were to play the prisoners of war befriended by Wily Halliday, arrived from Brisbane that morning, and there was a buzz in the air. It was a lay-off day, the unit wasn't to depart for Quoin Hill until mid-afternoon, and even the tired crew felt a renewed boost of energy, as if they were about to embark upon a new adventure.

The crew of the second unit, who had been busily filming background shots, the ships in Mele Harbour and aerial stunt sequences, were to remain in Port Vila and shoot a montage involving Sam, Elizabeth and the islander extras. The filming was scheduled for two days only, and Brett tried to persuade Sam to come out to Quoin Hill when she was free.

'You'll have a whole five days off, Sam,' he said, 'come and watch the POW stuff.'

It was lunchtime and they were welcoming the new members of the cast with a barbecue lunch by the pool, although clouds were gathering and any minute they'd have to run for cover.

'I'd like to, Brett,' she hedged as gracefully as she could. 'I'll see how I go after we shoot the montage.'

Brett cast daggers in Jason Thackeray's direction. Jason had arrived an hour ago and was chatting to Nick by the barbecue, but Brett had noticed him in earlier conversation with Sam. Something had happened, he thought.

'Yeah, well don't put yourself out, will you?' he muttered, and he left to join his new buddies who were all suitably impressed to be working with a Hollywood star.

Sam had been unable to disguise her pleasure when Jason had arrived, although she'd kept her greeting casual. She hadn't seen him since the night before last, and the kiss, which she'd found so distracting.

'Hello, stranger,' she'd said.

'Fancy a drive after lunch?' His response had been equally casual.

'Great. Will I bring my bathers?'

'Why not?' A look up at the threatening clouds. 'You like swimming in the rain.'

There was nothing at all different in his manner, she noted, not that she'd expected there would be, but she was beginning to think she'd imagined the kiss.

'Why didn't you come out to location yesterday?' She couldn't help asking, although it was none of her business.

He didn't mind. 'I visited some friends. We talked a lot like we always do. I didn't get back until late, everyone had gone to bed. Did you have a good night?'

'Yep,' she nodded brightly, 'had a great night.'

There was a moment's pause and she hoped he wasn't awaiting an account of the evening's events. She'd feel like an idiot saying her 'great night' was a hot shower and room service.

But he wasn't expecting her to say anything at all. 'My friends are very dear to me,' he said. 'They're the reason I come back to Port Vila every year. They were dear to Mamma Jane too, and I thought, perhaps, you might like to meet them.'

Friends of Jane Thackeray's! Did he need to ask? 'Is that where we're going on the drive?' she asked eagerly.

'No, I'd prefer to give them a bit more warning. They'll want to ask us to lunch.'

'I've got five whole days off soon.'

'Good. We'll make it a date then, shall we?' And he'd drifted off to chat to Nick.

Poor Brett, Sam now thought as she watched him at the bar regaling his new friends with Hollywood stories, he thought it was disloyal of her not to want to come to Quoin Hill. And possibly it was. But her loyalties lay in a

different direction. She was about to meet people who had
been dear to Jane Thackeray. People with a link to the
past. Yesteryear was beckoning, and Sam was unable to
resist. She didn't dwell on the fact that she was also
looking forward to Jason's company.

They left for their drive not long after the barbecue,
whilst the others were packing for the trip to Quoin Hill.
It was Sam's idea.

'Hate to be pushy,' she said, 'but why don't we go now?'
She didn't want Brett to see her leaving with Jason – she
could live without the withering looks.

'Sure.'

She'd give her bathers a miss, she decided, it really
wasn't a good day for a swim, and she met him at the car
with her wet-weather Drizabone.

'Good thinking,' he grinned, his own anorak slung over
his shoulder as he waited for her.

The shower that had threatened during lunch had
broken and been brief, but the wind was picking up now,
and darker clouds were rolling in.

'Looks like bad weather,' she said.

'It's always unpredictable this time of year,' he replied.
'If you try to wait for the right moment during the
monsoon season, you could be hanging around for days.
Oh,' it suddenly occurred to him, 'would you rather not
go? You're quite right, there might be a storm.'

'A storm! Hell yes, all the more reason.'

'Good. Tamanu's wonderful in a storm.'

Jason turned the car around and they headed off in the
opposite direction to the one Sam was used to, south-east,
away from Port Vila and the area of Mele Bay which she'd
come to know so well.

'Where did you say we're going?'

'Tamanu Beach Club. A little resort. It's a pity we've had
lunch, the food there's excellent.'

She laughed. 'Don't you think about anything else?' For

someone so lean and fit, Jason seemed obsessed with eating.

He took her remark quite seriously. 'I love good food,' he said. 'Quite frankly I'd rather not eat at all if the food isn't good. It's such a wonderful thing to share, don't you agree?'

'Yes, I suppose so.' Sam hadn't really analysed the social aspect of eating, she just ate when she was hungry, preferably a large steak. Pity they were going to a resort, she thought, she'd have liked to have seen a different aspect of the island.

The rain held off as they drove, but the clouds continued to gather and the sky looked ominous.

'Simon's been very lucky over the past two months,' Jason remarked, 'but his luck could be about to run out.'

'Oh no it's not, it's all going his way.' She smiled in response to his querying look. 'Simon's hoping the weather will be ghastly. He wants the Japanese POW camp to be a quagmire of muck. If there'd been big storms earlier, he would have altered the schedule and shot the POW stuff then.'

'How adaptable of him.'

'That's Simon, he's a genius.'

Tamanu Beach Club was nothing like she'd expected. It was like nothing she'd seen before in her life, and Jason smiled at her astonishment, having registered her reaction when he'd mentioned the word 'resort'.

They'd left the road and driven along a track to a remote part of the island's shore where, scattered amongst the hardy scrub, on a coastline of extraordinary beauty, five small cottages sat. Their tiny verandahs looked out across the sand to where low surf rolled over reefs onto a broad, white coral beach. Three of the cottages were constructed of wood, brightly painted and attractive, the other two were made entirely of coral. The small pieces of uncut coral, in their natural state of varying shapes and sizes, were cemented together, and the result was ornate and unbelievably pretty. Pandanus trees leaned in the wind, and strung between two swayed a hammock. On a grassy mound stood a restaurant, wooden-roofed and open to the elements. Tropical flowers adorned its white-clothed tables and a menu board leaned against a wooden post.

'I've stepped into a picture book,' Sam said. 'This isn't real, it can't be.'

'I thought you'd like it.'

'Understatement of the year!'

He introduced her to his friends who ran the private resort, a middle-aged Dutch couple to whom Sam took an instant liking. Jan was a burly man with twinkling eyes and a beguiling smile; his vivacious wife, Gerry, a strikingly attractive woman of Dutch-Indonesian descent.

Gerry was appalled that Jason hadn't brought Sam to Tamanu to dine. 'You have eaten?' she said with mock horror, although it was three o'clock in the afternoon, and hardly surprising. 'Then you will stay for dinner of course.' She clasped Sam's hand as though they'd been life-long friends. 'And you must stay for the night, it is the off season, we have very few guests, and then you must have eggs benedict in the morning.'

Sam shared a smile with Jason; he was obviously not the only one to whom food and conviviality were inextricably linked.

'I'm afraid we can't,' Jason apologised. 'Sam has a very early call in the morning.'

'A call?' Gerry still maintained her hold on Sam's hand, and in her brown eyes was a look of humorous bewilderment. 'What is this call?'

'It's movie speak,' Sam said, finding the woman utterly engaging.

Jason explained that Sam was playing the lead in the film that was being shot in Port Vila, and Gerry was most impressed.

'You are a movie star! All the more reason for you to stay at Tamanu. Tamanu is the perfect place for movie stars, no-one around to give you all that hassle. Isn't this right, Jan?'

Jan dutifully nodded agreement and gave Sam a wink, which said Gerry was being Gerry, and Sam thought what a wonderful relationship they appeared to have.

'Next time, I promise,' Jason said reassuringly. 'For the moment I've just brought Sam out to show her around,' and before Gerry could get another word in, he added, 'and now we're going for a walk.'

They left Jan and Gerry unfurling the plastic walls of the restaurant in preparation for the storm that was threatening, and, donning their wet-weather gear, they walked up the coast away from the beach club.

The sand soon turned to rocky reef right up to the shoreline, and they left the beach to wander along the well-worn track that wound through the coastal grass and shrubs. After ten minutes or so, they came to a tiny sandy inlet that led into a deep, wide well amongst the rocks, the surf breaking twenty metres beyond, a perfect natural swimming pool.

'I used to come here with my parents when I was a child,' he said. 'It's one of the clearest memories I have of the times we shared.'

They sat on the patch of beach, Sam taking off her sandals and digging her feet into the coarse sand.

'There were no buildings out here at all then, and the road was even worse than it is now, but Dad always indulged us. My mother loved swimming here too,' he added. 'She was like you, an absolute dolphin in the water.' He smiled, breaking off midway through his reminiscence, a little self-conscious. 'You should have brought your costume despite the weather,' he said, 'it's the ideal place for a swim.'

But Sam wasn't interested in swimming. She was

intrigued. It was the first time he'd spoken intimately of his parents. He'd mentioned them that night at Vila Chaumieres, which now seemed so long ago, but only briefly. He'd said that his father had died in an accident and that his mother had left not long afterwards, and then he'd continued with the story of Mamma Jane.

'Tell me about them,' she said, hugging her knees to her chest and leaning forward expectantly.

'Who?'

'Your parents.'

He hesitated. Did she really want to know? She'd only ever been interested in his grandmother, and how the story of Mamma Jane related to Sarah Blackston. But huddled there in the oilskin coat that seemed far too big, eyes wide, fair hair blowing untidily in the breeze, she looked engagingly childlike, and he found her eagerness gratifying. It was he whom she now wanted to know about, and the thought pleased him.

'I worshipped my father,' he said. 'He was a man of principle, everyone respected him, but what I remember most was the fun that we had. To everyone around him, Ron Thackeray was strong, he was a leader, they listened to his opinions, but to me he was like a big kid, full of energy. God, I loved him.' He smiled at his memories as he looked out to sea.

'And your mother?' Sam asked after a moment's pause.

'I barely knew her really. Oh I wanted to, but she didn't seem to have much time for me. All of her life was focussed on my father. I suppose she must have loved him very much.' He shrugged. 'Anyway, she disappeared three months after he died. She didn't say goodbye, and I never saw her again.'

How extraordinary, Sam thought, for a woman to abandon her child like that. 'Weren't you angry?'

'I suppose so, but I think Mamma Jane knew it was going to happen. Not that she ever told me she did, but she prepared me for it. I realised that a long time later.'

'Prepared you? How?'

'My mother told me she was going away for a while, I remember it quite clearly.' He looked out to sea again as he recalled the day, still vivid in his mind. 'She hugged me and said all the right things, that I was to be a good boy for Mamma Jane while she was gone. I believed she'd come back. There was no reason not to. Then Mamma Jane took me on a month's trip to Brisbane and the Gold Coast. I'd never been away from the islands, so it was pretty exciting. I was to go to boarding school in Brisbane when I was twelve, just like my dad had, so she was probably preparing me for that. And she was certainly trying to distract me. I missed my father terribly. It helped, I must say. We had a wonderful time together.

'But when we came home, just before the independence celebrations, my mother was still gone. I was amazed that she wasn't going to be there for the celebrations. Even at that age I knew it was going to be the biggest thing that had ever happened on the island. "Mami's going to miss the party," I said to Mamma Jane. That was all I could think about,' he gave an ironic smile, 'poor Mami, not getting to see the fireworks and everything, typical kid. And that's when Mamma Jane told me. I remember she was quite brutal. "Your mother's never coming back, Jason, and you have to get used to it," those were her exact words.'

'How awful,' Sam breathed.

'Not really, she didn't want me to live with false expectations.' Jason grinned. 'I told you she was tough. I asked if my mother was dead and she said no. She didn't offer any explanation, but she said it was just us now, that we'd have to look after each other. "We're a team, you and me," she said. She'd said the very same thing to me soon after Dad's death, so I think she knew right from the start that my mother would leave.'

Sam was enthralled, but one thing remained a mystery, and she felt compelled to ask. 'When you told me about Wolf Baker and your grandmother, you said that Wolf visited her because he'd heard about your father's death.'

'That's right.'

'But you never said how your father died.' She hoped she wasn't being presumptuous, but he was speaking so openly.

Jason didn't find the query presumptuous, but he paused for a moment's consideration before answering. Would he tell her the truth? Yes, he decided.

'It was a car accident. At least that's what they said. Late at night, he drove off the road, into a tree. A broken neck. His death was instant. I found out later that they said he was drunk, which was strange because according to Mamma Jane, my father rarely drank. But there was grog in the car, and all over him evidently, so they said it was an accidental death. That's how it was recorded anyway.'

'*They* said?'

'Yes, "they". Mamma Jane told me the truth fourteen years later, not long before she died. It wasn't an accident at all: my father was murdered.'

'Murdered?' Sam was shocked. 'Murdered, good God, why? I mean, who? How do you know?'

As if to mirror the drama of Jason's story, the day had turned bleak, and the storm was about to break.

'I think we should be heading back,' he said.

'Oh, I'm sorry.' She'd gone too far, she thought, she'd badgered him with questions and he found her intrusive. 'I didn't mean to pry, really I didn't. I'm terribly sorry, it's just that you were talking so . . .'

Her instant concern was guileless and charming, he thought. 'You're not prying at all,' he laughed, 'I'm enjoying myself, I'm indulging in the past.' He was, he realised. He'd never spoken to anyone as he was now speaking to Sam. 'But the storm's going to break any minute, we'll get drenched.'

'Bugger the storm, I want to get drenched.'

'You'll catch pneumonia and Simon Scanlon will kill me.'

'You don't catch pneumonia when you're wearing a Drizabone, that's what they're for. Go on, Jason.'

But he grabbed her hand and hauled her to her feet instead, and just as he did, a distant bolt of lightning streaked the horizon, flaring across the blackening clouds that rolled overhead.

'Quick! Put your sandals on.'

She did as she was told and together they started sprinting back along the track, Sam still protesting.

'I don't mind getting wet, I want to hear what happened.'

'You won't be able to hear a thing in a minute.'

He was right. They were fifty metres down the track when the storm broke in all its tropical magnificence, swift and ferocious.

They stopped running. What was the point? Beneath their protective clothing, their chests and backs were dry, but the rest of them was drenched.

'It's wonderful!' Sam yelled above the thunder's roar and the crack of the lightning that so brilliantly illuminated the now black sea. She hadn't bothered with the hood of her Drizabone, and she raised her face to the pouring rain.

Jason again grabbed her hand. 'Yes, yes, it's wonderful,' he said, 'come on now, hurry up.'

Fifteen minutes later, back at the beach resort, they dried off, Gerry insisting upon lending them a pair of tracksuit pants each, Jan's swimming on Jason's slim frame quite ridiculously. They drank steaming mugs of coffee and then they left, promising faithfully to return after the two days' filming.

On the slow drive home, over the rhythmic beat of the windscreen wipers, Sam was determined to pick up where they'd left off.

'So what happened?' she asked. 'With your father?'

He didn't regret telling her, but how could he put it succinctly? he wondered. There was someone else who could tell it all so much better. But he would give her the background, he decided. The background that he'd heard from Mamma Jane.

'My father inherited my grandmother's love of the islanders,' he said. 'Well, like Mamma Jane, he was quite simply one of them. He spoke their language, not just Bislama, but several dialects, and he married an islander. Although not from Melanesia,' he added, 'my mother was half Polynesian.'

Sam was surprised. He hadn't told her that before, but it certainly explained his intriguing looks.

'The local authorities, both the French and the English, didn't much approve of my dad. It was the 1970s and the Melanesians were starting to insist they could run their own country. The French, particularly, wanted to maintain some control in the islands after independence, and Dad was too free with his legal advice on how they should go about setting up the new constitution. By the late seventies he was a positive menace.'

Jason swerved to avoid a pothole; the road was treacherous, particularly in this weather. He slowed the car down to a crawl.

'The colonial administration had corrupted many of the local leaders. They'd appointed them as ministers, given them chauffeured cars and servants, and these chaps swanned around in luxury while their own people lived in miserable huts without electricity. The authorities were trying to sneak in a dodgy constitution that wouldn't allow freedom of the press, and would guarantee the corrupt islanders jobs in perpetuity. Dad was very vocal about the whole situation, and there were honest people around who listened to him, so the government couldn't do much about it, except agree to take him on board as a legal adviser in the drawing up of the new constitution.

But there were others who saw him as a very serious threat. Those from the private sector with business interests in the islands wanted to keep the locals in their pocket. So . . .' Jason gave a shrug and avoided another pothole.

'So they killed him?' Sam was surprised by the detached way he spoke of his father's death. It was as if he was talking about a historical figure from the past, she thought, as if there was no personal link.

'Yes, that's right.'

'Who? Do you know?'

'No. But I believe Mamma Jane did. When she told me, just before she died, that my father had been murdered, she said I mustn't live with any bitterness. She said that justice had been done, and his death had been avenged. Which I found rather strange at the time,' he added, 'because Mamma Jane wasn't a vengeful person.'

He glanced at Sam, who was willing him to continue. 'That's about it, I'm afraid. She didn't tell me any more.'

'So you don't know who killed your father, or who avenged his death, or how it was done?'

'Nope.'

Sam was astonished. Why wasn't Jason driven to discover the truth? She certainly would have been.

Jason was aware that his apparent nonchalance surprised her. He was willing to share the whole story with her, but the rest of it wasn't his to tell. She would find out soon enough, he thought.

The storm had abated a little when they got back to the Crowne Plaza, and they went to their respective bungalows to shower and change. That night they dined with the crew members; and the second unit director, an efficient young man called Steve, announced that if the weather hadn't cleared by morning, they'd postpone filming.

Jason walked Sam back to her bungalow, along the path that wound among the coconut trees, the two of them huddled beneath the huge umbrella provided by the resort. The wind had dropped now, and the rain was little more than a steady drizzle.

'If you're not working tomorrow,' he suggested, 'I'll arrange lunch with my friends, shall I?'

'Great, I'd love it.'

She was thoughtful when they arrived at the bungalow door. 'You know, it amazes me that you can be so . . .' she searched for the word '. . . so objective, so detached about everything, Jason.'

'About my father's murder, you mean?'

'Yes. Oh please don't get me wrong,' she hastily added. 'I don't mean to be critical, I'm just surprised.'

'It was twenty-four years ago, Sam, and the past is the past.'

'Yes of course it is.' She shook her head, perplexed. 'I suppose it's being here . . . making this film . . . Somehow the past seems so immediate, so tangible. I feel I'm a part of it.' She smiled apologetically. 'I'm sorry, that sounds silly, doesn't it.'

'It doesn't sound silly at all.' He enjoyed very much sharing his past with her, he thought, but he'd far rather share his future, and beneath the umbrella he leaned down to kiss her.

This time there was no mistaking the kiss for a polite gesture. Their bodies were close, his arm was about her and, as his lips lingered on hers, she returned the kiss. But she was astonished when, as they parted, he handed her the umbrella.

'Good night, Samantha,' he said, and he walked off through the rain.

In the morning, the debris of coconuts that lay scattered about the lawns of the resort was the only evidence that the storm had ever been. The morning was bright and clear and perfect for filming.

They were shooting in an actual village, which was just up the street from the Crowne Plaza. The film unit, for a hefty fee by local standards, had the official permission of the local government, and the village itself was to be well remunerated. The villagers, who would be used as extras, were to receive a cash payment at the end of the day, and everyone was very happy with the arrangement.

The principals' makeup van had accompanied the first unit to Quoin Hill, but Maz had remained in Port Vila to tend to Sam and Elizabeth. She did their makeup and hair at the resort and then, in costume, the women were transported to the nearby village in the Landcruiser.

'Geez, you're a blast from the past, eh?' Bob Crawley was impressed. He was accustomed to seeing Sam in shorts and a T-shirt; she looked quite different in her wig and the 1940s blouse and skirt.

Whilst the crew was setting up for the first shots of the day, Jason arrived. Sam was sitting in one of the canvas director's chairs near the catering truck, which was parked in the street by the wide, muddy drive that led into the village. Elizabeth was chatting to the cameraman nearby.

'When you weren't in the foyer I thought you weren't coming,' Sam said, pleased to see him, remembering last night's kiss.

'Wouldn't miss it for the world.'

Again his manner, so casual, was in no way different, and Sam once more decided that Jason Thackeray was a bloody enigma. He ran hot and cold and she had no idea where she stood.

'Hello, Elizabeth,' Jason called.

'Hello, Jason,' Elizabeth called back, then she returned her attention to the cameraman. She'd been having a steady affair with him since Mickey had left.

A runner arrived with mugs of coffee, and Jason sat in one of the director's chairs.

'How bizarre,' he said, looking up the muddy drive to

the village square where, amongst the squalid huts, the grips were laying camera tracks and the sparkies were rigging lights and reflector boards. 'Today meets yesterday, how truly bizarre.'

'Yes it is, isn't it,' Sam agreed. The director, Steve, had shown her the village square, and the particular hut where they'd be shooting, and she'd commented upon the excellent work of the art department. Although the location was an 'actual', she'd presumed that the set designer's additional dressing had created the authenticity of a 1940s village.

'We didn't add a thing,' Steve had said.

The fact had amazed her, and she told Jason so. 'I can't believe how primitive it is,' she said.

'How long before you're needed?' he asked.

'Oh.' The non sequitur surprised her. 'About twenty minutes, I suppose.'

'Let's go for a walk.'

He took her arm as they picked their way through the mud created by the storm, and they walked into the heart of the village.

The walls of the ramshackle pole huts were principally of corrugated iron that had seen better days, the roofs also, although some were thatched. Hessian was draped over open doorways, and children played in the central square where there were the remnants of a cooking fire.

'Just as it was in my grandmother's day,' Jason said.

They wandered amongst the huts, the children gathering happily around them, several taking Sam's hands, enchanting her with their smiles. Jason chatted in Bislama to the villagers, and Sam, proud that her lessons with Elizabeth had paid off, was able to understand much of what they said, despite the speed with which they said it.

She made a tentative attempt to join in now and then, and the villagers grinned, applauding her efforts even when she got it wrong. It seemed the adults were just as excited as the children that the 'pipol blong filem' had chosen their village.

It was not only the art designer whose labours had proved unnecessary in recreating the past; the costume department had also had it easy. Several villagers had been instructed to divest themselves of their brand-name shoes and logo-emblazoned T-shirts, but for the most part, sloppy shorts, shirts and bare feet or sandals were favoured by the men, and the majority of women wore Mother Hubbard dresses, just as they had in the colonial days.

'How extraordinary,' Sam said to Jason when they finally returned to the caterer's truck. 'It's as if time's stood still.'

'It's also rather shocking, don't you think?'

Yes, she supposed that it was, although the people seemed very happy, she thought. She waited for him to continue.

'This is actually quite a well-to-do village by some standards. A lot of these people are employed at the Crowne Plaza.'

She nodded. Even with her limited Bislama she'd gathered as much from the villagers' conversations. It had surprised her to think that they worked in such modern and opulent surrounds, and then returned to homes so primitive.

'There are many other villages that still don't have electricity or running water,' Jason continued, 'it's a disgrace. The Melanesians remain subjugated, and the corrupt ones amongst them continue to live the life of Riley. My grandmother had hoped that independence would achieve something better, but it actually created a monster worse than colonialism.' In his eyes there was a wealth of anger. 'And it was that monster that killed my father.'

Sam was silent, realising the inadequacy of any response. She also realised that she'd been wrong. Jason Thackeray was far from detached about his father's murder. And about those who had perpetrated it.

The second assistant director appeared, Sam was called to the set and the day's work began. Jason didn't stay to watch the filming and, to Sam's disappointment, he wasn't at the Crowne Plaza upon their return in the late afternoon. She showered and changed, eagerly awaiting his company in the dining room that night, she had so much to tell him.

The day in the village had had a profound effect upon Sam. She had made friends amongst the villagers, particularly the children, who had instantly adopted her. During the filming, the children had been instructed to mill about and call her 'Mamma Black', which they obediently did. But when 'cut' was called and a break was taken, they didn't stop. She continued to be Mamma Black and they displayed even more affection, the little ones vying to climb up on her lap, the others holding her hand or nestling against her. The children adored her, and she adored them in return. It was little wonder, Sam thought, that Jane Thackeray had formed such a bond with these people, and more and more, as the day progressed, she felt as if she had actually *become* Mamma Tack.

She longed to tell Jason what had happened, but he didn't appear that night, he was obviously dining elsewhere. Sam felt rather let down, there was no-one else with whom she could share her feelings.

He arrived on set the second day, however. Work was well under way, and he simply gave her a wave. They were standing by, Steve had not yet called 'action', but the children were already milling about playing with her. 'Action' meant nothing to them. Sam noted that, as Jason watched, his expression, although enigmatic as always, was somehow fond. Fond and distant. He was reminiscing, she thought. Aware of her appearance in full costume and wig, she presumed that he was thinking of the past and his grandmother. She was right, but only to a certain extent.

'Action!' Steve called, and Sam concentrated upon her performance. He was watching Mamma Jane, Jason was thinking. He was a child again, and he was visiting a village with Mamma Jane, watching her whilst she played with the children. He smiled at his indulgence. It wasn't Mamma Jane at all, he reminded himself. It was Samantha Lindsay, the woman he loved. And, very soon, he intended telling her so.

Jason didn't stay long. During a brief break in filming he said to Sam, 'See you at dinner', and disappeared.

At the end of day, the crew packed away the gear, the two-day shoot over. Sam hugged the children one by one.

'Siyu Mamma Black,' they said.

The villagers gathered around, many of them chanting the same farewell, having also taken to calling her 'Mamma Black' when the camera was no longer rolling. She promised them all that she would visit the village again before she returned to Australia.

Less than a week to go, Sam thought. In just six days they'd be heading home for Christmas. There was to be a ten-day break before they shot the final scenes at Fox Studios, and then it would all be over. The past two and half months on location seemed to have flown, and she was already sad at the thought of leaving.

That night, over dinner in the Crowne Plaza dining room, she let it all pour out to Jason. Her feel for the past, her affection for the islanders, her identification with Jane Thackeray.

'I felt as if I *became* her, Jason,' she said. 'As if I actually *became* Mamma Tack!'

He smiled. She hadn't drawn breath for twenty minutes and her meal was congealed on her plate.

'Well, you certainly looked like her,' was all he said.

After dinner, he once again saw her to her bungalow door.

'It's all arranged with my friends,' he said. 'Tomorrow, eleven o'clock, we're invited to lunch.'

'Great.'

She waited for him to kiss her. He did. And this time she sent him the strongest of signals in her response. Then, as they parted, she jumped in quickly.

'Would you like a nightcap?' she asked, and the offer was plainly for far more.

He didn't even hesitate. 'No thanks. I'll see you in the morning.'

'So where are we going?' she enquired as he held the car door open for her. 'I didn't bring my bathers.'

There was a frosty edge to her voice, which didn't seem to bother him.

'You won't need them.'

He climbed into the driver's side. 'You'll like these friends of mine,' he said. 'And I think you'll find out some answers today.' Answers to what? she thought.

'I do pry a lot, don't I?' she said with a touch of irritation.

'Yes, but I don't mind.'

Why did she find his manner patronising? Was it because he made a habit of kissing her and then disappearing into the night? Three times in a row now. And the last time, she couldn't have sent a stronger signal. She found it very insulting.

'Well, it's my job to pry,' she said, 'it's called research. After all, I *am* playing your grandmother.' She sounded scathing, and she meant to.

'I thought this film was only *based* upon my grandmother,' he said with a smile.

She'd been pedantic about the fact often enough, and the realisation that she was being hoisted on her own petard only irritated her all the more.

'Even *based upon* is enough to make it ironic, don't you think?' she said archly.

He realised that she was annoyed because he'd left without accepting her offer of a nightcap and all that it inferred. It was good that she was annoyed, he thought, he needed to be sure of how she felt about him.

'Don't be cross, Sam,' he said gently. He flashed a glance at her and smiled, then returned his eyes to the road ahead. 'There's a reason for everything, and we're just about to close a door on the past. I think that's right, don't you? With the film drawing to a close?'

He looked at her again. Bright green they were this time, she thought, those amazing eyes.

'When we've put the past to rest, we can get on with the future.'

Sam was confused. What was that supposed to mean? What was she supposed to say in response? She was at a loss, but she realised her irritation had completely disappeared.

'So who am I going to meet?' she asked, her interest piqued.

'My dad's best friend,' Jason replied. 'He's a retired school teacher, and he's been like a father to me since I was ten. His name is Pascal Poilama.'

# CHAPTER TWENTY

'Hello, Samantha, Jason's told me all about you.' Pascal Poilama was a good-looking man in his mid to late sixties. Strongly built, with flecks of silver in his close-cropped, steel-grey hair, he was well spoken and his handshake was firm.

'How do you do, Mr Poilama.'

'Pascal, please.' He smiled, the whiteness of his teeth accentuating the deep coal-black of his skin. 'Come in, come in, I've made us some coffee.'

He ushered them into the rear living room of the small weatherboard house. Open doors led out to a porch and a large, pleasantly untidy back yard with a chicken coop and vegetable garden. A hammock was slung between two cabbage palms, and a child's swing hung from the branches of a tree.

'Leia has gone shopping, she'll be back in about an hour, and then the troops will descend upon us for lunch.' He referred to his son and daughter, their respective spouses and his five grandchildren. 'They always do on a Saturday. Marie is coming today too, Jason. She insists upon meeting Samantha.' Pascal's sister, Marie, and her family lived in a village nearby. 'But for the moment we have the place to

ourselves. Do please sit down. How do you take your
coffee?'

They talked briefly about the film, and Pascal was most
interested. 'Jason tells me it's about Mamma Jane,' he said.

'Well, it's *based* upon her,' Sam said, with a smile to
Jason. 'The writer was inspired by the stories he heard of
Mamma Tack.'

'I must say you look very like she did as a young
woman.'

'Do I?'

'Most certainly.'

Sam was pleased. She was also intrigued that Pascal
Poilama referred to Jane Thackeray as 'Mamma Jane'.

'Pascal's parents were very close to my grandmother,'
Jason explained. 'He and my father grew up like brothers.'
He looked expectantly at the older man; he had asked
Pascal to tell Samantha about his father.

'Indeed,' Pascal replied, 'we were as close as any two
brothers could be. We rode, we swam, we canoed together,
everything was a race, as it is with boys.' He smiled at
Sam, and she felt very comfortable in his presence.

'When we were little I often let Ronnie win because he
was three years younger, but he never minded when
he lost. He just accepted that I was bigger and tried harder
next time.'

Pascal sipped at his coffee, happy to oblige Jason as he
reminisced about the past.

'But when we were teenagers, the competition became
not only tougher, it took on a new meaning. We were both
keen to shine in the area which was automatically perceived to be the other's domain. And we did. Ronnie could
handle an outrigger canoe far better than I ever could, and
I beat him at polo every time.' He gave a proud smile.
'Mamma Jane had bought us horses,' he explained, 'which
we kept in a paddock behind her house. She found our
competitiveness very healthy. She said we symbolised the

true equality we should all be fighting to achieve in the islands.'

Sam was finding the old man fascinating, but she wondered where it was all leading.

Pascal laughed delightedly. 'I'm not sure how Mamma Jane justified her equality theory when I was the only islander boy I knew who owned a horse, but in any event, Ronnie and I played our own version of polo and had our own gymkhanas. Ronnie was always the first to raise the bar, and I was always the first to make the successful jump. Again, he never seemed to mind, he just kept raising the bar to impossible heights. But then, that was Ronnie. To Ronnie, nothing was impossible.'

'We remained brothers throughout our lives,' Pascal said, 'and I still called him Ronnie even when we became men.' Once again, he smiled to Sam. 'I was the only one permitted to do so, apart from my mother and Mamma Jane.'

Pascal glanced at the clock on the mantelpiece. There was a great deal to tell, and he decided to get to the point. There would be no chance to talk at all once the hordes arrived.

'Jason tells me you are interested in the truth about Ron Thackeray.'

'The truth?' Sam asked, jarred by the sudden halt in his boyhood reminiscence.

'About his death.'

'Oh! Oh no . . .' She flushed with embarrassment. 'I mean . . . well, it's none of my business.' She darted a look at Jason. How on earth could he have said such a thing? She felt mortified.

'Forgive me, I put that the wrong way,' Pascal apologised, aware of her discomfort. 'It is Jason's wish that I tell you what I told him eight years ago, not long after Mamma Jane's death.'

*'He knows that his father was murdered, Pascal, no*

*more than that. When I am gone, tell him as much of the truth as you dare. Do not endanger yourself.'*

Pascal had questioned why Jason wished to share the past with Samantha Lindsay, and Jason's reply had been simple. 'Because I wish to share my future with her, Pascal, and I want no secrets between us.' To Pascal, a romantic at heart, the reason was a good one.

'I will tell you exactly what I told Jason,' Pascal said to her now, 'no more and no less. Just as Jason has asked me,' he added when Sam seemed about to protest, 'and just as I wish.'

Jason nodded encouragingly at Sam, and she felt her discomfort ease as she sat and listened to Pascal Poilama.

'I was very excited by the prospect of an independent, democratic government,' he said. 'I was a young man in my late thirties, an English teacher, educated when most islanders my age were not. I had a son and a daughter going to school; the world would be a new and wonderful place for them, I thought. Ronnie thought so too, and he inspired me from the outset, as he did many others. He warned us, however, that we islanders must take great care in the choice of our leaders.'

Even as he spoke, Pascal could hear Ron Thackeray.

*'There are already corrupt men who have accepted favours from the French and English to the disadvantage of their own people, Pascal. They will destroy you, divide you, the money will go into the pockets of the corrupt few. You must unite your people, select your political leaders with care.'*

'Members of the private sector disliked him even more than the government. Ronnie was one of the legal advisers in the drawing up of the new constitution, and a number of powerful businessmen were doing all they could to block the new law that only Efate people could own land.'

*'Marat is the ringleader, Pascal, your people must be made aware of that. Through his government contacts,*

*he's placed many islanders who owe him favours in posi-
tions of power. He's negotiating a land deal, with one of
them as figurehead, in order to bypass the new ownership
laws.'*

'Ronnie was perceived as a troublemaker by some of
those who were dictated by self-interest, but no-one
expected such a drastic measure would be taken to silence
him. Homicide is not a common crime in Efate, it never has
been, and certainly not amongst the white population.
When we heard of the car crash everyone believed that his
death was accidental. I believed so myself, as did Mamma
Jane. Until drunkenness was cited as the cause. Ronnie did
not drink. A beer now and then, but never heavy liquor. It
was a serious blunder on the side of those who organised his
death, it raised questions amongst we who knew Ronnie
well. Those questions were never addressed, however, and
the cause of death was reported as accidental.

'But I found out the truth one day not long after. I was
paying a visit to my parents, who were at that time quite
elderly.' Pascal gave a wry smile. 'Well, they were probably
around the same age as I am now, but they seemed elderly
at the time.

'They lived in a village on the outskirts of Vila, and my
father's cousin, a powerful man and one destined for a top
position in the hierarchy of the new government, was with
them when I arrived. I didn't like my father's cousin, he
was one of those who'd sold his own people down the
river, an ex-policeman who lived in a big house and had a
chauffeur-driven car. He rarely visited my father, they had
little in common, and I was interested, so I stood beside
the open door of the hut and listened. My father and my
mother and my father's cousin were talking intensely, they
had no idea I was there. And then I heard the Frenchman's
name.'

'*It was Marat, Savi,*' Pako Kalsaunaka said. '*We had
nothing to do with it, I swear.*'

'Then how do you know?' Sera hissed the question. Savi had remained silent, his elbows on the table, his head in his hands, shocked by the confirmation of Ron Thackeray's murder.

'I heard them boasting about it. Three of them. Out at Marat's property, full of kava, how they'd doused the car with whisky and how they'd poured more whisky down his throat after they'd broken his neck.'

A low moan emanated from Savi.

'Just dumb workers, that's all, he'd paid them a year's wages each, they had no real idea what they were doing.'

'Everyone knows what they are doing when they kill a man, Pako,' Sera said with loathing. 'So what do you propose to do about it?'

'I can do nothing, you know that.'

She had thought as much. Pako, for all his newfound power, would not risk his position and the promise of a bright new future. 'Then why did you come here? Why did you tell us?'

'Because I want you to know the truth, that we were not involved. Those I work with had no idea of Marat's plans.' Pako stood. 'I came also to warn you that you must look to Pascal. He has a big mouth, and I worry for him.'

Savi lifted his head from his hands and looked up at his cousin. It was the first time he had spoken.

'Is that a threat, Pako?'

'No.' Pako realised, possibly for the first time, the huge gulf that now existed between them. He did not rejoice in the death of Ron Thackeray, and it saddened him that his cousin suspected he did. 'But we are family, Savi, and Marat is a man to fear. Look to your son. Warn him.'

'I kept well out of sight as my father's cousin left the hut. And when he'd gone I confronted my father. I told him I'd overheard everything. I told him we must denounce the Frenchman to the authorities. I was outraged when he disagreed.'

'We cannot, Pascal. We cannot do that.'

'For God's sake, Papa, this is Mamma Jane's son! Ronnie was my brother! Marat must be brought to justice!'

Even Sera, who longed to agree with her son, could see the hopelessness of such an action. 'And what would we tell them, Pascal? That we heard a rumour that some of Marat's workers killed Ronnie? Even if we could persuade one of them to talk, Marat would deny everything. He would say he was not responsible for his labourers gone mad on kava. Savi is right, there is nothing we can do.'

'Then I'll go to the authorities on my own.'

'You will not, Pascal.' Savi rose from the table. 'Educated as you are, do not forget that you are still one of us. If Marat can kill Ron Thackeray with such ease, do you think he will hesitate at killing you? You're just another black to him.'

Pascal shook his head in resignation. 'I loved my father. Very much. But he was a man of the past, one who had spent his whole life serving colonial masters. I remember, when I was an arrogant young man, little more than a teenager, I perceived him as weak. I was wrong, Mamma Jane told me so, and I believed her.'

'Your father is one of the bravest men I know, you must never forget that, Pascal.'

Mamma Jane's tone was harsh, and he was aware that he was being put in his place.

'You mistake conformity for weakness. Your father has led a careful life. A life dedicated to his family's welfare. It takes true courage for such a man to throw caution to the winds and risk everything.'

Mamma Jane's eyes seemed to bore into his skull.

'Savi did that. And he did it for me. Do you have any recall of that day, Pascal?'

A fight. His father and the Bos. Yes, Pascal could vaguely remember it. He didn't know what it had been

*about, but he'd grabbed Ronnie's hand and headed for the
kitchen where they'd hidden under the table.*

'You were five years old at the time,' Jane prompted.

'Yes, I remember.' *That was when they'd left the plantation, he recalled. They'd come to the village and lived with
his mother's family until they'd built a hut of their own.
He'd virtually forgotten until now.* 'I remember, Mamma
Jane.'

'Good.' *She signalled the end of the conversation.* 'You
are one of a new breed, Pascal, and I'm proud of you, but
never forget that your father is a very brave man.'

'My father was not weak, but he was cautious by
nature, and I couldn't bring myself to trust in his judgement. To simply do nothing about Ronnie's murder was
inconceivable, so I sought advice from the only source
possible. Besides, it was right that she should know the
truth of what had happened. I went to Mamma Jane. She
had known Ronnie's death was no simple car accident, but
she had never considered the possibility of premeditated
murder. Such things didn't happen in Vila.'

'I warned him, Pascal. I warned him that one dark night
they'd set upon him, either the locals full of kava or the
colonials full of drink, and that he'd end up half bashed to
death. I warned him so many times to be careful.'

'Mamma Jane thought that some young bloods had
been out to teach Ronnie a lesson, and things had got out
of hand. That they'd killed him by mistake, then disguised
it, clumsily, to look like an accident. She was shocked
when I told her about the Frenchman.'

'Marat,' *she whispered, the blood draining from her
face.*

'He paid three of his men a year's wages each.'

*So Jean-François had revenged himself at last. After all
these years, and his many attempts to ruin her, he had
finally committed the ultimate act of revenge. He
had murdered her son.*

'*There was a land deal going through. Ronnie's interference was endangering it.*'

No, no, she thought, it was far more than that. *Marat was a sour old man, in his seventies now, withering alone on his property. It was common knowledge that his son, Michel, had no interest in inheriting the plantation. Michel lived with his wealthy wife in Paris, awaiting the death of his father so that he could sell off the property. And Marat knew it. Why would he go to such lengths? Why would he take such risks? Why would he wish to accumulate more wealth for his ingrate of a son? No, Jane thought, Marat had sought personal revenge, knowing that it would be convenient for others to ignore the true circumstances of Ron Thackeray's death.*

'*What should I do, Mamma Jane? Papa says I can do nothing, that Marat will have all the answers and that the authorities won't listen.*'

'*He is right, Pascal, they won't.*'

'*Then tell me how I can avenge his death!*' *Bitterness, frustration and anger gnawed at him. He'd wanted Mamma Jane to have the answers, or at least some plan of attack. Surely, with her influence, he'd thought, they could approach the authorities together, demand an investigation.* '*Tell me, Mamma Jane,*' *he begged,* '*tell me. I can't stand by and let Ronnie's death count for nothing!*'

'*I assure you, Pascal, Ronnie will not have died in vain.*'

*Never had he seen such a look on Mamma Jane's face. Her eyes were hard and her voice cold as ice.*

'*Marat will answer for what he has done. And he will answer to me.*'

'Mamma Jane's advice was the same as my father's. There was no point in going to the authorities, she said. We had no evidence but hearsay, and the Frenchman would deny it all.

'Ah,' Pascal rose from his chair as he heard the front door open. 'Leia is back from her shopping.' He left them, to reappear a moment later, laden with groceries, a pleasant-looking Melanesian woman in her sixties by his side.

'Jason.' Leia held out her arms and the two of them embraced.

Sam rose as Pascal introduced his wife. 'How do you do,' she said, and she was about to shake hands, but Leia embraced her instead.

'Samantha, we've heard so much about you.'

Exactly what Pascal had said. Jason had obviously been talking about her a great deal, Sam thought. Uncharacteristic, surely, for someone who made a habit of kissing and running.

'Are we ready to start on the lunch?' Pascal asked, rubbing his hands together in anticipation. One of the great joys he and his wife shared was the preparation of food.

'Not until I've unpacked the groceries.' Leia took the bags from him. 'I'll give you a call when I'm ready,' she said over her shoulder as she disappeared to the kitchen, leaving the three of them together.

'Why don't you get yourself a beer, Jason?' Pascal suggested. 'It's about that time, isn't it?'

'It certainly is, and I'd love one. How about you, Sam?'

'Oh.' Surely that wasn't the end of the story, Sam thought. 'Yes,' she responded automatically, although she didn't really want a beer at all. 'Thank you.'

Jason fetched a couple of Tuskers from the bar fridge in the corner, while Pascal took two glasses from the dresser. The Poilamas didn't drink but they always kept a healthy supply of alcohol for those visitors who did.

'So what happened?' Sam asked, as she accepted the beer and they all sat once again. Her earlier discomfort at being intrusive was completely forgotten. 'What happened to the Frenchman?'

'God moves in mysterious ways,' Pascal said. 'They

'were Mamma Jane's very words,' he added. 'The Frenchman was discovered only the following day. He'd fallen
from his horse, which was quite extraordinary, because
despite his advancing years, he was renowned for his
horsemanship.'

*'I will confront him, Pascal, and I will make him
account for my son's death. Marat fears the power that I
hold in these islands.'*

'The animal was found in the morning. It had returned
to the house, saddled and riderless, and the workers
mounted a search. It was midday when they discovered
him, he'd been riding in the plantation, as it seemed he
often did. And he'd had a fall.'

*Worried for her safety, he had insisted upon accompa-
nying her, and she had agreed that he drive her to Undine
Bay under the strict proviso that he play no part in the
confrontation.*

*'You must promise me, Pascal.'*

*He promised, knowing that if he did not, she would go
to the plantation alone. At least he would be with her if
there was any trouble.*

*They arrived in the late afternoon, but just before they
turned off the coast track, she made him stop the car.*

*'I will drive from here,' she said. And, when they'd
changed places, she instructed him to keep out of sight. 'It
is better if Marat believes I am alone.'*

*He slunk down low in the passenger seat as Mamma
Jane drove the vehicle up the main drive of Chanson de
Mer.*

*A Melanesian girl was leading a large chestnut gelding
out of the stables, which stood to the right of the house.
The animal was saddled and bridled, and the girl watched
the car's approach with interest as she led the horse to the
hitching post and mounting block twenty metres from
the front verandah.*

*Jane drove to the left, away from the stables and the*

main door of the house, and out of sight of the front
windows. Marat may have already seen the car, but if not,
she would prefer to surprise him. She knew that the girl
was the only other person she was likely to encounter. It
was common knowledge that the Frenchman kept just one
house servant these days, a local village girl who lived with
him in the big house and whom he demeaned in whichever
way he wished. The white overseer, who virtually ran the
plantation, lived with his family in a cottage which Marat
had built for them a good mile away.

'Stay hidden, Pascal,' she said, and when she'd alighted,
he slid out of the driver's side after her, to lie on the ground
beside the car.

She closed the door. 'Do not come to my aid unless it's
absolutely essential,' she instructed. She circled the vehicle
and Pascal, his cheek pressed against the rough grass,
watched from beneath the car's undercarriage as she
approached the girl.

'Allo,' Jane said.

The girl smiled a welcome, she'd recognised Mamma
Tack instantly, everyone knew Mamma Tack. 'Allo
Mamma Tack,' she said.

The girl was pretty, barely out of her teens, but Jane
could see the angry swelling beneath her left eye. She'd
been beaten, as she probably was on a regular basis. Jane
asked her name. It was Mela. They conversed in Bislama.

'Is the Masta inside the big house?' Jane asked.

'Yes, but he will soon go riding in the plantation,' Mela
answered. The gelding stood patiently beside her, reins tied
to the hitching post. 'The Masta always rides at dusk. I
must make the horse ready for him.' She bent and started
struggling with the girth strap, pulling on it with all her
might. 'I can never pull it tight enough to please the
Masta,' she said with a touch of desperation, 'I do not
have the strength.'

Jane put her hand to the girl's face and Mela looked up

*as she felt the soft caress of her fingers. Gently, Jane traced the swelling over her cheekbone.*

'You should go home to your family in the village, Mela,' she said.

The girl felt the quick prickle of tears. She longed to go home, but she was too frightened of the Masta. She had been proud when he had chosen her from the other village girls as his personal servant, but she hated him now. And she could not leave, she was trapped. The Masta would never allow her to go back to the village.

She quickly notched the girth strap in as firmly as she could, then straightened and faced Mamma Tack. She would tell Mamma Tack, and perhaps Mamma Tack could help her get away from the Masta, she thought hopefully. Mamma Tack was the only person who could.

But Mela froze, open-mouthed, a guilty flush suffusing her cheeks as she looked past Jane to the house. She was afraid that he might have read her very thoughts.

Jane turned. Marat was standing on the verandah twenty metres away, riding crop tucked under one arm, the silver-white of his hair a beacon in the late afternoon sunlight.

He'd been watching them for several moments. When he'd stepped out onto the verandah he'd been most surprised to discover Jane Thackeray in conversation with his servant; he'd seen no car arrive. He'd looked about and noted that the vehicle was parked far to the left, out of sight of the front door and windows. It appeared she had come alone.

'Madame Thackeray,' he said, his voice, still strong, still authoritative, 'what a surprise.' She remained a good-looking woman, he thought, yet she must be nearing sixty. No longer slender, her body had thickened, but it only lent her an added strength.

She stared challengingly at him, a power to be reckoned with, and he stared back, aware that he was a commanding *figure himself, as long as he remained motionless. Once he started to walk, his lameness was painfully evident, and he didn't wish her to see his strength so diminished.*

She'd paid little heed to her appearance, he noted, her hair was grey and her face was weathered, but there was no denying Jane Thackeray was a handsome woman. He hated her for it. He hated everything about her. He would far rather have killed her than her son, if he could have got away with it.

'To what do I owe this great honour?' he asked.

'I want to talk to you, Marat.'

'Marat?' he queried, his eyebrows raised in mockery. 'How very uncivil of you, Jane. Whatever happened to Jean-François?'

Jane strode the twenty metres that divided them and looked up at him where he stood on the verandah.

'I know that you killed my son!'

It came as a surprise, although he refused to be alarmed. How did she know? he wondered. Who had dared talk? It must have been one of those dumb blacks he'd hired. He'd paid them a year's wages for their deed and their silence, and yet one of them had run to his best friend Mamma Tack. Whichever black bastard was responsible would be whipped to within an inch of his miserable life, Marat thought.

'What a quaint notion, Jane. Wherever did you hear such a rumour?' She obviously had no proof, or she would have gone to the authorities.

'Several of your workers were heard boasting, full of kava, they were quite specific about the details.'

'So that's your proof, is it? A few blacks, mad on kava telling slanderous stories about their master?' She could do nothing, he told himself, but her manner was confronting, and he didn't like it.

'Now come along, Jane,' he tried to sound reasonable, although he would rather have taken his riding crop to her.

*He would have liked to slash that handsome face to a pulp. 'You know as well as I that I am not popular with my workers. I have never tried to be. They're lazy, all of them, it's in their blood. They need to be ruled by a strong hand if one is to get any work out of them. And they don't like my methods, so this slander is their way of getting back at me. Surely you can see that.'*

*Jane had fought to keep herself in check. She had intended to bargain with him, to blackmail him into agreeing to her terms. But the reasoning tone of his voice suddenly angered her beyond measure. 'You killed my son, you murderous bastard! And you'll pay for it!'*

*Her anger ignited his, and he dropped any pretence of civility. 'Just how will I pay?' he snarled. 'Who's going to listen to a bunch of drunken savages? Get off my property, you're trespassing. Go back to your black friends, bitch.'*

*Marat turned away and started towards the front door.*

*Mela, standing beside the mounting block, holding the chestnut's bridle, was worried and confused. She hadn't understood what the Masta and Mamma Tack had said, but she knew they were angry, and the Masta was about to go inside the house. Did that mean he wasn't riding today? Should she unsaddle the horse? Then she saw Mamma Tack race up onto the verandah and bar the Masta from the front door.*

*Marat's arthritic left hip rendered him virtually crippled, and Jane was too quick for him. In several swift strides she was up the verandah steps and between him and his escape.*

*'Get out of my way, woman.' He slashed at her with his riding crop, but she dodged easily to one side and, unbalanced, he staggered and almost fell, clutching at the nearby windowsill to save himself.*

*'You're not going to escape me, you evil bastard, you're going to answer for what you've done.' Jane had never felt such rage.*

*Pascal had crept from the car to the side of the house and, crouching low, he peered through the railings at the far end of the verandah. He was tempted to run to Mamma Jane's assistance. But he knew she would be angry if he did. The old man was feeble in his lameness and Mamma Jane had the situation under control.*

'You listen to me, Marat,' she hissed. 'I will not have my son die for no purpose. You will do as I say, or I will go to the authorities and expose you for the cold-blooded killer you are.'

'And who's going to listen, you stupid woman!' he roared. God, how he wanted to kill her. 'You have no proof!' He had to get away from her. He tried for the door again, but again she barred his way, and he didn't dare attempt to push her aside bodily for fear of falling. He wished he had his walking cane, but he never used his cane on the short distance from the house to the mounting block.

'Oh, but people do listen to me, Jean-François,' she said, the use of his Christian name vitriolic and mocking. 'Believe me, they listen. I am Mamma Tack, remember?'

Of course he remembered. She'd said that to him once before, all those years ago. She'd flaunted the weight of her ridiculous title, and it had worked then. It wasn't going to work this time.

'Mamma Tack!' he spat the name back at her. 'Mamma Tack? You're nothing but a whore and a nigger-lover.'

'Better a nigger-lover than a nigger-killer, Marat!' She screamed out the words. Her rage had turned to sheer hatred now. She'd never before experienced hatred, and she wanted to kill him with her bare hands.

'You've plundered and killed and raped these people for years, and you'll pay for it!'

He swung at her again with the riding crop. She grabbed it with both hands, and they struggled in a mad dance for possession, Marat's superior strength eventually throwing her aside, but again he nearly fell as he did so.

Behind the verandah railings, Pascal remained poised to run to her assistance, but something stopped him. It was the hatred he was witnessing in Mamma Jane's rage. Never had he thought to see hatred in Mamma Jane, and the power of it rendered him frozen.

Marat made his way clumsily towards the verandah steps. He had to get away from her madness, he had to get in the saddle. On the ground he was a cripple, but on horseback he was as strong as he had ever been. Keeping a firm hold on the railing, he took each step one at a time, cursing his infirmity.

Jane fought to control the insanity of her anger. She had come here with the intention to bargain, she must not let her hatred deter her from her purpose. She followed him, right by his side, worrying at him like a cattle dog would a recalcitrant bull. She must corner him, she must make him realise there was no alternative but to agree to her demands.

'There's a way you can save yourself, Marat,' she said, her voice still trembling with the rage she now battled to curb. 'I won't go to the authorities if you do as I say.'

He was barely listening as he started on the twenty-metre walk to his horse, his lame leg swinging out to the side on each alternate step, a clumsy, comical gait, his hip aching with the effort.

'Stop trying to block the new land ownership laws. Call off the others who are doing the same. You know that they'll listen to you, they'll do whatever you say.'

Mela watched their approach, terrified for Mamma Tack. She didn't know what Mamma Tack was saying, but no-one stood up to the Masta the way Mamma Tack was doing. The Masta could kill Mamma Tack. Mela's hands were shaking as she untied the reins from the hitching post and held onto the cheekstraps of the horse's bridle.

'Stop interfering with the rights of the islanders,' Jane continued relentlessly, encouraged by Marat's silence, *convinced she was getting through to him. 'Stop paying bribes to the officials you've put in power,' she demanded. 'And call off the others who are corrupting them too.'*

*But Marat wasn't listening. He was at the mounting block now.*

*Mela cringed in anticipation, worried for herself as well as Mamma Tack. The Masta was about to check the girth strap.*

*Stupid black bitch, Marat thought, as he pulled the strap a notch tighter. He would have given her a backhander but there wasn't time, he had to get in the saddle so that he could take command. On horseback he'd be able to deal with the demented woman who was driving him mad.*

*Mela held tight to the bridle whilst the Masta stepped up onto the mounting block. Obedient and well-trained as the chestnut was, if the horse made the slightest movement, the Masta got very angry.*

*His left hand upon the pommel of the saddle, Marat put his right hand beneath his knee and lifted his lame left leg into the stirrup, pain screaming through his hip.*

*'If you promise to do this, Marat, if you promise to stop impeding the progress of the new government . . .'*

*Jane Thackeray was continuing to harangue him, but he was nearly there now.*

*'. . . then I promise that I'll tell no-one you murdered my son.' It was what Ronnie would have wanted, she thought as she watched the Frenchman feebly attempt to mount his horse. Her son would not have died in vain. 'Do we have an understanding, Marat?' she demanded. 'It's your only way out, I swear it. Otherwise you'll answer to a murder charge.'*

*He heaved himself up, swinging his right leg over the horse's body with ease and, once in the saddle, the pain was gone. Mela fed him the reins and he gathered the horse in. He was beyond Jane Thackeray's power now, no longer a cripple.*

'You don't dictate to me, bitch! Get off my property!' He lashed out with the riding crop, landing a stinging blow across her shoulder, frightening the chestnut, which shied to one side. He swung the crop again, missing her this time, but alarming the horse further, the animal prancing on the spot, tossing its head. 'Get off my property right now, you nigger-lover!'

Jane's hatred returned with a vengeance. She had thought that she'd worn him down. She'd taken his silence as defeat, admission that he would agree to her demands. She lunged for the animal's bridle, grasping the ring of the bit firmly in her hand, balling her fingers into a fist around it, her rage once more insane.

'You'll answer for everything, Marat!' she yelled. 'You'll answer for my son's death, and you'll answer for your crimes against these people.' She was strong, and the chestnut obeyed the hand that held the ring of the bit in its mouth. It stopped prancing and tossing its head.

Marat cursed the gelding. He wished he was on the black stallion – the stallion would have trampled the bitch to death – but he didn't dare ride the stallion these days.

'Get away, you mad bitch!'

He ripped hard on the reins. The bit dug cruelly into the animal's mouth and as its head jerked up Jane was nearly pulled off her feet, but she hung on.

'You're a cancer to these islands, and you'll pay for it!' she yelled.

He lashed at her again and again with the crop. Pascal raced from behind the verandah railings. Mela screamed at the sight of the Masta beating Mamma Tack.

'No, Masta, no!' she wailed hysterically.

'You think you can beat me into submission the way you do her?' Jane hung onto the bridle with all of her strength as she felt the lash of the crop across her shoulders. 'You'll have to kill me first, Marat, it's the only way you'll be free of me!'

The horse, in pain and confused, circled on the spot, dragging Jane with it, whilst Marat continued to beat at her.

'I'll kill you all right, bitch, you can be sure of that!' As he slashed at her, he pulled the horse's head still higher, the animal's neck arched, its mouth open, its teeth bared.

The chestnut was terrified now. It screamed, a shrill whinny of fear, and then reared, hooves pawing wildly at the air. Jane felt her shoulder nearly pulled from its socket as the ring of the bit was ripped out of her hand. Then she was on the ground, Pascal beside her, dragging her away.

The horse seemed to freeze for a moment, poised on hind legs, forelegs extended, majestic in its terror, and Marat felt himself falling. As if in slow motion to start with, all he could see was sky, then everything spun crazily about him and the mounting block loomed before his eyes.

The chestnut's hooves crashed to the ground, narrowly missing Jane as Pascal dragged her clear, and the animal shied away from them, tossing its head, its mouth ripped by the bit, its eyeballs rolling in fear.

Pascal helped her to her feet and together they inspected Marat, Jane kneeling to feel for the man's pulse. He was dead. There was blood on the mounting block where he'd struck his head, but the wound was not the cause of his death.

'His neck is broken,' she said.

They were silent as their eyes met, both registering the significance. Ronnie's neck had been broken too.

'You must go for the police, Pascal.' She stood. 'I will stay here with Mela.' She put a comforting arm around the girl whose eyes were rolling fearfully, just like the chestnut's.

But Pascal made no move. 'There is no need for the police. I will take Marat into the plantation, it will look like an accident, that way there will be no investigation.' She hesitated, and again he insisted. 'There is no need for the police, Mamma Jane. Justice has been done.'

Jane agreed that justice had indeed been served upon the Frenchman, and she felt no remorse for the part she had played in his death. But there were complications to the simplicity of Pascal's plan.

'Mela is a witness,' she said.

'Mela saw nothing.' Pascal spoke to the girl in Bislama. 'The Masta is dead, Mela,' he said, and the girl nodded. The Masta certainly looked dead. With *Mamma Tack's* arm about her, Mela's fear had subsided.

'You do not wish Mamma Tack to get into trouble, do you?'

Mela shook her head vehemently.

'The Masta fell from his horse while he was out riding, Mela. You saw nothing.'

Mela nodded. 'I saw nothing,' she said, and she turned to Jane. 'I saw nothing, Mamma Tack.'

Jane looked at Pascal for a moment, then nodded.

Pascal calmed the chestnut, speaking soothingly to it and stroking its quivering neck, and when the horse was pacified, Mela held the reins whilst he heaved the body of the Frenchman over the pommel of the saddle.

He mounted the horse and, aware that the animal's mouth had been damaged, he barely used the reins as he rode towards the plantation. They were unnecessary anyway: the chestnut was a well-trained animal and responded excellently to the merest pressure of his knees.

Uninstructed, Mela fetched a bucket of water and a scrubbing brush and set about cleaning the blood from the mounting block. Jane watched in amazement as she scrubbed away, chatting happily.

She would go back to the village, she said, just like Mamma Tack had told her she should; she was free again now that the Masta was gone. She would find a nice young man, there were many in the village, and she would get married and have babies.

Mela was glad that Mamma Tack had killed the Masta

*and she was honoured to be playing her part in it all. She would boast of it to her family when she got back to the village. They would share in the secret and rejoice in the Masta's death. And when she had babies, she would tell them the story too. She would become a hero.*

*It was nearly dusk when Pascal returned. Carefully, he washed the offside shoulder of the horse, which was stained with the blood that had dripped from Marat's head wound. He would have liked to have loosened the girth belt, knowing it would cause the animal some discomfort being strapped tight throughout the night, but he dared not.*

*'You must not go home to the village tonight,' he said to Mela. 'You must stay here until they find the horse and send out a search party for the Masta. And you must be here when they return with his body.'*

*'I know what I must do,' Mela said with a hint of irritation. She didn't need his instruction, she was fully aware of the part she must play, and she was looking forward to it.*

*During the drive back to town Jane was silent. The situation had been taken out of her hands, it seemed. The islanders were her allies in crime, and she felt no guilt. They were rid of their enemy and her son's death had been avenged.*

*'God moves in mysterious ways, Pascal,' was all she said.*

'Investigation proved there were no suspicious circumstances,' Pascal continued. 'The Frenchman had been riding at dusk, it was presumed that something scared his horse, it shied, and he fell. Death was instantaneous, according to the report. Just like Ronnie, his neck was broken. Extraordinary, don't you agree?'

'Ready to start on lunch?' Leia popped her head around the door, and Pascal jumped to his feet.

'Can I help?' Sam asked, rising from her chair.

'Don't even think about it,' Jason interrupted before Pascal could reply. 'No-one's allowed near the kitchen when those two are cooking. We'll do the washing up.'

Pascal smiled. 'Help yourselves to another beer,' he said before he disappeared.

'What an amazing story.' Sam declined the Tusker Jason offered; she'd barely touched the first one. 'The coincidence of the Frenchman dying accidentally like that, Pascal's right, it's quite extraordinary.'

'The coincidence of the broken neck is extraordinary, I agree,' Jason said as they again sat. 'But the rest of it isn't.'

Sam was puzzled by his enigmatic remark, but he was quick to explain. Leaning forward, elbows on knees, beer glass clasped in both hands, he spoke quietly, conspiratorially.

'You notice that Pascal never mentioned the Frenchman by name?'

She nodded, the omission had been patently obvious.

'That's because he was a well-known tyrant in these parts for decades, and even now, to accuse him of murder would be unwise. There are powerful people in Efate to whom the name Marat still means something.'

'Marat!' Sam lowered her voice to match his, but her reaction was one of astonishment. 'The Marat plantation we used on location?'

'The very same. Jean-François Marat was his name.'

'Pascal told you it was Marat who murdered your father?'

'No. Not in so many words, but he's aware that I know. There are some things which are never mentioned between us. He's told me no more than he's told you, but it's understood that I know it was Marat. It's also understood that I know Marat's death was no accident. Pascal actually told me the Frenchman was killed, but he never said how, or by whom.'

He sipped at his beer, aware that she was waiting breathlessly for him to continue. 'He told me years ago that the islanders will never betray the Frenchman's killer.

It seems that many know who it was, but Pascal says they will not betray one of their own.'

Jason had never thought he would hear himself say the words out loud, but then he had never thought he would meet someone who meant as much to him as Sam, and it was important that she should know the truth.

'It was Pascal who killed Marat, I'm sure of it. I have no idea how he did it, and he'll never tell me, just as I'll never ask him. But he knows that I've guessed it was him.'

He put the beer glass down on the coffee table. 'The other day, when we were talking about my father on the drive back from Tamanu Beach, I couldn't tell you the truth. The story is Pascal's, it had to come from him.' Jason glanced in the direction of the kitchen. 'And right now he's aware that I'm telling you what I know. He hasn't said anything to me, but I have his permission.'

'Why?' Sam asked. She was puzzled. 'Why is it so important to you that I should know the truth of what happened?'

He wouldn't tell her the true reason now, he thought. He'd tell her tomorrow. 'Tying up the loose ends, I suppose.' He gave one of his easy smiles. 'We've shared so much of my family's past, I thought I'd trot out the last of the skeletons. Shall we go to Tamanu tomorrow?'

The abrupt change of conversation caught her off guard.

'We promised Gerry we would,' he prompted. 'Besides, we have to return the tracksuit pants. And then after dinner we can stay the night.'

He was propositioning her, she realised. And so casually. The cottages were designed for lovers; she'd changed into the tracksuit pants in one of them, and was impressed by how unbelievably romantic the room with its canopied double bed was.

The man was a chameleon, Sam thought. One moment he was repelling her obvious invitation, and the next he was openly propositioning her.

Jason smiled, and added reassuringly, as if to put her at her ease, 'It's the off season, you'll be able to have a whole cottage to yourself.'

'That'd be great.' She met his gaze evenly. She didn't want a whole cottage to herself, and he damn well knew it.

Saturday lunch in the Poilama household was rowdy. Pascal's son and daughter arrived with their families, and his sister Marie brought her tribe as well. Marie and her huge husband, Rami Samala, had two sons, both in their thirties, and four grandchildren between them. The Samalas were village people, the brothers fishermen, and they and their wives spoke little English. Bislama was the main language of the day and food was the predominant occupation. The children picnicked out in the back yard and the adults sat around the huge wooden table in the kitchen. The kitchen was the largest room in the house, and obviously the hub of the Poilamas' existence.

The variety of dishes was amazing, a mixture of French and island cuisine, and Leia unashamedly admitted to Sam that it had been Pascal who had taught her how to cook.

'His mother was a professional,' she said. 'I had to become a good cook to keep him.'

'And now she cooks even better than Mama did,' Pascal proudly proclaimed.

Much of the meal they ate with their hands, rolling soused fish up in the marinated leaves of green vegetables, or dipping pieces of chicken into a selection of sauces.

'You see what I mean?' Jason said to Sam, spooning another serve of poulet fish steamed in coconut milk onto his rice. He squeezed fresh lime juice over the top. 'It's a ceremony, food like this,' he said, 'a labour of love.' And Sam found herself agreeing.

During the lunch, Pascal watched the two of them. It was obvious that Jason loved the girl very much, and he wondered if the girl realised that she loved him back. That too was obvious to Pascal.

Jason would have told Samantha what he perceived to be the truth, Pascal thought, and he was glad. It was right that Jason should believe he, Pascal Poilama, had killed Marat. Mamma Jane's secret remained safe amongst the islanders, and they would honour it for the rest of their lives, as would the generations that followed.

They hugged her goodbye when she left, the children with whom she'd been playing in the back yard each vying to be first, then the adults embraced her and shook her hand with affection. She was warmed by their hospitality. It was as if she'd been welcomed into the family, she said to Jason on the drive back to the Crowne Plaza.

'Well they *are* family,' he said. 'They're *my* family. Mine and Mamma Jane's.'

Jason had been amused by the family's reception. He'd told no-one but Pascal of his feelings for Sam, and yet it had been quite obvious that the whole family knew he was in love with her. There were evidently some secrets that Pascal Poilama, an incurable romantic, simply could not keep.

'You will have this one, it is my favourite,' Gerry said as she ushered them into the coral cottage with its brightly coloured furnishings, the canopied four-poster bed the conspicuous main feature.

There was a moment's silence. It was obvious that Gerry had assumed they were lovers. Jason said nothing, but Sam was aware he was looking at her. The decision was hers. She addressed herself directly to Gerry.

'I love it,' she said. 'It's one of the prettiest places I've ever seen.'

'Yes it is pretty, isn't it? Come and look at this.'

She led Sam through the door at the rear into a narrow walled space open to the sky and the palms that towered outside.

'The bathroom,' Gerry beamed, 'no roof, isn't it divine?'

The walls of the bathroom, like those of the cottage, were made entirely of coral, forming an intricate pattern and smelling slightly of the sea, fresh and salty. Sam ran her fingers over them.

'Yes,' she said. 'It's divine.'

They had a light lunch. Jason had warned her. 'Save your appetite for dinner,' he said. 'Jan's told me there's a crowd booked in, it'll probably turn into a party.'

After lunch, they walked down the track to the swimming hole. They swam and sunbaked and then swam again, and, on the way back, Sam collected shells and pieces of coral from the beach.

In the late afternoon, when they returned to the cottage, they were pleasantly tired and, as Sam showered the salt off her body in the open-roofed bathroom, she gazed up at the palms and the blue, blue sky. It was the most romantic place in the world, she thought.

She wrapped a sarong around herself and sat on the verandah whilst Jason showered. She looked beyond the pandanus trees to where the low surf rolled across the reef, and she listened to the sounds of the sea and the palm fronds rustling in the breeze. She was in a Somerset Maugham story, she thought, or maybe a movie, based on a Michener novel. It was surreal and romantic, she was living a dream.

'It's two hours before we need to get ready for dinner.' Jason appeared at the door, a towel around his waist.

She rose and went inside, pulling the door shut behind her, to where the canopied bed beckoned and the filtered light shone through the shutters that he'd closed.

An hour later, she returned to the verandah. They'd dozed off after they'd made love, and he was still sleeping. She'd taken a hibiscus blossom from the arrangement that sat on the coffee table and placed it behind her ear – it seemed only right – and, wrapped in her sarong, she sat looking out at the sunset. The sea and

the rustling palm fronds had a different sound now, a
sound she was part of. She was no longer in a novel, it
wasn't a movie, and it wasn't a dream. She was living in
this very moment, here in this place, a part of it all, and
everything was real.

The sky was slowly flooding with colour, the deepest of
orange fanning out from the horizon to mingle with pinks
and yellows. The door behind her opened and she turned
to him, her face glowing in the rosy light.

'Oh Jason, just look at it.'

He pulled his chair up close beside hers and together, his
arm around her, they watched the sunset. Then he turned
to her.

'I love you, Samantha.'

It was an unemotional statement of fact, and she smiled.
She liked his directness; it was something they shared.
'They're green now,' she said, staring into his eyes.

'I think I've been in love with you from the moment we
first met.'

'You did a good job of hiding it. I found you quite
remote.'

'Yes, many people do, I believe. I've no idea why.'

'I love you too,' she said. The words came out with such
certainty that Sam surprised herself. What a relief it was to
admit it, she realised.

'I rather suspected you did.' He didn't mean to sound
arrogant, but he hastily corrected himself in case she thought
that he had. 'Well, I hoped that you did. That's why I played
the cat and mouse games, I wanted to be sure.' She raised an
eyebrow. 'You were so absorbed in the film and my grandmother, Sam. I needed to find out your feelings for *me*, rather
than my connection with the past. And let's face it,' he
shrugged, 'this film-making business is very . . .' he appeared
to struggle for the right expression '. . . very transient. I
needed to be sure that you wanted more than . . .' He left it
hanging, hoping that she understood. She did.

'A bit of a fling?' It was believable that he could have thought that was all she was after, she supposed, given the way she'd made her intentions so clear the other evening with the invitation for a 'nightcap'.

'Well, yes.'

It was normally all she did have, Sam thought wryly. Flings. This time she wanted much, much more. But she didn't tell him that. She smiled instead.

'So to make sure it was more than just a fling, you brought me to the most romantic place on earth.'

'Yes.'

'It doesn't seem a very wise choice to me, Jason.' She looked about at the exotic setting. 'Tamanu is designed for flings.'

He made no answer, but took his arm from around her and shifted his chair to face hers, his back to the sunset. His face was in shadow now, but he looked very serious, she thought.

'I've been practising medicine in a clinic for some time,' he said, 'in Bournemouth. But I recently left, I didn't enjoy the work, it was too hectic. Not enough time for personal contact with the patients.'

'Oh?' What a strange choice of topic, she thought, when they'd just made love and were watching a perfect sunset.

'Yes. I intend to set up in private practice,' he continued. 'Preferably a small town where I feel I'm really needed. I think Mamma Jane would have liked that.'

'I'm sure she would.'

'I inherited substantial wealth from her, you know. She set up a trust account for me after my father died and it's accumulated quite substantially, plus there are the properties she left me.'

'Good for you, Jason, that's really beaut.' He sounded so extraordinarily formal that she wanted to laugh.

He didn't appear to find her response facetious and continued in earnest. 'There are also some investments that afford a modest income, so I wouldn't be reliant upon my practice as a profit-making concern . . .'

My God, Sam thought, he's proposing, and in full Victorian style.

'. . . I'm thirty-four years old, I've never been married . . .'

'Is this a proposal of marriage?'

He came to a halt. 'Yes,' he said. 'Yes, it is.'

'Shouldn't you be on one knee?'

He recognised her facetiousness this time, but it didn't deter him. He got down on his knee and took her hand in his.

'Will you do me the honour, Samantha? Will you marry me?'

She burst out laughing. 'Oh for goodness sake, Jason, get up.'

He dragged his chair back close beside hers and sat with his arm around her once more.

'You don't have to think about it right now,' he said, 'tomorrow'll be fine.' Then he took her face in his hands and started kissing her gently. On the lips, the nose, her cheeks, her ears, whispering a quiet chant, over and over, 'Say yes, Sam. Say yes, say yes, say yes,' until her laughter subsided, and they went back inside.

They made love again, as naturally and as gloriously as the first time, and Sam didn't need to wait until tomorrow, she knew her answer, and so did he.

The crowd of twelve who'd booked in for dinner arrived from Le Meridien Resort in a mini-bus. They were on a corporate convention, they were in a mood to party, and the several guests staying at Tamanu joined in the festivities, Sam and Jason included. The fairy lights were on, the champagne was flowing, and, following a superb meal, the music blared at full volume and the night turned into a singalong over yet more bottles of wine.

It was around then that Sam and Jason decided to leave. The crowd was fun, but they hungered for each other's company.

'We're off for a walk along the beach,' Jason said, as they bade them good night.

Several of the crowd exchanged knowing looks; it was quite obvious that the young couple were hopelessly in love. Honeymooners probably.

They did walk along the beach, behind them the sounds of the merrymakers and the lights of the restaurant bizarre in the remote surrounds of the rugged coastline.

When they returned to the cottage, they didn't make love; they talked instead. Gerry had left the chilled bottle of champagne in its ice bucket on the table, as Jason had requested, and they sat on the little verandah, the sounds of the party more raucous than ever.

'Tell me about *you*, Sam,' he said. 'I know Samantha Lindsay, the woman and the actress, but I know nothing of your past, and you know all of mine. Which isn't really fair,' he added. 'I want to hear everything. What were you like as a little girl?'

She smiled. He was destined for disappointment, she thought; her past was hardly as fascinating as his. 'I was trouble,' she said. 'I wanted to act from the age of ten.'

She told him all about her childhood in Perth. 'Idyllic, overlooking the river,' she said, 'so beautiful. The Swan River was my playground when I was a kid. Swimming and fishing and crabbing and prawning, everything that kids did in those days, and I'm sure still do.'

She told him about the soap she'd starred in, and her mother's horror that she'd had to go to Sydney. '"Families and Friends" it was called, one of those soaps that idolised youth, and I was past my use-by date at eighteen.'

She told him about her first trip to London when she'd fallen in love with the theatre.

'All I wanted in the world was to star in a play at the

Theatre Royal, Haymarket. And I did,' she said proudly.
'Nine years later. Nora in Henrik Ibsen's *A Doll's House*,
it was the most exciting time of my life. And then I landed
this movie,' she grinned, 'and now *this* is the most exciting
time of my life.'

He leaned forward in his chair and kissed her. It was a
kiss of such tenderness, but it aroused her nonetheless, and
she wanted him to make love to her.

Jason, however, remained in the mood to talk. 'Have
you ever been in love before?' he asked. He wanted to
listen to her all night, to know everything about her.

She reflected for a moment, remembering Pete and the
pantomime at Fareham. 'I thought I had,' she said. 'Just
once. I was quite sure at the time that he was my great
love.'

In the light of the moon, and the soft glow coming
through the shutters from the lamp in the bedroom, she
looked at him. And as she did, she knew that she hadn't
really loved Pete. 'But it was infatuation,' she smiled, 'I
know that now.'

The crowd at the restaurant was leaving, noisily
climbing into the mini-bus. There were a lot of goodbye
yells to Jan and Gerry who were by now exhausted and
quite thankful to see them go, the Tamanu guests having
long since retired to their cottages.

'Tell me about him.'

'There's nothing to tell. I was young, eighteen, I'd had
one minor and very disappointing sexual experience.' She
shrugged. 'I think I was just desperate to find out what it
was like to be in love. Poor Pete,' she said with a rueful
smile, 'I literally threw myself at him. But somehow,' she
added thoughtfully as she recalled Fareham and Chisolm
House and the stables, 'everything around me seemed to
lend itself to romance. I remember it was the first time I'd
seen snow.'

That Christmas Day, it was so clear in her mind. The

view from the loft windows of the stables. The courtyard all clothed in white. The walk to Titchfield, Pete waiting for her when she'd returned. He'd rejected her that night, she remembered.

She broke from her train of thought and scoffed self-consciously, 'Oh really, Jason, you don't want to hear all of this.'

'I do, I do,' he said, enthusiastic, topping up their glasses. He was prepared to listen until dawn. 'I want to know everything about you.' He handed her the champagne. 'Go on, go on,' he urged, 'tell me about Pete, tell me about absolutely everything.'

He was irresistible in his eagerness, she thought. The remote man she'd first met was no longer there. Nor the enigmatic creature who had intrigued and even tantalised her. She was seeing the real Jason Thackeray now. This was the man who loved her, and whom she loved in return. She took a deep breath and started.

'It was my first time out of Australia and I was doing a pantomime in the south of England. *Cinderella* to be exact, and I was playing Cinders.' She gave a theatrical moue; he surely couldn't be interested. 'We were performing in an obscure venue called Ferneham Hall in an obscure place called Fareham. You wouldn't know it, I don't think many people do, but it's a little market town in between Portsmouth and Southampton.'

As she talked, the past flooded back. 'I loved it there,' she said. 'I loved everything about Fareham, its past and its present.' She'd forgotten her self-consciousness now. 'It's so pretty.'

'I agree,' he said. Then, amused by her surprise, he added, 'I visited the place in late 1994, just after Mamma Jane died.'

'Really?' Her look was one of incredulity. 1994, that was when she'd done the pantomime. What a remarkable coincidence, she thought, the two of them might well have been in Fareham at the very same time.

'I wanted to see where she grew up,' Jason explained. 'You're quite right, it's a very pretty town.'

'Jane Thackeray grew up in Fareham?' Sam put the glass down on the small wooden table, her hand felt shaky.

'Oh yes, she often talked about her childhood, and her life there as a young woman. Go on,' he nodded, 'so you met Pete doing the pantomime. Was he an actor?'

'What did she say about her childhood?'

'That it was poor but happy. That she lost her mother at an early age, but she adored her father, that she had a best friend called Phoebe. Go on, Sam, tell me about Pete.'

Jason waited for her to continue her story, but she didn't.

'Phoebe?'

Sam gripped the armrests of her chair. Phoebe Chisolm's friend Jane. She remembered her dream that night. Two young girls, not yet women. And the following day how she'd asked the housekeeper, Mrs M.

*'Did Phoebe Chisolm have a particularly close friend when she was a child? A girl about the same age?'*

*'Oh dear me, yes. Jane Miller.'*

'Her best friend was called Phoebe?'

'Yes, I never knew her last name.' Jason, so accustomed to Sam's obsession with his grandmother, reluctantly accepted the change of topic, although he would far rather have heard about Pete. 'Mamma Jane talked about her a lot. Throughout her life actually. They wrote to each other until the end of the war when Phoebe went to America. I think they lost touch after that, I don't know what happened. But Mamma Jane still talked about her. She said she owed her life to Phoebe.'

Sam remembered how she'd asked the old woman in the park about Jane Miller. Maude, that's right. Maude, who'd visited her during her hallucination that night saying, *'We're a team, you and I, dear.'* Old Maude with the pretty smile.

'*Jane had such lovely fair curls, just like you,*' Maude had said.

And outside the real estate office. She'd asked Jim Lofthouse.

'*What happened to Jane Miller?*'

'*She went to some island in the South Pacific. Nobody heard from her again.*'

The mysterious Jane Miller. Sam realised that her fingernails were digging into the wooden armrests.

'Jane Thackeray's maiden name was Miller, wasn't it.'

It was a statement, not a question, and Jason was surprised. 'How did you know?'

'Your grandmother's best friend was called Phoebe Chisolm.'

Jason suddenly noticed that she looked shaken. He was concerned. 'Are you all right, Sam?'

'Jason.' She clasped his hand, spilling his champagne. He put the glass on the table. 'Jason, I own Phoebe's house where they played as children. I've heard them. Two little girls. Your grandmother and Phoebe. I've heard them.'

The initial shock was receding, and Sam felt lightheaded, even euphoric. It was meant to be, she thought. Some force was at work, everything had been planned. The dreams she'd had, the voices she'd heard, the love that she'd felt in the old house. The house, which she now owned. Mamma Tack, Jane Thackeray, the movie, Jason, it was all meant to be.

The words tumbled out, and she told him everything as clearly as she could remember, each intimate detail of all that she'd experienced. Not only the voices and dreams and Maude, the old woman she'd encountered in the park, but, most important of all, the sensation of the past that she'd felt so strongly in the house.

'It was as though the past and the present were entwined,' she said. Sam was drawn back to their own present, to the rustling leaves of the nearby pandanus trees and the warm, salty breath of the breeze on her face. 'I believe there's a force at work, Jason, a force that's making things happen.'

Jason was surprised that someone as practical as Samantha had embraced the fanciful notion of a supernatural force; it was so out of character for her. Of course she'd been affected by the past, he thought, a modern young woman, an actress with a sense of drama, alone in an old Victorian mansion. But he didn't wish to sound dismissive.

'It's weird, I grant you,' he replied with his customary reserve, 'very weird that you bought the house which belonged to Mamma Jane's friend Phoebe. But it's a freak coincidence, Sam,' he said gently. 'That's all it is. Just a freak coincidence.'

'No it's not.' She was perfectly calm now. 'It's not a co-incidence at all. It's meant to be. Everything's happening by design. You, me, everything. And it's the house that's making it happen.'

He took her hand and they stood. 'Well, if that's the case,' he said as he drew her to him, 'then I'm very, very grateful.' And he kissed her.

'Make love to me, Jason,' she whispered, 'make love to me.'

# CHAPTER TWENTY-ONE

'Hey, Sam!'
The moment Sam walked into the lobby of the Quay Grand with Nick Parslow, Brett swooped on them. He picked her up bodily and whirled her about.

'Nick wouldn't let me come out to the airport. He told me he wanted you all to himself.' He put her down. 'Although why, I have no idea,' he said with a camp moue at Nick. No malice was intended and Nick took none, but he didn't bother responding. Brett Marsdon's heavy-handed humour simply wasn't his style.

'Man, it's great to see you, I've missed you. How was Perth? How are your folks? Did you have a good Christmas?'

Sam laughed. Brett was at his eager-puppy best and she was glad to see him too. 'Yes, I had a fabulous Christmas, thanks. How was yours?'

'The best! Sydney's one cool town, I tell you.'

Sam had spent the ten-day Christmas break in Perth with her family, but Brett had chosen to holiday in Sydney rather than return to the States. He'd never been to Sydney before, and a number of his Hollywood buddies who'd worked there had raved about the place.

'Let's do the bar thing.' He draped an arm around her shoulders and was about to drag her away, ignoring Nick altogether.

'I haven't booked in yet.'

'Later, later.' He waved a hand airily. 'Do that later.'

'You go and grab the best table with a view,' she said firmly, 'and I'll meet you there in ten minutes.'

'You're on,' he agreed. 'A Capriosca, okay? They make the greatest Caprioscas here.'

'Sounds fine.' She had no idea what a Capriosca was.

Nick bowed out of 'the bar thing'; he still found Brett Marsdon a bit much.

'Thanks for picking me up,' she said as she kissed him fondly. 'I'm glad it was just the two of us.'

'Me too. Congratulations, Sam, I'm happy for you, Jason's a really beaut bloke.'

'I agree.'

'See you at the studio tomorrow. Oh,' he turned back, 'and while you're chatting to Mr Hollywood, tell him to cut down on the partying. He hasn't stopped since he got here.' It wasn't a bitchy remark. Nick had realised since their return to Sydney that Brett Marsdon had a serious coke habit and he was surprised that he hadn't twigged earlier. It explained the man's erratic behaviour in Vanuatu, but it worried him. Brett wasn't required for filming until the end of the week but he'd been flying so high his brains would take some time to unscramble. 'It mightn't be a bad idea if he used the next few days to dry out a bit,' he said.

'Why do you think he'd listen to me?' she asked.

'You're the only one he *does* listen to, Sam.'

A 'Capriosca' turned out to be the latest fashion – vodka, fresh limes and sugar syrup, a refreshing drink with a kick in its tail – and Brett was astonished that she'd never heard of it.

'Hey babe, where have you been?'

The taste of the fresh limes reminded her of Vanuatu.

As they started on their second, he cosied up to her, thigh to thigh. 'So tell me, now that the Doc's off the case do I stand a chance?' He gave her the grin his publicist loved best, the furrow-browed one that magazines paid a fortune for, and because she wasn't sure whether or not he was serious, she decided it would be kinder not to laugh.

'I'm afraid the Doc's still very much on the case, Brett.'

'But he's gone back to England. Nick told me.'

'Yep, and I'm meeting him there in a week, after we finish filming.'

'Oh. That serious, huh? Well, we've still got a bit of time up our sleeve. You know?' He wiggled his eyebrows and looked her up and down lustfully. 'While the cat's away . . .'

He was joking, she realised, it was all right to laugh. And she did.

'We were married last week,' she said.

The comedy act stopped. 'You *what*?'

'We were married in Perth. At Christmas.'

'Oh.' He'd known when he'd returned from the POW filming at Quoin Hill that she and the doctor were an item, but he'd thought it was just a location fling. Hell, everyone had them, that's what locations were for, a regular love-fest.

'Married!' He could barely get the word out.

'Yep.'

Sam remembered the morning at Tamanu Beach when they'd lain entwined in each other's arms, discussing their plans.

'I don't believe in long engagements,' he'd said.

'I don't believe in engagements at all,' she'd answered.

Brett seemed in a state of shock, and Sam grinned. 'Married, for better or for worse,' she nodded, 'the whole box and dice.'

The expression on her face as she said it took Brett by surprise. He couldn't remember a time when he'd seen anyone look so completely happy. He wondered what it would be like if, some day, someone looked like that when they spoke about him. He envied Jason Thackeray.

'That's great, Sam,' he said, and he smiled. 'The Doc's a lucky man.'

The smile this time wasn't his publicist's favourite, and Sam thought that the genuine article, which showed just a little too much gum in the publicist's opinion, was infinitely more attractive.

'It's great, really great,' he said. 'I mean it.' He planted a brotherly kiss on her cheek, and eased his thigh away from hers as he raised his glass. 'Here's to you and the Doc then.'

'Thanks, Brett.' It was a pity so many misunderstood Brett Marsdon, she thought, there was a really nice bloke beneath Mr Hollywood. They clinked glasses. 'I could become addicted to these.'

The following morning, in the makeup room at Fox Studios, it felt strange to Sam, looking in the mirror and seeing Sarah Blackston. Over the past ten days the film had been the farthest thing from her mind.

But an hour later, when she entered the vast space of Sound Stage 7, it felt even stranger to be confronted by Huxley House, Sarah's childhood home, the eerie replica of Chisolm House.

During the three months since they'd shot the opening scenes, the set had been dismantled and kept in storage, and it had now been reconstructed for the final moments of the film. It had been a laborious and costly exercise, but Simon Scanlon, ever the perfectionist, had insisted from the outset that the procedure was essential.

'Bugger the expense,' he'd said to the producers who'd wanted to shoot the opening and closing scenes in the first several weeks of studio production. 'We'll make budget cuts elsewhere. The actors'll change on location, it happens every time. The relationship between them will develop, the characters they're playing will broaden . . .' Christ how he hated having to convince the money men of artistic necessity, he'd thought. 'The integrity of the film demands that we shoot in sequence!' He'd won, as usual. And, as usual, he'd been right.

Simon stood beside Sam in the deserted studio and together they looked at the house. He wanted Sam to explore it alone, and he'd ordered the lights up and the set cleared for the purpose. The crew, the other actors and extras were all drinking coffee outside.

'Take a look around, Sam,' he said, 'reacquaint yourself. Sarah has come full circle, she's back in the home of her father that was once so oppressive. But it's not going to be a prison any longer, she's decided. She's a fulfilled woman, she's changed. Take a look around, get the feel of it.' And he left her to it.

Sam did as he instructed, and she tried to see the house through Sarah's eyes as she wandered its rooms.

Sarah Blackston had returned to the family home, which she'd inherited upon her father's death, shortly after the war. She had opened it as a convalescent home for wounded soldiers, and devoted her life to the cause. The final scene, the 'Hollywood happy ending', as Simon so scathingly called it, and the one battle he had lost with the producers, was the return of Wily Halliday. Upon his liberation from the Japanese prisoner of war camp, Wily had traced Sarah and the two would be reunited.

Try as she might, Sam found that she could no longer see Huxley House through Sarah's eyes. Sarah had ceased to exist, and so had Huxley House. She was wandering the rooms of Chisolm House, and it was her own eyes she was seeing it through. She would be back there soon, she thought, sharing her life with Jason in the house that had somehow made everything happen.

She chastised herself. She must stop being subjective, she

must get into character, she must become Sarah. But, as she looked at the painting of Amelia Huxley above the mantelpiece, all she could see was the portrait of Phoebe Chisolm. Jane would have looked at that portrait, she thought. Phoebe's best friend, Jane Miller. And as she pictured Jane looking at the portrait, Sam suddenly realised how simple it was. In Vanuatu, Jane Thackeray and Sarah Blackston had become one. Sarah was not lost to her at all.

She caught sight of herself in one of the gold-leafed mirrors that adorned the walls, and the new Sarah looked back with all the strength and purpose that Jane Thackeray must have possessed. Sarah and Jane were still one, she realised, and again the house was helping her. It pleased her to think that, for one short while of film fantasy, Jane Miller would be returning as Jane Thackeray to the house she had known so well in her youth.

Over the first few days, they shot the scenes of Sarah's return, and the metamorphosis of Huxley House into a welcoming home for convalescent soldiers. The old stalwart actors, Anthony and Fiona, were reprising the roles they'd played in the opening of the film, the butler and housekeeper having remained in service after the death of their master to prepare Huxley House for the arrival of their new mistress. And in their eyes the transformation of the claustrophobic mausoleum mirrored the transformation they saw in Sarah.

*'Huxley House is to serve a purpose other than a prison,' Sarah said, ripping down the ancient drapes of the drawing-room bay windows. Sunlight flooded in. The servants, shocked, followed her as she marched into the next room. 'There will be love in this house.' She ripped down the drapes there too. 'As there should always have been.'*

It was a happy three days; Sam enjoyed working with Anthony and Fiona and the actors playing the soldiers whom Sarah befriended. And then the day arrived when they were to shoot Wily Halliday's return.

They were late starting that morning. The entire unit was waiting for Brett Marsdon who was still in makeup. He'd been partying until all hours in a Kings Cross nightclub, despite Sam's warning, or perhaps rebelliously because of it, and he'd arrived forty minutes late.

'So much for your opinion that he listens to me,' Sam said to Nick as they sat in the studio drinking their third coffee apiece. 'I tried, really I did.'

'Oh well,' Nick shrugged, 'so long as he comes up with the goods.' He couldn't be bothered discussing Brett Marsdon, who was a lost cause, in his opinion. 'Just one more day to go. I'll miss you.'

'I'll miss you too.'

'The little prick's still in makeup, I take it.' Simon Scanlon materialised beside them, steaming black coffee in hand, he'd been talking with the lighting director and the ever-reliable Kevin Hodgman, director of photography.

'I believe so,' Nick said dryly.

'Oh well, only one more day to go.' He echoed Nick's words as he plonked himself into a chair beside them.

Simon seemed in a remarkably good mood, Sam thought. Normally he'd be fuming about the loss of studio time.

'I want to shoot the scene in one take, if I can,' he said. 'We'll rehearse the buggery out of it first and we'll go in for the closeups afterwards, but I want to get the full impact in a two-shot, and I want you to give Brett all you've got, Sam. Save yourself during rehearsal and then sock it to him. We've got a two-camera setup and the lighting is superb.'

'Aren't you going to shoot Brett's stuff first?' She was surprised. Simon was adamant about shooting in sequence whenever possible, and there was a scene prior to the reunion where, unbeknownst to Sarah, Wily Halliday watches her through the bay windows.

'Nup. I don't trust him.' Simon drained his coffee, boiling as it was, and signalled a runner for another one. 'Black, three sugars,' he called. 'He's been out of touch too long, our party boy, and I'm relying upon you to fire him up. After the big scene, he'll be fine, he'll carry it through to the shots outside.'

Sam looked uncertain. She wasn't sure if she wanted the added responsibility, but Simon gave her a nonchalant wink. 'The little prick's a different actor when he's working opposite you, Sam. Don't give it a second thought, just take him up there with you.'

Sam started to feel nervous. She was already unsure of herself, and Simon's sublime confidence unnerved her even further. She couldn't seem to get into character today, all she could think of was Jason and the thought that she would be with him in two days.

Simon grinned, oblivious to any problem. 'So what are your plans, Sam?' he asked. 'You're off to join Jason in England, Nick tells me, and you're going to live in a divine Victorian mansion and he's going to open a medical practice.'

She eyed him with suspicion; he was taking the mickey out of her, surely. But he was leaning forward in his director's chair, elbows on knees, hands under his chin, giving her his undivided attention. 'It sounds idyllic.'

Sam looked at Nick, who shrugged in all innocence. 'You didn't tell me it was meant to be a secret,' he said.

'It isn't,' she assured him. She was amazed not by Nick's divulgence of her plans, but by Simon Scanlon's interest in her private life. Simon was interested in no-one's private life. Work was the only thing that mattered to him. Why wasn't he talking to her of Sarah Blackston and the scene they were about to shoot?

'Jason's a good bloke, I'm happy for you, Sam.'

They'd been Nick's very words to her, Sam thought, and once again she looked to Nick, who simply smiled back. He had a feeling he knew where Simon Scanlon was heading.

'So long as he doesn't demand you give up your career of course.' Simon knew Jason approved of Sam's career, Nick had told him that too.

'Oh no,' she countered eagerly. 'Even if we have a family, Jason's happy for me to keep acting. He says I wouldn't be whole without my career.'

'Understanding bloke.'

'Yes, he is.' Sam remembered the conversation they'd had in Perth.

'Why should I wish to change you, Sam?' Jason had asked. 'It was your passion about your work that first attracted me. Well, it worried me, I admit,' he'd laughed. 'It's quite terrifying to find that you're falling in love with your own grandmother.'

Sam was jolted out of her brief reverie. 'There's not many around who understand actors like that.' Simon was studying her so warmly that she felt encouraged to continue.

'Jason says that he doesn't want to turn me into a doctor's wife. He says that if he tried, he'd be changing the very person he fell in love with.'

Simon's eyes didn't leave hers, but in the background he saw the second assistant director arriving with Brett Marsdon.

'He must love you very much.'

She nodded.

'And you love him too, don't you?' She was glowing with it, he thought. He caught the signal from Kevin the DOP, and gave an acknowledging response with his right hand, which Sam didn't notice.

'Yes,' she said. 'Yes, I do.'

Her face was radiant. She looked exactly the way he wanted her to look.

'Then use it, Sam.' The mesmeric gleam was back in the pterodactyl eyes. 'Use it!' And Simon Scanlon left just as the second assistant arrived.

'We're ready for you, Miss Lindsay,' the second said.

Sam turned to Nick. 'I've been conned, haven't I?'

'Yes.'

*Sarah opened the door. A man stood silhouetted in the late afternoon sun. An emaciated man, she couldn't see his face. But she'd been expecting a new arrival that day. She looked for the hospital attendant who should have been with him, but the man was alone. Strange, she thought.*

*'Welcome to Huxley House,' she said. 'Please come in.' She closed the door after him and led the way into the drawing room.*

*'Would you like some tea before we settle you in to your new quarters?' she asked, about to ring the bell for Beatrice.*

*'No thanks, I'm fine.'*

*She recognised the voice.*

*'Wily.' She whispered the name, not daring to face him.*

*'Lieutenant Wily Halliday, at your service, ma'am.' He smiled, tentative, unsure of her reaction. He'd enquired and he knew she wasn't married, but there could have been someone in her life, it had been three whole years.*

*She turned. He was lean and weathered, a man twenty years older than his years, but the eyes were the same, and the smile, uncertain as it was, held a vestige of the old cheeky challenge.*

*'Wily.' She could have reached out and touched him, but she didn't. She stood breathlessly drinking in his image. 'That's short for William, is it?'*

*'Nope.' The smile broke into the grin that she knew so well. 'I was named after Wily Post.'*

*'First man to fly solo around the world,' she said, 'seven*

*days, eighteen hours and forty-nine minutes.'* Her eyes didn't leave his for a second.

'That's right. You remembered.'

'No. I looked him up at the library.'

*They stood motionless in the sunlight that streamed through the bay windows, the love between them palpable.*

'Cut!' Simon called. If the producers wanted a final clinch, they could get fucked, he'd decided, and he wasn't going to shoot one to give them the option. 'Well done, Brett, good stuff!' He smacked Brett heartily on the back.

'Yeah, it was great, wasn't it.' Brett had been knocked out by the connection he and Sam had shared, and he accepted the congratulations as his due. Man, but they'd soared, he thought. He gave her a wink. 'The A team, Sam,' he said.

Simon Scanlon was pleased. Just as he'd anticipated, she'd taken the little prick right up there with her.

He hugged her closely. 'I was right, wasn't I?' he whispered.

'Yes, you cunning bastard.' She'd thought of nothing but the love that she felt for Jason as she'd looked at Brett. She hadn't been Sarah Blackston and she hadn't been Jane Thackeray. It had been a total cheat, but it had worked.

'So this is Chisolm House.'

Jason had pulled the car up just inside the main drive and they stood, rugged up in their heavy overcoats, arms about one another, surveying the elegant facade and the front garden, stark in its winter nakedness.

'It's gorgeous,' he said.

'I knew you'd love it.' She grabbed his hand. 'Come on.' And together they ran to the front door.

They'd driven directly from the airport and collected the keys from the real estate office, Jim Lofthouse having good-naturedly opened early in order to await their arrival.

Sam headed straight for the front drawing room, Jason following, and there it was.

'Meet Jane's best friend, Phoebe Chisolm,' she said, and Jason gazed up at the James Hampton portrait of the girl with the tantalising smile, captured so perfectly in the shaft of light.

'Hello, Phoebe,' he said, 'you're very beautiful.'

They explored the house from top to bottom, Sam deciding which rooms could best be converted to Jason's surgery. 'Reception here,' she said, 'you'll need a secretary of course. A middle-aged one, very plain,' she grinned, 'and through here would be your consulting room.' She raced ahead and he followed her. 'Just like the drawing room, lovely and light, more bay windows, and the smaller room over here would be your examination room . . .' Jason caught her midway in her dash from one door to another.

'It's perfect, my love.' His arms were about her, beneath her open coat, holding her body close to his. 'Everything is just perfect.' They kissed.

'I'll show you the stables,' she said.

But she didn't give him a guided tour of the stables. She took him straight upstairs to the loft instead, and they made love on the bare mattress of the double bed.

Afterwards, she jumped up and grabbed a doona from the linen closet. 'I'm bloody freezing,' she said as she threw it over them and snuggled in beside him.

'Serves you right for being so wanton.'

'I forgot to switch the heating on.' She was about to jump up again.

'In a minute, my love, in a minute.'

They laughed as they rubbed warmth into each other, rolling about beneath the doona, and half an hour later they made love again.

'Why don't you sleep for a while,' he suggested, kissing her forehead. 'I'll pop out and buy some supplies.'

'No way.' She bounded instantly from the bed. 'I'm

coming with you.' She didn't want him out of her sight for a minute.

'You just got off a twenty-six hour flight, Sam.'

'Eight hours of which I slept like a baby. First class, remember?'

'There's such a thing as jet lag and body clocks, you know.'

'Bugger them both, I don't believe in them.' And she raced downstairs to turn the heating on. It started as soon as she flicked the switch. Thank goodness, she thought gratefully, remembering how the system had refused to operate that morning a lifetime ago when she'd left the stables. She recalled her fanciful notions about the house telling her to go, and she smiled to herself. I'm being welcomed back now, she thought happily. Then she ran upstairs to jump under the shower.

The next several hours were spent shopping and exploring the town, Sam delighting in sharing her favourite haunts, which included a beer at the Red Lion. When they returned, she still refused to give in to fatigue and he watched her as she happily set out the crockery and lamps and cushions they'd bought from the local interiors store. It had been decided they would stay there for the next month whilst they furnished the main house. Her energy seemed boundless, he thought, but she'd crash soon.

He insisted on preparing them an early dinner that night. Sam had discovered during their stay in Perth that he was an excellent cook, a fact that hadn't surprised her in the least.

'I'm hopeless,' she'd admitted. 'I suppose I'll have to learn.'

'Not if you don't want to. I enjoy it.'

It was cosy and warm, and as she curled up beside him on the sofa, she could barely keep her eyes open.

'Come on my love,' he whispered, 'bedtime, you're exhausted.'

'Mmm,' she agreed. 'I've crashed.'

He half carried her up the stairs and helped her into her pyjamas as he would a drowsy child, and the moment her head touched the pillow she was fast asleep. He returned to the kitchen where he cleared the remnants of their meal and did the washing up. Then he sat down with a book and tried to read, but he couldn't concentrate on the words. He was too happy, he realised.

Ten minutes later, showered and pyjama-clad, he slipped into bed beside her and watched her as she slept. She was so beautiful, he thought, so serene in her sleep. He wanted to touch her, but he didn't dare for fear of waking her. He had no idea how long he watched her, but when he finally drifted off himself, it was with a sense of sheer bliss.

Sam didn't know what time it was when she awoke, but he was sleeping soundly beside her. She didn't know what it was that had awoken her either, and she lay in the darkness listening.

There was someone downstairs, she thought. She could hear no movement, no creaking of floorboards, and the stable floor did creak, but she could hear a voice. Then another voice responded.

She sat up, about to wake him, but even as her hand went to his shoulder she stopped herself. There was something familiar in the voices. She'd heard them before, she realised. But this time they were not the voices of excited girls, they were the voices of two young women in subdued conversation. She strained to hear their actual words, but she couldn't make out what it was they were saying.

She crept out of bed, careful not to disturb him, and at the top of the stairs she flicked the switch that operated the downstairs light. The voices stopped, and she walked down the steps into the room that she knew would be deserted.

Perhaps if she sat quietly in the dark the voices might

return, she thought. She switched off the light and felt her way over to the sofa. Jason had turned the heater off before retiring, but the room still retained its warmth, and she curled up comfortably to wait.

The minutes ticked by, her eyelids felt like lead, and she knew she was on the verge of sleep. She was too comfortable, she told herself, and she abandoned the sofa for a carver chair, sitting straight-backed, jerking her head up each time she felt herself nodding off.

Then gradually she heard them, again not the words, but the voices; they came to her as if from the past, carried on the very air that surrounded her, and as sleep engulfed her she saw the images of two young women, one fair, one dark.

'*All things are meant for a purpose, Jane,*' *Phoebe said.*

*It was late in the afternoon, the day before Jane and Martin were due to depart for Liverpool, and from there for the New Hebrides. It had been Phoebe's decision that they say their personal goodbyes in the stables; there would be others around the following day.*

*Jane sat on the sofa. The very same sofa where Marty had proposed to her, she thought, and where he had tried to voice his misgivings about their marriage. 'You're young and strong, Jane . . .' he'd said. But she'd refused to listen, the decision had been hers and she knew she would never regret it. She rocked the baby gently, Ronnie comfortably asleep in her arms. Phoebe was right, she thought, all things were meant for a purpose.*

*Phoebe was sitting, straight-backed, in a carver chair, unusual for Phoebe, who liked to lounge in comfort, but Jane knew why. Phoebe was prepared for the discussion she'd been avoiding over the past three days. They'd spoken of everything else in such detail. The past and their childhood, the future and their aspirations, but the time had now come, and Phoebe knew it. It was why she'd suggested the stables and why she'd chosen the hard-backed chair. In customary style, she got straight to the point.*

*'You will tell him nothing, just as we discussed in Edinburgh.'*

*'I thought that perhaps it was too soon then Phoebe, too soon for you to know your own mind. Is it really what you want? Are you sure you don't wish me to tell him when he comes of age?'*

*'Quite sure. No-one but you and Martin must ever know. Least of all the boy.' She looked at the baby Jane held in her arms. 'He is your son, Jane. God meant it that way.'*

*Phoebe stared through the windows at the cobbled courtyard and Chisolm House beyond. She could have kept James Hampton's child, she thought, she was strong enough to have borne the stigma. But her mother wasn't and, although she knew her father would not have disowned her, it would have ruined Arthur Chisolm's career.*

*All things were meant for a purpose. She repeated the message to herself. She was a noble figure and she had played her part in an ingenious plan of God's doing. A plan that had been set in train the day Jane had nearly drowned and their lives had become inextricably bound. Martin Thackeray was unable to sire children, and giving birth to Jane's child had been her destiny, Phoebe told herself.*

*Jane sat in silence. She had never seen Phoebe look sad. Angry, yes, sullen and sulky, even morose on occasions, Phoebe was a mercurial creature. But never sad. Jane rose, the sleeping baby cradled in her arms.*

*'Phoebe?' she said quietly.*

*Phoebe stopped gazing out the window and looked up.*

*'Hold him.' Jane offered her the child.*

*'Oh good heavens no.' Phoebe laughed. 'I'm hopeless with babies, you know that.' She stood. 'Don't look so tragic,' she said and she smiled brightly as she kissed Jane*

*on the cheek, 'I'll have another child one day.'*

*She dropped the frivolity as quickly as she'd adopted it, preferring instead the drama of the moment. 'Isn't it wonderful, Jane, the way it's all fallen into place? You always said I could make things happen.'*

*'Yes, I did.' Jane wasn't sure whether she was agreeing because Phoebe wished her to, or whether she truly believed it. 'And you have, Phoebe. You have.'*

The room was cold and Sam awoke, freezing. She sneaked guiltily back upstairs and slipped into bed beside Jason, hoping that the chill of her body wouldn't wake him. He'd have every right to be annoyed that she'd sat up half the night in the cold, dreaming fanciful dreams of the past. But were they fanciful? she wondered. She knew he didn't believe there was any force at work in the house, that it was all in her imagination, and he was possibly right. But the images had been so clear.

She felt herself drifting off to sleep as the warmth of his body seeped into hers. Two young women, one dark, one fair, she could still see them. She wondered what they'd been discussing in such earnest.

It was mid-morning when she woke to discover him sitting on the bed beside her, a tray of tea and toast resting on his knees. 'You've been asleep for twelve hours, so much for a person who doesn't believe in jet lag and body clocks.'

She sat up and kissed him energetically, nearly spilling the tea. He put the tray on the floor, took off his shoes, and allowed her to wrestle him into bed.

But the images of last night were not forgotten. In the cold light of day they remained clearer than ever. There was a force in the house that had made it all happen, she thought as he kissed her. A benevolent force to which she would be eternally thankful.

# EPILOGUE

Jason had been touched by her present. Sam walked into the drawing room and looked at the photograph. She'd given it to him only yesterday.

'Mamma Jane and my father and old Godfrey,' he'd smiled, 'that's lovely of you, Sam, and how well it's come up, hasn't it?'

She'd sneaked the old photo from his wallet and had an enlargement made and framed in silver. She sat it on the mantelpiece beneath Phoebe's portrait, alongside the formal family picture of the Chisolms.

'I think it's right that Jane should be here with Phoebe,' she'd said.

'So do I, my love.' He'd nodded approvingly. 'So do I.'

He always humoured her about her fantasies, but the fact was they no longer existed. She no longer heard voices or saw visions. She no longer had time to be preoccupied with the past of the house; she was too involved in its future.

Sam looked about at the newly refurbished drawing room. She could hear Jason singing loudly in the shower upstairs. They'd done so much in just one month. The style of the house had been beautifully maintained; it was elegant, but it was also comfortable. A real home, she thought. And there was a tenant in the stables now. They'd leased the flat to a young lighting technician who was contracted to Ferneham Hall for a year. A man of the theatre – Sam found it wonderfully apt.

But today was the most important day of all: the opening of Jason's medical practice. The brass plaques had gone up last week, one on the stone pillar of the main drive, and one beside the front door. 'Doctor Jason Thackeray, General Practitioner', and underneath were listed the surgery hours. Mavis, his receptionist, would be arriving in half an hour, and the day was already fully booked with six consultations, Jason allocating at least an hour for each.

'I'll allow less time when I sort out the hypochondriacs,' he'd said with a grin.

Sam thought of the film script that had arrived from Reginald Harcourt last week. She couldn't get enthused about it, and he'd told her not to anyway. 'It's an average script, Sam,' he'd agreed, 'and when *Torpedo Junction*'s released at the end of the year you'll be the hottest thing on the market, Simon Scanlon tells me.'

Yes, her career could stay on hold for a while, she thought. There were more important things on the agenda at the moment.

She wandered over to the bay windows to look at the snow. She'd dragged Jason out of bed first thing this morning when she'd seen it from their upstairs window. A thick blanket had fallen during the night, silent and magical, everything draped in white, without a breath of breeze to disturb it.

Then, through the frost on the panes, Sam saw her. Standing by the fountain in the front garden. Maude. She was sure it was Maude. She rubbed at the windows to no effect. She contemplated running upstairs to get Jason. She had told him about the mysterious old woman in the park and she so wanted him to meet her. But her hesitation lasted for only a moment. By the time she'd fetched Jason Maude might have disappeared, and she desperately needed to talk to Maude.

She ran into the hall, grabbing her coat and throwing her scarf around her neck. She wasn't thinking clearly, but she felt Maude might have some answers. To what, she wasn't sure, but something told her the old woman held the key to the past.

She half expected Maude to have vanished by the time she'd raced up the main drive and into the garden. But Maude hadn't. When Sam arrived, breathless from the cold, the old woman was still standing by the fountain.

'Hello, Jane,' Maude said, as if she'd been waiting.

Sam didn't bother correcting her. 'Hello, Maude.'

'Maude?' The old woman seemed confused.

'Yes,' Sam nodded firmly, 'Maude.' There would be answers this time, she thought. Maude *who*? she was about to ask.

'Good heavens, how silly of me.' Maude smiled her pretty smile. 'I'm always so bad with names. Come closer, dear, where I can see you, my eyes aren't what they were.'

Sam crossed to the fountain.

'You're not Jane at all, I know that, it's just that you look so very like her, forgive me. Do your coat up, dear, you'll catch your death.'

Sam automatically did as she was told. The questions she'd been about to ask now escaped her, and she found Maude's eyes distracting. They were vivid for someone so elderly, and they seemed familiar.

Maude chatted on. 'I've noticed the plaques,' she said. 'Your husband is opening a general practice. How nice to have a family doctor back at Chisolm House. Just like the old days. Chisolm House has a fine medical history, you know.'

'Yes, so I believe. Would you like to come in for a cup of tea?'

'No, dear, thank you, I can't stay long.'

'But it's cold, please come inside.' The old woman wasn't even wearing a coat, Sam realised. She took Maude's arm, it was warm to the touch.

'I don't feel the cold,' Maude said. 'And don't you find,' she added, 'that after a heavy snowfall like this, the air is actually quite warm?' She smiled. 'It's as if the snow is a blanket, wrapping us all up in its warmth.'

'Yes, I do find that.'

'See this fountain?' Maude placed her hand affection-ately upon the fountain. 'So pretty, don't you think?'

'Yes, yes it is.' Sam rested her hand on the fountain beside the old woman's, her bare fingers not registering the ice-cold of the snow that shrouded the stone.

'Jane and I used to build a snowman over this fountain. Jane always said it was cheating, but I said, who cares, we have the best snowman in town.' Her laughter was girlish and stopped as quickly as it had started. 'Congratulations,' she said.

'On what?' Sam was mystified.

'Your baby of course.'

Sam stared at the old woman. How could Maude know? Two months didn't show at all.

'Oh my dear, one can always tell by the look in a woman's eyes.' Maude turned to the bay windows. 'And that is your husband, I take it?'

Sam turned. Jason was standing in the drawing room looking out at them, and Maude gave him a flirtatious wave. 'How very handsome he is.'

Jason smiled and returned the old woman's wave.

'Yes, I think so too, but then I'm biased,' Sam said as she waved back. 'Please, Maude,' she said, 'please come in and meet him.'

'No, dear, no I won't, as I said I can't stay. In fact you won't be seeing me any more.' Maude touched Sam's hand where it rested on the fountain. Her fingers were so warm,

Sam thought. 'I just wanted to say welcome home.'

She turned as if to go, then paused, pensive, her eyes focussed upon the fountain. 'Jane always told me I could make things happen,' she said. 'For others, it would appear, not always for myself, but then I have a feeling I may not have deserved it. No matter,' her smile was radiant as she looked at Sam, 'all is well now. Goodbye, my dear.'

Sam watched her walk away, healthy and strong. For a woman that age, there was no halt in her step.

She went inside. Jason was still standing by the bay windows.

'You see?' she announced triumphantly. 'I told you she was real.'

He didn't seem to be listening. 'You looked so beautiful out there, Sam,' he said.

'I tried to get her to come in and have some tea, I mean, she wasn't even wearing a coat, but she said she doesn't feel the cold.'

'Who? Who are you talking about?'

'Maude of course. She waved at you.'

He looked blank.

'You waved back at her, Jason.'

'I waved at you, Sam. You were standing in the garden leaning on the fountain, and you looked so incredibly beautiful. And you turned to me, and I waved.'

'I was with Maude. We both waved.'

'No, my love. You were alone.' He pointed through the bay windows. 'Look.'

In the deep fall of snow, there was just one set of footprints.

'Are you all right, Sam?' He was concerned.

'Oh yes, I'm fine. Really,' she said as she kissed him, 'I'm fine, just the last of the ghosts, that's all,' and she smiled.

She realised where she'd seen those eyes before. They were the eyes in the portrait. Goodbye, Phoebe, she thought. Perhaps she even whispered it as she looked out at the fountain and the clear imprint of her hand in the snow upon the stone, right where her fingers had rested beside Phoebe's.

**Judy Nunn**
*Territory*

*Territory* is a story of the Top End and the people who dare to dwell there. Of a family who carved an empire from the escarpments of Kakadu to the Indian Ocean and defied God or Man to take it from them. Of Spitfire pilot Terence Galloway, who brings his English bride Henrietta home from the Battle of Britain to Bullalalla cattle station, only to be faced with the desperate defence of Darwin against the Imperial Japanese Air Force.

It is also a story of their sons Malcolm and Kit, two brothers who grow up in the harsh but beautiful environment of the Northern Territory, and share a baptism of fire as young men in the jungles of wartorn Vietnam.

And what of the Dutch East Indies treasure ship which foundered off Western Australia in 1629? How does the Batavia's horrific tale of mutiny and murder touch the lives of the Galloways and other Territorians – like Foong Lee, the patriarch of the Darwin Chinese community, and Jackie Yoorunga, the famous Aboriginal stockman? What is the connection between the infamous 'ship of death' and the Aborigines that compels a young anthropologist to discover the truth?

*From the blazing inferno that was Darwin on 19 February 1942 to the devastation of Cyclone Tracy,* Territory *is a mile-a-minute read.*

**Judy Nunn**
*Kal*

*Kalgoorlie.*

*It grew out of the red dust of the desert over the world's richest vein of gold. Like the gold it guarded, Kalgoorlie was a magnet to anyone with a sense of adventure, anyone who could dream. People were drawn there from all over the world, settling to start afresh or to seek their fortunes. They called it Kal; it was a place where dreams came true or were lost forever in the dust. It could reward you or it could destroy you, but it would never let you go. You staked your claim in Kal and Kal staked its claim in you.*

In a story as breathtaking and as sweeping as the land itself, bestselling author Judy Nunn brings Kal magically to life through the lives of two families, one Australian and one Italian. From the heady early days of the gold rush to the horrors of the First World War in Gallipoli and France, to the shame and confrontation of the post-war riots, *Kal* tells the story of Australia itself and the people who forged a nation out of a harsh and unforgiving land.

'A huge and sumptuous novel . . . absolutely unputdownable. Nunn is mistress of the old-fashioned story we beg to hear.'
*Herald Sun*

**Judy Nunn**
*Beneath the Southern Cross*

'*A night of debauchery it was . . .*'
   *Thomas Kendall stood with his grandsons beside the massive sandstone walls of Fort Macquarie. He smiled as he looked out across Sydney Cove, '. . . that night they brought the women convicts ashore . . .*'

In 1788, Thomas Kendall, a naive nineteen-year-old sentenced to transportation for burglary, finds himself bound for Sydney Town and a new life in the wild and lawless land beneath the Southern Cross.

Thomas fathers a dynasty that will last beyond two hundred years. His descendants play their part in the forging of a nation, but greed and prejudice see an irreparable rift in the family which will echo through the generations. It is only when a young man reaches far into the past and rights a grievous wrong that the Kendall family can reclaim its honour.

*Beneath the Southern Cross* is as much a story of a city as it is a family chronicle. With her uncanny ability to bring history to life in technicolour, Judy Nunn traces the fortunes of Thomas Kendall's descendants through good times and bad, two devastating wars and several social revolutions to the present day, vividly drawing the events, the characters, and the ideas and issues that have made the city of Sydney and the nation of Australia what they are today.